C000059413

# THERE'S SOMETHING ABOUT EMILY . . .

# THERE'S SOMETHING ABOUT EMILY . . .

**Peter Jenkins**

Copyright © 2012 by Peter Jenkins.

Library of Congress Control Number:    2012907075
ISBN:          Hardcover              978-1-4691-2592-3
               Softcover              978-1-4691-2591-6
               Ebook                 978-1-4691-2593-0

All rights reserved. No part of this book may be reproduced or transmitted in any form or by any means, electronic or mechanical, including photocopying, recording, or by any information storage and retrieval system, without permission in writing from the copyright owner.

This is a work of fiction. Names, characters, places and incidents either are the product of the author's imagination or are used fictitiously, and any resemblance to any actual persons, living or dead, events, or locales is entirely coincidental.

This book was printed in the United States of America.

**To order additional copies of this book, contact:**
Xlibris Corporation
0-800-644-6988
www.xlibrispublishing.co.uk
Orders@xlibrispublishing.co.uk
303648

My thanks to Mark and Teresa Piddington, whose daughter, and my great niece, Emily, appears on the front cover. And a special thanks to my wife, as well, for putting up with all the hours I've spent in front of my computer keyboard.

# Prologue

As one of the few members of a million-year-old civilization that had evolved away from being anything physical, the alien entity no longer inhabited any particular world or planet. He now existed only at the very highest, spirit level, totally devoid of any earthly restraints, as we would understand.

His wholly peace-loving race are able to project their minds, to roam and explore the endless space, time continuum, seeking only the acquisition of knowledge and learning, this now being their sole purpose and very meaning of their existence, their *raison d'etre*. Like all the others, his mind had been programmed from its inception just to gather information, then to analyse, draw conclusions, and predict probable outcomes. Above all else, they needed only to learn from the errors made by other life forms. For wisdom and understanding was surely the ultimate power, if used correctly.

Detecting some form of minute transmission from a far distant galaxy, the alien followed his natural curiosity, and opened the section of his mind that enabled him to transport through the vacuum of space. He had been at rest, probably for a couple of thousand years on our earthly time scale, but even in this self-imposed catatonic state, during which time he analysed all his collected data, a part of his thought processes had still been endlessly scanning. He had been looking for something, anything new, to capture his attention. Now, he had detected a hitherto unknown, small magnetic anomaly in an insignificant, far distant galaxy, one that he was already very familiar with.

In the milliseconds that it took him to direct all his thoughts toward identifying and investigating the anomaly, he was simultaneously accessing all the known data on that particular section of the cosmos.

He already knew of the relatively tiny solar system, the complex of which comprised a single, small, declining sun that was being orbited by a total of eight minor planets and several comets. The only planet of any real interest was the third from the sun, which, for its small size, had a huge diversity of mostly carbon-based life forms.

Still in emergence, all the bio-life forms seemed to be intent on destroying each other in their endless struggles for dominance. It was from this tiny blue planet, that the new electro-magnetic anomaly was emanating.

The alien knew that one particular life form had emerged dominant and supreme since the planet was nearly destroyed by an asteroid strike that had polluted its fragile and unique atmosphere for an aeon. This specie was proving itself to be far more intelligent than any other that had previously inhabited their world. However, in apparent ignorance, not only were they intent on destroying each other, but also the very fabric of the environment in which they lived.

Their genus was called humanoid. They considered themselves to be superior to all the other life forms on their planet. Any lesser creature, they commonly referred to as 'animal,' and generally treated them all with a callous disdain.

In order to sustain themselves, this humanoid life form had learned to breed, nurture and harvest many of the other creatures on their planet. They generally believed that all animals had been created by a God, and put there solely for this purpose. Such indiscriminate actions and beliefs had, in many cases, already led to the total eradication and extinction of many other life forms, but they still they carried on, seemingly regardless of the consequences of their actions.

The humans were also intent on plundering all their other worldly resources, which in essence, were vital to their continued existence. Destruction of their environment in order to produce food, and the need to extract mineral resources to progress their civilisation, was apparently of no consequence, or of little consideration, to the long-term effects that it was having on their world. They were constantly hacking away at, and burrowing into, the delicate crust of their planet. Trawling the oceans until they were nearly empty of certain marine life species, and destroying with fire, huge areas of forestation, so vital to the quality of their planet's fragile atmosphere.

On their present course, the alien had already calculated that they had less than two thousand more of their years left to exist, before the tiny blue planet would reach a point where their specie would be totally wiped out, either from starvation, or from pollution to the fragile environment.

His data scans immediately detected and recognised that the humanoid evolutionary development had moved on considerably faster than expected since he, or any of the others, had last visited their world. On that occasion, choosing to interact, they had implanted certain knowledge into the minds of some individual humans. This had enabled them to design and erect peculiar structures that they called pyramids, which they had used to incarcerate some of their dead.

He and the others had long puzzled over the human obsession with death, and a belief in a life thereafter. They concluded that it was something common to most of this specie, and that previous mischievous interventions by others of their race, might have had some influence in this. The humans, it seemed, had realised that some extraordinary external forces, beyond their comprehension, were affecting and influencing their normal existence. Unable to understand, they perceived that it had to be some sort of divine intervention sent for spiritual guidance, something not too far removed from the truth.

To satisfy and control the curiosity of the masses, the leaders of their respective societies, set about creating many false images and names that became deified, and referred to as Gods. So powerful became the obsession to worship these Gods, it caused the human race to divide itself into many fragmented sects. Each sect identified itself by its particular following. Its disciples, as the followers came to be known, believed that theirs was the only true God, thus denying the existence of all others.

Religion, as it all came to be known, brought about many sacred rites and ceremonies, some involving barbaric forms of sacrifice of other humanoids and animals, made as a gift to a particular God. Such singular beliefs inevitably became the main causation for huge conflicts between the followers of differing religions.

The aliens had noted an obvious similarity between many of the religious followings, but had failed to understand why the numerous and diverse human races could not all live peaceably together, each worshipping their own God. Their observations were still ongoing.

Most of the previous alien visitors had found it all somewhat amusing and interesting. They had repeated their little experiments many times over just to observe and try to assess or predict any differing outcome. Greek, Aztec, Persian, Minoan, and many other civilisations, had all been interesting, in the differing ways that the humans had chosen to worship their particular God. He recalled that the most unpredictable of all, had been the carpenter's son, Jesus, who had declared himself to be the son of a God. He was considered a particularly strange happening, for this human had seemingly evolved without any of their intervention.

The man had lived his short life trying to persuade those that he met to love each other. The concept of love was not something that the aliens understood, for it seemed to have so many differing aspects, mostly relating to complex human emotions.

The happenings relative to the short life of the man, Jesus, had ultimately given birth to a branch of religion the humans named Christianity, but only after the humans had themselves, put the man to death for his beliefs. It was all totally beyond their comprehension.

Other similar efforts by the aliens to emulate this man, and to create another super being, or dominant race, had so far failed. Genghis Khan and Adolph Hitler numbered amongst many other similar tyrants they had created. These were seemingly ordinary little people that they had sought to elevate. All were subsequently considered by the aliens to have developed egotistical minds that had gotten out of their control, and necessitated a premature termination of the experiments before too much damage was done to the humanoid race.

The aliens, on their part, did not recognise any wrongdoing in their passive interference or interventions. Humans had been considered just another, minor, emerging specie bent on self-destruction in a relatively short period of time. So where was the harm? A few hundred million of their life form, eliminating themselves, had already benefited the rather appealing little planet by preventing an infestation of these curious little warlike creatures.

Although the alien thought that he understood all the concepts, he was no longer able to feel, or experience any real emotion. For feelings such as pain, joy, love, sadness, grief or compassion, had all been identified as weaknesses that influenced thought processes, and interfered with any logical judgement. In consequence, following their own worldly struggles, his ancestors had tried to totally eliminate all such emotions, expunging them psychophysically from their reasoning processes. To a greater extent they had almost succeeded, but in so doing they inadvertently created another problem for themselves, something that was about to become abundantly apparent to the visiting alien.

Association and interaction with his own kind had become largely unnecessary, for unless the individual alien chose to terminate, he could theoretically, live forever. Similarly, should he choose to replicate, he was able to split his mind to create another entity, an exact duplicate, or clone, of himself. All his thoughts and knowledge were automatically passed on, and they became common to all the others, as was theirs to him. The arrangement would appear to be little short of procreative perfection, but it did have certain drawbacks. There was no longer any need for communicative interaction. No argument, disagreement, or mutual enjoyment in being in another's company. Put quite simply, they had created loneliness.

Simultaneously accessing information contained in all the memory banks of the simple computers, and by intercepting the millions of telephonic broadcasts and communications, the alien was quickly able update his knowledge. He concluded that the human technological achievement had also progressed much more rapidly than he, or any of the others of his race, had envisaged. Scientifically, the humans had reached the point that now allowed the sending of information-gathering probes to the other celestial bodies within their solar system. Significant advances had been made in communications; there were now many primitive satellites in geo-stationary orbits around the planet. He noted a huge proliferation of rather primitive, mechanically propelled, transportation vehicles, most with highly toxic emissions, that were polluting the fragile atmosphere and quickening the destruction of all life on the little planet.

Strangely, the alien realised that he felt saddened by all of this, for he was now considering it to be a rather appealing and beautiful little world. For him, that in itself was something completely new, for a feeling of sadness was surely an expression of emotion, and something he should not be able to experience?

He turned his attention to the social structure now adopted by the humans. There seemed to be a widespread obsession associated with the accumulation of something called money, or wealth, as they called it. Money was used to barter for goods and chattels, or was given in remuneration for a skill or service rendered to another person.

The humans seemed to spend an inordinate amount of their short life span in gathering together many things that they desired, only to abandon, or give them all away, when they died. It was a very strange arrangement that piqued his curiosity even further.

Searching for the cause of the original magnetic anomaly that had prompted this particular visit, he found that the humans had begun experimenting in a very dangerous area of physics. They had constructed a primitive particle accelerator, that he was already aware, had suffered a catastrophic failure at its inception. Its very existence caused him some concern. For while his ancestors were still physical life forms, not unlike the humanoids, his own emerging race had recognised the dangers in this science and abandoned all similar projects. He concluded that if the humans continued to dabble in things, about which they had little understanding or knowledge, this too would serve to hasten the destruction of the planet. It might even have the potential to destroy this whole solar system?

The alien's newly perceived liking for this world prompted him to explore places his previous visits had overlooked. He was now in a hospital concentrating on a young humanoid mother in the act of giving birth to a brand new life form. The biological concept of human reproduction was understood, but he hadn't appreciated the depth of human emotion that accompanied the delivery of the infant child. He saw the pain associated with giving birth, then tears of joy in the eyes of both parents. He noted the obvious delight of the people engaged in cleaning and inspecting the newborn infant child, which was giving loud voice to the indignity of such handling.

He brain scanned the infant and found it to be perfect in every way. He was somewhat surprised to find that the infant had somehow detected his intrusive presence, and had suddenly gone quiet. As the newborn child was placed into its mother's arms for the first time, the alien detected the shared feelings of comfort and bonding that were taking place. This, in itself, left him with another hitherto unknown sense, one of pleasurable satisfaction.

He had found the tiny infant brain to be devoid of all but basic instincts. It had yet to be corrupted in any way. He likened it to an empty computer that craved input. Communicating telepathically, he placed a somewhat pleasing image of himself into the child's mind. Then, as a parting gift, added a small gem of learning into the memory banks of the infant. This was something that would later emerge to her benefit, for he had recognised she was a girl child. Satisfied, he was about to move on from this environment when he overheard the whispered conversation between the parents. There was tenderness in their private words of affection for each other, accompanied by the touching and hugging, and then the kissing. He wondered what such physical contact felt like. In his loneliness, he wondered what it must feel like to be part of such an intimate relationship. What was the driving force behind all of this emotion?

The door of the hospital ward was flung open and two more, older children, erupted into the room to be instantly gathered into the arms of their welcoming parents. He watched as they were introduced to their new baby sister, who, he now learned, was to be called Emily. Their father formally introduced the twins, Peter and Rita, to the infant. The mother looked on with obvious feelings of pride and affection for her family, this reflected in her tear-filled eyes.

The alien recognised that a whole new window of opportunity to interact was being presented to him. Hitherto long suppressed emotional feelings were suddenly clawing their way back from the deepest recesses of his mind and into his being. They were making their presence immediately apparent. For the first time, he too began experiencing feelings and desires.

He liked what he saw, and he wanted to be a part of it. He wanted to help this human family in their daily struggle to live a reasonable life. To impart certain knowledge, teach, guide, and perhaps try to show them the errors of their ways. He realised the endless possibilities of such an undertaking, and for the first time, was unable to predict any sort of outcome or conclusion. It would all need great care and consideration . . . There, two more emotions he was previously unaware of. He found another as well, a joyous anticipation, and excitement, at the prospect of it all . . .

# Chapter 1

David Morrison-Lloyd parked his beautiful new Mercedes Taxi, his silver dream machine, in the lay-by outside of the Chase-side headquarters of J P Morgan, Bournemouth. He glanced at the clock and realised that he was 15 minutes early for his pick-up. Reclining the driver's seat a little, he decided to shut his eyes. The spring sunshine, warm on his face, quickly induced a feeling of pleasurable contentment, for David was rather happy with his lot. Despite the recession, things had been going quite well for him just lately. He let his thoughts drift back over turbulent events of the past few years. He contemplated all the happenings, good and bad, and attempted to try and pinpoint the factors that had contributed toward all his recent changes of fortune.

David and his school-day sweetheart, Sue Lloyd, had been together, as a couple, for fifteen years. They had met at a wild, girls only, party that had been gate crashed by David and some of his mates. It was more or less love at first sight despite some of the hurtful remarks from her snobby school friends referring to David as her 'grease-monkey' or 'bit of rough.' Their relationship had withstood the test of time, and after six months, they became proper lovers to celebrate Sue's sixteenth birthday.

Sue's parents, both senior partners with a leading Chamber of solicitors and barristers, in the City of London, had frowned upon their only daughter's infatuation with the handsome young motor mechanic, then Grenadier Guardsman. They considered that she could do better for herself and nagged at her to terminate the relationship in favour of their preferred choice, a rather meek and mild, well connected young gentleman, a pupil barrister, working out of their offices.

Both parents had badly underestimated the will and resolve of their daughter in making her own choices. A blazing family row had ensued culminating in Sue accusing them of bigotry, and they cutting off her allowance after she stormed out of the large family home in the Surrey stockbroker belt.

Living only on her fast dwindling savings, Sue, and a hitherto unknown girl who had advertised for a flat-mate, had moved into a tiny, rented, furnished apartment over the top of a second hand clothes shop in Chelsea. It was a dreadful time for her. She could no longer afford the running costs of her beloved little BMW Mini Cooper, and reluctantly had to sell it to pay off her mounting credit card debts.

The word 'economise' was not in Sue's vocabulary. The concepts were beyond her comprehension. Never before had she ever had to cook, clean or do the household chores. Despite her good education, the only employment Sue was able to find, was as a waitress in a local coffee shop. She hated it, but at least she was able to be nearer to her beloved David, in his Wellington Barracks. The angry young Sue had shunned and refused any contact with her parents for nearly a year. She blamed them entirely for her predicament.

It was David, fed up with constantly getting his ear bent, and now having to supplement Sue's income, that in desperation, finally managed to bring about, and affect the reconciliation. He succeeded in persuading Sue to invite her parents to the party being held to officially announce their engagement. The Lloyd's had pretended only to reluctantly accept. Neither were prepared to express their immense relief, for truth be known, they were both very much regretting their actions and desperately missing their only child.

David and Sue had often laughed about the time that both sets of parents were introduced to each other. Sue's mother, Edith, dressed in all her finery for the party, had proffered her white-gloved hand only to have it vigorously shaken by a big-bosomed woman, dressed all in black, and smothered in tiny mother-of-pearl sequins, her shoulders draped with an imitation, fox-fur stole.

Edith Lloyd, her face a picture to behold, managed to stammer, "We are pleased to make your acquaintance, Mr Morrison, Mrs Morrison, how are you both?"

"How-do m'ducks, nice t'meet cher, I'm sure. It's lovely day for it, innit?" David's mother and father were Londoners, Cockneys, working class with their own dialect, and born within the sound of the bells of St. Mary-le-Bow church.

The buxom, fun-loving Josie Riley, had become Mrs Albert Morrison when she jumped over the brush with her rather diminutive, fifth generation, baker's barrow-boy sweetheart. Having just celebrated their silver wedding anniversary, they both now ran and lived over the top of their very own, prosperous, home-baked bread, coffee, and patisserie outlet, in fashionable Chelsea.

Regarded by many to be 'salt of the earth,' Albert and Josie were both dressed in the traditional costume of the pearly King and Queen. Immensely proud of their roots, they looked the world in the face, said it as they saw it, and owed not a single penny to anyone. They lived each day like it was their last. Honest, hardworking common people, with Christian principles, they were afraid of no one.

It took quite a few glasses of ale and bubbly before David and Sue saw that Albert Morrison was clutching fondly at the backside of a rather giggly Edith Lloyd on the dance floor. Mr Lloyd, George, it seemed, was getting an ear full from a life-long supporter of the Gunners, regarding the number of black and foreign players now playing in the first team. If he had understood half of what he was being told, he would not have been nodding his every approval to all the vociferous opinions of Josie Morrison.

George Lloyd was to be forgiven, for his attention was directed elsewhere at the time. He was obviously more than a little concerned about the attention being paid to his wife by Albert Morrison, but he was in no position to intervene, at least not until he too found himself on the dance floor and doing the Lambeth Walk with Josie Morrison. The Lloyds still shudder with embarrassment with all the memories of that evening.

Their class background being so different, it was a big surprise to both children that their respective parents quickly became such very good friends. Invitations were routinely exchanged to any social function or gathering. The Lloyds found that the Morrisons were the life and soul of any party and always requested that they came dressed traditionally, mostly to amuse their other, pre-warned, guests. Another small factor that might also have had some bearing, was the Lloyds having asked their private investigators to conduct discreet enquiries as to the social standing and financial status of their prospective future In-laws. David's parents, the Morrisons, were found to be of exemplary character, not short of a bob or two, and the land with the shop on, was probably worth a couple of £million at today's prices.

The Morrisons were similarly tickled pink at the prospect of having a couple of 'nobs' in the family. They loved the plummy, Surrey accents and affectations, amusing many of their friends in the local pubs by imitating and taking a rise out of the Lloyd's voices and mannerisms.

Both sets of parents desperately wanted grandchildren that would bear their respective family names. Together they secretly began to make plans for a big wedding, but the culture gap was far too wide, and neither family could agree on the venue, guest list, order of service, and many other similar essentials.

Six months later, just to keep the peace, and much to the disgust and disapproval of both sets of parents, David and Sue announced that they had chosen to have their own, private, millennium wedding. The ceremony was to coincide with the welcoming in of the New Year. Nobody was officially invited, they were just advised when, and where, it would all take place. Be there if you liked . . .

At dawn, on the Millennium New Years Day, they were to be found on the pure white sand of a sun-kissed beach, located on a tiny coral island in the South Pacific. There, they had gathered together with a dozen other couples of a like mind. David and Sue expressed, and made their lifelong vows to each other in the presence of several hundred witnesses, all total strangers. Having proclaimed and promised, they then sealed their devotional commitments with the traditional exchange of wedding rings. It had all been so deeply moving and romantic . . .

The island, one of two that straddled the International Date Line, was the chosen venue for a huge international gathering. The game plan was to celebrate the new millennium on one island, for it was the first place on the planet to be able to do so. Then towards the end of the day, everyone took to the boats, and to travelled the couple of miles across to the other island, which lay on the other side of the International Date Line. This little island being the very last place on the planet to be able to start the New Year festivities. The beach partying had been non-stop for forty-eight hours.

David smiled to himself with the fond memories of their first nights spent together as man and wife. Now, Mr & Mrs Morrison-Lloyd, the hyphenated name being adopted to please the whims of their parents, the young newlyweds had chosen to make love on a carpet of palm fronds spread out on a deserted beach, and under the stars. It had been so lovely, idyllic, but the grains of sand had gotten into everywhere. It necessitated hours of careful mutual exploration, grooming, searching and cleaning in an improvised seawater bathtub, just to get rid of it all . . .

David tried to picture the faces of all the new friends they had made during the following two weeks of their honeymoon. Living simply in a veritable paradise, they spent their days making love, walking the beaches arm-in-arm, just chatting, and making plans for the future. Both were accomplished swimmers and qualified scuba divers, and they had snorkelled together in the crystal clear waters, gathering shellfish and crustaceans to be grilled or baked in the dying embers of the camp fire, then shared with the other newly-wed couples, that had similarly stayed on.

David found that the passage of time was taking its toll. Their images and names were becoming somewhat vague to his memory. He made a mental note to renew some old acquaintances when he found some spare time.

He squirmed in his seat. The nagging, constant pain from his old wounds still bothered him. It was a constant reminder as to the horrors of war. This was a chapter in his past life that David wished had never happened, and, but for his frequent periods of discomfort, would now rather forget, if he could.

David had completed his apprenticeship as a motor mechanic, or technician, with a leading BMW dealership in Holland Park in 1997. Already a TA Reservist in the Royal Engineers, there had been a slight lull in his relationship with Sue. He couldn't now remember why, but fed-up and seeking change and adventure, he decided on the spur of the moment to sign up for the Regular Army. He was delighted and surprised that when Sue eventually found out, she had approved. She apparently had a thing about men in uniform . . .

Having completed his mandatory nine months with the 2nd Battalion, Grenadier Guards, Nijmegen Company, David was about to be transferred to the 1st Battalion for active service abroad. Thinking that it might prolong his stay in the UK, and to be closer to Sue for their impending wedding, David had made application for Special Forces and had been immediately accepted for the gruelling training.

Early in 2002, now SAS, he was operational in Iraq. Working closely with US Forces on operation Telic, his covert mission was mainly intelligence gathering in Basrah, but his units' presence had already been noted. One evening, the unprotected civilian vehicle in which he was a passenger, was blown up by a roadside IED. His best mate, Tommy Carr, had been blown to pieces, but Tommy's torso had somehow protected David from the worst of the blast. He had survived, but had taken multiple shrapnel hits to his lower body.

Medivacced back to the UK, he was in a bad way. There had followed a long stay in hospital to deal with his injuries. David found it all difficult to remember. His hitherto fit, muscled young body had been reduced to a hideously burned and scarred wreck. The musculature had quickly wasted away during the weeks of fevered pain and inactivity.

On the road to recovery, it had taken many weeks of painfully determined physiotherapy just to get him back on his feet. The surgeons finally announced that they had done their very best for him, but it was still touch and go as to whether or not he would ever be able to father a child. He looked at himself in the mirror and sadly wondered if his beloved Sue would still find him physically attractive enough to ever want to make love again?

For the second time in her life, Sue's strength of character had been badly underestimated. She was absolutely devoted to her David, and cared little what he looked like physically. Starved of his affections, she longed to be back in his arms and made this abundantly apparent from the outset.

Out of necessity, their lovemaking, previously wild and passionate, had become something needing much more careful experimentation. It was a whole new pleasurable ball game.

On his discharge from hospital David was summoned to meet his CO. He announced that he had chosen to leave the Army despite the Regiment's offer to find him a suitable administrative post. Both Sue and the parents were influential in the decision-making, for they had all been beside themselves with the worry. David had realised that he probably might not have gotten through his ordeal, but for their loving support, and constant bedside presence. He felt obliged to seek their views and advice before making such an important career decision. The thought of being a desk-bound pen pusher, horrified him, and he doubted that he would be able to stick with it. He also felt that he had given more than enough of himself to the service of his Country and considered that, if anything, they owed him big time.

The MOD, in considering his compensation award, unfortunately didn't quite see it that way. He hadn't lost a limb, was not severely incapacitated, and was seemingly making a full recovery. It was basically just down to coping with the trauma and disfigurements. His offers of compensation, on the sliding scale of entitlement, were woefully inadequate in his view. They took an even further decline when Sue joyfully announced that she had at last become pregnant. The whole family were delighted, more so when the scan revealed that she was carrying twins, but David's claim was reduced even further, because he had now proved that he was capable of fathering a child.

'Bastards,' David had thought, but he knew that with the MOD, he was dealing with the civil servant mentality where everything was either black, or white, with no shades of grey to argue about . . .

A gentle tapping on the driver's side window interrupted his thoughts, and brought him back to the present. He sat up with a start. A familiar grinning face was looking at him through the glass. He dropped the window and smiled back, "Hello Rory, I'm sorry sir, I was daydreaming."

"Hello David. Are you here for me today? I have to go to Heathrow Terminal five."

"I'm your man, sir," replied David as he hurriedly exited the car to put his passengers luggage into the boot. He liked Rory McGregor, one of his regulars. David knew that Rory was an Account Manager with J P Morgan, a bit of a fitness freak, and an all-round good egg.

"Lovely car David, is this a new one?" Commented Rory as he slid into the back seat. David closed his door and got back into the driving seat.

"Yes sir, I took delivery and got it plated only last week. I'm afraid I'm still running it in, so we won't be breaking any speed records today. Do we have plenty of time, Sir?"

"My flight is scheduled to leave at 1430 and I'm already checked in on line, so, yes, I think we're okay David."

"Thank you sir. Is everything alright with you, how's the family?"

David and Rory had children of roughly the same age, but David secretly envied Rory's lifestyle and, in particular, his beautiful house, set well off the beaten track, in the lovely Dorset countryside. It was in stark contrast to the ex-council house that David and Sue had purchased in New Milton, a small town in the New Forest.

The imminent birth of the twins, Peter and Rita, in the spring of 2003, had prompted them to seek and provide a better quality of life for their new family. David had previously brought Sue down to the New Forest for a long weekend. They had stayed in a modestly priced hotel in Brockenhurst, while exploring the area.

The couple liked what they saw. The newly declared New Forest National Park, together with the unspoiled coastline, reflected the different pace of life adopted by the mostly retired people, that lived there. David's modest compensation payout had been enough to put down the deposit on the 1960's built, fairly spacious, three-bed semi. There had been just enough left over to buy a Peugeot 406 Estate car, to kick-start his own little taxi business. David did his apprenticeship contracting to a couple of well-established local taxi firms, but picking up old ladies and ferrying drunks around was not to his liking. He applied for his own Operators Licence, traded the Peugeot against a second hand Mercedes, and moved up-market, concentrating more on the 'executive' type of work.

David, an excellent driver, carefully negotiated the traffic lights and roundabouts, then hit the dual carriageways that led up onto the motorways. He took the speed up gently and smoothly to 60mph, just under 2000rpm, then engaged the cruise control.

The in-car conversation with Rory touched upon their respective families, wives, the children growing up, sport, politics, the recession and all the usual things that two young fathers would normally discuss. Rory knew all about David's military background and the terrible wounds he had sustained. He expressed his delight that David's luck appeared to be 'on the up' what with a new car and all . . .

"I couldn't have done it without the help from my In-laws," David confided. "They have decided to give Sue a gift of three grand each year as part of her inheritance. Some tax avoidance thing that you probably know more about than I, Rory. It couldn't have come at a better time, though. Sue was going to have to get us another car to run the kids to school. We decided that she should have my old Merc, and

I should get a new one, lease hire, for the business. I still keep the old one plated, though, I might need to use it occasionally. Y'know, it's a funny thing Rory, but it seems that just when Sue and I find ourselves struggling a bit, something always seems to turn up for us. I reckon him upstairs must be looking out for us . . ."

David dropped Rory off at his destination with plenty of time to spare. His return trip was to pick up an elderly couple, coming back from a Bangkok holiday, into the South Terminal at Gatwick. The M25 drive of about forty miles to the other airport was largely uneventful, and he took it at a very leisurely pace. It also afforded him further time for his reflections.

David realised that his off-the-cuff comment he had made to Rory, about someone upstairs watching over him, could almost have been true. There had been several strokes of good fortune just lately. The first was shortly into the early spring of 2007, when Sue announced that she was again pregnant. They had been trying for another child for several months. Peter and Rita, by then nearly five, were still a bit of a handful, but they were just about to be starting school. Sue's pregnancy had gone particularly well and little Emily made her September entry into the world with the minimum of fuss and bother, an easy delivery. David had jokingly remarked to Sue that she was getting to be 'a bit of an old hand at it' and got a playful slap for his cheek.

Emily has blonde hair and beautiful, big brown eyes, like her Dad, while Peter and Rita are brunette and their eyes, blue/green, like their Mum. So little 'Em' as she came to be referred to by all the family, was always going to be a little bit different somehow. And so it was . . .

Sue had found difficulty in breast-feeding the twins. She found that she was unable to produce enough milk to satisfy her children's lusty appetites, and her nipples became very sore and painful in the constant effort. She had found that it was necessary to supplement their diet with powdered milk, eventually weaning them onto it completely.

Sue knew the importance of any newborn infant taking milk from its mother in the first few hours of life. Quite apart from the bonding process, she'd read somewhere that there were important anti-bodies or some essential substances in the mother's milk that would provide a natural resistance to infections. Little Emily, she found, was very gentle on the nipple and as she suckled contentedly, Sue whispered to her in terms of encouragement and endearment, like many mothers do.

There is a short period after a child's birth when the eyes appear to be watery and unable to focus properly. It varies in the time it takes for the child to overcome this, but one day, a parent will notice that the infant has achieved this milestone, and is actually looking at them properly through focused eyes. Recognition is born.

Not so with Emily, though. Sue had noticed from day one that her baby, while still sucking eagerly at the nipple, was also looking her straight in the eye, and seemed to be drinking in every little thing that Sue was saying. It was uncanny, even a little scary at times. She told David about it, and both sets of parents, amused and enthralled, watched the child as Sue cooed lovingly over her.

"She's probably only taking comfort from the sound of your voice, love. She is obviously far too young to be able to comprehend the meaning of your words, but it certainly looks as though she does. Keep on doing it though, try reading her little stories, or nursery rhymes. After all, it can't hurt can it? It might even help her later on, when she starts learning to talk, who knows?"

"You don't think there might be something wrong with her do you, David?"

"Like what, love?"

"Well, I don't know. This is not what you would call normal child behaviour, is it? Perhaps some form of autism or something? Should we get her tested, do you think?"

David, taken aback, had to think for a few moments.

"Sue, love, she's only six weeks old. I'm not sure that there is even a test for that sort of thing at her age. Look at her. To all outward appearances, Emily's a perfectly normal and very beautiful little child. Stop worrying for goodness sake; I'm pretty sure she's okay. Lets just carry on as normal for a while. She might prove to be a child genius, who knows?"

They both chuckled at the thought, and even discussed the possibilities of such a revelation. Emily, meanwhile, still sucking contentedly at the breast, just appeared to be listening.

*I am sensing that your parents suspect there is something wrong with you Emily. I think you should endeavour to behave more in keeping with a normal human infant, and try not to cause them concern.*

*'I don't know how a normal human infant should behave, Jojo. Can you teach me please?'*

*I'm not sure either, little one, but I will do some more research to see if I can find an answer to the problem. Meanwhile, it might help to watch Peter and Rita, perhaps, if their behaviour is normal, you could try to follow their example.*

*'Yes Jojo, I will try to do that. Thank you.'*

David slotted the car into a double parking space in the short-term car park at Gatwick South Terminal. He deliberately chose to park on the less busy upper levels, because of the several incidents of minor damage to the car paintwork in the past. That's the big problem these days he thought to himself, nobody seems to care about anybody else's property. The world would be a much better place if people were more polite and considerate toward each other. He took the stairway rather than the lift, and then the path alongside the moving walkway into the South Terminal. He felt better for having stretched his aching legs after the long drive.

A glance at the 'Arrivals' board told him that the Bangkok flight was 'baggage in hall' already. He smiled and congratulated himself for his timely arrival. The Hart's, Doug and Freda, would be coming through very soon now. He didn't need his name-board. They were regulars, and very well known to him. Settling on a good vantage point to see passengers coming through into the Arrivals Hall, he took the weight off his feet by hitching his backside up onto one of the high stools in front of the coffee shop. Someone had left part of a Sunday newspaper on the counter. David pulled it towards himself and idly scanned through the several pages. There was little of interest; it was full of the political parties squaring up to each other in the forthcoming election. He had little time for any politicians; they were all the same to him, a bunch of conniving, lying bastards, all out to feather their own nests at the expense of the taxpayer. If he had his way he'd sack the whole bloody incompetent lot of them, then find all the best brains in the country to fill all the Ministerial positions irrespective of their particular political leaning. Pay an attractive salary, put them on two-year contracts with fixed objectives. As for the one-eyed, Scottish slime-ball currently in No10, well, he'd be the first one up against the wall come the revolution . . . David smiled at the thought, and rubbed his aching thigh, 'damn them all' he muttered and pushed the paper away in his disgust. Whatever has happened to one of the greatest manufacturing countries the world has ever seen? Where did the slogan 'British is best' disappear to? "God I wish I was in charge" he murmured out loud. He realised his outburst had attracted the curious attention of another Taxi driver, similarly seated a few feet to his left. David smiled at him and indicated to the newspaper.

"Damned politicians. Sorry mate, but they make my blood boil. There isn't one with an ounce of honesty or integrity."

The man smiled back in understanding, "Yeh, that'd be right pal, that'd be right." He buried his nose back into his coffee cup in apparent disinterest at any further discourse on the subject.

Embarrassed slightly, David returned to his thoughts. 'God almighty, what is wrong with me today? I certainly got out on the wrong side this morning, didn't I. What's brought all this on? Come on Davy boy, snap out of it, let's think about something else instead.'

The Hart's came through pushing a huge pile of luggage. David moved to intercept them, they hadn't yet looked in his direction.

"I suppose you two would like a lift home, would you?"

They turned to the sound of his voice, their faces reflecting joyous relief at his presence.

"David, my boy. You don't know how good it is to see you. We have been through an absolute nightmare, I can tell you. Do you know we were both stuck in our hotel room for a whole week. Couldn't go out, it wasn't safe. We could see all the rioting from our window. It was terrible."

David took the luggage trolley from the effusive Mr Hart.

"Let's get you and Freda in the car then, Doug, and you can tell me all about it on the way home. You're both looking just about all-in, and I expect you'd very much appreciate a proper cup of tea, by now?"

"Got it in one. Lead on David, my boy, we're all yours . . ."

The journey back to Barton-on-Sea was largely plain sailing. It wasn't quite rush hour yet, but the M25 and M3 traffic was slowly building up towards it. David put the car in the nearside lane and set the cruise to 60mph. He only needed to move out just a few times to pass the occasional slower moving heavy goods vehicle. He knew that travelling in this manner was easy on both the car and driver. It was also amazing how quickly a steadily maintained speed gobbled up the miles.

He listened patiently while Doug and Freda narrated their nightmare holiday experiences. He made all the right noises in all the right places, but was somewhat relieved when it all started to tail off. They had never once asked him about Sue and the children, but what did it matter, they were a lovely old couple. He stole a glance in his rear view, and was pleased to see that they were both nodding off. The luxurious warmth and almost silent hum of the car, coupled with a lovely smooth drive, often induced that effect on his passengers. He smiled to himself and realised that he was quite proud in being able to provide that simple pleasure for the people that he liked.

His mind went back to the subject of his recent good fortune.

David was delighted when Sue had decided to return to her studies with the Open University and try again for her accountancy qualifications. At home, Sue was running the office, doing the bookwork and taking bookings for the taxi business. She was already a great help to him, and had even acquired her taxi badge, so that she too could drive if circumstances ever required it. Sue explained her decision pointing out that she would soon have more time to spare when the twins started school. She estimated that if she could devote about three hours a day to study, with luck, she would be able to qualify within two years. David knew better than to argue, but did question whether little Emily, now a toddler, might not up take more of her time?

"David, she is such a little angel. She is never any trouble. If I put her in her playpen, she sits there watching what I do, and listening to everything I'm saying. I swear she understands all that I'm telling her. I've even taken to doing a running commentary on all of my actions just to keep her amused. She never plays with toys like the twins used to. I've watched her pick up one of Rita's dolls, examine it carefully, and then put it to one side. I think she somehow worked out that it was something inanimate, and was therefore of no further interest to her. If I leave her alone in her cot, she doesn't worry about it. She will just lie down and gaze vacantly up at the ceiling. Sometimes I hear her chuckling to herself and gurgling unintelligibly. She still worries me a bit David, I'm sure there is something not quite right in that tiny little head of hers."

"Sue, we've been over all this before. Emily is barely a year old. Just look at her. Does she look abnormal in any way? Is she reflecting any of the classic symptoms of autism? I agree that her talking is a bit slow, and sometimes, I too wonder just what goes on in her tiny mind, but I am absolutely sure that we have nothing to worry ourselves about."

"She's teething David, her gums are looking very sore, but she doesn't cry at all. Okay, she won't eat anything hard at the moment, that's understandable, and she's a bit off with twins, that too. I just can't quite put a finger on it all, David, but it doesn't seem right to me, it just isn't normal child behaviour."

"Who are you comparing her to, Sue? The twins? They were a nightmare at her age. Do you recall your frustrations in trying to get Peter to crawl, and to pee in his potty? Or all those sleepless nights when we were trying to get Rita to sleep through, without crying to come in our bed? Yes, of course you do. Does Em do any of those things? The answer is 'No' and we should be thankful for it. She is a brilliant child, no trouble at all, but if it will put your mind at rest, let's try and make an appointment with a child psychologist, or behavioural expert, of some sort. You can't be concentrating on your studies if you are worrying like this, can you?"

"I wouldn't know where to start with anything like that, David. Dr. Salmon I suppose, but I hope she doesn't think I'm some sort of paranoid mother when I tell her how perfect Emily is. She might make an appointment for me instead."

They chuckled at the thought. David embraced Sue and kissed her tenderly. Emily watched her parents in silence.

*You need to develop your language skills Emily. It is important that you begin to communicate verbally.*

*'Why do I need to be able to do this Jojo? If I can learn everything from you and we can communicate with each other. I don't need to be able to speak, do I?'*

*We are communicating in a way that is no longer possible by most humans, Emily. From your birth, I opened parts of your mind to impart certain knowledge to you, and I made parts of me available for you to access. Yes, we can communicate, but you are reading my thought waves, and that does not require you to learn any particular language. You will be able to understand the thoughts of any human as soon as you can train your mind to lock on to, and interpret, their particular brain wave patterns. But you will still need to develop and master the spoken language skills, in order to communicate normally with others of your kind, Emily. This is something that you can only achieve for yourself, for I cannot help you with this. It is no longer possible for me to speak or communicate in this manner. Your intelligence quotient is already far greater than that of most humans and it is a fairly simple matter for you to learn to use vocal communication. Indeed, it is a skill that every normal human child will learn in the first few years of its life. I sense that your parents are concerned that you are not learning to speak, Emily. We should try and allay their fears, shouldn't we?*

*'Yes all right Jojo, I will try and learn to speak. I love you Jojo, you won't ever leave me will you?'*

*I will always be here for you Emily.*

Love was something the alien was unfamiliar with. His data banks contained little information on this hitherto little investigated human trait. He recognised only that it was something deeply emotional. His limited encyclopaedic knowledge told him that it was "to have a passionate desire, longing, and feeling for something" but he was left struggling when trying to comprehend the full meaning of Emily's words, when they were directed toward him.

His short relationship with this tiny infant humanoid had been interesting up until now. He had enjoyed carefully imparting tiny pieces of knowledge into the very limited capacity of Emily's mind, but he sensed that there was something else, much larger and beyond even his comprehension, in there as well.

What he didn't know was that his unique sensory perceptions had, so far, been unable to unlock the complex part of her mind that controlled all her basic feelings. This particular aspect of the brain was part of normal human development. It was to be shaped, nurtured, and guided by all the love and tenderness experienced by the child in her early, formative years.

Long suppressed in his own being, it was the very part of him that was now struggling to emerge. Coupled with it all came the realisation that there was so much more to learn about humans.

Emily sat quietly in her playpen watching Peter and Rita as they played on the floor beside her. The children had an old pack of playing cards all spread out, face down, on the carpet. They were playing a simple game called 'pairs.' This involved alternately turning over two cards to make a matching pair. If the player failed to make a pair, the cards would be replaced face down, in the same position. The secret was in remembering where, in the mass of cards, each number was to make the required pair.

Rita was always slightly better at this than Peter, who quickly tired of the game if he couldn't win occasionally.

David, comfortable with his feet up, was reading his paper, Sue sat at the dining table struggling to concentrate on some boring accountancy textbook. She glanced up at the children as Peter made some accusing comment to his sister.

"Come on you two, play quietly, or you can both take it up to your bedroom. Your father and I don't want to be listening to your incessant bickering all the time."

"But she's cheating, Mum. She knows where all the cards are."

"But that is the whole idea of the game, Peter. You must try and remember where you turned them over. Rita can't be cheating, she is just remembering better than you."

"She is cheating, Mum. Emily is telling her. I am playing against both of them, it's not fair."

"That is enough Peter. Emily is only a baby. She cannot possibly be doing what you say. She can't speak and probably doesn't even understand the game you are playing."

"She does Mum, she tells Rita if it's the right card by slapping her hands on her legs. It's not fair, I'm not playing anymore."

Peter got up from the floor and went to sit in front of the TV.

Intrigued, Sue left what she was doing and lifted Emily from her playpen. They sat down with Rita on the floor, Emily between her legs.

"Alright little one, let's see if Peter's right." Sue turned over a six. There were twenty-nine other cards left to choose from. She moved her hand slowly over the cards watching Emily all the time. As she reached the right hand extremity, Emily slapped her little legs and excitedly and made a happy gurgling sound.

"This one Em? You want me to turn this one over?" Emily slapped at her legs excitedly. Sue flipped the card over . . . it was another six.

"My God, she did it David, did you see that? Emily did it, she picked the right one. I swear she did it. Clever girl Emily, can you do it again? Watch this David."

David put his paper aside as Sue turned another card face up, this time it was the queen of hearts. Sue slowly moved her hand over the remaining twenty-seven cards while watching Emily all the time. There was no reaction until her hand got back to the face-up card. Emily again slapped enthusiastically at her little knees.

"What this one Emily, the card beside, is that the one I should turn over?"

Little Emily was beside herself with agitated excitement. Sue flipped the card; it was the queen of clubs. The colour drained from Sue's face as she gazed incredulously upon her tiny baby.

"No, it's not possible is it David? She's barely a year old. She can't be doing that at her age. Tell me its just coincidence."

"I don't know Sue. Here let me have a go with Emily, see if she can do it again, for me this time."

Sue and David changed places on the floor.

"Come on Em, do another one for Daddy." David reached forward and randomly turned over the ace of diamonds.

"I know that one, let me, let me do it, Dad," squealed Rita excitedly.

"Just a minute Rita, we just want to see if Emily can do it. Besides, it's still her turn, isn't it."

David moved his hand slowly over the remaining twenty-five playing cards looking all the time for some reaction from Emily, there was nothing. After about half a minute, David turned another card at random, it wasn't a match. Rita seized the opportunity and quickly matched the ace of diamonds with the ace of spades, but failed on her next go.

There were now twenty-four cards left on the table and it was Emily's turn again. Sue couldn't bear not to be involved. She was back on the floor with David and her daughters again.

"Come on Em, try and do another one for Mummy. Which card should I turn over first?" Sue moved her hand over the cards looking for her baby daughter to do something. There was nothing, no reaction at all. Emily was staring intently ahead, her mind seemingly elsewhere. Sue lifted her over and gently bounced her in her lap whispering her name.

"Emily, Emily . . . Come on baby, play with Mummy now, there's a good girl. Look at Rita. She wants you to play some more. Which card Emily? Tell me baby . . ."

Emily turned her tiny face and looked into her mother's eyes. She stretched up her arms obviously seeking a cuddle, as far as Emily was concerned, the game was over.

*Have a care Emily. You are displaying behaviour that is not what your parents expect of you. I can see that you are gaining some pleasure from this simple game, but it would be prudent not to show yourself to be too clever. Your parents already sense that you may be slightly different to your siblings. Perhaps it would be wiser not to make your advanced development too apparent until a little later in your life.*

*'Oh, Jo-jo, Mummy and Daddy are both enjoying watching me play, they think I am such a clever girl and I like that . . . Do I have to stop playing?'*

*Give your Mummy a cuddle Emily, she will like that even more. Demonstrate your affection, it will help to put her mind at rest. If you really want to please your parents, try to concentrate on learning to speak your language. I sense that this particular aspect of your development is causing them some concern.*

Emily's first birthday was celebrated in the traditional way with the single candle being extinguished with a rather wet-blown raspberry. It was a time of great excitement for all the family. Emily, much to the delight of everyone, had suddenly found her tongue. Almost on a daily basis, her vocabulary was increasing, as was her diction and enunciation. Baby words were not for Emily, with the guidance of her delighted parents, she was quickly learning to express herself in the proper way.

David loved to sit with the children, Emily usually on his lap, and read them a bedtime story. As he read the words, he moved his index finger across the page pointing to the particular word he was reading. In this way, David knew that the children would come to recognise a whole word, rather than having to break it down into individual syllables, in order to enunciate. It did not go unnoticed that little Em was following all of this very intently. David sometimes stopped on a particular word to see if the children would read it for him. It was not only a much-enjoyed little game, but also a measure of their concentration, comprehension and reading ability. If they got it wrong, he playfully chided them, but always corrected their error before moving on. Peter and Rita, always trying to outdo each other and impress their father, were soon able to read books meant for children far in advance of their age group. Emily, despite her considerable age difference, and unbeknown to her parents, was not that far behind.

Peter and Rita, now nearly seven years old, were eagerly anticipating starting at Junior School at the beginning of September. Their intellectual development had reached the stage where one of them was beginning to emerge as somewhat brighter than the other. Peter found that he was struggling to keep up with Rita in the sibling rivalry stakes. In the many games they played that involved thought and calculation, Rita usually emerged the victor. Much to his disgust, Peter couldn't even come close to Rita's score in a game of Scrabble, and rarely won at Draughts, or card games. Rita was definitely much quicker and brighter than her brother, and took great delight in the approbation of their parents whenever she excelled.

To compensate, Peter, fast becoming a bad loser, tried to excel in the physical. He was proving to be quite an accomplished little footballer, endlessly practicing his ball skills, alone, whenever he got the chance. It also meant that he could avoid playing what he now considered to be 'stupid board games' with his sister.

Rita rose to his challenge. She was determined not to let him get the better of her in any way, shape, or form. Her longer legs and lighter body frame allowed her to easily outrun her brother and she gave a very good account of herself in the frequent wrestling bouts that arose following a disagreement between them. Peter's superior strength would inevitably dictate the outcome, but he knew that his sister was no pushover and respected her as such.

Despite their rivalry, they remained very close, and loved each other dearly. Their relationship with each other could best be described as sharing and caring. They confided with each other in all their little problems, worries or secrets. One or the other instinctively knew if there was something amiss. Askance or enquiry as to the problem was unnecessary, for the first person that either would confide in was the other.

To the casual onlooker, this would hardly seem be surprising, for it is generally recognised that between many twins, there is some form of extra sensory communication. This phenomenon was much apparent between Peter and Rita, and had already been noticed by their parents and the rest of the family. Without even realising it, the children had developed some sort of unspoken rapport where it was possible for each to know, or be aware of, what the other was thinking or feeling.

Such togetherness can only be ascribed to children who have shared the same space in their mother's womb, and have grown up together since birth. It was not something that could easily be extended to include their younger sister, and they were both aware of this. It would seem that Peter and Rita, being twins, and a few years older, would never be able to regard Emily in the same light that they saw each other.

They had quietly talked about it and generally agreed that they loved having little Em as a sister, but both had recognised that there was something about her that neither could quite comprehend, or get to grips with.

During the summer of 2010, the erupting Icelandic volcanoes, closely followed by the British Airways cabin crew strikes, all played absolute havoc with David's little taxi business. Cancellations, re-scheduling, and late flight arrivals all became commonplace, and resulted in a considerable loss of earnings.

On the spur of the moment, with no bookings to fulfil, David and Sue decided to take a few days off during the latter part of the school summer holiday break. They booked into a small bed and breakfast, The Bide-a-wee, in Weymouth. They were allocated two spacious, and very comfortable adjoining rooms on the first floor of a very large, partially modernised, Victorian guesthouse in the Old Harbour. It was conveniently situated only a couple of roads back from the beach.

The elderly owners, Jim and Doris Cox, were lifelong friends of David's parents. The couple, when young newly-weds, had been forced to temporarily move out of London during the blitz when a buzz bomb, or doodlebug, destroyed half of the street that they had called their home.

After the war, Weymouth's historic charm and appeal had won their hearts, and, although they kept in touch, and visited neighbours in old London as often as possible, they never felt the desire to return to their Cockney roots.

Now well into their eighties, the couple had more or less passed the day-to-day running of their busy little Guest House over to their only daughter, Sharon. Thirty-five and unmarried, she had been fostered, and then adopted, by the Cox's as a teenager.

After the untimely death of her parents, in a tragic road accident, when she was very young, Sharon had had a very hard time of it. She had become a difficult child, handed back by foster parents on several occasions for being too unruly.

On reaching her teens, she had frequently run away from care and foster homes, and had even taken to living rough on the streets of Southampton. Inevitably, in order to eat, she had drifted into petty crime and drugs, before coming to the notice of the Police. After several appearances, the Courts, very limited in their options, had repeatedly placed her back into the care of the local authority and their disgusting institutions. It had been a never-ending circle of misery for her.

The final placement, with the Cox's as foster parents, was only meant to be temporary. Just until she reached the age where she could be regarded as an adult and support herself. The hard-pressed authorities were, by now, keen to discharge their statutory obligations, and wash their hands of her completely.

It had proved to be the best thing that ever happened in her hitherto miserable existence. The Cox's had shown her every consideration, kindness and regard, things she had never previously experienced. Being trusted, given a generous allowance and a comfortable home, were suddenly all hers, with no strings attached. With it, and above all else, came a genuine love and affection toward her.

In a show of heartfelt gratitude for being taken in, Sharon had reciprocated by devoting the whole of her life to the care of her elderly stepparents, and the running of their little business.

Now a very attractive, slim, green-eyed redhead, Sharon found that she was uncomfortable in the company of men. In the past, she had only ever been regarded as a sex plaything, for life on the streets had been hard, the memories painful. There had been many bad experiences. Shunning male company completely, she had struggled to come to terms with her sexuality. The fact that she despised men, led her into believing that she might have lesbian tendencies? As such, she had never experienced any meaningful relationship with anyone else of either sex, but it didn't seem to worry her that much. She buried herself in the day-to-day running of the B&B.

The Cox's, and Sharon, occupied the basement rooms of the B&B property together with Sharon's beautiful, three-year-old golden retriever, Sam.

From the moment that the children arrived, and were introduced to Sam, it was a mutual love at first sight. Sam absolutely revelled in all the extra attention being afforded to him, not to mention the added attraction of the many little titbits of biscuit that was surreptitiously slipped his way when Sharon wasn't looking. He reciprocated by seeking to spend all his time in the company of his newfound benefactors, whatever they chose to be doing. Dog and children quickly became virtually inseparable. The Cox's were only too pleased to grant permission when they were asked if Sam could come and spend some time with the family, playing on the beach.

Under David's watchful eye, the twins and Sam immediately took to playing in the shallows, throwing a tennis ball for the dog to retrieve, then digging great holes in the beach with buckets and spades.

Sue, holding her daughter by the hand, introduced Emily to the pleasures of paddling, making a game of quickly scurrying back, laughing and squealing, as the gentle swell threatened to engulf their legs.

The strength of the morning sunshine gradually increased prompting Sue to break out and administer large dollops of sun screening cream, and huge, stupid-looking floppy hats, much to the delight of the twins. The interval also afforded a convenient opportunity for everyone to partake of a large drink of luke-warm squash, and a gritty jam sandwich.

With dire warnings from Sue, Peter and Rita, who were keen to get back to their sandcastles, were forbidden to venture out of her sight under any circumstance. They scampered away, back down to the waterside, leaving David comfortable in a deckchair, to the quiet contemplation of the sporting pages of his newspaper.

Sue fussed over Emily. She busied herself in carefully erecting a large beach umbrella and arranging a beach towel so that they would be shaded. She then allowed Emily and Sam to curl up, close together, and shut their eyes to the rest of world.

Sue, finally satisfied with all her arrangements, pulled one of her accountancy textbooks from her bag. She turned onto her stomach, letting loose her bikini top back strap.

"Rub me in some cream, please David," she murmured. David willingly set to his task, both of them finding a mutual enjoyment in the erotic sensation of his tender ministrations to her back and legs.

"Have you noticed how much the children have enjoyed having Sam around, David?"

"Hmm, kids and dogs go together, don't they? I was the same with Dolly when I was their age. It broke my heart when she had to be put down, though."

David moved back to his deckchair, picked up his paper and shook off the sand. He tried to find the point where he had left off reading.

"Sam and Em seem to be particularly besotted with each other, don't they? I really think that having him around is good for her. Have you seen how he looks at Em, head on one side, almost as if he and she were communicating in some way? I was watching them last evening, it was all a little bit spooky really."

"Hmm, really? Can't say I noticed anything particular," David turned to a new page.

"Emily has some funny little ways, hasn't she David? Do you know that, sometimes, when I am alone at home with her, I get the strangest sensation that she is somehow messing with my head? I suddenly become aware that she is trying to get my attention. When I turn to look at her, she is always staring at me intently. The funny thing is, it usually means that she wants me to do something for her, and I even know what it is she wants me to do. I can't really explain it any better than that, but it happens all the time now. It is the oddest feeling, David, really weird."

David set his paper aside.

"Y'know, now that you come to mention it, Sue, I think that I've have had the same sort of thing happen to me, once or twice. I've not said anything in case you thought I was cracking up, heading for the loony bin, or something. Perhaps there is something she is able to do, what do you call it? ESP or something? If it happens again, it might be interesting for us to try and be more receptive, if that's the right word. Let's see where it takes us Sue. Can't do any harm, can it?"

Sue thought for a bit. "You don't think it might be something to do with autism, you know, what we talked about before, do you David? Em really worries me sometimes, she is so different, somehow."

David thought for a bit and Sue was aware that he was choosing his words carefully.

"We've been over all this ground already, Sweetheart. Emily is proving to be a very intelligent, beautiful, healthy little girl. Okay, she does things that, to us, appear to be a little bit odd, different somehow, to what we have come to expect, but I really don't think there is anything wrong with her. Her walking, talking and intellectual development has come on in leaps and bounds over the past few months. How about we both stop looking for problems that probably don't exist. Why not concentrate more on what we are both experiencing and see exactly what, if anything, our little daughter is trying to do. Let's see where, if there is anywhere, she is able to take us? This is unknown territory for us both, and I can't see that it will hurt to just go with the flow for a while, will it Sue? Who knows, we might both be pleasantly surprised?"

Sue thought for a bit then looked up and into the face of her husband.

"I love you David, you know that, and I trust your opinion and judgement in all things. OK, if you think this is the right thing for us to do, then I will go along with it. But can I suggest that we give it six months, keep a diary for reference, and, if at any time either of us feels in any way uncomfortable with anything, we immediately seek some sort of professional advice?"

"Sounds like a plan to me, darling, but you keep the diary, I've got quite enough to write about already. Running a taxi business generates more paperwork than enough. I was already thinking though, that it might be a good idea to get a dog of our own to start with? Obviously, we will need to sound out the twins, first, but I can't imagine they will say 'no' do you?" What do you say?"

Sue laughed, any reply to the suggestion was rudely interrupted by the untimely and mischievous arrival of her other errant offspring, and a bucket of cold seawater.

The precious few days were all spent in a similar fashion, the children quite content to amuse themselves playing on the beach, building ever more complicated sand structures, only to see them flattened by the incoming tides.

Playing in the warm seawater, Peter, already a natural little swimmer, encouraged Rita to discard her armbands, and to manage without them. Both parents watched with some trepidation, ready to move in at the slightest hint of any trouble, but by the third day, it was apparent that Rita was becoming nearly as competent in the water as her brother. The sibling rivalry, still very apparent, even in their play.

Sue found contentment in getting herself an even suntan while working at her accountancy books. This left David to amuse Emily playing in the sand, building sandcastles, which were immediately demolished by Sam, much to Emily's delight.

It had not gone unnoticed that she and Sam had become almost inseparable by this time. The dog was found one morning asleep on Emily's bed, her arms wrapped fondly around his neck as they slept. No one had been able to keep them apart, wherever they were, Emily seemed to be chatting away, unintelligibly, to Sam who sat staring at her intently. He would sometimes give a little bark, whine or whimper as if in response, which to the quietly watching adults, indicated that there must be some form of communication taking place that they didn't understand.

David, having settled Emily into her afternoon nap with Sam, found it difficult to concentrate on his paper. He gazed thoughtfully at his daughter wondering just what was going on in that tiny little head of hers? Try as they may, he and Sue had been unable to understand any of the words that Emily was apparently using to communicate, if indeed she was, with Sam. Their interaction was fascinating and slightly spooky to observe, indeed, even amusing. The dog was obviously concentrating intently on what Emily was apparently saying, even to the point of displaying differing expressions and responses to her words. Whatever was taking place, it was all totally beyond their comprehension. Sharon confessed that in all her years as a dog breeder and handler, she had never seen, or heard, of anything quite like it before. David began to feel a little apprehensive about the consequences of having to separate them when it was time to go home? He instinctively felt that something urgently needed to be put into place before that moment arrived.


Sharon had given David details of a lady friend of hers, another dog breeder, who lived close by in Whyke Regis. She had a litter of Springer Spaniel puppies that were about ready for weaning. A quick phone call had arranged an evening viewing.

Without telling the children where they were going, they all set off, ostensibly for a short walk just to help their dinner go down. Much to Emily's disappointment, Sharon had already taken Sam out for his evening walk, so that there was no danger of him wanting to tag along.

At first sight, the semi-detached house in Marlborough Avenue showed signs of needing a bit of a makeover to bring it back to it's former glory. The owner, Laura Dobson, a widow in her early sixties, was obviously expecting them, and was found pottering around in the small front garden. She quickly endeared herself with the children by introducing them to her own little companion, an overfriendly and slightly overweight, Springer spaniel named Judy. The children were immediately delighted and quickly became infatuated as Judy sniffed and danced all around their feet and legs in the manner common to the breed. Their joy knew no bounds, as they were conducted to a garage at the side of the property where inside, in a small caged off area, had been constructed a makeshift whelping pen. It was kept warmly illuminated by infrared lights, for there, huddled into a tangled mass, was a litter of seven delightful little bundles of mischief.

"Three dogs and four bitches," murmured Mrs Dobson to David and Sue, as she pointed out which was which, in the melee of excitedly little canine bodies, now clamouring for attention as the children squatted down offered their fingers through the wire.

"If you were to select one from the litter now, I can keep it for you for another couple of weeks. They haven't had all their injections yet, and I won't let them go until they have. What did you want, dog or bitch? Dogs will be cheaper. I will give you all the pedigree certificates. Are you going to breed? Do you want the tails docked, that'll be extra of course?"

"Whoa, slow down Mrs Dobson. We don't know anything yet. We are only here to see the litter at the moment. We were considering getting a pet for the children, that's all. As for exactly what we get, no decisions have yet been made. Sue and I will need to talk about this with the children before we make any more plans in that respect."

"Oh, I was under the impression that you were coming to choose one of the litter tonight, that's what Sharon said, I can't afford to wait too long. You are getting the first pick of the litter, Mr Lloyd, and I will be advertising them for sale very shortly. If you want one, you had better let me know ASAP, my litters always get snapped up pretty quickly. I have a good reputation in the dog breeding community, you know."

David had noticed that her attitude had subtly switched from being like a kindly old soul, to that of the hard-nosed businesswoman. He found himself taking a bit of a dislike to Mrs Dobson's attitude and turned away from her before saying something that he perhaps might regret.

"Look at Emily, David," whispered Sue. "What is she doing, do you think?"

Emily was kneeling down and staring intently into the eyes of one of the litter, which had separated itself from the rest. The little pup was standing on its back legs, with its front paws resting on the wire mesh, occasionally whimpering. David could see that the pup's attention was entirely focused on Emily, who was quietly muttering something quite unintelligible. It was as if pup and child were somehow communicating with each other.

Emily turned to look at her father, her face a picture of concern and consternation. David looked directly into her eyes. He squatted down to be nearer and took her little hand as a comforting gesture. As their eyes met, a thought and a picture had come into his mind. From that, he immediately knew that all was not what it seemed, something was very wrong here, somewhere. He looked questioningly at Em again, and received another image. He now knew exactly what it was. He lifted Emily up into his arms. Grim faced, and suddenly angry, David turned back to his host.

"Mrs Dobson, can you give me some information on the sire of the litter, please. Is it a working dog, a gun dog perhaps?" David saw her eyes reflect surprise at the question.

"The dog is a four-year-old champion, now put to stud. He belongs to a friend of mine. He has an excellent pedigree, and was second runner up to best of breed at Crufts last year. It will all be on the pedigree certificate, Mr Lloyd. Why do you ask?"

"Oh, you know, Mrs Dobson. One hears such horrendous stories about unscrupulous people and puppy farms in Wales and Ireland. I'm no expert on these things, but I've noticed that Judy, the mother, seems to show surprisingly little interest in her litter. I would have expected her to be more keen to get in the pen with them, instead of just sitting back and watching like that."

"The pups are being weaned, Mr Lloyd. I have started them on puppy food solids. I find that it is better for the litter, and Judy, for them to be kept apart at this time."

David had noticed a subtle change in her body language. Her comment to him was made as she stooped to fondle Judy's ears, a gesture that made it unnecessary for her to look directly at David when she spoke. She was uncomfortable with his questions, that much was evident, so, he decided to push it a little further.

"Tell me Mrs Dobson, how exactly does it all work then? You tell me that the pups are Judy's litter and that their father is some highbrow show champion, but how do we, as potential purchasers, know that this is all kosher and correct? Is there perhaps some sort of DNA testing that will verify this? If not, then the information, given by you on the pedigree, becomes rather meaningless, surely?"

"Mr Lloyd, I can assure you that as a very reputable dog breeder, I am dismayed to think that you would even think such a thing . . . Blah, blah."

She ranted on trying to show indignation at his suggestion, but David smiled inwardly, for he was no longer listening to her protestations, his SAS training had taught him to recognise when he was being lied to, 'Gotcha, you deceitful old bag' he thought to himself, 'I'll lay odds that this litter has come from somewhere other than Judy and the wonderful Crufts champ? Thing is, what do I do now? You'll not admit it, and I have no real proof, but, by god, I can, and will, make things as damn difficult as I can for you.'

He looked down at Em and found that she was smiling up at him in a knowing manner.

"Okay, little one, your Daddy's on to it, let's see what we can do," he whispered as he gathered her closer into his embrace. Mrs Dobson was still protesting vociferously, but David had heard enough.

"Come on kids, I think we've all seen what we came for, let's all go and get some chips or a big Mac or something, what do you say?" The pups were immediately forgotten as, with cries of excitement, the children exited the garage hand-in-hand with their slightly confused mother.

"Thanks, Mrs Dobson, we may be back in touch, but we need to talk things over a bit. I might want to bring a friend round to see the litter, and to help us choose a good healthy pup. He's a Police dog handler, knows all about these things, would that be alright with you?"

"All my pups are good and healthy, Mr Lloyd, I can assure that they will pass any inspection you think is necessary. If you wish to have a properly qualified vet check the health of any pup you care to choose, then I have no objection, but it will have to be at your own expense. Do I make myself clear?"

David had noticed a slight narrowing of her eyes as he mentioned the Police, but he had to hand it to her, she was good, damned good, at covering her all too obvious concerns.

"Crystal, Mrs Dobson, thanks again, and a very good evening to you."

As soon as they were a comfortable distance away, Sue, slightly miffed at being excluded from the conversation in the garage, confronted her husband.

"Mind telling me what all that was about, Mr Lloyd? What exactly are you up to, and who's this mysterious friend you have in the Police, all of a sudden?"

"The pups have come from a puppy farm or somewhere similar. They're not Judy's litter, I'd put money on it. She's as bent as a nine-bob-note, Sue, and lying through her back teeth."

"How do you know David, what proof have you? You're going to have to explain a bit more if I'm to believe you, that's for sure, come on, spill the beans?"

"How do I know she's lying? Body language, Sue, all the classic signs, might have come straight out of the interrogation training manuals, believe me, she's a bad 'un if ever I saw one. As for the pups, Emily told me."

David stopped in his tracks. The enormity of what he had just said suddenly becoming apparent. He looked at Sue, seemingly searching for words.

"Don't ask me how, it's what we were talking about earlier. Emily somehow placed a thought and a picture in my mind, I know she did."

David tried to rouse his baby daughter, perhaps seeking for her to confirm this absurd sounding assertion. But little Emily, content in her fathers embrace, had fallen fast asleep; her arms wrapped tightly around his neck, and her little head resting comfortably on his shoulder, as he walked along.

The rest of the journey back down towards the seafront was largely made in silence. David inwardly questioning himself as to exactly what had just occurred, and Sue, similarly seeking to make some sense out of his startling revelation. She somehow sensed that what he was saying was correct. Sue thought that she had herself, experienced much the same sort of thing. A thought or an image of something just seemed to appear from out of nowhere, and always, it had some connection with Emily.

They stopped to pick up some chips for the twins before resuming their leisurely stroll. Another thought occurred to Sue.

"This friend of yours in the Police, do I know him?"

"He's a figment of my imagination at the moment love, but by golly, he won't be for much longer if I have my way. That woman is definitely a fraud. I think she is probably getting litters of puppies from other dubious sources, and giving them a false pedigree to inflate their selling price. Think about it, she could pass off any number of pups as being out of Judy. Yes, her dog has certainly had a litter recently, that is abundantly apparent, but I doubt that the pups we just looked at were all the same litter. That means that the pedigrees she supplies are false and meaningless, but it will serve to push up the earning potential of the pups considerably, probably into the thousands. She is taking money from people by preying on their snobbish perceptions. It's probably theft, a criminal deception, I think. Trouble is, I'm not sure that Sharon Cox is not involved as well. It was she that recommended us to go to Mrs Dobson in the first instance, wasn't it. She also said that they were close friends. I wonder just how much deeper this goes, Sue? Let's see what Sharon's reaction is to what I am about to say to her. Don't be surprised at anything you might hear from me, I'm just fishing around to see what else might be in the muddy waters."

The rest of their slow walk back to the B&B was spent largely in silence, each of them deep in their respective thoughts, and trying to come to terms with the enormity and ramifications of David's suspicions. The realisation that little Emily was definitely able to communicate in some sort of telepathic manner, now becoming abundantly apparent to them both. It would also seem that, like a real life Dr Doolittle, she was somehow able to talk to the animals? How stupid does that sound? But the evidence was irrefutable, both to Sue and David. They had now seen and experienced it beyond any further doubt.

Sue found that now, far from being concerned about little Em being different in some ways, she felt rather excited and proud of her daughter's unique ability. The realisation of the truth had somehow come as an enormous relief, a weight lifted off her shoulders. She gazed lovingly at Emily, still asleep on her fathers shoulder, and wondered just what the future might hold for a person with such a wonderful ability. She vowed, inwardly, that whatever else might happen, she would seek to help Emily develop her talent to it's utmost, whatever that was, who knows?

David's thoughts were somewhat different, he was inwardly seething with indignant anger at Mrs Dobson's blatant attempt to deceive him. He wondered just how many times, over the years, she had similarly taken other good people for poor, unsuspecting mugs. He had a mental image of her rubbing her hands in glee, as she watched another happily unaware, and delighted family leave with a little dog. He could picture the avarice in her eyes as she greedily pocketed another five hundred odd quid for a pup probably worth just a fraction of that. He knew that, come what may, he was going to put a stop to it and to bring about her come-uppance, but as yet, he hadn't quite worked out how.

He again wondered just how deeply Sharon Cox was involved? She was a dog-breeder herself, and had already called Laura Dobson her close friend. He surmised that it was inconceivable that she could be totally ignorant of the scam. Sharon was a pretty astute cookie, she had to be to run the family business. Yes, she was definitely in on it, of that he was sure. David felt it was even more of an insult that she should seek to try and involve him in her shady dealings, given that their respective parents were such close friends. He wondered what the Cox seniors would say if they were ever to find out? Maybe they are in on it as well? 'Oh my God. Heaven forbid,' he muttered to himself at the realisation of what it would do to his own parents if he proved that they were.

"Did you say something?" asked Sue. They were just about to turn into the B&B and she caught his quiet, personal whisper.

"No, not really love, I was just thinking out loud. I was mulling things over and probably reading more into all of this than is actually there. Let's just play it by ear for the time being, shall we? We've only got three more days, so let's not spoil it for the kids by causing any bad feeling. We can talk some more when we are alone on the beach tomorrow."

Emily stirred from her slumbers at the sound of her father's voice. She became fully awake as the family went in through the front door.

A joyous Sam came bounding up to greet them as they entered. Standing on his hind legs, his forelegs on David's upper arms, it was plain that he couldn't wait to get as close as possible to Emily.

"Down Sam, there's a good lad, let me put her down first, you stupid animal."

Child and dog were reunited. Their apparent joy in each other's company knew no bounds as they rolled together on the floor of the hallway. Sharon came hurriedly through from the kitchen wiping her hands on a tea towel.

"Sam, Sam, that's enough, do you hear me? Get back, sit, and behave yourself . . . Sorry David, I don't know what's wrong with him today. He isn't normally this boisterous, but just lately he seems to be a different dog. He even ran away from me on our walk today. I found him here on the doorstep when I got back. He's never done that to me before. It seems he just wants to be with your children. They must be spoiling him. Can I get you all some tea or something, how did it go with Laura, the pups are lovely aren't they?"

"Tea would be nice Sharon, thank you. Perhaps we should all go through to the lounge, that is if we can separate these two into some semblance of order?"

"Sam, Sam, leave Emily alone will you, you'll hurt her. Leave, Sam, Sam, leave, do you hear me?" Her voice was going up in a rising crescendo as Sharon sought to impose her will and bring Sam back under her control. She finally grabbed his collar, and roughly pulled him away from Emily, who, if anything, was enjoying his attention by laughing and encouraging him to play with her. Sharon dragged the dog backwards toward her. Holding hard to his collar, she gave him a violent shake and sat him back onto his haunches. She moved around to his front, thereby putting herself between Sam and Emily. With her free hand she slapped his nose, not hard, but it was enough to provoke a reaction from Sam. The dog bared his teeth into a snarl at the chastisement, and gave a warning bark against any more such treatment. Sharon was clearly taken aback.

"Bad boy, bad dog. No, do you hear me, no? My god, what is the matter with you today, you bad dog. You don't show your teeth and growl at me my lad, bad dog"

She pointed her finger close to his head as she spoke. She again shook him roughly to further enforce her words. Sam's reaction was so fast that it took every one by complete surprise. A quick flick of his head, and in an instant, Sharon's finger was laid bare to the bone. She released him and stepped away, pale and horrified, as she hurriedly wrapped the tea towel around her bleeding finger. Sam, immediately contrite, sought to hide behind Emily, who gently fondled his ears in response. There followed a few moments of silence as everyone, dumbfounded at what they had just seen, tried to come to terms with it. David noticed that Emily was muttering something to Sam.

Sue broke the silence as she moved round to take a closer look at Sharon's finger and to try and comfort her obvious shock and distress. Peter and Rita, both frightened, moved closer to their father, holding on to his trouser leg, and putting him between themselves and the dog, a creature that they now viewed with suspicion, and saw in a whole new light.

"This is going to need a stitch or two, Sharon. Do you want me to phone for an ambulance?"

"No need for that Sue, I'll take her in our car. See to the children, they're a bit frightened, I think. Sam is okay with Emily, ask her to take him through and settle him in his bed. He will do what she asks, no problem."

"How can you say that Mr Lloyd? Emily is only a baby, how can she control a vicious dog? No, I won't allow it, take him out back, and lock him in the garage. He won't be able to hurt anyone else if he's in there. I'll sort him out when I get back, I'll give him what for, just you see."

"Sue, will you take the children away, please. Just do as I suggested, I'll deal with this. Come on Sharon, show me the way to your A&E, you're the one that needs sorting right now."

David took her by the elbow and steered her out of the front door still protesting.

It was a short drive to the Weymouth Community Hospital, the journey conducted largely in silence. David accompanied Sharon as she booked herself in at the desk of the Minor Injuries Unit where the Receptionist was apparently an acquaintance of hers.

"Dog bite? What, not Sam, surely Sharon?" Was the response from Pat, as she entered the details of how the injury had occurred?

"Fraid so, I don't know what got into him, Pat. I can't trust him anymore, that's for sure."

"I'm really surprised, Sharon, Sam always seemed to have such a gentle nature. Doctor will be able to see you straight away. Fortunately we're reasonably quiet tonight, so if you and the gentleman would care to take a seat just over there, he'll be with you shortly."

David and Sharon sat in an awkward silence for the several minutes that it took for the doctor to arrive. David was mulling over in his mind how best to broach the subject of Mrs Dobson's attempted deception. He realised that he had no real proof of his suspicions, certainly nothing that would hold up in a court of law. He trusted his own instincts though, and just knew that she was guilty as hell. How to get some form of concrete evidence that was the crux of the matter? He needed something irrefutable to either present to the authorities, whoever they were, or to put the fear of god into Mrs Dobson, and Sharon of course. He had nothing, but they didn't know that, did they? The ghost of an idea began to form and he smiled inwardly in anticipation.

With three stitches in her heavily bandaged finger, Sharon was complaining bitterly about how she could be expected to manage at the B&B with one hand out of action. Their short journey came to an abrupt stop as David pulled the car into an empty parking space on the seafront.

"What are we stopping here for, David. Is the car playing up, or something?"

"No, the car is just fine Sharon, I just need to have a little talk with you, while we are alone."

He saw a puzzled look come into her face.

"Tell me what you know about Laura Dobson, Sharon. You said she was a close friend, how long have you known her?"

"Ah, this is about the pups isn't it, you want to check on their pedigree background, is that it?"

"Well, something along those lines, yes. I was more interested in Mrs Dobson's standing in the dog breeding circles. Is she well regarded? It is always a good sign if her peers respect her, isn't it? What do you, personally, know about her?"

"Laura is well thought of by everyone. She is a member of several dog breeder societies, and has been asked to judge, on several occasions. She has bred several different breeds, German Shepherds and Poodles of all sizes, but she is best regarded for her expertise with spaniels, Cockers and Springers mostly, oh, and some Retrievers, they're the easiest to sell. Gundogs are always popular. She only has Judy at home at the moment, but I know that she owns several other dogs, as well. I think she has a brother who owns a lot of farm property somewhere up-country, and other people in Wales or Ireland, as well. I seem to remember her telling me that they all came over from over there originally. I guess that's where her other dogs are kept, but I'm not absolutely certain, so don't quote me."

"So how come she's a friend of yours, Sharon? There's a lot of difference in your ages, how long have you known her?"

"This is a small town, David, regular dog walkers all get to know each other. We go back a long way, Laura and me, probably twenty years or more. Sam is my third dog, I knew Laura when I had Shelley, my rescued Springer. We had her put to one of Laura's champion stud dogs. It produced a litter of seven lovely pups, I remember wanting to keep them all. Laura taught me quite a lot about dog breeding and things, and well, with the common interest, it was inevitable that sooner or later, we would become better acquainted. Besides, Laura and I, well we're very alike, we don't have men friends, if you see what I mean? I don't remember exactly when I met Laura, but it's quite a number of years ago, when I was just a teenager, and not long after I first moved into the B&B. We became quite close once, even planned to set up home together, but then there was Mum and Dad to consider. Well, I couldn't just leave them, could I?" She sighed wistfully. "Is that enough for you? Are you going to have one of her pups, then?"

"We've not entirely made up our minds yet Sharon. Sue and I are not entirely sure that the pups we saw today are Judy's litter. To that end, and to satisfy us that everything is okay, I am going to ask a close friend of mine, a Police dog handler, to come look at the litter, and help me choose the right pup. He will also do a DNA check for me while he's at it. It's a simple matter for him to have samples taken from the pups and their mother, to be expertly compared and verified.

I am assured that I will have the result back within 24hrs. There are some concerns that I need to be putting to rest, before we go much further with any of this."

David had chosen his words very carefully, and as they were delivered, he was looking closely at Sharon for some reaction. It was definitely there. A slight look of anxiety had shown, just fleetingly, in the eyes, of that, he was sure. He continued, trying to press home a small advantage.

"Of course, if it is found that my suspicions are correct, then I will not hesitate to inform all the proper authorities of the scam, but let's hope it doesn't come to that. She may well be kosher, Sharon, but my nose, and gut instinct, is telling me otherwise."

Sharon was definitely shaken, that was apparent, so David pushed it further.

"You're looking distinctly worried, Sharon. I hope this doesn't involve you in some way, does it? If you know something more than you're telling me, it might be better to say so before it's too late. I don't want to drop you in it, as well. We can always have a little rethink, can't we?"

There was a few moments of awkward silence before Sharon whispered, "I don't want to become involved, David. It would be the end of Mum and Dad if they found out."

"Just so we get this straight Sharon, are you telling me that my suspicions are correct?"

"Yes. She has been doing it for a long time. She thinks it's foolproof. She sells pups out of the litter and immediately replaces them with others of a similar age. Judy had a litter of seven pups and the Sire was a champion show dog. So if you phoned the dog owner for confirmation, she would have to say that it was correct. But nobody knows exactly how many pups are sold as being from the original litter, only Laura."

"So where do you come in, Sharon?"

"I get a small cut out of every pup sold by my recommendation. It's not a lot, but it makes it worthwhile, if you see what I mean. I knew someone clever, like you, would catch us out eventually. I'm sorry for getting you into this, David, but please don't involve me. I won't be doing it again."

She started to sob gently into her handkerchief. Crocodile tears, he thought.

David deliberately let her stew for a few minutes. To all intent and purpose, he was deliberating his next move. His next question took Sharon completely by surprise.

"What are you going to do about Sam, Sharon?"

"I don't know, why do you ask?"

"It cannot have escaped your notice that Emily and Sam have bonded in a such a way that they have become virtually inseparable. I am concerned as to what will happen when we go home in three days time. I'll cut to the chase, Sharon. I would like Sam to come home with us, is that going to be possible, do you think?"

Her eyes narrowed, "Is this going to be the price of your silence, David? Do I have to part with Sam, is that going to be the deal?"

"It's not a deal, Sharon, let's call it an amicable arrangement. I will pay you what I consider to be a fair price for a three-year-old retriever, with a dubious temperament. You, in turn, will organise a proper bill of sale, for a cash settlement. Sam after all, has bitten you, so it shouldn't be too difficult to explain Sam's departure to your parents. I don't foresee that there's any real problem, do you?"

"If I agree, how do I know you won't report us, anyway? I only have your word that you won't."

"And that is all you are going to get, Sharon. The word of a gentleman is enough in my book. You will also put a stop to Laura Dobson's shenanigans, as well. How you do it is entirely up to you, but if I get the slightest hint she is still at it, the gloves will come off, and I won't stop till she is behind bars, Do I make myself clear?"

"I'm not sure that it's possible, David. I know Laura to be in with some pretty nasty characters, I might be putting myself in danger, you too, come to that."

"We'll cross that bridge if we come to it. What I say still stands. Do we have an agreement?"

Three days later, David and his family set off for the long drive back to the New Forest with one extra passenger. Sam was more than content to squeeze himself in with the luggage. Anything was tolerable just so long as he was in a close proximity to his beloved little Emily.

# Chapter 2

The week following David's departure had not gone well for Sharon Cox. Her mind had not been on her work, and she had found herself close to tears on more than one occasion. She had been dreading this moment, but recognised that it had to be done. She picked up the house phone and dialled Laura Dobson's number. She had rehearsed the intended conversation in her mind a dozen times, but words seemed to fail her as soon as she began to speak.

"Hello Laura, it's me, Sharon, how are you?"

"I'm just fine, thanks, Sharon, what can I do for you? What have you got for me?" There was a little chuckle on the end of her question. "Does Mr Lloyd want one of the pups, perhaps?"

"No, I don't think so Laura, he's gone home now. It's a bit of bad news I'm afraid. I think we are going to have to stop doing this, at least, for the time being."

There were a few moments of silence on the other end of the phone.

"You had better come round and explain yourself, lady. Be here in twenty minutes."

"Laura, I can't, the B&B has new guests arriving this morning, and I have a mountain of work to get through."

"I said twenty minutes. You'll be here if you know what's good for you." The phone went dead.

Sharon quietly replaced the phone onto the cradle. She was feeling frightened and upset. This had been a terrible week for her, what with getting bitten and having to part with Sam, then having to explain why to her parents. Once again, she was very close to tears. In her own mind, she had convinced herself that she was very much the innocent party, having been sucked into it all by the persuasive Laura. She was beginning to regret the day that they had ever met, but one couldn't turn the clock back.

She had wondered how David had managed to cotton on so quickly to their little enterprise? He was certainly a very astute and persuasive character. She was distraught at having to part with Sam, but somehow knew that he no longer regarded her as his mistress. It was very strange how he taken to the child, Emily, so quickly? She had personally witnessed the interaction that had taken place between dog and child, otherwise, she would not have thought it possible.

For the present, she was under instruction to report to Laura, something she would rather not do, but the veiled threat was enough to convince her that she must. With apologies to her parents, who took over her chores, she excused herself by claiming that she needed to get some important items of shopping that she had forgotten. With some trepidation she hurried round to her meeting with Laura Dobson.

Shaun Riley sat, arms comfortably folded, with his backside hitched up onto the welsh dresser in the kitchen. He was quietly watching the woman who now called herself Laura Dobson. She was busy making pastry while bringing him up to speed with Sharon Cox. He had just heard what had been said between them, and could see that Laura was quite angry and upset.

As she spoke, Shaun still listened intently, but allowed his mind to drift back to the time, now thirty—nine years ago, when he had first met and worked with this woman. It had been during the time of the glorious struggle, when the IRA had been causing havoc by indiscriminately bombing cities on mainland Britain. Lara Dobbs, as he new her then, was the partner of his best mate, Ryan, and very much one of the team. Their reign of terror had all came to a rather sad and unexpected halt when Ryan, the bomb maker, accidentally blew his hands off while trying to construct a timer for a huge car bomb. In their remote location, Ryan had bled to death in Shaun's arms before any medical help could be summoned. The team had fragmented, taking refuge at various safe locations around the country, but staying loosely in touch with each other, while awaiting further orders.

Those thirty-odd years had taken its toll. Shaun was recalling just how much he had fancied her in those days. He did not find it difficult to remember how sexy she had looked even with her boyish appearance. He knew that she was a couple of years older than he, but what did that matter? She was still slim and her long auburn hair, now cut short, was tinged with iron grey. He recalled how she had usually dressed in her grubby, loose fitting army fatigues. Now, it was stretch jeans that accentuated her tight little arse without showing any visible knicker line. He concluded that she was either not wearing any, or perhaps just a thong? Her loose, transparent pink top, fell open as she leaned forward, allowing an occasional tantalising glimpse of her breasts. With the darker pink of the areola around her prominent nipples, poking at the flimsy material of her see-through her bra, it was all very nice, and Shaun was feeling decidedly horny . . .

In his fantasies, he had imagined forcibly taking her on many occasions, for Shaun liked a bit of rough. His sexual fantasy always culminated as he imagined his victim realising just how much she was enjoying his attentions. He could even picture her contorted face in the moment of their coital climax.

Lara had proved herself to be loyal, not only to the cause, but also to Ryan. She had repeatedly rejected his advances both before, and after, Ryan's untimely demise.

Shaun's lechery had not gone unnoticed. She knew exactly what he was thinking, and she tried to drag his mind back to reality. However, it left a warm, comforting feeling inside of her, to think that at sixty-four years of age, men still found her sexually attractive.

Shaun, a big man in every respect, had kept himself fit on his pig farm, situated in a remote area close to the Welsh borders. Now sixty-two, and standing a shade over two metres tall, he weighed in at seventeen stones, all of it muscle.

Shaun Riley would best be described as a great bull of a man with a huge sexual appetite. He didn't give up easily on any potential conquest, and wondered if Lara might still be up for it if he tried again now? Mind you, he could see that the years had taken their toll, but the vestiges of her former beauty were still apparent. 'Many a good tune played on an old fiddle,' he thought to himself as he detected the old familiar stirring in his loins and felt himself becoming aroused. He made no attempt to hide his erection.

"She'll be here in a minute, so get yourself out of sight and listen to what she has to say. If I think she needs sorting out a bit, or if I need help, I'll signal you in by banging the rolling pin down hard on the table. Alright?"

Shaun, disappointed at the interruption, grunted, and hid himself in the pantry. There was a gentle tap on the back door. Laura checked that he was out of sight, before unlatching the door to admit a rather breathless Sharon. Seeking to put her on the defensive immediately, Laura put the large pine kitchen table between them, and stared fixedly at Sharon for a few moments before sharply saying,

"You're five minutes late, girl, and I don't like to be kept waiting. I have some urgent business to attend to, so keep it short and to the point. What have you done that should necessitate us stopping selling the pups, as we are?"

"Laura, I haven't done anything. It must have been something that happened while he was here. He knows all about it. I didn't tell him anything, I swear. He told me that he was going to go the Police Laura, even blackmailed me into parting with Sam, what was I to do? I tell you he knows. He's told me that I have to stop you, as well. That's why I'm here. Laura, you've got to stop for a while, otherwise he will make sure that you go behind bars for criminal deception. That's what he said, and he means it Laura, he knows everything, we've got to stop doing it, I tell you . . ."

"Sam is one of our stud dogs, you had no right to part with him. Has money changed hands in this?"

Sharon bit her lip and gave a little sob. "He made me give him a bill of sale."

"For how much?"

"Five hundred."

"Five bloody hundred, is that all? You stupid little bitch, he's worth ten times that. Give the money here, now." She held out her hand expectantly.

"I don't have it with me, Laura. Its back at home in the safe."

"Then you will go and get it, right now, and be sure to get your little arse straight back round here, immediately, lady, do you hear me? You stupid little cow, you have no idea what you are messing with here. Get out of my sight while I think about what to do with this bloody mess. I'll sort our Mr Lloyd. What's his full name, where does he live?"

"He's called David Morrison-Lloyd, hyphenated, you know. He lives in the New Forest somewhere. I only have his business card, there's no address on it, but it has all his other contact details. He might have put his address in our register, I'll have a look for you when I get home."

"Do it girl, bring the business card, and the money, straight back here. I'll try and sort something out in the meantime. God, what a bloody mess, get out of my sight, go on, away with you now."

Shaun emerged from the pantry as the back door closed after Sharon.

"It would seem we have a bit of a problem," he murmured quietly. "The last thing we need is the Filth poking around in our affairs now that everything is looking all legit. Its not a good time either, given that we're expecting orders from above any day now, we could all be back in business very shortly. She's gonna have to be taken care of, seen to, before she starts gobbin' off all over the place, don't y'think now?"

Laura thought for a bit. "She's single, looks after her parents, and runs a little B&B. I doubt she would be greatly missed. She's a fairly frequent visitor here, fancies me a bit, I think. I can always deny that she ever came round here today, let's hope she hasn't been noticed. By the time anyone gets around to asking, it would be a little difficult to recall. My memory, after all, isn't quite as good as it once was. What do you have in mind?"

"The van's outside, and we have the big laundry basket I bought the pups in. It doesn't need a bloody genius to work it out. She'll be a contented pig's fart by this time tomorrow, just like the others."

He chuckled at his own macabre humour.

"I don't want you making any mess in here, Shaun, do you hear me now, I know what your like."

"I was thinking of perhaps having a bit of sport with her first, she's not a bad lookin' chick. Besides I've never shagged a lesbo before. Can't pass up on a golden opportunity like that now, can I?"

He thought he detected a gleam come into Laura's eyes.

"You're a bloody animal, Shaun Riley, but you'll not be doing it here, do you hear me now. Save it for Tiptree, where we can all watch."

They both chuckled at the prospect.

Sharon was deeply troubled. The conversation with Laura had not gone as she had thought it might. She had rather expected that given the news that her little scam had been rumbled, she would have reacted differently. Scared perhaps? More panicked? Certainly be a little more contrite and eager to try to cover things up in some way? Perhaps even take some sort of precautionary steps, just to give the impression she had complied with David's warnings?

Sharon knew that Laura would demand some of the money. She had hoped to split it equally, but that idea was apparently a non-starter? It was true that Sam had come from Laura's stock of puppies, but Sharon had always thought he had been given to her as an affectionate gift from Laura. She hadn't appreciated that he was only on loan, and earmarked to be another one of her stud dogs. Perhaps he was better off being with David? Sharon then realised that Laura probably intended to snatch Sam back somehow, maybe even inflict physical harm on David in the process? She recalled her words, 'I'll sort out our Mr Lloyd,' it wasn't just an idle remark, was it? No, she really means to do it . . . She wondered how? Thinking back, she knew that Laura was in close association with some pretty rough looking characters, travelling people, of the Irish gypsy type. She had seen them herself on more than one occasion. Laura would probably enlist their services, yes, that would be it. She must warn David to watch out for such people. God, how had this all started and got out of hand so quickly? She wished she had never got involved with introducing David to the damned woman.

She hurried along, completely preoccupied with her thoughts, and only narrowly avoided being hit by a cyclist, as she stepped into the road without looking. Ignoring his angry shouts of derision, she pressed on regardless. Breathless, upset, and now really worried, the thought of anything-untoward happening to David and his family horrified her. 'I must warn him, tell him exactly what Laura has said.' She instinctively felt in her pockets for her mobile, but it was at home in her shoulder bag.

Sharon slipped quietly in through the back door of the B&B, and listened for the location of her parents. She heard their voices, they were upstairs, obviously changing the beds in readiness for the incoming guests. Tiptoeing quickly through to her little office, Sharon found her keys in the desk drawer and retrieved the envelope containing £500 from the safe. She picked up her shoulder bag and crept out into the Hallway. The Guest Register was open on the last completed page.

In the address column, David had written only his postcode, BH25 5JU/8. Sharon sorted out his card from her purse and jotted it down on the back. She took out her mobile phone and was dialling David's home number as she slipped back out the way she had come in.

"Sorry, but neither David nor Sue are here to take your call at the moment, but if you would care to leave your name, number, and a short message, we will get back to you soonest." Sharon cursed. "David, this is Sharon Cox, I need to speak with you urgently. Please ring me back as soon as you get this message. I'll try your mobile as well, it's very urgent."

The same happened when she tried his mobile number, no reply, so she left a similar message on his voice mail.

Sharon wasn't to know that David had heard her, but he was on the motorway, passengers on board, and he never accepted phone calls whilst driving. It did cross his mind as to what could possibly be wrong. She said it was very urgent and her voice sounded so obviously distraught? Very curious . . . But never mind he would ring her back in about 25 minutes time, after he dropped off his passengers at Heathrow.


Not bothering to knock, Sharon burst straight into the kitchen where Laura was still talking to Shaun. He jumped up from his seat on the corner of the pine kitchen table and glowered at her, angry with himself, and her, for catching him unawares.

"This is my cousin Shaun, from Ireland, he's just brought me some more pups. You can talk freely, he knows about everything. Where's the money?"

As she spoke, Laura spotted the phone that Sharon was still clutching in her hand. She caught Shaun's eye, and saw that he had spotted it as well. Sharon was taken completely unawares as Shaun suddenly lunged forward and grabbed her by the nape of the neck, snatching the phone from her grasp as he did so. Laura grabbed her shoulder bag and up-ended it, spilling all the contents out onto the table. The envelope with the money went straight into her pocket, the amount unchecked. Next came her purse contents.

"His address, girl, where is it?"

Sharon's neck was being held in a vice-like grip, Shaun's fingers digging into her flesh unmercifully. The pain was excruciating, she found it difficult to speak. Shaun put his mouth next to her ear and hissed,

"The lady asked a question of you, where's the bloody address? Speak if you know what's good for you, bitch." He squeezed even harder, and shook her violently to reinforce his words.

"My purse, his card, its in my purse," she gasped.

Laura found what she was looking for. "Shaun, the phone, give it here."

Sharon could do nothing, she watched helplessly as Laura checked her phone for the last dialled numbers, against those on David's business card.

"What did you tell him? Shaun, hurt her a bit more if she doesn't answer me truthfully."

"I didn't get through, Laura, I haven't told him anything, honest, that's the truth. Please stop him hurting me Laura, there's no need for any of this. Please Laura . . ."

"You were going to warn him, am I right?"

"Yes, yes, I didn't want to see him get hurt. His family and mine go back a long way, Laura. Please stop this, there's no necessity, I'll answer your questions. Please, he's hurting me Laura."

"You were going to grass me up, so why should I care what he does to you. Where I come from, we have our own ways of dealing with informants. Shaun, the bad hand, let's show her what we mean."

Shaun, still holding her by the neck in one hand, and her left wrist by the other, forced her hand slowly down until it was flat on the table. The rolling pin, wielded by Laura, came smashing down on the backs of her fingers with a sickening crunch of breaking bones. Then immediately again, but this time on the fingernails. Sharon screamed and writhed in Shaun's grasp. He responded by smashing her head, face down, onto the wooden tabletop. Mercifully, Sharon immediately lost consciousness, so she didn't hear her mobile phone ringing to David's returned call.

Laura picked up the ringing phone and threw it against the stone wall, where it smashed into tiny pieces. Shaun had let Sharon's limp form drop to the flagstone floor. He saw that her mouth and face was a mess of broken teeth, blood and gore, but she was still breathing. He kicked her viciously in the ribs for good measure, now disappointed at being denied his 'bit of sport.'

"Let's get this mess cleared away Shaun, I think I'll be coming with you to the farm for a few days. I'll collect my things while you sort her and the pups out. Ready to leave in ten minutes, okay?"

Out of perceived necessity, Laura had always lived in such a way that she would be able to pick up her personal effects, and be ready to vacate in minutes, leaving little evidence behind.

The original team of bombers, the active service unit, had consisted of six people headed up by her late husband. They had all arrived separately in the UK, early in 1973. Based in Liverpool, while they got themselves organised, they all moved on to other remote farm locations, as soon it became practicable.

Needing arms and equipment, the group carried out an audacious hijacking, helping themselves to whatever they needed from a legal arms shipment, that was leaving Rotterdam, bound for the Yemen. Reputedly belonging to Monzer al Kassar, the stolen arms were never reported, officially, in Britain, but the identity of the thieves was somehow made known to the furious al Kassar. He swore never to conduct any more business with the IRA, and to get even by supplying its opponents, the Protestant Loyalists factions, with whatever they required.

Ryan's gang, as they became known, was just one of three similarly active terrorist cells, all working completely independently, their identities unknown, even to each other. They had all been sent over by the Ruling Council of the IRA, with orders to carry out bombings on carefully selected targets in mainland Britain. Listed amongst the successes of Ryan's gang, when they were most active in 1974, had been The North Star Pub, the Swiss Cottage Tavern, and later, the Houses of Parliament.

It was only the untimely demise of Ryan himself, in 1974, that brought about an immediate cessation to their activities, for the authorities of that time had absolutely no idea who they were looking for.

Another active service unit, the Birmingham six, had been blamed for some of the atrocities committed by Ryan's group. This had led to an enormously expensive and protracted trial leading up to their conviction, and wrongful imprisonment. Appeals, re-examination of the evidence, and a judicial review finally led to the convictions being overturned, on the grounds that the Police had fabricated confessions and some of the evidence. It had taken 16 years, and proved to be a huge and costly embarrassment to the British Government. As such, it was to be regarded by the IRA, as a successful operation.

Sinn Fein ordered them to cease bombings as part of a peace accord in 1975. One of the gang, Marty McCue, was immediately recalled to Ireland. At that time, he was the only one of Ryan's gang, with any sort of formal education. Having achieved a degree in Politics and Economic studies at Queen's University, Belfast, his considerable knowledge was required to help further the cause, by political means.

He was now an advisor, and Personal Assistant to the Deputy First Minister in the Stormont Assembly. It was generally accepted that all their orders and funding would now come indirectly through his auspices, but for security reasons, Marty's name was never mentioned, even amongst the rest of the cell. Since his departure, there had never been any further contact or communication with him. Where they were concerned, he didn't even exist anymore, and neither did they, to him.

Of the remaining five that were still in the country, Laura, or Lara, as the rest knew her, had assumed the role of leader, and now earned her living as a dog breeder, and dealer. It was an ideal cover that allowed her to move freely around the country on legitimate business. But greed had got the better of her, and, working with Shaun at Tiptree Farm, she had devised and developed the puppy scam.

With a carefully built, and well-organised collection and distribution network, it had earned many hundreds of thousands of pounds over the years. Most of her deals were conducted in untraceable cash, so she had assumed the role of Accountant as well.

Lara was responsible for the funding of nearly all their respective enterprises. Any excess profit from their various business enterprises was deposited into an anonymous, numbered account with the Bank of Ireland. On that account, there were never any bank statements or withdrawals, and she didn't keep any of the deposit slips, everything was immediately shredded. There were only two signatories on the account, hers and Marty's, but neither of them had ever conducted any transactions. Her only other record of anything, was contained in her own rather ancient, personal file-o-fax, which never left her possession.

Laura still believed that the money she was depositing, was to be used, back home, to further the cause that she, and the others, had dedicated their lives to supporting, that of a United Ireland. She had no way of knowing that none of the money had ever been touched. It was just sitting in the Bank of Ireland account, accruing interest.

Shaun Riley had been recruited into the active service unit, following the death of his father, who had been shot and fatally wounded by British troops, following protests against the Bloody Sunday Massacre. As an impressionable young lad, with a deep and smouldering hatred for the British, he sought only to wreak revenge and retribution for the death of his father. Little else was of any consequence, for he had no head for politics or religion.

Now, with a couple of trusted stockmen, Shaun ran Tiptree Farm as a very successful and lucrative pig breeding and weaner unit, raising some 4,000 animals a year, to their 70kg slaughter weight. Lara had originally purchased the remote farm property as a safe house. But over the years, Shaun had worked hard, and turned it into what it was now.

Being so remotely situated, the farmhouse and its extensive collection of barns and stables had been easily extended to include the ultra modern intensive pig unit now housed in three huge, windowless, purpose-built buildings.

Two of the original barns, adjacent to the farmhouse, had been allocated to Lara's dog breeding operations. Routinely, Shaun or one of his stockmen would drive around the country on legitimate pig business, usually picking up feed, or collecting piglets. They were easily able to combine this with collecting litters of pups, or taking in the dogs that had been stolen to order, and were to be used in the breeding program. Many of the stolen dogs were ones that Lara had supplied in the first place, and whose genuine pedigree, was already known.

Lara was still the brain behind the whole operation. She was in complete control of everything, and provided all the necessary computer generated paperwork for every puppy they sold, albeit that most of it was completely fictitious.

Dermot and Michael Close, the brothers, now ran a legitimate quarry business in Wales. Close Roadstone & Tarmacadam Ltd. supplied dressed Purbeck, Cotswold, and Portland stone for building. Granite for floors and kitchen worktops, and most recently, using all the crushed waste stone in tar macadam, for the surfacing of roads, paths and driveways.

Their business too had thrived, for a lot of their transactions were to the Gypsy tarmac layers, who only ever dealt in cash.

Once again, the remote location, in the foothills of the Black Mountains, had been originally acquired as another safe house. It was there, in their first quarry, that all the previously used bombs had been constructed, and where Ryan had died.

In the normal process of extracting stone from the quarries, explosives are commonly used. Both of the brothers were licensed to store and use such material, and they always made sure that they complied meticulously with the terms and conditions of their Licence. As such, no suspicions were ever aroused when the local Constabulary made their annual inspection of their premises.

What the authorities didn't know, was that there was a small arsenal of illegally held firearms stored in a small natural cave beneath the stone-flagged floor of the old quarry office, a double-garage sized, stone-built building, situated high on the cliff face, adjacent to the bungalow.

Since the closure and landscaping of the quarry, the office had been converted into a bird watchers hide.

The brothers were orphans, convent raised, without ever having known their parents. The nuns had told them that they had been killed by the wicked Protestants, beyond that, they knew nothing. As teenagers, they had run away from the convent, and had been found by Ryan Dobbs, living rough, in the Belfast slums. Through his indoctrination, they found a purpose in life, working for the IRA, who took care of them in their time of need.

The bungalow had been designed and built by the brothers on Bleanaway, this being the site of their first quarry working. The natural stone of the building, and all the landscaping was a thoroughly professional job. The brothers had chosen to replant only indigenous trees, shrubs and plants, resulting in tastefully designed, matured gardens, that served to compliment and enhance the natural beauty of the area.

The flooding of the gravel pit had created a large, deep lake, that covered Ryan's grave. It was now stocked with brown trout, and provided a haven for all sorts of other bird and animal life. The brothers liked nothing better than fly-fishing from their little rowing boat, afloat on their own private water.

Being surrounded by so much natural beauty, and in a wildlife habitat that they had created from nothing, Michael and Dermot were justifiably proud of everything they had done. With no public footpaths or rights of access to worry about, they declared it to be a private nature reserve, and jealously guarded it with some sophisticated electronic surveillance. Numerous 'Private property' and 'Keep out' signs threatened prosecution to trespassers.

Both brothers were still devoted to furthering the cause, whatever that might now be? For neither held any strong political nor religious views. It was something they had always done, and would continue for as long as they were able, mainly because they didn't like anything to change. The regular payments of cash, were collected by courier each month, and delivered by hand to Lara. The amounts were never questioned, it was all calculated as a fixed percentage out of their profits. They didn't ever begrudge or question the payments, they kind of regarded it as rent, or repayment of the original loan.

With the onset of old age, and as their health deteriorated, they took care of each other. Michael was not in good shape. He had developed a serious heart condition that would have benefited from bypass surgery, but for his allergy to most anaesthetics. Dermot had quite naturally slipped into the daily routine of becoming his brother's carer, their business being run as a secondary consideration. It wasn't something that he took any delight in doing, and, like many old men they were always bickering. He frequently referred to his brother as a 'great, useless, good-for-nothing lump' and received similar short shrift in return, but there was never any real malice. For after a whole lifetime of being together, neither could envisage life without the other. They were simply two old men, who wanted nothing more out of life than what they had already achieved.

Being so set in their ways, both regarded the life that they had made for themselves was their most precious asset. They just hoped and prayed to be left in peace to enjoy the tranquillity of their lovely home, for the rest of their mortal days.

In that regard, they both doubted that, should they ever be called upon to resume any of their old activities, neither of them would be of much use any more. They now they saw their role only as custodians of the cache of ageing weaponry, and as fundraisers for the cause. Anything beyond that they really didn't want to know about.

The last member of the team is perhaps the most surprising and unlikely, for Connor McCall was born and educated in England, and later, at Queen's University, Belfast. His mother, now dead, was part of the Irish community that had settled in London after the war. Connor had been recruited by Marty, only because of his extensive local knowledge of London, and the places frequented by people perceived as being likely targets. He had taken no real active part in any of the bombings perpetrated by the rest, but was innocently instrumental in some of the planning.

As his name reflects, his ancestry stretched way back to the old country. In his late teens, Connor had researched his family background. He found out that his great, great, great grandparents had fled Ireland in 1846, during the potato famine, when they were just children. Like so many others, hunger and the likelihood of starvation had forced them into abandoning their homelands. His family must have trekked to the coast where, under cover of darkness, they stole a small sailing boat from the Belfast docks. Against all odds, for none of them were competent sailors, they had somehow made the perilous crossing across the North Channel to land in Galloway.

Probably cold, wet, exhausted and close to death, local Parish records recorded that they had all been found, and given shelter, by a kindly landowner. He had them all nursed back to health, and provided for them, until they were able to repay him by working for next-to-nothing on his estates. But at least they were alive, which is more than can be said for the approximately three million other good Irish people, that had lost their lives to poverty and starvation.

Eventually, when the landowner died, and the estate was sold to meet the death duty, Connor's family were again made homeless. They were forced into becoming just another group of wandering Irish tinkers, eking a living by turning their hand to any task offered. When they couldn't find suitable work, they had to resort to petty theft, and poaching, in order to eat. Wherever they went, their reputation preceded them. They were looked upon as common criminals, and resented by the local gentry, who 'encouraged' them to keep moving by whatever means at their disposal.

The British Government were blamed then for doing nothing with regard to the Irish famine, and thus allowing it all to happen. The hatred for this act, and the deep resentment arising out of their subsequent treatment, had been passed on down the generations of travelling people. It still burned just as fiercely inside Connor to this day. For the Gaelic Irish is truly an unforgiving race of people, with very long memories.

Connor's burning ambition in life, was to see that all the land titles that had belonged to his family, being restored back to their rightful ownership. It was proving to be a long-term, complicated, legal project, that he had already been working on for many years.

Now, Connor cared little in regard to the concept of a United Ireland. He had finally come to accept that it was probably never going to be. He concluded that his adopted country would never be able to sustain itself, even if, by some miracle, it did happen, so why bother pursuing a hopeless dream?

'Williams, Thompson & McCall, Solicitors' was written on the polished brass plate erected on the entrance to their London Office, in Fulham. Tony Williams was the senior partner. Now approaching his eighty-second birthday, he considered himself to be only semi-retired. With his sharp mind for property and business law, the other two frequently called upon his considerable experience for advice. It was he that had innocently arranged the original purchase and conveyance of all the properties now occupied by the remaining members of Ryan's gang.

'Thompson & McCall, Solicitors and Attorneys at Law' was on the second plate at their Bournemouth Office. It was here, just outside of Bournemouth, near a small village named Downton, that Connor McCall had chosen to live with his beloved wife, and business partner for the past thirty years, Lizzy Thompson.

She knew nothing of his dark past. They had met at Queens University as young students, and quickly became lovers. Both had been studying politics, history and law. They had enjoyed attending and speaking at many of the heated, idealistic public debates and discussions, so common to their particular generation. But ban-the-bomb, and the Poll Tax, always came in as runners-up to the Irish situation, which was where Connor was at his most passionate.

They had lost touch when Connor, unannounced, had suddenly moved back to London.

Almost two years went past before a chance meeting in the High Court in London, had resurrected the relationship. No explanations were offered, they just picked up where they left off. The old flames of their previous passions were instantly re-ignited.

It had been a whirlwind romance. Lizzy was totally infatuated and completely taken in by her husband's wild, seemingly carefree spirit. They chose not to marry, but to jump over the broomstick in the manner of the gipsy folk, whose lifestyle they both admired, and sought to emulate.

Childless by choice, and now both in their late fifties, they too, had led a seemingly idyllic, somewhat Hippy lifestyle, on their smallholding property, at Downton in the New Forest. They chose to share their life with horses, goats, pigs and a host of pet cats, dogs, and any other waif or stray animal, that happened to come their way.

Connor and Lizzy would usually travel into their Bournemouth office on Connor's Harley Davidson if it was dry, or in his lovingly restored Morris Minor woody, if it was wet.

Once a year, when friends of Lizzy's came stay, and take care of the animals, they both took off in their old Mk1 Range Rover, towing an equally old, but immaculately maintained, little Sprite caravan. For a few weeks they chose to live the life similar to that of the travelling people, that numbered amongst their closest friends.

It is the problems and causes associated with these people that they had specifically chosen to champion and represent. It now formed the cornerstone of their thriving business. Both are well known and respected amongst the travelling people, who often travelled many miles just to seek their help and advice.

As Sharon slowly regained consciousness she had to fight firstly, the considerable pain that she was experiencing, and secondly, the claustrophobic effects of her confinement. It took her a couple of minutes of careful self-examination to reach the conclusion that she was lying on a dirty old blanket, in a foetal position, hands tied behind her back, and with a cloth bag tied over her head.

As there were a number of puppies crawling all over her, she had to move very carefully and tentatively. Exploring with her good hand, she felt the wickerwork of a basket, and realised that she and the pups were entombed together inside. She knew the basket, it being one used by Laura to house the pups when they were being transported. She had seen it many times before. Pictured in her mind, she recalled it is a big old laundry basket, with two heavy leather straps over the top to fasten it, and act as hinges for the lid. They were evidently on the move as well, this apparent from the swaying, and the noise of the van engine.

Fighting back the urge to scream at her predicament, Sharon set about trying to think logically as to how to affect her escape. Using only slow and tiny movements so as to avoid injuring the pups, she moved her hands down her back and under her backside. Now she had to get her tied hands under and around her feet so that they were in front of her. She kicked off her espadrilles, and by drawing her knees right up to her chin, one leg at a time, she was eventually able to accomplish this difficult manoeuvre.

Panting with the effort it taken in the confined space, she now needed to get the hood off her head in order to breathe more easily. By carefully exploring the knot and working only by touch with her good hand, she was relieved to find that it was not tightly tied. After a few minutes of fumbling, she was able to loose the drawstring and lift the bag enough to clear her mouth. Sucking in great lungfuls of slightly fresher air helped restore a sense of calmness. She pushed the bag higher, and could now see dim light for the first time, but it was not sufficient enough to make out the detail of the knotted rope around her wrists. Sharon had to resort to some more careful exploration, this time using her swollen lips and broken teeth. She nearly gave up several times, but willpower, anger, determination and resolve, all kicked in to encourage her to continue with her efforts.

Her loose and broken front teeth gave her agony as she vainly tried to chew through the rope one fibre at a time. She realised that her continual and repetitive movements were causing the rope to loosen slightly. Fighting the excruciating pain of her broken fingers, she changed tactics, now concentrating on trying to loosen them further.

Working her hands up and down, in and out, twisting them back and forth finally gave her enough leeway and allowed her to slip her good hand out of the restraining coils.

Turning slowly onto her back, Sharon reached up and tried vainly to push open the lid of the basket, but the straps had been fastened. She tried pushing out the ends of the basket with her shoulders and feet, but this only produced shooting pains in her side, where Shaun had put the boot in. She realised she wasn't going to get out until someone actually opened the lid of the basket.

She needed to plan for this eventuality, and closed her eyes and tried to think and calm herself. She started moving around as much as her confined space would allow, fighting cramp and trying to gather up her last reserves of energy in readiness, but for what, she didn't yet know.

As the time passed, Sharon found that things were getting steadily worse, if that were possible? For now, just to add to her problems, she desperately needed to pee. She groaned in painful agony at her predicament.

David was puzzled. His return call to Sharon had been cut off while the phone was ringing? Now driving back down the motorway he put the car in the nearside lane and set the cruise control at 60mph. It afforded him time to think. On impulse, he called home where he knew Sue was taking care of Emily. His call was answered immediately.

"Hello love, it's only me, I was just wondering if you've heard anything from Sharon Cox, at all? She's been trying to get hold of me, says that it's urgent."

"I took the twins to school, popped round to Tesco, and got back here about ten minutes ago. There's a message here, on the answer machine from her, saying much the same thing. She sounds a bit upset, David, what do you think is wrong?"

"I haven't the faintest idea, love. I tried her mobile, and it was cut off before being answered, now I'm getting nothing, number unobtainable. I was going to suggest ringing the B&B to see if she's there. I don't have that number in my phone, though. Will you do it please? Ring me back if it's anything really urgent. I'm M3, just past junction 3, southbound, so I won't be back for good hour or so, okay?"

"Hello Mrs Cox, it's Sue Morrison-Lloyd. Yes, we're all fine thank you. I know it's your busy day, but I wonder if it might be possible to have a quick word with Sharon, please? No, it's nothing urgent, just to do with Sam's feed, he seems a bit off colour at the moment, that's all."

Sue was deliberately playing it down, so as not to cause any unnecessary alarm to the old couple. She didn't yet know that anything definite was amiss, but Sharon had sounded rather upset and distraught on the answer-phone, not like her at all . . .

"She's gone to the shops, has she? Well, alright then, but when she comes back, will you tell her I called, please? Ask her if she would kindly give me a ring back. Thanks Mrs Cox, Oh, by the way, does she have her mobile with her, I could perhaps try calling her on that. What's her number?"

Sue waited while Mrs Cox went to consult her phone book for the number. She already knew it, but the short interlude had given her some more time to think. Sue painstakingly wrote down the number as it was dictated back to her.

"Thanks Mrs Cox, I'll let you get on now. Is Sharon okay? Keeping well, I hope? Yes, that's good then. Tell me though, isn't it a bit odd for her to be out shopping on a Saturday morning? It's changeover day for the B&B isn't it? You're usually so busy. How are you and Mr Cox coping, with her not there?"

Sue listened while Mrs Cox rambled on. Alarm bells were beginning to ring in her mind. Something was definitely not right down there.

"Hmm, nearly an hour just to go to the supermarket round the corner? Well I expect she's met up with someone and has gone for a coffee or something, but it's not like her to be so inconsiderate, is it? Yes, alright, Mrs Cox, nice to talk to you again, but I must get on, as well. Bye dear, regards to Mr Cox, bye."

Sue slowly replaced the receiver into its cradle, her brow furrowed in thought. She stood there motionless at the desk silently thinking, wondering, and mulling it over. The creeping tentacles of worry were beginning to emerge, and take a hold in her mind.

She was completely unaware of Emily and Sam staring at her intently, both of them party to her every thought.

*'I am sensing that there is something to do with Sharon that is causing concern for your parents, little one. I am going to have to leave you for a short time, in order to try and establish precisely what is giving rise to such concerns. Sam will look after you while I'm gone, but you will no longer be able to communicate directly with me, until I return. I will be as quick as I can, for it pains me for us to be parted, even for a short time.'*

The Alien entity thus began the relatively slow process of detaching himself completely from the body and mind of the dog, without causing injury to the animal. He had chosen to partially enter into Sam's being, in order to try to experience for himself, some of the physical enjoyment associated with being such an animal. He needed to be able to live in a much closer proximity to his chosen human companion, Emily. He had anticipated that it would also serve to further his understanding of the most powerful of human emotions that he was still seeking to experience, that of love.

He was not disappointed, being so close to Emily, feeling her tender touch, the sensations of being stroked, brushed and, groomed by her, and the others, had already awoken such deep feelings within him, that it had all become like an insatiable thirst never to be quenched.

He had quite easily come to accept and enjoy his subservient roles in that of being the family pet. He found great pleasure in being the focus of all the family's tender loving care. In return for all the kindness and affection, he reciprocated by trying to be the perfect example of what was expected of him, by bonding closely with every member of what he now regarded to be, his family.

Of course, it was only Emily that knew all of this, and with whom he could fully, and openly, communicate. As such, their bonding was complete. The pair had now become virtually inseparable.

In leaving Sam, the alien left enough additional knowledge implanted in the primitive animal brain, for him to be able to carry on without any noticeable difference in behavioural temperament. The alien knew that the dog would now rather lay down his life than let any physical harm come to anyone in the family. This was especially important with regard to little Emily, for she had rapidly become the first love in the alien's hitherto lonely existence.

Emily's development had moved on at a remarkable pace since Sam had come into her life. From the beginning, she had found it very easy to read the brain patterns of an animal, so keen to ingratiate and show affection. Direct communication had followed, as a natural progression, even more so, when Jo-jo had entered part of himself into Sam's body and mind. It was he that had taught her how to accurately interpret canine thoughts and sounds, to the point that Emily could now 'speak' their very limited, primitive, language.

Emily, still so young, had started to refer to Sam as Jo-jo, for it was only she that knew the truth of the matter. The alien had not sought to discourage this, for the image of himself that he had left in her mind when she was a tiny infant, was that of a big, fluffy, friendly dog.

He had calculated that being in Sam would certainly bring about a closer bonding and understanding between them, thus furthering his quest to physically try and experience emotional love. In many ways his assumptions were proving correct, for Emily certainly loved Sam, or Jo-jo, the entity that temporarily inhabits part of his mind and body.

Intellectually, Emily had now reached a point that, like a new computer that needs programming, she craved input, knowledge. Only just recently, she had found a veritable cornucopia of such knowledge contained in the family bookcase. Sue, one day thinking that all was far too quiet, had found her little daughter sitting on the floor, with Sam, completely surrounded by all the books.

She had chided her daughter, cautioning her against causing any damage, but seeing no harm in her apparently looking at the pictures, she had left her to it.

Sue hadn't even appreciated that Emily was already able to read, let alone speed read, which is what her tiny daughter was doing when she had found her. She, never for one moment would have guessed that Emily was already able to understand most of the content of what was contained in the books.

Emily, being so young and lacking any formal schooling, now needed to sort out the difference between fiction and fact, truth and fantasy, in all that she was reading. This process drew her ever closer to Jo-jo via Sam, with whom she was able to endlessly discuss all such matters by telepathic thought processes alone.

He in turn found it far easier to impart huge pieces of knowledge directly into her brain, rather than attempt to separate out that which was relevant at the time, as opposed to that which he knew would become more apparent, and useful to her, in the future.

Almost the entire contents of the set of junior encyclopaedias were imparted into the memory banks of her mind for future reference, along with the meaningless information contained in the collection of text and reference books that covered a diverse and wide range of subjects. Even those pertaining to Sue's current accountancy studies were not overlooked. Only works of pure fiction were set aside unread.

Not surprisingly, their greatest discussions concerned religion in all its differing forms. In particular, the content of the family bible, which was the hardest for Emily to understand, because it comprised both fact and fiction. Jo-jo advised that many of the stories were undoubtedly the result of myth and exaggeration, created over the centuries by their constant re-telling, but he confessed that where the man, Jesus, was concerned, his knowledge was somewhat limited. This man had proved to be a total enigma, his teachings and accomplishments, mystifying even the watching aliens.

Jo-jo urged Emily to accept all the basic concepts of his teachings, and to try and understand the differences between what is right, and what is wrong, in everything she did. Effectively, to embrace his Christian principles as her role model for guidance in future life.

Emily had already learned how to impart images and suggestion into the minds of her mother and father, but there still remained the seemingly enormous hurdle that involved opening the long dormant recesses of their respective minds, to enable actual communication by thought alone. Telepathy.

Emily had been assured by Jo-jo that it was possible. She needed only to find, identify, and lock on to, the correct miniscule thought waves that sometimes emanated when her parents were either asleep or deep in thought. She should then be able to immediately attune to that frequency, and be able to develop and teach them how to conduct a direct speech process, with her, by thought alone.

In seeking to achieve this, both her parents had already identified her probing presence in their minds. Not understanding what was happening, they had simply referred to it as 'sometimes messing with my head.' Emily was finding that they were now learning how to open their minds and become ever more receptive to her patient thought searching processes. She knew that it could only be a matter of time for her to achieve her goal.

Sharon could stand the agony no longer, and voided her painfully distended bladder in a torrent of warm blessed relief. The pungent smell of her own urine, mingled with that of the pup's faeces, reached her nostrils and caused her to gag. Lying on her back, she was forced to vomit. The content of her stomach finding a resting place around the bottom half of her face and in the small recess of her neck, just under her Adams apple. It wasn't much, but the filth, mess, and stench, added even further to her distress and discomfort. She was just about to try to wipe some of it away, when she realised that if she did, it would immediately be apparent when the basket was finally opened.

She knew now, that she was fighting for her very life. She had no idea why she had been so brutally beaten and kidnapped, it must be that she had stumbled into something far more serious than just the puppy scam, but what? It was also obvious to her that Laura and Shaun could never just let her go, they must have other plans for her, none of them good. The stark reality of her situation was apparent.

She sensed a change of movement in the running of the van. The driver had changed down a couple of gears, and she could tell that they were travelling uphill on a gravel track. She adjusted her position back to that she had been left in. The hood was pulled back down over her face smearing vomit along the bottom seam. She hid the rope that had tied her wrists underneath herself, and then placed her hands behind her back, hoping that it wouldn't be noticed that she was no longer restrained. She waited, heart beating like a sledgehammer, sensing every motion of the van, which had now slowed almost to a stop. There was a harsh meshing of the gears and a slight jerk as it went into reverse, and backed up a short distance. Finally the engine stopped. She heard the roller shutter of the van as it rattled upwards, and Shaun and Laura saying something, but she couldn't make out what. She nearly panicked, her espadrilles, they were off her feet. She located them both and managed to get one foot half inside one shoe, before she felt the basket being dragged backwards, and a waft of cool fresh air coming through the wickerwork. Sharon heard the roller shutter being raised further, and then there was a whining sound and a sensation of descending on the tail lift.

Someone stepped onto the platform and opened the lid of the basket. She heard Laura's voice.

"Oh my god, what a bloody stench. The dirty bitch has pissed herself, and it looks like she's puked up as well. Is she still alive, Shaun?"

"She's breathing, her chest is moving. You get the pups sorted out. I'll go and fetch a pallet truck from the barn. I'm not touching any of that, she can bloody well stay put for now. We'll sort her out tomorrow when the farmhands are not here. Hopefully she'll be dead by then, save us a job."

"Where do you want me to put the pups, Shaun, which cage?"

"Any of the empty ones will do for now. There's a pile of straw over there, that I use for bedding. Throw some of that in first, if you will. Water bowls are over that side, by the tap. They won't need feeding till this evening, but I expect they'll be a bit stressed and thirsty, they usually are. I'll put the kettle on while I'm over at the house."

Sharon heard his footsteps moving away across the gravel. After a few seconds, she sensed that Laura was removing one or two of the puppies from around her. She seemed to be putting them into another container of some sort. She heard her whispering little entreaties to each of them in turn. At last, there was a slight lift of the tail lift as Laura stepped off and walked away, it was now or never.

Sharon sat up, lifted off the hood, and had to squint her eyes in the bright sunlight. Ignoring the pain in her side, she quickly pulled herself onto her feet, and grabbed her shoes. Taking a moment only to slip them on, she was alarmed to see that she would be in full view if Laura were to turn round. She was busy arranging bedding for the pups, in one of a bank of wire mesh cages. Sharon had no idea where she could hide, but she must get out of Laura's sight immediately. She stepped down off the platform and crept round the blind side of the van. Moving towards the front, she now realised that she was in full view of the farmhouse where Shaun was apparently putting on the kettle. The only place left to hide was in the cab of the vehicle. Without a seconds thought, she climbed quickly and quietly up and into the passenger side, where she crouched down on the floor and eased the door shut behind her, locking it on the button in the process.

The seconds passed, giving Sharon time to take stock of her situation. The keys? Where were the keys to the van? She groped round the steering column, and was elated to find that they were still in the ignition.

Voices, she could hear voices, Shaun was apparently returning with the pallet truck. She risked a quick peep over the driver's side door and into the shed where Laura had last been seen. Shaun was standing with his back to her, and he was passing over a cup of something to Laura. Sharon ducked down again and reached over to lock the driver's side door, as well. The mechanism gave an audible click as the button was depressed and Sharon held her breath in anticipation. She need not of worried though, the dogs and puppies in the shed had all become aware of the human presence, and had set about yapping excitedly. Finally Shaun could be heard moving round to the back of the van dragging the pallet truck.

"Shit, she's gone, Lara. Lara, come here quick, the bloody little bitch has escaped somehow."

"Christ, how the hell? Well, she was here less than three minutes past, so she can't have gone far. Get the guns and the dog, while I go down the lane a-ways, and see if I can see her. She'll stick out like a sore thumb in that white top she's wearing. Quickly now, do as I say . . . away with you, man."

Sharon saw Shaun running back towards the farmhouse as she positioned herself in the driving seat of the van. She eased the gear stick into first gear position and kept the clutch pedal depressed. Easing off the handbrake, she depressed the accelerator pedal halfway down and waited till Shaun disappeared into the house, before turning the engine over on the key. As it roared into life, Sharon immediately lifted her foot off the clutch and, with wheels spinning on the gravel, put the vehicle in a tight right hand turn.

As she became lined up with the gravel track, she saw that Laura was about fifty yards ahead, and staring back, dumbfounded, as the van now sped toward her. Sharon lined her up and pushed the pedal right to the floor. At the last moment, Laura, realising what was about to happen, held up her hands and screamed something at Sharon. At the very last second, she tried to dive out of the way. The nearside front quarter of the van hit her a glancing blow on the left shoulder, and she was flung aside like a rag doll being thrown from a pram. Sharon stole a glance in her nearside rear view, and was delighted to see her lying motionless in a tangled heap in the long grass beside the track.

"Have some of that, bitch," she muttered. She also noticed that the tail lift was still down and occasionally dragging along the uneven ground. It was slowing her down, so she would need to stop before much longer in order to raise it.

After a mile or so, Sharon eased back to a more sedate speed, and slowly brought the van to a halt, stopping the engine. She painfully got out and went back to raise the tail lift. The wicker basket had gone, presumably, it had fallen off somewhere? She briefly wondered if the little pups were alright?

It took all her strength to set the tailgate upright, and pull down the roller shutter, so that it could be properly latched. Panting with the exertion, she heaved herself back up into the drivers seat, and wound down the window for some fresh air. She took stock, checking the fuel gauge, it showed half a tank, but she had no idea where she was, or where she was going. Home was out of the question, for that would be the first place they would look to find her. She was filthy dirty, injured, and badly needed some medical help. She thought of David, he must be warned. She needed to speak with him. He would help, of that she was certain . . .

Sharon heard the distant sound of a noisy, high-revving engine, coming from behind. She had stopped the van just round a blind bend in the track. She smiled to herself and quickly put on her seat belt before re-starting the engine. Selecting reverse gear and building up the revs she held it all at biting point on the clutch.

A Land rover came hurtling round the bend, the driver immediately having to slam on its brakes to avoid a collision. The moment Sharon saw it in the rear view mirror, she dropped the clutch and sent the van hurtling backwards toward it. There was a sickening crunch, as the Land Rover crumpled into the back of the van. The impact jolted Sharon violently backward, then forward, in her seat, but the headrest and seatbelt had ensured that she received no further injury. She had already calculated that most of the impact would be absorbed by the heavy tail lift on the rear of the van.

In the comparative silence that followed, she stopped the engine and got out to take a look behind. The whole front of the smaller vehicle was a tangled mess, with steam, oil and petrol seeming to be coming from every part of the engine. Shaun and another man were both slumped unconscious in the front seats. They were bleeding heavily from facial cuts and head wounds. Sharon saw that neither had been wearing seatbelts. Shaun also looked, and sounded, to have chest injuries as well. He was already showing signs of regaining consciousness, but his breathing was laboured and stentorian.

There was a large, black, Alsatian dog in the caged area at the back of the vehicle. With it's back twisted and broken, the animal was obviously dead.

"Clunk, click every trip," Sharon muttered to herself.

Looking around the interior, she noticed two shotguns in the passenger foot well. Both were broken at the breach, but there were cartridges already inserted into the barrels, ready for use. She shuddered at the thought of the damage they might have inflicted upon her. Moving swiftly on, she saw the corner of what looked like a mobile phone, in the glove box, on Shaun's side. Eying him carefully, she reaching inside to take it, but first had to move something heavy out the way. Curious, she withdrew whatever it was from the glove box, as well. She gasped as she recognised that it was a pistol, wrapped in an oily yellow duster, and in a plastic bag. She took both the phone and handgun with her back to the van, which she saw, had extensive damage to the rear. After a quick inspection she decided that it was still driveable. It had to be, for she had no other option . . .

Sharon took a few moments to decide on her next move. Before starting the engine and driving off, she dialled 999 and asked for police. Ignoring the questions from the operator, and in a panicked sounding voice, she reported hearing a large explosion. The phone, with the line still open, she then dropped out of the window, onto the soft grass verge, before driving away.

Sharon knew that the abandoned emergency call would be treated as 'very urgent' and be quickly traced back to this location. She hoped that the police would be very interested in what they found. The most important thing now, was for her to put as much distance as possible between this godforsaken place, and wherever she was going, and to do it as quickly as the accident-damaged van would allow.

The lane emerged at a T-junction onto a single-track tarmac lane. For no apparent reason, Sharon turned right, and continued on for several miles, the van taking up most of the width of the winding road. She hadn't yet seen any other vehicle, or sign of life. Another T-junction, another right, she decided. This time the road was a narrow two lanes, and a small white marker told her that she was on the B4215. Sharon looked around the cab to see if there was a map, or something to tell her where she was. She saw a holdall sticking out from beneath the centre seat. Her damaged left hand prevented her from dragging it out, so she pulled the van into the side of the road, and stopped in the entrance to a gateway, leading into an empty field.

Hefting the heavy bag up onto the seat beside her, Sharon saw that it was divided into two compartments, with three small side pockets on one side. Made entirely in black leather, it was an expensive looking piece of kit. Unzipping the main compartment, Sharon was delighted to find that it contained women's clothing. These were obviously Laura's things. The bag must belong to her.

Sharon quickly sorted out a change of underclothes, a pair of jeans, and a sweatshirt, that looked about her size, a toilet bag and a bit of make-up. Not bothering too much with the rest of the bags contents, she set about tidying herself up as best she could, while using the blind side of the van as her changing facility. Bundled her own soiled clothing into a supermarket shopping bag, found in the glove box of the van, she stuffed everything else back into the holdall.

The other compartment of the bag proved to be a veritable treasure trove. Her own purse and wristwatch, together with some of Laura's jewellery. A Laptop, some CD's, a file-o-fax, several paperwork files, a bank bag containing the envelope with Sharon's £500, and several other bundles of banknotes sorted into their respective denominations. They were all held together with elastic bands that had parcel labels attached, showing the totals. A quick mental tally-up revealed something in excess of £10K. Delving further, Sharon found another pistol, similar to the one she had taken from the Land Rover, but with a spare ammunition clip taped to the handle. There were three, old style, Nokia mobile phones in separate plastic bags. They looked to be comparatively unused, except for a piece of masking tape stuck to the back of each phone. Written on the tape were three differing names, and another mobile number. Sharon shoved it all back into the bag, started the engine, and pulled away.

Her mind was in turmoil, what had she gotten involved with? Nothing made sense anymore? One thing was certain though, she needed to get to somewhere safe. She also needed to dump this van, if she were to be stopped by the Police, highly likely, considering it was stolen and badly damaged, how could she possibly explain being in possession of loaded firearms, and a whole heap of cash?

The road sign indicated that she was about to join the A40, and travelling eastbound, would take her to Cheltenham. 'Cheltenham? That's in Gloucestershire . . . Christ, I'm miles from home. The A40? That goes straight across country towards London, I'm sure? Yes, it's the A40 that's called the Westway, or something, it goes straight into central London, I'm sure . . . Now I know where I'm going.'

Sharon put her foot down.

Jim and Doris Cox were beside themselves with worry. Sharon had walked out of the B&B around nine that morning. It was now five in the evening, and they had heard nothing from her. The new guests had arrived and been made comfortable, but now they needed their evening meal. Alternating between bouts of frustrated anger, and genuine concern for her whereabouts and well being, they set about looking after their guest's immediate needs. They were in the middle of dishing up when the phone rang. It was Jim that answered the call.

"Dad, it's me. No don't talk, I need you to do something urgently for me. Yes, I'm alright, but I won't be home for a few days. I'm sorry, but I'm sure you'll manage without me. No, I can't explain now, I'm on a public telephone, and I don't have much money. Dad, just listen. I need you to find David Morrison-Lloyd's phone numbers for me. I need to speak with him very urgently. No, his card is not in my desk, I've lost it somewhere, that's why I'm ringing. Try directory enquiries, or ring his parents, or something. Do whatever it takes, Dad, it's very urgent. I'll ring you back around 9pm, okay? Love you both . . ."

There was a click, and the line went dead leaving Jim standing there and wondering what on earth was going on?

Laura lay in the grass and carefully moved each limb in turn. Slightly dazed, her left arm and shoulder was already bruised and aching. She knew that she had been hit by the van, but luckily she had been off her feet as she tried to dive to one side. In consequence, it had caught her only a glancing blow, the impact spinning her round. and throwing her up onto the soft grass verge. She slowly managed to sit upright, but then had to quickly draw in her legs and slightly roll out of the way as the Land Rover, driven by Shaun, hurtled past in pursuit of the van. He acknowledged her only with a lift of his hand.

Remarkably, she found that she had sustained very little injury. Apart from the aching shoulder and a few minor grazes to her arms and knees, everything else seemed to be in working order. She pushed herself to her feet and took a few tentative steps back, up towards the farm.

There was a tremendous crashing sound from behind, and she instinctively knew what it was. The Land Rover had found the van . . . Lara turned and started back down the other way, now moving with a sense of urgency, and some concern as to what she would find. Her left shoulder and now her ribs bothered her as she moved, but it was of little consequence, the pains being somewhat overcome by her seething anger. She had little idea of how far she would have to go, but it was all downhill and the going was fairly easy. A couple of minutes, and she began to get out of breath, but fortune was in her favour as the other stockman, Dennis, came up behind, driving the big farm tractor. He too had heard the crash and had come to investigate in the only other suitable vehicle. He stopped to pick up the breathless Lara before continuing. Rounding a sharp bend, they had to slew violently off the track to avoid hitting the stationary Land rover blocking their path. Lara let out an expletive and quickly moved in to take stock. She found that both men, Shaun and Michael, had just about regained consciousness, but were still sitting in the wrecked car, their faces a bloody mess. Shaun appeared to be holding in his chest and was having some difficulty with his breathing. Seeing Lara, he gasped,

"She took my bloody phone and a gun, but I saw her throw the phone out of the van window, it's down there on the grass somewhere. Find it, quick . . ."

"In a minute Shaun, let's get you sorted a bit first, shall we?"

Shaun snorted in anger, "Lara, get the bloody phone woman. Do it now I say. Turn the bloody thing off before they trace the call. I'll bet she's purposely left the line open. Do it now Lara, before we have the damn Filth crawling all over us."

He gasped in pain at the effort he had put into his demand. "And get Dennis to hitch up the tractor to the front of this blasted car, drag us back up to the barn. We've got to hide this vehicle and cover our tracks. Do it Lara, do it now. Quickly, do as I say, woman."

Lara didn't argue, she knew he was right. The phone still showed the 999 open line before she switched it off.

Sharon knew that she was pushing her luck. Pedal to the metal, she had been hurtling along the A40 just about as fast as the little Iveco box van would go. Common sense was telling her to slow down, but the need to put as much distance as possible between herself and wherever it was she had just come from was paramount. She saw a Police patrol car up ahead, and, rather than pass it and show the damaged rear of the van, she chose to take the next exit slip road. It led up to a T-junction where for no apparent reason she chose to turn right. The A415, the road she was now on, took her back under the A40 and onto a roundabout. In negotiating her way round, she spotted a sign pointing the way to the Witney Four Pillars Hotel. Sharon decided that was for her . . .

Twenty minutes and a couple of phone calls later, she had what she wanted most.

"David, David is that you? Oh, thank God, this is Sharon. I've been desperately trying to get hold of you. No just listen to me for a minute, please. I think you're in great danger. It's Laura Dobson and another man, they beat me up and kidnapped me, but I've escaped. I stole their van to get away. David, they've got guns. I think they're coming to get Sam back, maybe to hurt you as well . . ."

"Whoa, slow down there Sharon, don't say anything more, this is a public telephone line. Just answer me a few questions, will you?" Ignoring his plea, she ranted on, almost unintelligibly. "Yes, okay, but tell me first, are you badly hurt?"

He listened grimly to her now tearful replies. "And where exactly are you now, Sharon?"

He wrote it down on his desk blotter. "Do you have any money Sharon? Christ, how much? No, don't explain now, just listen for a minute, here's what I suggest you do." David was thinking on his feet. "Book yourself into the hotel for one night under a false name. If they ask for ID, just offer to pay for the room in advance. Cash on the table usually works. Next, book a local taxi to take you to Terminal 4 Heathrow. You will need to get there for 0930, tomorrow morning. I am going to meet you on the ground floor of the short-term car park, next to the car park payment machines, got that? What have you done with the van?"

"There's a housing estate about half a mile up the road. I backed it up into a dark corner of a big car park. I locked it and threw the keys into the bushes. You'd have to drive right into the car park to see it. I think it will be okay there for a while . . ."

"That all sounds good, well done. Now, quickly run over the plan again just to see that we haven't missed anything?

Sharon did as she was asked.

"That's it, you've got it, I'll see you tomorrow morning then. In the meantime, I'll talk to some people and see about getting you some private medical help, and a safe place to stay. We need to figure out what all this is about, and that will dictate our next move. Ring your Mum and Dad, Sharon, tell them you've got to go away for a few days or something, but on no account mention anything about what's happened, me, or your injuries. What they don't know can't bother them can it? Oh, by the way Sharon, if it's any consolation, I'm sorry to have gotten you into this, love. I feel a bit responsible, if you see what I mean . . . ? I've just had another thought. Bring everything in the bag exactly as it is. We'll look at it together. There might be some significance in the way things are set out, so probably best not to touch anything else for the time being. Okay, I'll see you tomorrow as arranged, then. Take care, bye."

David replaced the receiver, thought for a few minutes, and then dialled another couple of numbers.

He was unaware that Emily and Sam had been listening closely to his conversation with Sharon, and to those calls he made subsequent to hers.

*I have located the lady Sharon, little one. I have locked into her brain pattern, so that I will be able to find her again, instantly. I have detected that she is distressed and has some injuries to her body that require attention, but she will be well again when they are healed. She is thinking that there are some evil people that mean to do her more harm if they find her whereabouts. I do not yet know who they are, and Sharon is asking for some help from your father. I am sensing that she considers there is some danger to you and your family, as well. We will both need to be vigilant where strangers are concerned.*

*I think it would be better for you all to change location until the danger is past. I can put this idea into the mind of your father, but it might be less confusing for him, if it were you that suggested it, Emily . . .*

"Sue, I want you to go and pack up a few things for yourself and the children. Put them in the other car, and take yourselves off to your parents for a while."

"What? Why, David, for God's sake? What about the twins going to school?

Sue, please don't argue, love, just do as I ask. I know all about their schooling, but this has to be regarded as being a lot more important. It's all a bit of a wild story that involves Sharon, who is telling me that I might be in danger. I'm not sure that I've got the whole story yet, but, if there is any substance to her concerns, I would feel a lot better if we were all away from here for a while. At least until I know the score, and I can see what she's getting at?"

David didn't want to alarm Sue too much, but she could see right through him. Her questions reflected her concerns. Why hadn't Sharon gone to the Police yet? Who were these people that she was so afraid of? What was he planning to do to help her? Was there any danger to her and the children?

David was struggling and getting exasperated, there was so much that he didn't know, and couldn't tell her. He finally had to give it to her straight. She just needed to trust his instincts, and please do, as he suggested, do it now, with no more argument. Given the circumstances, he thought, it had to be the most sensible thing.

Lara struggled to support the weight of Shaun as they slowly made their way from the barn to the farm cottage. Dennis was similarly helping Michael, the other stockman, who had been sitting beside Shaun in the accident. Shaun was cursing under his breath at his own inability to stand up and walk properly. His whole left side was very tender from armpit to pelvis and shooting pains in his ribs had already convinced him that one or more were broken. He knew he was going to be out of action for several days; maybe even a week, but he had faith in his own body's powers of healing and recovery.

Shaun refused to be put into his bed and preferred his favourite armchair in the lounge. Lara set about cleaning up his face and, at his insistence, used ordinary superglue and pieces of sticking plaster to repair the worst of the superficial cuts to his face and forehead. He sat silent while she fussed over him, only speaking when she was between ministrations. He was thinking out loud more than addressing her directly. She noticed that his speech was slightly slurred at times, and looked at the pupils of his eyes. One was definitely slightly larger than the other. She suspected that there may be a concussion, but Shaun denied having any sort of headache, and refused any proper medical examination.

"Just give me a couple of days to get back on my feet then we'll go find that little bitch. I'm am personally going to enjoy slowly shagging the arse off her, before wringing her scrawny neck, and mincing her up into tiny pieces to feed to my pigs"

Laura shuddered at the thought. She knew that he meant every word.

"Shaun, she dialled 999 and called the Police, they could be here any minute. We are going to have to get away from here PDQ. I think we should go to the other safe house and let some of the dust settle on this bloody mess. I'll ring Dermot and ask him to come and get us."

She fished her phone out of her jacket pocket, but realised that their number, for security reasons, was not listed on her personal mobile. Her file-o-fax, that's where . . . Then came the awful realisation. Her file-o-fax was in her bag that was tucked under the middle passenger seat of the van, which was now, God only knows where?

The enormity of it hit her like a sledgehammer. Everything was contained in that bag. They were all in deep trouble unless they got it back intact. Lara tried to convince herself that perhaps Sharon wouldn't notice it, but she remembered that it had been too big for the space and had protruded forward from under the seat. It was too much to hope for.

"Shaun, we don't have time to wait for you to get better, we've got to act now, otherwise we're finished."

His eyes narrowed, "What are you talking about woman?"

"I'm talking about us, Shaun, the whole gang, all of us. Unless I get that bag of mine back, intact and unopened, we are all dead meat. Caput, finito, am I getting through to you now, you great lummox?"

Shaun didn't appreciate being spoken down to in this manner, and but for his injuries, he would have reacted violently, giving her a backhander. Instead, he hissed,

"Explain yourself woman, and mind your tongue, if you know what's good for you."

"Shaun, I'm sorry, I didn't mean any disrespect, forgive me, please. It's my bag, my holdall, it's in the bloody van. It's got everything in it. My laptop, my purse and credit cards, CD's with all the transaction records, my file-o-fax, paperwork on the safe houses, my gun, details of all our previous operations, together with our identities, press cuttings and a whole host of other pieces of paper that I saved from way back. It even has Marty's contact details. Shaun, we must get it all back immediately, before anyone else gets a chance to look at it."

"Holy shit, woman, what in gods name possessed you to keep records like that? And to be carrying them all around with you as well? You stupid cow, I aught to be shooting you myself. Sit down over there, we need to think this through. The bitch won't get far in the van, it was probably too badly damaged. She didn't have any money, so my guess is she will be either phoning home, or that Lloyd bloke. Worst case scenario is that she goes straight to the Filth."

"Oh my god . . . Shaun, the money. There's over ten grand in that bag as well. Money from Dermot. I hadn't had a chance to bank it."

Shaun waved his hands in the air in despair, and immediately regretted doing so. A shooting pain in his ribs caused him to clutch at his side again. He struggled to overcome the pain and recover his composure before carrying on.

"That settles it then, we will have to go to Dermot's place, and call a conference with the others. Michael and Dennis will take care of this place for the time being. How is Michael by the way? Is he alright? You'd better go and check on him while I think this through."

Lara did as she was bidden. She was relieved to temporarily get out of Shaun's company. There was no knowing what he might do when he was angry. Laura realised that for the first time, she was no longer in control, and that she was becoming frightened of Shaun.

The stockman, Michael, was on his feet. His face was decorated with two pieces of surgical plaster and his right eye looked puffy and swollen. He would soon be sporting a black eye, that much was evident. Apart from the obvious, a sore head, and feeling a bit shaky, he declared himself to be relatively unscathed.

Asked if they were okay to run the farm for a while, Dennis and Michael, both of whom had families, reluctantly agreed to move into the farmhouse, until Shaun was fit enough to return. Nothing was mentioned regarding why he was vacating, Lara let them assume that Shaun needed better medical attention to his injuries.

Laura's biggest regret was in regard to all her dogs and puppies that were being kept in the barn. There was no time to arrange for them to be removed elsewhere and neither of the stockmen were willing, nor capable, of taking care of them as well. There was no alternative, they would all have to be destroyed. "We'll have to turn them all into pig swill," was how it was callously put it to her. She was horrified, and racked her brain for some alternative solution, but in the available time left to her, she was unable to come up with anything viable. Reluctantly she had to agree to their demise. It hurt, for Laura, despite all her other evil ways, loved her animals . . .

Seething with anger and fighting back the tears, she cursed her own stupidity and blamed it all on Sharon talking to her Mr David double-barrel, bloody Lloyd.

David sat in his car in the short-term car park of Heathrow terminal four. He was watching the lift areas expecting to see Sharon arrive any minute. It was just after 9.30am and she should have been there by now. The minutes dragged by, and he kept checking his watch. David was a stickler for timekeeping, and considered it to be rude not to be on time for an appointment. At last, a woman looking a lot like Sharon, came out of the lift and looked uncertainly around her. David watched her carefully. Even at a distance he could see that her face was a bruised mess, and her left arm was carried high in a sling. She had a black, heavy looking holdall in her right hand. She saw him sitting in his car and walked toward where he was parked. David cursed silently under his breath. He had wanted to first check that she was alone and not being followed, before picking her up. Too late now . . .

He got out of his car and moved toward her. He noticed that two smartly dressed men appeared to be watching her from the lift area. They looked a bit out of place somehow. He took the bag from her and murmured,

"Don't look round, but I think you're being watched. Get in the back seat and belt up, we're going to be moving fast."

David threw the holdall in the boot, and gently closed it. Getting into the car, he took one last surreptitious look toward the two men, and he saw that they were walking purposefully toward the exit road. David decided to play for time, and got out of his car again. He walked over to the payment machines, and went through the motions of paying for his car parking time. He watched out of the corner of his eye as the two men got into a waiting blue Ford Focus.

David drove slowly toward the exit barriers and saw that the Ford had already passed through ahead of him. It appeared to be waiting at the junction. He cleared the barrier and drove slowly up behind the Ford, there was no way that he wanted to pass it, better to have it in front, it gave him more options. The driver of the Ford waved his arm out of the window for him to pass, but David ignored it. The seconds passed and another car came up behind David's. The driver of the Ford was looking at David in his rear view. The driver of the car behind David, impatient with the hold-up, sounded his horn. It prompted the Ford into pulling away with a screech of tyres, David followed. At the second roundabout, the driver of the Ford committed himself on the dual carriageway, and headed towards the M25, expecting David to follow. But he did a sharp left, and headed down towards Staines, putting his foot down. He'd lost them for the time being.

He smiled to himself and glanced over his shoulder at Sharon sitting quietly in the back. It was his first chance to get a closer look at her face, and to speak to her. Black eye, thick lips and her nose looked a bit crooked and painfully swollen.

"My God, Sharon, you look as though you've done a few rounds with Mike Tyson, tell me what they did to you, and why?"

He listened quietly as she tearfully related everything that had happened to her. He only interrupted to clarify a couple of points, otherwise he left her to let it all pour out. It seemed to be helping her, the release of all that pent-up emotion and anger? Sharon finished her story and they both sat in silence for a while, each with their own thoughts.

"Sharon, those two blokes in the Ford, have you seen them before?"

"No, do you think they've been following me? It doesn't seem possible, how would they have known where I was, or where I was going?"

"Well, they were certainly interested in us, that much was obvious. They'll know that we've rumbled their cover, so we had better watch out for anything suspicious in the future. I don't for one minute suppose that they will just give up and go away. God only knows what all this is about, Sharon. Are you sure that you've told me everything? This has got to be more than just a scam involving selling a few dodgy puppies. You mentioned something about guns, where are they?"

"In the holdall, two small hand guns, pistols, I suppose you'd call them. I don't know anything about guns David, so I haven't touched either of them, at all. And yes, I can't think of anything I haven't told you that's relevant to all of this, except that I am bloody scared stiff, and just about at my wits end. Where are we going, by the way? I need to get some medical treatment as soon as possible."

"I was going to take you to Sue's parents, but now that I've seen the state of you, I've changed my mind, I'm going to get you some of the very best medical help available. These people we're going to are some very good friends of mine, the ones who got me through all of my injuries. They're considered to be the very finest in their particular fields of medicine. They'll take good care of you, and get you fixed up again, so stop worrying on that score. As for the rest of this mess, I think it might be time to call in some help, don't you?"

"Not the Police David, please. I couldn't bear to face Mum and Dad if I was going to be prosecuted for anything. It would just about break their hearts, I know it would."

"Sharon, this is something far more serious than just the puppy-dog scam. These people are armed criminals of some sort. Laura Dobson and this other bloke, Shaun, are obviously mixed up in something that we don't yet know about. It would seem that the threat of reporting them to the Police was enough to trigger them into doing what they've done to you. You've already said that they may be after me, as well, and I've got my family to consider. We may have no other option than to pass it all over to the proper authorities to deal with. We're way out of our league here, don't you understand?"

Sharon bit her swollen lip, bowed her head and cried, her emotions no longer under control. David pulled a packet of tissues from the glove box and passed them to her. They travelled the next ten miles in comparative silence. Except for Sharon's occasional sob and nose blowing, each was party only to their own thoughts.

"Do you think that Laura was going to kill me, David?"

"Probably not Laura herself, more likely that bloke, Shaun. But that's not to say that she wouldn't have gone along with it. They probably had no other option, Sharon. How could they just let you go? So, yes, I think the bastards were going to kill you . . . You were lucky to get away like you did."

David thought for a bit. "Tell me again what you remember about the location of where they took you. A farm of some sort, you said.

Picture it in your mind again, Sharon. Did you see evidence of any farm animals, milking sheds, cattle byres, feed stores, you know, that sort of thing? What about muck on the ground? Every cattle farm I've ever seen has some of that around?"

"There were sheds, big ones, small barns, I suppose. They were all around a central courtyard, which was quite big, about the size of two tennis courts? The cottage, or farmhouse was just ordinary. Quite old looking, not modern, it's red brick, and probably 1930'ish, if I had to guess its age.

I saw a tractor and the front of a larger truck sticking out of one of the buildings. Then there was the Land rover, and a quad bike, I think. They were parked in a cleared space beside the same building. I didn't see any other animals, only the dogs and puppies in the cages. I'd guess there were about fifty of them altogether, all in the one shed. There was definitely a smell about the place, an animal smell, typical of a farm, but as I say, I didn't see any other farm animals.

The yard was a bit muddy. I only had my espadrilles on and they were caked. I had to wash them in the hotel bathroom sink. The farm itself is up a long gravel track, well off the road, maybe two miles or more? I drove several miles down country lanes before I even got to a B road. The B4215, was that it?"

"If we were to try and backtrack your route, do you think you would be able to find it on a map, Sharon?"

"I'm not sure, but I'm willing to give it a go. How much further is it David? This girl is badly in need of the ladies room."

"Not far now love, about ten more minutes, okay?"

# Chapter 3

Shaun Riley sat in a comfortable armchair, a large glass of Bushmills' Irish whiskey clutched in his right hand. His left arm, he held in such a manner so as to lend support to his painful ribs. The late evening car journey from Tiptree Farm to Bleanaway Quarry had been absolute agony for him, despite the luxury and comfort of the brother's Range Rover that had come to fetch them. By the time that they arrived at the Quarry, Shaun looked decidedly pale, and very much the worse for wear. He was forced to lean heavily on Lara again, as they slowly made their way from the car to the bungalow. At his insistence, she had to lower him carefully into an armchair, instead of putting him straight to bed. Chiding him for being so damned awkward and stubborn, and for refusing to go to hospital, Lara tried to cover the fact that she was deeply concerned for him. She suspecting that he might have something more seriously wrong than just cracked ribs. In her eyes, Shaun had always been a tower of strength, and it frightened her to see him reduced to something as weak as a kitten in this way.

The brothers still had no idea why Lara and Shaun had suddenly demanded to be brought to Bleanaway. Lara was a fairly infrequent visitor, but they hadn't seen Shaun for more than thirty years.

Michael made them very welcome and set about preparing a late supper, while Dermot, for Shaun's benefit, proudly launched himself into a potted history of everything that they had achieved since his last visit, just after their 'days of glory,' as he put it. As he spoke, he watched Shaun help himself to another glass from the bottle of Bushmills, left on the table. He looked questioningly at Lara for some explanations. Before she could speak, Michael came through with the sandwiches and salad he had prepared, and they set the table for supper.

They ate in comparative silence, Shaun, although hungry, found difficulty in sitting upright in a dining chair, and in swallowing his food. He contented himself with seeking only to empty Dermot's bottle of Bushmills' the effects of which, were becoming apparent. Excusing himself from the table, he painfully retired back to the easy chair where he stretched out and closed his eyes. In a few minutes, his snores proclaimed him to be dead to the world. The rest of them, dog tired, turned in to sleep fitfully. There still hadn't been any reason or explanation offered as to why they were at Bleanaway.

At breakfast, Dermot could contain his impatience no longer.

"So tell us why you've come here Lara? And what's the matter with Shaun? Why have you not contacted us in the proper manner as we all agreed? You've put all our carefully planned security measures in jeopardy. Why?"

"We have an urgent problem that requires immediate attention. Shaun and I think that our cover may have already been compromised. We couldn't stay at Tiptree or Weymouth, so that's why we're here. At this moment, Dermot, nobody else but you can possibly know of our whereabouts, so we're safe here for the time being. But unless we get some of my property back, we might all be in bad trouble very soon. I'll try to explain . . ."

Talking quietly and answering the occasional question, Lara recounted everything that had occurred. She omitted nothing, neither taking any blame, nor apologising for any of her actions.

It was Michael that broke the silence following her revelations.

"So, let me see if I've got this right. This Sharon woman is in possession of your holdall, which contains not only some of our money, but also your gun. Worst of all, there's a file that contains all the planning details relating to some of our previous operations, is that how it is?"

"Yes Michael, that's exactly how it is, and now you must appreciate why it is so vitally important that we get it all back before she realises what she's got, and decides to hand it over to the authorities. If that happens, I'm afraid we're all finished."

"Alright, I'm not even going to ask why you decided to keep such a file, the stupidity of it is beyond my comprehension. We can talk more about that later. So, what have we got on her present whereabouts? And, more to the point, what have you and Shaun done already?

"At this moment we don't know where she is, so we need to locate her. Shaun was talking to a couple of his men last evening, while we were waiting for you to pick us up. He's told me that they're bloody good and don't mess about. He's promised them a £10K incentive for the return of the holdall and all its contents. There's a similar bonus for proof of the demise of Sharon Cox. We know her home address in Weymouth, it's a little B&B, but I very much doubt that she would be stupid enough to go back there. She might have contacted her parents and told them where she is though. Shaun's men will already be looking into that aspect. We know that she was trying to contact a taxi driver by the name of David Morrison-Lloyd. He's some sort of family friend to her adoptive parents. We have his business card and we will soon know exactly where he lives. I would anticipate that Shaun's men would certainly be talking to him in the near future, as well. They're probably already on to it, even as we speak. We need to trace the damaged van as quickly as possible. There is just an outside chance that my bag might still be under the centre passenger seat undiscovered, but somehow, I doubt it. I've already put the word around to some of my associates in the travelling community, it might be good if you could do the same, please, Dermot." He nodded his agreement.

"We know that the van had half a tank of fuel, so theoretically it could be anywhere within 200 miles. However, it must be quite badly damaged at the rear, so I don't think she would have chanced driving it too far away from Tiptree.

Shaun is obviously out of action, and neither of us has any other transport. Apart from a few pounds in my pocket, we have no money, and I have no means of access, to get at any more. My bank cards are in my purse, and all my accounts details are in my file-o-fax, both of which are in the holdall."

"Transport is not a problem, Lara, you can use my Range Rover if necessary. We keep a float of £500 here, you are welcome to that if you wish, but what would you want cash for?"

"Thanks Dermot. We may have to express gratitude, grease a palm or two, who knows? I'm a bit worried about Shaun, though. Is there any way we can get him some medical help without him having to go to hospital?"

Shaun, on hearing mention of his name, awoke from his alcoholic stupor. The act of pulling himself upright in the armchair where he had spent the night, made him gasp in pain. He hissed through gritted teeth,

"I've already told you woman, I don't need no medics prodding me around. Give me a couple of days and I'll be back on my feet, it's just a couple of cracked ribs, that's all. Paracetamol and some more Bushmills, that'll do for me."

He tried to stand, but the effort was too much. He waved the empty glass at Dermot and pointed to the nearly empty bottle.

"Fill me up again please Dermot, there's a good chap. I've heard most of what's been said, now it's my turn. As I see it, we have no other option but to stay here for the time being. We are probably safe enough for now, but if the worst happens, it won't take long for the Filth to cotton on to this place. We need to contact Marty and the other guy, what's-his-name, Connor, that's it. Warn them about what's happened. Do we have their phone numbers?"

"We have them," Dermot murmured, "But, not on secure lines. Marty shares an office in Stormont now, so we would have to go through the switchboard to speak with him. I doubt that he would even accept a call if he knew it was from us. He's a very important man now, Shaun, a Personal Assistant and advisor to the Deputy First Minister, Martin McGuinness. He would definitely have the most to lose if this fiasco gets out of hand. The political ramifications don't bear thinking about. My inclination is to leave him out of it completely, unless we are forced into telling him.

As for Connor McCall, he's now a Solicitor with offices in London and Bournemouth. We do have both office numbers, but, as far as we know, nobody has spoken with him since Ryan's death, thirty-six years ago. That is, unless either of you has?"

"I'm in touch with his senior partner, Tony Williams. He has acted for me in several personal matters. I don't think he knows anything about Connor's involvement with us, though. So it's probably better that we try to keep it that way. Let's try for a home number for him instead. Do you two have a computer terminal here somewhere? It shouldn't take long for me to find him."

There was a moments silence while each of them wondered sort of 'personal business' it was that required Lara to engage the services of a rather prominent London Solicitor? No doubt explanations would follow, or perhaps she might make it apparent in the fullness of time, but for someone supposed to be keeping a low profile . . . ?

Dermot conducted Lara to the small office extension to the bungalow. It was from here that the brothers were able to run their business. Shaun turned to Michael, who was sitting opposite him in a similar easy chair, eating a dish of porridge.

"What do you have in the way of guns, Michael? That damned woman took my pistol as well. I'm feeling naked without it."

"We don't keep anything here Shaun, unless you count Dermot's little .410 garden gun that he uses to shoot crows on the reserve. The cache of arms is safely buried and well out of harms way, best leave it that way, eh?"

"Well, we're going to be digging them up again then, aren't we? For right now, I'm needing another gun and they're no damn good to anyone buried in the bloody ground. Get Dermot on to it immediately. Do it now, do you hear what I'm saying, do it now?"

Dermot walked back through from the office. "We can all hear what you're saying Shaun, but it's not quite that simple. The guns and ammunition have been in the ground for thirty-five years, or more. So who knows what state they're in? For all we know, they could all be rusted out and useless by now? Secondly, I'm with Michael on this one. I too think it best to leave them where they are. This is our home, not the OK corral. Nobody is going to be allowed to start any shooting in this place, and that includes you, Shaun. Lastly, people who carry guns usually end up getting shot themselves. Our days of death or glory are long behind us now. We value our lives too much to throw them away in the pursuit of what we both now perceive to be a lost cause. If the Police turn up here to arrest us, then so be it. I for one, will not be putting up any resistance."

"Well said, Dermot, that goes for me, as well. There's probably more chance of the Pope turning to Judaism than in us ever seeing a United Ireland. Even our own people can't seem to live peaceably together, can they? Surely, even you can see that it's a lost cause now, Shaun? It's certainly not one worth dying for, is it?"

Michael, setting his empty dish to one side, got up out of his chair and approached Shaun with the intention of re-filling his glass again. He leaned forward towards Shaun indicating that he should hand him the glass.

For an injured man, Shaun's reactions were lightning fast. His left hand shot out and grabbed the back of Michael's head dragging him down and off balance. The glass in Shaun's right hand shattered as it was rammed into Michael's face. His scream was stifled as Shaun viciously thrust the palm of his right hand up under Michael's chin and hurled him backwards onto the floor. Shaun hadn't even moved out of his chair, but Michael, his face already a bloody mask, was down, and totally out of it.

Dermot gave a strangled cry and leapt to his injured brothers side.

"My god Shaun, what've you done, what was that all about? Michael's an old man with a bad heart, no harm to anyone. Lara, Lara, here, quickly. Bring some towels from the kitchen, quickly now . . ."

Shaun was wrapped in agony with the effort. Through gritted teeth he hissed his vehemence.

"He's a fucking coward, a traitor to the cause, like you. What's happened to you both for Christ's sake? Where's the boys I once knew, the ones that risked their lives for the cause? Are you both just going to sit here and wait for the British scum to come and take you? Because, by god, that's never going to happen to me. If this is where I am to die, I'll be making damn sure that I take as many of the bastards with me as I can. Now, fetch me a fucking gun."

Lara, on hearing the disturbance, came hurrying through from the office.

"What's happened, what's going on? Oh, my god, Michael, how did this happen?"

"Bloody Shaun . . . Quick Lara, fetch me some clean towels from the linen cupboard before he bleeds to death." Dermot was carefully extracting pieces of broken glass from his brother's face and trying to reposition his bottom lip, which was almost severed.

"Steady Michael, easy now old lad, don't try to speak, there's a good chap. don't worry yourself, we'll soon get you fixed up again. You'll be all right, you'll see . . ."

Lara arrived with an armful of assorted clean towels and knelt down beside Dermot who began applying them as pads pressed firmly over the wounds to staunch the bleeding. With his back to Shaun, he whispered to Lara.

"We need to get Michael to hospital immediately, he's in a bad way, I think. Damn Shaun to hell, there was no necessity for this. If the Police don't kill him, then by Christ, I will. The man's a raving bloody lunatic. Here hold on to this, I'm going to phone for an ambulance."

He started to rise, but never quite made it. The near-empty bottle of Bushmills smashed down onto the back of his head and sent him sprawling on top of his brother.

Two smartly dressed men had made a quiet entry through the open front door of the B&B. One, tall, slim, fair-haired and with a neat moustache, signalled to his companion to remain silent by placing his finger to his lips. A nod of understanding and a raised eyebrow from the other shorter, darker complexioned, and stockily built man, was enough. The first man pointed to the Visitors Book and Register on the table, and they both started to turn back the pages, the shorter man taking notes.

"Can I help you Gentlemen?"

They both looked up, startled, and moved guiltily away from the table. Jim Cox, wiping his hands on a tea towel, was standing behind, and eyeing them both suspiciously. His keen hearing had detected the sound of the loose, creaking floorboards in the hallway, as they had made their entry. He had already noticed that, apart from a document case under the arm of the smaller man, they appeared to have no luggage, but it might be in a car outside, perhaps? They were definitely not his normal run-of-the-mill type of B&B customer.

"Sorry, we were just looking to see if there were some favourable comments in the book. We were considering taking a room for the night, do you have any vacancies?"

Jim decided that he didn't like what he saw. There was nothing that he could quite put a finger on, they just didn't seem to ring true. He made a show of checking the Register, knowing already that there were two vacant doubles, but with Sharon away, he and Doris had been run off their feet coping with the two families they already had booked in for the week.

"No, sorry gents, it would seem that we're fully booked with some new people due to arrive later this afternoon. If it's any help, I could recommend a couple of other similar establishments, or a very reasonably priced local hotel, nearby."

"That's a pity, Mr Cox, we were recommended to come to you by a friend of yours. She spoke very highly of your establishment, and felt sure you would be able to accommodate us." The fair-haired man spoke with a slight accent that Jim couldn't quite place, Scottish, or Irish perhaps?

Surprised that they already knew his name, Jim politely enquired, "And this person would be . . . ?"

"Laura, Laura Dobson. I believe you know her, yes?"

"I know of her, but I wouldn't have numbered her amongst my friends. More a passing acquaintance, really, but I will thank her for her recommendation when I see her."

"I don't suppose you would happen to know where she is at the moment would you Mr Cox? She's not at home in Marlborough Avenue, and I would so much have liked to see her. I'm her nephew you see, and my colleague and I, well, we're down here on business and I haven't seen Aunt Laura for some years. She's not answering on her mobile, either."

"No, I have no idea where she might be. She's better known to my daughter, Sharon, but she's away for a few days, as well, so I can't ask her for you."

"Would that be Sharon Roberts? I think my aunt has mentioned her before. Could they possibly be somewhere together do you think? I am really keen to speak with Aunt Laura before we go back up north. Can you perhaps ring Sharon and ask her for me?"

Jim became even more suspicious. He didn't want to be rude, but he now felt the urge to tell them both to bugger-off. He didn't like being questioned in this manner, and Sharon hadn't used the name, 'Roberts' since he and Doris had formally adopted her back in 1990. Whoever these people were, they were not being straight with him, that much was apparent. He'd heard enough . . .

"My daughters name is Sharon Cox, so you must be mistaken. Why are you asking me all these personal questions anyway? I really am a very busy man, and I don't have the time to stand around chatting, so if there is nothing more, I will bid you both a good day if you please."

Jim moved to the front door and took out the wedge to enable it to be closed. He meant it to be a clear signal for them to leave.

"Sorry Mr Cox, we understand completely. I wonder, would it be too much to ask for Sharon's mobile number so that I could ring her. It can't do any harm, can it? She might be with my aunt, perhaps?"

"No sorry, that is not possible. My daughter is travelling abroad and her mobile phone is here with us. She is non-contactable. I wouldn't give her number to a total stranger anyway. Goodbye gentlemen."

Jim watched them leave, an uneasy feeling playing on his mind. Sharon was evidently in some sort trouble, but where, how, what and why, were all the unknown factors. Could the Dobson woman be involved? He wished Sharon would just phone and let him know. Whatever was wrong, he was sure that he and Doris would be able to sort it out for her . . .

Late that evening, David and George Lloyd, Sue's father, were carefully laying out the contents of the holdall on the covered billiard table at the Lloyd's Surrey home. Before an item was removed, its position in the bag was recorded and it was given an identification label. David had no idea why he was doing this, it was something deemed to be the correct procedure in his previous training. Besides, it did no harm, and might prove useful later.

First out were various items of women's clothing in a poly bag. Some of it was soiled and bloodstained, so this was identified as belonging to Sharon. The remainder, which was clean, was assumed to belong to Laura Dobson. It was put into two separated piles.

Next came a laptop computer. No attempt was made to turn it on, it was just given a label with the make, model and serial number recorded. George was making a separate list of the items as they worked. The evening wore on, and they stopped for a break surveying their progress so far. The tabletop was now getting a bit crowded with everything laid out separately. His list read,

1. Two fully loaded handguns together with one spare ammunition clip and a total of 39 live rounds.

2. Eight assorted CD's variously labelled, and seemingly relating to dog breeding and animal sales.

3. Two passports in different women's names. One Laura Dobsons. The other, of Irish issue, is in the name of Lara Dobbs. (The photographs are similar. There is little doubt that this is the same person.)

4. Four files of paperwork relating to two differing bank accounts drawn on the Bank of Ireland.

5. A cloth bank bag containing £10,350 in bundles of used banknotes of different denominations.

6. Three identical Nokia, old style, mobile phones. Each has a name and number stuck on the back.

7. One very modern, top-of-the-range Samsung touch-screen mobile phone and charger. Probably Laura Dobson's?

8. One purse/wallet containing cash, credit cards, receipts and other personal paperwork in the name of Laura Dobson.

9. An old file-o-fax belonging to Laura Dobson.

10. A bag of make-up and personal toiletries.

11. A large bunch of sixteen assorted keys.

12. A box file containing copies of three property title deeds and paperwork relating to the purchase of the said properties.

The bottom of the bag was now all that was left, and sticking out from underneath the stiff base insert was the corner of another file. It proved to be the most startling revelation of all the contents. David and George spent the rest of the evening, and well into the early hours studying and discussing its content in apparent disbelief.

They finally retired, their minds reeling, knowing that the information in their hands was so sensitive that it should immediately be passed on to a very senior Police Officer for proper investigation. However, after some discussion, they both felt that there were some issues that needed addressing first.

George Lloyd had recognised the name 'Tony Williams,' the solicitor's signature that featured on several of the legal letters and documents in the files. He and Tony had been more than passing acquaintances over the years. They had studied Law together and qualified more or less at the same time. Now, as members of the same Gentlemen's Club, they frequently enjoyed a glass or two in each other's company. George refused to believe that the Tony Williams he knew, would knowingly be involved with anything untoward. He therefore felt that he owed it to Tony, as a lifelong friend, to have a quiet and discreet word in his ear, before submitting everything to the proper authorities for investigation. To that end, he made a note in his diary to ring Tony early the next morning, and to arrange to meet up with him at his earliest convenience.

David got very little sleep that night, there was too much to think about. He wished that Sue, quietly slumbering beside him, would wake up so that they could talk it through. He glanced again at the luminous dial on his battered old Rolex Submariner. 0340hrs, he remembered that he was due to pick up at Heathrow at 0710hrs. Two JP Morgan executives to go back to Chaseside. He also needed to call in at home and pick up some more odds and ends that they had forgotten in their hasty departure.

His mind kept drifting back over everything that had taken place, trying to make some sense of it all, and put the events into a chronological sequence. It dawned on him that he really should be making some contemporaneous notes as he had been trained to do. He resolved that he would address this at his earliest opportunity. He then realised that it had only been a little over a week since he and the kids had been playing on the beach at Weymouth with not a care in the world. Now, it was as if there was just too much taking place for him to cope with alone.

He heard Sam give a little bark, something that he rarely did. Curious, David slipped out of bed, picked up his dressing gown, and padded across the landing to the children's room. They were all fast asleep, but Sam was standing at the window looking intently through a gap in the heavy curtains. He heard David's approach behind him and turned his head toward him in acknowledgement of his presence. Kneeling down beside him, David parted the curtains a little so that they could both see. Fondling Sam's head and ears he whispered, "What is it boy, what's bothering you?" The dog whimpered and pawed at the window. David stared out focusing all his attention on the moonlit back garden for a full minute. Everything seemed to be all right, but he was not about to dismiss the dog's heightened senses without further investigation.

"Come on then lad, something is obviously bothering you, let's go see what it is, shall we?"

Man and dog moved quietly downstairs to the kitchen. With Sam eager to get outside, David, as silently as possible, unlocked and slowly opened the back door. Sam pushed his way past David's legs and shot off across the garden toward the bushes in the corner, barking loudly as he went, David followed, vainly trying to get into his dressing gown as he ran barefoot in the dew-wet grass. There was some commotion in the bushes, and David thought he heard someone curse, and Sam give a yelp before it all went quiet again.

"Sam where are you boy? Sam, here boy . . ." David was blundering around blindly in the bushes wishing he'd had the foresight to bring a torch. On the other side of the fence, he heard an engine start, a diesel, it sounded like a small truck, but he couldn't be sure. It pulled away with a screech of tyres and disappeared, unseen, into the night. He found Sam lying on his side, unconscious in the bushes.

Gathering him up in his arms, David ran awkwardly back across the lawn shouting to rouse the rest of the house as he went. He reached the kitchen and with one sweep of his arm cleared everything off the granite worktop. He gently laid Sam down, and as he did so, all the house lights came on. George, in his dressing gown, Sue in her nightdress, both stared uncomprehendingly at the scene before them. David was listening at Sam's chest and trying to establish if he was still alive. There was some blood that looked to be coming from one of the dog's ears.

"George, we need a vet, now. Get on the blower. Find me an emergency practice somewhere local. Sue, I need a blanket, some old towels and warm water . . . quickly love, he's alive and breathing, but he's taken a blow to the head. There were some intruders in the garden."

David heard another sound behind him. The three children and Edith were all standing in the doorway. David looked into Emily's eyes, the telepathic message he received from her was as clear as if she had spoken. Without even having to think about how he should reply, he had answered her question in the same manner. In the heat of the moment, the full significance of it failed to register.

'I think he'll be just fine, Em, but we need to quickly find someone special who can help make him all better again. Daddy will see to it.'

George and Sue set about their allotted tasks, David was making a show of fussing over Sam for the children's benefit. Inwardly he was seething with rage, for all this was becoming very personal now.

George quickly managed to find a veterinary practice that operated an emergency animal ambulance service. In response to the call, Sam was on his way to undergo treatment within an hour. By that time, to everyone's relief, he was already showing signs of regaining consciousness, but the family were taking no chances, he needed urgent attention. George, together with an anxious Sue and Emily in his car, closely followed the ambulance to the vet clinic.

The rest of the family, the twins and Edith, went back to their beds, but David had a shower and readied himself for work. As soon as it was daylight, he carefully went over the ground where Sam had been found injured. Two differing sets of footprints coming from the back fence showed the point of entry. It was apparent that Sam had given a good account of himself as there was an area of flattened grass and shrub where a scuffle had taken place. A two-foot long piece of 20mm iron reinforcing bar, was found discarded nearby, probably used to hit the dog he thought to himself? David left it in situ, he wasn't sure whether or not he was going to call in the Police yet.

Over breakfast, he sorted out a small notebook for himself and started to jot down a few things.

There was little doubt in his mind that all of this was somehow connected with what had happened to Sharon, but as yet, he had no definite proof. The very fact that there were people trying to get into the Lloyd's house was enough to convince him that, whoever it was, had already tracked him down. It was a reasonable assumption that this was as a result of his recent association with Sharon. The only people who knew of this were the men who had seen him pick her up at Heathrow, but who were they? Did they also know where he had taken her for treatment? He thought not, but he needed to warn her to be on her guard and to lie low for the time being.

One thing was for sure; he now needed to take urgent steps to protect his family. It was time to go on the offensive and he needed a definite plan of action. Collecting his thoughts, he set about planning his strategy.

Rule one, identify your enemy. He mentally started to assimilate what he knew so far.

Laura Dobson, AKA Lara Dobbs. She lives alone in Weymouth in a house that she apparently owns? She is either the sister, or the wife of Ryan Dobbs, who, according to the file, seems to have been the leader of an IRA terrorist unit, back in 1974. Lara's last known location was at Tiptree farm, the property identified from copies of deeds on file, and the probable location from where Sharon escaped.

Shaun Riley, close accomplice of Lara Dobbs, the person responsible for inflicting Sharon's injuries. She described him as being, Irish, in his sixties, big built and very strong. He may be injured from the accident engineered by Sharon during her escape? He was last seen at Tiptree Farm as well.

Marty McCue, mentioned only once in the file, and whose name was on the back of one of the three mobile phones. Present whereabouts unknown.

Dermot and Michael Close. Probably brothers? They may be living together at a place named Bleanaway Quarry, from where they may now be running a business named Close Roadstone & Tarmacadam Ltd. Their names being on some deeds, and another of the three phones. (Present location needing verification. NB—Try looking them up on the net, they might have a website?)

Connor McCall, mentioned in the file as being a source of intelligence gathering. May be a junior partner in a firm of solicitors 'Williams, Thompson & McCall' a fact yet to be verified by George? His name being on the last of the three phones. Present whereabouts unknown.

Then there were two or three more unknown male persons, briefly seen two days ago at Heathrow. Nothing else known.

OK, so that made a total of eight people that were definitely not to be regarded as 'friendlies.' Their primary target was obviously Sharon Cox, probably because of the information that had inadvertently come into her possession? He must now look upon himself as being their secondary target because of his known association with her.

His next consideration was what information and resources he had currently available to him, and how best to use them. This needed a bit more thought. David set off for his Heathrow pick-up, the journey affording him plenty of time to ponder.

His latest acquisition of the two identical 9mm Browning revolvers was obviously uppermost in his mind. He was well acquainted with this particular weapon. It was standard Army issue in many countries around the world. He thought that the ones that he had, were originally Belgian Army issue, and probably forty years old? It was apparent that neither pistol had been used very much, as both looked almost brand new. The ammunition was of a similar age. Several of the brass shell cases were showing traces of verdigris oxidisation. In normal military circumstances these rounds would have to be rejected, but these circumstances were anything but normal.

David knew that in keeping the guns, he laid himself wide open for prosecution if they were to be found in his possession by the Police. For the time being, he was prepared to risk that eventuality. The protection of his family, and Sharon, far outweighed any other consideration. He had secreted one weapon in his car. The other was back in George's under-floor safe. George knew how to use it.

David would have liked to gain access to the contents of Laura's laptop, but a brief inspection revealed that it was protected by a password. For the time being it had been set aside, but Sue, who was far more adept on the computer than he was, had promised to have another go at it when she found time. The password might be contained somewhere in the old file-o-fax? Something else that needed more careful study . . .

He assumed that Laura Dobson and Shaun Riley would have moved location from Tiptree Farm, given that Sharon was very likely to report them to the Police for her abduction and assault. That left Bleanaway Quarry as one possible location for them, but there may well be other 'safe houses' that he wasn't aware of?

He had the house keys to Laura's place in Weymouth. Perhaps another discreet and unannounced visit there might prove fruitful? Once again, he would be risking prosecution should he be found trespassing on premises.

His phone rang; it was Sue giving him an update on Sam. He had taken a nasty blow to the head, as suspected. X-rays revealed that he had sustained a hairline fracture of the bone over his right eye, and a small cut in his left ear, that was also badly bruised. The vet thought that the flesh of the dog's ear had padded the blow, and might have saved him from a far more serious injury. They were going to keep him in for observation for 24 hours, but Sue and Emily were having none of it, they had brought him straight back home with them. David was much relieved. He knew that if anything more serious had happened to Sam, little Emily would have been absolutely mortified.

With all these thoughts going through his mind, David's driving had been more or less on autopilot. Junction 13, M25, the A3113, was his exit, and he checked his mirror to move off to his left. Hitting his left indicator he started to change lane. Another glance in his mirror showed a silver coloured Ford Mondeo, three cars back, now doing the same thing. He recalled that it might have been behind for some distance, but its presence had failed to fully register in his preoccupied thoughts. Damn, he cursed his own inattention and stupidity.

A glance at his watch showed that he had only twelve minutes to spare before the scheduled flight arrival that he was due to meet. The Mondeo, he could see was three-up, and remained separated from him by two intervening vehicles. From the A3113, he took the 'T5 only' spur, and slowed right down to the regulation 40mph speed limit, something that very few other cars ever did on this particular road. He had expected that if the Mondeo were not following, then it might have overtaken at this point. The two other cars took the opportunity to pass, but the Mondeo stayed where it was, about 100yds back. David smiled to himself, time for a little bit of fun, give them the old run-around.

At the entrance to terminal five car parks, David hung around for a few seconds before taking his ticket to lift the barrier. This gave the driver of the following car time to catch up, he wanted them to see him park. The spiral descent to the next level down, level 3, David took at a very sedate pace allowing the driver of the Mondeo plenty of opportunity to see that he had exited onto that level.

After driving slowly around the one-way system, David finally reversed into a vacant space in amongst a group of already parked cars. His choice was governed by two factors. Firstly, it was within thirty yards of the exit spiral, and secondly, there were no other similar spaces in the same row. The Mondeo driver was forced to park much further away than he would have liked.

David made a show of collecting his name board and phone, and, while resting on the boot of his car, pretending to be writing a name on the board. He was surreptitiously watching the occupants of the Mondeo, who seemed to have chosen to remain in their car, probably waiting for his next move?

Pretending to be talking on his mobile, David made his way slowly across the car park to the lifts. In doing so, he deliberately passed within two car lengths of the Mondeo. The occupants deliberately kept their heads turned away from him, but it was enough for him to see that these people were different to those that had followed him when he had picked Sharon up previously.

David entered the lift and descended only one level. He ran as fast as he could across the parking area of level 2 and then back up the spiral road to level three. He quickly moved to his car noting that there were now only two people in the Mondeo. Without any further ado, David was into his car, engine started, into gear and he was moving swiftly away down the exit spiral. He very much doubted that anyone in the Mondeo would have even seen him go. The whole thing had taken only a few seconds.

He only went down as far as level 1 where he quickly found another space. This time, it was well out of sight of the exit spiral. Moving quickly over to the glass walled staircase, he sprinted upstairs to level 3 again. He couldn't wait to see the reaction of the occupants of the Mondeo when they suddenly realised that his car was no longer there.

He wasn't disappointed, from his vantage point in the staircase, he saw a man run from the lift area, to the Mondeo, and leap into the back. With a screech of tyres it headed for the exit. Laughing heartily to himself, David went to meet his passengers in the Terminal 5 Arrivals Hall.

Sharon thought she was in a seventh heaven. The attention and kindness being shown to her by all the clinical staff was little short perfection. Almost immediately after the admission formalities, she had undergone a whole series of X-rays and clinical assessments. She had then been introduced to a rather handsome looking gentleman. His surgery door name plaque identified him as,

Surgeon Lieutenant Malcolm Blackmore MD FRCS RNVR.

Quite informally, he had tenderly held her good hand while she tearfully related how she had sustained all her injuries. In seeking to comfort, he had embraced her, allowing her to cry on his shoulder. He advised that he was to be her own personal physician and surgeon for as long as it took to make her fit and well again. He explained that his specialist fields were in facial reconstruction and cosmetic surgery. An hour later, sitting on her bed, and again holding on to her good hand, he painstakingly detailed the surgical procedures that she would shortly have to undergo. He was trying to put her mind at rest from the outset.

Sharon found that she was completely at ease in his company, and quickly warmed to his charming bedside manner. Malcolm recognised that he was getting through her highly emotional state, and started to lighten the mood with some humour.

"We can't have a pretty girl like you sporting a Stephen Fry look-alike conk, can we? Leave it with me, sweetheart, and I will have you looking even more beautiful than you could possibly have imagined. I can see that your rather lovely elfin, heart-shaped face, definitely lends itself to something a little more pert and sexy up front, don't you agree?"

Sharon had blushed and stammered her way through all her replies. He had spent another hour showing her photo-fit type pictures, of slightly differing shaped noses, inviting her to select how she chose to look. After much amusing discussion and advice, she had made her choice. Without any further delay, it was off to surgery to reset three broken fingers, and to give her a new nose. This clinic operated flat out, 24/7.

Next morning, now in recovery, Sharon found she was sporting a facial cast, and a couple of black eyes from the nasal surgical procedure. Despite this, she had been assured that her operation had been a complete success.

With so much time on her hands, she found herself eagerly awaiting Malcolm Blackmore's every visit. In the short time that she had come to know him, Sharon was completely smitten. She couldn't expunge from her mind the memory of his tender embrace, and the exciting, musky, male odour of him.

Talking with the nurses, she found out that he was a widower with two teenaged daughters. His wife had apparently died of cancer some three years previous. He didn't date with any of his nursing staff despite being asked out on several occasions.

With all his kind and comforting words, he had managed to make her feel special, somehow . . .

There was now little doubt in her mind that Mr Malcolm Blackmore was quite 'a dish,' a compliment that she had never attributed to any man before. Inexplicably, she found that his gentle, understanding, bedside manner had hit upon, and awoken within her, many hitherto unknown and dormant feelings. It was all a bit confusing for a girl who thought she was a man-hater, and a bit of a lesbian.

When Malcolm had clinically examined the bruising to her ribs, he had gently probed the area under her partially exposed breasts, gently feeling for broken ribs. His examination had then moved down to her exposed lower abdomen, where Shaun had kicked her. Although it had been slightly painful, Sharon found that she had rather enjoyed the experience of being touched by him, even in this clinical manner. His gently probing fingers had even caused her to become sexually aroused, her sudden wetness embarrassingly apparent in her paper underwear. It had been the first such occurrence for her, in many a long year.

In the days of her recuperation, whenever he visited, Sharon did her best to keep Malcolm Blackmore at her bedside for as long as she was able. Slipping easily into first name terms with each other, she found herself confiding and talking about many things with him. Now, it being her time of the month, they had even touched upon the most delicate and personal of female subjects, he inquiring if her period, in the light of her injuries, appeared to be completely normal?

Sharon realised that these were things that she would never have dreamed of discussing with any man before, but Malcolm's kind, professional, and understanding nature, had completely overcome all her inhibitions. In no time at all she had developed such a complete trust in him that she knew, for the very first time, she was falling in love with a man . . .

Sharon's next scheduled piece of surgery was to repair her broken front teeth. The facial swelling from the nasal surgery and the stitches to cuts inside her lips, had yet to subside before any more work was possible. She was allowed out of bed, and spent a lot of time with the other patients listening to their sometimes-harrowing stories of how they had sustained their injuries in the various theatres of war.

Up until then, she only had the clothes she had been wearing when admitted to the clinic. Clean, white, disposable, paper underwear had been provided for her on a daily basis, but it was all very basic and none too flattering for a girl seeking to impress. A chance remark to one of the nurses resulted in a visit from a lady describing herself to be a 'personal shopper.'

David had already told her that all her private care would come out of the money in the holdall, but she had no idea how far this would stretch. What the hell, she thought, live now pay later? It summed up her ever more carefree attitude. Selecting from various catalogues and brochures, she ordered an extravagant selection of nice clothing for herself.

Her only regret was that she was forbidden to have contact with anyone but David outside of the clinic. She would have loved to speak with Jim and Doris, if only to let them both know that she was okay.

The sudden realisation that her sexuality might be normal had served to raise her optimism regarding her future love life. She was certain that Malcolm found her attractive and, in response, she had even started to flirt with him a little. A flutter of the eyelashes, a 'Lady Di' sideways glance from a deliberately introduced double-entendre, audaciously showing him all her new sexy underwear, Malcolm had taken it all in good humour, ever the professional gentleman.

After a week, Sharon was getting a little frustrated, and longed so much for him to reciprocate to all the signals that she was giving out. Just to give the tiniest indication to show that he understood her feelings toward him, was all that she longed for. And then perhaps, a few words of encouragement, to indicate that he had similar feelings for her. It would have made her day. But at the moment, it just wasn't happening . . .

Dermot had slowly regained consciousness; he had the mother of all headaches. It took him a good few moments to work out why it was that he couldn't bring up his arms to lift himself from the floor. He realised that his hands were tied behind his back. He lay there for a further minute or so, while the waves of pain and nausea coursed through his brain. Then, he finally remembered how he came to be in this position. Rolling onto his back, and with a supreme effort, he managed to raise himself into a sitting position, only to find himself staring down the barrels of his own .410 shotgun.

Shaun, who was far from sober, was waving it menacingly under his nose. He had Michael's mobile phone pressed to his ear, and was giving orders to someone on the other end. Dermot remembered . . . Michael, where was he? He looked desperately around but couldn't see his brother anywhere; he had been moved out of the lounge.

Shaun ended his phone call and sat in the chair staring malevolently at Dermot. He began to gently prod the gun into his face.

"I would think that a gentle little squeeze on this trigger would be sufficient to blow your fucking head off at this range, would it not, Dermot?

"Shaun, please. Michael? Where is he?"

"Lara has him in the bedroom, seeing to him." He laughed at his own macabre humour.

"Shaun, listen to me, please. Michael is an old man with a bad heart. He's in a bad way and needs proper medical attention. Please, I beg of you, call an ambulance, get him to hospital, man . . ."

"He'll be alright for the time being. Lara knows what to do; she'll make sure the old bastard doesn't bleed to death. Now, where are those guns hidden?"

The mobile phone in Shaun's hand rang. He looked at the display and accepted the call.

"Yes, John, what have you got for me?" He listened intently. "Tell them to give it another day or two. If she doesn't show up by that time, we'll burn the place. Yes, that's what I said, burn it. Make it look accidental. That should be enough to flush the bitch out of her hideout. Any news on the van yet?"

Shaun again listened intently to what he was being told.

"Well, keep looking . . . What about the taxi bloke, have we found out anything more about him yet?"

He listened again and gave a snort of derision.

"If he's not there, then get inside, man. Search the place. I want names and addresses of all his friends and family, anywhere else that he might have taken her. God almighty, I'm not paying you good money to give me all this negative crap. Get back there, get inside, I want to know if the bitch has been there. If she hasn't, you will burn that one as well. They'll soon get the message, do I make myself clear, now?"

There was some more conversation from the other end before Shaun ended the call with a terse,

"Call me back when you've got some good news, not until then, I don't want excuses, I want results . . ."

He threw the phone onto the couch in apparent disgust.

"Idiots, I'm surrounded by incompetent fucking idiots. God damn them all to hell . . ."

He turned his attention back to Dermot who had been listening to the conversation.

"Not going too well, is it, Shaun?"

Shaun scowled and looked at his watch. Dermot wanted to score points.

"It occurs to me that if this woman has already gone to the Police with the holdall, then they will know where we are by now, our address is inside the bag, is it not?"

"Yes, go on . . ."

"All the approaches to the sanctuary are covered by CCTV and intruder alarms. We have some very rare and exotic birds nesting here, Shaun. None of the alarms, or cameras, has been set at the moment. Michael has turned them all off, because we were expecting you. Don't you think it might be a good idea to reset them again?"

"Yes. Whereabouts are the control panels?"

"In the office. But you will need me to show you the setting sequences, Shaun. You will not manage it alone, man. It's quite a complicated procedure, with different key settings for each alarm. Here, untie me, and I'll gladly show you."

Shaun's eyes narrowed, he was obviously giving the matter some thought.

"Shaun, I can't imagine that the Police will come here anything less than mob-handed, and armed to the teeth. If we are going to stand any chance at all of defending ourselves, any small advantage we can gain is vital. Come on man, we're wasting valuable time here, cut me loose."

Shaun heaved himself painfully to his feet and fished in his pocket for his penknife.

"No tricks Dermot, or so help me, I'll blow you into the middle of next week. Turn around now . . ."

Dermot felt the ropes, tight around his wrist suddenly go slack. He shook his hands free and for the first time in many hours, he was able to move his arms back to his front. Massaging his wrists and shrugging his shoulders to get some movement going again, he took stock of his position. He was in no fit state to tackle Shaun even if he was injured. The shotgun was still pointed in his general direction; he needed to get it out of Shaun's possession.

"Shaun, you're obviously in pain with your ribs, man. Why not let Lara put some strapping on for some support. It worked quite well for me some years back when I fell, and broke two of mine. I've got some wide crepe bandages in the first aid chest, the ones I used. They're clean and ready for use again, should I get them for you? There might be some other things in there that she can use to help Michael as well?

"Give them to Lara, and send her through as soon as she's finished seeing to Michael. Then I want the guns, Dermot. Whereabouts are the guns stashed?"

"Shaun, even if I told you, it would be of no use. You would need at least three strong men, and probably some heavy lifting gear to get at them. I tell you what, you let me see to Michael while Lara straps you up, and then I'll show you where they are, that's a promise . . ."

"Are they here, somewhere close?"

"They're nearby, Shaun, not too far away, just a short walk."

"Dermot, if you're bullshitting me, you're a fucking dead man walking, is that clear enough?"

"Shaun, on Michaels life, I swear I'm being straight with you, man."

"Do it then. Set the alarms, get the stuff for my ribs and give it to Lara, but if I get the slightest hint that you're double-crossing me . . ."

His words were already falling on deaf ears, for Dermot was striding out of the room, hurrying to his brothers bedside.

A half hour later, Michael's mobile rang again. Shaun picked it up, looked at the caller display, and hit the receive button.

"Shaun, it's John. Good news, we've found the van, and one of my lads has just turned over the taxi drivers place. We've got a few more addresses to check, but he also found that he'd scribbled down "Sharon, 4 Pillars, Witney" on his desk pad. Anyway, I knew immediately where it is, and I'm on my way over there now. Luckily, I'm only a few miles up the road. Your van's apparently parked in the corner of a private housing estate car park, near to that location. My blokes say that it's locked, and that they can't see anything inside. What do you want us to do with it now?"

"I want you to get inside the van and check around properly. If the bag's not in there, then get rid of the damn thing, make it disappear, it's yours to do what you like with. Check thoroughly around the area, the bitch can't be that far away. I want both her, and that bag. Do whatever it takes to get them. What is the Four Pillars, Witney, anyway?"

"It's a hotel, just off the A40."

"Check to see if she's there, or if she's been there. She can't be missed, a redhead with a messed up face, someone will have seen her. Get back to me when you've got something. Oh, and John, well done mate, I owe you. One last thing before you go, I may be needing three or four big strong lads over here very shortly, can that be arranged? Good man, I'll get back to you as soon as I know more."

Dermot and Lara whispered to each other at Michael's bedside. His face, despite being heavily bandaged with towels to soak up the blood, was a complete mask of red.

"He's in a pretty bad way Dermot, I can't stop the bleeding. He's slipping in and out of consciousness with the pain and loss of blood. We must try and get him to a hospital urgently. What's happening with Shaun, why has he untied you?"

"I persuaded him to let you strap up his ribs, and I've come to get the crepe bandages for you to use. I've just finished turning off all the alarms, but he thinks I've been turning them on. You're to go through and see to him as soon as you've finished here with Michael. Lara, where do you stand with all of this? Are you going along with Shaun, or are you with Michael and me? I need to know . . ."

"Dermot, I'm truly appalled at Shaun's behaviour, and I'm really sorry for what he's done to Michael. I feel that I'm partially responsible, by bringing him here. I'm not sure that we are strong enough to go up against Shaun, even though he's injured. What have you got in mind?"

"We need to get the shotgun Lara. I was hoping you would be able to distract him long enough for me to creep up behind him and grab it before he realises. Are you up for it?"

"I will try and do what you ask, but if it all goes wrong, I want no part, and I will deny all knowledge. He will kill us both of us if he thought we were against him. I may even have warn him when I see that you've already got the gun, just to let him think that I'm still on his side. Now, where are those bandages you're talking about?"

"Lara, where are you woman? Get your arse in here now, you hear me?"

Lara hurried through from the bedroom.

"Sorry Shaun, Dermot was just sorting out the bandages while I was seeing to Michael. Shaun, listen to me, please. Michael is in a really bad way. He needs a blood transfusion and should go to hospital immediately. I think he will die if he doesn't get one soon. Let Dermot take him in the Range Rover, or something. We can get some of your friends to pick us up, we can't be staying here much longer, that's for sure."

"We don't go anywhere until we get our guns, Lara. Dermot and Michael are the only ones who know where they're buried. There's still time to sort out this fucking mess before the shit hits the fans. We've found the van, and I reckon we're close to getting the damned girl as well, I'm waiting on an update from John now."

"My bag, was it in the van?"

"No, not that John could see. But he hasn't been able to check properly yet, he said the van was locked. I've told him to break into it, and then get rid. He's also checking for the girl in a hotel very close to where it was found. We'll have her soon, you'll see. Now what do you want me to do so that you can get some strapping round these damned ribs of mine?"

"You'll need to get your jacket and shirt off, won't you, you great lummox, I can't put bandages on top of that now, can I?"

Shaun carefully laid the gun down across the dining table. He painfully shrugged off his jacket and unbuttoned his shirt. Lara saw that the whole of his left ribcage, from armpit to abdomen, was black and blue with bruising. She helped him off with the shirt.

"My god Shaun, this needs more than a bit of strapping, man. Try putting your arms up above your head while I see what we're dealing with here. How many ribs do you think are broken?"

"How do I bloody know, for Christ's sake woman? More than one, I can feel them all moving. Just get on with it . . ."

"Shaun this is going to hurt. Promise me now that you won't be hitting me, because if you do, so help me I'll smack your ribs so hard, you'll wish you'd have died . . . Deal?"

"Do it woman. Do whatever you've got to do."

As gently as possible Lara probed with her fingers, trying to assess the extent of the damage to his ribcage. It wasn't good. As far as she could make out, all of the ribs on the left side were broken, and possibly a fracture of the sternum as well, but without a proper X-ray?

"You're right, there's more than two, maybe three or four? It's too difficult to tell, exactly, with all that muscle in the way." She was deliberately playing it down and seeking to humour him.

Shaun smiled at her suggestively, "I've got others you've yet to be acquainted with, you know."

"Down boy, behave yourself, I doubt you're in any fit state anyway?"

"You wanna try me woman? Don't go writing me off just yet."

"Come over here by the window where there's more room, that's it, now hold still, and keep your arms up. Just breathe in for me while I get the first turn or two on these bandages. You're to tell me if you think it's too tight."

Securing the end of the bandage to his torso with a couple of pieces of plaster, Lara began walking round Shaun carefully and tightly layering the bandage from the bottom upwards, as she went. She saw Dermot watching from the bedroom, biding his time, and waiting his chance.

"Keep your arms up man, breathe in and raise your ribcage, this needs to be tight if it's going to do you any good." Lara was speaking to distract Shaun's attention. Dermot was tiptoeing towards the gun on the dining table. On her next turn around Shaun, she saw that Dermot was reaching for the gun, he'd made it. She stopped in front of Shaun and looked him straight in the eye to catch his attention. Whispering and indicating by eye movement to the area behind Shaun's right side, she said,

"It's Dermot, he's got the gun Shaun, he just crept in and took it, I'm sorry . . ."

Shaun smiled at her and without turning round, he addressed Dermot.

"It might be better if you just put the gun back down on the table, Dermot, it's not going to be any use unless it's loaded."

Shaun slowly lowered his right arm and produced two cartridges from his right trouser pocket. He held them tauntingly in the air for Dermot to see.

Dermot broke the gun open and looked at the empty chambers.

"Damn you Shaun Riley, but you'll never get to use this gun again, that's for sure."

Dermot reversed his grip so that he was holding the gun by its barrels. He raised it up as high as the confines of the room would allow and smashed it down onto the floor. The gun flew apart, the wooden stock broken at its thinnest point. He threw the barrels onto the floor with the rest of the gun and stormed off back to his brother's side.

Shaun hadn't moved, nor had he shown any sort emotion following Dermot's outburst. He looked Lara in the eye and smiled.

"Damn thing was no good beyond about ten yards anyway. And these are only bird shot."

He returned the two cartridges to his trouser pocket.

Sue sat down at her father's desk and fired up the laptop. She didn't get far with it, entry being denied to her unless she had a password. Laura's file-o-fax consisted of about 150 pages of cramped handwriting and notations, most of which were meaningless to anyone but Laura herself. Sue was vainly looking for something that might be a password.

Two pairs of eyes were watching her intently, from the other side of the room.

*I sense that your mother is seeking to gain access to some information contained in the machine, little one. She is seeking a sequence of characters that will then permit her to see what she wants. I am going to help her by telling you what she wants to know. Place these characters into her mind. "qpwo1029"*

Sue had set the file-o-fax aside. It was a hopeless task trying to find anything in there. She stared at the keyboard and a series of characters just popped into her mind. Her fingers automatically pushed the keys in sequence, and the computer responded with a "good afternoon Lara" written across the desktop page.

Sue turned to look at Emily. "Did you just do that, Em? How did you know?"

There was absolutely no doubt in Sue's mind that Emily was responsible. The correct password characters didn't just magic themselves into her head, but how did Emily know what she was looking for? She didn't need to ask the question.

"Jo-jo told me, mummy. He knows everything."

Jo-jo again . . . ? This was something that neither she nor David had quite got to the bottom of yet. Emily frequently mentioned Jo-jo, and they had both come to assume that he was just some figment of her rather vivid imagination, a little friend she had invented in her mind. The twins, when asked, had both said much the same thing. Jo-jo is Emily's make-believe friend. Strangely though, they had all noticed that whenever his name had cropped up, all the right things seemed to happen, as in this instance.

"Well, will you thank Jo-jo very much for me Em. I don't know how he knew what I wanted, but he has certainly been very helpful."

Sue set the matter aside for the time being, and concentrated on accessing the available data on the computer, making notes as she progressed. The afternoon wore on and Sue, totally engrossed, lost all track of time.

The full extent of the puppy scam was becoming abundantly clear now. The discs reflected that there had been many hundreds, indeed thousands of transactions, many going back more than thirty five years. The scale of it all was absolutely astronomical, involving hundreds of people, and many thousands of pounds. Animals that had been passed off as being pedigree bred, attracted inflated prices, and genuinely sold, top pedigree animals, were frequently stolen back from their owners, and reintroduced back into the well organised breeding programs. There seemed to be dozens of dog breeders on Laura's records, many of them probably unaware that they were part of a massive fraud?

Sue turned her attention to the bank accounts, but once again found that they were protected by passwords, and other security measures. Sue looked at Emily and Sam; both were sitting quietly in the corner of the room apparently 'talking' to each other.

"Em, will you ask Jo-Jo if he can help me with these other passwords and security devices, please. I'm having some problems in accessing the data that I want to look at?"

Sue had no idea if this would work? Up to now, she had never even acknowledged the existence of Jo-jo, let alone ask him for assistance, but she figured that must be worth a try?

Sue watched in fascination as her daughter stared at Sam for a few seconds before slowly and painstakingly answering her request. In her little baby voice, she said,

"The account numbers are, 42739905 and 42761103, Bank of Ireland, the sort code is 08-01-96. They both have the same security answers, O'Hare, 22/09/49, postcode DT4 0PX." The user names, passwords, and numeric codes are identical for both accounts. Jo-jo says they are all written down on page 15 of the file-o-fax book, where all the personal data for Lara Dobbs is recorded."

"Hang on a minute Em, I am going to need to write all that down. Can you just say it all again for me,

please sweetheart? Only say it all a little bit slower this time . . ."

Sue wrote everything down as her little daughter dictated it again for her. It was as though Emily was reading from a page of script, there was no hesitation in her little voice, everything came across exactly as Sue would have wished.

She stared at the notepad in utter disbelief, and then turned up the relevant page of the file-o-fax. Everything she wanted was indeed there, but how had he known?

Emily's assertion that 'Jo-jo knows everything' was beginning to look a distinct reality . . .

"Thank Jo-jo again for me Em, will you please?" Then more or less as an afterthought, she asked, "Where exactly is Jo-jo sweetheart, is he here in this room with us?"

Emily's answer was even more confusing, for it seemed that Jo-jo was everywhere, all around. He was even inside Sam, if that were possible?

"How do you speak with Jo-jo Em, can I speak with him as well?"

"Look at me mother. Can you understand the thoughts that I am sending to you now? If you can, then you may be able to speak with Jo-jo, if he will let you."

Sue looked incredulously at Emily. The message from her was coming through loud and clear although no actual words were being spoken. Emily smiled. She got up from the floor and walked over and into her mother's arms. Direct telepathic communication with both of her parents had now been established.

David, having dropped his passengers off at Chaseside, made his way home. He had nothing else in the diary for that day, and, despite everything else that was going on, he needed to catch up on his paperwork and submit his September accounts, otherwise, there would be no money coming in.

The empty house seemed cold and unwelcoming without the rest of the family. He shrugged off his jacket and hung it on the back of his office chair before going through to the kitchen to put the kettle on for some tea. Waiting for the kettle to boil, David noticed a movement of the window blind caused by a draught. The transom window was unlatched and slightly open. Without a seconds thought, he pulled it tight shut and secured it properly.

Cup in hand, he went back through to his office and went to turn on his laptop. It was open, he never left it like that, he always closed the lid down after leaving it on 'hibernate.' He hit the 'on' button and it slowly came to life, but it had been shut down completely by a previous user. David was puzzled, Sue had her own laptop, she never used his computer unless it was something to do with the business that she needed to look at? He thought back, the last person to use it was himself, when he got the details for the job he had just completed, very strange . . .

He noticed the light flashing on the answer phone indicating that there were messages for him.

"This is Carl, Concierge at the Chewton Glen, Mr Morrison-Lloyd. I have two gentlemen who need to go to Southampton Airport this afternoon. Could you ring me ASAP if you are available please. If I haven't heard from you by 1100 this morning, I shall have to make an alternative arrangement. Thank you . . ."

David glanced at his watch, 1050. This was a nice little job that would fit in with going back up to Godalming. He reached for his card index of phone numbers. It was open. His hand hovered momentarily while he glanced at where it was opened to. His parent's address? Why on earth would Sue be wanting to look at that? Alarm bells began to ring in his head.

He dialled the Chewton Glen number and asked for Carl. Picking a pencil out of his desk tidy, he pulled his scratch pad towards himself in readiness. He was still thinking about the inconsistencies he had found. An idea occurred to him and he thoughtfully turned his pad over before recording details of his pickup.

As soon as he had hung up, he turned his pad back over and held it up to the light. He could see distinct impressions of someone else's handwriting on the otherwise blank page. Using the side of his pencil point, he carefully shaded over the area of the writing. He stared at the result. His parents address, Sue's parent's address, Sharon, the 4 Pillars Witney . . . How had they found that one? Of course, it was written on the corner of his desk blotter. There was some other indistinct writing that was impossible for him to decipher, but he had seen enough.

Whoever they were, they now knew where to find him. This would probably account for the intruders last night, and his followers this morning? He reached for the phone to call Sue, but hesitated on realisation that it might be bugged. 'No, best to call her on the mobile when I get in the car,' he muttered to himself.

He sat back, thinking about what to do next. This was all getting out of hand, he really needed to speak to the Police, despite Sharon's pleas for him not to. He knew that it would take some hours to explain it all to a Police Officer, and right now, time was something he didn't have much of. Besides, it would be better to get approval from George and Sharon first. In his mind, the matter was again put on hold.

David climbed the loft ladder and dug around in the piles of junk in storage. He finally descended carrying his old Bergen containing most of his army kit that had never been handed back. A quick sort out was necessary to discard items that he didn't need, before putting the whole lot into a small wheelie suitcase, so as a further disguise to its content. He placed it in the back of his car, and again checked that the pistol was close to hand and ready for use.

He made himself a toasted cheese and onion sandwich and another cup of tea, which he consumed while trying vainly to complete his accounts, but the necessary concentration just wouldn't come. He went out into his back garden and called Sharon first.

The call lasted about five minutes, she doing nearly all the talking, and going on about some dishy doctor who was obviously taking very good care of her. Not wishing to burst her euphoric bubble, David contented himself by firmly reminding her not to speak to anyone else outside the clinic but him. He would only call her on this mobile number. That prohibition must now include his own family, even if she believed the calls might be genuine or urgent. She was to accept absolutely no calls, except those from his mobile. She must also tell the clinic to deny that she was even a patient there, should they receive any such enquiry. He stressed that the measures might seem draconian, but they were necessary for her continued safety. He was glad that she didn't see fit to question his judgement and accepted everything he said.

He decided not to tell her anything about the IRA related file, found in the holdall.

His next call was to Sue, who was very excited and eager to update him on her progress in accessing the information contained in the laptop. He started to ask how she had managed to break through all the security measures, but she had silenced him with a single remark.

"Not now David, you would find it very difficult to believe me, even if I tried to explain, and I'm not sure that I'm clear on it myself yet. Best leave it all till later. You know Emily better than all of us, so you'd be better talking it through with her. If I am understanding her correctly, it seems that we might have inadvertently acquired a somewhat invisible house guest from somewhere down the line?"

It made no sense at all, but he didn't have the time to push it any further. David briefly outlined his concerns regarding the break-in at their home, and the information that he knew had been gained from it. Reassuring her that nothing else seemed to be missing or damaged, he left it with her to tell George and Edith, and then to ring his own parents, and try to put them fully in the picture as well.

His last call was to Jim and Doris Cox. He spoke with Jim and struggled to put his mind at rest regarding Sharon's absence. He reluctantly had to tell him that Sharon was undergoing some minor medical treatment to rectify a few personal problems she had encountered. If all went well she should be back with them in a week or ten days, to explain everything. The questions all had to be sidestepped. No, he didn't think that it was anything serious. No, she was definitely not contactable while she was receiving treatment. The specialist clinic was a secret location. Yes, it did have some connection with Laura Dobson, but Sharon definitely wasn't with her now. It was difficult, and he desperately wanted to end the call, he hated having to deceive the old couple in this way.

He was on the verge of ringing off when Jim went on to telling him about the two men that had recently asked after her and Laura Dobson. Listening carefully to the descriptions, he was fairly sure that it was the same two men he had seen at the airport when he picked up Sharon. He finally terminated the call and stood, hands in pockets, staring thoughtfully at the flowerbeds.

"Hello David, lovely day. We haven't seen you, or the family for a while. Is everything alright?"

It was his elderly next-door neighbour speaking over the garden fence.

"Oh, hello, Mrs Clasby, yes everything's fine, just a bit of a minor family crisis, that's all. Sue and the children are up in Surrey, helping her mum out for a few days. Tell me Mrs Clasby, has there been anyone round in the last couple of days, there seems to be some footprints in my flower beds?"

"That would probably have been your window cleaner, David. He came round early yesterday. I've paid him for you. You owe me ten pounds, by the way."

"Thanks, Mrs Clasby." David extracted a £10 note from his wallet and handed it over. "I forgot they were due this week."

He regarded his windows, which didn't look particularly clean. "Not much of a job is it Mrs C? Can't get the staff these days, can we? I think I'll kick them into touch, and do it myself in future."

"Oh Mr Lloyd, I'm sorry. I paid him without checking the work first. It never occurred to me."

"No, no, Mrs C, you did the right thing, thanks again." He pointedly looked at his watch, "My goodness is that the time already? I'm sorry, I would love to chat some more, but I've got to go. There are two gentlemen waiting for me to pick them up from the Chewton Glen."

"Alright for some, isn't it, David?"

He laughed and went back indoors. Window cleaner, cheeky bastard, even got payment for breaking in. He looked at the kitchen worktop under the window, and sure enough, there was a slight muddy scuffmark. Probably went out through the front door, he thought to himself as he walked through into the passage. He collected the mail off the doormat, and there, was part of a muddy footprint, imprinted on the corner of one white envelope. Looking through the rest of his mail for anything important, and finding nothing, David threw it all onto the dining table for sorting out later.

David loved driving into the grounds of the Chewton Glen. It is one of only two five-star rated, country hotels in the south of England, and often frequented by Royalty and top politicians. The sweeping driveway led down to a horseshoe shaped, paved area, that served the main Reception. Although he was five minutes early, his two gentlemen were awaiting his arrival in the entrance hall. With a nod from Carl to indicate that he had the right people, David made his approach.

"Gentlemen, good afternoon to you both, I'm David, your driver."

They both stood up and shook his hand.

"Have you completed the formalities, are we ready to leave? If so, my car is this way, please."

They followed him outside.

"Your luggage gent's? Do you have anything to go in the rear of the car?"

The taller, fair-haired man replied, "No, we're travelling light. It's just these two pieces of hand-luggage which we would prefer to keep with us, if you have no objection?"

"No problem, gents . . ." David opened the rear doors of his car for them. He had already noticed that the man he had spoken to, was wearing an Irish Guards Regimental tie. He now caught sight of the seven-pointed star and shamrock motif, on his tiepin and cufflinks. He was smartly dressed in a dark blue pinstriped suit, white shirt and highly polished black brogue shoes. Every inch of him screamed that he was a military man.

His companion, or colleague, could not have been more the opposite. Shorter, very dark complexioned, almost Arab looking, thought David. He wore a rather scruffy dark grey suit, no tie, an open neck blue shirt, and cheap looking brown shoes, that looked as though they had never seen any polish in their life.

David got the distinct impression that he had seen both of them somewhere before.

They set off and David opened the conversation.

"Excuse me asking, sir, but isn't that an Irish Guards tie you're wearing? I was in Afghanistan with some of the Micks. Were you there, perhaps?"

"I was, but it's not something that I care to talk about, thank you, Mr Morrison-Lloyd."

"Excuse me, sir, but how do you know my surname? Have we met before? You both look a little familiar?"

"Look, we're apologising for this little bit of subterfuge, Mr Morrison-Lloyd. This is a genuine fare for you, though. My colleague and I are both wishing to go to Southampton Parkway Station approach if you please. There is a car waiting for us there."

He produced a wallet from his jacket breast pocket. Opening it up, he held it so that David could see the warrant card, reflected in his driving mirror.

"We are both Police officers, Mr Lloyd, and you have been giving us a bit of a headache over the last few days. I am detective chief inspector Charles Ferguson, and I am with Scotland Yard serious crime investigation department. My colleague here is detective sergeant Ahmed Suffajji, of the west midlands regional crime squad."

In his mirror, David saw the other man's warrant was being similarly displayed.

"You're the two that were following Sharon at the airport, and the same ones that have been asking questions about her at the B&B in Weymouth, perhaps?"

"Yes to both of those, Mr Lloyd, you're remarkably observant, and very well informed. Only we were not following Sharon, our interest lies with you. Mr Cox, unfortunately, never let us get that far."

"You were following me? Why, for gods sake?"

"Cards on the table Mr Lloyd. Can you tell us please, what exactly is your involvement with Shaun Riley and Laura Dobson?"

"Before I answer that, can I ask what your particular interest is, please? There is a great deal that I can tell you about Riley and Dobson. You've actually saved me a job, as I was on the verge of giving it all to the Police anyway. What I have is extremely sensitive, and will need a lot of careful consideration."

"Go on then, Mr Lloyd, we are all ears. What is it that you have, can you give us the gist of it, perhaps?"

"We don't have the time now gents, and most of what I have is of a written, documentary nature. If you can both come to this address tomorrow evening, I will show you everything we have, and gladly try to answer as many of your questions as I can, but I warn you both, it may take a very long time."

David gave Mr Ahmed one of George's business cards from his wallet.

"Now it's your turn, what is your interest in all of this?"

They two Policemen looked at each other and Ferguson nodded. The other man spoke for the first time in a slightly accented Asian voice.

"Mr Morrison-Lloyd, we have reason to believe that Shaun Riley is connected with the disappearance of three women, prostitutes from the Cheltenham, Gloucester and Worcester areas, respectively. We were beginning to think that he was grooming Laura Dobson to be his next target. A far as we can make out, Riley was the last person to visit her. She too, has now completely disappeared."

David gave them both a wry smile,

"Gentlemen, with all due respect to you both, I know nothing of the three women that you speak of, but where Laura Dobson is concerned, I think you are definitely barking up the wrong tree. From what I know of her, she's a very tough cookie, and is more likely to be Riley's long-term accomplice, rather than his next victim. I have proof of this, but you will both need to come to my in-laws home, again, for me to be able to show it all to you."

"Mr Morrison-Lloyd, you say 'again,' meaning perhaps that we have been there before? I can assure you that neither of us has ever been anywhere near your in-laws address. In point of fact, we didn't even know where they lived until you just gave us that piece of information."

"If it wasn't you guys that my dog disturbed last evening, then we have another problem, gents. For it would seem that there is almost certainly another team on much the same track as yourselves. They may even be slightly ahead of you in the game."

Mr Ahmed sounded a little indignant.

"This is not a game Mr Morrison-Lloyd, we believe it is almost certainly a murder enquiry, but as yet, we have found no bodies. Without them, we have only circumstantial evidence to substantiate all of our theories. We sincerely hope that you can be of some real assistance in the further pursuit of our enquiries."

"I have a distinct feeling that might well be the case gents, but I very much doubt that the information I am about to give you, is quite what you are both expecting?"

Late that evening, at Bleanaway, Shaun, again much the worse for more of Michael's Bushmills, listened intently to the latest update from his search team leader, John. Neither man was happy.

"Yes, a woman answering her description stayed at the Four Pillars three nights ago. She booked a local taxi to take her to Heathrow, and left at 0730 next morning. We've spoken to the driver. He dropped her at Terminal four. We must assume she's probably somewhere abroad by now Shaun."

"The bag, did the driver say what she was carrying?"

"Yes, one black holdall, and a shoulder bag, that was all."

"She must have met someone, she didn't have her passport with her, and she couldn't have checked-in with the guns in her possession. The bag must have either been given over to someone else, or deposited somewhere, till she comes back for it." Shaun was thinking out loud. "Is there a Left Luggage depository at the airport, John?"

"I don't know, Shaun, do you want me to check? It seems a bit pointless, even if there is, we could never hope to get anything out of there, anyway."

"Shaun, listen to me . . ." Lara had been ear-wigging in on their conversation. Shaun looked her way questioningly.

"Shaun, Sharon doesn't have a passport. She can't get one because she doesn't have a Birth Certificate. She told me only recently that she has never been abroad. She must still be in the country somewhere. I'd lay odds that the taxi driver, Lloyd, met her. Think about it man, he would have immediately taken her to somewhere for treatment. Tell John to forget the airport, concentrate on finding where he is. He's the key to all this. He will have my bag, and the girl won't be too far away."

"Did you hear that, John. The girl doesn't have a passport. You heard what Lara said? Okay, so let's just do as she says. Do we know where the taxi driver is now? The in-laws, but the girl isn't there, are you sure, have we been inside? What, attacked by the bloody dog, Jesus Christ, John, what am I paying you for? Get those fucking idiots replaced, we need to keep watching the place. What about his parents place in Chelsea? Okay, well keep watching there, as well. I tell you what John, I've just had a little idea that might just flush her out for us. Let me run this past you. You remember the other day when I mentioned burning her out? Yes, well here's what I think we should do . . ."

In the early hours of the next morning, long after everyone had gone to bed, one of the families staying at the B&B did a moonlight flit. Before leaving, the man crept quietly downstairs and into the kitchens. With a large adjustable wrench, he unscrewed the gas pipe connection to the cooker, allowing the gas to escape. He then lit a small candle and placed it on top of an upturned bucket in the corner. Closing all the external vents and shutting the fireproof kitchen door tightly behind himself, he covered the gap at the bottom of the door with a wet towel, thus making everything inside the kitchen virtually airtight.

He and his wife, together with their two teenaged sons, proceeded to quickly, and silently, let themselves out of the unlocked, back door emergency exit, and out into the night. A car was waiting to meet them just up the road.

The kitchen and dining area of the old Victorian building are situated immediately above the basement living area of Jim and Doris Cox. Both were absolutely exhausted from their hard days work. They slept soundly and heard nothing.

The subsequent explosion occurred nearly half an hour later. The force from the blast took the lines of least resistance, outwards and downwards. Blowing the kitchen door off its hinges, a huge fireball of burning gas swept out into the hallway and up the staircase setting everything ablaze in its path.

The down-force of the explosion ripped it's way straight through the terracotta tiled kitchen floor, and pushed the floorboards and heavy oak joists out of the wall hanger brackets on one end of the building. The whole lot came crashing down onto the bedroom below, where Jim and Doris Cox, were sleeping. Doris died instantly, as the corner of one of the ceiling joist beams smashed through her chest crushing her ribcage and pulverising her heart. Jim, barely conscious, lay trapped under the rubble in his smouldering bed, trying vainly to beat out the flames with his bare hands.

Eventually, help arrived, and he was immediately rushed to hospital. A little later, a spokesperson described his condition as being 'very poorly' and his injuries as 'potentially life-threatening.'

# Chapter 4

"And in the local news, Dorset Police, together with the County Fire and Rescue Service, are still at the scene of what is believed to be a large gas explosion, that occurred in Weymouth this morning. One person is known to have died, and another is said to be critical, following the explosion, which has severely damaged a popular small guesthouse premises. A Police spokesman stated that the investigations into the cause of the explosion were still in the preliminary stages, and that they are treating the incident as suspicious."

David was on his way down the M3 having just joined from the A31, at Winchester. His car radio had automatically tuned into the local radio station, Radio Solent. The hairs on the back of his neck stood out, and a feeling of dread clawed at his insides as he commanded his hands-free phone to dial Sue's mobile number. It rang for what seemed like an age before Sue picked up the call,

"Hello David, what's up?"

"Sue, I just heard on the local radio about a gas explosion at a guest house in Weymouth. They didn't name the place, but I just have this god-awful feeling. Can you ring Jim and Doris? I don't have their number on my phone. If there's no reply, try the local Police in Weymouth, or better still, the news desk at Radio Solent. We need to know if they're alright. Ring me back as soon as you know anything . . . Thanks Love."

He broke the connection and realised that he hadn't been concentrating on his driving again. Indicating left he had to move out of the way of a rather indignant BMW driver, who, wishing to overtake, was impatiently flashing his headlights from behind. The other driver glared at him as he passed, and David raised his hand and mouthed an apology.

A glance in his mirror told him that the two-up, green Toyota Corolla, that had been tailing him since leaving Godalming, and all along the A31, was still about 100yds back with two other cars in between. David assumed it was the Police still on his case, but couldn't be sure? Anyway, what did it matter? He thought that their presence could be regarded as somewhat reassuring.

If, on the other hand, they were the opposition, he took comfort in the presence of the loaded pistol, now out of sight under a folded yellow duster, in his driver's door pocket.

He was on his way to pick up three people from Highcliffe, booked to go to the Southampton Docks. Then it was straight down to Bournemouth Airport to meet two people from an incoming Tenerife flight, and to drop them off at Lymington. Last job would be 1700, two regulars from Barton-on-sea to the Heathrow Hilton Hotel. His now scheduled 2000 meeting with the Police at the in-laws in Godalming made for a very full day, but at least it kept his mind occupied, which right now, was exactly what he needed . . .

Sue was frantically trying to establish some sort of contact with, or news of, Jim and Doris Cox. All her phone calls so far, had been frustrating. The guesthouse number had been totally unobtainable. Two calls to Dorset Police Headquarters had produced nothing but her call being transferred from one department extension to another, until it was inevitably lost. After the second attempt, she gave up on the Police completely.

That left only the Radio Solent newsroom. They tried to be helpful, but could add little to their original broadcast. They did however confirm, that the guesthouse was the 'Bide-a-wee,' Jim and Doris's place.

After Sue made it clear that she was a concerned relative seeking information on her loved ones, she was kindly given an update on the previous broadcast, with as much information as was currently available.

Preliminary indications were that the deceased person was believed to be Doris Cox, but no formal identification of the body had yet been made. Her husband, James Cox, was now in Poole Hospital, intensive care unit, suffering with breathing difficulties from the inhalation of smoke. He remained poorly, but stable.

An appeal was about to be broadcast regarding the whereabouts of Sharon Roberts, the stepdaughter of the deceased. Police were urgently requesting her to come forward in order to assist them with their enquiries.

Sue replaced the receiver gently into its cradle, her mind in turmoil. She glanced at her watch, David would be en route to the docks with his first fare, best call him in about half an hour or so, after his drop. She thought about contacting Sharon, but remembered David's warnings not to. Well, someone was going to have to tell the poor girl . . . No, probably best to leave it to David, he had been quite adamant about not speaking with Sharon.

Was there anything else that she could do to further things along? Only ring David's parents and put them in the picture . . . Her dad as well, he was meeting with Tony Williams at their gentlemen's club for lunch today. He would probably appreciate being put fully in the picture, she was sure. She dialled his mobile number first.

Sharon was scheduled into surgery for the first of some dental work to repair her chipped and broken front teeth. Sitting in her private room reading a popular women's magazine, she felt apprehensive. Like most people, she hated dentists, but her fear was somewhat tempered in the knowledge that Malcolm Blackmore had promised to hold her hand, and assist in all the procedures.

She wondered how her parents were coping without her at the B&B, and tried to recall the booking register entries for that week. They wouldn't come to mind, but this was the last few days of September, and with the children all back at school, she took small comfort in assuming that it would be fairly quiet, and not too much work for the old couple. For some reason, she found herself thinking about them a lot that morning, and wished that she could just give them a call to reassure them that she would soon be home again.

Shutting her eyes and daydreaming, she could imagine their reaction on being introduced to Malcolm.

'Oh, Mum, Dad, this is my fiancé, Malcolm. He has just asked me to marry him, and I am so happy. Malcolm, please say hi to my parents, I do hope that you will come to love them as much as I?'

She could picture their beaming smiles, and Jim vigorously shaking his hand, Doris, wiping away tears of joy. Malcolm in his

Navy uniform, looking so tall and handsome by her side . . . Their wedding would need some careful planning of course. Nothing too elaborate, perhaps a civil ceremony, a simple exchange of vows in a suitably romantic setting? The Seychelles or the Maldives? Sharon had only ever seen brochure pictures of these exotic locations. Now, quite unashamedly, she longed to feel the warm tropical sun, while frolicking naked, on a deserted beach with the man she loved. It would seem to be the most natural thing in the world for them to be doing. She felt herself becoming aroused and smiled, wicked girl . . .

How many children would they have? Two seemed to be a nice comfortable family. Not too far apart, of course. A little girl first? Yes, that would be nice, and she would look so pretty dressed in her little pink baby cloths. Her parents strolling, no promenading, that was the word, along the seafront at Weymouth on a sunny Sunday morning. Would she be fair, like her mother, or dark like Malcolm? Did it matter? Not really, but I think I would prefer her to look like me, and her brother to be more like his father . . . It was at this point in her contemplations that she was dragged back to reality . . .

"Come on then, young lady, let's be having you. This is no time to be sleeping, we need to fix your central eating . . ."

Sharon laughed at Malcolm's little joke, and took his outstretched hand, as he helped her out of the armchair. Sliding her hand under his arm, she pulled herself towards him, deliberately allowing her unfettered breasts to come into contact with his forearm. Sharon was wearing only a nightdress and lightweight dressing gown. She had taken considerable care with her appearance that morning. An early shower, and herbal shampoo, before drying and brushed her hair until it gleamed like burnished copper. After a light breakfast and a thorough scrub at her tender teeth, she had carefully applied a little make-up. Not too much, it was difficult enough what with the fading bruises, and only being able to use her one good hand. Just the faintest hint of eyeliner and a little shadow, then a little blusher to her cheeks. A touch behind the ears of her favourite Givenchy Irresistable, and she was satisfied that her trap was set.

As they walked arm in arm along the corridor to the Dental Suite, Malcolm was again going over the intended dental procedures, but Sharon's mind was somewhere else entirely. She finally pulled him gently to a halt and stepped round to his front. Smiling, she reached up and put a single index finger onto his lips.

"Kindly hush your mouth, if you please, kind sir. This little lady has heard all that she wants to hear regarding her impending dental treatment. What she would appreciate is a little reassuring hug from her ever-so-handsome doctor, if that is not too much to ask?"

Malcolm smiled and quite naturally took her into his enfolding embrace. Sharon quickly moulded her body against his, thrusting her hips slightly forward in a suggestive manner. Standing in an otherwise deserted corridor, they managed to hold the embrace for only a few seconds. It should have gone on quite a bit longer if Sharon had her way, but they were interrupted by the sound of a door being opened further along the passage. A nurse, pushing a trolley, emerged from a side ward and broke the spell. Sharon cursed under her breath, she was just about to present her lips inviting a kiss. She had to content herself by stepping back still holding his hand. Giving him her best beaming smile and the slightest little curtsy, she whispered,

"Ooh-la-la Mr Blackmore, you certainly know how to give a girl reassurance . . ."

She gazed into his eyes looking for some positive reaction, but disappointingly, he was just smiling back in his usual way. 'Damn the man,' she thought. 'Just how much 'come-on' does he need?'

They linked arms again and continued their slow walk towards the Dental Suite.

"Tell me Malcolm, I know that you're a Naval officer, but do you ever have to wear a uniform, at all?"

He laughed, "Yes, of course I do, but thankfully only when I'm on official functions, now. The uniform is not very practical here in the clinic. One finds it rather difficult getting all the blood off of the white shirts, you know. Why do you ask?"

"Oh, I was just trying to imagine what you would look like in uniform. We girls like that sort of thing, a smart-dressed, brown-eyed, handsome man, don't-you-know?"

He chuckled again. "I can show you some photos, will that suffice?"

"For the time being, Mr Blackmore, for the time being . . ."

She delivered her words with a sidelong glance and a rather sexy, suggestive, knowing smile.

"We're here," he said, gently breaking their arm-in-arm contact, and opening a door for her to enter.

The dental surgery was much the same as any other, except that there seemed to be a lot more of it. Impressively, all the polished instruments were laid out in various dishes in glass fronted cabinets. The chair, a huge maroon-padded leather affair, was umbrella'd by the usual array of drills and airlines, and flanked on either side with spittoon sinks, and instrument stands. Softly played classical music emanated from a hidden sound system, and there was a television screen looking downwards from the ceiling. The whole thing smacked of an opulent efficiency.

The masked technician, busily gathering together various items onto a nearby worktop, turned to greet them. Lifting the mask, Sharon was surprised to find that she was looking at the face of a startlingly beautiful young Negro woman.

"Sharon, I want to officially introduce you to Liutenant Moira Pinckney of the United States Marine Dental Corps. Moira specialises in oral and maxilofacial surgical techniques. Behind that radiant dark smile that she gives us all, there's the brain of a surgical genius. It was Moira that put all the tiny stitches into your mouth the other day while we were busy sorting out some of your other little problems. She will be looking after you today, and I will be very privileged to assist her. I have to say that in my opinion, you couldn't be in better hands. Moira, this is Sharon."

Moira peeled off one of her surgical gloves and the two women shook hands.

"Malcolm is such a smooth talking son-of-a-bitch, isn't he? Snaps knicker elastic at twenty paces with those looks as well. But on this occasion, Honey, he's probably right. You are in good hands."

Moira's soft American accent was a delight, and it seemed to be so natural to her vivacious personality. Her dark skin and radiant smile accentuated her own beautiful white teeth.

"In a couple of hours from now, Honey, you're going to be walking out of here with as near perfect set of teeth as you could ever wish for. I've been studying your X-rays, and I can't foresee any problems, most of what we have to do is cosmetic, which is my particular speciality. We have state-of-the-art equipment and the very finest materials to work with. I am confident of complete success. So, if you'd just like to hitch your little butt up onto my chair, and make yourself comfortable, we can pop in a couple of little preliminary injections and give them a few minutes to take effect. For entertainment, we can both watch

Malcolm suit-up, eh. Come on, Tiger, get out of those strides and into your surgicals. Flash us your boxers, lad."

Malcolm smiled and obliged. He took it all in good part as both women laughed uproariously at his favoured CK tartan underwear. He had recognised that it was a deliberate ploy, from Moira, designed to put Sharon entirely at ease, for what he knew, was not quite as simple a procedure as she was making it out to be. He was quite happy to go along with it.

George sat quietly reading his newspaper in the lounge area of the City of London Gentlemen's Club in Old Broad Street. He was anxiously awaiting the arrival of his old friend and colleague, Tony Williams. He felt the vibration from his mobile phone in his breast pocket, and walked toward a nearby phone booth to accept the call in more privacy, it was Sue. George listened to what she told him without making any interruption or comment. He jotted down a few salient points on the booth scratch pad as an aide-memoir, while she spoke, but Sue's account of what had happened in Weymouth that morning was accurate, concise, and needed no clarification. He thanked her for the call, concurred with her intended course of action in speaking only to David's parents, and broke the connection.

He walked grim-faced back to his seat and took a large slurp of his yet untouched whiskey sour. George had never met either Jim or Doris Cox, but he was aware of how highly they were both regarded by those that knew them. The anger and indignation for what had happened to them was now seething and boiling within him. He saw the unsuspecting Tony Williams handing over his hat and coat to a staff member in the Club entrance hall. George was about to ruin his day.

Tony walked through to the lounge area glancing at his watch as he did so. It would tell him that he was already ten minutes late for their 1230 arrangement. Spotting George across the room, he put on his best smile and walked towards him, weaving through the other seated members.

"Hello George, nice to see you again, old chap. How are you?"

His hand was outstretched for the traditional handshake. George half rose from his seat and gave only a perfunctory, limp-wristed, response.

"Tony . . . Yes, I'm quite well, thank you."

Both men then had to wait while Tony ordered a drink from the steward. George declined the offer of another.

The two men made small talk regarding the weather and the cricket scores, while awaiting the drink. George's

somewhat grim attitude was puzzling Tony, and as soon as the steward left the table, he cut straight to the point.

"There's obviously something that's bothering you, old man. Would you care to enlighten me?"

"You're right, Tony, but it's a matter of a very delicate nature, and in the circumstances you would be perfectly entitled to choose not to discuss it under the rules of client confidentiality. However, I come to speak with you today, with my personal assurance, that because of our lifelong acquaintance, I have only your best interests foremost in my thoughts. I wouldn't be doing this for anybody else but you, Tony. Do I make myself clear?"

"Clear, yes George, but this is all very mysterious and obviously quite serious, judging by your demeanour. Come on, old man, get to the point, what's wrong?"

"Tony, there are some questions that I need to ask of you, and they cover two differing aspects of what seems to relate to terrorist activity going back to the 1970's decade. They both involve you."

"Good Lord, man. What on earth are you talking about?"

George held his hands up to silence his protestations.

"I have very recently seen documents, and title deeds of properties, that you did all the conveyancing on, for a certain lady. This would have been back in 1974 and 75. I have the exact dates in my diary, but they're not that important to what I have to say."

"And the lady's name is?"

"Lara Dobbs, also known as Laura Dobson. Ring any bells Tony?"

"Aah, well yes, I am well acquainted with the lady. I have had the privilege of acting for her on many occasions for over thirty years. In fact, I am still acting on her behalf even as we speak, a recent consultation. So if this conversation would involve a conflict of interests, then perhaps we should say no more, George?"

"I don't see it that way, Tony, so please allow me to continue."

"Go on then, George, but if I see us getting close to the knuckle, I will call a halt. Agreed?

"Agreed. The documents that I refer to, were contained in a holdall belonging to Laura Dobson, as she calls herself now. There are other documents that leave me in no doubt that this woman was a part of an IRA terrorist group that were responsible for bombing London at that time. Most recently, she has undoubtedly been responsible for hundreds, if not thousands of cases of criminal deception and fraud, on a huge scale. In the past week, a young woman, a friend of my son, was kidnapped and violently assaulted, by Dobson, when she got close to finding out about her crimes. If she hadn't managed to escape, I fear that she might even have been murdered to prevent her from revealing what she knows."

George took another sip from his whisky to give himself time to rally his thoughts. Tony Williams sat in apparent stunned silence, his hands gripping, white knuckled, to the arms of his chair.

"How did you get to see these documents George? Where are they now?"

"They were all contained within a holdall, that was in a vehicle, used by the young woman, when she escaped from her kidnappers. The holdall, and its contents, will be passed over to senior Police officers this evening. My son-in-law has them stored at my place for the moment."

Tony Williams nodded in understanding, but said nothing.

"So, how well do you know Laura Dobson, Tony? Tell me about her, what is she to you now?"

"She is my client, that is all she has ever been. I have acted for her, as you well know, but our relationship has only ever been entirely professional. I would have to consult my files as to exactly which properties I had a hand in, but I seem to remember that they were farms, or something similar. Most recently, well about eighteen or more years ago, I recall that it was a house in Weymouth, where she now resides. I have always believed her to be a very respectable person in the dog-breeding world. Crufts and all that, you know? In point of fact, I bought a cocker spaniel from her myself, once, when we reached completion on her house. Damn thing mysteriously disappeared from my garden though, wandered off and got lost somewhere, I suppose?"

George found it difficult to stifle a grin. 'Yee gods, the irony of it, even her own solicitor,' he thought.

"Gentlemen, your table is available now, and lunch is being served. If you would care to come this way please." The steward fussed over them until their luncheon order had been placed.

The two men sat facing each other and George found himself struggling to find the correct words to drop the next bombshell on his old friend. There was little doubt in his mind that what he was about to tell Tony would certainly spoil his meal, and might even do irreparable damage to their professional and social relationship. He decided to avoid the subject until they had finished. No sense in spoiling a good filet mignon, served with fresh vegetables and duchess potatoes.

They ate in comparative silence, each wrestling with their thoughts. Tony kept trying to lighten the mood by attempting small talk, but he soon gave up, sensing that there was a lot more to come from George. It was almost a relief when they again retired to their lounge chairs to continue their conversation. The steward brought them two more drinks, and George took a sip at his whiskey before continuing.

"Tony, tell me a bit about your junior partners, if you will. How did you come to meet them? What were the circumstances of you entering into a partnership with Connor McCall and Elizabeth Thompson?"

"Is this part of our previous conversation, George? I don't see any connection to anything we have previously discussed. If we're just chatting, then I would prefer to continue where we left off, if you don't mind."

"This is difficult, Tony. It rather depends on what you tell me, as to whether or not it has any relevance to what I've already told you. But you must let me be the judge of that I'm afraid. You will have to trust me on this one. Now, tell me George. How you came to meet Connor McCall?

"Connor is either my nephew, or my son. At least I think he is. He's certainly family, of that, there can be no doubt. Now I know that probably sounds a bit stupid, but it's complicated. I will try to explain.

My brother, Thomas, was married to Connor's mother, Mary McCall, as was, back in the early fifties. Tom was in the Army, and on leave. It was during the Suez crisis as I remember. It was all a bit of a hurried wedding, because Mary had suddenly announced that she was pregnant, you see? I should say that before the wedding, Mary was sort of working for me at the time. I was just a lowly articled clerk back in those days. She was like a breath of fresh air in the office. I loved having her around, and I managed to put small, menial tasks her way, just to keep her near to me. I knew that she and Tom were engaged, and saving to get married, and I wanted to help them in some small way.

George, she was lovely. A brown-eyed brunette with all the right attributes in very good order, if you catch my drift? She was vivacious, intelligent, incredibly sexy, everything a man could possibly want in a woman."

George nodded in understanding, and took to gently polishing his glasses with his table napkin.

"Anyway, when it came to Christmas, Thomas had just gone back to his unit. Mary, whose parents lived in the Catholic part of Enniskillen, was a bit wary of going home, because of the usual troubles in Ireland. That particular area of County Fermanagh, was not a good place to be living, if you were a Catholic, it seemed.

I had just bought my first house in Bethnal Green, and needed a hand in getting it all fixed up. It was a bit of a wreck, you know? It badly needed a lot of repairs, complete redecoration, new lino, and all that sort of thing. On the spur of the moment, I invited Mary to come and stay with me, never thinking that she might accept, but she did. And then she stayed on for another three months after Christmas, as well. Told me she was saving a fortune by not having to pay board and lodgings, it seemed to justify our unusual relationship. You will understand that a man living with his brother's fiancée was not exactly *de rigueur* in those days, was it?"

George smiled and took another sip from his glass. Tony was in full flow now and he wasn't about to interrupt and spoil it.

"Well, I suppose it was inevitable that Mary and I would, well you know . . . It was only the once, mind you, and we were both mortified with guilt afterwards. She moved back into lodgings that same week. Our relationship after that was never quite the same. I got the feeling that she thought that I had taken advantage of her, and that she blamed me entirely for what had happened. I hadn't, for what we had done was what we both wanted at the time, but she just didn't quite see it that way. George, if only I could turn back the clock . . . but there it is, the dirty deed was done, and I'm the one that has had to live with the consequences.

I was Best Man at the hurriedly organised Registry Office wedding, and I met Mary's parents only the once. I got the distinct impression that they were all too aware of what had transpired, and I got very short shrift from them both.

The baby, Connor, was due to be born in the July of 1954. Thomas was killed in action in the April, so Connor never ever knew his father.

Mary was eventually thrown out of army-married quarters, and I invited her to come and live with me, but she refused. Instead, she moved into a squat with an Irish group, living in Camden. I lost touch with her after a couple of years.

The next thing that happened was in 1969, when I received a letter from a young man asking if he could meet with me. He was claiming to be my son. I was flabbergasted, of course, but somewhat intrigued, as well. I had been in several relationships, but I have never got anywhere near anything serious enough to warrant marriage, or setting up home with anyone. I was reasonably certain that I had never put any girl in the family way, yet here was this young chap? I just had to see him."

Tony beckoned for the steward to bring another round of drinks, and they waited until he left.

"George, from the moment that he walked into my office, I knew that he was family. The resemblance was striking. It transpired that his mother had used her maiden name on his birth certificate, which is why he is called McCall, and not Williams. He told me that his mother, Mary, had died an alcoholic. On her deathbed, she had told Connor to seek me out, and to say that she was sorry for not telling me that I had a son.

I was still not sure, we didn't have DNA testing, or anything like it in those days, and I wasn't certain that I would have pursued it even if we had. I was by then, a rather lonely man, George. I was grateful to find that there was someone else with whom I could relate.

So there it is, Connor is either my nephew, or my son. Personally, I care not which, and I really would prefer not to know. I offered to take him in, to come and live with me, but he refused. He had his mother's caravan on one of those travelling gypsy sites, and lived with an elderly lady, that they had befriended. He had no source of income, so I gave him a generous monthly allowance, and eventually paid for the rest of his education. I frequently invited him to come and stay with me, but he was always too busy, and I only got to meet him very occasionally.

Connor went to university in Belfast, which is where he met, and subsequently married, Lizzy Thompson. They now lead a rather Hippy type of existence, which I don't altogether approve of, but he feels that he has a debt of gratitude to the Irish travelling people, that took he and his mother in, during their time of need.

He and Lizzy are currently living on a smallholding property, in a place called Downton, which is fairly local to Bournemouth, and where they now have their own office. Connor is keen on tracing his family heritage, and seeking the restoration of land titles that were lost during the great potato famine. I've tried to advise him that it might all be a bit of a lost cause, but he will not be swayed from it. Is that enough for you, George? Oh, I suppose that I should add that I took he and Lizzy on as partners, soon after they both matriculated and got their Degrees. It seemed the right thing to do at the time, to give them both a bit of a leg up, so to speak . . .

My understanding is that they're both very good at what they do, George. Championing the causes of the people that Connor grew up with, that is. I don't profess to like it, I feel uncomfortable in the presence of these rough types, and I rather tend to shy away from getting directly involved with most of their work. That's why we agreed that they should open the second office in their name only. That's about it in a nutshell, do you need anything more?"

George took another sip at his whiskey, and steepled his fingers, just to give the impression that he was deep in thought. He held the moment for perhaps a full half minute, knowing that he was about to deliver the final, knockout punch.

"Tony, you say that you gave Connor a generous allowance. What period would this cover, please?"

"Well Connor was born in 1954, and I first met him shortly after Mary's death in 1969, so, from then to when I took them into the business which was in 1979. That ten-year period give or take a few months, I suppose. Look George, where is this going, why are you so interested in Connor?"

"I am sorry to have to tell you Tony, that I have seen irrefutable documentary evidence, that to proves beyond any doubt, that Connor was also a member of that same terrorist cell I previously mentioned. They were all involved with bombing targets in London, and perhaps elsewhere, as well. It is apparent that the targets to be bombed were those identified by Connor, who passed on all the relevant details to the gang. All this took place during the first half of that period that you have specified. Shall we say, broadly, from 1969 to 1975? It would seem that during that period, he was being paid by the IRA, as well."

Sitting back in his chair, George watched the look of shock, incredulity, and then horror, slowly appear on the face of one of his closest friends. He hated himself for what he had done, but he knew that he couldn't now stop himself, the rest of it still needed to be said.

"It doesn't end there, I'm afraid, Tony."

His friend looked grimly at him again.

"Things have moved on, and have become even more serious in the past few days. The documents that I refer to, will be passed over to the Police this evening. It is apparent that Laura Dobson, and the other members of the terrorist cell have been trying to prevent this from happening. They kidnapped Sharon Cox to silence her, and but for her resourceful escape from their clutches, I think she would almost certainly have been murdered."

"George, that is a supposition. You cannot say, for certain."

"You are correct, of course, Tony. But it is a reasonable supposition, considering the extent of the injuries she has sustained. And, we have good reason to believe that they have already murdered at least one other innocent person, to achieve their aims."

"To what are you referring now, George?"

"In the early hours of this morning, the bed and breakfast establishment in Weymouth, The Bide-a-wee guesthouse, which is owned by the girl's parents, was blown up. Her stepmother was killed in the blast. Her stepfather is now in intensive care."

"Oh my God. Are the Police sure that it was deliberate, and not a terrible accident?"

"Too early to say, but according to the news, they are treating the explosion as suspicious. More than that I cannot add."

"Do you know if Connor is involved with any of this George? If he is, I need to know."

"I don't know Tony, but given his previous involvement with the terrorists, it is very likely that he will have been alerted, at the very least. What do you think?"

"I think that my son is in deep trouble, George, and I'm not sure that I can, or should, do anything to help him. There is one small point that might be of concern to me though. This young woman, Sharon Cox you called her. Could she also be known as Sharon Roberts, or any other name, given that she's adopted?"

"Once again, at this moment, I don't know. I could easily find out for you, but does it have any relevance to what we are discussing, Tony?"

"It might. Some of my past work for Laura Dobson has mention of a Sharon Roberts. It may just be that it's entirely coincidental, but if it isn't, and they are one and the same person, it would shed a whole new light on what you believe. I cannot say any more than that, we are getting into the realms of client confidentiality, which is where I will not be compromised. I would be grateful if you could see your way into letting me know though, George, what is it that is going to happen this evening? You mentioned that the documents were going to be passed to the Police. Do you have a meeting arranged?"

"Indeed we do, Tony. Senior Police officers from Scotland Yard are coming to meet with my son-in-law and me, at eight tonight. In the light of what I have told you, as an old friend and colleague, I must urge you not to do anything that would compromise either of us. Indeed, we should probably not be having this conversation at all, but I just felt that I owed it to you."

"For which I shall be eternally grateful, George. You have my word that what you have told me will never be revealed to anyone outside of the confines of these four walls. Here, shake my hand, man, as gesture of my sincerity."

"Hello, yes, this is David Morrison-Lloyd. I wonder if it might be possible to have a word with Malcolm Blackmore, please? I am sorry to be troubling you like this, but it is rather urgent . . ."

"Hello Mr Morrison-Lloyd, this is Sonia on the switchboard, I remember you, how are you now?"

"I am very well thank you Sonia, I remember you, as well. A man doesn't easily forget a rather lovely blue-eyed, blonde bombshell, even when he's poorly . . . Sorry love, but I need to speak with Malcolm, urgently please."

"He's doing his rounds somewhere, David, I've paged him for you, even as we speak. Ah, here he is now, I'm just putting you through, byeee."

"Malcolm Blackmore speaking."

"Hello Malcolm, David Morrison-Lloyd. Sorry to be troubling you, but I have some awful news regarding Sharon's parents, one of whom is dead. I was rather hoping that you might be the right person to gently break it to her?"

"Sharon has just come out of the last of her dental surgery, which all went quite swimmingly. She's making excellent progress, and is in good form at the moment, David. We were thinking that she would probably be fit for discharge in a couple of days. This sounds as though it's going to be a huge setback for her, and might just be too much. She's been through such a terrible ordeal. Physically, she's well on the mend, but mentally, is still quite vulnerable."

"I appreciate that Malcolm, but her stepmother died in an explosion at their guesthouse this morning. Her stepfather is in Poole hospital ICU, and very poorly. She will have to be told at some stage. Is she up to it, do you think?"

"You had better give me the details and a contact phone number, David. Best let me choose the moment to tell her, though. She's really quite smitten with me at the moment, but God only knows what this will do in that regard? It's quite a common occurrence for a patient to imagine himself, or herself, to be romantically attached to their physician. We don't respond to it of course, that would be deemed to be taking advantage and thoroughly unprofessional. I'll confess to finding her devilishly attractive, though."

"I know, she never stops talking about you. According to her, you're somewhere between Superman and Valentino. Oh, and the sun apparently shines out of your jacksy, as well."

Both men chuckled, but their humour was overshadowed.

"Seriously though, Malcolm, Sharon already has my mobile number, but for her own security, she has been forbidden to make, or accept, any other calls except to and from my number. This is even more vital now, given what has just happened. As for her being discharged, this would be a big problem. I don't have anywhere safe to take her. Can she stay there, in the clinic, for a while longer, perhaps?"

"This is a busy facility David, we desperately need all the bed spaces. Leave it with me; I'll see what I can do. Now, give me those details, if you will . . ."

Tony Williams was deeply concerned. As he drove home, his thoughts revolved endlessly around everything George had told him. He tried to picture his son's complicity with a gang of terrorists. In his troubled mind he imagined a darkened room with a group of scruffy individuals, all standing around a dimly lit table, studying a street map, planning their next atrocity. One of their number was to one side. He was busy constructing the bomb. There, standing in their midst, his face shining like that of an angel, was his son, Connor. Tony could see that Connor's arm was being viciously twisted up his back and he was screaming in agony. He was being tortured into giving the gang all the valuable information they needed.

Yes, that was definitely the case . . . Connor was acting under extreme duress. He was being forced into helping them . . . Connor desperately needed his father's help.

Forgetting his promise to George, he hit Connor's speed-dial number on his in-car mobile.

Late that afternoon, Shaun, walking painfully with the aid of a stick, made his way with Dermot, down the front lawn of the bungalow. They stood together on the southern edge of the lake. From there, they could see the bird-hide situated about a hundred metres up a steep gravelled path roughly hewn out of the granite cliff face, to the west. The hide commanded a spectacular view from a point over thirty metres above the lake, an ideal location for watching the many different species of waterfowl that lived there. Pointing out the path, Dermot spoke quietly, as though he was not wishing to disturb the peace and tranquillity of the picturesque surroundings.

"The arms cache is under the floor at the far end of the hide, Shaun. Walk in the door, go to the end of the hide and look at the floor. Centre flagstone is the largest; it's about a metre square and about 120cms thick. It weighs an absolute ton, man. On either end of the big stone there are two smaller ones, that you can easily remove with a pickaxe. You will then see that there are steel loops at each end of the big flagstone. Hook a sling through those, and two or three strong blokes, working with a big lever, should be able to lift it out.

Michael and I put it in that way 34 years ago, but we wouldn't be strong enough to move it now. You will definitely need to get some muscle up here if you want to get the stuff out."

"What's under the flagstone? There was more boxes of stuff than will fit under a square metre?

"Yes, you're right, Shaun. The flagstone covers a circular hole that's plenty big enough for a man to get comfortably through. Then he has about an eight-foot drop down into a natural cave, that we had to enlarge a bit to get everything in. It was all loosely packed in straw, and bone dry when we sealed it over, but heaven only knows what state we'll find it in now? Do you want to try walking up there with me, take a little look for yourself, see what you might need, man? There's a sort of handrail all the way. When it was used as our site office, Michael put the power cables through a galvanised steel conduit pipe that's secured to the cliff face. It's good and strong."

Shaun eyed the slope dubiously, undecided. His whole being wanted to see him striding purposefully up the steep slope, entering the hide, and ripping up the floor single-handed, just to show this smug little git what a real man could do. He hated the state that he was in now, and fervently longed to lay hands on the little bitch that had done this to him. His rage, coupled with the excess of Bushmills, was clouding his judgement.

Dermot knew that there was nothing to be gained by them going up to view the hiding place, but with the germ of an idea in his mind, he suggested it anyway. He hoped that Shaun would see it as a challenge, and he was not to be disappointed.

"Yeh, why not? Lead on, I'll follow in your footsteps, but no tricks now, Dermot . . ."

"No tricks Shaun, I'll help you up, if necessary. I will just need to go and turn off the alarm, and get the door key. It's hanging up in the office. Stay here man, I'll be back in just a minute."

Giving Shaun no time to think or object, Dermot trotted back up toward the bungalow leaving him alone by the waters edge. Bursting in through the front door he called for Lara, who was busy tending to Michael.

"I'm to take Shaun up to the bird hide. He wants to see where the guns are buried. Keep an eye on our progress up the slope. As soon as you see us go in the hide, and we're out of sight, get Michael into the car and drive down to Abergavenny. Go out the back way, just follow the track till you come to a big iron gate. The gate will be open and the alarms will be off. I'll leave the gate unlocked, we may need to use it again. The road will take you down to a little village called Mardy, where it is signposted to the A465, and Abergavenny. My mobile phone is in the hands free cradle in the car. Use it to call for an ambulance. I suggest you do it from a pub car park, and let them come to you. It will be easier than trying to find an A&E hospital unit. Have you got all that?"

"Michael is very weak Dermot, and he's a big man as well. I might not be able to manage him. Besides which, Shaun has the car keys in his pocket."

"There's a spare set in the top left office drawer, Lara. Think positively woman, for god's sake. This might be our only chance to do something for Michael. Take the opportunity to get away yourself, as well. Otherwise, I can see us all ending up dead."

Lara thought for a few seconds, she was looking for obvious problems.

"What about Shaun, he'll likely wring your neck when he realises what you've done, Dermot?"

"Just you leave him to me, woman. In his present state, I think I could get the better of him in a struggle. One good punch to those ribs should do it, don't you think?"

"Don't ever underestimate Shaun Riley, Dermot. I've seen him in action countless times. I know what he's capable of. Believe me, if he's riled, he'll be like a wounded tiger. There will be no stopping him, even if he is severely injured."

"Lara, Michael will likely die if we do nothing, and I cannot live with that. We've been gifted this one opportunity. Now go for it, please, I'm begging you."

Lara walked over to the lounge window and looked down to the lakeside, to where Shaun was waiting. She saw him reach into his jacket pocket and take out Michaels mobile to accept an incoming call. He turned his back to her as he started speaking to someone.

"Alright Dermot, let's do it. Quickly now, Shaun's busy on the phone. Turn off the alarms, and open the gates. Get me the car keys, and I'll get Michael wrapped in a blanket. Get him as far as the back door for me, and keep Shaun occupied for as long as you can. I'll do my best for Michael, I promise. I'll say goodbye now, Dermot, and good luck. I hope this mess gets sorted and we can perhaps meet again, but somehow, I don't think that . . ."

Dermot interrupted her. "Here's my wallet, it has some money inside. My debit card pin number is 4-7-11. Use it to get some more if you need it. Good luck, Lara, and thank you."

Shaun sensed that Michael was up to something, but couldn't quite work out what. He'd already checked that he had possession of the keys to the Range Rover, the shotgun was broken beyond repair, unless there was another gun somewhere? He started to walk back towards the bungalow, but the phone in his pocket started to ring and distracted him. Shaun fished it out and stared at the caller's number on the display. It wasn't one that he recognised, but he decided to accept it anyway. He pushed the button and held the phone to his ear saying nothing.

"Hello, Michael, are you there, hello . . ."

"Who's speaking please?"

"Ah, Michael, is that you? This is Connor, Connor McCall, I need to speak with you urgently."

"Hello, Connor, this is not Michael, it's Shaun. How are you, man? It's been a long time?"

"Shaun, thank God it's you. Look, no time for niceties, we have a big problem. I've just gotten off the phone from my father. He's been telling me about someone he knows that has a file detailing all our past operations. Apparently, it's all going to be handed over to the Police this evening. If that happens we're all finished, we've got to try and prevent it happening."

"Connor, calm yourself, we were about to ring you and warn you of the same thing. We are aware of the existence of this file, it belongs to Lara and was stolen from her. We have been desperately trying to locate its whereabouts in order to retrieve it. Do you know where it is now, for certain?"

"Shaun, according to my father, it's in the possession of a Solicitor friend of his, named George Lloyd, and his son-in-law. He has an address somewhere in Godalming, Surrey."

"I know that address, it's one of the places we are currently watching. Are you absolutely sure that the file is inside? I don't want to be sending my men in on some wild goose chase if it's not there."

"According to my father, senior police officers are going there this evening to be handed the file. He is usually right, Shaun. So, yes, I'd almost stake my life on it being there."

"Okay Connor, thanks for this call, I'm going to break off because we haven't much time to get anything properly organised, but we'll do our best. I have your number now, so I'll call you back as soon as I have anything positive."

"Shaun, have you spoken to Marty about this?"

"Marty? Hell no. We thought it best not to, unless we really need. So don't you go contacting him yet, okay."

"Well, alright then Shaun, but I really think that we should. After all, Marty probably has more at stake than the rest of us. This mess is a potential killer to the present peace accord. Christ, I'm not exaggerating when I say that it could have international repercussions if any of it gets out."

"Connor, I said, no, we wait. That is a direct order from Lara and me."

Shaun broke the connection to prevent any further discussion on the subject. He was sure Connor would comply. He immediately selected his next call while noting that Dermot was now coming back down the lawn toward him.

"John, who have we got watching the Godalming address?" He listened to John's reply.

"Only the two, eh. Tell me, are they good men, able to handle themselves, do you think?"

John was very keen to defend the abilities and integrities of his men, especially after incurring Shaun's wrath after the embarrassing fiasco with the dog. He felt reasonably certain that the two men he had in place could probably be relied upon to deliver the goods, but immediately started to regret his assurances, when he heard what Shaun was intending.

"I now have it on very good authority, that the holdall and all its contents are inside that address, John. There is no time to lose; I want you to act immediately. You will order your men to force entry by any means at their disposal, and without regard for anyone in the house. They are to take possession of the holdall and all it's contents. You will then be responsible for seeing that it is brought straight over here to me. We cannot afford to fail on this John, the police will be there this evening, so we need to act right now, is that clear?"

"Christ, Shaun, you don't want much do you, man? This is a lot to ask of them, even coming from me. It's going to cost you big time, you know that?"

"There are ten thousand good reasons already waiting on the bags safe return, John. I might be persuaded into paying an additional bonus to a good team leader, though. What do you think, do we have such a man?"

Shaun listened to John's final assurances and broke the connection. Dermot was standing a couple of paces away, eying him up. Shaun smiled at him and moved to take his arm.

"We've just located the holdall, Dermot. I'm anticipating that it will be back in safe hands very soon now."

"I got the gist of it, Shaun. It's good news. We may not need to dig up the guns after all. Shall we go back inside instead?"

"We'll be digging the stuff out irrespective of everything else, Dermot. I need to arm my men, and what's surplus to our requirement, will immediately be sold on for cash. We will need to pay for the return of the holdall, and for all the help we've been getting. So, lead on, man. Onwards and upwards . . ."

Shaun chuckled to himself. Despite the pain, his mood was definitely lightening.

The yellow Ford Transit flatbed truck was parked in a small lay by in Munstead Heath Road. Marked up as a Highways Maintenance vehicle, with amber flashing lights fitted on the cab roof, it attracted very little attention from any passers-by.

It had, however, been carefully positioned to afford a good view of the front entrance to George Lloyds extensive property. The two men, Kevin and Danny, were dressed in hi-vis jackets over dark green boiler suits. They had set out a few roadwork signs and bollards to give the impression that work was taking place to the roadside ditching.

Having spent most of the last three days seated in the cab of the vehicle, just watching and reporting back on who they saw coming and going, they were understandably bored. The reasons for their presence had never been properly explained, but that was their orders, and they were getting well paid for doing it.

Like most surveillance jobs, it was extremely tedious, and they both now longed for something significant to happen. One of them was just about to nip down to the town centre to top-up on their dwindling food supply and to pay a call of nature, when the mobile phone they were sharing, started to ring. Kevin picked it up and accepted the call.

He put the phone on loudspeaker, so that both of them could hear what was being said.

They listened with growing trepidation as to what John was now instructing them to do. The call ended and they looked at each other apprehensively. Neither of them was keen to make the next move, despite being told that they should act immediately. They knew that two women, three children, and a vicious dog occupied the house that they had been instructed to forcibly enter. They also knew that both of the men that lived in the house, had separately driven away earlier in the day. Other members of the gang were tailing them, and latest reports had put them both many miles away. A plan of action was still needed to cover all eventualities, and they sat discussing their options for a further ten minutes.

Edith and Sue were both in the kitchen giving the children their tea when Sam gave a warning growl and padded out of the kitchen towards the front door.

'Hello, what's the matter with Sam?' Sue was thinking to herself. The answer popped into her mind immediately. She was rather getting used to this now. Emily had been communicating with her mother like this all day, getting her used to it.

'There are two men in the driveway. They are approaching the house. They are dressed like workmen. They're both carrying tools.'

Sue looked at Emily who was still tucking into her salad, seemingly quite unconcernedly. How did she know?

'Is it Jo-jo who's telling you this Em? Does he detect anything else?'

'Jo-jo will tell me when he knows more, mother. He says that Sam should be brought back here to protect us if necessary.'

Emily had only once glanced up from her meal during this short telepathic exchange with her mother, nobody else in the room was aware of anything untoward.

The doorbell rang and Edith got up from the table muttering, "Who can that be at this time of the day?"

"I'd better bring Sam back in here before you open the door, Mum. I'll shut the kitchen door while you see who it is. Sam, come here, boy."

Sam padded reluctantly back to the kitchen. He sensed a presence in the porch way and gave a warning bark.

"Hush Sam, come here, boy, there's a good lad. Sit over there with Emily, there's a good boy."

Sam did as he was bidden, but his whole attention was focused on the now closed kitchen door.

Edith put the security chain across, and cracked open the front door as far as the chain would allow. Two men, similarly dressed in hi-vis yellow jackets, yellow helmets, and dark green boiler suits marked with the familiar Surrey County Council logo, confronted her.

"Sorry to bother you missus, but I wonder if you'd mind if we fill up a couple of buckets from your tap. We're working on the drains just up the road, and we need to knock up some cement. My mate here just realised that he's forgotten to fill our water drum on the truck this morning?"

"Yes, I think that will be alright. We have an outside tap round the back. If you'd just like to go through the side gate and walk down the path, it's located on the first corner just before you get to the kitchen window. You can fill up from there."

"Thanks missus. We heard your dog bark, is it safe for us to go into the garden? Don't want to get bitten now, do we?"

"We have Sam in the kitchen with us, it will be quite safe for you. Please shut the side gate on your way out."

Edith shut the front door and walked into the lounge to peer through the net curtains, and to follow their progress to the back of the house. About a half-minute passed, and one of the men came back and knocked gently on the window. Edith pulled up the net to see him shrugging his shoulders and pointing at the tap. He was mouthing, "no water" at her.

'Stupid man, what's the matter with him?' Edith muttered as she walked through to the back of the house, and unlocked the back door. She opened it to go outside. Stepped carefully down over the threshold onto the path, an arm came around her neck, grabbing her from behind. Before she could scream, a rough and calloused hand was clamped over her mouth and nose, severely restricting her breathing. She was petrified.

"Easy now missus, just give us what we've come for, and nobody will get hurt, will they?"

Edith rolled her eyes to signal compliance. Her both hands had come up to try and pull at the hand covering her mouth, she desperately needed to breath. The man in front of her brought up the points of the garden prong he was carrying and prodded her under the chin with it.

"My friend told you to take it easy. Just one sound out of you, and it will likely be your last. Do I make myself clear?"

Edith nodded as best she could. There was little doubt in her mind that this thug meant what he said, and the thought of her head being impaled on a garden prong had now reduced her to a terrified, quivering wreck. To her extreme embarrassment, she felt her bladder spontaneously empty itself. It didn't go unnoticed by her captors, who smirked at her discomfort. Sensing that she was about to collapse completely, the man behind moved his grip over her mouth just enough to allow her to take a breath. Prodding her under the chin again, the one in front, Kevin, put his face right up to hers and hissed,

"The black bag that was stolen from us, where is it?"

'Mother, look at me.' Sue turned away from the cooker to look at Emily. 'Nanny is being threatened by the two workmen. Jo-jo says to lock the kitchen door, don't let Sam out. He says that he will take care of Nana.'

Sue knew better than to question what she was being told by her daughter. So as not to alarm the twins, she moved purposefully round behind them to the already closed kitchen door, and silently lifted the handle to lock it. She then turned the key on the double deadlock as well. Sam, sensing that something was amiss, had followed her. He now stood with his nose right up against the frosted glass panel trying to see through. He quietly growled his warning.

"Quiet Sam, it's only some workmen. Sit and stay, there's a good lad."

Edith felt the hand over her mouth slowly ease enough to allow her to answer. She gasped in another breath of air and somehow found the strength to speak.

"In the games room, on the billiard table. It's all in there." She whispered hoarsely.

"Which way, missus, don't piss me about now?"

"Through the door, turn left, end of the hallway, the door facing you . . . Don't hurt me any more, please."

"Stay with her Danny, if she, or anyone else, tries anything funny, break her scrawny bloody neck. I'll get the bag."

Edith felt the man's arm tighten round her neck and the hand came back tightly over her mouth again. She tried to pull on the hand, desperate to breath, but the man's grip only tightened further, and he lifted her until she had to stand on tiptoe. Danny was enjoying feeling her futile struggles, and cared little what pain and suffering he was inflicting on the old bitch.

Kevin burst into the games room and cursed when he saw that the contents of the bag were all neatly laid out on the billiard tabletop. Indiscriminately grabbing everything to hand, he quickly threw it all into the holdall in an untidy mass. He had no recollection of what the original contents were, so there was no way that he could check if he had everything. He seemed to remember being told something about some files and CD's, women's clothing, and some mobile phones, was that it? Yes, he certainly had all of those . . . A laptop, where's the bloody laptop, for Christ's sake, and the two handguns as well? He glanced desperately around the rest of the games room, but there was no sign of anything else.

'Fucking hell, and damn the bloody woman,' he thought. He realised he would have to go back and question her further. He rushed back to where he had left his mate holding on to Edith.

Running out of the back door he had to leap over Danny who was inexplicably rolling around on the ground holding his hands to his head, and moaning, as if in pain. Edith was standing a few paces away, her hand to her mouth watching him in transfixed astonishment. Throwing the bag down on the grass, Kevin quickly took in the scene, trying to work out what had happened. The fork and spade were still where he had just left them, and there was nobody else, except Danny and the woman. He went down onto his knees beside his stricken accomplice. Slapping gently at his cheeks he tried to establish a rapport.

"What the fuck have you done to him, missus? Danny, it's Kevin, get up mate, what's wrong with you, boy?"

With Danny now lying on his back, Kevin could see that his mates face was a mask of smeared blood. His whole expression, one of fear and agony. He saw that Danny had bitten through his top lip, it was bleeding profusely. For some reason, he was holding his hands clamped tightly over his ears, and repeatedly muttering, "No, no, no, take it away, please God, take it away . . ."

Kevin thought Danny was having some sort of fit. With a Herculean effort, he heaved him upright and across his shoulders into a fireman's lift. Grabbing the holdall with his spare hand, he staggered as quickly as he could back out of the gate, and down the drive to their truck. They had left it with the engine running, ready for a swift departure, if necessary. Kevin dumped Danny unceremoniously over the tailgate, straight onto the flat bed of the vehicle. He winced as he heard his head hit the steel floor.

"Sorry mate," he murmured as he threw the bag in beside him. Pausing only to drag one side of a heavy tarpaulin over both, to hide things temporarily, he leaped up into the cab. With the tyres scrabbling for grip on the gravel, Kevin sent the truck hurtling out onto the quiet Munstead Heath Road, and away.

Edith, now in shock, was still standing in the garden when Sue came to find her. Emily had told her mother that the men had gone, and that it was now safe to open the door. Putting her arms gently around her mother's shoulders, Sue led her back indoors. She sat her down and set about making a fresh pot of tea. The twins were staring at their nanny, frightened and confused. They had no understanding of anything that had happened in the past five minutes.

Emily got down from her chair and walked round to stand in front of her Nana. Putting her arms out in the usual way that a child does when wishing to be picked up. Edith automatically accepted her up onto her lap and cuddled her to her bosom. Sue, busy pouring the tea, failed to see exactly what was happening behind her, but on turning round, she saw that Em had reached up, and was gently touching her Nana's face, causing her to look down into the eyes of her little granddaughter. They held on to the eye-to-eye contact while Emily was seen to be quietly whispering something, that only her Nana could possibly hear. The change in Edith's face was quite remarkable to behold. The pained and worried expression, usually associated with a person in shock, seemed to melt away. The pallor disappeared as colour returned to her cheeks. The slightest hint of a smile, always there on Edith's face for the children, was seen to slowly return.

Edith broke the spell. With both arms, she wrapped little Emily closer into her loving embrace. Kissing the top of her head, she returned the whispered terms of endearment, and murmured thanks to her tiny little granddaughter.

Sue was not able to understand anything of what she had just seen, but she was getting rather used to this by now. It would seem to be just another miraculous demonstration of the power contained in Emily's little mind.

Dermot, with Shaun close behind, trudged their way slowly up the steep incline towards the bird hide. The path, cut into the cliff face, was too narrow for two people to walk side-by-side. The steep incline was hard going, even for Dermot, who had done it hundreds of times before. He could hear Shaun's laboured breathing behind him, and smiled to himself as he imagined the pain and discomfort that he was must be experiencing. He paused on a particularly slippery part of the path, and turned to see how Shaun was coping. It also afforded him a chance to look back to the bungalow to see if Lara had made any move with Michael yet. To his consternation, he saw that she was in full view. She was struggling, with Michaels arm draped around her shoulders. As they slowly made their way towards the open door of the car, Dermot knew that if Shaun was to look round now, he couldn't fail to see them.

"How are you doing then, Shaun? We're just over half way, and this is probably the worst bit. The path isn't quite so steep from here on. Watch your footing, though. Try and avoid the mossy bits, just there and there."

He pointed in an effort to get his full attention. "They're very slippery. Best keep a tight hold on the handrail until we're past that big rock just up ahead. From then on, it's fairly good going again."

Shaun looked up, his face pale. The sweat glistened on his forehead. Dermot could see flecks of dried blood in the corners of his mouth. He was pleased to see that the climb was taking its toll on him. He would be easier to handle if there was any trouble.

"How did you and Michael manage to carry the gear all the way up here, for gods sake? More to the point, how the hell are we going to get it all back down again?"

Dermot chuckled, "We were all young and fit back then, Shaun. And besides, this path was once wide enough for a Jeep. We quarried a lot of stone off the cliff face before we landscaped it all. As for getting the stuff down, we can easily fix up a block and tackle and lower it all down onto the shoreline. It'll be a doddle, man, you'll see."

Shaun grunted, and they both continued their slow ascent. As the path levelled out and widened, Dermot was able to walk backwards while talking to Shaun. His aim was to offer encouragement, while distracting his attention away from looking back. He could see that Michael was now in the car, but Lara seemed to be faffing about, fetching and carrying things from the bungalow.

They finally reached the entrance to the hide, and Dermot fished around in his jacket pocket for the key. His last look back had seen Lara climbing up into the driver's seat of the Range Rover, and he prayed that Shaun wouldn't hear her start the engine. He need not have worried, though, fate was on his side. The phone in Shaun's pocket gave a shrill ring, even as Lara turned the key in the car ignition.

Dermot breathed a sigh of relief as they both entered the hide. His last glimpse was of the car disappearing up the path behind the bungalow. Shaun was busy on the phone, and had seen nothing.

"Shaun, great news, Kevin and Danny have got the bag back. I've told them to rendezvous with me at Chieveley Services on the M4. I'll be bringing it straight over to you after that, OK?"

"Well done, John. Was there any trouble? Was the girl there?"

"No trouble Shaun, nobody got hurt, they were in and out in five minutes, according to Kev. There was no sign of the girl, I'm afraid, do you want us all to still keep looking?"

"Damn right I do. The bitch will have to surface sooner or later, and I want her fucking head on a plate when she does. This whole operation goes on until I get her, is that clear?"

"Whatever you say Shaun, you're the man. I'll get the Godalming address back under surveillance again immediately."

"John, bring me four good strong lads, each with a pickaxe and a big strong lever. It looks as though we'll also need a twelve-foot scaffold pole, or something similar, to use as another lever. I'm looking at what we might need to get at the stuff right now. If there's anything else, I'll ring you back."

"No problem, Shaun."

Breaking the connection, Shaun looked at Dermot and grinned. He was standing on the big flagstone arms on his hips and ineffectually stamping his foot trying to detect any movement. Dermot could see that the news from John had been like a shot in the arm for Shaun, his injuries forgotten, he had seemed to have acquired a new lease of life. Dermot knew that it would also make him a very dangerous proposition when he realised that he had been duped.

"This doesn't look too difficult Dermot, old lad. How heavy do you reckon this stone might be?"

"Probably close to half a ton, Shaun. Michael and I used a fork-lift when we laid it down, but I daresay it'll come up with a bit of sweat and leverage."

Shaun moved over to the observation point, a long narrow window that opened inwards, and latched up to afford a view over the lake. He poked his head out and looked down the thirty-five foot drop to the narrow piece of stone ledge that formed the shoreline of the waters edge.

"Do you have a suitable block and tackle, Dermot?"

"In the shed behind the bungalow. It's old, but still serviceable, I think. We'll have a look when we go down . . ."

Even as he said it, Dermot was immediately regretting his words. He had inadvertently made reference to the bungalow, thereby causing Shaun to look that way. It was as though everything was happening in slow motion. Shaun was still leaning out of the window when Dermot saw his whole body stiffen, and he ducked his head back inside. The murderous look on his face left Dermot in no doubt as to his intention. Shaun made an immediate lunge toward him, growling in anger. Dermot knew that his life was in the balance, and he had to defend himself. Balling his fist as tightly as he could, and in the split second before Shaun's hands grabbed his throat, Dermot delivered his best punch into his ribcage on the injured side. He knew that it had been a telling blow, as a gasp and a grimace of extreme pain, shot into Shaun's face, but he still came on, he was virtually unstoppable.

Dermot felt himself violently slammed back against the cliff face that formed the back wall of the building, the back of his head impacting heavily against the unyielding stone. Shaun's hands were grasped around his throat, his thumbs seeking to apply pressure onto his Adams apple to squeeze the life out of him.

Dermot felt himself beginning to black out. He frantically continued to rain blows into Shaun's ribs, and tried to bring a knee up into his groin and genital area. With his left hand he tried to gouge at his eyes, but he couldn't reach properly. With one last supreme effort, Dermot again smashed his fist into Shaun's ribs. Even through the thick material of Shaun's jacket and the strapping, he felt them all move under the impact of his punch. He sensed that the grip on his throat had loosened very slightly. Encouraged, he tried again, and again, pummelling the blows in continuously until, with a roar of pain and anger, Shaun had to release and step back clutching at his injured side. Blood trickled from the corner of his mouth. Both men stared malevolently at each other gasping for breath. Shaun doubled in pain and holding his ribs, Dermot massaging his throat and gulping in lungfuls of air.

"I should have killed you when I had the opportunity two days ago," Shaun growled.

"But you didn't, and now you're paying the price. Lara has taken Michael to hospital. Did you think I was going to just sit back and watch him die at your hand, you murdering bastard? I'm giving the orders now, you'll do as I say, or, by God, I promise you, I'll kill you myself."

"You're forgetting that I've got five of my blokes on their way here. So just how long do you think you're going to last when they arrive, Dermot? If you're going to kill me, you'd better get on with it now, while you can."

"Don't tempt me, Shaun, I might just do it yet. Now give me that bloody phone, Lara needs to know that we've got her bag back."

"Lara doesn't have a phone."

"She has my phone, it was left in the car when you arrived. Now give me that one, so that I can ring her."

Shaun was not about to part with his only connection with his henchmen. Instead, he called up the directory and scanned it for Dermot's own number. Finding what he was looking for he hit the 'call' button and put the phone expectantly to his ear.

Dermot moved threateningly toward Shaun, his fists clenched. Shaun backed away until he was cornered in the far end of the hide. Slipping the phone back into his pocket, he took up a defensive stance against Dermot's expected attack, turning his injured ribs away from him.

In his present condition, there was little doubt in Shaun's mind that Dermot, given the opportunity, would be able to beat him in a stand up fight.

Dermot waded in throwing roundhouse punches at Shaun's head and kicking at his shins and kneecaps in an effort to bring him down. Forced to defend against the onslaught, Shaun was content to fend off as best he could, but his cunning mind was already detecting a pattern to Dermot's relentless attack. Six punches then a kick, three times now . . .

Dermot aimed his next kick at Shaun's groin, but it never landed, Shaun was ready and waiting. His swinging leg was grabbed as it came up, and forced on upwards. Dermot lost balance and fell heavily onto his back. For the second time in two minutes, the back of his head hit the stone, only this time, it was too much, and he was knocked senseless. Shaun waded in with repeated kicks to the head and body, each blow knocking Dermot's limp body along the stone floor of the hide, towards the open door. A sickening crunch of broken bone as his boot hit the back of Dermot's head, told Shaun that he had broken his neck, but he gave him two more vicious head kicks, just for good measure. Shaun finally stood back breathing hard, his lower face smeared with his own blood.

"You should have fucking killed me when you had the chance, Dermot, old lad. Now you can go say a hello to Ryan for me . . ."

Grabbing one of his arms, Shaun dragged Dermot's lifeless body outside, and with one final kick sent it over the edge of the cliff to bounce once on the stone at the waters edge, before plunging, and slowly disappearing, into the depths of the murky green water. Shaun stood swaying on the very edge of the precipice, staring down at the ripples as they spread out over the surface. His pain was forgotten; there existed a gleam of self-satisfaction in his eye. Revenge had never tasted sweeter.

Lara dialled 999.

"Emergency, which service please?"

"I need an ambulance. I've come across a man with some serious facial injuries."

"Can I have your name please?"

And so it went on.

"Can I reconfirm your location again, please? Is it the Crown Inn at Pantygelli, that you're saying?"

"That's the name on the pub sign, I'm a stranger to this area, I've just pulled into the car park to make this call. Look, can you hurry up, please. This man is bleeding all over my car seats and I'm late for an important meeting."

"An ambulance is on its way to you now, I just need to take a few more details, so if you would please be patient for me. Now, can you briefly tell me where it was that you found this man?"

Lara broke the connection. She got out of the driver's seat and went round to open the front passenger door.

Michael was slumped in the seat, his whole head wrapped in towels wet with his own blood. He was barely conscious.

"Come on Michael, we need to get you out of the car. An ambulance is coming for you, and I can't afford to be here when it arrives."

Michael mumbled something that Lara took to be in general agreement with her wishes. She was trying to swing his legs round to get him out of the car, but it needed a lot of effort in his weakened condition. He put his arm around her shoulders, and she accepted his weight, as his feet slipped down onto the ground. Turning him round, she gently walked him a few paces, and sat him down on the retaining wall of a nearby flowerbed. She stood in front of him, holding both hands on his shoulders to support him, and listening for the two-tones of the ambulance.

She bent down to speak into his ear. "Michael, I'm sorry, but I'm going to have to leave you when I hear the ambulance approaching. Dermot will need me back at the quarry. You know that I can't be found here with you, don't you?"

Michael nodded and mumbled something through the bandages.

"Alright, take it easy, Michael, don't try to speak now, just try to relax, it won't be long now."

Michael grabbed and shook both her hands in frustration. Whatever it was that he was trying to tell her, it must be something important. She bent closer to him, again trying to catch his whispered, distorted words. They came slowly, each one enunciated as clearly as his painfully damaged mouth would allow.

"Tell-Dermot-not-to-forget-the-wire."

"What wire, Michael? What are you talking about, is it important?"

"Yes. Dermot-knows . . ."

She could hear the ambulance in the distance; it was time for her to leave. With a tear in her eye, Lara said her last goodbye to Michael. She doubted they would ever see each other again. Leaving him seated on the wall in full view, he looked a pathetic figure with his head swathed in bloody bandages.

She drove out of the pub car park and headed south, back down toward the A465. Lara was going back to the only place she really felt safe, her home in Weymouth.

David pulled into the drive at Godalming, and parked the Mercedes behind Georges Jaguar. He glanced at his watch, it told him that he had just about enough time to take a shower and grab a sandwich before the Police arrived. He knew nothing of the earlier events of that afternoon. Sue, realising that David was probably well on his way to Heathrow, with passengers on board, when it happened, and had thought it better not to worry him. After all, apart from the holdall being taken, very little harm had occurred, except for Edith being very frightened. Looking at her now, laughing and playing a game of scrabble with the twins, she appeared completely back to her normal self.

George had arrived home an hour ago, and had already been told, but somehow, Sue sensed that something else was troubling him. He seemed preoccupied with another matter, and hadn't quite appreciated the ordeal that his wife had been through. He had made all the right noises in all the right places, and even gave Edith a comforting cuddle, but to Sue, who knew her father well, he just seemed to be struggling to do and say the right things. His general demeanour seemed to lack his normal warmth and sincerity. She watched him pour an overly large scotch and soda, then, rather than spend time with the children, as was normal, he retired to his study for some peace and quiet.

The sound of David's key in the door always prompted the children into running to greet him. He, in turn, always made sure that he made a fuss of them all, by sitting himself down and allowing each to tell him of their day. It was always Emily who claimed his lap position. She being the smallest and youngest, it was kind of regarded as her privilege by the twins. Their conversation naturally revolved around the excitement of the afternoon's events, and David had already gotten the gist of what had transpired before he ever got to talk to Sue and Edith.

Getting out of his chair, with Emily still in his arms, David walked through to the kitchen to where Sue was preparing a couple of rounds of sandwiches for his tea. He put his arm around her shoulders in a comforting manner, already sensing that she was keeping a tight lid on her emotions.

"Sounds as though you've had a hell of an afternoon, love. Care to tell me about it?"

The moment began to get the better of Sue. She felt her lip quivering as she tried to stifle a sob. David hugged her closer to his chest, and the three of them went into a huddle, wrapping their arms around each other.

With their heads now so close together and with emotions running so high, it was the perfect opportunity for Emily to take the next progressive step in trying to teach her parents how to communicate with each other, telepathically.

Using her own mind as a sort of catalyst, or unscrambling device, for their thought processes, she introduced her mother's brain pattern into the mind receptors of her father, and visa versa. She also ensured that as soon it was clear that they had grasped the concept, the information was implanted into their memory banks, as an automotive function. This now ensured that each would be able to call upon the other, telepathically, should they wish to do so.

Emily had been doing exactly this with Jo-jo, the alien entity, since the day of her birth, so she no longer needed to converse with him in a normal speech mode, as was still necessary with her parents. With Jo-jo, her own mental capabilities had developed to a point where whole blocks of information could be imparted or exchanged, in an instant. Emily knew that this was a skill that could only be acquired with constant practice. A great deal of further development and refinement was needed to fine tune and enhance her parent's exchange of thought processes. This would be something she would have to actively encourage.

Emily, working in tune with Jo-jo, had been brought up with it, but she appreciated that there was so much more still available to her. She was now in the process of being introduced to another of the enormous dormant powers contained in the recesses of her own brain. The latest being telegnosis, the ability to acquire knowledge regarding distant events, the main power used by Jo-jo. He had already explained the concepts, and established that the basic requirements to enable its performance were contained within her relatively primitive little brain. He had assured her that it was possible for her to be able achieve, she only needed to learn how, under his guidance.

His teachings always reflected that there were absolutely no limitations to the learning ability in an intelligent healthy mind. It was only the degenerative processes associated with the physical ageing of the brain that would inhibit its ultimate development to the point that he, and the rest of his race, had reached.

Emily, still so young, had come to realise that having Jo-jo as her mentor, made her absolutely unique, and effectively, set her apart from all others. He had assured her that he would always be there for her, and she took this literally to mean, for the rest of her mortal life.

For a two-year-old human child, her knowledge and intelligence quotient (IQ) development was already far beyond that of most adults, but she still aspired to achieving greater things, if only to justify what she perceived to be, his love and dedication toward her. She wasn't to know that this was precisely the emotion that he still wished to physically experience for himself.

She had sought his advice before taking this step with her parents, questioning whether or not he thought it was right? In his enigmatic way, he had put the ball straight back into her court by telling her,

*'Child, you will need to make many such decisions in your life. Some will be right, some will be wrong, but all will be made on the basis of it being the best way to proceed, with good intent. That is your criteria for living.'*

Such wisdom left Emily to ponder the possible consequences for a considerable time. The conclusion that she finally reached was that the benefits would, in all probability, far outweigh any possible drawbacks. Her decision made, she had only been waiting for a time when both her parent's minds were closely in tune with each other. Today, with all it's heightened emotions, and all the feelings of mutual love and tenderness being expressed between them, had presented itself as the perfect opportunity.

Exactly how it happened was just as mysterious as when Emily first made contact with them in this manner.

David slowly became aware of Sue's voice in his mind. The revelation caused him to pull back from the huddle slightly, and to look searchingly into her eyes to see if she was getting a similar response from him. The smile on her lips, and the triumphant look in the face of little Emily, was enough to convince him that she was. What had just occurred was a wonderful gift from his daughter. He formulated a trial message to that effect in his mind, and attempted to convey it to Sue, by thought alone. Her reply came back loud and clear, she agreed with him entirely.

They joyfully went back into their close huddle, and remained that way for several minutes, experimentally revelling in their newfound ability, to converse by telepathic means alone. When they finally broke apart, Emily took great delight in witnessing how such a simple thing for her to impart, had added to the already strong bonds that existed between her parents. That factor alone had seemingly justified her decision.

Metaphorically, Emily had only just opened the doors for them. It was now down to her parents to push them farther, in order explore the possibilities of what lay behind. They also needed to establish if any boundaries existed in relation to just how far they could go.

None of them quite realised just how much this would alter their lives, and how soon they would need to be putting their new unique ability into practical use.

The front doorbell rang and David glanced at his watch.

"God almighty, where does the time go? That must be the Police here already. Give George a call will you please, Sue. I'll show them through to the games room, it'll be quiet in there. Come on Em, you can stay with me. Tell me what you think of these two Policemen."

With his daughter in his arms David opened the front door.

"Evening gents, you're a bit prompt, I've not long been in myself and was just about to take a quick shower before you arrived. Never mind, you're here now, come on in will you?"

"Good evening Mr Morrison-Lloyd. Apologies for being a bit early, it was a long drive for us, and it's always better to be early, rather than late, isn't it? Is this your daughter? She's a little cutie, what's her name?"

"This is Emily, she can be a bit shy with strangers. Are you going to say hello to these nice gentlemen, Em?"

Emily turned away and hugged her father's neck in the way children do when they are unsure. The men laughed.

"This way then gents. Tell me, do you have families?" They followed David into the hall and then along the passage to the games room where George and Sue were just turning on all the lights.

"Ahmed is a family man, David, but I'm still single. Is it alright to address you by your first name, sir? It's going to be a long evening, and it might be easier for all of us if we dispense with the polite formalities. Please call me Charles, and this is Ahmed."

"That's just fine, Charles. May I introduce my wife Sue, and my father-in-law, George Lloyd. You are in his house. Sue and I live down in the New Forest, as you are probably already aware?"

"Yes, David. How do you do Mr Lloyd, Sue, pleased to meet you both."

The introductions complete, there was an awkward pause while each waited for the other to make a start on the business in hand. It was David who set things in motion.

"Gents, since I last spoke with you, there have been some certain unfortunate developments. This afternoon, while George and I were out of the house, two men, posing as council workmen, wishing to fill a bucket with water, managed to force their way into this very room. They were after, and have taken, the holdall containing all the documents, and other evidence, that I was about to hand over to you tonight."

The two Policemen looked at each other.

"We're sorry to hear that David, was anybody hurt, at all?"

"George's wife, Sue's mother, Edith, was roughly manhandled, and was a bit traumatised, but fortunately, she seems alright now."

"This is serious incident David, have you reported it yet?"

David felt Emily tighten her grip on his neck to attract his attention.

"Excuse me for a moment gents, what is it Em, do you want to go to Mummy, darling?"

It was a little distraction that allowed her time to communicate a message to her father.

'I am sensing that there is some deceit in the way that these men are acting, father. They are not being entirely truthful, and they are here for some other purpose.'

David passed his daughter over to her Sue, who caught his eye and nodded slightly, indicating that she too was aware of what had been passed.

"Sorry gents, where were we? Oh yes, I remember . . . Yes, we have reported it to our local Police, and we are just waiting on the arrival of the CID, who said they are coming to interview us, and take statements. I told them eight o'clock, the same time as you, so they should be arriving any minute. We thought it best to get you all together, and save us from having to keep repeating ourselves. Can I perhaps offer you both a drink while we're waiting?"

"This puts a slightly different complexion on our lines of enquiry, Mr Lloyd. Will you excuse us both for a minute please, I need to have a confidential word with my colleague."

They retired to the far corner of the room and with their backs turned, could be seen to be talking in animated whispers. There was obviously something that they could not agree upon.

David grinned at Sue and Emily. George, confused, sidled up to him and whispered,

"What's going on David? What's all this about the CID coming?"

"Trust me George, I'll explain later. A fiver says that those two will be out of the front door within the next three minutes . . ."

"Mr Morrison-Lloyd, my colleague and I were expecting to come here tonight to receive certain information that you claimed would further our enquiries into the three missing females that we suspect might have been murdered by Shaun Riley. We now find that two unknown males have allegedly removed the documents we were promised, this afternoon. While we sympathise with what has happened, we feel there is little point in us both sitting in on the interview with your local Police, on a matter that is clearly out of the scope of our main enquiries. We can easily apply for copies of your statements, and they will be on my desk first thing in the morning. I have your phone numbers should there be anything that I wish to clarify with you, but from what you have told us, we're both beginning to think that there will be little here to further our particular lines of enquiry. We have a long drive back to our office in Worcester, so if you are happy to leave things like that, we will bid you all a good evening?"

"Okay gents, if that is how you see it, then I can only apologise if you feel you've had a wasted journey. If you would care to leave me your contact phone numbers, I'll ring if I think I have anything more for you."

"Certainly, David. I will leave you with my personal card. Please feel free to contact me, direct, at any time. It will be a lot easier than going through our switchboard."

Ferguson produced a card from the lapel pocket of his suit, and placed it on the table. He picked up his coat and briefcase, and both men started towards the door. David followed them both down the passage to the hall, where he opened the front door to let them out.

Wishing them both a curt, "Good evening," he watched as they got into the now familiar silver Ford Focus and quickly reverse it away down the drive. Smiling to himself, he walked back to his waiting family.

"What in God's name was all that about, David? I thought that we were going to hand this sorry mess over to senior Police officers this evening. Why have they just walked out on us?"

"I'm not sure, George. Perhaps those two were not real Police officers. We have Emily to thank for recognising that there was some subterfuge taking place, and communicating it to Sue and me, before anything was given over."

"Emily? Good God man, she's only two years old, how can you possibly rely on anything that she tells you? And how did she tell you anyway? I didn't hear her say a word."

"George, you are just going to have to believe us. You have a truly remarkable little granddaughter here. Sue and I, as her parents, are still struggling to understand the complexities of her little mind. If I tell you that she can sense things in other people's minds, that you or I could never detect, it would sound rather stupid and far fetched. But she can, believe me. Not only that, but she doesn't even need to speak to us in the normal way to tell us something. We have just recently, learned to understand her thoughts. I know it all sounds quite incredible, but believe me, it's true, isn't it Sue?"

Sue looked at her father and nodded. Emily, still in her mother's arms, gazed wide-eyed at her grandfather, giving nothing away.

"It's true, Dad. We don't know how she does it, but she can transmit her thoughts to us, and we have just learned how to answer her back in the same way. As for her being only a child, yes, that is correct, but Emily can already read, and hold an intelligent conversation, in the same way as you or I. She will probably beat you, hands-down, in a game of chess, backgammon or cribbage, as well. We've never had her tested or anything like that, we don't need to. We already know that we have a child genius. Her intelligence quotient will probably be off the measurable scale?

Even now, I am sensing that Emily doesn't wholly approve of us telling you all of this, but you are bound to find out sooner or later. It's better that we tell you, and Mum, and ask that you don't ever tell anyone else. David and I, well, we both fear that if it ever got out, Em would never be allowed to live a normal life. So, now you know, can we count on your discretion?"

George was lost for words. He had a dozen questions that he would have liked to ask, but felt that this was not the right time. Sue had previously talked with her parents, expressing concern that her baby daughter was somehow different, but this latest revelation just beggared belief. He caught Emily's gaze and she smiled at him. He reached out and playfully squeezed her little nose.

"I always knew that you were a clever little tyke, but I can't imagine that you're ever going to beat me at cribbage. You're little secret is safe with me and your Nanna, little'un, but it will cost you a cuddle or two starting right now, little lady, come and give me a big hug, and perhaps teach me how to mind-read as well. It would be right handy in Court sometimes."

The light-hearted remark broke the tension, and everyone laughed. Emily went willingly into the outstretched arms of her grandfather who she loved, trusted and felt safe with. She responded to his request for a cuddle, but was not quite ready to share anything else with him. For right at that moment, she was sensing that there was something that was deeply troubling him, something that might have been related to what had happened that afternoon, but she couldn't be sure?

Later that evening, the two men shared the last of George's best Johnny Walker Blue Label single malt.

"So where do we go from here, David? It's time for a rethink on what's happened, how do you see the situation now?"

"I'm not sure, George. When they come to realise that what they've taken back in the bag is of little significance, I'm surmising that they're probably going to come back for the rest, that's fairly obvious. On that basis, we need to put everything we've still got, beyond their grasp, at least until we can arrange something better. Any ideas?"

"Well let's recap on exactly what it is that we've still got. There's the computer, and the file relating to their terrorist activities. The personal bits and pieces belonging to the Dobson woman. What else? What have I missed?

"Only the guns, mustn't forget those, George."

"Hmm, I'm not too comfortable about having those in the house, David. I'd rather they were disposed of as quickly as possible. Why can't we just hand them over to the Police in the normal way? In fact, why not just give the local police a call right now, and give them everything?"

For reasons best known to himself, David chose to ignore the suggestion.

"It occurs to me that we may well have already become targets for elimination, in order to prevent us passing on what we know. We've established that the two blokes that were here tonight were probably not *bona fide* policemen, so who were they? How do they fit into the equation? They're obviously not after any of the stuff that we've still got, otherwise, I think they would have acted quite differently earlier today, when I first mentioned the file, and they had the opportunity to lay hands on it sooner. The fact that Ferguson left me his calling card, leads me to believe that they're to be regarded as something other than 'the opposition,' am I making myself clear so far?"

"Assuming that the card is genuine, then, yes, I would have to agree?"

"Alright dad, so what else is there that could possibly be gained out of all of this? My brain hurts with just keep thinking about it. The other thing that is bothering me is the danger that my meddling has put onto my family. If I could somehow convince them that it was just me that they should be after, it might take away some of the threat to the rest of you. Let me just run this idea past you, then tell me what you think . . ."

# Chapter 5

The late autumn sunlight streaming through the window of her private ward was making Sharon feel particularly good. She had just finished her breakfast of scrambled eggs on toast, and was on her second coffee when the morning newspaper arrived. After a quick perusal, she tossed it onto her bedside table and glanced at the clock. Malcolm would be starting his rounds about now, so it would be a good twenty-five minutes before he got to her. Plenty of time to take a shower and put on a bit of slap to make herself look presentable . . . Grabbing her toilet bag and a couple of fresh bath towels she headed off to the bathroom just down the corridor.

Sliding the 'engaged' sign across, she closed the door. There were no door locks fitted on any of the facilities in the clinic, but it didn't worry her, for her room was located in the female surgical wing. Stepping out of her nightclothes, Sharon stood naked in front of the full-length mirror and critically examined herself. The bruising to her ribs and abdomen had faded to a red, blue and yellow tinge on her otherwise milky white skin. Apart from a very slight bit of discomfort when she turned over in bed, it no longer bothered her. The swelling and bruising associated with the assault, and her subsequent facial surgery, was similarly fading. She was particularly pleased with her new nose, it seemed to take several years off her appearance.

Cupping a breast in each hand, she tested their firmness and elasticity and probed carefully for any lumps. Sharon knew that she had been gifted with nice looking breasts. They were not too big and pendulous, just nicely proportionate, rounded and firm. With evenly located, slightly large, pink nipples that were just pert and dark enough to show attractively through her underwear, she considered her breasts to be her best feature.

Malcolm had given her an exercise routine to prevent her muscles from getting flabby during her stay, but despite a twice daily workout, she found to her dismay, that she was still able to pinch an inch of flab around her midriff. Mentally castigating herself for allowing it to happen, she resolved to increase her fitness regime, and watch her diet.

Stepping under the warm shower, and soaping herself all over, her thoughts revolved around how she was going to persuade Surgeon Lieutenant Malcolm Blackmore that he should be seriously considering dating her in the foreseeable future. All her attempts to pull him, had seemingly failed up to now, and time was rapidly running out. Having been advised that she could be discharged from the clinic any day, Sharon found that she was dreading the thought of being parted from him. On the other hand, it would be nice to get back home and see Jim and Doris, her adopted parents, for she had so much to tell them.

She realised that the future was still uncertain, of course, the problems with Laura Dobson and that horrible man, what was his name? Shaun, her nephew, Laura had said, still existed. She was relying on David to somehow sort that one out for her. She had no idea how he was to achieve this, and simply blocked it from her mind entirely, by not even thinking about it. For the time being, she preferred to look at her world through rose tinted spectacles . . .

Vigorously towelling herself down and applying some of her newly purchased Victoria Beckham body lotion, she set about making herself as attractive and sexy as possible for Malcolm's routine visit to her bedside. There wasn't time to do very much with her hair, so she satisfied herself by simply wrapping it in a hand towel and making a turban on her head. A vigorous scrub of her lovely new teeth was followed up by a quick application of just a trace of pink lippy. The hint of a green eye shadow and a little blusher to enhance her pale cheeks was all she had time for. It was the best she could do for the moment, her trap was set . . .

Malcolm was dreading his round that morning. He deliberately left Sharon to be his last patient having already advised the rest of his staff that he needed to break some devastatingly bad news to her. None of them envied him his task, for it had become quite the topic of clinic gossip, that Sharon Cox had a thing for Malcolm Blackmore, and possibly, he for her? Everyone hoped so, for it had been quite some time since the untimely death of his wife, and Sharon was perceived to be an ideal candidate for his affections.

With one eye on the clock, Sharon, dressed only in her new, black lace underwear and her pale pink terry-towel dressing gown. Carefully arranging herself in her window armchair, so that her gown fell apart to exposed rather more of her thighs than would normally be deemed appropriate. She was keen to give the impression of being caught napping when Malcolm arrived.

A full half an hour passed, and she was beginning to perspire in the heat of the morning sunshine. She got out of her chair to pull the sunshade down a little, thereby spoiling her pose. Damn the man, where was he? He was never usually this late on his round, he must have had some sort of emergency? Picking up her newspaper, she had just sat back down again when there was a polite knock at her door, and Malcolm entered, but without his usual entourage.

Sharon gave him her best smile and rose out of her chair to greet him. Walking round the end of the bed, she looked up into his face for some sort of reaction, trying to gauge his mood. Something was troubling him . . .

"Good morning, Mr Blackmore. Is this to be a pleasant social call? Have you purposely managed to mislay all the rest of your nursing staff somewhere, just so that we can be alone? What a lovely idea."

"Hello Sharon. I don't need to ask how you are this morning, do I? You're looking positively radiant and particularly lovely, if I may be so bold?"

"You may be as bold as you wish, kind sir. It does a girl a power of good to be appreciated, but I can see in your eyes that there is something amiss. Have you had a bad night? Come and talk to me for a while."

She linked her arm into his and walked him the few steps towards her window, and the two armchairs.

He pulled the two chairs closer together, so that they could sit facing each other. Reaching out to gently take both of her hands into his own, he carefully avoided squeezing her broken fingers.

"Sharon, I spoke with David yesterday, and he has asked me to pass on some news to you. I have been struggling all night to find the right words, but there is never an easy way to break bad news, it always hurts.

I am sorry to have to be the one to tell you, but there was a gas explosion at the guesthouse in Weymouth early yesterday morning.

Both of your parents were in bed at the time, and the whole kitchen floor came down into their bedroom.

"Oh my God, Malcolm, are they . . ."

"Jim is being transferred to the burns unit at Odstock, and is described as being very poorly. Doris, I'm afraid, died instantly in the blast. Sharon, I'm so terribly sorry. I'm aware of your love and regard for them both, and it goes without saying, that I will do anything, and everything within my power to see you through all of this. Come here, let me give you a hug, I think that I need one just as much as you, right now."

Sharon stood and allowed herself to be enfolded into his embrace. The shock and grief were yet to kick in, but for the moment, she found some solace and comfort in the arms of the man she loved.

Shaun, was awakened by the sound of Michaels phone ringing on the bedside table. He reached out, picked it up, and pressed the acceptance button without first looking to see who it was that was calling. Painfully pushing himself upright into a sitting position, he tried to swing his legs round, and over the side of the bed.

"Hello, who's that?" he growled into the phone.

"Is that Mr Michael Close I'm speaking to, please?"

David immediately suspected who he was talking to, but deliberately kept the conversation overly polite.

"He ain't here at the moment, what is it you want with him?"

"He doesn't know me personally, but I just wanted a word with him on a private matter. My name is David Morrison-Lloyd, I'll perhaps try again later. Any idea when he might be available, please?"

Shaun couldn't believe his ears, and was very nearly lost for words. It took a few seconds for him to collect his thoughts. He angrily replied,

"I know who you are, Lloyd, you're the bastard that, until recently, had some property that didn't belong to you. You've caused us all a whole lot of trouble. What do you want with Michael?"

"To whom am I speaking please, what I have to say is rather personal. I was rather hoping that we might be able to come to some arrangement concerning the return of some more of the property that is still in my possession."

"This is Shaun Riley, you will recognise who I am from what you've seen in the holdall. Why should you be wanting to return anything to us, and what is it you think is so important, that we would be wanting to trade anything for it?"

"Ah, the infamous Mr Riley, no less. The murderer, fraudster, kidnapper and woman beater. Killed any more young women lately, have you? Well the net is rapidly closing on you now, you cowardly piece of shit. I don't even want to be discussing any of this with you, you're just scum. However, it is abundantly clear to me that you haven't got Laura Dobson's bag back yet, otherwise you would know exactly what items I have to trade. Well, you now have my mobile phone number, so if one of you wants to get back to me later, we'll no doubt be able to come to some arrangement. But I'm warning you, Riley, I will not be brokering any sort of deal with you or Lara, Laura, or any other bloody name she chooses to call herself. I can think of a few choice ones that would be more suitable. No, I will speak only with Michael or Dermot Close, who I am reliably informed, are now both to be regarded as reasonably honourable and trustworthy gentlemen, despite what you all did back in 1974."

"And what if they refuse to speak to you Lloyd. What then?"

"Tough shit. I will give you just three more days, that should be plenty enough time to contact Connor, Martyn and Ryan, and to agree to my terms. Otherwise, by this time next week, you'll all be history and probably looking at the world from behind bars. In the meantime Riley, if I get so much as a sniff of any more of your thugs anywhere near Sharon Cox, or any of my family, I promise you that I will shoot them, and then you, using your own pistols. I won't be killing anyone; I will be doing a kneecapping job, just like your murdering IRA scum used to do, all those years ago, is that clear?

"You haven't said what you want out of this, Lloyd."

"Half a million pounds, Riley. Not one penny less. That is the price of our silence, and buys back the remainder of the contents of the holdall. Ring me back only when you're ready to do an electronic transfer into an account number that I will give you. Three days, starting from now. The clock's ticking . . ."

The line went dead leaving Shaun fuming with rage and indignation. He struggled to get off the bed and hurried into the toilet to void his bowel, such was the effect that the conversation had on him. Sitting quietly, he tried to recall exactly what had been said. The reference made by Lloyd with regard to the women he had killed, had really shaken him. How the hell had he found out about that? There were never any witnesses, of that Shaun was sure, and yet here was this arsehole . . . There was obviously much more to this bloke than he was giving credit for? Why, all of a sudden, did he want to trade the files and information for cash, instead of just handing them over to the police? And where in Gods name could he be expected to raise half a mil at short notice? He needed to speak with Lara, she had all the purse strings, but even she'd run out on him . . .

For the first time in his life, Shaun Riley felt alone and afraid. He knew that by his own vicious stupidity, he had lost the support of all of his comrades. Now he was on his own, threatened, badly injured, and very vulnerable. He wished that he could have turned the clock back a couple of weeks to when he was quite contentedly tending his pigs, without a care in the world.

The phone in his trouser pocket rang again. This time he looked first to identify the caller.

"Yes John, where the bloody hell are you, man? You were supposed to be here last night."

"Sorry Shaun, a bit of a problem with Kevin and Danny, the lads that got your bag back. They're asking to be paid off, and refusing to go back and watch the Godalming address. I'm having to draught in some more blokes to replace them. I'm just leaving now with the lads, and gear that you asked for, we should all be with you by early this afternoon."

"Quick as you can then John, I want to be well away from this place, by tonight, if possible."

Shaun broke the call and, hands in pockets, gazed thoughtfully out of the lounge window towards the lake. It was a beautiful morning and the sunlight reflected off the ripples thrown up by the gentle breeze. His eyes narrowed as he spotted something floating on the surface. He guessed what it was.

"Damn you Dermot, damn you to hell, even when you're fucking dead, you won't go away, will you, you bastard?"

He slowly and painfully made his way out to the garden shed thinking to find something to weigh the body back down. On finding that the substantial door was securely locked, and that he had no idea where the key was, Shaun's anger and frustrations began to boil over to the point that they were clouding his better judgement. Instead of returning to the bungalow to look for the key, he started to kick at the door, trying to force his way into the shed. He hadn't even noticed that the door opened outwards, and that all the energy put into his efforts, was entirely futile. The door remained solidly closed.

The pain and physical exhaustion inevitably took its toll and he collapsed onto his knees, his lungs heaving for air, bloody spittle falling from his mouth. His whole body was so wracked with pain that he was barely able to stay conscious, but he started the long and painful crawl back up to the bungalow. His mind was going. The sole thought was the realisation that he needed to get back in contact with Lara again. She would know what to do, she would help . . .

"Hello David, this is Malcolm. How are you, is everything still okay?"

"Malcolm, yes, everything's fine this end. How's our girl? Have you told her yet?"

"This morning. So far she's not shown too much reaction, but I suspect that will probably come later when the full realisation has time to sink in? Look, David, the main reason for ringing you like this is to put a little idea to you."

"Go on then Malcolm, I'm all ears."

"David, my girls are on half term hols next week, and I've booked some leave to be with them. How do you feel about our lady coming to stay with us for a while? You said that you had nowhere else suitable, and with her home in Weymouth in ruins, I presume that she is effectively homeless, am I right?"

"That just about sums it up, Malcolm. I was thinking of bringing her here, to Godalming, but I'm fairly certain we're under surveillance, and I didn't really want to endanger her safety. Frankly, I'm running out of options. I could get her into a nice comfortable hotel somewhere, but then she would be on her own, and that's not going to be any good for her either, is it?"

"No, she's still emotionally very vulnerable, David. Physically, apart from her broken fingers, she's ready to face the world again. The clinic wants her bed space, and it's two-fifty a day for her to remain here, you know?"

"Christ, I didn't think it was that much, Malcolm. Any idea what the cost of her treatment comes to so far?"

"Probably twelve grand, maybe even a bit more? I can find out for you, but I will need her discharge papers approved first, which kind of brings us full circle, doesn't it? What do you think about her coming with me? My leave starts the day after tomorrow."

"Where will you be taking her Malc? I don't actually know where you live?"

"Do you really need to know, David? You're conversant with security measures, it might be better for all of us if that information was kept on a need-to-know basis. I live in Hampshire, will that suffice? You will have both of our contact phone numbers, after all . . ."

"Yes, you're right Malcolm, thanks for reminding me. I presume our girl has no objection to any of these arrangements?"

"I haven't actually put it to her yet, David, but I am getting the distinct impression that it will gladden her little heart somewhat? Do I take it that I have your approval?"

"Absolutely. One last thing though, there has been an autopsy on Doris Cox and her body has just been released for interment. There will have to be a formal inquest, of course, but they're satisfied with the cause of death. I've provisionally given the job to a local, Weymouth undertakers, but I'm still waiting to hear about a funeral date. I will keep you posted. Jim Cox is now in Odstock, and is showing signs of slight improvement. If you're thinking of taking our girl on a visit, Malcolm, take great care, mate, the opposition might still be around, if you get my drift?

"Alright, David, my thanks for that. I'll look after her, don't you worry. If there's any problem relating to what we've just discussed, I'll get straight back to you. Cheers for now."

David broke the connection. He had no concerns about Sharon being with Malcolm. That was to be regarded as a stroke of luck and solved a big problem. The thing that really did concern him was the size of her medical bill, for which, he had already accepted responsibility. Thinking that the money from the holdall would cover it, and now to find that it was totally inadequate, was certainly another big headache. God knows what Sue was going to say, they didn't even have that sort of money in their joint savings? No, it's got to come from another source. Time for yet another re-think . . . Hands in pockets and deep in thought, he walked through to their bedroom to where Sue was busy making their bed.

"Sue, didn't you tell me that Emily and Jo-jo had helped you access Laura Dobson's bank account details?"

"Yes, why do you ask?" She finished smoothing down the bed and replacing the pillows as she spoke.

"Do you think we have enough information to be able to transfer some funds out of her account, perhaps?"

"I don't see why not, apart from it being totally against the law, of course. What are you scheming up now David Morrison-Lloyd?"

"I can see a bit of a cash crisis looming, and I was just trying to think of how we could lay hands on enough money to cover the expense of Sharon's medical treatment, Doris's funeral, and give us a bit of spare capital to work with, when Jim comes out of hospital. I don't see why the money shouldn't be paid by those responsible for all the troubles in the first place, do you?"

"I can see the logic in your reasoning, David, but it's still totally against the law, surely?"

"Just think about it for a minute, love. If we did manage to do it, transfer some money that is, and Dobson found out about it, what could she do? She can hardly go to the Police can she? It's the same with the ten grand of hers that we already have, she can't report it stolen, otherwise, she would have done so already?

I think that provided we keep receipts and records of how we spend her money, and, we take no personal gain from it, we could not be criticized. In fact, I think that we would be perfectly justified in doing so. Am I making any sense?"

"If you put it like that, then yes, it makes sense. How about we run it past my dad to see what he thinks before we get too carried away?"

"How about you get Laura Dobson's computer fired up and we see how far we can get with this first? No sense bothering him if it's not possible."


"As far as I can make out there are two accounts drawn on the same Irish bank. One is obviously her current account that she uses to pay all her daily living expenses. The other, I'm not sure about. I rather suspect that it is set up to automatically transfer money in excess of a set amount, straight into another high interest savings account. Her current account shows a nice healthy balance of £25,302.65

The other is showing an immediately available balance of just £3,000, but I haven't been able to access any information with regard to how much is held in savings. I don't think the necessary security passwords are contained in her file-o-fax."

"OK, so let's just see how far we can go with this . . ."

Sue worked away for several minutes accessing the current account, using passwords and other security devices from Laura's file-o-fax. She got to the point where it became necessary to provide information regarding the account the money was to be transferred into, and with a little prompting from David, she put their own joint account details forward.

"How much, David?"

"We don't want to clear the account completely, it might arouse suspicion at the bank. Go for £25K, see what happens . . ."

Sue entered the figures and pressed the 'proceed' key. A message flashed up to say 'transaction completed'

"My God, I think we've done it David. It was too easy, surely?"

"Give it half an hour, then get a balance on our account, we'll soon know . . ."

Feeling rather pleased with himself, David picked up Georges newspaper and retired to the empty games room for some peace and quiet. The days events kept going round in his mind, he still had the distinct impression that he was missing some vital piece of the puzzle, somewhere?

He had decided that for the time being, he would say nothing to Sue about his phone conversation with Shaun Riley. It had been something of an idea that he had put to, and discussed with George, the previous evening. He was thinking to go on the offensive, and try to buy them all a bit of breathing space.

On the spur of the moment, and against George's better judgement, he had made the blackmail demand for half a million pounds.

Now, on reflection, he doubted that his demand would ever be met, where would they ever be able to raise that sort of money at such short notice? He was rather surprised that Riley hadn't scoffed at the idea completely, though? Perhaps it wasn't so stupid after all? One thing was now certain, he could hardly go and give it all to the Police, for there was far too much money involved. If he handed over the files, he could kiss goodbye to the £10K of their money that he already had, and probably the £25K that he and Sue had just transferred into their own bank account, as well.

He was financially liable for Sharon's care, Doris's funeral arrangements, and poor old Jim, when he came out of hospital. Sharon didn't have anything now. No home, no money, and the old chap would obviously need considerable support to get him back on his feet again. All of a sudden, £35K was looking a decidedly paltry amount, all things considered?

Insurance? The revelation came to him. Sharon would know, of course. He glanced at his watch intending to ring her and then remembered that it probably wasn't such a good idea at that time? He resolved to talk to her as soon as possible though. The insurance papers were probably languishing in a drawer, somewhere in the burned out guesthouse in Weymouth? They were important documents, and needed to be retrieved before they were irretrievably lost.

David fished in his pocket for his diary and pulled out his notebook as well. Diary first, and it told him that there was very little taxi work in the coming week. The October half-term breaks were always a quiet period. No bad thing really, he thought, it gave him a few days to devote to the matters in hand. A trip to Weymouth to get the insurance papers could be turned into an ideal opportunity to have a discreet look around the inside of Dobson's house? Yes, that would be good, there was still something missing in all of this, something he didn't yet know about? There might be some clues contained in her private papers?

His thoughts kept coming back to Ferguson and his sidekick, what's-his-name, Ahmed. If they're not policemen, then who the devil are they, and how do they fit in? He eyed Ferguson's card and phone numbers, tossing up whether to just phone him and ask? But, in the end, he decided against it. He hadn't noticed the usual tail car that day. Perhaps Ferguson's lot had called off their surveillance? But then there was still Dobson's crowd? It was still far too early to make any rash assumptions in that respect, let's just assume we're still being watched 24/7, and plan accordingly . . .

David retrieved his old Bergen from under the billiard table, emptied it, and laid everything out, kit inspection fashion. He shrugged off his jacket and trousers and stepped into his fatigues. They felt good, a little on the big side since he had lost a couple of inches off both waist and chest, but that was of no real consequence. His boots were US Army issue, traded for a couple of bottles of scotch when he was in Helmand. They were highly prized by the British troops because of

their superior quality and comfort. David's were already well trodden
in when he got them. They had belonged to a Staff Sergeant in the
US Army Marine Corps, with whom, he had gotten very drunk one
night. David smiled to himself at the fond memory. They had sworn
everlasting comradeship, but the man's name now eluded him . . .

There was a little mildew showing white on the surface of the soft
leather. He frowned and wiped it away with his thumb and forefinger
before slipping his foot inside. A bit loose, but then he only had thin
socks on. He set about applying a bit of dubbin with an old yellow
duster kept for the purpose. A greasy mixture of tallow and linseed
oil, contained in an old screw top Marmite jar, it was still good
considering that he had mixed it together himself, all those years ago.
It would serve to soften and waterproof the leather.

The very act of putting his combat gear back into good order was
enough to induce the old feelings of pride and resolve. The need to
'kick arse' and to show the enemy who's boss, was boiling in his
blood. It was time for some positive action.

Lara waited until dark before parking Dermot's Range Rover
several doors along from her house. She walked quietly back, looking
around constantly to see if she was being observed. Satisfied that
nobody was watching her house, she retrieved a spare door key from
under a garden flowerpot and let herself inside. The place smelled
musty, and there was something decidedly smelly in the kitchen
somewhere. Her nose led her to a half carton of milk that she had
forgotten to put back in the fridge during their hurried departure
over a fortnight ago. Wrinkling her nose against the putrid smell, she
washed the contents away down the sink and sprayed an air freshener
around. Without turning on any lights, she boiled a kettle and made
herself a cup-a-soup, which she took through to the front parlour. Her
easy chair felt so good and comfortable after the long drive back to
Weymouth, and she shut her eyes in contentment. It was good to be
home again . . .

A rattle of post coming through the letterbox awoke her with a
start. The mantle clock told her that it was nearly eight o'clock. The
cold soup was on the coffee table where she had put it last evening, it
was untouched. She dragged herself out of the chair and headed for
her bathroom.

Shaun awoke to the sound of someone shouting his name. It took him a few seconds to work out where he was, for he found that he was lying on the floor in the lounge of the bungalow. He glanced at his wristwatch, it was 1035, but what bloody day? And who was calling him? He tried to push himself upright and the pains shot through his ribcage causing him to grimace and roll over onto his back. That was how John found him.

"Shaun, Shaun, what in God's name? Are you alright, man, what's happened?"

"John, help me up will you, I've cracked a few ribs. I'll explain later. Here take my hand, and just ease me up gently, will you?"

John did as he was asked, and helped Shaun to sit down on a nearby dining chair. He couldn't help but notice the deathly white pallor, and bloody spittle that had dried on his chin and beard. It didn't take a genius to see that Shaun was in a pretty bad way, and probably needed some urgent medical attention. This was out of the question of course, at least not until after he'd been paid. He'd had a dozen blokes pestering him for some money for the past weeks work. As far as he was concerned, Shaun owed him big time, and he was expecting to be paid, there and then. Shaun's physical condition was of little consequence to him. Just as long as the cash was forthcoming, he couldn't care less. He needed to get him back on his feet though, otherwise, they'd be getting nowhere . . .

"Shaun, can I get you a drink or something, man? I've got four blokes outside waiting for you to tell them what you want doing. Here's your bag, by the way. I'm not sure that we've got everything that was in it originally, but we did our best."

"Tip it out on the floor, John, let's see what's inside."

John upended the holdall and the contents spilled out. Shaun reached for Michael's walking stick and poked around in the pile of women's clothing, pushing it aside to reveal very little else but the mobile phones and a few CD's.

"Fucking rubbish, there's nothing here but junk. Where's the computer, the cash, the guns, the files? This is just some of Lara's clothes, and some old mobile phones. Stuff of no value; I'm not paying you for this, John, I tell you now. This is not what I expected."

"Shaun, my blokes broke into a house to get this lot. They said that they had to pick it all up, and quickly bundle it into the holdall. They took everything they could see. It's not our fault if half the stuff is missing, how are we expected to know? Come on man, be reasonable, I can't tell them you're not paying, can I? I can understand that you're pissed-off about it, but you still owe us."

"You were going to be paid out of the money that was in the bag. The deal was that it be returned to me intact. That's not what's happening here, is it, John? Without that money, I can't pay you, can I? There's no money here, and I can't immediately lay my hands on any until I speak to Lara. She's taken another of our group to hospital."

"So when does this Lara, get back here then, Shaun? And how long will it take for her to get our money? I'm warning you, we're not leaving here without it."

"You don't threaten me, John. I've told you how it is. If you have to wait a couple more days, then that's tough. In the meantime, there's probably a hundred grand's worth of guns buried just up that hill outside of this place. Let's see if we can't broker some sort of deal with a few of those thrown in, shall we?"

John was not a happy man. He stood threateningly in front of Shaun contemplating his next move. He could see that Shaun's injuries had rendered him relatively helpless. He would not have dared stand up to him if he'd been his usual fit self. John had seen Shaun lift a man clean off his feet, and lay him out cold, with one swipe of his backhand. Shaun's ruthless reputation against those that had dared to double-cross or argue with him was the stuff of legends. There were obviously others in this group of Shaun's that might be just as dangerous? The body floating in the lake had not gone unnoticed on their arrival, and Shaun was the only one here. If he was still capable of killing a man in the state he was in, he was not to be regarded as a pushover. John concluded that he had little option but to go along with Shaun's wishes for the time being. A hundred grand's worth, Shaun had said. Well that'll do nicely if the opportunity presented itself.

"What exactly is involved in this then Shaun? Where's the stuff buried, are you going to show us, or what?"

"No, I'm in no fit state to be doing any heavy lifting. I'm going to stay here and make a few phone calls to see if I can arrange to get you some cash. You can handle this one, John, it's not going to be too difficult for your lads, I promise you. Here, I'll draw you a little sketch plan of where you need to go, and a diagram of how I think it would be easiest to lift out a single heavy flagstone. Did you bring the stuff I asked for? If you did, it should be no problem."

"We did, now show me, but I warn you, if you're bull-shitting me about this, Shaun, then there's five of us here who are not going to be any too pleased with you, do I make myself clear?"

"On my mothers grave, this is kosher, John. Look out of the window. You see that bird hide up the cliff beside the lake? Well the stuff is in there, under the floor at the far end. There's just the one big flagstone that covers the entrance to an underground chamber. You'll need to lift it clear, but it has lifting eyes at each end, which should make it a lot easier for you. Now, I suggest that if you hook a rope through one of the lifting eyes, and use the long pole as a lever, your lads should be able to . . ."

Half an hour later, fully briefed, John and his lads began lugging all their gear up the steep narrow path to the bird hide.

That evening, David set off to Weymouth. He had spoken to Sharon who confirmed that Jim and Doris had kept all their important papers in a locked, fireproof deed box, in the bottom drawer of the office desk. A quick phone call to the local fire service, had arranged for an officer to be present, and if necessary, to assist in the recovery of the box. He was due to meet-up with him at 0800 the next morning.

David kept checking his mirrors, looking for any sign of a tailing car. He even stopped at Fleet Services for a few minutes, carefully observing the vehicles that followed him in. For the time being, he was satisfied that nobody was following. He stayed on the M3 as far as junction 8, where at the very last minute he veered over to the nearside lane, and exited onto the A303 to take him as far as Andover. From there his route went through the Wallops to Salisbury, there to pick up the A354, which ran all the way down into Weymouth.

The warm autumn evening had brought out the locals to all the seafront bars and restaurants that were busy making the most of the warmest October on record. David found a bit of free parking in a quiet back street, and set out on foot to recce first the guesthouse, and then Laura Dobson's place. Her house keys were in his jeans pocket. He had dressed in dark clothing, and had a black nylon ski mask and an old, service issue Swiss army knife, in one back pocket, and a small Maglite pencil torch nestled in the other. He left all other unnecessary items locked in the glove box of the car.

The guesthouse was much as he expected. All the windows and the front door had been boarded over, and some scaffold erected, presumably to shore-up the building? He was relieved to see that the back door, the one he had a key for, appeared undamaged, and that no one had yet tried to break in and loot the place. It gave him some optimism for being able to get his hands on the deed box. Sharon had also mentioned Doris's jewellery box, usually to be found on their bedroom dressing table. But judging by the state of the building, David thought that the possibility of its retrieval was unlikely.

Hands in pockets, he slowly made his way back along the seafront towards Whyke Regis and Marlborough Avenue. David walked straight past the house noting that it was in complete darkness. He walked another hundred yards before stopping to re-tie a shoelace, looking about himself all the time. He turned round and walked back. A single car passed him going in the opposite direction. David kept his head down and was sure the driver had not seen him. Ten yards before the house, he quickly pulled the black ski mask over his head and face, just before stepping over the garden wall onto the lawn. Tiptoeing quickly up to the front door, he carefully pushed what he had surmised was the right key, gently and silently into the door lock. It fitted and turned, but he was met with a solid resistance, the door was bolted inside. Cursing under his breath, he remembered the back door. In the dim glow of the street lighting, examining the bunch of keys to choose the right one, he made his way up the side of the house.

The mortise lock unlatched with an audible click, and the door pushed inwards with a loud squeal from the unoiled hinges. David stepped inside and quietly pushed the door shut behind him. He guessed that he was standing in the kitchen, and this was confirmed as his eyes slowly became accustomed to the darkness. He stood absolutely still, examining his surroundings by using all of his senses, as he had been trained to do. There was no sound that he could detect, but there was a faint odour of some sort of perfume, which seemed a bit incongruous in a kitchen environment. He could see that the window blinds were down, so he risked a quick flick around with his pencil torch. There were two other doors. One, he discovered, led into a large pantry, the other took him out into the entrance hallway, and a staircase to the upper part of the house. There was enough light filtering in from the street to allow him to see where he was going, as he tiptoed quietly over bare polished floorboards, that creaked under his weight, to another door.

The antique polished brass doorknob rattled slightly as he placed his hand around it. In the comparative silence of the old house, the noise had sounded positively deafening. He winced at his own clumsiness and pressed on, he could feel his heart pounding. The heavy curtains were drawn and the interior of the room was a stygian blackness. Another flick around with his torch revealed that he was in some sort of parlour, or lounge. The beam came to rest and spotlighted what he was looking for, a large open bureau in the far corner of the room.

It was evident that Laura Dobson was meticulous with the organisation of her desk and it's contents. Everything was laid out neatly in all the cubby-holes and drawers, but there was nothing of interest for David. He spied a two-drawer, steel filing cabinet on the floor beside the bureau, but found that it was locked when he tried to open it. It occurred to him that the key was probably one of those on the bunch in his pocket. He fished them out and started going through them one at a time, the maglite held between his teeth.

There had been no sound, but some sixth sense detected another presence behind him. Without even thinking, he threw himself to one side and in doing so, narrowly avoided being struck over the head. He sustained a glancing blow with some heavy implement that landed painfully on the point of his left shoulder. Instinctively, his balled right fist came up to where he perceived the person's head and face to be. It was a solid punch, David felt his knuckles hit the forehead of whoever his attacker was, and his assailant went down onto the floor. David immediately followed up his advantage by dropping his knee heavily into the area of his solar plexus. He heard the air go out of his lungs in a painful gasp. David's hand came up ready to deliver the killing chop across the throat and carotid artery, but for some reason he held back.

The light glinted off some sort of weapon held in the right hand, so he stamped hard on their wrist, causing the person to cry out in pain, and drop whatever they were holding. David picked it up. It was a heavy ornamental brass-handled poker. He dreaded to think of the consequences of it making contact with his skull. He threw it onto a nearby sofa, out of reach.

The sound of the voice was the giveaway, David knew instantly who it was on the floor, and he lit up the person's face with his torch. A very frightened looking Laura Dobson stared wide-eyed back at him.

"That's enough, Mrs Dobson, I don't want to hurt you any more, but I will if necessary."

"Who are you, what do you want, how do you know my name?"

David realised that the ski mask had so far hidden his identity and muffled his voice. He also had the advantage of shining the torch into her eyes in the darkened room. He took a few seconds to decide his next move, and held out his hand to help pull her up into a sitting position. He pushed the ski mask up clear of his face, reversed a dining chair, and sat down facing her.

"Stay where you are for the moment, Mrs Dobson, I'm not here to steal anything. I'm merely looking for information to help me with a few unanswered questions. You will know what I'm after if I tell you that my name is David Morrison-Lloyd."

"You . . . My God, you've got a damn cheek coming here, Mr Lloyd. You have no idea of the trouble you've caused, meddling into my affairs. It's a good job Shaun's not here, he'd wring your bloody neck and feed you to his pigs."

"What, like he did to the three young women he's suspected of murdering previously, Laura? Is that how he disposed of their bodies, then?"

David knew that he had scored a home run. The look on her face in the torchlight, was sufficient. She knew that she had just said far too much for her own good. She tried to bluff it out.

"I'm sure I don't know what you're talking about, Mr Lloyd. I was merely speaking figuratively. I know nothing about Shaun murdering three women, and I doubt that there's any truth in such an accusation."

"Try telling that to the two Police Officers from the West Midlands Regional Crime Squad that I spoke to only a couple of days ago. In point of fact, they were looking for you, Laura, concerned for your safety and well being. They thought it very likely that you were to be Shaun Riley's next victim, that is, until I put them straight on a few things."

Her eyes narrowed and she pulled her knees up wrapping them in her dressing gown. She shuffled back against the bureau into a more comfortable sitting position. There was an angry looking bruise rising on her forehead where David's fist had made contact. She touched at it tenderly. David switched on the angle poise lamp on her bureau, and resumed his seat.

"Shaun would never hurt me Mr Lloyd, we go back too far, and besides, he needs me. What did you tell these two policemen, then? You obviously haven't disclosed anything about our previous activities, otherwise you wouldn't be here now, and demanding a half a million pounds from us?"

"So far, I have managed to stall them, and disclose very little, but I won't be able to do so for much longer. You've obviously spoken to Shaun. It's good to hear that he's taking my demands seriously. When do you think you will you be ready to transfer the money over?"

"Shaun rang me this afternoon and put me in the picture, but I don't understand you, Mr Lloyd. One minute you're all high and mighty, seeking retribution and justice, the next, you're attempting to extort money from us by blackmail. You're no better than we are, isn't that the truth, now?"

"I have my reasons Mrs Dobson, all of them financial. I cannot change what you've already done, can I? If I hand you all over to the Police, it will inevitably lead to a very expensive public trial, putting vast sums of money into the pockets of Lawyers and Solicitors. The inevitable outcome will see you all serving a very long time behind bars, all paid for by the British Taxpayer, in the name of Justice. I see no advantage to anyone in any of that, do you?"

"No, but then that is the way of things, surely?"

"The money I am demanding will be split between Sharon, in compensation for her injuries and the loss of her home, and Jim Cox who has lost his wife, his home, and just about everything else he has ever owned. These are things that took him a lifetime of hard work to acquire. I personally, will take nothing but my expenses out of this, Mrs Dobson, on that, you have my solemn word. On reflection, perhaps half a million pounds is not nearly enough when weighed against their losses, what do you think?"

"Your reasoning is sound, and your intentions magnanimous, Mr Lloyd. What you ask is neither an impossible, nor an unreasonable amount. However, if we were to pay, we would need to have some sort of guarantee that everything you have will be returned to us intact. How will we know that you will stick to your end of the arrangement?

"You will not be getting the guns back, Mrs Dobson, and I will be demanding that you cease swindling innocent people with your puppy scam activities. The ten grand of your money has gone. It was put towards paying for Sharon's injuries. You will all undertake to have no more contact with Sharon Cox, me, or any of my family. As a form of insurance, a sealed envelope with a copy of all the relevant documents relating to your crimes, will be lodged in a safety deposit box held by my bank. My instruction will be that it be passed on to the Police in the event of anything-untoward happening to any of us. I haven't quite worked out all the final details yet, but that's the gist of it, so far. Am I to assume that we are still in agreement?"

"I will need to consult with the others before I can agree to anything, Mr Lloyd. Do I take it that you are now happy to deal with me in this regard? You told Shaun that you would only speak with Michael or Dermot."

"I hadn't anticipated us ever having this conversation, Mrs Dobson. I still have the distinct feeling that I'm missing something else in all of this, which is the reason why I am here tonight, looking for some answers."

"I'm sure I don't know what you mean, Mr Lloyd, you will find little else here. What you have from my holdall is pretty damning evidence that I regret ever having kept. I should have destroyed that file long ago. As for the puppies, well I realised over thirty years ago just how really stupid people can be about their pets. I did it the first time, and managed to sell fifteen pups from a pedigree bitch Springer Spaniel that had whelped a litter of only five. I pocketed a cool £350 in clear profit out of that. It was just too easy, money for old rope. God only knows how much I've made over the years, Mr Lloyd, but I've had a good living out of it, and I can just about afford to pay what you ask. You will need to return all my bank account details and my file-o-fax forthwith. Without those, I am not in a position to do anything.

I heard from my bank manager this afternoon, he rang me to ask when I was expecting to deposit some more money into my current account. With my mortgage payment due in a few days, I've had to borrow from Michael and Dermot's business account, and then arrange a temporary overdraft facility to tied me over. So, I'm already aware, and rather surprised, that you have already managed to transfer funds out of my current account, Mr Lloyd. But you will never be in a position to get anything from the other savings account, so don't bother even trying. There are only two people that have access to that account, and the security access codes are not recorded anywhere. They are only in my head, and that of only one other of our group. It will do you no harm to return some of my property if this arrangement is to proceed."

"This other person, would that be Ryan Dobbs, or perhaps Marty McCue? I wonder if the First Minister knows of McCue's past involvement with an active IRA terrorist cell? Should I perhaps be the one to advise him, do you think, Laura?"

"You would effectively kiss goodbye to the half million pounds if you were to do such a thing, Mr Lloyd. The money withdrawal and transfer from that account needs authorisation from us both. Marty will certainly want to retain his position and standing with the First Minister, and because of that, he will probably agree to your demands. So why would you want to jeopardise the arrangement before it even gets off the ground?"

"I don't. I was merely pointing out another of the options available to me if the money isn't forthcoming, Mrs Dobson."

"We are all well aware of the delicate position we find ourselves in, Mr Lloyd. The past couple of weeks have been likened to having the Sword of Damocles hanging over one's head. If there is any amicable arrangement to be found, you can rest assured of our full co-operation in that respect. The only stumbling block, as far as I can see, will be getting Shaun Riley to agree. The man is a law unto himself. It was he alone that ordered the firebombing of the guesthouse. None of the others were consulted, or given the chance to have any say in the matter. He has been badly injured by Sharon Cox, and humiliated by you, Mr Lloyd. Shaun is a very vindictive and dangerous individual to have as an enemy. I'm glad not to be in your shoes. Tell me a little about Sharon, if you will. Is she alright now, were her injuries that serious?"

"Why should you care about Sharon's welfare, Mrs Dobson? It was you, after all, who was partly responsible for her injuries in the first place?"

"In her respect, there is more to this than you know, Mr Lloyd. But it bears no relevance to the matter in hand, and needn't concern you. I know that it sounds far-fetched, but I effectively saved her life on that day. Shaun Riley was intending to rape, and then murder her. He gets his greatest thrill from taking a woman by force, and climaxing as he chokes the life out of them. Yes, I am prepared to confirm that there have been others in the past. If the truth be known, probably more than the three that you mentioned? I decided to accompany him to the farm hoping, that at some stage, I might perhaps get him to spare her life. Believe it or not, nobody was more elated than I, when she managed to get away from us, but for obvious reasons, I couldn't show it, could I? It was just a pity that I'd left my holdall in the van. It is that one mistake on my part, that has led us to where we are now."

"But you smashed her fingers and nails with a rolling pin. Shaun Riley broke her nose, smashed four of her teeth and gave her ribs a good kicking. She has been in a private clinic undergoing reconstructive surgery, since the day after her escape. Physically, I'm told she is now doing quite well, but mentally, it is feared that the damage is irreparable. She may be psychologically affected for the rest of her life, especially after learning of the murder of her stepmother, and the loss of her home. I would think it reasonable to assume that, yes, she was badly hurt. Does that answer your rather stupid question?"

In the dimming torchlight, Laura Dobson bit her lip and hung her head, stifling a sob. David was almost beginning to feel some compassion toward her. He had to remind himself of just what a hard-faced, conniving bitch, he was really dealing with here. Talking to her, one would have thought that butter wouldn't melt in her mouth, but only five minutes ago, she had nearly smashed him over the head with a poker. He massaged his aching shoulder at the thought. No, she definitely didn't deserve his sympathy.

The minutes ticked by, each was deep in their own thoughts, considering the implications of what they had discussed.

"So where do we go from here, Mr Lloyd? Am I to have some of my property returned, if so, you can start by handing me back my keys, please?"

She held out a hand in expectation. David smiled and tossed them onto the floor at her feet.

"Your file-o-fax, and the documents relating to your properties, together with your purse and credit cards, will all be returned along with any other items we consider irrelevant. Your computer, the file relating to your bombing activities, and all the remaining CD's will stay with us until I see the money has been paid into my nominated account. Have I missed anything? Oh, yes, you can tell Shaun Riley from me that he is to call off his surveillance team. Tell him he's wasting his time. He will never locate Sharon Cox, and as I now hold all the aces, if I get the slightest hint of any non-compliance, or double-cross, I will let the Police have everything I know about him."

"I will tell him, but I cannot make any promises that he will heed what you say, Mr Lloyd. As I said, Shaun is a very dangerous individual to make an enemy of. How and when do you intend to return my property?"

"I shall be attending the service of remembrance for Doris Cox, which will be held at 2pm next Monday at the little Baptist Church on the Esplanade. Do you know it?"

"Yes, I do. Look, would you mind if I paid my respects as well, Mr Lloyd? Doris was a lovely lady and I liked her a lot. She didn't deserve to die like that."

"I am in no position to refuse you Mrs Dobson, it is a public service for all her family and friends in this area. There will no doubt be a large contingent of local people, and as we are the only ones that know of your true involvement, if it can be called that, I don't see any difficulty with you being there. I will hand you a carrier bag after the service. Will that be okay?"

"That will be fine, but be sure to bring my computer with you, I will need to use it to transfer the money over. The interim couple of days will afford enough time for me to talk to the others.

One last question please, Mr Lloyd. I have been puzzling myself ever since the day you brought your family to see my litter of pups. You seemed to sense almost immediately that Judy was not their mother. Nobody else has ever been able to do that in all the years that I have been breeding dogs. My curiosity is aroused. Just tell me, please, how did you know?"

David smiled to himself, the memory of that evening was still vivid in his mind. He was not about to reveal to anyone that his baby daughter was a little child genius, gifted with the ability to communicate with animals. He had to think fast. The truth would sound even more far-fetched than the explanation he was about to offer.

"They taught us many things in the Special Forces, Mrs Dobson. Recognition of characteristic animal behaviour was one of the more obscure lectures given by a prominent animal psychologist. I never thought for one minute that it would ever be of any benefit to me. But when I saw that your dog, Judy, wasn't displaying any of the usual instinctive maternal behaviour toward her litter that one would have normally expected, I picked up on that. And then, with my suspicions aroused, I homed in, and played a hunch. Your own demeanour and body language, when I posed a few awkward questions, was the giveaway, Mrs Dobson. I knew immediately that you were lying to us."

"You were in the Special Forces, Mr Lloyd?"

"I was SAS, and I still have access to many of their considerable resources, Mrs Dobson. There are many of my colleagues who would be absolutely delighted to make the acquaintance of you, and your little band of cowardly thugs, so don't ever make the error of underestimating me, will you? A couple of phone calls and you will all wish you had never been born. Psychopathic maniacs, such as Shaun Riley are what we in the Regiment most enjoyed coming up against. They make a much more of an interesting challenge than the ordinary, run-of-the-mill terrorist idiots. However, they are still afforded the same utter contempt, and tend to get quickly squashed, much like the proverbial cockroach found in ones kitchen. Do I make myself clear?"

"It would seem that we have all seriously underestimated you already, Mr Lloyd. I will pass on your comments, and your somewhat colourful analogy to the others. Now if our business is concluded, I would like to retire back to my bed. May I be allowed to get up from the floor now, please?"

David stood and moved the chair back out of the way. He held out his hand to assist her, but she ignored it and pushed herself upright in a surprisingly sprightly manner. Laura Dobson had kept herself very fit, David concluded. He indicated for her to go ahead of him, he was not prepared to allow her out of his sight for a second. Without another word being spoken, he exited the house the same way that he had come in, via the back door. He heard it being locked and bolted behind, as he walked back down the drive.

It had been an interesting and seemingly productive evening. His mood was buoyant and distinctly more optimistic. Hands in pockets, and deep in thought, he set off back along the seafront to find his car.

If he'd had the presence of mind to take the same amount of care leaving, as he'd taken entering, David might have noticed the blue Ford Transit panel van parked almost opposite Laura Dobson's house. He might also have noticed the unusual looking aerials and other attachments on the roof of the van. He would not have been able to see the two men inside, quietly shutting down their array of sophisticated audio and visual surveillance equipment that had been set to try and capture everything that had taken place inside the house that evening. They had only been partially successful though, their equipment having missed quite a lot of the conversation due to the muffling effect of the heavy curtains.

The next morning, after an uncomfortable night spent sleeping in his car, David met with a Dorset Fire and Rescue Officer at the Bide-a-wee. He explained exactly which items he was seeking to retrieve, and their probable location within the building. He asked for permission to enter, and to look for them.

The Fire Officer was adamant that the building was unsafe, but then offered to have a brief look for himself. He stressed that he wasn't about to put himself into any danger just for the sake of a few items of jewellery, and some pieces of paper, but he was sympathetic to David's predicament with regard to the insurance documents.

Ten minutes later, David was handed the deed box, but the jewellery casket was nowhere to be seen in any place that was easily accessible. David came away, having been advised that the building would, in all probability, have to be totally demolished.

Connor McCall was a very worried man. Since his telephone conversation with Shaun, he had been waiting on tenterhooks for the return call. Lizzy had found his mood swings almost unbearable. For the past couple of days, he had been brooding over something personal, that he absolutely refused to discuss with her. It was so out of character for her usually happy-go-lucky, laid-back partner.

Today, their journey from Downton, to their Bournemouth office, had been conducted almost in silence. Even their new litter of beautiful little Kune Kune micro-piglets, his own pet project, had failed to enthuse him. They had all been farrowed late last evening, and while they had both assisted in the deliveries, his mind was obviously not on the matter in hand. Three days ago, he had been like an expectant father, and so looking forward to his prize sow giving birth. What on earth had happened in the interim? Lizzy was totally at a loss. Try as she may, she couldn't bridge the communication gap. She'd never seen him so preoccupied and jumpy. Every time the phone rang he quickly snatched it up, but when he realised it wasn't the call that he was so obviously expecting, he was terse and short with whoever was on the line, almost to the point of being rude. It was as if he couldn't wait to get rid if them.

She couldn't allow things to continue in this vein for much longer and resolved to get to the bottom of it. Today, given the opportunity, she was going to speak to Tony. Perhaps his father could throw some light on whatever it was that was troubling Connor?

Connor knew that he was upsetting Lizzy, but he couldn't help himself. There was no way that he could let on about his past life before they'd met. Her parents had both been Protestant, where Connor's background had been decidedly Catholic. He had effectively abandoned his religion to marry Lizzy. Then there was the question of their different political leanings. Lizzy's Irish sympathies now leaned more in favour of the Democratic policies, rather than those of the Republicans, which she considered to be outdated.

That aside, their marriage and partnership was one based entirely on love for each other, and their shared common interests. On virtually everything else, they had to agree to differ.

The teenage Connor had been recruited into the group by Marty who, with his magnetic personality, had easily taken up with, and been accepted by, the local Irish community in London. Slowly gaining Connor's friendship by buying him drinks, and loaning him a few quid when he was skint, Marty had introduced him to the others, only after he had boasted about knowing many of the soldier's local drinking haunts. They had led him to believe that Shaun was a semi-professional bare-knuckle fighter, who liked nothing better than to pick a fight with a drunken squaddie, and then make a few side bets with his mates to make it more interesting. It had all sounded like a bit of a laugh, and perhaps an easy way for him to make a few bob on the side? Slowly, his indoctrination had begun. Marty was very clever in delivering all the political rhetoric and poison clichés against the British Government's continual 'rape of Ireland' as he paraphrased it. The gullible and impressionable, Connor, believed his every word.

Driving his mothers old green Commer panel van, with everyone piled in the back, he had been only too pleased to show them around his manor, and to help find them temporary accommodation in various bed-sits and caravans.

Connor now realised that he had been unbelievably naïve in those days. Even on Christmas Eve, 1974, when the bombs had exploded in two pubs in Hampstead, he still hadn't made the connection. The group had all visited The North Star, and The Swiss Tavern, as well as a few other pubs, in the fortnight previous.

Following the bombings, there had been a period of intense Police activity, and Connor had been invited by Marty to accompany him over to Ireland for a few weeks, ostensibly to meet some of his family. But the real reason was to temporarily get away from the heat. Only when they were in Belfast did he finally learn the truth from Marty, but by then it was too late, he was one of the group. Marty had become his best friend, the others, his comrades-in-arms. They were all united in a common cause.

Connor eventually returned home, but did nothing more than keep his head down, get on with his studies, and say nothing to anyone. The full realisation of his involvement, and the seriousness of what he had helped to bring about, was apparent in all the media releases covering the investigations into the atrocities. He was now running scared, and had been for the past thirty-five years.

The only other contact that he'd had from the group was during late summer of 1975, when Marty phoned and told him that they were all back on mainland Britain. He had declined their invitation to join them on a farm somewhere in south Wales, citing his commitment to his further education as the main reason.

Twice in the period leading up to Christmas, he had met up with Marty, and stayed with him in Belfast for the New Year. It had been he, that had suggested to Connor, the idea of trying to restore the lost Irish land titles to their rightful owners, and had promised to help in any way that he could.

Over the ensuing years, each had followed the others career with interest, corresponding and visiting each other occasionally, particularly when Connor was at Queens University. True to his word, Marty had helped Connor in his quest for land titles, for he now worked at Stormont, and had access to the finest, and most comprehensive archives and records, available in the whole of Ireland.

With all this in mind, Connor felt that, despite Shaun's direct order to the contrary, he should advise Marty of the latest developing crisis that threatened them all. To that end, he had twice left messages, via the Stormont telephone switchboard, for Marty to contact him as a matter of urgency. Two days had passed and he was still yet to make contact. He wasn't to know that Marty was on a working holiday in the USA, and not due back for more than another week.

Sharon sat quietly in the passenger seat of Malcolm's BMW X5 as he drove down the A31 from Aldershot towards Winchester. The full realisation of her present circumstances had dawned on her as she struggled to come to terms with the death of her adopted mother, and the news from David, that the Bide-a-wee guesthouse would, in all probability, require complete demolition.

Once again, she was homeless, almost penniless, and left with no foreseeable future. There were insurances on the building and contents, and joint life policies between Doris and Jim, made in favour of each other, so as far as she was aware, none of it was seemingly coming her way. She thought it highly unlikely that Jim would want to start up another B&B when he eventually got out of hospital, or rather, if he ever got out of hospital? For he was still in the ICU at Odstock, and still described as 'very poorly.' It was important for her to get to see Jim as soon as possible.

"Malcolm, I know it's a lot to ask of you, and I don't want to be a nuisance, but I really need to see my father in hospital. Do you think that we could perhaps arrange a visit? Sometime this weekend, if that's possible? I don't have any money for a taxi, though . . ."

"I was rather anticipating you asking me that one, Sharon, and yes, I think we might be able to pop over to the hospital. I'll take you. It's not too far removed from where I live, a nice half hour-run through the countryside, if I stick to the back lanes. I will have to see what my daughters have arranged, but I'm sure it won't be a problem. They tend to go off and do their own thing now. Probably riding, or golf lessons, that's what usually happens on a Saturday if it's dry. Swimming, gymnastics, or squash, down the local sports centre, if it's wet. They cost me an absolute fortune with all their extra-curricula activities. All entirely their mothers fault, of course. She was very keen that they should both grow up with a good education, and with all the basic skills one would expect of young ladies of quality and substance. My late wife was a terrible snob in that respect."

"Thank you, Malcolm. You're very kind. I'm sorry if I'm not very good company for you at the moment, I've had rather a lot to think about in the last day or so. It's so difficult for me to see exactly where my life is going at the moment, and I really need to speak with my dad, if he's well enough to talk to me, that is?"

"Don't expect too much, Sharon, Jim's in intensive care, which by its very nature means that he is probably struggling. If it's of any help, you are welcome to stay in my house for as long as you wish. I'm sure that you and my girls will get along like a house on fire. Excuse the pun. It was inappropriate given the present circumstances. What I mean is, that it's been nearly three years since Elizabeth died, and it's about time we, as a family, all tried to move on a bit. I'm sorry to say that you will find that my place is still full of her memories. She is everywhere. Up until now, I suppose to the greater extent, I have been responsible for this. I felt that by not getting rid of any of her things, it was as if she was still there, somehow? Well, you know . . . I suppose this was done both for my own, and the girl's sake. They both took it very hard, as you can appreciate."

There was a few seconds pause as he pulled himself together, and thought about what he wanted to say next.

"I'm not sure that any of us are over her death, even now? When I'm away, at work, it's not so bad, I can sink myself into my job, but as soon as I get back home, the memories all come flooding back again. I still lie awake at nights whispering her name, longing for her touch and comforting warmth beside me . . .

Sorry, I didn't mean to sound so maudlin, but I need you to understand that I might not be quite ready for another serious full-on relationship just yet, Sharon. So lets just try and keep our relationship on a purely platonic basis for the time being, can we, please? You are a very attractive lady, and I make no secret of the fact that I'm warming to your company. I've been getting the distinct impression that you are perhaps feeling the same about me? There may well be a future for us, but right now, it's far too early for me to say. Is that all alright, with you?"

"Malcolm Blackmore, I think I fell in love with you on the first day that we met? Call it love at first sight if you like. I have been putting out all the signals and longing for you to give me just the slightest little hint that you felt something toward me. There have been times in the past fortnight when I could have screamed at you in frustration, for seemingly ignoring me. Now, when we're trundling along the road in a motorcar, you choose for the first time, to talk about the possibility of us getting together. You do pick your moments, don't you, Mr Blackmore? Why couldn't we have had this conversation while we were enjoying a glass or two of wine, over a slightly romantic candlelit supper? I might perhaps have been in a better position to influence your feelings a little? You're an absolute cad, sir, for toying with a girls emotions."

Malcolm was surprised. For a fleeting moment he genuinely thought that he had offended her. He glanced over in her direction, and their eyes met. He caught the mischievous gleam in her eyes, and the fleeting little smile on her lips. For the first time in many hours, they both managed a little laugh. The ice had seemingly been broken.

"Tell me a little about your daughters, please Malcolm. Apart from their names, Charlotte and Michelle, aged fourteen and fifteen, I know nothing more about them. You've just told me that they like horse riding, golf, swimming and what else? Oh yes, tennis and gymnastics. They sound awfully fit, I'm not sure that I can keep up with any of that. I'm a bit of a couch potato, apart from dog walking, and the occasional dip in the sea during the summer, that is."

Malcolm laughed. "No worries, Sharon, I can't keep up with them either. Elizabeth was the athlete of the family. She was the one responsible for all of their interests. She taught them both how to ski, sail, and play a very decent round of golf, and tennis, as well. The horse riding and golf are something we all did together, as well as play tennis. We'd play doubles, either kids versus parents, or father and daughter, well you know . . . Then there's the fishing and sailing, of course, but those are usually reserved for when we went on holiday. I don't suppose we'll be going anywhere again this year. Life without Elizabeth seems so empty now. We haven't been able to play anything together since she died. Do you play anything, Sharon?"

"I've played a round of golf or two with Jim, but I'm not much good. I don't have a handicap or anything. Tennis, I last played at school. So, I'm a bit out of practice. Who looks after the girls when you're working, Malcolm? They're still too young to be looking after themselves, surely?

They both go to a boarding school. The Canford, down near Wimborne. I expect you've heard of it?

Sharon nodded.

"They're both really quite clever, according to their tutors, but don't ever tell them so. Their mother would never have approved. She would always want to push them to the absolute limit in everything. She would always urge them into trying to do better, no matter how good they'd done, or what they'd achieved. They're also fiercely competitive with each other, as you will soon see.

We have an elderly couple that look after the house, Mr and Mrs Carter. Elsie and Dave, but we always refer to them by their surnames. They have been with us for donkey's years, and were in service to Elizabeth's parents before coming to us. Mrs Carter was appointed as the children's Nanny, and now she's my housekeeper. Carter is the butler, but he also does a lot of the routine maintenance and gardening, looks after the cars, and takes the children to and from school for me. There's a whole host of other people that come in to help do all the cleaning, but we rarely see them. They tend to come and go while the house is unoccupied. They work for the Courtenay Estate Management Company, who are kept advised with regard to what needs doing around the house, by the Carters. In all other matters, they're supposed to take direction from me. However, they're so good at what they do, that I rarely get bothered. And that is exactly how I like it. The Carters are wonderful people, salt of the earth, and I don't think we could manage the house without them. They live in the west wing, while we have the main building. You can have the east wing, or the guest rooms as we refer to it. It's the most recent addition, and very warm and comfortable, you will find."

"West wing, east wing, main building, my God Malcolm, just how big is this house of yours? I was expecting just a nice little run-of-the-mill three or four bed, with a little bit of garden. How much is the Navy paying you?"

Malcolm laughed again. "Probably not enough, I could certainly double my salary in private practice, but at the moment, it suits me to stay put for the time being. At least until the girls finish their education and can stand on their own two feet. No, the house belonged to Elizabeth's family, and came as part of her inheritance from her parents. It will never be mine, I just have it in perpetuity, or until I either voluntarily relinquish my right of habitation, or I die. It will all be going to the girls eventually. It is Elizabeth's money that pays for everything. Unbeknownst to me, she set it all up when she knew that she was going to die. There are no terms or conditions, I am free to remarry and continue living there, if I so wish, but I have no say in how the girl's inheritance, or the fortune in cash, stocks and shares, that they have held in trust, is to be administered when they come of age. It makes for a somewhat easy life for me. I just okay the expenditure, and sign all the household cheques on a monthly basis. The Accountants department of Devon Estate Management do everything else for us."

"Am I to assume that your late wife was some sort of titled lady, then, Malcolm?"

"Lady was the effective word, Sharon. For Lady Elizabeth Margaret Courtenay, as she was before we married, was what you would call 'old money.' Her family tree is well researched. I can show it to you if you're interested. It goes all the way back to the thirteenth century to one Margaret Beaufort, Countess of Devon. Probably beyond that as well, but the records get a bit scarce before then, what with the Norman conquest and all that.

I have absolutely no idea of the full extent of the family fortune, Sharon, but it includes several farms and estates in Devon and Cornwall, properties and offices in the City, this house, and another similar sized one on Guernsey, that has recently been converted into a four-star hotel. Those are just some of the ones that I am aware of. There are probably others in Scotland, where there is a considerable forestry interest that belongs to the family, and in France as well, where her brother lives. He's a vintner and connoisseur of fine wines, by the way. You mentioned enjoying a nice glass of wine, well, we have a well-stocked cellar that rarely gets opened these days. Personally, I prefer a good old pint of English ale, but you're welcome to fill your boots with the stuff if you like it. The girls don't drink wine yet, and the Carter's are teetotal, I think?"

"I'll bet they do, Malcolm. The girls I mean. Don't go kidding yourself in that respect. There aren't many teenagers that don't enjoy experimenting with alcohol these days. I'll lay odds that the girl's dormitory is almost as well stocked as your wine cellar."

Malcolm chuckled. "Well if they do, I can't stop them, can I? I just hope that they have sense enough to know when to call a halt. This is where their mother's influence is missing so much. That, and the fact that they are both nubile young ladies now, it's enough to drive a man to drink, I can tell you . . . We're nearly there now."

The car pulled off the narrow country lane onto a gravelled drive approach to the house. In the remaining light of the late evening, Sharon could see that all the lawns and garden flowerbeds on either side were immaculately laid out and beautifully tended. The front of the house illuminated itself as the car activated the PIR sensors, and the main doors opened, as if by magic.

A gentleman dressed as a butler came out to open the car doors wishing them both a good evening. Malcolm was addressed as 'Mr Malcolm, sir' and Sharon as 'Madam.'

"Good evening Carter. May I introduce Miss Sharon Cox? She will be staying as my guest for a while. Are the east wing guest rooms prepared, please?"

"They are sir, Mrs Carter saw to it all this afternoon. Welcome to Oakwood, Miss Sharon, please call me Carter, my wife and I are at your service. Please feel free to ask for anything you need during your stay. Will you be taking a little supper, Mr Malcolm, Mrs Carter has a light meal prepared if you so wish?"

Sharon was impressed, especially so when Carter made a slight bow in her direction before walking round to the back of the car to get her bag.

"Are you hungry, Sharon? Mrs Carters cooking is to die for, believe me. One of her light meals would be called a banquet anywhere else, isn't that right Carter?"

"If you say so, sir. Mrs Carter would be flattered to hear you, I'm sure."

"I'd like a cup of cocoa, and perhaps a couple of digestive biscuits, or a small sandwich, please Malcolm. Beyond that, well, I don't think I could manage anything heavier at this late hour. Would that be alright Mr Carter?"

"Certainly Miss. I will get Mrs Carter to prepare something a little special for you. And what about you, Mr Malcolm?"

"A small glass of my draught ale, and whatever Mrs Carter has prepared, please Carter."

"Yes sir, thank you sir. Should I be serving in the dining room, or would you perhaps be more comfortable in the conservatory? It is such a beautiful evening."

"The conservatory will be fine, but give us half an hour, please Carter. I will show Sharon to her rooms. Tell me, please, where are the girls?"

"Miss Charlotte and Miss Michelle are in the library Mr Malcolm. They asked for a plate of sandwiches to be served while they went about their studies. Mrs Carter says they are both hard at work, and obviously keen to complete all their homework assignments, in order to leave the rest of their holiday week free. Shall I tell them that you've arrived home, sir?"

"No, don't bother them now, Carter. They will have probably have heard us arrive anyway. I expect we shall see them presently. Now, if you will just let me take those bags, Carter. It's this way Sharon."

Sharon awoke to the sound of the dawn chorus and glanced at her bedside clock. It was 5am. She stretched herself out and turned onto her back, luxuriating in the warmth and comfort of her king-sized bed. She listened intently for any indication of someone being already up and about, but could hear nothing. Of course not . . . she had the whole of this part of the house, three completely self-contained apartments, all to herself. She slipped out of bed and padded quietly into her en-suite bathroom to relieve herself.

The concealed lighting switched on automatically as she entered. She squatted and took in her surroundings, casting an expert critical eye over everything. The corner mounted, full-length mirrors, carefully angled to show three images. The gold plated heated towel rails and taps, fitted on the entire bathroom suite. Her matching bath, shower, toilet, bidet, washbasin, all were quality items, tastefully selected, and finished in an ivory-flecked, pale yellow background colour, with a subtle little wild flower decoration to break up the monotony. The floor was of a similarly coloured, slightly mat-finished, non-slip Italian marble, streaked with complimenting colours to match the flowers depicted on the suite. The floor felt lovely and warm under her bare feet, so she assumed that there must be under-floor heating, as there were no radiators to be seen. The air conditioning hummed almost inaudibly, but she couldn't see any extractors.

Rising from her toilet pedestal caused it to automatically silent flush. The same thing occurred a second or two after she positioned herself over the bidet. It continued to flow until she took her weight off of the polished wood surround. Impressive . . . it was obvious that a lot of thought had gone into everything, and the overall effect was one of functional opulence and luxury. She washed her hands, exited the bathroom, and silently crawled back into bed, thinking about the previous evenings events.

Malcolm had given her a quick tour of the main house before they had enjoyed a quiet supper together. He had not understated anything when he had told her that Elizabeth was to be found everywhere. All her pictures, photographs, trophies and personal effects were still positioned exactly as she had left them nearly three years ago. Her coat, hat and boots were still hanging in the hall closet, alongside her riding hat and crop.

The orangery, where she grew her beloved orchids, was exactly as she had left it. Only the passage of time reflected the fact that she was no longer there to nurture the delicate flowers. They badly needed a little TLC to bring them back to their former beauty. Sharon thought she might give it a go herself, a bit later perhaps?

The girls had finally come through to greet their father and to be introduced to Sharon. They had both obviously just showered and readied themselves for bed, as they were in their dressing gowns, with hair wrapped in towels.

From the outset, Sharon had sensed an underlying hostility toward her. It was made blatantly obvious by the attitude of both of them. She got the distinct impression that she was there under tolerance. The handshake from Michelle, the elder of the two, had been limp-wristed and totally insincere, but Charlotte had at least managed a smile, albeit accompanied by a quick critical appraisal of her clothes and appearance. Their first meeting and greeting had certainly lacked any genuine regard for her, and Sharon wondered if Malcolm had spoken to them of her predicament?

After only five minutes of rather strained and polite conversation, during which they outlined their plans for the weekend, the girls excused themselves and retired to bed.

Malcolm had looked slightly embarrassed, and started to apologise, for none of their plans was to include anything in the company of either their father, or Sharon. She held up her hand to silence him.

"It would seem that I have a few bridges to build before I can earn the respect of your daughters, Malcolm. We can't expect them to just accept me into their home, and take me into their lives, without getting to know me first. The death of their mother has left a huge void to be filled, and I'm not sure that we will ever be able to achieve it.

There may have to be some compromises here. I cannot ever replace their mother and I'm not even going to try. I would rather they see me exactly as I am, just a friend of their father's. It is up to you to set the ground rules, so to speak, and advise them accordingly. For if we are to have any sort of future relationship, you will need to speak to them, and sooner, rather than later, I think."

The conversation continued in much the same vein for perhaps another fifteen or twenty minutes with Malcolm in tacit agreement of her assessment of the situation, and suggestions as to how to resolve it.

Carter came to clear the dishes and effectively brought things to an end. Sharon rose from her seat and moved toward the door with Malcolm following. Taking her arm and straining to make conversation, he'd accompanied her through the house, until they reached the entrance to her suite. He'd pointed out a few ornaments, pictures, and slightly interesting architectural details, on the way, but there had been a distinct atmosphere of awkward silence between them, on the things that really needed to be said. Each was left thinking that Sharon's presence in the house might have been a mistake, but neither was prepared to say it. After a slightly less than passionate kiss goodnight, Sharon had shut the door behind her, and quickly began readying herself for bed. Her first evening at Oakwood could have gone better she thought. The house was stunning. There was more luxury here than she could ever have dreamed of, but with it, came a whole host of problems. As she had undressed, showered, and slipped comfortably into bed, the events of the evening, and their previous conversation, kept going around in her mind, and sleep just wouldn't come. She was already beginning to realise that her perceived love for Malcolm, was perhaps more of an infatuation directly associated with the confines of the Clinic, and his care for her during her treatment?

Now, in the early morning light, the naïve simplicity of her relationship with him, was in stark contrast to the reality now becoming more apparent. Things were certainly not going to be as simple as she would have wanted. She hadn't for one moment thought that Charlotte and Michelle would prove to be a difficulty. She had imagined that, as children, they would do as their parent told them? But the girls were no longer to be regarded as children. They were young adults, adolescents in every respect, and they damn well knew it.

Her first impressions of Malcolm's daughters from last evening, was that they were spoiled little brats that could both do with being properly put into their place, but was she the right person to be doing it? Most definitely not . . .

At Bleanaway, the work on removing the arms cache from beneath the stone flagged floor of the bird hide, was not going too well. The scaffold pole, that had been brought to use as a lever, proved to be totally inadequate for the job. John's men had set everything up as Shaun had suggested, but as soon as lifting pressure was applied, it had buckled in the middle, the heavy stone slab remained unmoved. John left them hammering away at the cemented stone surround with large cold chisels. They were trying to clear enough space around one end of the adjacent big flagstone, to enable them to drive a big lever bar under one edge. He was thinking that if they could just get a wedge or two under one end, then with a little patience and a lot of sweat, they might be able to raise it a little at a time? To facilitate this, John needed to find some baulks of timber and cut some more wedges. He was heading down to Michaels and Dermot's shed, hopefully to find what he wanted?

Shaun, unable or unwilling to face the steep climb up to the hide, was waiting for him to give a progress report. In the meantime he was looking around the bungalow trying to find something suitable to eat. With no one to take proper care, the place had become a tip. There were dirty dishes and crockery piled in a stinking heap in the kitchen sink. The larder and contents of the fridges and freezer were now almost exhausted. There was no booze left anywhere, and, to his disgust, Shaun was reduced to having to use some sort of horrible tasting powdered milk in his tea and coffee, both of which would soon need replenishing. All the bedrooms were untended, the bedclothes, and bandages soiled with Michael's blood, were still littering the floor. Shaun's dirty underwear was piled on the bed, and he was now reduced to wearing Dermot and Michael's pants, but none of their other clothes fitted him, so he hadn't had a clean shirt, or a bath, for nearly a fortnight.

The lounge looked as though a bomb had hit it. Along with all the broken glass, beer cans and empty bottles that littered the floor, Shaun had made up a bed for himself by pushing two armchairs together. It was the only way he could get comfortable. The table had been thrown across the room, and now lay broken in the corner. The curtains, torn off the hanging rail in a fit of anger when he saw Dermot's body floating in the lake, he now used for bedclothes. They were left where he had discarded them that morning, just another untidy heap on the floor. A foul, rank and stale smell of bad food, and body odours, pervaded throughout, despite the opened doors and windows.

Shaun found half a pack of stale digestive biscuits, and started to stuff them greedily into his mouth as he went back outside to meet John.

He listened with a growing frustration and anger as John outlined what little progress they had made so far. When Shaun told him that the shed was securely locked and the key was nowhere to be found, John realised that he would have to make the long climb back up to the shed to bring down some tools and levers to force it open. He was not a happy man, either.

On a stroke of inspiration, John pulled his mobile from his pocket and rang one of the lads in the hide. He explained what he wanted and asked for the requisite tools to be brought down. He and Shaun retired to the bungalow to make as cup of tea while they were waiting.

Fifteen minutes later, the tools arrived, along with all four of the men who also fancied a cuppa. They produced some proper milk and biscuits from the truck, and for the next three quarters of an hour, they all sat around drinking tea laced with cheep brandy. They discussed and arguing amongst themselves how best to get the big slab up and out of the way, but talking was never going to get the work done, was it.

Shaun could take no part, he had to move away lest his anger and frustration boil over and he would say, or do, something he might regret. He was convinced that he was surrounded by incompetent idiots. He fervently wished that he didn't need to rely on them so much, but in his present physical state, that was not the case. Sitting in the garden, he tenderly probed at his ribcage. It had been more than a fortnight since he had sustained his injuries, and things had gotten no better. In point of fact, he thought they were probably worse?

The strapping that Lara had applied had helped, but now it slipped down and worked loose. It needed re-doing. But he couldn't manage it alone. He wished she were here to help.

The phone in his pocket rang to break his thoughts. He looked at the caller ID and recognised her number.

"Hello Lara, I was just thinking about you. I was just about to call, and here you are. What can I do for you, my dear?"

"Hello Shaun, how are you?"

"About the same, you know . . . I've got John and some of his lads here at the moment. They're trying to get at the guns, but not having too much luck at the moment. Fucking idiots, the whole damned lot of them, God, how I wish I could just . . ."

"Shaun, listen to me, it's important. When I dropped Michael off, he whispered something to me that I didn't quite understand. I asked him to repeat it. I'm sure he said, 'Tell Dermot not to forget the wire.'

I asked him what he meant, and he just said, 'Dermot will know.' Shaun, you need to remind Dermot, it might be something to do with the guns. They might be booby-trapped or something. Is Dermot there, let me speak with him?"

There was a long silence on the phone.

"Shaun, are you still there? Speak to me, man."

"I'm here, Lara. I was just thinking about what you said. Dermot isn't here any more, so I can't ask him."

"Well, is he contactable then? Where's he gone, Shaun, did you let him go?"

Even as she was talking, the awful truth began to dawn. She knew that Shaun would never have willingly let Dermot go. The consequences of his complicity in helping to organise her and Michael's escape meant that he had probably met his ultimate demise at Shaun's hands. She changed tack.

"Shaun, is Dermot alright? You haven't . . . killed him?"

"He's gone Lara. We had a fight. He lost."

Lara immediately broke the connection and fought back the tears. First Michael and now Dermot, where would it all end? Shaun was totally out of control. Damn the bloody man, he was beyond her contempt, and now to be regarded as nothing less than a psychopathic monster. There was little doubt in her mind that she would probably be next on his victim list, she knew too much about him. He would soon be coming after her, of that she was sure, she must get away, put as much distance as possible between them.

Deep in thought, she made herself a comforting cup of tea. The phone call to Shaun had originally been to tell him of her plans to retrieve the contents of her holdall, but with news of Dermot's death, things had now changed somewhat. She took her tea through to the garden seat, and with a pencil and notepad, set about working out her plans for the immediate future.

First she needed to get her computer, paperwork and passports back. To achieve that, the arrangement for Lloyd to be paid half a million pounds needed to proceed without a hitch. She had told him that the transaction would need authorisation from the others, but this was a lie. She had complete autonomy over the bank account, and as such, could do whatever she wished. She doubted that Marty McCue, the other signature on the account, had even bothered to look at it for years? Anyway, it was a chance that she was going to have to take. After paying Lloyd, she would close the savings account, transferring all the funds into her current account. She could then clear all her debts, and pay off her recently arranged overdraft.

Next, she would need to put the house and contents on the market at a ridiculously cheap price in order to get a quick sale. Her little collection of arty bits and pieces could go separately to a local auction house. They were quite valuable, so no real problem was envisaged there . . .

The next heading was Tiptree Farm. The title deeds to the property were in the name of a holding company that she and Ryan had set up. It named her as the Chief Executive, and sole shareholder, so she didn't envisage much of a problem in that regard either, but it would need to be sold as a profitable going concern in order to realise its full market potential. She needed to take some advice from Tony Williams, her solicitor, on how best to approach that one.

Bleanaway was a little more complicated. She owned the title deed to the quarry, but she had granted Michael and Dermot a fifty-year leasehold on their bungalow. She calculated that there was probably another twenty-something years left on the lease? Oh well, give it to Tony to sort out . . . He'll know what's best. In point of fact, she could probably appoint him to oversee the disposal of everything in her absence? Grant him a power of attorney and let him deal with it all. On completion, he could simply transfer the cash, less his fees, into her account. It might take a few months, but it would certainly save her an awful lot of worry. He didn't even need to know of her whereabouts. Just give him a contact mobile phone number. She could be anywhere in the world.

She mentally went through everything again, looking for problems and pitfalls. A little smile crept across her lips when she pictured Shaun's reaction on receiving a letter informing him that his farm was up for sale. She would love to be a fly on the wall.

She glanced at her watch. Tony would probably still be at his desk, so she went back inside to make the call.

Sharon had dozed off again, but was awoken by the sound of voices and the clip-clop of horse's hooves. She slipped out of bed and peered through a crack in the curtains. Michelle and Charlotte were to be seen riding across the back courtyard of the adjacent stable block. They were heading for a field gate that would take them out on to a meadow bridle path that stretched around the perimeter and down towards some distant woodland. Two Jack Russell terriers and a black Labrador were playfully running circles around them. She could hear their voices and laughter, but couldn't quite make out any of the words. They cleared the gateway, and set the horses off, side by side, on a gentle canter with the dogs barking excitedly as they ran alongside, their passage through the grass left a pattern of tracks in the silvery morning dew. Bathed in the autumn sunshine, it was an idyllic picture and Sharon drew back the curtains and opened the window to drink it all in. She stood for a few minutes sucking in the fresh morning air, and wondering about her future. She was wishing that she could somehow become an integral part of life in this beautiful house, and that of the man that lived here.

She showered and dressed in her brand new jeans and sweatshirt, pleased with the snug fit around her bottom as she critically viewed her images in the three way-mirrors. Brushing her hair until it shone, and applying a small amount of make-up, she was finally satisfied with her appearance.

Making her way back through the house to find the kitchens, her intention was to seek Malcolm out, and perhaps go for a short walk before breakfast. Following the sounds and delicious smells that were emanating from below stairs, Sharon walked straight into a huge utility room, and food preparation area, that led on into the kitchens. A rather plump, grey-haired, jolly looking lady, bright blue eyes and rosy cheeks, looked in her direction. While drying her hands on a tea towel tucked into her apron strings, she walked forward to greet her, wearing a big smile on her face.

"Good morning, m'dear. You must be our guest, Miss Sharon. I'm Mrs Carter. Did you sleep well? We were just about to bring you some tea on a tray. Carter, where are you man, Miss Sharon is here and seeking some breakfast, no doubt?"

Sharon smiled and held out her hand to be shaken. She had immediately taken to Mrs Carter, recognising in her, the same endearing qualities as those in her own parents. Mrs Carter took her outstretched hand and bobbed a polite little curtsy. Sharon was tickled pink.

Carter came through from the pantry looking slightly flustered, and shrugging himself into his butler's jacket.

"Pardon me, Miss Sharon, you've caught us unawares. Good morning Miss, have you had a comfortable night?"

"Very, thank you Mr Carter. If it's not too much trouble for you both, may I have some coffee and two rounds of lightly scrambled egg on toast, please? And if you have a glass of chilled fresh fruit juice, any one will do, that too, would be very nice."

"Yes Miss, but will you be waiting for Mr Malcolm to join you? He asked me to advise that he would be taking his breakfast at eight in the conservatory. He hoped that you would joining him."

Sharon glanced at her watch it was just after seven.

"Is Malcolm not about yet, Mr Carter? I rather thought that he would be an early riser."

"Oh yes, Miss. Mr Malcolm was up at dawn. He has taken his fishing rods down to the river to see if he might take a couple of trout on the morning rise. He should be back very soon now, the sun is just coming up over the trees, and the fish tend to stop feeding as the water warms up."

"Point me in the general direction of the river please, Mr Carter, I shall jolly well go and spoil his fun. Serve him right for not inviting me along."

Carter smiled. "Yes miss, certainly miss. But you will need some gumboots, over trousers, and a thorn-proof jacket. If you would like to come this way, I will fit you up with the necessaries from the hall closet."

Five minutes later, Sharon was walking purposefully along the same bridle path as that taken by the girls earlier. It led down towards a line of trees that bordered either side of the river. A well-trodden and tended pathway went up and downstream along the bank. Sharon stopped, uncertain of which way she should walk. Her hearing detected the faint sound of voices coming from somewhere upstream. She headed that way toward a sweeping bend in the river. A short-cut path through the undergrowth clearly presented a quicker route and Sharon moved away from the riverbank. The voices ahead of her were getting louder as she got closer. She stopped to listen. The tone of the voices had changed, someone was clearly angry and delivering a dressing-down. She crept forward seeking a position to view what was happening, without being seen.

A dense intervening Hawthorne bush, and the trunk of a large spreading chestnut tree, got her to within thirty metres, undetected. Sharon peeped round the tree trunk and through the bank-side foliage. From the raised bank, she was looking down on the river.

Malcolm was standing ankle deep, mid-stream, in the shallowest part of the river. Sharon guessed that it was a crossing point for the animals. He was holding on tightly to the reigns of the two horses as they impatiently tossed their heads. Charlotte and Michelle, still mounted in the saddle, were having a heated exchange with their father. The dogs splashed around, chasing each other in the shallows, occasionally barking. Together with the noise of the faster moving water, it was difficult for Sharon to hear exactly what was being said. She could only make any sense of their words even when voices became raised in anger, but after twice hearing her name mentioned, she knew that she was the topic of their disagreement. She dropped to her knees, and crawled a little closer, hidden from view by the high ground. Malcolm was in full flow.

"Ashamed of you both . . . Crass, boorish behaviour . . . downright rudeness unbecoming of you both . . . What do you think your mother would say?"

Michelle appeared to be speaking for them both, and shouted angrily back at her father.

"Mother would not have approved of you bringing one of your floozies into our home . . . As far as we're concerned she's your guest, not ours, and the sooner she's gone the better . . ."

Sharon was shocked. Floozy? Well, that was a new one. She'd never been called that before, and was not even sure that she knew the full meaning of the word?

Malcolm was clearly deeply insulted, and his words came over loud and clear.

"How dare you speak to me in that manner, young lady. I am your father, and you will show me due respect and consideration at all times. I do not have to explain myself, or my actions, to you, nor anyone else for that matter. You seem to forget yourself. What is more, you have just demonstrated to me that you are still to be regarded as just a rather stupid little child, this being clearly evident by your arrogant, rude, and immature behaviour. As for what your mother would, or would not have approved of, you are in no position to make any such judgement in that respect young lady, for you still have much to learn. Your very words are an insult to her memory. Sharon would still be a guest in our house, irrespective of whether or not Elizabeth was still here. She, at least, would have understood and extended the hand of human kindness to someone in distress.

On this occasion I am somewhat prepared to overlook your appalling behaviour, purely on the basis that I have not made you fully aware of Sharon's present predicament. Well, that is my fault and I apologise for the oversight. So now, you will both listen to me while I briefly relate why it is that she is here to stay with us at Oakwood.

You have both recently lost your mother after a prolonged illness, and we are all fully aware of the pain and grief associated with her loss, but at least we were able to prepare ourselves for the inevitable. Well, Sharon too, has only just lost her mother. She was brutally murdered when her home was firebombed, a little less than a week ago. Not only that, but as a result of the same incident, her father now lies critically ill in the burns unit at Odstock Hospital. We are planning on going to visit him this afternoon. The fire resulting from the explosion, has burned her home to the ground. She has lost nearly all her clothing and possessions, and at this moment in time, has very little money available to enable her to replace them.

You will now then begin to get some idea of the terrible ordeals that she has recently been subjected to. Can you both, just for one minute, picture yourselves being in that same situation?

Sharon is still one of my patients. In the past fortnight she has had to undergo both facial and dental reconstructive surgery, following a particularly vicious assault. You must have noticed that her left hand is heavily bandaged. Well, she has three broken fingers and the beds of two of her fingernails are crushed. It will take many painful months for those to heal properly, and in all probability, her fingers will be disfigured and scarred for life.

Despite everything that has happened to her, Sharon still comes across as a stoical individual, prepared to face up to everything, and anything, that the rest of the world throws at her. She is charming company, very worldly wise, and, if I am honest, a much needed breath of fresh air in my life. You may also have noticed that apart from the colour of her hair and eyes, there is a somewhat startling resemblance to the image of your mother. I certainly noticed it from the moment we first met. It is one of the many things about her that I find particularly attractive. Having said all that, I can assure you, that at present, there is absolutely nothing going on between us. I am the one not yet ready for any sort of relationship, and I have told her so. For the time being, Sharon and I have tacitly agreed that we are to be regarded as just good friends. Sharon will continue to be made very welcome in our home, at least until she is able to find her feet again. She is my guest, and you will show her the sympathy and respect she is entitled to. That is what Elizabeth would have wanted, and would have expected of you both. Do I make myself abundantly clear?

The two, quietly acknowledged their father's words.

In conclusion, I think that you could both learn a lot from Sharon. She stands out as a shining example on how to conduct oneself when, through no apparent fault of your own, the whole world in which you live inexplicably collapses into ruins around you.

Heaven forbid that anything like that should ever happen to any of us. But then, three weeks ago, Sharon would probably have said the same thing? So I suggest you both take a little time to reflect upon it, for who knows what destiny has in store for any of us? It has certainly taught me that, in this life, we should never take anything, or anyone, for granted. For me, Sharon has demonstrated a quite extraordinary strength of character. She has shown so much bravery in the face of extreme adversity, and still manages to come up smiling. I want you both to know that I tried to apologise to her for your behaviour last night. She came straight back at me, actually defending your corner. The lady deserves a medal, but they don't give them out for that sort of thing, do they?

I think you both owe her an apology. Do either of you have any questions? Have I made things clear?"

From her position, Sharon had heard, or pieced together, every word, including the contrite and mumbled apologies from the girls to their father. The revelation that she closely resembled Elizabeth Blackmore had come as a little bit of a shock. She made a mental note to study some of the family photos back at the house. She peeped through the undergrowth and saw that Malcolm had let go of the reins, and was watching the girls, who were now moving slowly away toward the far bank of the river. Malcolm stood mid-stream for a full two minutes, watching them go out of sight. He finally turned and made his way up the bank towards her position of hiding.

Keeping the tree between them, Sharon remained out of sight until he was well along the riverbank. Only then did she start back, hurrying out of the woods and cutting diagonally across the meadow, taking the most direct route back to the stable block at the rear of the house. She walked quietly along the side path of the house and round to the front entrance, where in the porch, she shed her boots, over trousers and coat, before admitting herself.

The bell contacts over the opening door had made her presence known, and Carter quickly appeared from the direction of the kitchens. He set about picking up her discarded clothing.

"A pleasant walk, Miss Sharon? Did you manage to find Mr Malcolm?"

"Very nice, thank you Mr Carter. No, I didn't find Malcolm, I must have gone the wrong way at the river?"

"Ah, I'm sorry Miss, perhaps I should have advised you. Mr Malcolm will always be found walking upstream. He prefers the upstream nymph method of fishing for his trout."

"That would be it then Mr Carter, I went downstream."

"Please call me Carter, Miss. Everybody does. I'm Carter, she's Mrs Carter, it avoids confusion."

Sharon laughed heartily, and held on to his arm while putting on her slippers.

"Does it Carter? How about you just call me Sharon, then?"

"Oh no, Miss, that would never do . . . We below stairs have to acknowledge our position and your social standing here in Oakwood.

It is the accepted and orderly way of things, but I thank you for suggesting it.

Ah, here comes Mr Malcolm now, if I'm not mistaken. Perhaps if you would be so kind as to stay and greet him for me, Miss? I will need to help Mrs Carter prepare the breakfast trays."

"Morning Sharon, how goes it? Did you have a comfortable night? You have a bit of colour in your cheeks, have you been out yet? Look what I've caught, do you like fresh trout?"

Malcolm held out a brace of plate-sized wild brown trout hanging from his fingers. They looked truly magnificent with the sunlight sparkling off of their wet iridescent flanks, and with the profusion of black ringed orange and white spots, so characteristic of wild, chalk-stream browns.

"Whoa, there boy, one question at a time. Let me see, yes, yes and yes. So that's a 'yes' to everything, isn't it? I was very comfortable, thank you. I slept well and awoke when the girls left for their morning ride.

I've walked down and along the river looking for you. I was about to deliver a severe telling-off for you're not inviting me along. I just got back a few minutes ahead of you. I must have walked the wrong way?

And lastly, I love all fresh fish, Malcolm. I prefer it to red meat really, but don't let that ever deter you from treating me to a bit of rare fillet, or rib eye, occasionally, will you? Are those two lovely little brownies destined to become our dinner tonight? They look so pretty, it seems almost a pity to have to eat them."

"If you so wish ma'am. I will give them over to Mrs Carter with instructions to prepare them in any way she sees fit. Let her surprise us . . . Are you hungry yet? Personally, I'm famished. Breakfast in the conservatory, how does that sound?"

"Carter already has my food order, Malcolm. I need to powder my nose, so I'll see you in ten minutes. Are we still going over to the hospital later on?"

"We are, but let's talk about it over breakfast. Ten minutes then?"

# Chapter 6

David sat quietly in the comfort of the customer waiting area of the Mercedes Benz Garage in Southampton. The car was in for its first service, and he had arranged for it to be done while he waited. He was passing the time by reading the sporting pages of the complimentary copies of the morning papers. Occasionally, he looked down through the large viewing window to watch the technician that was working on his car in the workshop just below.

He noticed that the man was peering intently and shining his torch at something that had caught his attention under the rear of the car. He saw him call to his Supervisor to come over, and he pointed out whatever it was. They both clearly looking very puzzled. David saw the other man reach up and carefully detached something small from beneath the bodywork of the car. Both men were looking at the object intently, turning it over and over, and examining it from all angles. David's curiosity was aroused and he tapped on the glass to attract their attention. The Supervisor looked up and saw him. He indicated his intention to come up and speak.

"Hello Mr Morrison-Lloyd, we're almost finished, sir, won't be keeping you much longer. I'm pleased to say everything is just fine and dandy with the service, except that the technician has just found this little object attached to the underside of your car. It appears to be magnetic, heaven only knows what it is, but it's certainly nothing to do with the car?"

He dropped a little circular disc, about the size and thickness of a ten pence coin, into the palm of David's hand. There was a slightly raised, sealed plastic face on one side and a powerful little magnet glued on the other. David knew immediately what it was, but he bluffed it out.

"How very odd. Well thank you for bringing it to my attention, I'll have a closer look when I get home, maybe prise it apart, see if I can see what it is?

He popped it into his pocket, and from his wallet sorted out a five-pound note.

"Here, tell your man that I'm grateful, and ask him to accept a little drink from me, will you please?"

"Yes, Mr Morrison-Lloyd, thank you sir, all part of the service, sir. Now if you'll just excuse me, I'll bring your car around to the front just as soon as it's finished, and had a wash."

David returned to his seat with the ghost of a smile on his face. So that would explain why there hasn't been any car visibly tailing him for the past few days. He fished the object out of his pocket again and magnetically clamped it on to a two-pence piece before putting it into an empty compartment in his wallet. He was not familiar with this particular type, but he rather suspected that it needed to be earthed to another ferrous source for it to be activated, and to work properly?

During his time in the Special Forces, he had used many similar little devices himself, and located them after the enemy had surreptitiously attached them to his own unit's vehicles.

The object that now nestled in his wallet was undoubtedly a GPS transponder. It had been continuously broadcasting his cars exact whereabouts for heaven knows how long. David tried to work out when and where it might have been attached. His best guess was the night that Ferguson and his sidekick Ahmed had come to George's place to see them, but he couldn't be sure?

He now needed to work out if there was any way that he could turn things around, and use the transponder to his own advantage, rather than just destroying it, and thereby alerting the opposition to it's discovery. For the time being he decided that he would replace it somewhere on the car. He had no real problem with Ferguson knowing of his whereabouts, it was almost to be regarded as a comforting advantage, somehow, but the man was still a bit of an enigma, another part of the puzzle that didn't seem to fit in anywhere?

The thought prompted David into fishing out his little pocket-sized notebook, and again going through all his now copious notes that covered everything to do with the case. Trouble was, they had been randomly jotted down as he had come across them, so they were in no particular chronological or sequential order of events. Trying to make some sense of it all, from reading his cryptic notes, was proving practically impossible.

He closed the book with a sigh and let his mind wander. He wondered if Ferguson was aware that Laura Dobson was now back in Weymouth? Should he perhaps tell him? It would certainly give him an excuse to do a little more probing in that area, try and establish exactly where Ferguson's interest in her, came into the equation? No, perhaps not such a good idea, there was definitely too much at stake there now. The deal with the half million pounds was far more important . . .

On impulse, he decided to make a couple of phone calls.

"Hello Malcolm, it's David. Are you okay to talk?"

"Sure, Sharon and I have just finished breakfast, she's gone up to her rooms to get ready to go and see her father. What's up, David, nothing else wrong, I hope?"

"No, it's nothing really, I was just phoning for an update, and to see how you two are getting along?"

"We're alright, David, I think Sharon is beginning to settle in a little now. Any progress or developments at your end?"

"Well, you can tell her that I've retrieved all the insurance documentation, and Sue is getting on to it over the weekend. Unfortunately, her mother's jewellery box seems to be buried under a whole heap of rubble. It will have to wait till they can start clearing all the stuff out of the way. The fire officer reckoned that the whole building is structurally unsafe. He wasn't too keen on both of us going inside, made me stand at the door and shout directions to him. God, you should see it Malcolm, it's a miracle anyone got out of there alive, I can tell you. The good news is that if everything goes as planned, I might be able to put some substantial money her way very shortly. I'm not going to say too much, it's all a bit airy-fairy at the moment, but keep your fingers crossed for me. You said you were off to see Jim. Any idea how he's progressing?"

"I phoned last evening and spoke to a colleague, Gilbert, he's a senior consultant at Odstock. He was able to tell me that Jim is conscious, lucid, and his condition is now stable. His vital signs are showing significant improvement, and the doctor in charge is optimistic. He will have to remain in ICU for the time being, but they may move him to something slightly less than high dependency, early next week.

All things considered, it sounds to me as though he's on the mend, David, but I haven't told Sharon yet. I thought it better that she see him first, and then find out that his condition is improving. He's not going to be a pretty sight I'm afraid, I'm told his hands and face are quite badly burned."

"Jesus, Malcolm. I don't envy you this one mate. Look, give her all our love will you, please. She and Jim are constantly in our thoughts and prayers. They don't deserve any of this."

"I know. Sharon is a quite remarkable woman, David. She is so strong in the face of extreme adversity. You can be sure that I will be endeavouring to take very good care of her, that's a promise."

"Thanks Malcolm. Look, be on your guard, mate. You will need to keep your eyes peeled and your wits about you all the time. They're almost certainly still looking for her, and it's no secret that Jim is now in Odstock. It was widely reported in all the local papers. So it stands to reason that it will be one of the places being kept under surveillance?"

"I have a couple of ideas in that respect, David, leave it with me. I've got to go now. I can hear our girl coming. I'll ring you back later."

The phone went dead before David could say anything more. He sat staring at it for a minute or two, trying to assimilate his thoughts.

He scrolled down the list of names in his phone directory until he found what he was looking for. He got his diary out of his pocket and flicked through to the page marked 'personal details' and then hit the call button on his phone. It rang for a good half minute before the receiver was lifted in acceptance, but nothing was said on the other end.

"Hello Mrs Dobson, is that you? It's David Morrison-Lloyd."

"Oh, it's you. What do you want, Mr Lloyd?"

"I was wondering if you'd had a chance to speak with the others yet, in regard to my proposal, that is?"

"We are all in general agreement, Mr Lloyd."

"Excellent. In that case, I am in a position to give you the details of the account into which the money should be electronically transferred. Do you have a pen handy?"

"Go ahead, Mr Lloyd."

"Santander. Sort Code 09-01-26. Account No 031655 48529337 in the name of DML Holdings. Do you want to read that back to me?"

She read it back to him correctly.

"And when can I anticipate you completing the transfer Mrs Dobson?"

"With the return of my computer, I shall be in a position to do it immediately, Mr Lloyd."

David thought for a few seconds. He was keen to get everything done as quickly as possible, but to return her computer meant taking a trip back up to Godalming, and then back down to Weymouth. He decided to play an ace.

"Okay, then. What if I were to come down to Weymouth and return all of your property this afternoon. Would you be able to make the transfer while I was present? I could then verify that everything was in order by checking my bank account in your presence, just to make sure that it had all gone through."

"I could ring my Bank to see if this would be possible, Mr Lloyd, but bearing in mind that it's Saturday and the Banks usually close for business at midday, it may complicate things somewhat. If I have a word with the Manager, I may be able to set it all up so that I can complete the transfer with a password sent from my computer? That is the only stumbling block as far as I can see. But why all the sudden hurry? We had an arrangement for Monday, isn't that soon enough for you?"

David had to think fast. "There have been certain developments unrelated to this, which might make it difficult for me to get down to Weymouth next week, Mrs Dobson. I am eager to get all of this out of the way as quickly as possible. There is also a fairly urgent need for me to get things back to normal for all of my family, as I'm sure you'll understand. You probably feel somewhat similar in regard to the return of your property, am I right?"

"Yes, Mr Lloyd. Perhaps if you will give me an hour and then call again, I might be in a better position to confirm the arrangement?"

"I'll do that, Mrs Dobson. Bye for now."

David was feeling pleased with himself, it had been a fairly productive ten minutes. He glanced at his watch, it was a little after nine-fifteen. An hour and ten minutes back to Godalming, fifteen minutes or so to swallow a coffee, and collect her stuff, then two and a half hours to Weymouth. Say, one-thirty or thereabouts. He decided to ring Sue and put her in the picture. He knew she would be delighted, for she couldn't wait to get back home, and had even started to bend his ear about it. He had to agree with her though, staying with George and Edith was alright, but from a business point of view it was proving a bit awkward, and there's nothing like the comfort and convenience of one's own home . . .

"Your car is ready now, Mr Morrison-Lloyd. If you would just like to accompany me down to Service Reception area, we can complete the paperwork for you, sir. This way, please."

At Bleanaway, things were at last beginning to show some progress. Much to Shaun's frustration, John's gang had been reluctant to do any more work the previous evening. They had merely contented themselves with forcing open the door on Dermot's shed with a spade, and then ransacking the contents in their search for useful items. Their best finds were a two-ton capacity toe jack, and a large block and tackle, both of which were checked over, and laid out on the lawn ready to be transported up to the hide.

Deciding to stay overnight, they sent one of their number out in the truck to get some stores. He returned an hour later laden with fish and chips, pizzas, two bottles of brandy and several six-packs of assorted ales and lagers. They all made themselves comfortable and switched on the TV, and that was effectively it for the rest of the evening.

The next morning, it was a bleary eyed gang that, after tea and toast, began to lug all the tools and heavy gear back up the narrow path to the hide.

Shaun had decided not to say anything in regard to the warning that Lara had given, to the effect that the arms cache might be booby-trapped. He had given the matter a little thought, and concluded that passing on the warning would almost certainly call a halt to any further work. There was too much at stake to risk that happening. This was the sole factor that influenced his callous decision. He, after all, was not in any imminent danger, so he was perfectly prepared to let them, in their complete ignorance, shoulder all the risk.

Shaun contented himself with sitting quietly outside in the morning sunshine watching the ripples occasionally emanating from around Dermot's floating body, as some of the lake's fish started to feed on his decaying flesh. He nursed a tumbler, half filled with the last of the cheap brandy, and reflected on his plans for the immediate future.

He decided that he must try and broker a deal with John whereby no cash changed hands. He needed every penny of the money in his floor safe back at Tiptree. That, and any other cash he could possibly lay hands on . . . He started to consider his all his assets and options.

Tiptree? Yes, perhaps he could move some stock to slaughter? Turn them into cash. He calculated that there was a batch of animals that must be pretty close to 70kgm slaughter weight by now, that is if Dennis and Michael, his stockmen, have been doing their job and feeding them correctly in his absence? He decided to give them a ring for an update, and dialled his own home phone number.

He listened with growing frustration as it rang and rang. There was obviously nobody there in his office to answer, and neither the answer-phone, nor the call divert, were switched on, as they should be if the office was unmanned.

"What a bloody fiasco, fucking idiots, the pair of them, so they are." He muttered. It did nothing for his temper. He tried to recall from memory either of their mobile numbers, but apart from the first five digits, they too eluded him. Lara probably had them in her phone, but that was amongst the items still missing from the bloody holdall.

"Shit, shit, and more bloody shit." But even the spontaneous string of angrily delivered expletives hadn't helped, it seemed that just about everything was being stacked against him.

Up in the bird hide, John had at last managed to get a couple of substantial levers under one edge of the huge granite flagstone. The combined weight of four men on the levers had raised it just about high enough to be able to slip the toe of the jack under the edge as well. They were now carefully jacking up one end of the stone, seeking to get it high enough to position one of the levers under, and across, in such a way as to act as a roller. A task made more difficult not only by the confined workspace, but also by the tendency for the angled jack foot to want to slip out from under the enormous weight of the stone.

After another fifteen nerve wracking minutes of heaving and pushing, they finally achieved their goal and they all sat back to take a well-earned breather before tackling the next manoeuvre. It proved to be a relatively simple process to lever the stone forward over the roller, a fraction at a time, until it rolled clear of the hole.

John, on his knees, put his head down and shone a torch into the hole. The disturbance of the air inside threw up an oily, chemically smell, that caused him to draw back. Standing astride he looked again. He thought that it was probably a six foot or more, vertical drop down to where he could see nothing but a layer of old, grey straw. They were going to need to clear that out of the way first, but how? The hole was barely large enough to admit a well-built man on a pair of steps or a small ladder, neither of which they had with them anyway. There was no way that he would be able to work in such a confined space, either. No, he would have to be lowered down, headfirst. As far as he could see, there was no other viable alternative.

"Anyone got any bright ideas?" He murmured. They could all see the problem and each was waiting for one of the others to volunteer himself. After the previous evenings session of binge drinking, none of them were feeling quite ready to be hung upside down over the hole.

"There's supposed to be a hundred grand's worth of guns and ammunition in the bottom of that hole." John muttered. "And it's probably going to be ours for the taking. We just need to get it out, somehow. I reckon that if we could fix up the block and tackle above the hole, and tie a rope around someone's ankles, the rest of us could lower him down to shift some of that loose straw. At least then, we could get some idea of what we're up against? Anyone got a better idea? No, well who's going to be first then, or do we need to draw straws? Think about it while we get this tackle rigged over the hole. C'mon lads, we can do this, now where's that length of bent scaffold tube? That'll do for a starters; if we can just wedge it up in the roof over the hole somehow, we'll have something substantial to hang the pulley block from."

They set to making the most of what little kit they had available. The final result was far from ideal, but it looked as though it might work? It was John's baby, so he volunteered to act as guinea pig, and be the one lowered, feet-first, down to the bed of straw. They tied a loop in the rope and John, taking a tight hold, gingerly put his right foot into it before letting his full weight slowly come to bear. Stepping out over the hole, they lowered him down very easily, his fourteen stone being no problem for the lads manning the pulley.

His feet touched bottom and came up against a solid resistance under the straw. He scraped it aside with the edge of his boot and stamped his foot. The sound told him he was standing on a wooden box or crate of some sort. Stepping out of the loop, he was able to turn round in the hole, but there was insufficient space for him to crouch down. He contented himself by tracing around the edges with his foot trying to gauge the size of whatever it was that he was standing on? He concluded that there were two similar sized boxes, side by side. Standing on one, he was able to move the other slightly with his foot, so they were not excessively heavy. He was relaying all this information to the others as he went along. When he was sure he could achieve no more, they easily lifted him, bodily, out of the hole again.

John was both enthusiastic and optimistic, this wasn't going to be as difficult a job as he first imagined. If they could just get a rope around, and lift out, one of the two top boxes the rest would become easier as they started to clear some space.

So keen was he to get things moving again, John started to tie the rope around his own ankles while the others watched on, bemused. Sorting out an additional twenty-foot length of suitable rope, one end of which he had tied to the scaffold pole, John instructed them to carefully hoist him up aloft and then lower him headfirst into the hole.

The oil and chemical smell was almost overpowering, but he persevered, working by touch only. Running his hand all around the end of one of the boxes, he was elated to find that there was a substantial handles to which he could attach the rope. He slipped the rope end through the handle, and while still holding on to the end, ordered that he be pulled up again. Two minutes later the first box was hoisted out onto the floor of the bird hide. The others gathered around, waiting for it to be opened by John, who whilst undoing the rope from his ankles, eyed it with eager anticipation.

He dusted it off and saw that it was heavily constructed, with steel reinforcements around the corners. Despite its long incarceration underground, the box was still bone dry. It was painted olive green with yellow, stencilled markings denoting the contents to be some type of grenade ordnance.

He unsnapped the fasteners and slowly lifted the lid. It was immediately apparent that the box interior had been completely altered, for it contained not grenades, but pistols. Divided into ten compartments, each separated by thin plywood, and tightly packed in with straw, there were two pistols and two spare magazines in each section.

Twenty, 9mm Browning semi-automatics, still oil-coated, and wrapped in waxed protective paper. They were looking as good as the day they'd left the factory. John whistled his appreciation as he removed one from it's packaging. He calculated that with ammunition, it would easily be worth five hundred smackers on the black market, and so far, he had twenty.

He passed it round to the others who were all similarly impressed. They talked excitedly as they familiarised themselves with workings of the weapon, and took careful aim at imaginary targets. John finally retrieved the pistol and carefully rewrapped it before putting it back in the box.

"C'mon lads, there's lots more goodies to be had yet, let's see what else we've got down here."

The second box proved to be identical to the first, the contents exactly the same except for the addition of five silencers for the pistols. John was thinking that he now had forty pistols, easily twenty grand's worth, given that there was some ammo down there somewhere?

He wasn't to be disappointed, the next layer of four wooden boxes all proved to be exactly that. Of a slightly larger size to the first two, they were much heavier, because each was tightly packed with boxes of 9mm cartridges, hundreds of them, and of two slightly differing types.

It was hard work carefully manoeuvring the heavy cases out of the ground, so they decided to take a break, and to go and give Shaun an update on their progress. John took two of the pistols and two differing boxes of ammunition back down with him.

While they set about brewing some tea, Shaun, already familiar with the workings of a Browning pistol, unwrapped one from the waxed paper, and wiped off the surplus oil from the surfaces of the weapon. He selected one of the boxes of cartridges, broke it open and carefully slotted the rounds into the magazine. The others watched on with growing interest, and excited anticipation.

He snapped the full magazine into the handle, primed the weapon and stepped outside. The others watched on as he took aim at Dermot's body floating in the shallows approximately a hundred yards away. Shaun squeezed the trigger once, to gauge the accuracy and range. The bullet splashed into the water just beyond the target. He then fired off another ten shots in quick succession, most of them hitting home and causing the corpse to shudder and roll over in the water. It was an impressive demonstration of both marksmanship and weapon capability. Grinning, he looked at John and waved the gun in his direction. John visibly paled . . .

"And there's still another two left in the mag before I need to reload. So, I'll have these two, and we can do a deal on some of the rest if you like?"

"What about the rest of the boxes then Shaun? What's in those?"

"They might be a bit too tasty for you, John. You might have some difficulty in disposing of some of that stuff. Best let me deal with all of that. I know exactly the right people to talk to, they'll jump at it."

John didn't like his reputation as a wheeler-dealer being belittled in front of his men, but Shaun was the man holding the gun, at the moment.

"So, am I presume that you don't need me and the guys any more then Shaun? You want me to leave the rest of the stuff in situ, down in the cave, for you to get out yourself?"

Shaun recognised the sarcastic veiled threat. He walked menacingly towards John and stood directly in front of him, choosing to stand deliberately too close for comfort. John's eyes were following the gun in Shaun's hand as it slowly came up until the barrel rested in the middle of his forehead. He could feel the warmth of the metal on his skin, he saw Shaun's finger tightening on the trigger. He backed up a little; his hands held out in a clear demonstration of submission and supplication. His legs were beginning to shake and he sensed a movement in his bowel. From the murderous look on Shaun's face, and in his eyes, he knew that he was only a whisker away from having his head blown off.

"Easy, Shaun, take it easy man. I didn't mean anything, we're here to help, remember?"

"Don't mess with me, John. You will finish what you came to do, and then we will come to a mutually agreeable financial settlement whereby you will take away a quantity of arms and ammunition in lieu of your fees. Is there anyone else here that doesn't want to see things my way?"

His question was met with total silence. Although they would far sooner be paid in cash, none of them fancied their chances in arguing the point with Shaun, gun in hand, and in his present mood.

"Right then, perhaps if you've all finished swilling tea, you might like to get on with what I'm paying you for. And just in case any of you've forgotten, you're supposed to be up there, getting the rest of my stuff out of the cave, and bringing it all down here. I want it all stacked in the shed before you leave. By this time tomorrow, it will be on its way. So come on then, you lazy buggers, get yourselves bloody moving, the day's a'wasting."

Tucking the pistol into his jacket pocket, Shaun nonchalantly turned his back on them, and casually walked back into the bungalow to make himself another brew. He was smiling to himself as he went.

He knew that they wouldn't dare go against his wishes now that he was armed, and had adequately demonstrated his ability and prowess with the weapon. It was easy for anyone to hold a loaded gun, but to point it at someone, and be fully prepared to pull the trigger, knowing that you were about to take a life, well, that took a lot more guts and ruthlessness than he gave any of them credit for.

John, his fear having now turned to anger at his humiliation, trudged back up the slope closely followed by the rest. He could overhear their whispered conversations as they discussed what had just taken place, and he didn't like what he was hearing. His previous respect for Shaun had been based on years of friendship during which time he had earned many thousands of pounds through various nefarious schemes and highly questionable activities. Up until now, Shaun had always been straight with him, but now, John was beginning to sense danger, and even a double-cross somewhere in the offing?

Ever looking to gain an advantage, he wondered if Shaun knew exactly how many weapons there were in the cave? They had, after all been hidden for thirty-odd years. He hadn't even asked how many pistols had been recovered, so it must be assumed that he probably knew how many there should be?

He still didn't know what else he was going to find in the cave, Shaun hadn't told him, but he was damn well going to find out, that was for certain. And what's more, if there was the slightest opportunity to turn things to his advantage, he was bloody well going to take it, and Shaun Riley could go rot in hell.

The next layer of boxes in the hole were all slightly larger again. With the two top layers removed, there was now room for a man to get right down in there, and be able to work in the confined space around the stack, tying on, and helping to guide the boxes carefully up through the narrow opening. It became apparent that the stack was roughly pyramid shaped and consisted of eight layers with the biggest crates at the bottom.

The next box out was carefully manoeuvred into a clear space and untied. John looked for the now familiar side catches to open the box, but this one was different, it had been nailed together all round. It would need to be levered apart, and broken open to reveal its contents. John hesitated, weighing up the risk of further antagonising Shaun, but with some encouragement from the others, he reached for one of their smaller levers, and carefully set to work.

Three minutes later, with a final groan as the last nails gave up their grip, the lid was lifted off and set aside. Taking great care not to disturb the packaging too much, so that it could all be reassembled, John lifted off the top layers of straw, to reveal the contents. It was once again apparent that the interior of the crate had been cleverly modified to accommodate a greater number of items. This time it was Sterling submachine guns, complete with two spare magazines for each weapon. They were laid out in such a way that each layer of the crate comprised two assembled guns, and four extra magazines. All had been heavily coated in a light, corrosion resistant wax-oil, before being additionally wrapped in a waxed paper. Resisting the temptation to delve any further, and despite comments of disappointment from his lads, John carefully replaced the packaging and lid, locating all the nails back into their original holes before tapping them back down into place with the flat end of the lever.

John had already worked out that each crate contained ten weapons. So that meant thirty, with ammo. He guessed that their total value was probably in excess of £50K in the market for illegal firearms?

In his mind, he went over what he knew about machineguns. They were classed as prohibited weapons, so nobody, other than military personnel, could legally possess one. As such, their black market value was relatively astronomical when weighed against the price of an ordinary handgun. Even deactivated weapons, re-modelled to enable them to work again, fetched over a grand and that was without ammo . . . So a brand new one, supplied with say 500 rounds? What was the rate of fire for one of those, and how accurate were they? He didn't know. So where would be the best places to offer them for sale to get the best money? The London drugs gangs? Manchester and Glasgow were good bets, as well. He had several contacts in all of those potential outlets. John revised his original estimate of their value to something over £60k, and started to look for some way to wrest them away from Shaun. He decided to test the water first.

"Liam, will you and Davey start getting some of these boxes down to the shed for me, please. They'll have to be manhandled down the path unless you can think of an easier way? Have a look around while you're down there, see if you can find some wheels of some sort. These ammunition boxes and the machineguns are really heavy lumps. Take the pistols first and steer well clear of Shaun, crazy bastard is just as likely to shoot, as soon as look at you."

His phone in his pocket rang to an incoming call. He pulled it out and walked out of the hide.

"Hello Kev, what's up mate?"

"John, that bird that Shaun was looking for. Is he still after her, do you know?"

"As far as I know he is. Why, have you located her?"

"I might have. That old guy that's in Odstock has a couple of visitors at the moment. One of them is a woman with red hair, reckons she's his daughter. It's got to be her."

"Hang on there Kevin, I need to talk with Shaun. I'll ring you back in a couple of minutes."

John thought for a minute. This might be the lucky break, the slight edge that he was looking for? If indeed it is the woman Shaun's after, who knows? He called Shaun.

"What now, John?"

"Shaun, that woman you're looking for, I think she's just come to light. Do you still want her?"

"Too bloody right I do, where is she?"

"Apparently, she's visiting her father in hospital, even as we speak. I've got two blokes waiting for me to call them back with instructions. What do you want to do?"

"I want her here. I don't care what it takes, or how you do it. Just get her here, to me."

"There's a lot of risk here, Shaun, snatching someone away like that. What are you offering by way of incentive?"

"We've been over this already, John. It's £10K, but it will now be paid in collateral rather than cash, being as you've already failed to get it back for me. So don't push it, John. I'm not in any mood for any of your bloody shenanigans, so you'll just get on and do what I say, if you know what's best for you."

"Look Shaun, you need to stop talking to me like that, man. You know full well that without me nothing's going to happen, is it? You're in no position to be threatening me, so that's enough, you hear. Any more of it and I pack up my gear, take what I think I'm owed, and I'm out of here leaving you to get on with it, all by yourself."

There was a long silence on the other end of the phone. John had never spoken to Shaun in that manner before, he wouldn't have dared to do it face-to-face, but things were different now, and he was holding all the winning cards.

It was crunch time, either Shaun would capitulate, and reluctantly have to accept his point of view, or he was a dead man walking? He let the silence continue, it was Shaun's move. The answer, when it finally came, was delivered in very conciliatory terms.

"Yes, okay John, you're right. Look, I'm sorry, mate. I really had no call to speak to you in that manner. It's been a difficult and painful couple of weeks, and I'm fast getting to the end of my fucking tether. I'm very grateful for everything you've done so far, and I will be generous when we come to settle up. As for that damned woman, it was her that did this to me, and I want her to pay dearly for it, before I wring her scrawny bloody neck. So, just get her back here, as one last favour, will you, please?"

John had never heard Shaun sound so contrite. He didn't think the word 'please' was even in his vocabulary.

It could all be a ploy, of course, to make him think that Shaun was being genuinely sorry and remorseful, just until he got his own way? He would need to remain vigilant, expecting the double-cross, but for the time being he decided to appear to be going along with it.

"That's better, Shaun. Now for the time being, let's try and work together again, shall we? I will ring Kevin back, and pass on your instructions. He's a good man, and if it's possible, he will get it done, believe me. I've just told Liam and Davey to start bringing some of your stuff down, so if you could just show them where you want it, that would be a great help. The rest of the boxes in the cave are all much larger and look to be a bit of a tight fit. They may be more awkward to get out of the hole? We are just about to make a start on some of those, Shaun, so I'll keep you posted on our progress."

Without waiting for any further comment or reply, John broke the connection, and immediately returned the call to Kevin.

Meanwhile, David had returned to Godalming. He was busily collecting together all the items to be returned to Laura Dobson, and stacking them on the billiard table. He was ebulliently having a shouted conversation with Sue in the kitchen, as he worked. The children were all playing in the garden with Edith and Sam.

"And with any luck, we should all be able to return home tomorrow, and get the children back to some semblance of normality. It won't be over of course, there are still a few more loose ends to tie, and Sharon and Jim's finances to sort out, but I think we can safely say that we won't be in any danger any more."

"What about those guns, David? Mum and Dad are uncomfortable with having them in the house, and I don't like having them around either. While you're at it, can't you get rid of those as well?"

David hesitated in what he was doing. The gun from his car, was now in his Bergen. He'd taken out while the car was in for service. The other one was still in George's safe. David went through to the study to get it. Sue was right, they were a dangerous liability to have around. He would have to think about how best to dispose of them, but for the time being, they could safely be hidden in his garden shed at home. Tucking the second pistol, and spare ammunition clips into his Bergen, David put it in the boot of his car. He packed all Laura's things into an old sports bag, and put that in as well. With a cheery goodbye to everyone, and while tucking into a hastily prepared sandwich for his lunch, he set off for Weymouth.

Malcolm and Sharon, driving in Elizabeth's beloved little red BMW Mini convertible, with the top down, arrived at Odstock Hospital. So as not to attract too much attention, Malcolm had insisted that Sharon choose some things from his late wife's enormous collection of unworn clothes. Now suitably attired, rather demurely, in beige slacks and a Harris Tweed country jacket, and with her hair completely covered by a white silk headscarf, knotted under her chin. Sharon, with her sunglasses, completely looked the part of being a smartly-dressed lady from the country set.

Having parked close to the building, in one of the spaces reserved for hospital staff only, Malcolm took her arm, and keeping their heads down, they quickly entered through the main entrance, where he noticed there was some building work going on. Already familiar with the hospital layout, he steered her towards the Burns Unit on level 4. They rang the bell at the entrance to Radnor Ward, and Malcolm breathed a small sigh of relief. He had been constantly on the lookout for anyone that looked as though they might be taking a particular interest in them, but so far, he had seen nothing to arouse his suspicions.

Before being allowed in, the male nurse that opened the door to the ward, and enquired which patient they wished to visit, asking for their relationship to the patient. Sharon asked for Mr Jim Cox, and identified herself as being his stepdaughter. Malcolm, having given his name, was then recognised by the nurse who greeted him as a colleague. They exchanged a few pleasantries as he conducted them both to Jim's bedside.

No one had taken the slightest notice of the woman hospital cleaning operative, busily working a floor polisher in the corridor, but as soon as Malcolm and Sharon entered the ward, she abandoned her task and hurried out of the building to make an urgent telephone call to her brother, Kevin.

Sharon was really quite shocked at the first sight of her stepfather. It didn't take a genius to work out that if he was in a burns unit, then there would be a strong likelihood of some burn injuries, but she was totally unprepared for the reality. She barely recognised the frail looking old man, head swathed in bandages, and whose eyes filled with tears as soon as he recognised her. A bandaged hand reached out to her in a gesture of supplication, as she moved closer to his bedside, and leaned over to kiss his one bare cheek.

"Hello Dad," she whispered.

"Sharon, where have you been, girl? We've been so worried about you. Are you alright, love?"

The voice, normally so vibrant, sounded croaky, and waveringly weak.

"I'm just fine now, Dad. I'm sorry for neglecting you, I've had a few little problems myself, but I'm here for you, now. Dad, this is my friend, Malcolm, he's been helping me to get through some of this."

She stood aside to allow Malcolm to come forward and gently shake Jim's hand.

"How do you do, sir, I'm so pleased to make your acquaintance. Sharon has told me a lot about you, but I'm sorry that we should have to meet under these difficult circumstances. May I ask how you are progressing?"

The formal niceties being conducted between the two men gave her a few moments to stand back and take another look at her father. The big strong man that she so fondly remembered, was no more. The flesh had seemingly melted off of his frame, and he now looked but a shadow of his former robust, jolly self. She had already seen that the colour and sparkle had faded out of his normally twinkling blue eyes. They now looked a dull, watery grey, and tinged with sadness. She wondered if he had been told of Doris's death? She recalled him saying, "We've been so worried," as though she was still there? The thought that he didn't yet know was filling her with sadness, and her emotions were in danger of taking over completely. For his sake, she couldn't allow it to happen.

She moved to the other side of his bed and pulled up a chair, thinking that the next fifteen minutes of conversation was going to be very difficult. She needed to know if he was yet aware, and looked vainly around for someone to speak to. She caught the eye of the nurse that had admitted them and he smiled at her. Sharon excused herself, and went over to speak to him.

Malcolm watched her out of the corner of his eye while still carrying on his sympathetic conversation with Jim, who was giving him chapter and verse on what he remembered occurring at the B&B. He saw that Sharon appeared more than a little agitated, as the nurse consulted notes and shook his head, shrugging his shoulders. It was clearly evident that he was unable to answer her questions. Concerned, Malcolm was about to go over and see what it was all about when Jim himself dropped the bombshell.

"And they won't tell me how Doris is doing. I don't even know where she is."

Malcolm realised the significance of what he was being told.

"Hang fire Jim, old son, I'll go and speak to someone, see if I can find out for you."

He walked over to where Sharon was having her now, heated exchange, with the male nurse. He didn't wait for them to acknowledge him. He butted straight into the conversation.

"Can you tell me please, why it is that Mr Cox has not yet been advised of the death of his wife? The poor chap has just let slip that he can get no information about her, and doesn't even know of her whereabouts. This is an appalling state of affairs, who's in charge here?"

Sharon looked at him tearfully.

"Thank you Malcolm, you've just asked my same question. I gathered from the way Dad was speaking that this was probably the case, but this nurse was unable to confirm it one way or the other."

The nurse looked embarrassed, and shuffled the notes back into a neat stack before returning them to a folder.

"Look, I'm sorry, but it's really nothing to do with me. I'm just a nurse, and I follow routine procedures and instructions regarding the care of patients, as issued by the doctors and surgeons. I'm afraid you will need to speak to one of them. There must be some good reason for keeping it from Mr Cox, but there is nothing here in the patient's notes, to indicate anything. Would you like me to see if there is someone from the senior medical staff who is free to speak with you, sir?"

"I think that would be a good idea, please nurse. I'm sorry if I appeared rude, but this really isn't good enough. As you can see, it is clearly causing distress, not only to the patient, but also to his immediate family. Good God, man, there's a funeral service scheduled for Mrs Cox tomorrow, and her husband doesn't even know she's dead yet."

The nurse, clearly flustered, got onto his phone immediately. Sharon decided to leave Malcolm to it, and returned to her father's bedside.

Knowing that news of the death of his beloved wife of over sixty years would be devastating for him, she wasn't about to say anything, until she got the okay from the medical staff, who could perhaps cushion the blow by administering a sedative, or something. She sat down beside his bed and avoiding his gaze, took his hand gently between her own. She struggled to fight back the tears. Jim noticed the strapping on her fingers.

"You've hurt your hand, love. How did that happen?

Sharon didn't know what to tell him. It was all getting too much for her. She needed to get away for a few minutes, just to think, and to try and pull herself together.

"Dad, I need to use the loo. Any idea where it is, please?" She whispered.

"I've seen people coming and going from the corridor, love. I'm guessing it must be out there somewhere?"

"Thanks Dad. Just excuse me for a few minutes will you, I'm getting desperate."

Sharon let herself out of the ward, and set off in search of a public toilet. She didn't really need one, but her mind was in turmoil, and it would be a good place to sit quietly for a few minutes, and gather her thoughts. One of the three operatives, still cleaning and polishing in the corridor, helpfully pointed her in the right direction.

David parked his car in Marlborough Avenue, just up the road from Laura's address. He removed the old sports bag from the boot, and without any more ado, made his way straight up to the front door of her house. His arrival had been anticipated, the heavy oak door swung inwards to admit him, even before he had a chance to ring the bell. The hallway was dark and gloomy after coming in from the bright sunshine, and David didn't immediately see Laura, until she stepped out from behind the door and closed it quietly behind him. She got straight to the matter in hand.

"Good afternoon Mr Lloyd. I see that you are carrying a bag, which I presume contains all my things?"

"Hello, Mrs Dobson. Yes, I have with me all the items we agreed I should return. Have you managed to set up the transfer?"

"I have. My Bank Manager has agreed to complete the transfer on receipt of a password E-mailed from my computer, and sent immediately following a telephone call from my house phone, to his personal mobile. Any variation to what he and I have arranged, and the transfer will not happen. It is all highly irregular, and he is doing it purely as a personal favour to me, as one of his most valued customers.

He is waiting in his office for my call, so shall we get down to business immediately, Mr Lloyd? I wish to see what you have brought with you first, please. So come through to my parlour, you can empty your bag onto my dining table. Give me my laptop first. I need to be setting it up."

They worked in silence. Laura took her laptop and placed it on her bureau. Familiarly connecting the leads for power, wi-fi, printer and telephone, she glanced at David, still carefully laying out her things on the table. She reached over for her file-o-fax, about to take it without asking. He grabbed her wrist and looked at her questioningly . . .

"I need some information that I have written in here in order to access my account."

He thought for a second or two before releasing her, and nodding in agreement. He was thinking to himself, 'So much for not having the security codes recorded anywhere,' an assurance he remembered being made to him during conversation at their last midnight meeting. It beggared the question as to how she had managed to set up the transfer, if that vital bit of information hadn't been available up until now? Her Bank Manager must indeed be a very accommodating sort of chap? David, ever the sceptic, was beginning to smell a rat.

"Tell me Mrs Dobson. Did you have to offer any explanation to your Bank Manager as to why you needed to transfer half a million pounds so urgently. It cannot be an everyday occurrence for him?"

"He thinks that I am involved in some property investment deal, Mr Lloyd. The idea came from the name of your account, DML Holdings. It sounded just like some big investment brokerage, or something. I've told him that as part of the agreement, I needed to put a substantial amount up front as a gesture of commitment and good faith. It all sounded rather glib, but he seems to have accepted it. His only real concern was that I get over to see him, sometime early next week, to sign some papers confirming the transaction. Typical Banker mentality, don't you think? There now, the connection is made, the amount and the recipient confirmed, and the password is ready to be sent. I just need to make the telephone call and hit the 'send' button immediately after I hang up. The money should then be winging its way over to your account."

In his pocket, David's mobile phone started to ring.

"So let's get on with it then . . . Excuse me while I take this call."

Sharon stood at the wash hand basins letting the luke-warm water trickle over her hands without wetting her bandaged fingers. A few minutes sitting quietly in one of the cubicles had been enough for her to bring her emotions back under control. She was now deep in thought, trying to work out what she was going to say to her father should he ask about Doris.

She heard the door open behind her, and glanced over her shoulder. It was one of the cleaners, a young woman.

"Sorry to trouble you missus, but we'll be cleaning in here in just a minute, I need to bring in my trolley."

"That's alright, carry on, I'll be out of here in a couple of seconds."

Sharon shook the water off her hands and moved to the air-dryer on the wall. The motor hummed loudly into life as she placed her hands under the machine. It deadened any noise from behind.

The large, blue canvas bag came down over her head and was pulled all the way down to her knees and ankles before she could react. She screamed and tried to move, but a hand clamped down over her mouth and she felt herself being lifted off her feet by someone else grabbing her lower body. She kicked and struggled, but the bag was severely hampering her movements. The next thing she was aware of was being dropped head first into some sort of container, and landing on her back and shoulders as she hit bottom. She tried to kick upwards with her legs but the bag had already been pulled tight and secured over her feet. For the second time she found herself incarcerated. Trapped, frightened, upside down, and unable to breathe properly, she started to scream and cry.

Nobody took any real notice of the two hospital porters pushing a trolley marked 'hazardous clinical waste' out of the hospital to a waiting nondescript white, hi-top Transit van. The noise of the alteration works in the hospital entrance, precluded anyone from hearing the desperate muffled screams coming from within the trolley, as two men lifted it up into the van. Three minutes later, the van had cleared the hospital grounds and was being driven away up the road.

Sue watched the children playing in the garden as she prepared lunch. The twins were supposed to be helping Edith clean out the fishpond, but the discovery of lots of baby goldfish had sent them scurrying into George's shed in search of fishing nets and jam-jars. The nets, when finally located, unfortunately hadn't seen daylight for several years, and the net material was rotten and falling to pieces. Edith, rather than disappoint the children, had cut the legs off of a pair of her tights, and sewn it round the wire frame to form a bag. She was now busily stitching up the second net for Rita, while Peter tested out the first one. He already had a half dozen of the hapless little fish swimming around in his jar, much to the disgust of his sister who had yet to get her chance.

Emily and Sam, as always totally inseparable, were down the far end of the garden where Edith had laid out an old blanket on the grass. Emily was stretched out on her tummy with her head in a book. Sam, lying opposite with his head towards her, was enjoying the sun's warmth, and the comfort of just being with her.

Sue could see that they were occasionally communicating with each other, either telepathically, or by their language of guttural growls, clicks and quietly muttered unintelligible noises. This was something that the whole family had by now come to accept as being quite normal, but it never ceased to amaze Sue who fondly wished that she could understand, as well. She saw them both suddenly sit bolt upright and seem to stare into space for some reason. Sensing something was amiss, she spoke to her daughter telepathically.

'What is it Em? What's bothering you?'

The answer came back immediately. 'Jo-jo is sensing that the lady, Sharon, is in some distress mother. She is very frightened and upset. We are both trying to find out the reason, but she is a long way away.'

Sue didn't hesitate, she immediately reached for her phone and rang David. It was answered on the fourth ring. She didn't wait for him to acknowledge her, time was of the essence.

"David, it's Sharon, Emily says she's in trouble. Frightened and upset is what she said. Do you know where she is at the moment?"

He glanced at his watch. "Probably still at the hospital with Malcolm. Ring off now, love. I'll call him."

David scrolled through his numbers muttering to himself in anxiety and agitation. He hit the call button and put the phone to his ear. He was now pacing up and down behind Laura.

"Come on, come on, answer Malcolm, damn you, its urgent . . ."

"The person you are calling is currently unavailable, but if you would care to . . ."

"Of course he is, you stupid tart, his bloody phone is switched off. He's in the damned hospital, isn't he."

David killed the call. He had been shouting at his phone in exasperation. His sudden unexpected outburst had interrupted Laura as she was in the process of making her call. She stopped dialling and looked at him, a little smile of amusement had crept onto her face.

"Trouble Mr Lloyd?"

"Damn right, its trouble. Bloody Sharon again. She's got herself into some other sort of fix. She's supposed to be visiting her father in hospital in the company of her boyfriend. My wife says she's frightened, and upset. I need to get in touch with Malcolm, her boyfriend, to see what's wrong, but his bloody phone is switched off, presumably because he's still inside the bloody hospital building."

The smile had disappeared off of Laura's face, and had been replaced with a look of puzzlement.

"Mr Lloyd, how do you know she's in trouble? Your wife is presumably at home? You are here, so where did you get your information from?"

"You're going to have to trust me on this one, Mrs Dobson. I can't tell you how I know, but be assured, my source of information is absolutely impeccable. There can be no mistake, she is definitely in trouble."

"What are you going to do, Mr Lloyd? If it's Shaun's people, they will probably be taking her to him. He will almost certainly take his revenge, and kill her in the most diabolical manner that he can devise. Mr Lloyd, we can't let that happen. Please, we've got to stop him."

David stopped his pacing and looked at her in surprise. Her concern for Sharon's safety sounded genuine enough, but why? Time for that later . . .

"Do you know where Shaun Riley is holed up Mrs Dobson? Is it Tiptree Farm, or the other place, what's-it-called, Ble-something?"

"Bleanaway Quarry, Mr Lloyd. It's in Monmouthshire, South Wales. A good three hours drive away. Where did you say Sharon was last at?"

"Odstock Hospital, Salisbury, that's a bit nearer, and they've got a head start on us. I need directions to get to Bleanaway, Mrs Dobson, can you help me, please?"

"I can do better than that, Mr Lloyd, I can take you there myself. Besides, even with directions, I doubt that you would ever find it on your own. It's situated well off the beaten track."

"Look, I don't know why you are doing this Mrs Dobson, helping me that is, but I'm very grateful for your offer. Leave whatever it is that you're doing, and let's get going immediately. Every minute counts, are you ready to go?"

"I just need to change my clothes first, Mr Lloyd, so in the meantime, go and grab anything you need from your car. We'll take mine. It's a four-wheel-drive, and recognisable to Shaun, so he won't be too concerned if he sees it coming on the CCTV system."

"Christ, why should you want CCTV in an old quarry works? What's there that needs protection?"

"It was installed by Michael and Dermot Close, the brothers, as we call them. They turned it into a wildlife sanctuary, and installed the system to detect intruders after rare birds eggs and the like. It's a beautiful place Mr Lloyd, wait till you see it, I'm sure you'll be impressed. Now, shoo with you, let me get changed. Three minutes, and I'll be out front."

David hurried out to his car and retrieved his Bergen from the boot, glad now that he had thought to bring it with him. On impulse, he took the transponder from out of the glove box as well. He still didn't know who, or what, Ferguson's interest was, but it was time to find out. He pulled out his wallet and found his card. His phone was answered after only one ring.

"Mr Ferguson, David Morrison Lloyd. Look, I don't have much time for explanations, but I need your help, urgently. Shaun Riley is holed up in a place called Bleanaway Quarry, somewhere in Monmouth, South Wales. I have reason to believe that he has just kidnapped Sharon Cox, or Roberts, as you know her. We believe he intends to kill her. I'm in Weymouth, and just about to set off to try and stop him, but he's three hours away. Are you perhaps any nearer?"

"I'm not sure, probably, but I will have to look up the location to be certain, Mr Lloyd. Do you by any chance have a postcode, or is that too simple?"

"No postcode, I'm afraid, but if all else fails, track me on your transponder, I'm taking it with me."

There was a chuckle on the other end of the line.

"I told Ahmed he was wasting his time with that. How long before you found it?"

"No time now for that now, Mr Ferguson. I'm to be travelling with Laura Dobson and she's just coming out to the car, so I've got to ring off."

"Dobson? But I thought you told me that she's in league with . . ."

David cut him off mid-sentence, there was no time for any explanations, and besides, the reasons for her involvement weren't even clear to him yet.

Laura, except for the trainers on her feet, was dressed entirely in camouflaged army combat fatigues. She carried a sports holdall, and strode purposefully straight past him.

"This way Mr Lloyd, it's the Range Rover parked just up the road. Who were you talking to?"

"I was trying to get through to Malcolm again, but his phone is still switched off. I left another message for him to ring me back, but I was wondering if they've got him as well?"

The Range Rover unlocked by the remote as they approached, and David threw his Bergen onto the back seat and climbed in after it. Laura threw her bag in the back as well, but took the drivers seat.

"Are you not riding up front with me, Mr Lloyd, my driving is not that bad, I can assure you?"

"I want to change into something similar to what you're wearing. It'll be easier for me back here, but I'll wait till we get out of town first, I don't want us to get arrested for my indecent exposure before we've even got started."

The car moved smoothly away from the kerb, and was noticed only by the two men in the blue van, who as a result of the phone call they were just conducting with Ferguson, were hurriedly stowing things away in readiness to follow the Range Rover at a discreet distance.

Malcolm sat in the office of one of the hospital consultants, Mr Gilbert Townsend. Coffee had been served and they were still discussing Jim Cox. Malcolm and Gilbert were well-known to each other, having previously worked together as colleagues, and socialised on several occasions.

"So, I can categorically assure you Malcolm, that Mr Cox is fully aware of his wife's demise, but staff have noticed that he just refuses to accept it. Whether or not this is a side effect of the drugs being administered to aid his recovery, is purely speculation and open to discussion, but my own view is that there is some sort of mental problem that we may have to address later, when his physical condition allows."

Malcolm placed the file of notes back on the desk in front of him and took a sip of his coffee.

"Jim Cox is well into his eighties, Gilbert. You're far more experienced in dealing with the elderly than I am, what are his chances of getting through this?"

"At the moment, the prognosis is fairly good. He is strong and responding to treatment, but his age has some bearing, and the healing processes are somewhat slower. I anticipate he will be remaining with us for some considerable time yet, and will continue to be heavily dependent on the painkilling drugs, at least for the next week or two.

You know as well as I, that some patients can adopt a positive attitude, and quicken the healing process considerably, while others, well, they just seem to give up, and never fully recover, do they?

It rather depends on Mr Cox. If he responds to his treatments in a positive manner, apart from the scarring, he could conceivably make a full, physical recovery, and be out of here in, say five weeks? As to his mental state, well I'm just not qualified to comment in that respect. Does that sufficiently answer your questions, Malcolm? I'm sorry, but it's very difficult to be any more precise."

Malcolm, suddenly aware of how long they had been chatting, glanced at his watch. He stood up to leave.

"Thanks Gilbert, I'll pass it all on to his daughter. She may be able to influence him in some small way. I'd better get back before she begins to think that I've deserted her."

They shook hands and Malcolm walked out of the office and back towards Jim's bed. He saw Sharon's coat left draped over the back of the chair, but of her, there was no sign.

"Where's Sharon, Jim?"

"She went out to the loo about fifteen minutes ago. I would have thought she'd be back by now?"

"Fifteen minutes, you say? I'd better go and see if she's alright."

Malcolm tried to look casual and unconcerned, but he had a feeling something wasn't right. He exited the ward and saw the cleaner woman, polishing the floor.

"Did you see a red-haired lady come this way a few minutes ago, please?"

"She was looking for a toilet, sir. I sent her that way."

With a nod of her head, she indicated behind herself and resumed her work. Malcolm walked the route back to the hospital Main Entrance checking all the public areas. He walked outside, and to his car. Nothing, no sign of her . . .

With a feeling of dread, he pulled out his phone and switched it on. It immediately pinged up the two 'missed calls' from David, made during the last ten minutes. He hit the 'return call' button.

"Malcolm, what's happened to Sharon, she's in trouble?"

"What . . . how do you know? I was just about to ring to say that I can't find her. She left Jim's bedside and went out to the loo about fifteen to twenty minutes ago. She's disappeared off somewhere. Has she been in touch with you then, David? How do you know she's in trouble?"

"No time for explanations, Malcolm, just take my word for it. We're assuming the worst, that the opposition has grabbed her. If that's the case, she's most likely being taken to the bloke that hurt her before, Shaun Riley. The scumbag's currently holed up in some old Quarry workings in South Wales. We're just leaving Weymouth, and on our way there now. We're hoping we might be able to intercept them, or get there before he can do her any more harm. Are you with us on this one, Malcolm, we may need some more help?"

"The Police, David, call the Police, it's a kidnapping, and they'll need to be involved. Tell me what you want me to do. Where do I go?"

"Already done Malcolm, they're on their way as we speak. Look mate, start making your way up to the M4 and head for the Severn Bridge crossing. I'm trying to picture your best route . . ."

"I know my way, I'll give you another call when I'm over the bridge, we'll need to meet up somewhere on the other side. We shouldn't be too far apart by then. Are you packing any hardware?"

"We're fairly adequately equipped, what about you?"

"My twelve-gauge over-and-under is in the boot."

"Nice one, but let's hope we don't need it. What are you driving?"

"Elizabeth's little red and white Mini convertible."

"Nothing that stands out too much then?" David chuckled at his own humour. "We're in a dark green Range Rover, so we'll have to find somewhere safe to leave your car, and then you can come in with us. Catch you later."

David broke the connection without waiting for confirmation of his arrangement. He looked up and saw that Laura was staring at him via the rear view mirror. He assumed her to be requiring an explanation of his telephone conversation.

"That was Sharon's boyfriend, Malcolm Blackmore. He's a Naval Officer, and might come in handy if the going gets rough. Do you know how many more there are up at the quarry besides Shaun Riley and the two brothers, Laura? I know the whereabouts of Marty McCue and Connor McCall, but what about Ryan Dobbs, where is he now?"

"You had better get yourself changed, Mr Lloyd, and then come and sit up front here with me. I don't suppose you and I will ever be in a position to regard each other as anything but people on opposing sides, but we have been thrown together by this common circumstance? I was thinking that there is still a lot you don't know, and I see no point in keeping you in the dark any longer. Besides, with the Police getting involved, it will all inevitably come to light, anyway. I am hoping that you might want to adopt a slightly different view of things if I put you fully in the picture? It is going to be rather a long story, but we do seem to have plenty of journey time on our hands, so when you're ready . . ."

Sharon struggled to control the waves of nausea and claustrophobic panic that were sweeping through her and threatening to push her mind over the edge. Eventually, realising the futility in wasting her energy, she ceased her kicking and screaming, and instead, set about thinking about how best to improve her situation.

She knew she was inside a slippery-sided container of some sort that was barely large enough to contain her. She was still lying awkwardly on her head and shoulders with her feet and legs drawn up tightly to her chest in an inverted foetal position. She needed to get upright to aid her breathing, and prevent herself from getting cramped.

By using the movements of the vehicle to assist, she shuffled her shoulders back until she was able to complete a forward roll in the confined space. With a bit more pushing and shoving, she at last managed to get herself sitting upright, albeit with her knees drawn up nearly to her chin. In this position she was more comfortably able to shuffle herself around. She patiently gathered together the slack in the canvas bag bringing it all to the top. This allowed more freedom for her head and face. Breathing through the closely woven fabric was proving difficult, but it was at least possible. She told herself that she was unlikely to suffocate.

The physical effort was causing her to perspire, and her heartbeat and respiration had increased to the point that she was getting out of breath. Sharon knew that she must get everything back under control.

She sat quietly for a few minutes, trying to breathe evenly and slowly, willing herself to calm down. She used the time to take stock, to see if there was any way of escape.

With her good hand she felt around the neck of the bag at her feet. She was looking to see if she could untie the drawstring, but she could only get two fingers out through the remaining hole, and she couldn't locate the knot.

The van swayed as it went round a bend and Sharon concluded that she was facing backwards. At the next bend, as the van swayed, Sharon threw her weight in the same direction and felt the whole container begin to topple, but it rolled back upright as the vehicle straightened up again. With a little more effort, she was confident that she could get it to topple over if she wanted to, but to what advantage?

She concentrated all her senses trying to establish if there was anyone else within a close proximity. She couldn't detect anything, but curiously, the image of a child's face kept coming into her mind. Sharon didn't know why, the child looked vaguely familiar, but it wasn't anyone she was immediately able to recognise.

However, the phenomenon certainly seemed to bring about a calming and reassuring influence in regard to her present predicament, and she found that she was able to gain a little comfort from it.

For the time being, she concluded that there was no alternative but to accept the situation. She needed to focus her mind on staying alive, and to conserve all her remaining energy in readiness for any sort of small opportunity that might present itself. She thought about Malcolm and wished he were were there to help . . .

'I am sensing that the lady, Sharon, is much calmer now mother, but she is imprisoned in a box with a bag over her head. It is very dark, and there is not a lot of room for her to move. The box is on a lorry or in a van that is being driven along the road. They are a long way away, and not getting any closer. Jo-jo is unwilling to influence the mind of the driver while the vehicle is moving.'

Sue looked at Emily as she communicated telepathically. She was sitting on the floor with her knees drawn up under her chin and her hands clasped behind her knees. It was an uncharacteristic position for her to adopt, and Sue assumed that she was emulating Sharon's circumstance in some way? Her eyes were closed and she seemed to be breathing heavily. Sam, lying in front and facing her, was intently watching her every move, as though he too was sharing the same experience.

By now, Sue should've been quite used to the power of her tiny daughters mind, but this demonstration of telegnosis was simply astounding. Was she really able to project herself into Sharon's mind, to see what she was seeing? There was no other logical explanation for it. How else could she be so precise?

Sue had also come to finally accept that, far from being a figment of Emily's imagination, Jo-jo was very much a reality. She had worked out that in some way, he was very closely associated with Sam. That much was abundantly apparent from just observing what was taking place at that very moment. Sue suspected that Jo-jo might somehow have taken over a part of the dog's mind, but the idea sounded so far-fetched and preposterous, that she hadn't yet dared to discuss the possibility with anyone else?

Following the incident involving the two workmen, and Edith being assaulted, Emily had told her that it was Jo-jo, not her, that had turned the man, Danny, into a frightened quivering wreck. She explained that Jo-jo had apparently entered the section of his mind that contained all the man's worst fears and nightmares. Extracting them from these deepest recesses, he had then presented them all back to him again, simultaneously and continuously, to be perceived in a more heightened sense of reality.

The explanation, when given, had defied her imagination, but Edith had confirmed that she had been instantly released when the man suddenly collapsed to the ground and rolled into a frightened huddle. She said he was crying out, and covering his face, obviously in some considerable distress. Not understanding, or knowing the truth of the matter, Edith thought he might have been having an epileptic fit?

As if any further confirmation of Jo-jo's mysterious existence was needed, it came in the form of the help she had received when trying to sort out the code words to access Laura Dobson's bank accounts. The security information given to her had come from Emily. But Sue immediately realised that she was only repeating verbatim, something that was being put into her mind. Emily was obviously in touch with someone, or something, else, at the time. It had to be Jo-jo.

Telepathically, she acknowledged her daughters help, deciding for the first time to try and establish a contact with Jo-jo herself.

"Thank you, Emily, and you too, Jo-jo. Will you tell me if you are able to detect any further change in Sharon's circumstances, please? I may need to pass it on to David. I'll ring him now, and tell him what you've said."

She waited to see if there would be any response, but nothing was forthcoming.

Work at Bleanaway was progressing well. The first four boxes, the ones containing the pistols and some of the ammunition, had been carried down to the bungalow. At Shaun's direction, they had deposited in the kitchen. The change of plan came about when Shaun realised that he had little or no recollection of the full complement of arms stored in the cave. He sat staring at the boxes, wracking his brain, trying to remember exactly what they had stolen thirty-seven years ago. It was he, after all, together with Ryan, that had selected and manhandled them from the hold of the ship, and transferred them over to the old fishing boat.

He knew there were pistols and submachine guns, and a couple of RPG's and a box of warheads, but wasn't there a crate containing some old, Mills bomb type, hand grenades as well? Yes, and another of phosphor bombs. He remembered Ryan telling everyone that they were highly volatile, and to be extra careful when handling them. He wondered what state they might be in now? It crossed his mind that perhaps he should warn John, who he knew was busy hoisting the stuff out of the cave with a block and tackle?

His phone rang in his pocket.

"Yes John, what's up now?"

"Good news Shaun. I just heard from Kevin and Danny. They've got the woman, and are on their way here. They should be with us in a couple of hours with any luck. They're not sure of our location, so we'll probably have to send someone up to the road to meet them. They're to ring me again when they think they're close."

"Are they sure it's her, John. I won't tolerate any more cock-ups?"

"Red-head, mid-thirties, overheard to say that Jim Cox was her father. Does that answer your question?"

"Excellent, and is the bitch unharmed? I want to be the one to lay it on to her. We've a score to settle."

"That I don't know, you'll have to wait and see for yourself, Shaun. Look mate, we're pretty busy up here, so I'm going to get on with it now. We'll talk some more when we've finished."

"Yeh, okay John. Take it easy handling the bottom layers, mate. There's still some RPG's and warheads to come out. They might perhaps be a bit more fragile, so don't go dropping anything or banging the boxes around too much, will you?"

"Leave it with me, Shaun, We'll be taking extra care. Some of this stuff is mine remember, and I want to be around to enjoy selling it."

John broke the connection before Shaun could say anymore.

Shaun felt the better for having cautioned him as to the potential danger. He smiled grimly, things were beginning to go his way again. He amused himself by trying to think up something diabolical to put the girl through. Perhaps after he'd shagged the arse off her, he'd let the others take a turn as well? What then, slit her throat? Drown her in the lake? Tie her to a stake and use her for target practice? No, all too quick. How about burying her alive in the cave? No need to tie her up, just chuck her in the bottom and put the big stone back. If she didn't suffocate first, she'd probably take weeks to die of starvation? There would be no body, so, no worries . . .

His phone rang again. The caller ID identified it as Dermot's number? He briefly contemplated ignoring it completely, but at the last minute curiosity got the better of him. He accepted the call, but chose to remain silent. He suspected it might be a trap, and waited for her to speak first.

"Shaun, is that you? Speak to me, man."

"Lara. What do you want? I thought you'd given up and run out on me?"

"Not yet, I haven't. You've still got my holdall and some of my things, remember? And I expect that you've managed to get your hands on the guns by now? I need a replacement for mine before you dispose of them all, so I'm on my way over. How're your ribs, by the way. Are they any better, yet?"

"Not much, the bandages have worked loose and slipped down. They need strapping up again. Are you planning on joining up with me? I'm on my own here, and I could really do with some help. John and four of his blokes are bringing all the stuff down now, but I've no readies to pay them with. If I have to do a deal in exchange for some guns, I'm gonna get really screwed. Any chance you can quickly lay your hands on a few grand in readies?"

"No chance, Shaun, not till I've done the deal with Lloyd. He's still got my computer, and all the account details. I can't access any money till I get them back, and that won't be till Monday at the earliest."

"I might be able to help you there. I've got something arriving very soon that he badly wants. How long before you get here?"

"I'm just about to leave Weymouth now. I'm bringing Dermot's Range Rover back, so we can use that for transporting some of the gear back to Tiptree. I'm curious, tell me what you have, that Lloyd wants so badly?"

Shaun chuckled wickedly. "You'll see when you get here. Call me again, when you're closer."

Laura ended the call and slipped the phone out of the car hands-free loudspeaker cradle, and into the top pocket of her jacket. She thought for a moment.

"Well, Sharon's obviously on her way, but not there yet, so we're still in with a chance. Also, he reckons he's got something that you badly want, which sounds as though he might be prepared to do some sort of a deal for her return? I don't think he'd be stupid enough to be doing her any real harm if there's the slightest chance that she might be worth a large bundle of cash. What do you think?"

"That's how I see it as well, Laura. It leaves us room to negotiate and stall for time. I'm wondering if we should be telling Ferguson's lot about this, and bring him up to speed?"

"This man, Ferguson, Mr Lloyd. Tell me a bit about him, if you will. He doesn't sound like your normal run-of-the-mill plod. How did you come to get involved with him?"

"Funny you should ask about that . . ."

David explained how he had first turned up at the B&B ostensibly looking for her, claiming to be some long lost nephew. Then there was the brief sighting at the airport, when he picked up Sharon after her escape. The incidents of his car being followed, and then the meeting in his taxi, when they finally introduced themselves as Detective Inspector Charles Ferguson and Sergeant Ahmed Suff . . . something or the other? He omitted the evening meeting at Godalming, when Emily recognised them as not being entirely honest? And their seemingly hasty retreat, when they learned of the imminent arrival of the local Police CID.

"So if you suspected them of being bogus police officers, why have you chosen to get them involved now Mr Lloyd. It makes no sense?"

"Shall we settle on Christian name terms please, Laura. I would feel easier now that we are being open with each other . . . In answer to your question, I have been puzzling myself for weeks, trying to work out how they fit in, exactly? Whoever they are, they seem to know a great deal about Shaun Riley, and you as well, for that matter. They told me he that is suspected of committing several murders involving prostitutes, and you have since confirmed it. I'm not sure that they know about Tiptree Farm yet, and they certainly have no knowledge of Bleanaway, that much is apparent. I'm thinking that there must be another aspect to all of this that I have either missed completely, or something that I'm completely unaware of? Now it's my turn for a question. You mentioned something about him getting his hands on some guns, what's all that about?"

"It may be the answer you've been looking for, Mr Lloyd? Sorry, David . . . This man Ferguson, is he a tall, fair-haired, smartly dressed military man?"

"You've got him exactly. Do you know him then?"

"I do now. He's Scotland Yard anti-terrorist squad, or at least he was until he got mixed up with a man named Monzer al Kassar, drugs smuggler, and illegal arms dealer. I suspect he might still be on his payroll, even now? This other man, his sidekick, is he a short, scruffy looking Arab type?"

David nodded, "He is."

"He's spoken to me about Shaun before. He's definitely kosher. He was busy on a murder enquiry, at least three years back. Shaun's name had cropped up somehow, and he'd been followed to my place, while making a delivery. I denied all knowledge of anything untoward, explaining that he just delivered a litter of puppies to me. They seemed satisfied, and left me alone after that. We must assume he's still a Police Officer, until we know anything else to the contrary, David. It's interesting that they've managed to join forces, though. I wonder how that came about?"

"The guns Laura, does any of this have any relevance?"

"Very much so, but the story goes all the way back to the early part of 1973, when we were all sent over together, as an IRA Active Service Unit, and we were seeking to arm ourselves. We were routinely passed any intelligence reports regarding movements or shipments of arms, both legal and illegal. We decided it would be better to target the foreign illegal stuff. Less hassle, if you see what I mean?"

David nodded in understanding.

"However, that all changed when we found out about a legitimate cargo of mostly small arms, was being loaded in Rotterdam, and was bound for terrorist groups in the Yemen. It belonged to Monzer al Kassar, an arms dealer, who in those days was rather unscrupulous in his dealings. The IRA had apparently been negotiating with him for the shipment, and had almost reached agreement on the deal. But at the last minute he got a better offer, and sold it all away from under their noses without another word. The Ruling Council were furious, so it was they, that passed the details on to us.

Anyway, to cut a long story short, the boys hired an old fishing boat, and set off for Holland. In the early hours of the morning, Ryan and Shaun were put ashore in Rotterdam, close to where al Kassar's shipment was being loaded. I don't remember the full details, I wasn't there, but apparently, Ryan held the crew captive, while Shaun helped himself to some of the boxes in the hold. The brothers pulled the fishing boat alongside the freighter, and it was all passed over the side, and loaded onto our vessel.

Shaun then disabled the ships engines, so that they couldn't be followed. Ryan locked the crew in the engine room before leaving the ship. They motored back across to Lowestoft, transferring everything into fish boxes on the way. Landing in the early hours, we simply transferred it all into a waiting van hired by Marty, and brought it to where we were renting a warehouse, on the outskirts of London.

It was all so simple that it was almost laughable. It was Monzer al Kassar's turn to be absolutely furious. He obviously suspected that the IRA was responsible for the highjacking. Well it didn't take a genius, did it? Ryan and Shaun had made no secret of their Irish identities. But what did we care, we had what we wanted, and we felt that al Kassar had been taught a lesson, not to mess with us. He vowed never to do business with the IRA again, but to supply the opposing factions, instead. He's been after us, and whatever remains of his arms shipment, ever since."

"My God, that's thirty seven years ago, is he still alive?"

"As far as I know. The last I heard, he had been extradited to the United States to face trial on charges connected with the supply of illegal arms, drugs, and money laundering. But you can be sure that his criminal empire is still operating in his absence, and that Ferguson is probably still working for him."

"So, do you think we should trust him, Ferguson, that is?

Laura thought for a few moments before answering.

"As I see it, our common enemy is now Shaun Riley. We want to secure the safety of Sharon. Ferguson probably wants the arms shipment returned to al Kassar. The policeman, Ahmed what's-his-name, as far as we know, is after nailing him for the murders of three call girls. So basically, we're all on the same side. Shaun has five men and a whole arsenal of weapons at his disposal, and we're relatively unarmed. So you would have to say the odds are not in our favour. The only real thing we've got going for us, is the element of surprise. Shaun thinks I'm going to be helping him, and will probably be pleased to see me. We must plan to exploit that small advantage, and not allow Ferguson, or anyone else for that matter, to make any move until Sharon's safety is secured. Do you agree?"

"On the face of it, well yes. But it is difficult to formulate any sort of plan until we know exactly what the score is at Bleanaway. It all depends on whereabouts she is being held. I don't know the layout of the place at all. Where do you think he would keep her? Let's assume she's physically alright, but he's tied her up. Where do you think she would be imprisoned?"

"She could be put almost anywhere, but my best bet would be either the tool shed, or the office. Let me tell you a little about the layout of Bleanaway Quarry. As you know, it effectively belongs to me. I purchased the property back in 1974, and the title deeds are more or less in my name.

Officially, it is an abandoned stone quarry working that extends over one hundred and seventy-six acres of what is now a designated wildlife sanctuary. The sanctuary has been created entirely by the brothers, Michael and Dermot Close, who guard it jealously.

I granted them a lease on the property, that enabled them to build for themselves, a rather lovely, spacious, three-bedroom bungalow, with a small extension that is their works office. There is a car park at the rear of the bungalow, that is served from the first gate into the quarry. Southgate, we call it. The gate itself is very substantial and remotely operated, electronically, from the office. The Northgate is similar, and gives access to the northern half of the sanctuary, all the woodland behind the granite cliff outcrop. The whole place has a sophisticated CCTV surveillance system, but Shaun doesn't know how to work it, so it might be switched off."

"What about Michael and Dermot, surely they must know how it works?"

"In a minute, David, I'll come to that in a minute. Now, the bungalow looks down over an artificial lake of about three acres. The brothers created it by putting a clay liner into the huge hole that had been excavated during quarrying. They filled it by diverting a stream to feed in at a point furthest from the bungalow. The water flows continuously through the lake, and out via a small dam with a decorative paddle wheel at a point some sixty yards to the left of the bungalow. The paddle wheel also serves to drive a small electrical generator that provides all their power. It is all very picturesque. The brothers have devoted the whole of their spare time and retirement, thirty years or more, into its creation and landscaping.

Looking from the bungalow out onto the lake, one is looking east. Immediately to the north and forming the shoreline, there is a granite cliff face, an escarpment, that rises almost perpendicular out of the water, to a height of sixty or seventy metres.

Set into the cliff face, a little over half way up, is what used to be the old quarry office and explosives store. The brothers have landscaped it to blend into the cliff face, and turned it into a bird-watchers hide. Access to the hide is via a narrow footpath cut into the cliff. The path begins at the far end of the lake.

Michael told me that beneath the stone flagged floor of the hide, there lies the entrance to a small natural cave that holds the cache of arms. They've been there, undisturbed, for thirty-six years, so we don't know what sort of state they're in now? Shaun and his men are getting them out, even as we speak."

"What sort of weapons is there in the cache?"

"From memory, probably forty or fifty handguns, a couple of dozen submachine guns, sniper rifles, a few RPG launchers and warheads, Mills bombs, phosphor grenades and plenty of ammunition suitable for everything. We sold off quite a bit of it back in the seventies, so I'm not too sure of what we have left. Michael and Dermot packed it all, so only they will know exactly."

"My God, that's enough to equip a small army. We've got to stop that lot getting into the wrong hands, Laura. Imagine it getting onto the streets, and into the possession of the London drugs gangs. They'd be the ones to buy it. No wonder Ferguson wants it back. That settles it, then. We've got to accept for the time being, that he's one of the good guys, and keep him in the loop. Do you agree?"

"Well, we could certainly do with all the help we can get. You'd better speak to him and put him fully in the picture with regard to the arms, and also our intentions concerning getting Sharon out first. If he turns up with an armed Police Tactical Support Group, and they go in mob-handed, we might end up getting shot ourselves."

David remained silent, deep in thought. It was a lot for him to consider. There were still a few things that were not quite making sense . . .

"Laura, tell me about you and Sharon. You've told me twice now, that there is more than I need to concern myself with, or words to that effect. Were you and Sharon in some sort of relationship?"

Laura was clearly taken aback, and David thought she was going to tell him to mind his own business, or something. He saw that she was uncomfortable, agitated, and either looking to avoid his question, or she was searching for the right words.

They were on the Dorchester bypass, and she had to negotiate the car past some heavy goods vehicles, so it gave her some time to think.

"I think we're being followed, David. There's a blue van, about a hundred yards back, behind the two lorries I just passed. It's been with us since Weymouth. It looks like the same one that's been parked in the driveway of a bungalow nearly opposite my house. I'm going to stop when we get to Yeovil, give it a chance to pass. I need to use a loo, and buy a couple of bottles of whiskey for Shaun, so it'll be a good excuse."

David was craning his neck looking back, but apart from the occasional glimpse of blue, the van remained out of his view.

"I expect it will be Ferguson's men again. Don't worry about it, they're not doing us any harm. Tell me Laura, why would you be wanting to buy whiskey for Shaun Riley?"

"Shaun was quite badly injured when Sharon reversed the van into his Land Rover. He's certainly got at least three broken ribs, and I rather suspect that one may have punctured his lung, as well. He's been coughing up blood. He might even have a ruptured spleen? He loves his Irish whiskey, and it may be the best peace offering I could possibly give him, given the circumstances of my departure."

"What circumstances? Why would you need a peace offering? I thought you and he had been talking about my demand for half a million? Come on Laura, stop feeding me bullshit, let's have the whole story. Start off by answering my first question. Tell me about you and Sharon."

"You are very persistent Mr Lloyd. Alright, you asked for it, but we'll need to go back to 1973 again . . ."

David's phone rang in his pocket. He hurriedly pulled it out and accepted the call.

"Yes love, any more news?"

He listened for a minute to what Sue was telling him, making only the occasional grunt of understanding.

"Okay love, I'm with Mrs Dobson and we're on our way to try and intercept them. No, I'll explain later. I don't know, but yes, Malcolm is aware, and the Police, yes. Look love, we've got to get on, I'm ringing off now, I'll call you back as soon as I've got any news. Ask Em and Jo to keep at it please. Bye, love you . . ."

David switched off his phone, and returned it to his pocket. Laura looked at him in askance."

"Sharon is apparently trapped in a box, with a cloth bag over her head. She was panicking, but is calmer now. She is either on a lorry, or in a van, and travelling in a direction that goes away from where she was kidnapped in Salisbury."

It was Laura's turn to look sceptical.

"Mr Lloyd, David . . . How on earth can you possibly know? That must be the biggest crock of bullshit I've ever heard. If you want me to believe you, then you'll need to explain to me how you come to know all this."

David smiled, "You tell me yours, I'll tell you mine . . . You first. Go on then, Laura, what happened back in 1973?"

She thought for a minute, "If I start by giving you our reasons for being sent over from Ireland, it may help you to understand how we came to be active in London, and trying to target establishments frequented by British Troops.

Back home, the Irish Catholic people were still being subjected to all sorts of atrocities by the British troops sent to Ireland as peacekeepers. I was one of those particularly hard hit. First there was my brother. He was one of those arrested and interned without trial, in 1971. Then my father was killed, shot by a British soldier, while peacefully demonstrating in Derry, on what came to be known as Bloody Sunday. That was January 1972.

Ryan, my boyfriend, and some of his family, had suffered somewhat similarly, so the urge to inflict harm in retribution, burned equally strong in us both. As far as we were concerned, we were waging an all out war on the British Establishment, being run by the Heath administration.

Back home, Irish politics were in a hopeless turmoil, but Ryan's uncle, himself a Republican Provo and heavily into direct action politics, eventually emerged onto the governing Council of Sinn Fein under Ruairi O'Bradaigh. It was he that secretly instigated our cell being sent over to England to replace Gerry Kelly and Delours Price, both of whom had been arrested at Heathrow in March of that year. We all arrived separately in the country in May. Our only remit was to further the cause, that of a United Ireland, by any means at our disposal. We were promised funding, but very little of it was ever forthcoming. In the beginning, we were forced to beg, borrow, and steal just to live, but it made for an exciting life."

Laura smiled as she recounted the glory days during the troubles.

"I must tell you about one of the scams we pulled, it was so utterly audacious. It began when Ryan noticed that Securicor regularly picked up the days takings from a busy supermarket in Manchester.

We hadn't long been in the country, and we were all crammed into a tiny little bed-sit, hungry, and nearly broke.

From an old black suit he bought second-hand, he had me alter it, and run him up a uniform looking similar to theirs. I even had to hand-make the insignia with coloured pens, to sew onto it. The finished result didn't look too bad, and would bear scrutiny, from a distance.

He, wearing the suit, and with Shaun following, they calmly walked through the Supermarket, and into their office area. It was timed to perfection, they intercepted the real Securicor Guard as he came in through the back entrance, and bundled him into the staff toilet. They nicked his ID badge and helmet, and Shaun twisted the poor man's arm up his back, forcing him into giving away the password needed to collect the cash. They left him tied up in one of the cubicles.

Three minutes later, they walked out with over sixteen thousand pounds in untraceable used notes.

'Providentially given over in an act of extreme generosity,' was how Ryan jokingly described it, when we celebrated our success in a local pub later that evening.

We fled Manchester after that. But it had given us our first working capital, and marked our beginning.

Ryan had handpicked his team from the many waifs and strays that roamed the streets of Belfast and Derry, just looking for trouble. Shaun Riley, the Close brothers, Marty McCue, we all responded to his call to arms.

Ryan was nothing short of inspirational, Mr Lloyd. Tall, fair-haired, very handsome, and gifted with a silver tongue, he was a natural born leader of men. When Ryan spoke, you shut up, pinned your ears back and damn well listened.

He and I were inseparable. We had been lovers for many months before being sent over to England. The others all looked up to him for guidance. Only Marty ever dared make any challenge to his orders, and then they would sit down and discuss it together, before coming to any final decision.

Ryan respected Marty, for he was the clever one amongst us, the strategist. Ryan was the bomb maker, Shaun the muscle, and the brothers, well they just did as they were ordered, without question. We were a good team, with a good leader."

"What about Connor McCall, where does he come into it?"

"Connor? Oh, he was just some punk kid, with local knowledge, that Marty recruited into helping us. I never took to him, he was never really one of us, but he had his uses, finding us safe lodgings, food, transport, that sort of thing. In fact, it was he that recommended Tony Williams to be my solicitor and do all the conveyance work when we bought Bleanaway. Then came Tiptree Farm, and finally my house in Weymouth. Tony has acted for me for over thirty years, now. Connor always reckoned that he was Tony's illegitimate son, but I have my doubts. Tony is a real gentleman. Connor? Well, he's just a slime-ball in comparison . . .

Anyway, getting back to 1973, circumstances required me to take a step back from what the boys were doing. I fell pregnant, you see? Ryan, to get me away, bought me a little car, and ordered me to scour the countryside looking for suitable places for us to build a safe hide-away. I found Bleanaway first. It was still a small, privately owned, working granite quarry then, but rapidly coming to the end of its resourceful life.

Being located so far off the beaten track, I thought it was ideal. They all came to visit, and agreed with me. Within a month, or so, we had negotiated a deal, and with cash up front, it was ours. Michael and Dermot were quick to put a couple of those big residential caravans on the site. They moved into one, and Shaun and Marty shared the other. What remained of our cache of arms went with them.

The brothers decided to make a few pounds on the side by selling off what remained of the stone yet to be quarried. That's how their business, Close Roadstone, got started.

Ryan was forced into sending me away again after that. By then, I was visibly pregnant with his child, you see, and he didn't want any of the others to know. We both felt that it was better to keep it that way. Ryan told them I was going back to Ireland to care for my sick mother. In fact, I was lodging with an English couple in Bristol. Going home was totally out of the question, my mother hated Ryan's family, you see . . .

Ryan, needing to pay for my care, was living and working with a group of travellers doing tarmac drives. He visited me in Bristol, as often as he could.

So that the child would be born in wedlock, he and I went through a quiet, civil marriage ceremony, in the Registry Office in Bath Guildhall. That was July 1st, 1973.

My baby was born in December, 1973. A beautiful little girl, the image of her father. Ryan held her in his arms for the first time, three hours after her birth. I can see them even now, she, unusually wide-eyed and looking up at him, and he, the proud father, with a tear in his eye, waltzing her around the room.

We decided that she should be named Sharon-Louise Dobbs, after his mother."

Laura glanced across to David who was staring at her incredulously.

"Yes, Mr Lloyd, Sharon-Louise, with a hyphen, that is her proper name, and she is my daughter."

"But why haven't you told her? Ferguson told me her name used to be Roberts before Jim and Doris Cox adopted her. How come?"

"Her Birth Certificate is with other documents, left for safe keeping, with Tony Williams. There are also the original copies of mine, and Ryan's Birth Certificates, our Marriage Certificate, and even his old expired passport. They're all in an envelope, together with some old photographs of her father and me, pictured together. From those, her true identity should never be in any doubt.

Sharon-Louise was born on 7th December 1973, in Penn Street, Broadmead, Bristol. She weighed, 6lbs 7ozs, had bright green eyes, and a mop of ginger hair. Barbara Roberts delivered her, herself a midwife, and one of the couple I was lodging with.

I registered her birth myself at the same Registry Office where Ryan and I were married. I gave an address in Lansdown Road, Bath, so as not to confuse things. Ryan and I had lodged there briefly, around the time we got married.

The Roberts' were a lovely couple, totally devoted to each other. They had been married several years, but for some reason they were childless. When I asked if I could leave Sharon-Louise in their care while Ryan and I continued with our careers, they were delighted. Ryan led them into believing that we worked in London, and that we were saving hard to raise enough money to put a deposit on a house. Something not too far from the truth, was it?"

David nodded and smiled.

"Well, history reflects that we hit both the Swiss Cottage Tavern, and the nearby North Star Pub in South Hampstead, on Christmas

Eve. Our intended targets were some senior British Army officers, known to be dining in both establishments, on that evening. We were moderately successful. The true casualty figures were never released, but we knew, all right.

Things got pretty hot in London after that. You only had to speak with an accent, and order a pint of Guinness, to become a suspect. We all retreated back to Bleanaway, after buying another caravan to house Ryan and me, as well. Sharon-Louise stayed in the care of the Roberts. We thought it better for her.

By far our biggest problem was always our rapidly dwindling funds. We all came to realise that we had to find a way of supporting ourselves, without drawing any undue attention. In short, we needed to start some sort of legitimate business enterprise.

Ryan and Shaun both came from farming backgrounds. My father had worked in the Belfast shipyards, and my mother had bred dogs all her life. The Close brothers were orphans, with very little formal education, so they had only ever worked as unskilled labourers. Marty was a college graduate, and was unwilling to get his hands dirty. Our only asset real was Bleanaway, and we had about five hundred in cash left from the Manchester supermarket job.

Around that time, there was an outbreak of foot and mouth, and then swine vesicular disease, that swept the Country. The Ministry of Agriculture slaughtered many thousands of animals. As a direct consequence, the farming journals, that Ryan and Shaun used to read, were chock-a-block with farms that had gone bust, and full of cheap equipment from bankruptcy sales.

Ryan and Shaun found Tiptree Farm. Once again, it was an ideal location for us, because of its remoteness. We negotiated a price with the elderly owners, and I borrowed heavily from the Bank of Ireland. Using Bleanaway Quarry as collateral, we finally managed to scrape together enough money to buy it outright.

Ryan, Marty, Shaun and me, all moved into the cottage, and immediately set about trying to make it pay. I told you that my first puppy scam was in 1974, well, Tiptree was where it all started. I effectively set up a puppy farm, selling on as pedigree pups, any decent litters that I could lay my hands on. My mother had done it back home for years, so it was easy for me. It was my money that largely kept us all going at first.

Ryan and Shaun took advantage of the mess and chaos that the pig breeding industry had been thrown into by the all the swine vesicular emergency measures. There were thousands of fine, healthy animals under the threat of slaughter, and many farmers desperate for it not to happen. The animals could be bought for a song.

With a beat up old box van, hurriedly adapted by Shaun to carry livestock, he and Ryan scoured the country gathering together his first stock of mainly pregnant sows, and litters of young piglets. All highly illegal of course, they had no Movement Orders, or any other sort of documentation for that matter, but both Shaun and Ryan knew their stuff when it came to buying good animals.

It was hard work, David. Everyone had to help, even Marty, who just wasn't cut out for it. We set up a pigswill cooker, and most days, we were all up before dawn, either out collecting food waste, or actually making the stinking pigswill, with which to feed them. It was relentless, but eventually, as the swine vesicular outbreak was brought under control, we set about making ourselves legitimate. With our first batch of animals being sent for slaughter, the cash started to roll in. We paid off our all our debts, and became solvent within a year. There was a light appearing at the end of what seemed a very long tunnel.

Meanwhile, we had to make sure that we never lost sight of our original purpose. Marty had come up with his most audacious plan yet. He had worked out a way to smuggle a bomb into the Houses of Parliament. Such an enterprise would first need approval from the ruling Council of Sinn Fein. They were sending someone over to see us, but it all took time, and we had to wait patiently."

Laura paused for a few minutes to concentrate on a tricky little overtaking manoeuvre.

"With all this going on, we had very little time to devote to Sharon-Louise. Both Ryan and I would have liked her to be with us, but a working pig farm was just no place for a young baby. We both appreciated that for the time being, she was better off being in the care of the Roberts.

We're just coming into Yeovil, David. I'm going to stop off at one of the town centre supermarkets. Watch out for that blue van, its some way back, but still behind us somewhere."

"No worries, Laura, I'll give Ferguson a buzz while you're shopping, he needs to know about the guns. I expect it's his guys, anyway. Don't be too long, will you. Oh, and a can of diet coke would go down well please, I've had nothing since breakfast at seven this morning."

She smiled and hurried off. David watched her into the supermarket. He was beginning to see Laura Dobson in a completely different light, somehow? Almost warming to her company. He thought that despite all her past criminal activities, here was a woman that had worked hard, and obviously endured considerable hardship and grief in her life. In some way, and for reasons now becoming apparent, she now seemed to be seeking to make amends for the neglect and cruelty she had, by circumstance, been forced to inflict upon her daughter. Is that how it is? He couldn't be absolutely sure, but he decided that he was going to trust her, take her into his confidence, and respond to her admissions by being equally as open and frank with her, when the time came.

His thoughts were interrupted as the blue van moved past in a queue of slow moving, town centre traffic. He glimpsed two young men who gave no indication that they were in any way interested in the Range Rover. Laura emerged from the supermarket carrying two plastic carrier bags, which she carefully laid down in the rear passenger foot wells. Climbing back up into the drivers seat, she produced a can of coke and a prepared sandwich from her pocket. She deposited both into David's lap.

"Sorry, it's only cheese and tomato, choice was a bit limited, I'm afraid."

David smiled his thanks and broke open the pack to offer her one, but she declined and pulled the car out into the slow moving traffic.

"The van is about three minutes ahead of us by now. Two young blokes who didn't seem too interested as they passed. They might be waiting for us up ahead somewhere?"

"Did you phone Ferguson yet?"

"Jeez, no I forgot. Too busy looking for the van. Sorry, Laura, I'll do it now. Here give me your phone. I'll dial it up, then we can both listen to him on the hands-free loudspeaker. See if you recognise his voice?"

She handed him the phone and he passed it back as soon as he had punched in the number. She put the phone into the cradle, and pressed the green connect button. The phone rang audibly.

"You have reached the messaging service for Charles Ferguson. I am sorry, but I'm busy at the moment, etc etc."

"Mr Ferguson, It's David Morrison Lloyd. Please give me a ring back as soon as you get this message, we have some vital information regarding this present oper . . ."

David never managed to deliver his full message. The phone came alive.

"David, it's Charles. Sorry mate, I didn't recognise the number."

"I'm on Laura Dobson's phone, and we have you on the in-car loudspeaker, Mr Ferguson. The reason that I'm ringing, is to bring you up to speed with what we know, and also, to prevent anyone from getting themselves unnecessarily shot. Is sergeant Ahmed bringing his armed support group, do you know?"

"He is, David. We're in touch with each other, and he's just told me that he's about twenty-odd miles away. All being well, he should be there within the hour."

"Mr Ferguson, far be it from me to try and tell you how to do things, but there are a couple of considerations you should take into account. Firstly, Sharon Cox, we know she is being taken against her will to the same location. As far as we are concerned, her safety is paramount, and we would like to try and secure her release before your lot move in to do the mopping-up. We have a bit of a plan and the added advantage of being able to get right in, past all the CCTV that covers the place."

"We were not aware of the CCTV, David, thanks for the warning. Is there anything else we should know?"

"Shaun Riley is heavily armed. He, and half a dozen others, are busy digging up a huge quantity of arms even as we speak. This is serious stuff we're talking about, Mr Ferguson, there's . . ."

"I know what's in the arms cache, David, I've been after it for many years. I can quote the full inventory from memory, by now. Tell me a bit more about your plan to try and rescue the woman."

"Mrs Dobson, as you know, is an associate of Shaun Riley, and has spoken with him earlier today. She is expected. Riley thinks she is coming over to join up with him again. I'm travelling with her in the same car. It's a dark green, 07 plated, Range Rover. She is going to drop me off in the grounds as soon as we've cleared all the CCTV cameras. From there, well, we'll need to play it by ear, I'm afraid. It will largely depend on where Sharon is being held. I am expecting to have her boyfriend, Malcolm Blackmore, with me to help. He's RN and pretty handy. We will both be armed, but we will throw down our weapons and lie flat on the ground immediately the TSG gets involved. We don't want to become the targets of friendly fire."

There was a long silence on the other end of the phone.

"Okay, David, given that we decide to go along with your little plan, and I'm not for one second promising anything. What did you envisage as being our part in this."

"Secure the perimeter. Stay out of sight. Allow all vehicles to enter and none to leave. Ten minutes after you see our Range Rover enter, assume we've turned off all the CCTV and come in, quickly, quietly, and mob handed. Fire a warning shot in the air and declare yourselves. Anyone not lying prone on the ground must be assumed to be the enemy, and be eliminated, or dealt with accordingly. How does that sound?"

"Like you've done it all before . . . I'll talk to Sgt Ahmed and see if he and the TSG Commander will wear it. Do we know what sort of vehicle Sharon Cox is travelling in, or how far away they are?"

David looked at his watch; it was just before 1400. He did some rough calculations and was thinking out loud for Ferguson's benefit.

"From Salisbury, where she was snatched at 1300'ish, it must be the best part of 110 miles to Bleanaway. So given that she's in some sort of van, their probable journey time, across country, will in the region of two and a half to three hours? We're just leaving Yeovil, so we're now about the same distance away, I would think, but they had a fifteen-minute head start on us, as well. I reckon they will get there slightly more than half an hour ahead of us, say around 1600. We're not going to be there much before 1630, what do you say Laura?"

She nodded her agreement.

"That's my best estimates, Charles. Whereabouts are you?"

"Me, personally? I'm three-up in an unmarked car that is westbound on the M4, and just coming up to the Severn Bridge. I reckon Ahmed will be within spitting distance very soon, so I'd best be speaking with him immediately. I'll ring you back."

"One last thing before you go, Charles. The blue transit van that's been tailing us, is it one of yours?"

"Yes. They were told to stay with you. They're the tracking unit."

"No problem then, tell them to slot in behind us, please, we'll show them the way. Order them not to follow us any further when we reach the destination. I will signal them back. They are to get out of sight and await further orders from either you, or Ahmed."

"Consider it done."

The phone went dead, and David leaned across to set it back on standby. They sat in silence for a few minutes, each with their thoughts.

"Laura, your gun is in my Bergen. Remind me to give it to you when we stop, will you please."

She looked at him and smiled.

"Your newfound trust in me is gratifying and appreciated, David. For what its worth, I'm sorry that you and your family have inadvertently got involved in all of this mess. If I could only wind the clock back a month, none of this, well, you know . . ."

"Do you want to tell me about Ryan, Laura? What's he doing now? You're obviously no longer together."

She bit her lip, and David sensed she was getting a bit emotional. He sat silently waiting for her to find the right words.

"Ryan died in the late summer of 1974, at Bleanaway, David. I wasn't there at the time, only he, Shaun and the brothers. They had acquired an old car, a Vauxhall Velox, that they were planning to turn into a car bomb. The brothers were preparing the explosives, carefully weighing out and mixing it up from various chemical fertilizers and the like.

Shaun was busy doing some work on the car to accommodate the bomb, ensuring that everything would be out of sight, and it would stand up to a cursory inspection if necessary.

Ryan, working in one of the caravans, was supposed to be constructing a simple, delayed fuse detonator, to be connected up to the clock in the car. None of us have been able to work out exactly how it happened, but Ryan accidentally managed to blow himself up. The side of the caravan was blown out, together with Ryan. He died in Shaun's arms, mercifully, without ever regaining consciousness. He is buried in the bottom of the lake, interred there, before it was flooded.

I was with Marty over at Tiptree when it happened, so I didn't even get the chance to say goodbye to him. They told me later that he'd made a good job of it. His body was a bit of a mess. The others thought it was better that I remembered him as he was.

To say that I was devastated would be an understatement, David. We all were. Ryan was our lynchpin. Without him we were nothing, or so it seemed. I retreated back to Bristol and stayed with the Roberts' and Sharon-Louise. I told them Ryan had been killed in action abroad. They understood and respected my grief. They couldn't have been kinder, David.

It gave us all time to reflect on what we were doing, I think. It was all very well for us to be bombing other people, but when it happens to one of your own, and the carnage is there to see, well . . .

The Houses of Parliament bomb, planted as planned by Marty, had been only a moderate success. Marty was unable to place it exactly where he wanted, and had to settle for the Westminster Hall, as his secondary choice of location.

Nevertheless, the British Establishment had been hit at its most sacred and vulnerable point, in the very heart of government, so we all felt we had accomplished what we set out to achieve.

The Ruling Council back home was secretly delighted with us, and was pushing for more of the same.

The Police had absolutely no idea who was responsible, despite all their rhetoric and filibuster to the contrary. This was very evident when they actually charged the wrong people with crimes associated with us. Probably under pressure from all sides, they were obviously fabricating evidence to obtain convictions against those they suspected, but we were the only ones that knew this, of course.

As a group, we laid low, and just got on with our various legitimate business enterprises, always looking for the next opportunity. But, without Ryan, the previous drive and initiative just wasn't there anymore.

David was sensing that Laura was beginning to struggle with her emotions again.

"Tell me a bit more about Sharon and the Roberts.' How did she end up being taken into care so young? Was it something that you instigated?"

"Good Heavens, no, Mr Lloyd. I would never have willingly parted with my daughter. She, to me, was everything I had left in the world. Her separation from me came about as the result of another tragic accident, that happened in the New Year of 1975.

The Roberts' were Scottish, their parents both lived in Aberdeen. I had spent Christmas with them in Bristol and had asked me if they could take Sharon-Louise to Scotland to celebrate Hogmanay with their family. I was due back at Tiptree to help out, so I agreed. What I didn't know was that the Roberts' had allowed their parents to believe that Sharon-Louise was their child. God only knows what they were thinking, but it caused me to lose touch with her completely.

I subsequently found out, years later, that the Roberts' had both been killed in a road traffic accident in Aberdeen. Their baby, my Sharon-Louise, had survived, and after a spell in hospital, had been taken in by Barbara Roberts' parents, in the belief that they were caring for their own granddaughter. Their surname is Dewar, so it made subsequent efforts to trace Sharon-Louise's whereabouts, very difficult indeed.

I knew nothing of the accident, of course. My first inkling of anything being amiss was when the Roberts failed to answer their phone at Bristol. At first, I wasn't too worried, there was a strong bond of trust between us, and I was confident my baby was in good hands. But as the weeks went by, and there was still no news, I became increasingly concerned. I went to Bristol and was shocked to find that their house had been emptied of furniture, and there was a 'For Sale' board outside.

The Estate agents flatly refused to divulge the identity of the vendors, but the young girl, perhaps looking for a quick sale, had already let slip that the property was a bereavement sale, on behalf of the executors of a Will.

I feared the worst of course, that the Roberts' and Sharon-Louise had been killed. I desperately wanted to go to the Police for help in finding out the truth, but how could I? I wanted to tell the others, but they were still unaware of Sharon-Louise's existence, and I'm not sure they would even have approved, let alone given their help, in the circumstances.

Eventually, I reluctantly came to accept that Ryan and Sharon-Louise had both been cruelly taken from me. It shook my faith to my very soul, David. I even renounced my Catholic religion, for all my prayers and grief had been seemingly ignored. I quickly became a bitter, vindictive, hard-faced bitch, very lonely, and unwilling to enter into any sort of meaningful relationship with anyone, for fear of getting hurt even more.

We would have to wind the clock forward another ten years now, David. A chance remark made during a meeting with Tony Williams, prompted me into letting him hire a PI, to really dig around, and find out the truth about Sharon-Louise. I was making out my own Will, you see, and we needed to know, beyond any doubt, that she was definitely deceased. An initial search for a Death Certificate had so far failed to come up with anything, but I still didn't hold out much hope. It had all been too long, Sharon-Louise would be nearly eleven by then, and if she were alive, she would be calling someone else, Mum, surely?

The months dragged on, the PI was good, but he was having a hell of a time in dealing with the bureaucracy of the Scottish Child Welfare authorities. He eventually found the Dewar's, one of them, anyway. She was in an old folks home and suffering from dementia, but she rambled on about her granddaughter, named Sharon, being taken into care when she was a baby. Well, at least it was a start, and it gave me some hope . . ."

David's phone rang in his pocket, it was Malcolm.

"David, I'm just about to cross the toll bridge, where are you?"

"About an hour behind you, I reckon. We're just passing through Shepton Mallet. Can I suggest you continue on to junction 24, and get off onto the A449 to head up towards the A40 and Abergavenny. At the first available roadside lay-by, stop and wait for us there. Make sure your car is clearly visible Malcolm. I will ring you back as soon as we are on the same road, okay?"

"First lay-by on the A449. Yes, alright, David. Is there any more news on Sharon yet?"

"Nothing of any significance. I'll fill you in fully, when we pick you up. I have to ring off now Malcolm, we're expecting the Police to call us back any minute."

"Yes of course. Sorry David, cheers for now."

The line went dead.

"He's made good time, I'll bet he's not too far behind whatever vehicle Sharon-Louise is being transported in?" He observed. David used her proper name for the first time in deference to Laura's feelings. The significance of it didn't go unnoticed and she smiled at him.

"It trips off the tongue and rather suits her personality. I can quite see where she gets all her guts from as well."

"She is the image of her father David, both in looks and personality. She has even inherited some of his mannerisms, even though they never really got to know each other."

"So how did you finally get to find her? Tell me more, it's a fascinating story, Laura."

"Sharon-Louise was a wild child, David. She obviously didn't take kindly to being fostered. The PI traced her through at least three families that couldn't cope, and had handed her back into care.

It was Tony that came up with the idea of checking to see if she had any sort of criminal record. He established that her last appearance was in the Southampton Juvenile Court, charged with shoplifting and aggravated assault. The Court had remanded her back into care, with a recommendation she be kept in a more secure accommodation.

By this time Sharon-Louise would have been twelve. I desperately needed to see her, if only to verify her identity, but her placement could not be revealed by the authorities, even to Tony Williams. It was a very frustrating time for us all, and another eighteen months slipped past, without any further developments.

Correspondence between Tony Williams and the Child Welfare people continued with repeated requests for them to reveal her whereabouts, but on my insistence, he was not able to reveal why.

He finally had a one-to-one telephone conversation with her case officer, and was advised that she had run away from care, yet again. After another three months, the Police had apparently found her sleeping rough on the streets of Southampton. For her own safety, she had been taken back into custody. Tony was advised that she was to appear before the Juvenile Court, yet again, for another formal review. If I was to see her, this was to be my one and only opportunity.

I stood outside of the juvenile Court one cold, wet morning, waiting patiently for her to arrive. I was not to be disappointed. A car pulled up and she got out of the back, her face a picture of defiance and hatred for the rather severe looking woman, who held on tightly to her arm, and led her into the building.

It was only ten seconds, but there was no doubt in my mind, that for the first time in nearly fourteen years, I had just seen my daughter.

I telephoned Tony immediately, and asked him to declare an interest in her welfare, but it was too late for the present Court proceedings.

Tony, and her newly appointed Social worker, continued to correspond. He telling her, that Sharon was mentioned as being the main beneficiary in a Will that he was drawing up. She advised that Sharon Roberts, as she was now named, had been put into the charge of an elderly couple living in Weymouth, as a final placement. If she chose to abscond again, she would almost certainly be put into a secure accommodation until she came of age. It was her very last chance.

The rest is history, David. Sharon-Louise was the one and only reason for me to buy a house and move to Weymouth. I desperately needed to get to know my daughter all over again."

"But you've never revealed yourself to her. Why, for Gods sake?"

"By the time I moved into Marlborough Avenue, Sharon-Louise had settled into her new home. I used to meet her out dog walking, and she eventually told me of her background, and how happy she was living with the Cox's.

We became quite close, but for different reasons. I wanted to express maternal love, but she mistook it for love of the other kind. She came on to me, and wanted to take it further. It was a very difficult and delicate situation. On the one hand I wanted her company, but I obviously couldn't respond to her in the way she would have liked. I had to let her down very gently, and back off."

"My God, I can imagine. Only recently, she told me that you and she were not the type to be interested in men friends. All the more surprising now that she seems to have fallen for Malcolm, wouldn't you say?"

"I can assure you that there is nothing wrong with my sexuality, David. But after Ryan, I chose not to seek anyone else in that respect. It has been that way for the last thirty-six years, and that is how it will stay. As for my daughter, I am delighted that she has at last found herself a man that she can trust. She's had many bad experiences, I'm afraid. This Malcolm must be quite something, I can't wait to meet him."

"That moment is not too far away now. I can tell you that Surgeon Lieutenant Malcolm Blackmore, MD FRCS RNVR is considered to be a man at the top of his profession, Laura. He has been taking care of all Sharon-Louise's injuries inflicted by you and Riley. So it might be a rather strained meeting if you get my drift? Do you want him to know that you are her mother, and why you saw fit to hurt her in that way?"

"Does he know it was me that hurt her then, David?"

"I cannot say for sure, but I rather suspect that he does, so don't be too surprised if you get rather a cold shoulder, will you?"

"Best keep my true relationship strictly between ourselves for the time being then, please. I will need to find the right moment to tell her myself, but God knows how?"

# Chapter 7

Detective Sergeant Ahmed Suffajji, of the West Midlands Regional Crime Squad, was not a happy man. He hated being involved in operations that didn't have any serious planning beforehand, and this was one of those. A telephone call from Chief Inspector Charles Ferguson had put him right on the spot, and he'd had to respond as best he could. Fortunately, the TSG were planning a drugs bust that morning, and he was able to get them diverted from their intended task to come and assist in this operation. He left it with his own Operational Commander to square it with the Dyfed Powys Heddlu, the Welsh Police, and let them know they were going to be working on their ground.

Sitting in the front passenger seat of the armoured personnel carrier, he was trying to brief the TSG Commander, Inspector Bob Taylor, with what little information was available to him. Both men, on the in-car loudspeaker, had heard the second call from Ferguson, outlining the potential hostage situation.

The new information put a completely different complexion on things, for the safety of the hostage was of paramount importance, and took priority over all other considerations. It also complicated everything.

The situation was exacerbated by the fact that they were going into unfamiliar territory. There had been no time to dig out any Ordnance Survey material, or to arrange some aerial photographs from the force helicopter. They were just going to have to 'wing it' and this was not something that either of them relished.

The plan put forward by David was reluctantly agreed upon, only because they could think of nothing better, and Ferguson had assured them that the man, David Morrison-Lloyd, was an ex-SAS soldier, and was therefore to be trusted insofar as his experience meant that he probably knew what he was doing?

Their part of the plan, to observe, secure and contain, at least afforded them a breathing space in which to make a more positive assessment of the developing situation.

The sat-nav in their vehicle declared them to be just three miles from the intended destination, so the TSG commander ordered that they slow down to a more sedate pace, and turn off the blues. A recce of the gates was their first intention, and this was to be achieved by a slow drive past.

The plan went straight out of the window, when from a distance of half a mile, they spotted a male standing on the grass verge near the southernmost gate. He appeared to be waiting for someone or something. It was too late to stop, for to do so would surely draw attention to their vehicle.

"Everybody down on the floor, get out of sight immediately, do it now . . ."

There was a scramble in the back of the van as ten bodies hit the deck, and Bob Taylor dived into the passenger foot well on top of Ahmed's feet. Hopefully, only the driver, who had removed his headgear, and Ahmed, his civilian passenger, would be visible as they passed the man. Bob gave instructions to Ahmed.

"If he looks at you, just smile, try not to look as though you're clocking him. This is a marked Police vehicle, so there's no way he'll miss it. We've got to convince him that our passing is purely coincidental. Don't change speed, just carry on until we are out of his sight, then we'll stop somewhere up the road and have a rethink on our next move. Christ, what a bloody fiasco this is turning into."

Sharon squirmed uncomfortably, for she had been in the same cramped position for over two hours, being rocked around by the movement of the van. Her backside was numb and her legs, feet, back and shoulders, ached intolerably. She was beginning to need a toilet.

The atmosphere inside the bag had become stifling and she could feel a dull headache coming on. Probably due to a lack of oxygen, or a build-up of carbon dioxide, she thought. Either way, it was bad news for her. She fingered her wristwatch clasp and squinted at the luminous dial for the hundredth time. How much longer? She would need to do something positive soon, her situation, already bad, was deteriorating by the minute. She felt that she needed to be doing something, anything, that might serve to improve her situation.

Perhaps if she could just make a hole in the bag material, it might make breathing a bit easier? It would also serve to focus her mind away from the pain and discomfort, giving her something positive to aim at.

She slipped off her watch and with the edge of the metal clasp, started to scrape at the coarse nylon reinforced material, held taut in front of her face by her bad hand. Working away on a small area for about five minutes, patiently scraping with the edge of the clasp, she began to sense that the material was getting weaker and the threads were beginning to part slightly, it spurred her on . . .

The clasp began to catch on individual threads and she felt the first one part, then another and another, she was winning. Sharon pushed hard on the clasp and it slipped through a tiny hole in the material. She gently pulled it back and probed at the hole with her finger enlarging it further. Now two fingers and pull the sack material down against the pressure exerted by her head and knees. The material gave reluctantly, but now she had a hole big enough to get three fingers through. She pulled the hole up to her face and took a few breaths of the slightly less polluted, and cooler air, from outside of the sack. The sense of achievement served to raise her spirits.

Laura and David had reached the point where the A37 merges with the A4, just south of Bristol.

This being familiar territory for Laura, she negotiated her way quickly through a series of rat runs to avoid the town centre traffic, and entered onto the M32 at junction 3, with the intention of joining the M4 at junction 19.

The driving now became easier and she turned to David.

"Come on now, David, I've been telling you all about my life for the past two hours. How about you tell me a bit about yours?"

David went straight into his early life with Sue, and a little about his military service. He made it clear that it was a period in his life he was anxious to forget, or at least put behind him, as it involved so much pain, suffering and heartbreak.

By far his greatest joy was to be found in being a good husband to Sue, and father to his three wonderful children. He went on to expound in great detail about all the little differences in their personalities and characters.

"Little Emily though, is a complete revelation to us. She is so different to the twins. Where they are boisterous and noisy, Emily is quiet and reserved. The twins will wolf down every scrap of food put in front of them, while Emily will pick out only what she considers to be nutritious and beneficial. It took us ages to work it out, but she seems to be aware of the benefits derived from a healthy, balanced diet, and the importance of not overeating."

"How old did you say she is, David?"

"Emily is only two, but don't take any notice of that, Laura. Emily is a truly exceptional child, and way beyond her years."

"How so?"

David wondered if he should be telling her these things, and decided to play it down a little.

"Emily can already read and communicate without using baby words. She doesn't say very much, but when she does, you would think you were having a conversation with another adult. Yes, she has a child's voice, but all her thought processes are obviously way beyond her years. She can draw conclusions, make observations, and even predict reasonable outcomes based on any factual information made available to her.

In many ways, physically that is, she is still very much a two-year-old. Her coordination and physical development, for instance, are much as one would expect of a child of that age. It is her IQ that is off the scale.

She worried us for some time. Sue even suspected she that might be autistic. But now, we realise that she is just an exceptionally gifted child. We wonder what's going to happen when the time comes for her to start school? At her present rate of mental development, it will be her that will be teaching the teachers."

Laura chuckled, "Have you ever had any proper assessments made on her potential, David? I believe there are special arrangements that can be put into place for such gifted children."

"Sue is of the same opinion as me, Laura, we're not so sure that it's a good idea. Speaking personally, I would prefer to have Emily growing up as normally as possible, and in the bosom of her family. Formal schooling doesn't teach a child the difference between good and evil, right and wrong, or the love and respect that should be accorded to her parents and siblings, does it? There are many other things that we, as parents, inadvertently pass on to our children. Things that mould and shape their characters, and ultimately turn them into, well-adjusted, good people, or so we would hope.

My concern is that Emily's rather unique abilities will be exploited to the point that she will be regarded as some sort of techno-freak, guinea-pig-swat, or something. If she needs to have special education, that will cost a great deal of money, and Sue and I are not exactly loaded. Our parents may help of course, but nothing has ever been discussed, as yet, and I'm not sure that I will even allow it, for they have worked hard all their life to get themselves into the financial comfort zone.

I keep telling Sue that we should just accept what we have, a rather clever, beautiful little daughter, who almost daily, comes up with yet another little surprise for us to ponder. Time is on our side in that regard, and time will eventually dictate what is best for Emily, of that, I am certain."

"You said you would explain how you got to know that Sharon-Louise is in a box with a bag over her head. Is this something to do with Emily as well, David?"

David was caught out. There was no alternative other than to tell the truth, difficult as it may be . . .

"If I reveal this to you, Laura, you will be the first person outside of my family to know. Before I say anything more, I need your word that you will never reveal what I am about to tell you to another living soul. If you make that promise to me, I will trust you?"

"It all sounds very mysterious, David, but if that is what you wish, then yes, I will give you my word."

"Very well, but you will probably find it difficult to believe, I certainly would. It's a job to know where to begin really, but ever since Em was a tiny baby, we've all had the distinct feeling that she was able to communicate her thoughts. Messing with our heads, we eventually called it.

For example, Sue or I would be busy doing something around the house, completely independent of each other, and we would suddenly become aware that Emily, herself alone in another part of the house, needed her nappy changing, or that she wanted her dinner. Without thinking, we would go to see to her, only to find that the other of us was already there for the same reason. It happened too many times for it to be a coincidence, and what needed doing, was always correct. We used to laugh about it.

I'll give you an example that involves you directly. You remember when we came to look at your pups, and you asked me how I knew they weren't from the same litter?" She nodded, "Well, I didn't. It was Emily that knew, somehow?

On that occasion she sent a couple of pictures into my head, I can even describe them to you."

David shut his eyes and began speaking while Laura listened in growing astonishment.

"I'm seeing a large wooden shed with double doors. Inside is a bank of wire cages, three high and five long, along the far wall. There is a pile of hay and straw bales, on a pallet to the left side, and a pile of stainless steel dishes beside a water tap to the right. In four of the cages there are litters of puppies, but there are no adult animals in with them. The adults, three bitches and one dog, are housed separately in the bottom cages. Does any of that mean anything to you, Laura?"

My God, you've just described our holding facility at Tiptree Farm."

"Right, my next image is of a very big, bearded man, taking the puppies from one of the cages and putting them into a large wicker basket that is on a pallet truck. The man is wearing a dark coloured corduroy peaked cap, brown tweed jacket and brown corduroy trousers. He has light brown boots. Does that mean anything, Laura?"

"Shaun. You've just described what Shaun was wearing when he came to deliver the pups you looked at. The basket is our delivery container, the one that he put Sharon-Louise in when we took her back to Tiptree.

My God, David, that is truly astonishing. How on earth can she do it?"

"It goes beyond that now, Laura, for we've only just learned that our little daughter can communicate with us, and we with her, telepathically. Sue and I have only just learned how to do it, and our technique needs a lot of refining for us to be anywhere near as proficient as Emily. But nevertheless, we can now effectively communicate with each other, without saying a single audible word. Clever, or what?"

"So how does it work then, David? How do you talk telepathically?"

"Don't ask me, I'm only a beginner. You posed the question, and I'm now 'thinking' my answer to you, like I would with Emily or Sue. Are you getting anything?"

"No."

"I thought not, I would be surprised if you did. I can only assume that it's because your brain is not attuned to mine. It's the same at home. Sue and I can talk telepathically if we're close to each other, but we haven't been able to get through to the twins yet. I suspect we will eventually, though?"

"So what about Sharon-Louise having a bag over her head? How does that come into it?"

"Well that's the proverbial sixty-four thousand dollar question, isn't it? And the short answer is that I don't know how she does it. I can only assume that she has the ability to project her mind over great distances. Perhaps even seeing things through the eyes of another? How did she send me the pictures of Shaun in the puppy shed, if she wasn't somehow there to describe it? I've wracked my brain for a plausible answer, but it all comes back to the same thing. The only possible explanation would be that she was somehow able to communicate with the puppies themselves, and possibly, extract images from their minds?

Before you scoff at the idea, we know that Emily has the ability to communicate with dogs. My God, you should see her talking with Sam. They speak a language all of their own. It sounds like lots of little mutters, clicks, whimpers, yaps and whines. All totally incomprehensible to us, of course, but they obviously understand each other. It's truly amazing to behold.

Getting back to Sharon, I have come to the conclusion that Emily must have projected her mind, and seen the world from, in this instance, Sharon's viewpoint. She may possibly be able to actually experience, whatever it is that Sharon is experiencing, as well? There is no other logical explanation for it, is there?

The one thing I know for certainty, though, Laura, is that Emily is never ever wrong about anything. The power contained in that tiny little brain of hers, is nothing short of phenomenal."

"So it would seem, David, so it would seem . . . I think if I had heard all this from anyone else but you, I would not have believed it."

She thought for a few seconds. "There is one other thing I don't understand, David. I seemed to remember your wife, Sue, mentioning someone called Joe, who's this person?"

David laughed. "We have come to the conclusion that Jo-jo is Emily's little imaginary friend. She will quite often come out with some startling revelation that she will then attribute to Jo-jo rather than herself.

'Jo-jo thinks that . . . or, Jo-jo senses that . . .' and then some little gem of information that we might have been searching for, and it always proves to be accurate and correct.

We've all gotten rather used to it by now, and Sue and I have even started to go along with it by acknowledging his presence, if only for her sake. We think that Emily would be upset with us if we were to try and deny his existence. So what harm can it do?"

"Toll bridge coming up, David. We'll need £5.70. Do you have it? If not, look in my purse, will you please."

Malcolm negotiated his way onto the A449 and pulled over onto the grass verge approximately half a mile north of the roundabout. He glanced at his watch; it was a little after three. He decided to give it ten minutes before ringing David again. Reclining his seat a little, and shutting his eyes, he let his mind go over the day's events. Only a couple of hours ago, he had been in Salisbury, now, it was as though he was half a world away, somewhere in south Wales, and seemingly on some wild goose chase.

He pondered the circumstances of Sharon's disappearance from the hospital, puzzling over how it had been achieved. How was it possible to snatch someone, presumably against their will, from a busy hospital building or grounds, without arousing suspicion? Who knew of their presence there? There was nobody that he could specifically remember, other than the nursing staff. But as soon as Sharon had stepped out to go to the toilet, she had been taken. The cleaner woman had seen her, but as far as he was able to ascertain, there had been no one else. It had been a pretty slick, well-executed operation. That much was apparent . . .

David said she was in trouble. How in God's name did he know? He pulled himself upright and reached over the back for her jacket. Her mobile phone was in the pocket. He scrolled down through the last dialled numbers, but they were all to David, and several days old.

He thought about his feelings toward her now, and realised that he wanted nothing more, other than to have her back in his arms, safe and sound.

His phone rang to break his thoughts.

"Hello David. I'm on the A449 about half a mile up from the roundabout. Where are you now?"

"About five minutes away. Laura will give you a couple of flashes as you come into view. She says to pull in behind us, and follow to Abergavenny. She knows a car park where you can safely leave your car, and then come in with us, okay?"

"Okay. Any more news yet?"

"No, nothing more, but don't let that bother you. Anything significant would have be passed on to us immediately."

"Dare I ask how you know?"

"Not now Malcolm, just trust me on this one. See you in a few minutes."

The white van carrying Sharon slowed down to pick up the man standing in the entrance to the south gate. It accessed a gravel track leading off from the Old Hereford Road. He climbed up into the cab alongside Kevin, and the vehicle continued on up the drive. Its progress was watched from a distance until the van went out of sight over the brow of a hill.

Eleven figures, all dressed in black, paramilitary garb, stood up and emerged from the undergrowth on the other side of the road. They stayed exactly where they were, ready to duck back out of sight if necessary.

David's phone rang.

"Hello Mr Ferguson, we're on some sort of back road shortcut that will bring us into Abergavenny in about twenty minutes according to Laura."

"OK David, I've just joined up with Ahmed. His team are in position and awaiting your arrival. He tells me that a white Transit van entered the south gate to the property, about ten minutes ago."

"Nothing we can do for at least another three quarters of an hour then, Charlie, unless you feel confident enough to risk letting the TSG infiltrate the target area, and take up offensive positions?"

"I might do a little recce, myself, David, get the lie of the land. Can Mrs Dobson give me any indication as to where the CCTV cameras might be located?"

David consulted with Laura, who reached over and angrily snatched the phone from him.

"Mr Ferguson, despite what Mr Lloyd thinks, I would urge you to wait for our arrival, please. There are cameras and PIR alarms all over the grounds. The chances are that they might already be turned off, but are you prepared to take that chance? This is a young woman's life at stake here. Riley will certainly kill her if he gets the slightest inkling that something is wrong. Give me a chance to get in there first, will you. I know that I can turn everything off with the flick of one switch located on the wall of the works office."

"I hear what you are saying Mrs Dobson, but time is of the essence, and rather against us. We will be losing daylight in an hour from now. I will wait as you suggest, but I would urge you to get here ASAP."

"I'm not exactly hanging around, you know. How about you organise a Police escort for us from Abergavenny. For what it's worth, it might save us a few more minutes?"

"A dark green, 07 plated, Range Rover wasn't it? Leave it with me, I'll see what I can do."

Laura threw the phone back into David's lap, her anger apparent.

"That was the most stupid thing you could have said, Mr Lloyd. I keep telling you not to underestimate Shaun Riley, he is a very dangerous man, even in his injured state. The other day, he was seated in an armchair when, without warning, he glassed Michael Close in the face, and then hurled him across the room like a child's rag doll. Michael is a big man, sixteen stone at least.

I also fear that he may now have killed Dermot as well, and he would've been no pushover, believe me."

"My God, why would he have done that?"

"They didn't want him to dig up the guns, so he killed them. It's as simple as that. Shaun Riley is now to be regarded as a psychopathic killer. He is totally out of control. The only person he will listen to is me, and only because and he thinks I'm coming to help him.

He doesn't know that I'm only here for one purpose, to ensure that my daughter, Sharon-Louise, is not going to be his next victim. That is my one advantage over him, and I will not stand to see it compromised. So you, and your gung-ho pals, had better not be getting in my way. Is that abundantly clear? Because if it isn't, you can damn well get out of this car and start walking, right now."

"Easy Laura, we're on the same side, remember? I'm sorry. You're absolutely right, of course, I just wasn't thinking . . ."

Sharon was aware that the van had stopped, and picked someone up. She also sensed the change of road surface. They were driving on gravel now. The van was rocking violently as it negotiated potholes in the uneven ground. She could hear men's voices and laughter, and guessed that they were nearing their destination. She began to try and massage some life back into her stiffened joints, readying herself for action, should the slightest opportunity present itself.

After about five minutes, the van rolled to a halt and she heard the ratchet of the parking brake being applied immediately before the engine stopped. Doors slammed as the driver and passengers got out, she heard some shouting, but couldn't quite make out what was being said. She sat quietly in anticipation, all her senses alert and focused.

The rear doors of the van were pulled open and Sharon felt the vehicle moving as someone climbed up into the back. She felt the trolley being manhandled. Someone lifted the lid of the box and prodded at her head. She recoiled angrily.

"Is the bitch is still alive, then, Kev?"

It was a voice she recognised immediately. Shaun.

"Alive and kicking. What do you want done with her?"

"Stick her in the shed for the time being, Kevin. I'll, wait for Lara to arrive. We'll sort out what's to be done with her, later. Make sure she can't get out of the sack, though. She's already managed to escape from us once before. Tip her out of the trolley and bring it back with you. It'll come in handy to help bring the stuff down from the cave. Be sure you barricade the shed door as well, will you, just in case she does manage to get free."

Sharon felt the trolley being dragged over the grass and manoeuvred through a narrow door of some sort. Without warning, she felt herself being upended. Forced into doing a back somersault, she landed heavily on her knees, on what felt like a rough concrete floor. Seconds later, the door of the shed was slammed shut and she heard wedges, or props, being set and knocked into place.

Kneeling as she was, Sharon slowly pushed herself upright to see how far the bag would allow her to move. The small hole she had made came dimly into view and admitted the first gusts of fresh air. It was like a breath of spring, and she took a few moments just to breathe.

She raised herself up onto the balls of her feet, but her head came up against something solid above. Reaching up, she explored whatever it was, by feeling through the material of the bag. A substantial piece of wood, solidly fixed, possibly the edge of a bench, or something? She felt along it, moving toward the doorway, until her hand came up against something else fixed to the wood.

Her thighs began to protest at being held so long in the half-raised position, so she sank back down onto her knees to relieve the tension in her muscles. Crawling was awkward in the bag, but she managed to shuffle herself along a foot, and then gather all the slack in the bag to bring it to the top. Holding on to the piece of wood with her good hand for balance, she brought her head down to peep through the hole in the bag.

In the dim light, she could just make out the handle of a woodworkers vice attached to the bench. An opportunity to escape from the bag had presented itself . . .

Holding on to the bottom of the steel vice handle through the material, Sharon threaded the knob on the top through the hole in the bag. She pushed it on through until she could take a firm grip on the handle from inside the bag. The bag was now effectively hanging from the vice handle, which provided a secure anchor point.

Very slowly, Sharon began to move herself around, trying to bring her full weight to bear on the weakened material around the hole in the bag. It was awkward, she couldn't release her grip on the handle for fear of the material sliding off again, but eventually, she found a position that allowed her to apply all her weight. By pulling up on the handle, she was able to bounce herself up and down.

The tough, nylon-coated, hessian type material, slowly and reluctantly, began to tear around the hole, a couple of strands at a time, but the physical effort needed to achieve it was taking its toll. Sharon stopped to rest, and to examine her progress. The hole in the bag was now large enough to get her whole hand through. She pushed her hand and arm out and reached blindly up onto the bench top. A bench and a vice meant there were probably tools as well? A chisel or a file, anything with a blade that would cut, was all that was needed. Her fingers touched something loose on the bench and knocked it away slightly. She felt again for whatever it was, carefully, for it was now at the full extent of her reach. Touch told her that it was something made of metal, small and narrow, her fingernails just managed to reach far enough to drag it back into her grasp. She brought it back into the bag to examine it more closely. A piece of broken hacksaw blade about five inches long, that'll do nicely . . .

Abergavenny, and Laura stopped the car in the car park of a small Conference Centre, to allow Malcolm to park the Mini. He quickly gathered together his things and climbed up into the back of the Range Rover. The car was already moving as he fastened his seat belt. Emerging out onto the road, a Police Traffic motorcyclist, coming towards them, clocked the car, and did a quick U-turn. He drew up alongside, acknowledged Laura, and signalled for her to follow him. Both vehicles took off at speed. It was ten more miles to the entrance to Bleanaway Quarry. They were all done at breakneck speed, along narrow country lanes.

David hit the re-dial button on his phone to speak with Ferguson. His call was answered immediately.

"ETA two minutes, Charles. Call off the Police escort and the blue van now, please. Give us a clear ten minutes after we arrive. If you haven't heard anything else from us in that time, come in guns blazing. If we manage to disable the alarm, I will give you a single ring on your phone to let you know, okay?

"Sounds like a plan. Good luck, David."

"One last thing, Charles. Make sure that the TSG knows not to shoot at anyone lying flat on the ground. We're the good guys, alright?"

"They've already been briefed, but I will reiterate it just to hammer the point home."

"Thanks, Charles. Join us for a beer after, you're paying . . ."

The Range Rover swung into the gravel drive, and Laura brought the speed right down to a sedate pace.

"I'm not going to stop the car, you must be ready to jump out as soon as I give you the word. There's a window of opportunity coming up in about one minute, a bend not covered by any cameras. Move off to your left and follow the stream up as far as the back of the bungalow. I will park the car in such a way as to give you some cover to cut across over to the other side of the track. Hide in the bushes and watch for my signals. I will point to where Sharon-Louise is being held. If I take my hat off, it means that the power is turned off. Any questions, have I missed anything?"

Malcolm, already busy putting together his shotgun and pushing a box of cartridges into his pockets, asked inquisitively,

"Sharon-Louise? I assume we're talking about Sharon here, are we?"

"No time to explain anything now, Malcolm, the clock's ticking. I'll explain it later. Ready mate?"

"As I'll ever be, but I wish I'd thought to bring some camou gear, like you two."

Laura, hands off the steering wheel, quickly shrugged off her jacket.

"Here take mine. Give him my gun as well, David. I'll be sure to get another from Shaun as soon as I get there. Now listen up you two. Our sole aim is for us all to drive out of here with Sharon-Louise safe and sound. Everything else is of little or no consequence. We watch each other's backs. If Shaun Riley makes one false move toward any of us, shoot him immediately. Shoot to kill, anything less than a killing shot will be no good where he is concerned, believe me. Good luck, you get out of the left side of the car as I go round this next right-hander. The bungalow is on your right, two hundred yards further up. To avoid the camera, stay off the path all the way."

David and Malcolm exited the car as directed and rolled down a slight heather-covered embankment. Immediately onto their feet, they raced through the copse of silver birch trees that lined the stream on either side.

Laura drew the car to a halt behind a large white van. She guessed that it was the one that had transported her daughter. She was elated to see that there was a fresh set of wheel tracks through the lawn grass that led directly over to the garden shed. No prizes for guessing where Sharon-Louise might be. She hoped that the others would see it as well.

Reaching over the back seat, she retrieved the carrier bag containing the two bottles of Bushmill's whiskey, bought as a peace offering for Shaun. She was about to pick up the other bag as well, but at the last minute, another idea came to mind, and she decided to leave it in situ.

A glance at her watch confirmed that four minutes had already elapsed since she had entered the gate. Shaun emerged from the bungalow and saw her, a sub-machinegun hung from his shoulder. She smiled and waved in his direction.

"Lara. It's good to see you, again."

She walked toward him, shocked at his dishevelled state, and how much weight he appeared to have lost in the past week. His face was now pale and thin, his eyes red-rimmed, and tired looking. He was filthy dirty and carried himself in an uncharacteristic hunched-over position that obviously favoured his injured ribs.

"Shaun. How are you today? How're the ribs?"

"Bloody awful Lara. I don't think they're healing properly, at all."

"You're probably overdoing it you great lummox. Come on, let's get you back inside, I'll take another look and get you strapped up again. Here, a little present to help dull the pain . . ."

Shaun removed a bottle from the bag and quickly unscrewed the cap. He drank deeply straight from the bottle, some of the precious contents finding its way out of the corners of his mouth. Pausing only to wipe the back of his hand across his bearded chin, he quaffed at the bottle again. Half the content of the bottle was gone already.

"Aah, that feels so good, woman. You certainly know how to gladden a poor man's heart, to be sure."

Laura laughed, and moved forward to link arms to walk him back inside the bungalow.

"Now what's this little surprise you've got for me then, Shaun? Something that Lloyd wants badly you said."

"The woman. I've got her locked in the shed. I'm thinking we can do a deal for her safe return in exchange for the rest of your stuff, Lara. There's still a way for us to come up out of this mess, smelling of roses."

"Sharon? Is she all right? You haven't hurt her . . . ?

Shaun's eyes narrowed. This unexpected display of concern for the bitch's welfare was touching, but why?

"She's okay. A bit tied up at the moment, that's all. Why the concern?"

"Concern? No, I was just thinking that if we're going to be handing her back, she should be unharmed, that's all. Come on now, get that jacket and shirt off while I see if there's any more clean dressings in the first aid box. If not, I've brought a few things with me in the car."

Laura moved through to the office while Shaun went into the lounge. She wrinkled her nose at the stench of the place, and wondered what Michael and Dermot would've thought if they could have seen their once beautiful home reduced to a stinking tip. She felt the need to use the toilet again, but one look inside was enough to convince her that she was able to wait a little longer.

The office was piled high with the boxes of arms and ammunition stacked haphazardly. Laura glanced round to see where Shaun was, and reached over to the cupboard containing the fuse boxes. It was open, but the ammunition boxes stacked in front, prevented her from gaining access to the inside. One quick look was enough, there was absolutely no way she was going to be able to get in that way.

"I'm just going out to the car to fetch a few things in Shaun. I won't be a minute . . ."

Laura hurried round to the back of the bungalow. She prayed that the outside box containing the Fireman's Switch would be accessible. It was, and she turned the knob that cut off all power from the generator to the bungalow. She moved out into the open, and removed her hat from her head, stuffing it in her pocket. Walking to the car, she pointed at the shed as she moved. Retrieving the other carrier bag from the back, she walked back toward the bungalow, once again pointing at the shed.

"That's it Malcolm. She's done it, and she pointed to the shed. Sharon must be in there."

David hit the call button on his phone, already dialled up to Ferguson's number. He let it ring once and then immediately killed the call. His watch told him that it had been nearly eight minutes since they had entered the south gate, and so far, everything was going to plan.

From their position in the bushes, on slightly raised ground, they had a panoramic view over the whole area. The bungalow partially obscured the near left corner of the lake, but he could clearly see the whole cliff, the bird hide, and the footpath leading up to it, at the far end of the lake. There were two men awkwardly trying to manhandle a wheeled trolley up the steep path. He could see there were two boxes awaiting collection outside of the hide.

His attention was drawn to a disturbance around something floating on the surface of the water. From his present position, it looked very much like a body, but the distance was too great to be sure.

He surveyed the terrain, noting that there was plenty of natural cover around the perimeter of the lake, but anyone up at the hide would have the advantage of looking down from the high ground. Not good from a tactical point of view. He knew that the TSG were coming into unknown territory, and decided that it might be advantageous if they were met, and briefed, before they tried to move in.

David estimated that it would probably take the TSG another ten or twelve minutes to get themselves properly organised into offensive positions around the property. He whispered his thoughts to Malcolm as they formulated their next moves.

Up at the hide, work was progressing well. John now had six men at his disposal and he had already detailed Kevin and Danny onto shifting the heavy boxes of arms down to Shaun at the bungalow. This gave the two guys that had been doing it, Liam and Davey, a chance to rest up, and take it a little easier for a while.

The three relatively heavy boxes of machineguns were out, the first two having already been manhandled and carried down to Shaun. Now, with the aid of some wheels, John hoped to speed things up a little. He was already resigned to the fact that, with the daylight going, they were going to have to call a halt very soon. The prospect of having to spend yet another night in Shaun's company, and the shit-hole he was living in, didn't excite him at all.

The next layer comprised four identical boxes, all slightly longer than anything previously removed. Bill, working down in the hole, hefted the end of one to test the weight. He shouted up to John that it felt a bit lighter, but that its length, and the absence of proper lifting handles, would make it slightly more awkward to manoeuvre out of the hole. After some discussion it was decided that they should first try and remove the centre two boxes from the layer. Bill clambered up on top of the stack and by kneeling first on one, then the other, he managed to move them slightly apart. Next came the tricky part. Bill needed to lift the end of a box one handed, and with his other hand, pass a slip loop of rope over the end that was nearest to the hole. With the limited space available, it was something he had to achieve alone, for there was insufficient room for anyone else to be able to help. It was during this delicate part of the operation that the lead-light suddenly went out . . .

With the aid of the broken hacksaw blade, Sharon had finally managed to cut herself free of the sack.

Out of the dire necessity to relieve herself, the first thing she did was to pee in the furthest corner of the shed. She spent the next few minutes doing some vigorous stretching exercises to ease her cramped muscles and get herself back into shape.

Now, feeling quite a lot better, she was taking stock of the contents of the shed. The only light was from a small wire-covered transom window, mounted high over the workbench. Kneeling on the bench and peering through the dirty glass, she could see a bungalow about thirty yards away, but little else. The window was far too narrow for her to crawl through, even if she managed to remove the wire mesh. The only way out was via the door, which she knew was securely wedged on the outside.

She was thinking that she needed something to use as a weapon. All along one wall there were various boat bits. A pair of oars, a boat hook, some anchor warp, fenders, a pair of rowlocks, but nothing that looked remotely suitable. A drawer under the bench contained a few files and chisels, an old plane and an electric drill. Her best find so far was a carpenter's claw hammer, which she placed readily to hand on top of the bench. In the opposite corner to where she had relieved herself, there was a selection of gardening tools. Best of the bunch was a small garden prong, and that too went onto the bench top.

Her plan of action was simple. The next man to come through that door would find himself impaled on the business end of the garden fork. The hammer was there for backup. Immediately the door was clear, she would take her chances and make a run for it. As far as she could see, there was no other option.

David watched as Malcolm ducked back out of sight of anyone in the bungalow, and crossed back over to the other side of the drive. They had agreed that he should make his way back to the stream and come up on the blind side of the shed, to try and make an approach. As soon as he was out of sight, David made his way back, hoping to make a rendezvous with the TSG.

Malcolm, his heart in his mouth, moved swiftly along through the bushes. He took some comfort from having the pistol clutched tightly in his left hand, and his shotgun in his right. He reached a point that he judged would put the shed between him and the bungalow, and crept forward on his stomach to the edge of the bushes, to recce his position. He estimated a distance of twenty metres over open ground to the shed. To his left, he could see the cliff escarpment and realised that in order to cover the open ground, he would be in clear view of anyone that happened to look in his direction. The two men were still struggling to pull the ungainly trolley up the narrow path, and were facing in his direction. They were the obvious danger at the moment. He'd have to wait until they'd completed their climb before making any move.

Laura handed Shaun a Cornish pasty that she'd bought in the supermarket. He wolfed it down as she unwound the soiled bandages from his torso. She wrinkled her nose at his unwashed body, he stank like a polecat.

Naked to the waist, his injury showed no sign of any improvement; the whole of his left ribcage was still an angry mass of black, blue and yellow bruising. Her gently probing fingers detected that there was still a lot of movement in his broken ribs. He hissed at the pain of her touch, but said nothing.

"Shaun, you need proper hospital treatment, man. These are serious injuries that need professional attention. If you're not careful, you may end up with a punctured lung."

"Tomorrow, woman. Hopefully, we'll be on our way out of here by then. So just get on and strap me up for the time being, will you."

She tried to make small talk as she worked, but soon realised that his mind was elsewhere, so she lapsed into silence.

"Michael? Lara. What did you do with Michael?" He suddenly asked.

"I pulled into a pub on the way to Abergavenny. From there, I phoned for an ambulance, and left him in the car park to be found."

"Is the old bastard still alive? Where is he now?"

"I don't know, Shaun. I haven't made any enquiry to try and find out. I would hope that he makes a full recovery. Michael is such a lovely man, a gentleman. He didn't deserve what you did to him. He will probably be wondering why Dermot hasn't been in to see him yet."

"Dermot won't be seeing anyone anymore, Lara. He's out there, floating on the lake. The bastard is haunting me, he won't go away."

"Did you really need to kill him, Shaun? Dermot was of no real threat to a man like you, was he? I'm beginning to wonder where it will all end. Are you perhaps planning to kill me, as well?"

"It was him or me, Lara. He would've killed me if he could. As for you, well, you've crossed me once, Lara, but I understood your reasons. I'll give it to you straight, shall I? You won't get away with it again, woman, even though I've always had a soft spot for you. So think on before trying to do anything like that again."

Laura's blood ran cold. If he were to find out her real reason for coming back . . .

"And what about the woman out in the shed then, Shaun? How are we going to do a deal with Lloyd if you're planning to head back over to Tiptree tomorrow? I don't think it's a good idea to take her with us in the car, besides there's probably not going to be enough room."

"The car isn't big enough to take everything from here, anyway. I'm hoping to persuade John into putting some of it into storage for us."

"For which you're going to have to pay him. Shaun. You're not thinking, man. Why not just leave the stuff where it is? It couldn't be safer, could it? This place is like Fort Knox, what with all the alarm systems. Why bother moving it at all? Apart from a couple of guns to replace ours, we don't actually need any of it, do we? What is this obsession with you, in wanting to shift it all of a sudden? We don't need the money if we can do a deal for the woman. So just sell off a few guns to pay John what he's owed, and then we can bury this whole sorry mess, and try to get back to some semblance of normality, can't we? "

Shaun lapsed into silence. The idea simply hadn't occurred to him. He had been so determined to see everything dug out and brought down, that he had completely overlooked what exactly he was going to do with it all. Lara was right of course, the only real problem, as far as he could see, was finding someone trustworthy to be around and keep an eye on the place. That would need a bit of thought. On reflection, it wouldn't be too much of a job to put the big stone back over the hole and cement it all back into place. If he just took what was already out, and a sample of everything he intended to sell, the rest could stay in situ until he found a suitable buyer. The more he thought about it, the better it seemed.

Lara secured the strapping into place with a few strips of sticking plaster and stood away from him. He slowly lowered his arms. Feeling a lot more comfortable, he murmured his thanks as he shrugged back into his filthy shirt and jacket.

She could see that he was mulling things over, and decided to leave him to it for a few minutes. Walking out into the kitchen, she started to clear away some of the mess to enable her to make some tea.

Shaun reached a decision. He fished his phone out of his jacket pocket and called John.

Up in the bird hide, with everything plunged into darkness, they were still busily trying to hoist the first of the longer boxes out of the cave, by touch and feel, alone. With Bill down in the hole, steering the bottom, Liam and Gus on the block and tackle, and John holding on to Andy's legs as he guided the top of the box, the last thing that was needed was any unnecessary interruptions.

There was an audible groan from everyone when John's mobile gave out its shrill ring. Everyone stopped what they were doing while John took the call. He looked at the caller ID.

"It's bloody Shaun again. What does he want now, fer Chrissakes?"

He hit the receive button and put the phone to his ear.

"Yes, Shaun." He deliberately tried to make it sound as though he was a bit peeved.

"John, sorry to interrupt you again, but Lara and I have been having a bit of a re-think on what we're doing. Lara has suggested that it might be better if we leave the rest of the boxes where they are for the time being, just until we find a buyer. What do you think?"

John, phone to his ear, moved over to the hide observation window, and looked down toward the bungalow.

"I seem to remember suggesting exactly that, to you, yesterday, but you took exception to it, and threatened me with a gun, told me not to mess with you, remember?"

"Yeh, well, I'm sorry for that John. Perhaps I misunderstood exactly what you were getting at?"

Some movement caught John's attention. Down by the shed, a man appeared to be about to open the door. A quick glance out of the door of the hide established that it was neither Kevin nor Danny, so who . . . ?

"Shaun, shut it for a minute, this is important. I'm watching some bloke who's just about to open the door of your shed. He's not one of mine, so who is he?"

Shaun let out with a single loud expletive that was clearly heard by Laura in the kitchen. He dropped his phone, grabbed the machine gun from where it was lying on the couch, and headed for the front door. Laura was just in time to see him disappear outside. With a feeling of dread, she chased after him, pausing only to grab one of the two pistols, lying side by side on the dining table.

Malcolm saw that the two men, Kevin and Danny, were now out of sight on the far side of the bird hide. Now was the opportunity he had been waiting for. He sprinted from his hiding place to the blind side of the shed. A quick glance round the door end was enough to see that it was barricaded shut with three props and a wooden wedge jammed under the bottom of the door. To remove them would put him in full view of anyone coming out of the bungalow, and anyone looking down from the cliff. It was a chance he was going to have to take.

He had to assume that Sharon, if she were inside, would probably be bound and gagged. He would need to untie her, and might even have to carry her? Tucking the heavy pistol into the back of his belt, and leaving his shotgun on the ground, he made his move.

Kicking aside the three props and throwing them aside, he squatted down onto his haunches and removed the wedge. The door was now free to open. He whispered, "Sharon," and was just about to stand up when the door flew open and hit him full in the face, knocking him off balance. He caught the fleeting glimpse of a garden fork heading in the direction of his head, and instinctively rolled to one side. The prongs buried themselves in the ground inches from his face.

"Sharon, no, it's me, love."

"Malcolm? Oh, thank God."

She was on her knees beside him lifting his head, anxiously holding his face and kissing his lips.

"Are you alright, talk to me, Malcolm. My God, I nearly killed you."

"Jesus, lady. If that's how you're going to say hello, we're seriously going to have come up with something else."

Out of the corner of his eye, Malcolm caught sight of Shaun emerging from the bungalow, gun in hand. He was behind Sharon, so she was totally unaware of his presence. In one continuous movement, Malcolm rolled away from her, and up onto his feet. He grabbed both her wrists and bodily dragged her behind the shed out of Shaun's view.

Shaun brought the gun up and fired a 'tap'—three rounds that stitched diagonally across the open shed door, splintering the wood and piercing through the corrugated iron panel. Moving forward to a better position, he fired another, this time through the open door and out through the far side of the shed where he anticipated Malcolm and Sharon would be standing. Fortunately, they were flat on the ground.

Laura saw what was happening and screamed at the top of her voice.

"Shaun, no . . . Stop, leave her . . ."

The pistol in her hand automatically came up, and she squeezed the trigger as it lined up on him. The first round narrowly missed his head. Shaun felt the wind of it pass in front of his eyes. Snarling in anger, he did a quarter turn to face her, and brought his own weapon round to bear. Firing from the hip, he sent another tap in her direction. Lara fired a second, more accurate round, simultaneously.

From his position in the trees, David had seen the situation suddenly turn nasty. Without hesitation, he stood up and walked forward, the pistol held in the classic two-handed grip, at arms length in front. He estimated a distance of forty yards to his target. To guarantee any accuracy with a weapon he hadn't used for eight years, he preferred to be a bit closer. He shouted his warning as he moved forward.

"Riley, drop your weapon now, or I will fire."

His warning fell onto deaf ears, the noise of the machine gun being fired at Laura, and her return shot came at the same time as his shout. David started firing at Shaun, as did several other members of the Police TSG, who had now identified him as their primary target.

Shaun Riley died in a hail of gunfire that only ceased after his already lifeless, twitching body, hit the ground. In the silence that followed, everyone waited to see what would happen next.

Laura was under no illusions. She knew that she had been mortally wounded. Shaun's first round had smashed the bones in her left ankle. The second had hit her in the groin severing the femoral artery. The third had passed completely through her right lung and exited out of her back leaving a gaping hole.

As she went down, she'd had the satisfaction of seeing her own round hit him high on the left side of his chest. She sincerely hoped that it had passed into his cold bloody heart. Her only wish now was to see her daughter, one last time, and to say her goodbye. She could already feel the edges of darkness beginning to enfold her.

A loudhailer made the expected announcement.

"This is the Police. We are armed, and you are surrounded. You men in the building up on the cliff. You will throw down your arms, raise your hands and walk out, one at a time, to where we can see you. Do it now, or we will open fire on you. You have five seconds to begin complying with this order."

David, Malcolm and Sharon all threw aside their guns and lay motionless on the ground. Malcolm whispered an explanation of what had been agreed and was occurring, to Sharon.

Up in the hide, everything had stopped. With the exception of Bill, who was still stuck down in the cave, they had all witnessed Shaun being shot to death. John knew the game was up, and he was making one last phone call to his wife to tell her. The others immediately started to move out, as directed.

David, anxious for Laura, started shouting.

"Ferguson, can you hear me, Ferguson . . ."

"We hear you Mr Morrison-Lloyd. What is it?"

"We have a man down here, Ferguson, one of ours. We need to attend to her. I'm asking permission for Dr Blackmore and me, to get up and go to see to her, please?"

"Go ahead, David, but at the first sign of any trouble you are to take cover."

"Understood. I'm getting to my feet now. Malcolm where are you?"

"Right behind you with Sharon, we're coming too, David."

They all rushed to Laura's side and Malcolm made a quick assessment. He looked pointedly at David and shook his head imperceptibly. Sharon stood back in confusion. She couldn't understand why the two men that now figured most prominently in her life, were paying so much attention to this damned woman?

"Malcolm, David, this is Laura Dobson, the bitch that hurt me, the one who broke my fingers. She's the cause of all this. I don't understand why you're . . ."

David didn't look up. He was holding Laura's hand and looking into her eyes to see that she understood what he was saying. She met his gaze as he spoke.

"You don't understand Sharon-Louise. When this is all over, I will explain everything to you. I promise."

David saw a look of understanding, and gratitude, come into Laura's eyes. She turned her face to Malcolm and started to try to talk. Taking her other hand, he bent closer to catch what she was trying to say. She squeezed his hand in the effort it took to get her words out. It was to be the last thing she would ever say, her dying wish, was how Malcolm interpreted it.

"Take good care of her for me please, Malcolm. Tell her I'm sorry for everything . . ."

"Why did you just call me Sharon-Louise, David, I don't understand?"

From somewhere in the deepest recesses of Sharon's mind, the name had seemed somewhat familiar. It was a shock to hear it being used again. It evoked some long forgotten memory from her childhood . . .

"Later, Sharon-Louise, I'll explain it all later. This lady is . . ."

Malcolm cut him off.

"Dead, David. She's gone, I'm sorry . . ."

David gently lowered her hand, whispered something, and stood up. With his head bowed in obvious grief, he took Sharon-Louise by the hand, and silently led her away.

After carefully closing her now lifeless eyes, and covering her face over with her own jacket, Malcolm followed a few paces behind, as they made their way back towards the car. Each was alone with their individual thoughts.

Up in the cave, Bill, still down in the hole, was beginning to panic. He'd heard all the gunfire and the Police loudhailer, but he was trapped by the box jammed in the shaft. Unable to get out, he called for John to come and help him, but his pleas fell on deaf ears. John was already walking out with the others, hands on head, in surrender.

In the half-light of the cave, Bill heaved and pulled at the box, trying to move it, but it was to no avail.

Realising that he was getting nowhere, he stopped for a breather. In the confined space, he studied the problem. He concluded that the only thing to do would be to try and collapse the stack somehow. This would give him more room to manoeuvre the end of the offending box out of the way.

He stood with his back braced against that wall of the cave and placed his boot against the corner of another box in the second layer. He started to push and felt the box move slightly. He took a deep breath and tried again. The box moved six inches and he heard a distinct audible 'snick' from somewhere within the stack.

From that moment, Bill, and all the others, had six more seconds to live.

Back in 1974, when Michael and Dermot had been carefully repacking everything into smaller boxes ready to pack it all into the cave, they discussed the possibility of the arms cache being discovered, and falling into the wrong hands. To alleviate this eventuality, Michael had devised, and set, a simple booby-trap.

He'd taken one of the M26 fragmentation grenades, fused it, and wedged it into a box of No76 Special Incendiary grenades. A wire attached to the grenade pin, was fed out of a hole in the side of the box, and left dangling until all the other layers of boxes had been placed on top.

The whole bottom layer of the stack was comprised of the highly volatile phosphorus incendiary grenades.

Packed in batches of twelve, there were four heavily reinforced boxes, each containing ninety-six grenades. A total of three hundred and eighty-four in all.

The next layer was entirely comprised of the latest M26 fragmentation grenades. Similarly packed in batches of twelve, but being slightly smaller, there was a total of four hundred and eighty, less one.

The third layer was made up entirely of other oddments. Boxes of grenade fuses, six Lee Enfield L42 sniper rifles, together with telescopic sights, and several boxes of 7.62 ammunition. Then came four type 69 RPG launchers, together with some HE anti-tank grenade warheads.

The fourth layer was comprised entirely of similar RPG launchers, and dozens of grenade warheads.

Michael, after laying down this fourth layer in the stack, carefully brought the wire attached to the grenade, up the outside of the boxes, and he stapled it securely into place onto the top corner box of the fourth layer.

With everything covered in straw to hide it, only he and Dermot were aware of its existence. They would be the only ones able to disarm the device, thus enabling the safe removal of all the HE content of the cache. Their trap was set.

It was this fourth layer that John and the boys had been working on when the Police arrived.

The box stuck in the tunnel contained four RPG launchers, but Bill was totally unaware of this. In trying to collapse the stack, he had unknowingly triggered the booby-trap device, set by the brothers, thirty-six years previously.

It was all happening exactly as Michael and Dermot had foreseen and intended. The outward movement of the box had stretched the wire until it pulled the firing pin from the grenade. The released striking lever then automatically ignited the seven-second fuse.

In the milliseconds following the fragmentation grenade detonating in amongst the incendiary devices, they all combined together to produce one massively prolonged explosion.

In an instant, the temperature in the cave had reached a staggering two thousand two hundred degrees as the mixture of white phosphorus and benzene, came into contact with the air. It was more than enough to cause everything that contained any explosive content, to spontaneously detonate.

Bill was instantly blown to tiny pieces, and his body incinerated. No trace of him would ever be found.

Outside of the hide, where John and the other five were standing with their hands on their heads, awaiting further instructions from the TSG Commander, the blast incinerated them all. Their fragmented body parts being scattered to the four winds. Huge pieces of granite stone, the entire construction of the hide, was hurled high into the sky, and out, towards the unsuspecting TSG, still positioned in cover, on the other side of the lake. The shock wave from the blast lifted most of them from their feet and threw them backwards, further into the trees.

Plumes of burning phosphor rained down to burn clothing and flesh, and to start brush fires wherever it came to earth. The hail of boulders that followed, landed all around. They indiscriminately broke bones and caused many minor cuts and bruises amongst the hapless TSG.

Several boulders went crashing down through the roof of the bungalow. Another totally destroyed the shed in which Sharon-Louise had been imprisoned.

David, Malcolm and Sharon-Louise were furthest from the blast, but even they were blown over. They all managed to quickly scramble under the shelter of the truck as the debris from the blast began falling all around. A few seconds passed before those that could still hear anything, became aware of the sound of stone being cleaved apart, as if by some giant, unseen hand.

From the depths of the cave, the sudden extreme temperature, coupled with the force of the blast, had sent a series of fracture lines radiating deep into the cliff face, weakening the whole edifice. Eventually, gravity took over, and the structure could no longer support itself. In another instant, some ten thousand tons of stone became detached from the cliff face, to fall into the lake below.

From underneath the truck, with the last of the blast debris still falling, the three of them watched the unfolding spectacle.

The instant displacement of water, caused by ten thousand tons of stone, sent a plume of spray high into the air, and generated a mini tsunami. A ten-foot high wall of water swept out in all directions to engulf and swamp everything around the lake. It swept up the lawn to pick up the lifeless bodies of Shaun and Laura, smashing them headlong into the front of the bungalow, before slowly drawing them back again as the water receded.

Dermot's decomposing body was deposited far into the tree line, together with many of his beloved trout. Many of the fires that had been started by the burning phosphorus were thankfully extinguished, but several of the TSG found they were floundering in a tidal wave of water, that pushed them even further back into the trees.

The water wheel that powered the generator, was torn from its mounting, and sent rolling downstream, its progress hurried along by the many thousands of gallons of water, suddenly released from the collapsed dam. The contents of the lake were quickly draining down to a level some twenty feet lower than it was before the blast.

David, Malcolm and Sharon-Louise had the presence of mind to scramble out from under the truck, and up onto the flat bed just before the advancing wall of water sloshed its way underneath, but by this time the force of it was largely diminishing. They all had to grab hold of each other as they felt the truck begin to move, but after a few feet, it thankfully came to a halt again, two of its wheels now hung over the edge of the embankment leading down to the raging turbulence, that seconds earlier had been the gentle stream.

In the relative silence that followed, all that could be heard was the movement of numerous torrents and rivulets of water draining away to find their new levels. David was first to make a move. As soon as the water receded, he jumped down from the truck and called for Ferguson. A weak voice answered him from somewhere to his right. He fished out his phone and tossed it to Sharon-Louise who was standing looking totally bewildered.

"Make sure we have all the Emergency Services attending if you would please, Sharon-Louise. This place is called Bleanaway Quarry, and we're somewhere in Monmouthshire, I think? Just tell them there's been a big explosion, and that some people are hurt. Don't try to explain anything, otherwise they'll never let you get off the damned phone. Are you all okay with that, love? Malcolm and I will see what we can do for the others."

"I'm alright with it, yes, David. But why do you keep calling me Sharon-Louise, all of a sudden?"

"I'm sorry, but it will take a while for me to explain. If you would prefer that I just call you Sharon, it's not a problem, but Sharon-Louise is the name that appears on your Birth Certificate, your real name. Which do you prefer?"

Malcolm came quietly up behind her, and slipped his arms around her waist. He had been listening to what they were saying. Nuzzling affectionately at her neck, he whispered in her ear.

"I like Sharon-Louise, it suits you better."

"Sharon-Louise it is then. But where did you find my Birth Certificate, David? I wasn't even aware that I had one."

"Not now please, love. Malcolm and I have pressing work to do here. Just get on and make that call for me, if you please, and then come and find us. C'mon Malcolm, let's go find Ferguson first. This is his shindig after all's said and done."

They worked tirelessly until the arrival of all the emergency services. There had been only one serious casualty amongst the TSG. The Commander, Bob Taylor, had suffered a broken arm and collarbone after being hit by a large boulder, and after having been thrown against a tree by the blast. Several of the others had sustained nasty little cuts, bruises, and many had minor burns, but all things considered, with their body armour for protection, they all seemed to come out of it remarkably well.

As darkness fell, David told Ferguson that they were leaving in the Range Rover to return to Abergavenny. He explained that they needed to pick up Malcolm's car, and then they all had a long drive ahead of them if they were to get home. Ferguson was having none of it. He booked them into the four-star Angel Hotel, in Abergavenny, all expenses paid. He reminded them that they were owed a beer, and he was paying.

It was well past eight by the time they arrived at the hotel. Dirty, dishevelled and lacking luggage, the Hotel Receptionist looked dubiously at them, and verified the reservation before finally booking them in.

"One double room and one single." She intoned as she placed the two key cards on the counter and glanced up at the clock.

"I'm sorry, but you're a little too late for dinner, but I'm sure Chef will be able to put a tray together for each of you, should you so wish. Would you care to order something now?"

Malcolm looked at her disdainfully. Sharon-Louise sensed that he was about to explode, and stepped in.

"That's fine, thank you, miss. I would like two rounds of ham, lettuce and tomato on white granary bread with a pot of strong, freshly ground, Columbian coffee. Mr Blackmore will have . . ."

"Smoked salmon, or smoked cheese, on brown bread, two rounds, with four bottles of Newcastle Brown ale, and a bottle of a good single malt, with a carafe of iced soda water, please. David, what's yours?"

David smiled at Malcolm's order, but it sounded just the ticket.

"A generous ploughman's, and four bottles of Stella Artois, will do for me if Mr Blackmore will share some of his malt?"

It was Malcolm's turn to chuckle, his mood lightening, he nodded his assent and slapped David on the back in a gesture of friendship. The Receptionist scribbled down their order.

"Have it all served in our double room in an hour, if you please. We're all in need of a shower, first. Do you have a valet facility for our soiled clothing? Oh, and some suitable dressing gowns as well, please?"

"There will be no problem with any of that, Mr Blackmore. The dressing gowns will be sent up to your rooms, immediately. Please phone down to reception when you are ready to hand over your clothes. The Night Porter will see that they are all back with you before morning. If there is nothing more that I can do for you, your rooms are up on the first floor. Up the stairs behind, to the first landing, and turn left. Breakfast is served from seven till nine in the Dining Room. Enjoy your stay with us."

David languished under the hot shower. He was sitting cross-legged in the shower tray and wishing that the cascading water would somehow serve to wash away the horrors of the day. Laura's death had hit him hard. In their relatively short acquaintance, he had come to quite like, and respect her.

He recognised her commitment and dedication to the furtherance of her beliefs, and the resulting hardships she must have suffered in the days when the cell was active, and she lost touch with her child, Sharon-Louise. He tried to picture it happening to him, but couldn't even begin to imagine what it must have felt like.

There was also a degree of secret admiration for her cunning exploitation of people's stupid obsessions with regard to their animal's pedigree. Yes, what she did was totally illegal, but in the perpetration of her crimes, nobody really got hurt, did they? The only evidence of it all was contained in her computer and on the CD's he was in the process of returning before . . .

To protect Sharon-Louise, he resolved that they would all die with her, as would her file detailing all their past exploits. To hand it over to the Police now, would serve no useful purpose whatsoever.

The whereabouts of the computer served to jog his memory. Doris's funeral service was scheduled for tomorrow, and there was a lot to get through if they were all to attend. Sue would have to make her own way if she was going to come, so he needed to speak with her first. Then he needed to speak to Sharon-Louise. He owed her an explanation, and that, was going to take some time.

He reluctantly pulled himself to his feet and switched off the shower. After vigorously towelling himself dry, he donned the voluminous white towel robe supplied by the hotel and folded his soiled clothing before placing it all into a plastic bag provided for the purpose. A glance at his watch told him that it had been fifty minutes since their arrival, and he was feeling hungry. He made his call to Sue.

David padded barefoot along to the other room and knocked lightly on the door, which was immediately opened by Malcolm. He was similarly attired.

"Ah, there you are, David. I was just about to send out a search party for you. She's still in the bathroom trying to make herself look pretty again, I guess."

"I heard that, Doctor Blackmore. Are you looking to get your ears boxed, or something?" Shouted a voice from the en-suite.

"I'll settle for the 'or something.' Come on, lady. You've got two semi-naked men sitting on the beds out here, just waiting for you to join them. What on earth are you doing in there?"

"Pour the drinks and make a start, I'll be with you in a few more minutes. This hair dryer is about as much use as a chocolate fire-guard."

David flopped into the armchair and self-consciously pulled his dressing gown around his badly scarred legs in an effort to keep them covered. He sat awkwardly with his legs to one side, trying to keep the gown in place. Malcolm noticed his predicament.

"Here, sit yourself up on the other bed, David, you'll be more comfortable with your feet up. I imagine you've got rather a lot of explaining to do tonight, am I right?"

David moved up onto the bed, making a backrest for himself with the pillows. He replied to Malcolm's question as he worked.

"We've got a lot to talk about, Malcolm, a few decisions to make, and quite a lot of forward planning to do. Let's see where we are when I've brought Sharon-Louise up to speed a little. Now where's that food, I'm bloody starving. Stomach thinks throat's been cut."

Sharon came through to join them. She was a delight to behold. Her hair was burnished with the constant brushing, and it hung loose to her collar. She wore no make-up she didn't need it. Both men could both see that beneath the dressing gown, she was so obviously naked. The pale pink, ankle-length gown might have been made for her to pose in. Tied only at the waist, it fell apart as she walked to give tantalising glimpses of her legs and thighs. Her ample breasts seemed to be moving in rhythm to all her movements.

Seemingly unconcerned at how much of her body was on view, she sat herself down in the armchair just vacated by David, deliberately giving the boys another flash of thigh. She was well aware that both of her men were looking at her in obviously appreciation, and she was thoroughly enjoying the moment.

Drawing her dressing gown snugly around herself, she pulled her legs up to sit with them sideways, as only women can. She smiled knowingly and fondly at them both.

"You can both wind your eyeballs and tongues back in now, if you please, gentlemen. Before either of you gets any other bright ideas, all this little lady requires tonight, is a stiff drink, some food, a quite chat, and a good nights sleep, preferably in that order. Anything else you might have in mind is deemed to be strictly off limits."

"Do you mind, madam, I can't think what you might be suggesting. I'm happily married man, don't-you-know? I was just about to remark to my good friend here, how much that colour of your dressing gown, suits your fair complexion. Am I right, Malcolm?"

"Well said, sir. I agree entirely. And have you perhaps noticed how the fluorescent light catches the colour of her hair? It's really quite magnificent, wouldn't you say?

Sharon laughed heartily for the first time. Reaching over, she affectionately took Malcolm's hand into her own. She knew when she was beaten.

"Alright, I believe you, and I'm to assume that butter doesn't melt in either of your mouths, does it? C'mon you two, let's eat. Pass me a glass of something nice, please Malcolm."

As they ate, David started his narrative on Sharon-Louise's past. It was based on everything that Laura had told him in the car. They both listened, largely in silence, but with the occasional question on any point requiring clarification. David realised there was an awful lot of it that he had already forgotten, dates and other similar details, but he never envisaged having to do any of this. He wished that Laura could be there to do it herself.

His phone rang. David took the call and relayed the conversation to the others as he spoke.

It was Ferguson making his apologies for not being with them. He was apparently still at the scene as a large quantity of firearms and ammunition had been discovered in the bungalow. It all needed to be catalogued, labelled and made safe before removal. Floodlighting had been brought in, and he thought he might be there for the rest of the night.

He told them that Sergeant Ahmed Suffajji was the officer-in-charge of the crime scene, pending the arrival of his Senior Officers, to whom he is rather anxious to pass over the whole thing. He's rather keen to get back to his original enquiry, in regard to the missing call girls. He's just found out about the existence of Tiptree Farm, from paperwork found in Riley's pockets. Now, he wants to get over there with a forensic team, in the hope of locating remains of their bodies.

He's asked me to thank you all for your help, and to remind you that he will eventually need to take detailed statements. He went on to say that at the moment, they had no idea how many people had been killed by the blast, as there were only three bodies that were identifiable. Riley, Dobson and one other, who it appeared, might have already been dead for several days. All the rest were just fragments of charred body parts scattered over a wide area. There was even talk of having to drain the lake, a mammoth task even if it were deemed feasible. A fingertip search was being organised for the morning, but it might well take several days, even weeks, before they had any clearer picture. A lot of the identification would rely solely on DNA samples taken from bits of body found at the scene.

Ferguson recalled there were at least six other men that had emerged from the cave, and he asked David if he could help with the body count. Did he know how many people there were in the cave prior to the explosion? David replied that he didn't.

There was a slight pause in the conversation, and Malcolm took the opportunity to chip in, asking for the phone to be passed over to him.

"Charles, I'm Malcolm Blackmore. Look, if your lads come across a Holland and Holland twelve-gauge over-and-under shotgun, it's likely to be mine. I last had it by the shed just before we got Sharon-Louise out. I think that the big wave washed it away, so it might be downstream from there somewhere? It's got some sentimental value, as my late wife had it custom-made for me. Would you kindly make sure it doesn't get mixed up with everything else for me, please? I would very much appreciate its safe return."

"No problem Doctor Blackmore, I'll see to it personally."

Malcolm passed the phone back to David, a look of puzzlement on his face. He whispered to Sharon-Louise,

"He called me Doctor Blackmore. How did he know my profession, unless David told him?"

David was winding up the call, but he'd heard Malcolm's concern.

"Yes, okay then Charles, we'll all be down in Weymouth tomorrow to attend Doris Cox's funeral service and to have a poke around in Laura Dobson's house, as well. We'll be looking for her personal papers so that we can start to wind up her affairs and make her funeral arrangements. Yes, that's right, we will. Laura was Sharon-Louise's mother, but regrettably, we've only just found out. I've reason to believe that the house in Marlborough Avenue will probably be part of Sharon-Louise's inheritance, subject to the reading of Laura's will, of course. We'll be getting on to her Solicitor, Tony Williams, first thing in the morning, to get things moving. Can I use your name, should he need any verification of her death? Oh, that's great, thanks Charles.

Well, you know how to get hold of us, should you need. No, we're just having a chat over a drink. Yes, very comfortable thank you. Catch you later . . .

David killed the call and looked at Malcolm.

"Sharp cookie, our Charles Ferguson. Laura was convinced that he was working for some big-time arms dealer named, Alkassar, or something similar to that? But whoever he is, he certainly carries some clout where the Police are concerned. I've never let on to anyone about your profession Malcolm, what with the security issues. So Ferguson must have established it from elsewhere? I expect we'll find out eventually?"

Sharon-Louise had been patiently listening to their conversation, but there was a question she had been dying to ask.

"David, you mentioned something about an inheritance. What's all that about?

"Ah, I was wondering when we would get around to that one, love. Unless I am very much mistaken, I have reason to believe that you may be in for quite a pleasant shock. It would seem that your mother was quite a wealthy woman. From the conversations we had, I was given the impression that you were her next of kin, maybe even her sole living relative. I know for a fact that you are definitely mentioned in her Will, but to what extent, remains to be seen. You may have inherited, her place in Weymouth, a pig farm, an old quarry, some property in Ireland, and a hell of a lot of money, certainly a figure in excess of half a million pounds.

Sharon was speechless. With her hand over her open mouth, and her eyes wide in shock, her emotions were in turmoil. She didn't know whether to laugh or cry . . .

"A pig farm? What farm? Where is it? And what am I going to do with a pig farm? I don't know the first thing about pigs, except that they make good bacon. And as for the Quarry, I don't ever want to see it again . . . Oh, Malcolm, what am I going to do?"

"Let's not be counting all your chickens just yet, love. Wait and see exactly what you've inherited first, shall we? You might not know anything about pigs, but I've got a whole Estate Management Company who can move in and take over, almost at a moments notice. They will carry out an assessment. Believe me, if the business is any good, they will know almost immediately. If it isn't, they will handle the sale for you. The same goes for the Quarry. The land alone will at least have some considerable value. So you need have no worries on that score. David, tell me, how did you know about the money?"

"Remember me telling you last week that I might be getting my hands on a substantial amount of cash to help Sharon-Louise and Jim? Well, half a million pounds was what Laura was prepared to pay for the return of all her property contained in the black holdall. Minutes before we learned of Sharon-Louise having been kidnapped, I was in Weymouth with Laura, and we were just about to complete the deal. It was all hurriedly abandoned as soon as we learned of her plight. Laura has an account held by the Bank of Ireland. I have all the account details, but it is protected by security passwords, and Sue and I weren't able to gain access to get a balance. Tony Williams, her Solicitor, will be the man to find out for us. I will get my father-in-law, George, to speak with him tomorrow. They've been friends for years."

They all fell into a thoughtful silence. The enormity of it all was too much for everyone to comprehend. With the added complication of the Police involvement, it was going to take a lot of sorting out. It was Malcolm that broke the silence.

"Look David, with so much going on, we need to be able to talk to each other. I've been thinking that it might be a good idea for you and your family to come and stay with us at Oakwood for a week, or so.

The children are on their half-term break, and, like you with yours, I need to be spending some time with them. They'll have a whale of a time, I can assure you. My girls will see to that. What do you say?"

"Do you have enough room for all of us? I don't want to be putting you out in any way?

Sharon-Louise laughed, she was already warming to the idea.

"Enough room? My God, David, you should see Malcolm's place. He could easily turn it into a five-star country club, if he wanted to. There are acres of space, do please say yes."

"I will obviously need to speak with Sue first, but I don't see any real problem. I have a couple of taxi bookings for next week, but I think I can work those in all right? Are you sure Malcolm, the twins can be a bit boisterous at times? And we'll need to bring Sam as well. He and Emily will not be parted."

"We have dogs, horses, fishing, tennis, archery and a golf driving range. And if that's not enough, we can all go sailing out of Lymington, before I lay the boat up for the winter. The kids can help us with that, as well. They'll love it.

I can see that Sue and Sharon-Louise will be good company for each other for some shopping trips, and all the other girly things. As for you and me, we can either enjoy ourselves with the kids, or just chill out doing whatever you like. Sue won't have to worry herself with any household chores, the Carter's like to see to everything, and they love having a house full of people. You will be the first houseguests since Elizabeth died, so it's about time the old place got back to how it was. If it's going to be of any help, bring your in-laws as well, in fact, invite the whole family, we've plenty of rooms for them all, isn't that right, Sharon-Louise?"

Sharon was on her feet in excited anticipation.

"Oh yes, David, do please say you'll come. We both owe you so much already, and nobody knows more about all of this sorry mess than you do. I never really got to know Sue and the children when you had your weeks holiday with us in Weymouth, and I would love to see Sam again, I miss him so much."

"I think you'll find that Sam has changed his allegiance now Sharon-Louise. As I said, Emily and Sam are never apart. He sleeps at the foot of her bed, they eat together, play together and you should see them talking to each other, it's unbelievable. Okay, I'll ring Sue first thing tomorrow, and see what she says. I'll also speak to George regarding your inheritance details. I take it you're both coming with me to Weymouth tomorrow? I've got to get my car back, then you can have your Range Rover."

"My Range Rover? It's not mine, surely?"

"I rather think it is, love. There's also a fairly new Nissan Micra in the drive of the house in Marlborough Avenue. It's Laura's car, so that's probably going to be yours, as well. However, Malcolm was right to point out that we shouldn't be counting chickens just yet. But I would think by this time next week, you may find yourself to be a very wealthy young woman. Am I right Malcolm?"

"On the face of it, I would have to agree with David's assessment, Sharon-Louise. But let's take one day at a time."

He started to list things on his fingers.

"We've still got Doris's funeral to attend to, and now Laura's to organise. There's Jim still in hospital, we can't be ignoring his needs, can we? Then there's the insurance on the guesthouse to sort out, and the Police statements, all of which are handwritten, and that takes time. It all adds up to a whole mountain of bureaucratic paper to plod our way through.

I'm thinking that it might be better to put it all into the hands of David's father-in-law to sort out for us, always assuming that he will agree of course, David? He does have the advantage of quite a lot of prior knowledge of everything, so there will be no need to brief him, will there?

If he and his wife would like to join us at Oakwood for a few days, I will put my study at his disposal, to work from without interruption, and we will all be on hand to assist him with any of the details. It would seem to be an ideal arrangement. Will you ask him if he will act for us, please, David?"

"I will ask him in the morning. In the meantime, it's gone midnight and we've all had a long day, let's hit the sack. We can pick it up again over breakfast. I'll give you both a knock around seven-thirty, alright?"

Sleep wouldn't come easy for Sharon. So much had happened over the past five weeks that she found it all a bit difficult to fully comprehend. Quite apart from all the pain and discomfort she had been forced to endure arising out of the vicious assault, she was now being asked to believe that Laura Dobson was her mother, and that she did it to prevent Shaun Riley from raping and murdering her? If that was an example of her mother's maternal care and affection, well . . .

The next revelation, quite apart from discovering her true sexuality, was falling in love with Malcolm. Five weeks ago, she would never have dreamed of sharing a hotel room with any man, yet here she was wishing that he would wake up and come into her bed. Lying there naked, she smiled at her own wickedness, and listened to the rhythm of his breathing.

Sharon-Louise? It would take her a while to get used to being called that again. It had been no real surprise, for as soon as she heard it, she recalled something from way back in her childhood. Someone had used that name before, but try as she may, she couldn't remember whom, or where, it was?

Thinking about Laura brought about a whole host of differing emotions. She recalled their first meetings, while dog walking in Weymouth. That would have been while she was still in her teens.

If everything David had told her was true, then Laura had moved to Weymouth just to be near her. So why hadn't she declared herself? There had been twenty wasted years when they could truly have been mother and daughter.

"You stupid, stupid, bloody woman. Why didn't you tell me?"

She whispered to herself, while fighting back tears of regret mixed with anger. She recalled their rare moments of affection, when Laura had put her arms around her, or kissed her cheeks. Now, she realised that these were maternal endearments, but then, she wasn't to know, and she'd mistaken them for . . . whatever one calls that other sort of love? It was little wonder that Laura had seemingly gone cold on her when she wanted to take their relationship a step further. Now, she understood why.

The tears were flowing freely now, as she cried and sobbed silently into her pillow. The pent-up emotions were no longer under control. She pictured her mother's face as she lay dying, shot by that animal, Riley. She wished that she'd said goodbye, but hatred for what Laura had done to her, and ignorance as to who she really was, had dictated her own cold-hearted attitude, at her death.

Now, it was too late. Her mother was gone. She was never going to know what it would feel like to be loved, or to love, in that manner. It induced a sense of deep loneliness . . .

The remorse and self-recriminations continued until she was all cried out. Only then did sleep finally creep upon her, to ease her troubled mind.

Malcolm awoke to the dawn chorus. He glanced at the luminous dial of his old Rolex Submariner, and slipped quietly from between the sheets to pad over into the bathroom. The sound of his relieving himself caused Sharon-Louise to stir and open her eyes. She heard him wash his hands and brush his teeth. The bathroom light was extinguished, and he crept back towards his bed. She saw that he was naked. In the half—light of the dawn she caught a glimpse of his well-honed muscular body. She liked what she saw.

"I'm awake," She murmured.

"Good morning, lady. How are you feeling this beautiful morning? I've just had to scrub my teeth, my mouth felt like the bottom of a budgie cage. Damned whisky, it always does that to me. I should know better by now. Did you sleep well?"

"Not really, a bit fitful, too much on my mind, and this bed is not really to my liking."

"Mine's alright, what's wrong with yours?"

Sharon-Louise stretched out her hand to him across the gap between the beds, exposing a breast.

"I'm not sure, perhaps it needs a man to come over here and make a proper assessment. Would you care to volunteer your services, please, Mr Blackmore?"

Malcolm didn't need asking twice. They had an hour to kill before their scheduled knock from David. It was too good an opportunity to pass up.

David showered, shaved, and retrieved his freshly laundered shirt and underwear from the hallway where the Hall Porter had left them. He glanced along the corridor towards Malcolm and Sharon-Louise's room. Their clothes were still outside the door. It was seven-fifteen. He dressed and readied himself for breakfast.

At seven-thirty, on the dot, he left his room and went to knock up the other two. Their clothes were still outside of the door. He paused before knocking, he could hear giggling and laughter coming from inside.

He smiled to himself. 'No need to ask what you two have been up to,' he thought, 'well, good luck to you both, you deserve each other, and I'm not about to spoil it for you.'

He walked quietly away from the door and down to the Dining Room to breakfast alone. Twenty minutes later, David was halfway through his full English, when they came in, arm in arm, looking decidedly flushed and rather too full of each other. David stood, smiled, and wished them both a good morning. Malcolm, ever the gentleman, seated Sharon-Louise before taking his own, next to David.

"I thought you were going to give us a knock?" He whispered as he studied the menu.

"I didn't like to interrupt," He whispered back.

Malcolm looked at him and saw the knowing little smile on his face. He felt slightly embarrassed.

"Thanks mate, we kind of lost track of time for some reason? Sharon-Louise, my dear, what do you fancy?"

She hadn't missed the exchange between her two men and decided to join in.

"Right now, I'd like some breakfast, please Malcolm, but if you'd care to ask me again, after . . ."

It was enough to send all of them into a hearty chuckle.

"It's nice to see you two getting on so well, and I hate to be the one to spoil it by pointing out that we have a big day ahead of us. Look, I'm going to leave you to eat. I've a couple of phone calls to make if you remember. Is your offer still open Malcolm? No second thoughts on inviting my clan over to yours?"

"Of course not, David. You will all be made most welcome."

He left them to it, and went out into the morning sunshine.

# Chapter 8

Sue and her parents had readily accepted Malcolm's invitation to stay at Oakwood, but only after David had assured them that they would all be very comfortable, and listed the facilities available to amuse the children. George had very little work scheduled for that week, and nothing that couldn't just as easily be handled from Oakwood. He much appreciated being asked to represent all of Sharon-Louise's interests. David went on to explain to him that there is a file of papers lodged with Tony Williams that they were anxious to see, as it would prove who her parents were. According to her mother, the late Laura Dobson, Sharon-Louise is the name that is on her Birth Certificate, a document that she had never seen, and until yesterday, didn't even know existed.

David gave George the contact details for Charles Ferguson. He asked if he would pass on to Tony Williams the news of Laura Dobson's death. He added that Malcolm Blackmore and Sharon-Louise Cox, were going to be handling the funeral arrangements, just as soon as the Police released the body, but a death certificate would obviously be required first, so could he set about getting it organised, please.

He asked that a tentative enquiry be made regarding the content of Laura Dobson's Last Will and Testament. She had already mentioned to David, that Sharon-Louise was her main beneficiary. Depending on the content of the Will, David and Malcolm both thought there might be several matters regarding the Farm, the Quarry, and Laura's house, that may need addressing rather urgently? An open and frank discussion between Solicitors, who were old friends, might be the better way to handle things?

George was a bit sceptical, but he had agreed to give it a try.

Malcolm, passing telephone instructions to the Carters, to make Oakwood ready to receive more guests, was the main topic of conversation during the drive back down to Abergavenny. He told them to make sure that all the guest suites were made ready, and to move Miss Sharon-Louise's things from her suite, to the second bedroom in his own suite.

His next call was to Charlotte and Michelle, to outline his plans for the coming week. He left instruction that should any of his guests arrive in his absence, they were to receive and entertain them on his behalf.

He finished the call and smiled to the others.

"That'll give those two little madams something to think about. They've been getting ideas far above their station, just lately. It'll take something like this to make them buck up their ideas a little."

"They're teenagers Malcolm, young ladies, you can't expect them to act like adults. You're too hard on them. Give a little, they'll soon respond."

"And you're far too kind and understanding, Sharon-Louise. If they want to be treated like adults, which they do, then they've got to learn to act that way. I will not tolerate their childish tantrums and rudeness, and nor would their mother, if she were here. I am their father, and until they come of age, and even beyond that, I expect them to obey my wishes. It all comes down to a question of respect and discipline, both of which are entirely my responsibility. As their sole remaining parent, it is down to me, and me alone, to address the problem, and to see that it's put right.

As for now, let's just concentrate on getting through today, shall we? I can't see any of us getting back to Oakwood much before seven this evening, and that makes for a very long day.

Ah, there's my car now, David. Sharon-Louise, are you travelling with me in the Mini, or with David in this old jalopy?"

She thought for a few seconds.

"Would you mind if I travelled with David for a while, please Malcolm? I have a few more questions about my mother, that I would like to ask of him."

"Of course, I'll catch you up, David. Try not to lose me as we get into Weymouth, I don't know where we're going, remember."

"I'll stop on the A354 when we get on the outskirts of the town and let Sharon-Louise transfer back into your car. I expect I'll be fed up with her bending my ear by then, anyway."

Sharon-Louise cuffed him playfully round the head. "Beast!"

"And in the local news, mystery still surrounds the cause of a huge explosion that occurred yesterday afternoon in a remote abandoned quarry working, some twenty miles north of Abergavenny. Preliminary reports suggest that a number of people, believed to be caving enthusiasts, are missing, and may have been killed in the blast. A Police spokesman has told our correspondent that forensic officers are at the scene and that a further statement will be issued later. And finally, the weather today will be . . ."

David clicked off the radio.

"I suppose it was inevitable that we should expect some sort of spin would be put onto it. They can hardly let it be known that a bunch of IRA terrorists, with enough arms to start a small war, have been holed up there for the past thirty-odd years, can they? It would do little for public confidence in the Police efficiency stakes."

Sharon-Louise made no comment. David had noticed that she'd been unusually quiet up to now. He was rather grateful, as he needed to concentrate on getting out of Abergavenny, and on to the southbound A40. Now, with the driving easier, he checked his mirrors and saw that Malcolm's little red Mini was two cars behind. He took the speed up to a comfortable seventy, and engaged the cruise control.

"So come on then Sharon-Louise, what was it you wanted to ask of me?"

She thought for a bit before speaking.

"I couldn't help noticing that when Laura, my mother, was lying there shot and dying, that you . . ."

She sobbed and fumbled in her pocket for a tissue or handkerchief.

"Sorry, David. This is a bit difficult for me."

She was still looking for something to wipe her nose.

"It's alright love, I understand. That bag on the back seat was your mothers. See if there's something in there."

Sharon-Louise reached over and brought it forward on to her lap. She snapped it open and immediately found what she was looking for, a small pack of tissues. She took a few moments to compose herself while examining some of the other contents of the bag. In one of the side pockets, there were some old photos. They were all pictures of her, taken over the past twenty years. Each one evoked a memory and induced more upset for her. She couldn't help herself, the tears were flowing again.

David said nothing. He considered that it was probably better for her to express her grief in this simple manner, rather than to try and bottle it up. He, himself was no stranger to the kind of emotions that she was now experiencing. Laura's passing had filled him with similar remorse, but up until now, he had managed to remain stoical, and control his feelings, as a man should. The sight and sound of Sharon's grief was beginning to reduce him to the same level. He needed to do something positive before the situation got beyond his self-control.

"Do you want me to pull over and stop, Sharon-Louise? Perhaps if you were with Malcolm?"

His voice was tremulous, right on the very edge of breaking. She wiped her eyes, sniffed hard, and struggled to get her words out. The sentences were interspaced with sobs.

"I'm sorry, David, it's all been a bit too much for me. The sight of these pictures that she must have been carrying around with her for years? Why in God's name didn't she tell me she was my mother? All that time wasted. I can't help thinking that things could have been so much better."

"I can't answer you with any certainty, love, but she must have had her reasons. If it's of any consolation, your mother was aware of how happy you were when Jim and Doris adopted you. Perhaps that might have had some bearing on it? I can only imagine that she perhaps didn't want to complicate things any further for you."

"Did you like my mum, David? I seem to recall that it was only a month ago that you wouldn't have had a good word to say about her."

"Your mother and I have spent quite a bit of time in each others company since then Sharon-Louise. Shall we say that since I got to know her better, then yes, I came to quite like, and respect, her? She was a very tough lady, of that, there can be no argument. Sadly though, she seemed to have spent the majority of her life on the wrong side of the law. But in saying that, I have to confess to a secret admiration for her exploitation of people's stupidity, in regard to the pedigrees of their pets. She managed to make a fortune out of it without really physically hurting anyone. Sue and I have looked briefly into the extent of her puppy scams, and, you can believe me when I say it was astronomical. If you're interested, I'll show you one day, when this is all over."

"I'm not really interested, David. I'm ashamed for ever having been involved. I feel that I've let Jim and Doris down, betrayed their trust in me. Was my mother involved with the explosion at the guesthouse, do you think?"

"She assured me that she wasn't. Laura said that she quite liked Jim and Doris, and approved of their being your foster parents. She could see how happy you were with them. Your mother was even planning to come to today's service for Doris, to pay her last respects.

She told me that it was associates of Shaun Riley that caused the explosion. They were acting on his direct orders, without any consultation or approval, from any of the other members of their terrorist group. It was meant as an act of malicious retribution, perpetrated in an effort to force you into coming out of hiding. They were desperate to get the holdall and its contents back before it was handed over to the Police.

Think about it, Sharon-Louise, and you will realise that the loss of that holdall was an absolute disaster for them all. It put everything they had achieved in jeopardy. The Farm and its pig business, the Quarry and the tarmac business, all their identities and hundreds of thousands of pounds in bank accounts, not to mention the buried cache of arms. You were never meant to take that holdall when you escaped from Tiptree in the van. It was a dreadful mistake, an oversight, on your mother's part."

"You make it sound as though my escape was somehow orchestrated? I can assure you that it wasn't. I saw the opportunity to get away, and took it. They came after me as soon as they realised I was gone. Shaun Riley, and my mother, they both wanted me dead."

"I think you're wrong there, Sharon-Louise. Shaun Riley, yes, but not your mother. She was desperate to keep you out of his evil clutches."

"I don't understand. If that were true, why did she hurt me, smash my fingers, and then allow him to tie me up and shut me in that basket? It doesn't make any sense."

"Tied up, injured, kidnapped and imprisoned. None of it good, I'll grant you, but at least you were still alive, Sharon-Louise. But for your mother's intervention, Shaun Riley would have raped and strangled you, there and then, on her kitchen table. He planned to dispose of your body by dismembering it and feeding it to his pigs. Putting it bluntly, you would have been turned into pigswill. And if you think that sounds far fetched, let me assure you that he'd done it several times before. He was a psychopath. Rape and simultaneous murder by strangulation, it's how he preferred to take his women."

Sharon-Louise shuddered at the thought.

"But she smashed my fingers, David. Why do that to me?"

"Shaun Riley again. He was hiding in the larder when you first turned up at your mothers, and you told her about me. Unfortunately, he overheard everything that you said. As soon as you left to go and get the money I gave you for Sam, he told your mother that you were going to have to be 'seen to.' You're fate was in the balance from that moment on.

Your mother was thinking on her feet. She couldn't show any sign of weakness in front of Shaun, for fear that he would kill her as well. Obviously she had no wish to see you raped, and was desperately looked to find some way of preventing it. Knowing that Shaun liked his women to put up a fight, she pretended to go along with his plan, having already worked out that it would be less likely to happen, if you were rendered unconscious. With that in mind, she was looking for an easy way to knock you out. She didn't want to hit you around the head, the most obvious way, for fear of causing you serious injury. Nor did she wish to inflict upon you, anything permanent. It is fairly common knowledge that there are more nerve endings in the fingers and hands than in any other part of the human anatomy. That is why for centuries, the hands have been the main targets for torturers. Thumbscrews, nail pulling, burning of the palms, these are all excruciatingly painful, and will usually cause a person to faint in agony.

You will recall that your mother hit you twice with a rolling pin, a blunt instrument. Once on the fingers, but when that didn't achieve the desired affect, she had to hit you again on the beds of your fingernails. What she didn't expect was Riley, to smash your face down onto the tabletop. She had to watch your unconscious body slip to the floor, and then Riley putting his boot into your ribs.

Laura told me that hitting you, in that manner, caused her just as much pain as she knew she was inflicting. She was sick with worry, but couldn't show it. Her only daughter was lying badly injured on her kitchen floor, from injuries that she, herself, had helped to inflict, and she was unable to do anything to help her.

Think about it, Sharon-Louise. Put yourself in your mothers position, how would you have felt?"

She was unable to say anything, for there were more tears for her to cope with.

"As for your escape from Tiptree, Laura told me that when the basket was opened, she noticed that you were conscious, but pretending not to be so. Would that be right?"

"Yes, but how did she know?"

"Your shoes, apparently you had one on the wrong foot, and the cord that had tied your hands was sticking out from under your hips. Would that be correct?"

"I think so, but it's hard to remember, exactly."

"Well, she decided to give you the opportunity to get away by pretending to be fussing over the pups. She thought you would make a run for the woods, and escape that way. She didn't expect you to take the van, and that's where it all went wrong. The rest is history. Incidentally, did you try to run her over?"

"Yes, I drove the van straight at her, but I think she managed to jump aside at the last minute?"

"Yes, that's what she said happened. But was she was trying to speak to you? She said that she was she holding up her hands, and shouting at you to stop, just before the van hit her?"

"I think so, but I wasn't about to stop for her, was I? As far as I was concerned, she was my enemy."

"So you knew that she wanted you to stop, then?"

Sharon-Louise nodded.

"Well, it's too late now. She said that she was trying to tell you to stop, for her, so that you could both get away from Shaun Riley. But as you say, with murder in your heart for what she'd done, you weren't to know that."

There was a long silence as she thought about what she'd been told. Everything that David said was exactly as it had been, so the version of events could only have come from her mother. Rather reluctantly, she was going to have to accept the different interpretation being put on to what had actually occurred.

Believing that what her mother did was for her benefit was the most difficult part. Thinking back, Sharon-Louise remembered that she could just as easily have used the carving knife on her, instead of a rolling pin. She recalled that both had been on the kitchen table on that dreadful day. Did that give it some credence and justification? She nursed her bad hand. It had been more than a month now, and the pain was slowly subsiding. Malcolm was optimistic that she would regain full use of her fingers, and that her fingernails would eventually look normal, but it would take many months, even years. Her thoughts were interrupted.

"Of course, there is one good thing, perhaps two, arising out of this mess, isn't there, Sharon-Louise?"

"I can't think of anything, David. My mother is dead, Doris is dead, Jim is in hospital, I'm hurting, both mentally and physically, and you tell me there's something good. Where, for God's sake?"

"Well, you would never have met Malcolm, for one. And in the near future, you're very likely to find that you've suddenly become a rather wealthy young woman. Doesn't either of those prospects please you?"

"Malcolm, yes, but as for the money, no. I would still rather have my mother, and my home with Doris and Jim. They were everything to me, all I had. All the money in the world isn't going to bring them back, is it, David?"

"I think you've reached a crossroad in your life, Sharon-Louise. Your past has caught up, and you've just found out who you really are. The circumstances are somewhat tragic, I'll grant you, but you must try to be more positive, and move on from all of this. I felt much the same when I was nearly blown to pieces by a roadside bomb. Coming to terms with it was the hardest part, but I'm still here and I have a wonderful family to lean on occasionally. You have Malcolm, and me, if you like. So you're not alone. In fact, it's just occurred to me that you've probably got a whole host of relatives in Ireland as well? People related to your parents, that you didn't even know existed. Why not get a Solicitor on to tracing some of them? Better still, make a project of it for yourself. You could even get Malcolm's two girls to help. Call it a bridge building exercise. I'm sure they'd respond if you asked? I'm optimistic that we'll all know a lot more by the end of this week. So, chin-up, lady, dry those lovely eyes, you've a public to face today, and we need you to be looking your very best."

She dabbed at her eyes with a tissue and searched through her mothers bag for some make-up.

"I'm worried that I don't have anything proper to wear, David. I don't want to appear disrespectful to Doris's memory, I should at least be in something black."

"You're about the same height and build as your mother, except for a couple of rather obvious points. Perhaps you will find something of hers to get you by? While you and Malcolm have a look through her wardrobe and belongings, I'm going to call in at the Police Station to see if anything has been handed in from the B&B yet. They were advised about Doris's jewellery box. If the workmen have started shoring up the building, they may well have recovered it by now."

The rest of the journey was mostly taken up with small talk and explanations. David told her all about the cache of stolen arms, and related the stories told of her mother's involvement. He reiterated his, and Laura's suspicions regarding Ferguson not being completely straight, and again went over the uncompleted deal he had negotiated with Laura, with regard to the return of her property.

He outlined all the troubles that Shaun Riley's henchmen had put his family through while she had been in hospital. They spoke briefly about the amount of money that was owed for her treatment, and Doris's funeral arrangements. She was staggered at the enormity of it all, and promised to reimburse him as soon as her financial position became more apparent.

Just before pulling over to allow her to transfer into Malcolm's car, he gave her his final thought.

"If it's alright with you, Sharon-Louise, I intend to take possession of Laura's computer, and all her personal files. I'll keep them somewhere safe. I'm getting the distinct feeling that all this isn't quite dead yet. There are still two, possibly three, members of the original gang of terrorists that are unaccounted for. I doubt that they will be giving us any trouble, but it's good to have some insurance, just in case. I see little point in pursuing them in the name of justice. It will achieve nothing except for an enormously expensive trial, and a few pensioners being committed to prison for the rest of their life."

"Of course, David, you must do what you think is right. Up until now, I hadn't realised just how much trouble and inconvenience you and your family had been put to. In the circumstances, sorry, doesn't sound adequate enough for me to express myself. You can be sure that I intend to do everything I can to make it up to you, and that's a promise . . ."

The late afternoon drive out of Weymouth in slow moving traffic gave David plenty of time to reflect on the day's events. He concluded that it had all gone very well, all things considered.

Doris's jewellery box and contents were there to be collected, but they had to be claimed by the next of kin. David produced adequate identification, and tried to explain to the Station Officer that Jim Cox, her husband, was in still in hospital and that he was acting on his behalf, but the man on the desk was not having it. He would need to see a letter of authorisation to that effect. David left the Police Station less than happy.

He called round at Marlborough Avenue to give them the news, and to get his car back. He found Sharon-Louise and Malcolm enjoying a pot of coffee, while busily poring through the contents of the bureau and filing cabinet in Laura's lounge. Her meticulous filing system made everything easy for them. Malcolm decided that the best thing to do would be to load the complete cabinet into the Range Rover, and take it all back to Oakwood, for George to look at.

Sharon-Louise disappeared upstairs to have a look through her mother's wardrobe. David poured himself a coffee, and gratefully sat down in the sumptuous old leather sofa to take in the surroundings. He noticed that there were several rather nice looking pieces of silver, porcelain, and china, in the corner display cabinet, and three paintings on the wall that deserved a closer look. He finished his coffee and dragged himself to his feet. After a minute or two, he gave a low whistle.

"Have you seen these, Malcolm?"

"What, the paintings? Nice, aren't they."

"Nice? They're bloody magnificent. This little one here, of the horses, is a Jack Butler Yeats. The other two landscapes are purportedly, by Paul Henry. If they're genuine, they're worth a small fortune."

Malcolm came over to join him, and started to take a closer look at the paintings. He found a small magnifying glass in the bureau, and looked again at the signatures.

"I'm not sure that I would know an original from a forgery, if it got up and bit my backside, David. My knowledge of art is limited to what I've seen on the Antiques Roadshow. But I would have to agree with you, these do look genuine, too good to be just decorative splodges."

David said nothing. He'd already turned his attention to the display cabinet, which was locked, so he couldn't actually touch anything.

"I'm no expert either Malcolm, but it doesn't take a genius to recognise quality, does it? Look at some of this silver. It's beautiful.

And those two pierced, creamy-white coloured dishes, with the shamrocks, they look like Belleek to me? My parents have something very similar. And look at those plates along the back, they're definitely Moorcroft, as is that little pair of pink-coloured vases with the fishes on. My God, there's another fortune in collectables in here.

I wouldn't mind betting that most of the silver is Irish, probably from the Dublin Assay Office? Apart from the Moorcroft pieces, there seems to be a bit of an Irish theme to all of this."

Sharon-Louise came back into the room. She had found for herself a rather nice fitting pair of black, slightly flared-bottom slacks, and a white, loose-fitting satin material blouse, trimmed in lace at the collar and cuffs. On her feet, she was wearing a very smart, comfortable, pair of half-healed, black suede, sling-back shoes. A loosely tied, black and white silk headscarf, completed the ensemble. With the careful application of a little make-up, she looked stunning. Giving them a little twirl, she could see that her men were clearly impressed and appreciative. It served to raise her spirits.

"Is there any more of that coffee left in the pot? If not, I'll put another on? What have you two boys been up to, then?"

"We've been admiring your mother's taste in *objets d'art.* Some of these things are quite magnificent, and probably quite valuable, Sharon-Louise. Laura certainly had very good taste."

"Hmm, her jewellery box reflects much the same thing. There are some lovely rings and earrings, and I found this little gold locket, with a picture inside. I was wondering if the picture could possibly be of my father?"

She undid the clasp, releasing the chain from around her neck, and Malcolm took it from her. He briefly studied the little photo with the magnifying glass.

"I would say there is little doubt on that score, love. You're the spitting image of the man depicted in this little photo. Same coloured hair, squinty green eyes, and a facial bone structure like Shrek's. Everything's definitely there. Come and take a look David, ugly looking bugger, wasn't he?"

They all collapsed into laughter as Malcolm ducked the roundhouse swing of the handbag aimed at his head, and the kicks aimed at his backside as she chased him around the room. He stopped suddenly, and caught her into his arms, before she could attempt another playful swing. With her arms pinned to her sides, he firmly planted a kiss onto her lips to silence her squeals of indignation, but it quickly melted into something a bit more passionate . . .

"I'd better go and make that coffee," chuckled David, feeling a bit superfluous. He left them to it.

The Service of Remembrance for Doris was very well attended. It was a warm sunny afternoon and the little Chapel was packed, a reflection of the popularity, and high esteem, in which the rest of the Weymouth community held the Cox's.

Soon after the start of the Service, there was a short interruption as Jim Cox himself, arrived. He was being escorted, and ready to be assisted, by two male nurses, flanking him on either side. Leaning heavily on two walking sticks, but otherwise unsupported, he managed to walk slowly into the Chapel.

With his head and hands swathed in bandages, he was not immediately recognised by anyone but Sharon-Louise. She was quickly out of her seat and ran up the aisle to greet him with a hug. Only then did the rest of the congregation realise who it was. They all came to their feet to give him a spontaneous round of sympathetic applause. David gave up his seat next to Sharon-Louise in favour of Jim. He moved to the back of the Chapel, where he found himself standing alongside Charles Ferguson. The two men nodded their greeting to each other as the service resumed.

David was beginning to feel a little uncomfortable. He had been on his feet for nearly twenty minutes, and his legs were beginning to ache. The atmosphere was stuffy and claustrophobic, and he could feel beads of sweat beginning to run down his face. He quietly slipped out of the Chapel, and thankfully found a nice cool seat on the shaded side of the building. Sensing another presence, he looked up to see Charles Ferguson was standing slightly behind him. David shuffled across the seat to make room, and indicated for him to sit.

"Too warm in there for me, Charlie, and my legs are giving me gyp, as well. Nice to see you, though, it's good of you to come. Thanks for that."

"Least I could do, pay my respects, that is . . ."

They sat in silence for a minute.

"David, I was hoping that you might be able to help me?"

"What, more than I already have, you mean?"

"Well yes. It goes without saying that we are very grateful for all your help up until now, but there are still a few loose ends that need tying. Incidentally, we've recovered a considerable amount of arms from the quarry site. They've all been positively identified as coming from a legitimate shipment, stolen in Holland back in the seventies, by people believed to have been members of the IRA."

"I know, Charles. Laura told me all about it."

"Did she give you the names of all those responsible, David? I should tell you that there is a substantial reward on offer for information leading to the recovery of the arms, and the apprehension of those responsible for the theft."

"Really, how much exactly?"

"Fifty thousand pounds. The owner of the shipment was Monzar al Kassar, a wealthy arms dealer. He put up the reward all those years ago. I'm pretty sure it would still be on offer, should the right information be forthcoming."

"And what is the right information that you seek, Charles?

"A detailed list of names of those responsible, of course."

"But surely, you know that already? You were about to list the stolen arms shipment when I spoke to you yesterday morning?"

"I have been after those guns for more than thirty years, David. Shaun Riley's name only cropped up in other enquiries, which you already know about. I'm guessing that the people that owned the quarry, what was their names . . . ?"

"Michael and Dermot Close."

"Yes, that's them, were they involved?

"They were. Would you like to know the whole story, Charles? If I tell you, can I claim the reward?"

"If the information proves to be correct, then I will put your name forward with a recommendation. That's the best I can offer, David."

They got up from their seat to stroll slowly around the perimeter of the little Chapel. David related the story given to him by Laura, in relation to the theft from the arms shipment. He detailed how it was planned and achieved, pausing only for Charles to verify that what he was being told, was a correct account.

He left nothing out, except for the identities of those responsible. The two men halted in front of the Chapel, and Charles took out his Police pocket book to record the names that were about to be given to him.

"Shaun Riley and Ryan Dobbs, were the two men initially put aboard to rob the freighter. Michael and Dermot Close were handling the fishing vessel, and they helped to offload the cargo of arms and transport it back to Lowestoft. The man waiting in the van to meet them, was Martyn McCue.

I believe that McCue now works out of Storemont as a PA to Martin McGuinness, the Deputy First Minister in the Irish Assembly. It's a fair assumption that the Minister probably has no knowledge of his assistant's previous involvement with any IRA terrorist activities. It would be an enormous embarrassment if it was proved that he did, don't you think?"

"Jesus Christ, David. This is a red hot potato. You must give me your solemn word not to say anything to anyone else, and that includes other Police Officers, as well. I'll shall need to take advice on this one at the highest level."

"Of course, Charles. But to finish my story, you're already aware that Shaun Riley, the Close brothers and Ryan Dobbs, are now dead. The late Laura Dobson, was also known as Lara Dobbs. She had two passports, one of them Irish. Laura or Lara, was Ryan Dobbs' wife. Sharon-Louise Dobbs, Roberts, Cox, or whatever name you know her by, is their daughter.

As far as I'm aware, the only man still alive, and directly responsible for perpetrating acts of terrorism in this country, is Martyn McCue. He, according to Laura, was the principal planner and strategist for their group. I'm given to believe it was he alone, that planned, and was responsible for, the bombing of The Houses of Parliament back in seventy-four. Laura told me that their group also did the Swiss Tavern, and the North Star bombings, as well. So, the people that were subsequently put up before the Courts were definitely there as a result of Police fabricated evidence."

"Christ, David. This cannot be allowed to get out. The repercussions would be enormously embarrassing for the Government, Police, and the whole Criminal Justice system. The press and media would have a field day. The Establishment, as we know it, would probably crumble into disarray. Who else knows about this?"

David decided to play the ace that had just magically appeared in his hand.

"Apart from you, me, and Martyn McCue, nobody, as far as I know, Charles. However, there is a file detailing everything. It is now back in my possession. It is the same one that I referred to, when you and Ahmed came to my father-in-laws, a few weeks ago. I've just managed to retrieve it again, and I shall be keeping hold of it, at least until I hear from you, that the information I have just given, is of some financial worth. Then we can burn it, together, if you like? I've been wondering what such a file would fetch, if I perhaps offered it to a Sunday newspaper?"

Charles Ferguson stopped writing, and looked him straight in the eye.

"You're getting into very dangerous territory there, David. I should tread very carefully if I were you. There are forces available, that work to sort out embarrassing problems such as this, and in the simplest way possible. You don't want to get on the wrong side of them, believe me."

"And are you part of those forces, Charles? Laura had her suspicions that you are not quite what you claim to be."

"She was very astute woman, David. Who I work for, and what exactly my job description entails, depends largely on what the situation demands, and how I see it. I am prepared to tell you that I answer only to the people that appointed me, and they are not governed by anyone else, except the Monarchy. If necessary, I have it within my power to enlist the resources of every Police force in the Country, as well as any of HM armed forces. They are all at my disposal, should I need to use them. In that respect, and purely for convenience sake, I carry the honorary ranks of Army Captain, and Detective Chief Inspector of Police, but both are meaningless. They only serve to put me in a recognisable position of authority within the Armed Services, and Police, rank structures.

That is about as much as I'm prepared to tell you, David, except that I'm definitely to be regarded as one of the good guys. Up until now, that was my assessment of you as well, so please don't spoil it for the sake of a few pounds, it's really not worth it. You will be well compensated for your troubles, I will see to that."

Their walk brought them back to the church entrance, and their conversation was effectively ended, as the congregation, headed by Sharon-Louise, Jim Cox, and Malcolm Blackmore, slowly made their way out of the Chapel. A private ambulance car slid silently to a halt behind David and Charles, and they stepped aside to allow Jim easier access. He glanced in their direction, and David saw a look of confused recognition come into his eyes when he saw Ferguson. He paused and stood erect to look straight at him. David thought that he was about to say something, but the moment passed, and Jim continued on his way to be helped into the car, closely attended and fussed over by Sharon-Louise.

People were standing around talking, and renewing old acquaintances, as is usual at such a gathering. Ferguson turned and whispered into David's ear.

"I would appreciate being properly introduced to the lady, please David. I need her assistance as well."

David waited while Sharon-Louise kissed her stepfather goodbye. She stood back and quite naturally linked arms with Malcolm. They came to stand alongside David, shaking hands with, and thanking all the people that were leaving after the Service. As the last ones bade their farewells, David saw the opportunity, he touched their arms, and they looked his way.

"Sharon-Louise, Malcolm, I don't believe that I have formally introduced you both to Detective Chief Inspector Charles Ferguson. He's the officer-in-charge of all the enquiries that are now taking place.

Charles, may I introduce Miss Sharon-Louise Cox, and Surgeon Lieutenant Malcolm Blackmore of the Royal Navy Medical Corps. Is that the right title, Malcolm?"

"It'll do David, it'll do nicely. Mr Ferguson, Charles, please to meet you properly, sir."

The two men firmly shook hands. Sharon-Louise offered her hand only to find that it was being kissed on the back. She was tickled pink.

"Miss Cox. It's a pleasure to meet you at last. I'm at your service, please call me Charlie, everyone does."

"Thank you Charlie, I'm Sharon-Louise."

"Yes. Look, I want to thank you all for the sterling work you did in assisting my men after the explosion yesterday. I'm pleased to report that apart from Inspector Bob Taylor, they're all back to work this morning. I don't need to ask if you are all okay, I can see that you are. But your kidnap experiences must surely have been quite frightening ordeals for you, Sharon-Louise?"

"They're not something I would care to repeat, Charles, and no doubt I will have a few nightmares. Apart from a couple of broken fingers, and a few bruises on my butt, I'm physically very well now, thank you."

David stifled a grin and chipped in.

"Charles, you mentioned that you needed Sharon-Louise's help with something. Would you care to elucidate?"

"Ah yes, thank you for reminding me, David. It's to do with Tiptree Farm. Armed with a warrant, a team of officers went in at dawn this morning, to carry out a full search of the premises. The investigation concerns the activities of the late Shaun Riley, who was strongly suspected of having murdered several call girls. We are looking particularly for any human remains that might be present following the disposal of their bodies."

Charlie referred to his notebook.

"Two men were found on the premises, Dennis Bailey and Michael O'Rourke. Both claimed to be stockmen in the employ of Shaun Riley. We would like to take both of these men into custody for questioning, but we have a problem, in as much as they are looking after some two thousand animals, mostly pigs, but there are a couple of goats, and forty-six chickens, to be exact. If we decide to detain these men, there will be nobody to see to the welfare of all the farm animals."

"I can see that, Mr Ferguson, but what has it to do with me?"

He again consulted his notebook.

"I talked with a solicitor this morning, Miss Cox, a Mr Anthony Williams, who acted for your mother. We had quite a long conversation regarding the circumstances of her death. My enquiries have established that your mother was the sole owner of Tiptree Farm. Shaun Riley was her tenant farmer. Following their deaths, and with all the animals to consider, I needed to know who is now responsible for the property.

Tony Williams told me that, he'd been in contact with another solicitor, a Mr George Lloyd, who acts for you. I think he's your father-in-law, isn't he, David?"

David nodded.

"The outcome of all this, Sharon-Louise, is that under the terms of your mother's Will, the Farm has been left to you. I am therefore seeking your permission to put some experienced people in to care for your animals. I'm not sure where we get them from, there must be some procedure in place to cover this eventuality, but if it can be arranged through you, it would considerably simplify things?"

"My animals? My farm? Malcolm, can you help me here, please?"

Malcolm was already making a call on his mobile. He turned and walked away while speaking for several minutes. The others looked on and waited patiently. He verified the full address of Tiptree Farm with Charlie, and then continued to give his instructions. Finally breaking off the call, he returned back to them.

"Right Charles, there will be a team of six people from my Estate Management Company arriving sometime early this evening. These will all be volunteers, gathered from around the Estate farms. They will be there to work with the Police, and to assess what needs to be done with regard to the animals. There will be three experienced stockmen in their number. They will be completely self-sufficient, in three caravans that they will bring with them. I have instructed that they stay for as long as is deemed necessary for you to complete your work. Please ensure that your officers extend them every courtesy and consideration, otherwise, if there is any friction, I will withdraw them immediately, and you can make your own arrangements, is that clear?"

"Absolutely. Thank you Doctor Blackmore, and you too, Miss Cox, this is very much appreciated. I will immediately advise my Sergeant, Ahmed Suffajji, the officer-in-charge at the scene, of your arrangement. Thanks again."

"Now there's a little something you can do for us, Charlie."

"Name it, if it's within my power, then it's yours, David."

"Give the duty Sergeant at Weymouth Police Station a ring, and instruct him to release Doris Cox's jewellery box to me. I tried to get it this morning, but they said I would need a letter to confirm that I was acting on behalf of the next of kin. I don't have time to be messed about by some petty bureaucratic nonsense, Charlie."

"Well strictly speaking he was correct, David, but I understand your frustration. Leave it with me, I will endeavour to get the box, and bring it over to you later this week, if that's all right?"

"Okay by me, but I think you will find us all at Malcolm's address until next weekend. So you will need to clear it with him, first. Malcolm . . . ?"

"Fine Charles. We're all planning a week of winding down. So just let me know when you're coming and you can eat with us. Breakfast, lunch or dinner, it makes no odds. You can even stay the night at Oakwood if you wish to have a drink or two. How's your golf?"

"Not as good as I would like, unfortunately. Can I see how I'm fixed when I get back to my office and then come back to you? A day or two's rest and relaxation sounds just the ticket."

He glanced at his wristwatch as his car stopped a few yards away.

"Right, I've got to go. I'll bid you all a good afternoon, and I will definitely get back to you as soon as I'm in the office tomorrow morning, Malcolm."

"One last thing before you leave then, Charles. We intend to remove all the files and personal papers from Laura Dobson's house and take it back to Oakwood for the solicitors, George Lloyd and Tony Williams to refer to, in winding up her estate. There is also a considerable number of, what we believe to be, quite valuable pieces of *objets d'art* in the house, as well. As the house will be empty for the foreseeable future, we intend to remove and put them into storage for security reasons. Obviously, they are going to need careful handling and proper packing, so with Sharon-Louise's approval, it is my intention to get my Estate Management to attend to this, as well. Do you foresee any problems in that respect?"

"Not really, Malcolm. A courtesy call to Weymouth Police to put them in the picture, wouldn't go amiss, but if you do come up against anything untoward, then just refer them directly to me, okay?"

They stood and watched his car disappear into the distance, before walking arm-in-arm back to where David had parked his car. He dropped the others back round at Marlborough Avenue, leaving them to follow at their leisure. He guessed that they might want to be alone for a while?

Jim Cox sat quietly in the comfortable back seat of the private ambulance. The soothing effects of painkilling drugs was beginning to wear off now, and he was beginning to look forward to receiving his next dose of medication.

Despite the discomfort, he'd asked the driver if he would just drive him slowly past the Guesthouse, so that he could see for himself how it looked. The driver did better than that, he stopped the car, and allowed him a few minutes to get out and have a proper look. Standing on the pavement outside of the old place, it looked in a sorry state, with all the smoke-blackened brickwork, and windows boarded over, with scaffold erected to stabilise the structure of the building. It struck him as being poignantly quite sad, that the old Bide-a-wee Guest House sign, had become partially detached from the wall, and now hung by one screw at a drunken angle. He noticed that the Victorian leaded-glass panel, over the entrance, had somehow survived the explosion and managed to remain intact, although it was now blackened by smoke, and the colours of the glass were no longer discernable. The panel had been a particular favourite of Doris's, and she'd insisted on cleaning it every week. Even the lead itself had a polished sheen by the time she'd finished. She would be mortified if she could see it now.

He smiled at the memory of her standing on their rickety old wooden steps, while he held them steady for her. Reaching upwards would cause her dress to rise and expose a little of her thighs, an opportunity too good to for any normal, red-blooded man to miss . . .

They had been happy days, made all the better when Sharon had come into their lives. Childless, due to Doris having some womanly complication, that he had never quite understood, they had nearly reached their sixties, and had nearly given up on the fostering and adoption people. They were beginning to think that perhaps they might be considered too old to take on a child?

The unexpected placement of Sharon in their care, as a problem teenager, proved to be the best thing that ever happened for all of them. It took time, and patience, but they could see that she was responding to the respect and affection that they afforded her. Jim and Doris liked to think that in the first two formative years, they managed to turn her around completely. She eventually became the cherished and loving child that they'd always longed for.

It was always their intention that she should inherit the Guest House, but looking at it now, Jim wondered if it was really worth trying to resurrect it again? With Doris gone, living there would never be quite the same, somehow. The terrible memory of her death would always come back to haunt him. He shuddered as he recalled that dreadful night, flames all around their bed, and her lying dead beside him.

For him, it was definitely time to move on. He realised that the final decision on the Guest House would ultimately have to be his, but he would only make it after talking with Sharon. It needed to be based entirely on whatever she wanted to do.

"Mr Cox, if you're ready, sir. We really need to be making a move if we are to beat the rush hour traffic."

"Yes of course, lads. Sorry. I was daydreaming. Let's get away from here, there's nothing left for me now."

Back in the car, he was alone with his thoughts again. He remembered very little of the days following his rescue and admission to hospital. It was a period of intense pain and suffering, eased only by the powerful drugs that clouded his mind, as well as easing the pain. He was well aware that Doris was gone, taken from him, but the soporific drugs had the effect of making it all better. Under their influence, she was still there, alive in his thoughts and dreams, at least until the effects began to wane. Then, the reality of it all came back with a vengeance.

Solace and comfort was surely just another shot of morphine away? The dream world was preferable to that which was real. It had crossed his mind that this was how a drug addict must feel, when desperate for his next fix? Sinking ever deeper into the depths of pain and despair, longing to be rescued by another shot of the magic potion, was that how it is? If so, he could now empathise, whereas before, he would have scorned.

He shook himself free of his morbidity, for it did no good to dwell on such things. He tried to think more positively.

The service had gone very well, and all things considered, the Reverend had managed to give a surprisingly accurate précis of Doris's life. He wondered where he had gathered his information? Probably Sharon, but she seemed to know a surprising amount about their time before taking the Guest House? Clever girl, that one . . . Looks a bit different somehow? That new boyfriend's influence, I suppose? What was his name again? Malcolm, yes, that's it, Malcolm Blackmore. He seemed a nice enough bloke.

Something jogged in his memory. Jim quietly and carefully withdrew his medical file from the pocket in the back of the drivers seat. Putting on his glasses, he skipped through and ignored the technical gobbledegook, and turned to the last page that had been added.

Handwritten by the Consultant, Mr Gilbert Townsend, it detailed the circumstances of his release from hospital that morning. Even with his glasses, reading the writing in the moving car was a bit challenging, but he made out enough to see that he was to be transferred into private medical care. All future treatment was to be under the supervision of someone named Mr Malcolm Blackmore. Interesting . . .

He closed the file and slipped it back into the seat pocket. The male nurse in the passenger seat caught the movement out of the corner of his eye. He turned to Jim as he removed his glasses, and sat back in his seat.

"Alright, are we, Mr Cox? Are you comfortable, sir?"

"Medication's wearing a bit thin now, lads. How long before we're back at the hospital?"

"Probably a good hour before we get to our destination, sir. We can stop for a little shot of painkiller if it gets too much for you. Do you think you'll be able to manage for a while longer?"

"I'll give it a go, lads. Tell me, Mr Townsend said something about me being transferred to somewhere else this morning, but I didn't take it in properly, the old medication, you know? Anyway, where exactly are we going now? Is it back to the hospital, or is it somewhere else that you're taking me?"

"You're a very lucky man, Mr Cox. You're going into private medical care. We're taking you to a private clinic now. Its somewhere in Hampshire, near Winchester, a place called Oakwood. Neither of us has ever been there before, so we've first got to find it. We've got directions, but apparently, it's a bit off the beaten track?"

"Any idea who's going to be paying for this, lads? I can't afford private medical care, that's for sure?"

"That information is not available to the likes of us, Mr Cox. But rest assured, we wouldn't be taking you unless everything had been put into place beforehand. I suggest you sit back and just enjoy the ride, safe in the knowledge that tonight, you will be somewhere a whole lot better and more comfortable than Odstock."

Sharon-Louise followed Malcolm northbound up the A354. She was driving his Mini, he the Range Rover, loaded up with things from her mother's home. The evening light was fading into dusk, and they still had about another fifty miles to go. She was feeling tired and hungry. Neither of them had eaten anything significant since breakfast in the hotel that morning.

After David had left, they'd spent an energetic hour making the most of being alone in the empty house. She was not sure that her mother would have approved of the use they had made of her bed, but hoped that if she was up there watching, she would understand, and forgive them their moments of new found pleasure in each other?

The Service had gone quite well, she thought. The unexpected arrival of her stepfather had been a wonderful surprise, and the approbation of his presence by everyone in the congregation, had almost reduced her to tears again. The Reverend had grilled her for five or ten minutes immediately before the Service, to find enough information to put together something in regard to Doris's life. It had all come over rather well, in the end. She knew that Jim approved, as he had given her hand a little squeeze in gratitude during and after the address.

'She thought how frail he looked, but at least he was up, and walking unaided. It had to be regarded as a step in the right direction, surely?

She hadn't asked, but she suspected that his presence at the Service was in some way down to Malcolm's influence? Private ambulances are not conjured up from nowhere, and she thought it highly unlikely that the NHS would be footing the bill?

She had noticed that Jim seemed to have come to terms with, and now accepted that Doris was gone. His previous mental state had worried her a lot. Malcolm had told her that it could be down to the medication he was receiving, and it would seem that his assessment might be correct? She hoped so . . .

The next problem was going to be where he would go on release from hospital. She examined her options.

Laura's house was the obvious place, but she was not sure how Jim would feel about it. She couldn't just leave him there alone, he was certainly going to need some additional care before he was to be regarded as fit and well. She wondered if she would be able to cope with him herself, but didn't really relish the prospect, as it would seriously infringe upon her relationship with Malcolm. Was she being selfish in that respect? Well probably, but right at this moment, she was prepared to fight tooth and nail to hang on to her man . . . No, she would have to get him some private nursing help, or perhaps consider placing him into a retirement home with nursing facilities? She hated those types of places. 'God's waiting rooms' Jim and Doris had jokingly called them, when they themselves had visited old friends in that situation. 'Lonely old people being given the minimum amount of care necessary to see them through to the end of their mortal life.' And, 'Shut away, out of sight and out of mind, by uncaring relatives who frequently jib at the cost of such care.' Sharon-Louise could picture Doris saying it, even now.

The decision was made for her. There was no way that she would ever allow anything like that to happen to Jim. His care was her responsibility now, just as he and Doris had cared for her. At the earliest opportunity, she must talk it through with Malcolm to see if there was any sort of compromise that could be reached? If not, then their whole future together was going to be thrown into jeopardy.

She tried not to think about it any more, and glanced over into one of the roadside fields. It was filled with free-range pigs, and all their little shelters, or sties. It reminded her that she now owned some pigs, as well. Two thousand of them, Charlie had said. My God, that's an awful lot of bacon sandwiches . . .

She couldn't even picture in her mind what that many animals, all together in one place, even looked like? Perhaps it might be interesting to get over to Tiptree Farm, and have a look for herself? She would ask Malcolm what he thought.

She wondered about the logistical and financial implications of owning such a place.

What do pigs eat? Pigswill, she already knew about. She remembered the trucks coming to take away the leftovers from school dinners. But two thousand pigs would tuck away an awful lot of leftovers, what else did they eat? There must be some form of supplementary pellet food, or something? That in turn meant that there must be a feed bill associated with their keep, and then a wage bill for the stockmen that looked after them. Utility bills, Council tax, did farmers pay Council tax? She didn't know. What else was there? Farm maintenance, vehicles, veterinary inspections, they didn't come cheap, one dog was bad enough, let alone two thousand pigs, two goats and forty-odd chickens . . .

She sighed at the prospect. Did she really need all this worry and responsibility foisted onto her at this difficult time? No, she didn't. Perhaps Malcolm might be able to come up with some simple, quick solution?

Sharon-Louise realised just how much she was beginning to rely upon Malcolm for guidance and advice. She would need to be very careful in that respect. He might just get fed up with it all, and begin to regard her as a tiresome burden, being thrust into his already busy life schedule. If that were the case, might he decide to take steps to rid himself, accordingly? She hoped not, but it made her consider just how quickly things were moving along between them.

They'd known each other for only a month or so, and already, despite their tacit agreement to remain 'just good friends,' the relationship had already become full on, and intimate. She knew that the initial excitement and lust for each other would soon settle back into something slightly less physical, and more loving, especially if the girls, Charlotte and Michelle, were anywhere around.

It was only a couple of days ago that she'd heard Malcolm assuring the girls that there was nothing going on between them. Would he now want to correct himself, and admit to their intimate relationship? She thought it unlikely. She'd overheard him instructing the Carters to move her belongings into the second bedroom of his suite. Never having been in that part of the house, she had little idea of the layout, but even as she heard him, it crossed her mind that his daughters might not approve. They might perhaps accept that their father's changed domestic arrangements to be only a temporary measure, made in order to accommodate all the guests over the coming week? She fervently hoped that they would sensibly see it that way. She certainly had no wish to do anything that might give them cause for any further disagreement with their father.

She realised that there would be very little she could do in that respect. Malcolm had already made it abundantly clear that the discipline and upbringing of his daughters was entirely his responsibility, and effectively warned off any interference, but she saw it as an extremely delicate situation that needed more careful consideration on both sides. As to whether she should be getting involved? Well, only time would answer that one. She recognised the need to get 'on side' with the girls without giving the impression of acting like a parent, thereby compromising Malcolm's perception of sole parental responsibility.

It was a situation that, if handled wrong, could effectively drive a wedge between them. She spent the remainder of the journey mulling the problem over, and over . . .

Malcolm kept checking his rear view to make sure that Sharon-Louise was still behind as he negotiated the transfers from the A354 onto the A36, and almost immediately, onto the back lanes through the Deans towards Mottisfont. He glanced at his watch, it was nearly 8pm, and he too was tired and hungry. He decided to give the house a call and tell them all that they were only about ten minutes away. He imagined that they were perhaps waiting for their arrival before starting dinner? He dialled up the house number on Laura's phone, left in the car's hands-free cradle.

The phone rang twice before Carters familiar voice answered the call. Uncharacteristically, Malcolm sensed that he was chuckling as the receiver was lifted to his ear.

"Carter, are you alright, man?"

"Ah, Mr Malcolm, good evening, sir. Yes, I am perfectly well thank you, sir. Please forgive me, but I'm watching Mrs Carter receiving some . . . assistance, shall we say, from the children in setting out items on the sweet trolley."

The sound of the children's excited laughter could clearly be heard in the background. Mrs Carter was scolding Peter, who apparently had his fingers in the chocolate gateaux. Malcolm had to smile as Carter himself, was suddenly reduced to great guffaws of laughter. It was several seconds before he came back on the line and even then, Malcolm could hear that he was still literally crying with laughter.

"Oh, Mr Malcolm, please forgive me, sir. It's Mrs Carter, she's got a cherry stuck to the end of her nose, courtesy of Master Peter . . ."

The laughter was infectious, and Malcolm began to chuckle as well. He couldn't recall ever having heard Carter in such high spirits, and he had certainly never known him to be reduced to tears of mirth before.

"Carter, are you still there? Carter . . ."

"Yes, Mr Malcolm. Are you nearing home, sir? Your guests have decided to wait for you to join them before dinner is served. The food is all prepared and ready, sir."

"Ten more minutes, Carter. Would you kindly tender our apologies, we got caught in traffic. If Mrs Carter can manage to lose her cherry, then perhaps dinner for eight-thirty, might be the order of the day, do you think?"

"Oh, Mr Malcolm, that's very good sir, but I fear that Mrs Carter may have already lost her cherry many years ago . . ."

There were more guffaws of laughter as Carter broke the connection, without realising that their conversation was not yet over. Malcolm wanted to enquire if Jim Cox had arrived, and been made comfortable, but it would have to wait now?

Malcolm smiled to himself again, picturing Mrs Carter with a cherry stuck on the end of her nose. She'd always had a way with the children. He recalled that Elizabeth, as a child, and then Charlotte and Michelle, had all idolised and adored their nanny. Mrs Carter could always be relied upon to find something to amuse the children while they were left in her care. It was apparent that despite her advancing years, she hadn't lost her touch in any way. The children still revelled in her company.

On reflection, he hadn't intended the *double entendre* regarding the cherry, it had just slipped out, but he was glad that Carter, normally to be regarded as a bit straight-laced, had found it so amusing.

It was good to hear the sound of laughter in Oakwood again, and Malcolm couldn't wait to get home.

The cars pulled to a halt in front of the house and Carter was there to meet them, a smile still on his face.

"Mr Malcolm, Miss Sharon, welcome home. I trust that you've both had a pleasant journey?"

"We're fine thank you Carter. Give us a few minutes to freshen up, and then we can start dinner. My apologies to Mrs Carter for the late hour, but it has been unavoidable. It's been rather a long day. Have all my guests been made comfortable?"

"Yes, sir. They are all gathered together in the lounge awaiting your arrival. I have served canapés, and an aperitif. Would you and Miss Sharon care for anything, sir?"

"I'll have a glass of my German lager, please Carter. Sharon-Louise?"

"A very large vodka and tonic, ice and a slice, for me please, Carter."

"Yes, certainly miss. I will serve your drinks in the lounge for you."

Malcolm and Sharon-Louise went straight through to Malcolm's suite. He carried for her, a small suitcase of items of clothing that she had selected from her mothers extensive wardrobe. The two identical en-suite bedrooms, were on opposite sides of a passageway that led straight out onto a secluded garden patio at the rear of the house. It was the only area common to both bedrooms, and could be accessed by the French windows from both rooms. The remainder of his suite comprised another bathroom and sauna, and a small sitting room, that gave access to his other private study, or office. He explained to Sharon-Louise that Elizabeth's suite was on the other side of the partition wall on his side. It is a mirror image of his own and could be accessed through by a door from his bedroom leading directly into hers. From the patio, she could see that her bedroom, gave access to the second bedroom, in exactly the same way. There was a light on in the far bedroom, and the French door was slightly ajar.

"Who's in that one, Malcolm?" She whispered.

"I'm not sure. Why don't we go and see? Come on, its my house, after all."

He took her hand and led the way. The heavy curtains were drawn, so he tapped gently on the glass of the door.

"Hello inside. Is anyone home?"

"The curtain was drawn back by a rather attractive woman dressed in a nurses uniform. A smile of recognition lit up her face when she saw Malcolm.

"Hello Jacqueline, sorry if I startled you. You remember Sharon of course?"

"Yes, hello Sharon, how are you, now?

Sharon-Louise recognised her as one of the nurses who had taken care of her at the clinic.

"Hello Jacqui, nice to see you again, but what are you doing here? I'm all right now, surely?"

Jacqueline looked enquiringly at Malcolm.

"It's alright, I haven't told her yet. It was meant to be a surprise. How's our patient?"

"Mr Cox is more comfortable now, Malcolm. I gave him some medication as soon as he arrived, and he's managed to eat a light meal. He's a little confused and keeps asking to be allowed to join the other patients. For some reason, he thinks he's in a private clinic? I've tried to explain, but perhaps one of you might care to enlighten him?"

Sharon-Louise had heard her mention of 'Mr Cox' and gave a little squeal of delight. Without any further ado, she pushed her way past them both, and into the bedroom. Her stepfather was comfortably propped up in bed.

"Dad, Dad, it's me, Sharon."

She was at his bedside, and holding on to the fingers of his least damaged hand.

"Sharon, is it really you? Hello my dear, its good of you to come and see me, but what are you doing here at this late hour? Is there something wrong?"

"No Dad, nothings wrong. In fact, everything is perfect, just perfect . . . Thank you, Malcolm."

Malcolm smiled as she stood and came forward to embrace him. He unashamedly enfolded her into his arms and gently kissed away the tears of gratitude that were rolling down her cheeks. This, their first open display of affection for each other, was to set the tone for the coming week. He anticipated that by the time his guests had to leave, they would be under absolutely no illusions as to his intentions in that regard.

Driving from Odstock to Bleanaway, alone, had given him plenty of time to think. Malcolm had made a conscious decision that, no matter how much it was frowned upon by anyone else, this woman was destined to be part of his future. In the past few days, with all the traumatic experiences they had shared, he'd come to realise that he truly fallen in love with her. The thought that she might be going out of his life again, to take care of her stepfather, was too difficult to imagine. Malcolm could see only one solution to his problem. For the foreseeable future, Jim Cox would have to come and live at Oakwood.

He'd set about persuading Gilbert Townsend to allow Jim to be transferred from Odstock Hospital, directly into his private medical care and supervision. The arrangement was finalised only that morning, during the journey down to Weymouth. After the Service, Jim was to be brought directly to Oakwood.

There still remained a few papers to sign, just to tidy up the loose ends, but it was nothing that couldn't wait until Malcolm found some time to call in at the hospital.

All things considered, Malcolm was feeling rather pleased with himself. For it had been an inspirational idea, all cobbled together, over the phone, in only two days. But by far the best thing was, that it had all been expedited, with the minimum of fuss and inconvenience to his new patient.

The room now occupied by Jim had originally been adapted to care for Elizabeth during her prolonged illness, so there was very little that needed doing in that respect. Jacqui was to be allocated Elizabeth's other bedroom as soon as Malcolm could organise the removal of all her personal belongings.

Nurse Jacqueline Strong, a single lady in her early forties, had been recruited to his Clinical staff three years ago. He had conducted the interviews for the position personally, so he knew her to be dedicated to her chosen profession, very efficient, and totally reliable. When, on the spur of the moment, he outlined to her, a possible new position, working for him at Oakwood, and suggested most weekends off, normal hours, live-in accommodation whilst remaining on a similar pay scale, she had jumped at the opportunity. For in the nursing profession, those sorts of fringe benefits, and idyllic work conditions, made the job too good to pass up. She was owed some annual leave, so, by handing in her resignation, she was able to start in her new role of private nurse, immediately.

Malcolm was planning to ask George Lloyd to draw up a proper contract of employment to seal the arrangement. It would be awarded only after a month trial period in case there was any conflict of personality between nurse and patient.

After all the formal introductions, everyone sat down to a very convivial dinner. The food was trolleyed into the dining room, and Sharon-Louise, Charlotte, and Michelle, all set about assisting Carter in serving it to the guests. The talk over the table inevitably revolved around the events of the past couple of days. It became apparent to Malcolm that there was some confusion in the sequence of events. The only people present that knew the whole background to the story were David, and Sharon-Louise.

They all retired back into the lounge for a nightcap. Charlotte and Michelle bade them all goodnight and went to their rooms. Malcolm, rather than let the conversation go on into the early hours, suggested a full, after-breakfast conference. He asked for both David and Sharon-Louise to be prepared to relate everything that had taken place. A joint explanation, made together, for the benefit of everyone, so that they all understood everything that had occurred. With all the key players present in one room, he suggested that as each person's name came into the story, they too should be allowed to give their version of events. Everyone agreed that it was an excellent idea, especially George, who as well as taking notes, wanted to record the whole thing. He asked if he might be allowed to ask questions to clarify any point.

Everyone laughed, for he was generally perceived to be taking it all far too seriously. Did he imagine he was still in Court examining the evidence?

"You're certainly not going to be cross-examining me, George Lloyd," came the tongue-in-cheek response from Edith. "It will be as it's always been. I talk, you listen . . ."

He smiled, readily joining in with the light exchange of banter with his wife.

"Yes dear, of course, dear. I only wished to point out, dear, that if I am to be preparing your statement to hand to the Police, I will, in all probability, need to clarify certain matters arising out of anything, and everything, that you say. I usually do, don't I, dear?"

"George. Shut up. I've heard it all before. This is me you're talking to, remember? Now, be a good boy and take me to my bed, this instant."

To the amusement of everyone, Edith linked arms with him, and they strode purposefully towards the door.

"Good night, Mum. Night Dad," Sue called after her rapidly disappearing parents.

"Night everybody," Edith and George called back. Both gave a cheery wave without turning round.

Their exit left everyone chuckling, and effectively signalled the end to the evening. Malcolm looked around, suddenly realising that there were some other guests missing. With a look of consternation, he asked,

"The children? Where are the children? I've only just realised they're not with us . . ." He wasn't addressing anyone in particular, his question was directed to everyone left in the room. Sue answered him.

"Mrs Carter kindly offered to give them their meal in the playroom, and then put them to bed for me. Apparently, they're all sleeping together, Indian fashion, in a tepee erected for them by Charlotte and Michelle, who apparently loved doing it when they were younger?"

Malcolm smiled fondly at the memory of his own two little ones, dressed as Indian squaws, a'whoopin' and a'hollerin' as they war-danced, with their mother, around their makeshift coat-stand totem pole.

"My God, I'd nearly forgotten about all that. Yes, they did. Inflatable cushions, pillows and blankets all over the place, I seem to remember. The playroom is adjacent to the Carters living quarters, so the children will be well taken care of. You need have no concerns, there."

"Sam's in with them, as well. He won't let anything happen to Emily. He'll bark if anything's wrong, and if Sam lets rip, the whole house will hear it, believe me," chuckled Sue.

"Shall we look in on them, to see if they're okay?" suggested Malcolm. "Come on, its this way . . ."

The four adults tiptoed through the corridors leading to the west wing of the house. Malcolm halted at a door that was left slightly ajar. With a finger to his lips to caution silence, he gently pushed the door inwards. The nightlights dimly lit the interior of the huge playroom. There were toys strewn all over the place, but the large conical tent in the middle of the room dwarfed everything.

Stepping carefully, they made their way to the flap entrance, which was buttoned up in the open position. In the gloomy interior, Peter and Rita were asleep in each other's arms on one side of the tent, Emily and Sam on the other. Sensing the intrusion, Sam opened his eyes and lifted his head, but he made no sound as he recognised Sue and David. With a single wag of his tail, he settled his head back onto Emily's outstretched arm and closed his eyes again.

Satisfied that all was well, the adults quietly withdrew to leave the children to their slumbers. In the hallway, just after midnight, they all wished each other goodnight and retired, exhausted, to their respective rooms.

Sharon-Louise awoke to the sound of someone tapping gently on her bedroom door. She threw back the duvet and looked at her bedside clock as she leapt out of bed, it was just after five.

"Who's there?" She whispered through the unopened door.

"It me, you daft thing, who do you think it is? There's only you and me in this part of the house."

She opened the door and blinked in surprise, it clearly wasn't what she expected him to be knocking for.

"Malcolm, you're dressed, what's happening?"

"Come on then, sleepy head. You said you wanted to go fishing. It's a pleasant enough morning and there's a couple of trout, with our name on, just waiting to be caught. Are you coming?"

"Give me five minutes, I'll meet you in the porch. Sort me out some boots, will you please, darling?"

Their footprints left a meandering trail through the heavy dew, as they walked hand in hand through the grass. The dawn chorus was heralding the start of another beautiful autumn morning. The cool air seemed to be scented with the faint whiff of rotting leaves and fruits, mingled with wood smoke from some far distant hamlet.

As they made their way down to the riverside, Malcolm quietly explained that the River Test had split itself into two, a bit further upstream. The riparian rights of the east tributary belonged to the Malcolm, and the Oakwood estate. This was his jealously guarded, private, unspoiled fishing. He pointed out that the bank sides were deliberately left overgrown, only the riverweed was ever cut to prevent it taking over completely. To fish this water with a fly rod, one needed to be wading in the water and casting upstream, which is exactly how he preferred to fish.

In the half-light preceding the dawn, Malcolm stood stock still on the bank looking upstream for the first signs of movement on the water. His rods, already assembled and ready for use, he held in his left hand, their butts resting on the ground. His right arm was slung loosely around her waist.

"Shouldn't be long now, love. There's usually a couple of fish in that deep glide on the far side of the bend where the water smoothes out a bit, can you see where I mean?"

He was whispering. She sensed that their surroundings dictated that this is how it should be. Speaking in normal tones would surely constitute an intrusion into the peace and tranquillity of this beautiful, wild place.

A dimple on the surface of the water marked the demise of a newly hatched fly. It's passing left an expanding circle of water with a bubble in the middle.

"Grayling," he whispered. "They always leave a bubble. Nice eating, but they tend to be a bit small in my water. I think we'll wait till we see a decent trout to aim at."

He relapsed back into their patient, silent vigil. A small disturbance in the vegetation below caught her attention. Sharon-Louise watched in fascination as a tiny little water vole emerged from the bank under her feet. Totally unaware of their presence, it set about cleaning its whiskers and grooming itself.

A splashy rise at the head of the glide prompted an unseen heron to lift off from the cover of the reed bed.

Seeing the two human figures, the bird gave out with a harsh squawk of alarm and protest, before majestically drifting away on the wind, heading upstream, and away from them.

Sharon-Louise watched the little vole take to the water, and commence to furiously paddle its way diagonally across to the far bank of the river. The little creature had almost made it when it disappeared in an enormous swirl. One second it was there, and the next, it was gone. She gasped and pointed at the water.

"Malcolm, did you see that poor little . . . . ?"

"Pike, and a big one, by the look of him. That's something new to my water. I hope he doesn't decide to gobble up too many of my fish. Come on, love, let's move upstream a bit. I doubt there will be any trout feeding on this section of the river while he's around."

They walked quietly along the footpath through the trees to the next vantage point. The river widened out, and the water moved faster over the shallows on their side. There were several fish to be seen rising in the deeper water on the far side of the river.

"Here we go then. Give me your hand and tread carefully and quietly, we're going wading now."

He left one of the rods, and his wickerwork creel on the bank, and stepped gently down into the ankle deep water. With a little help, achieved by holding on to the belt of his waxed jacket, she followed as he moved slowly into a midstream casting position.

Malcolm stopped and motioned for her to move behind him, and to his left. He unhooked the fly from the retaining ring on the rod handle, and stripped off a few yards of line, letting the current drag it out straight downstream and to his right.

A fish rose confidently about eight yards upstream and Malcolm set about covering the rise. Lifting the line off the water, he made two false casts and then dropped the fly exactly where the fish had last showed.

The current brought the fly and floating line back towards him. He gathered it back through the rod rings to stay in touch. He let it come two or three yards, and then lifted the line off the water with a back flick of the rod. Two more false casts to get more line airborne, and he dropped the fly a yard beyond his first cast.

The little fly dimpled the surface as it hit the water, and there was an immediate swirl where it had landed. Malcolm waited for a second before lifting the rod and setting the hook. The fish tore away upriver stripping line off the little reel.

"Here, quickly, take the rod from me. You do it."

Stepping quickly round behind her, he thrust the pulsating rod into her hands at the same time showing her how to apply a little resistance on the rim of the reel with her index finger, to slow down its spinning motion. Guiding her hands into the right position to hold the rod and control the reel, and with the minimum of interference, he allowed her the first thrill of feeling a fish on the line.

"That's it, its better to control the line by stripping it back through the rings with your left hand, while keeping the rod held high, to allow the bend and flex to absorb the pulls of the fish. That's good. If he runs towards you, you'll need to strip the line back as quickly as you can. You must try to stay in touch with him and keep a tight line, otherwise he'll throw the hook. If he goes away from you, give him line, but make him work for it. That way he's fighting you, and the river. Taking into account your bad hand, you're doing very well at the moment, love. Not bad for a beginner, I would have to say . . . What about you, is it exciting, or what?"

Before Sharon-Louise could answer, the fish made a leap into the air, catching her unawares. With a sickening snick, the leader line parted at the fly knot, and everything went slack. Crestfallen, she looked helplessly at Malcolm, and started to apologise for losing the fish. He laughed and took the rod back from her to wind the line back onto the reel.

"Don't worry about it, Sharon-Louise, I wouldn't mind a pound coin for every fish I've ever lost in that manner. His leaping like that allowed him to bring his full weight to bear on the weakest part of the line, the hook knot. As this leader is only four pounds breaking strain fluorocarbon, it just couldn't take it. Never mind, love, he'll easily shed that hook, and no doubt come again another day, so let's go catch his big brother instead."

They clambered out of the water, and he carefully tied on another fly before continuing their slow walk upstream round long sweeping bend, watching for any rising fish.

"I think you're going to have to give me a few casting lessons, Malcolm. You make it look very easy, but I know that it isn't."

"There's an awful lot of literature been written on the subject, love, and many anglers and writers have elevated it into a science. Fortunately, on my water, there is no real need to be able to cast long distances. In fact, there aren't many places on the river where it is even possible. Eight or ten yards, I have found to be perfectly adequate for me, although I can cast further if I need to, but not with these little rods. These are only seven and a half foot, five-weight, brook rods. They're not designed for long-distance casting. I'll show you some other rods later, and explain the differences and terminology used to identify them. Do you think you're going to like fly fishing, then?"

"I've not caught anything yet, have I, Malcolm? But, so far, I've loved every minute of just being part of this wild and beautiful place. For me, I think the actual catching of the fish might just be a secondary consideration. Look, there's a big rise just over there. Show me how it's done, Malcolm. I'm happy just to watch you from here, this time."

Malcolm studied the position of the rising trout. It looked to be a very good fish.

"That's an awkward one to get a fly over, Sharon-Louise, I would need to be standing in the deepest part of the river to make room for the back cast, unless . . ."

He made his way through the bank-side vegetation until he reached a point judged to be nearly opposite to where the fish was rising. After pushing his way through more brambles and stinging nettles, and with the rod held high, he sat down on the four-foot high bank, and gently slithered down on his backside, until his feet entered the water. Moving very slowly, Malcolm stood up and quietly waded out as far out as his wading boots would allow. It was only about a yard, but it just about put him clear of the bank side vegetation. Sharon-Louise was intrigued, she couldn't see any way that he could possibly cover the fish with a normal fly-casting technique.

Malcolm stood and waited to see the fish rising confidently again before making any further move. Very slowly, he started to strip line from the reel allowing the slow moving current to pull it downstream. She could see that he was gauging the distance to the rising fish. It appeared to be about six yards away, and directly opposite to where he was standing. The next rise was very close to the reeds on the furthest side of the river.

Malcolm knew that he was only going to get one chance at this fish. The cast had to be exactly right. Too short was no good, as it would put the fly on thick surface weed. Too far would put it into the reeds. With utmost care and concentration, he readied himself. Waiting until he saw the fish rise again, he counted five seconds, and with a quick sideways flick of the rod, he sent the fly line from directly downstream to directly upstream. As the current brought it back towards him, he slowly raised the rod tip, causing the heavy line to hang in a 'D' shape with the water. Gauging the split second when the line was in the right arc he rolled the rod tip over and down, with a deft flick of his wrist. The loop of line sent out over the water took the little green-drake fly on its way. As the line straightened out, the fly dropped onto the water just as he would have liked. It was a perfectly executed roll-cast, and the satisfaction of seeing the fly land exactly where he'd aimed it, was part of his reward. One second, two seconds, and the water seemed to hump up, as the fly was sucked under with scarcely a ripple to mark its passing. He saw the floating line begin to move and he lifted the little rod to set the hook.

The water erupted as the fish felt the pull. Uncharacteristically, it turned and raced off downstream, the line cutting through the water at an amazing speed. Malcolm saw all the thirty-five yards of bright green fly line disappear off the reel in an instant, and the forty yards of white backing line were quickly beginning to follow. He set about chasing after the fish in an effort to get some line back. The depth of the water was forgotten, after only two or three strides, both of his waders were full of water.

Floundering along up to his crotch in the water, while frantically trying to prevent the fish from taking any more line, seemed almost futile, for he knew that he was heading back down to the deepest part of the river, just on and around the bend, where there was ten-foot of water. On reaching the bend, it would become difficult, if not impossible, for him to follow any further.

"Sharon, run ahead with the net, try and get ahead of him if you can. Just before the bend, jump down into the water, and make some commotion, do anything you can think of to stop him. He mustn't be allowed to get as far as the bend in the river, otherwise I'll lose him."

She grabbed up the landing net and sprinted back along the path for seventy or eighty yards, all the time looking through the bank side vegetation for any sight of the bright green fishing line. There was a gap in the bushes up ahead, and without thinking about the consequences of where she would land, she took a blind leap of faith off the top of the four-foot high bank, down into the water.

It proved to be a little deeper than she would have liked, and with a tremendous splash, Sharon-Louise found herself up to her crotch in the water, but thankfully still standing upright. With no time to consider her position, she looked upstream for the telltale fishing line that should be coming towards her.

Malcolm saw her come flying out of the bushes just short of the bend. He took a sharp intake of breath, watching as she hit the water. He was already convinced that his next sighting would probably see her floundering up to her neck, while desperately trying to get her feet back onto the bottom. But no, there she was, still standing, net held at the ready, and frantically running and jumping up and down on the spot to create a disturbance. He wished he had a camera . . .

There was a slackening of the pull through the rod, and he managed to get half a dozen turns of line back on to the reel. The water was now up to his thighs as he continued to chase down the fish.

Sharon-Louise, breathless with excitement, was looking to see where the angle of the line cut into the water to try to pinpoint the fish's position. Allowing for the invisible five-foot fly leader, she reckoned it to be still four or five yards upstream of where she was, and in the slightly deeper water to her left. She took two steps in that direction and was immediately up to her waist, the buoyancy of the air trapped in her clothing was beginning to lift her slightly. It made running on the spot more difficult, but she tried her best.

Malcolm continued to make headway, by putting as much strain as he dare onto the line, and by moving downstream toward the fish, winding line back as he moved. Thankfully, it had stopped running, probably due to all the commotion in the water ahead, and was now swimming in dour circles, in the deeper part of the river. He realised that unless it chose to swim back upstream toward him, there was no way that he could gain anything more. What with the deeper water, and the pull of the current, it had virtually become a stalemate situation. He also knew that if the fish chose to run downstream again, he would certainly lose it, for only Sharon-Louise stood between it, and the bend in the river now.

He applied as much pull on the little rod as he dared, before quickly lowering the tip and winding down. Very slowly, he was gaining on the fish, and was relieved to see the first couple of turns of green fly line were back on the reel. He found that by walking very close to the bank, where the water was slightly shallower, he could get closer. Sliding his backside against the steep bank aided his balance, and made progress slightly easier. But he constantly needed to move in a curious sideways stepping motion, keeping his back tight to the bushes, to avoid slipping down the underwater slope into the very deep midstream water. Eventually, he and Sharon-Louise were only about ten yards apart, and he began to feel slightly more in control of things. The fish seemed to be tiring as well.

"Stop jumping up and down now, Sharon. I'm going to try and lift him towards the surface. If you see an opportunity to get the net under him, then do it, but try not to hit the line, or you might dislodge the hook."

She ceased her running on the spot, and stood ready with the net, intently watching the point where the line entered the water. She saw Malcolm raise the rod as high as he could reach with his right hand, and carefully start to pull the line down through the rings with his left. The leader knot appeared and rose slowly out of the water as the fish was reluctantly drawn upwards. The water boiled as he made a dive for the bottom again, causing the little rod to buck, and forcing Malcolm to relinquish a bit of line back to him. This give-and-take battle went on for another minute or two, but each time the fish was drawn ever closer to the surface. Sharon-Louise twice caught a glimpse of a golden flash in the water as she eagerly waited for her chance with the net.

"I can see him Malcolm, my God, he's huge . . . Coming up this time, I think?"

The fish rolled on the surface a yard or two upstream of where she was standing, and for the first time, they both got a good look at him.

"I don't think he's going to fit in the net, Malcolm?"

"He's got to. Put the net in the water, and let me try to steer him into it tail first. As soon as his tail is in far enough, scoop the net forward and then up. Ready now, woman?"

"I'm ready. Go for it, man."

He smiled to himself at her immediate retort, and tried to concentrate on the matter in hand. Very carefully, applying as much strain as he thought the line would bear, he brought the fish back to the surface again where, for the first time, it lay on it's side, gasping, and nearly beaten. He watched with bated breath as Sharon-Louise quickly positioned the landing net immediately behind the fish, and just under the water.

At exactly the right moment, he brought the rod tip slowly down allowing the fish to drop backwards in the current. He held his breath in anticipation as she took a single step forward to push the net around the fish.

The surface of the water erupted into a cloud of spray as she struggled to lift the great fish upwards and out.

Malcolm could do absolutely nothing to help her. The hook-hold on the fish was no more, everything had gone slack, if she dropped the net now, the fish would be lost. He frantically gathered in the rest of the line as he quickly floundered down to where she stood, in the middle of the river.

With a whoop, she two-handedly held the net aloft, with the fish writhing in the mesh bag.

Together, up to their waists in the water, with the fish now safely theirs, they were laughing, hugging and kissing each other, joyous in their moment of triumph.

They made their way to the bank and Malcolm helped her out of the water. She still carried the net with the struggling fish, refusing to hand it over. Sharon-Louise gently laid the net down on a thick bed of wet grass and knelt to take a good look the fish. Nearly as long as her arm, and a full hand-span in depth, the fish lay gasping in the folds of the net. Malcolm came and knelt down beside her to admire his catch.

"Wild brownie. Cock fish, see the kype, this hooked bit on his lower jaw? He only gets that as he comes into breeding condition. This is a good fish, love, I'll bet he'll go well over six pounds maybe even seven? There's enough there to give us all a good feed of poached

Salmo Trutta. Where's the priest? Oh damn, I've left it in the creel, I'll just nip back up and fetch the rest of the gear."

Pausing only to tip the water out of his waders, Malcolm started to make his way back along the path upstream.

Sharon-Louise, still on her hands and knees, gazed at the beautiful creature as it lay there gasping, trying to breathe properly. Running her fingertips lightly over the slippery golden flanks caused the fish to quiver and give another little struggle.

"Alright my beauty," she whispered, "I'm not about to let him hurt you. Come along, let's get you back to where you rightfully belong."

She picked up the net and carried the fish back down into the shallows of the river. Carefully placing everything in the water, so that the fish's head faced upstream, she eased away the restraining folds of net from around him. Sensing that he needed to be held upright to recover, she knelt down in the water and held him with the palms of her hands gently supporting his weight from underneath. They stayed like that for a full minute, as the life-giving water again flowed through his gills. She sensed, rather than felt, the energy slowly returning, and whispered little encouragements for him to hurry up and swim away, before the wicked fisherman returns to turn him into his dinner.

Eventually, with a little flick of the tail, the fish moved away from her grasp, and slowly swam across the current into the deeper water. She watched him out of sight, whispering a slightly sentimental goodbye while shedding a little tear. Sharon-Louise knew exactly what it felt like to be held captive like that.

Malcolm returned to find her sitting on the bank with her feet in the water. The empty landing net, beside her, needed no explanation. He sat down and looked into her face, noticing the tear.

"Why?" he asked. She smiled and took his hand in hers.

"We had a little chat while you were gone. He told me that he had half a dozen Salmo Trutta Sheila's, just waiting for him to come along and father their babies." She paused. "Truth is, Malcolm, he was just too beautiful. I'm sorry, but I couldn't let you do it."

"My God, lady. That was the biggest fish I've ever seen come out of my stretch of the river, and now I've got to tell everyone that the crazy woman that I love, went and put it back. They'll never believe me . . ."

"So don't say anything then, Malcolm. Let it be our own little secret. Elmo won't be letting on, will he?"

"Elmo?"

"Yes, I just gave him a name, Elmo Trotter,"

"Elmo Trotter, Salmo Trutta, I've got it now." He laughed uproariously and planted a kiss on her lips.

"Come on lady, let's go hit the showers and get some breakfast, I'm starving. I expect it'll take us some time to get all the leaches off, so we had better get a move on."

"Leaches? What leaches?"

"Oh, didn't I mention them before? Sorry love. There are millions of the horrible little bloodsucking blighters living in the river, and they get into everywhere. We usually have to get them off in the traditional way, just a little touch with a lighted cigarette end, it makes them let go."

"You have got to be kidding me?" Sharon-Louise was looking at him in shock-horror, none too sure . . .

"Do I look like a man who would kid a lady about such a serious thing? No, of course not. I shall definitely need to give you a good looking over in the shower, and then you can do the same for me. Any leaches found, will need to be dealt with accordingly. Do we have a deal?"

She finally cottoned on and made out to take a playful swipe at his ear.

"Malcolm Blackmore, you're a beast, a cad, and a charlatan, sir. Yes alright, it's a deal . . ."

# Chapter 9

Malcolm and Sharon-Louise looked particularly happy and smug with themselves as they entered the dining room arm-in-arm. Wishing everyone a good morning, they saw that their guests were already tucking into breakfast. Carter seated Sharon-Louise beside Malcolm, and took their breakfast order. He was about to leave when Malcolm enquired after the whereabouts of the children.

"Mrs Carter has set a table, and is giving them all breakfast together in the old still-room, sir. I understand that Miss Charlotte and Miss Michelle are planning to take them pony riding later this morning. They are all in very high spirits, sir. Master Peter has been at the face paint already. He thinks he's big chief Sitting Bull, and Miss Rita is his Morning Cloud. In the circumstances, Mrs Carter thought it better to give the adults a little peace and quiet. Is that in order, sir?"

Malcolm looked enquiringly at Sue and David, and then Edith and George. They all smiled and nodded their approval of the arrangement.

"We've washed and dressed, Emily and she couldn't wait to re-join the twins, who were up with the lark. Your girls certainly seem to have hit it off with my family, Malcolm."

"Well alright then, Carter. Please pass on my thanks to Mrs Carter for her thoughtfulness. When Charlotte and Michelle have finished their breakfast, I would like a quick word with them before they all go out on the warpath, please Carter."

"Yes Mr Malcolm, I will pass on your wishes, sir. Will that be all, sir?"

"Yes, thank you Carter."

Several minutes had passed without any conversation, and it prompted David to set aside his morning newspaper. He looked across to Malcolm and Sharon-Louise who were huddled, heads together, chuckling and whispering like a couple of love-struck teenagers.

"Am I to presume that you two have already been out this morning? I heard a lot of giggling and laughter earlier on, and Carter was outside washing off some muddy boots when I came down for breakfast."

"We were out at first light, David. Malcolm took me fly-fishing. I'm sorry if we disturbed you, but we both managed to get a little wet in the process. Malcolm was just helping me out of my wet boots and trousers."

"Hmm, I'm sure he was . . ." David smiled and looked at Sue. "If a little fishing has that effect on two people, hadn't we better be giving it a go ourselves, love?"

Sue chuckled and nodded her agreement. "Would it be too much to ask if you had any luck? With the fishing, that is . . ."

"One that got away, and the fish of a lifetime that madam here, sneakily decided should be returned to the river, while my back was turned. Otherwise, we might all have been dining on fresh trout for dinner tonight."

"Oh Malcolm, don't be such a beast. There are still two fresh trout in the fridge that you caught the other morning. Besides, Elmo was far too handsome a fish to kill, just so that you could indulge yourself."

David, Sue and Edith started laughing, and George set aside his paper as well. There was obviously a little story here.

"Elmo, the handsome fish? This all sounds rather intriguing, come on Malcolm, spill the beans, just what have you two been up to this morning?"

"Well, okay, but let's start with the fishing, shall we?"

Now everyone was laughing, and he received a playful slap from Sharon-Louise who was clearly seen to be blushing in apparent, or feigned, embarrassment.

Malcolm related all the details of their early morning adventure. Much to the delight of everyone present, he proved to be a particularly skilled raconteur, offering little embellishments in exactly the right places to keep the listeners enthralled.

". . . He made off down-river like an express train, nearly wrenching the rod from my hands . . ." and, ". . . The sight of Sharon-Louise flying out of the bushes, and descending like a sea eagle onto the water sending it cascading everywhere, will haunt my memory forever. I fear that part of my river will never fully recover from it all, especially so after seeing all of her river-dance moves, made to create a disturbance."

". . . And then when I got back, there was this crazy woman, sitting on the bank, calmly emptying her boots of water, and no sign of my fish anywhere." He paused for a sip of his coffee, thus keeping his audience on tenterhooks.

"I couldn't believe what I was hearing. Elmo Trotter, she'd named him. They'd apparently been having a bonding session while I was away? He'd spun her some fishy tale about his harem of oversexed, Salmo Trutta Sheila's, apparently all queuing up to have his babies? And she'd let him go. Well, I ask you, what is a man to do with such a woman?"

He threw his hands in the air in a theatrical gesture of despair to finish his story. By this time, everyone was laughing heartily, even Carter. He had quietly placed their breakfast plates in front of them both, without causing any interruption, and had stayed on to hear the end of the story.

"Anyway, when we got back from the river, all wet and muddy, well, that's when it got really interesting . . ."

Sharon-Louise had heard enough. She picked up her table knife, and was seen to be testing the sharpness of the blade with her thumb. Suppressing the urge to laugh, she tried to sound menacing and serious.

"Malcolm Blackmore, if you still value your wedding tackle, I suggest you call a halt right there, am I making myself understood, mister?"

This time, everyone was laughing, even Malcolm, and this was how Charlotte and Michelle found the mood of the dining room as they came in answer to their fathers bidding. Malcolm rose from his seat and, leaving his breakfast unfinished, he went to greet them both with a kiss on the cheek. He turned to his guests.

"Please excuse me for a minute or two, everyone, I just need to have a private word with my daughters."

He placed an arm around each of their shoulders, and led them out of the dining room and into the library, shutting the door behind, for some privacy. They looked expectantly at their father, both wondering what they'd done wrong this time?

He smiled, "Don't look so worried, I'm about to thank you for the sterling effort you are both putting in for our guests. I was particularly impressed when you helped Carter serve dinner last evening, and I'm appreciative for the time you are devoting to keeping the children amused."

It was a relieved Michelle that spoke for them both.

"Oh, daddy, it's been such a hoot, really. I think we had both forgotten how to play, and enjoy ourselves. We've never had a little brother, and Peter is such good fun. He is the dominant one, and has a very vivid imagination. Rita as well, but she always seems to be competing with her brother. It reminds us of how we used to be with each other. Perhaps we still are, sometimes?"

Malcolm smiled and sat down in his favourite reclining reading chair, inviting his girls to sit opposite.

"The other reason for wishing to speak to you is a little more serious, I'm afraid."

They looked at him questioningly. He held up his hand and indicated towards the area of the house that used to be his wife's domain.

"It cannot have escaped your notice that I have an elderly gentleman patient in what was your mother's suite. He is Sharon's father, Mr Jim Cox, the man that I told you about, the one that was firebombed out of his home. Well, I've had him transferred here, into my care, and he will be staying with us until he is well again. The nurse taking care of him is Jacqueline Strong. She was on my staff at the clinic, but now works privately for me. The thing is, I need her to be on hand 24/7 to see to Mr Cox. It would be wholly inappropriate for her to be sleeping in the same room as her patient, which puts me in a rather difficult position. In short, I have decided that today, I'm going to clear your mother's suite of all her personal effects, and to allow nurse Strong to occupy that bedroom."

He held up his hands as he sensed that they were both about to protest.

"I anticipated that my decision would upset you, but there can be no discussion on the matter. That is how it is going to be. Now, I can either ask you if you wish to pack your mothers things, or I can get one of the people sent from the estate management company to do it. It goes without saying that you can both select and keep any items that you cherish from your mother's belongings. The rest will be properly packed and stored in the basement, until I can make a decision on their final disposition.

Believe me when I say that this is as difficult for me, as it is for you. Before I proceed any further with this, I would like to hear anything that you have to say on the matter. Michelle, would you care to speak first?"

She looked at her sister before speaking.

"I think I can speak for us both, daddy. Naturally, we are shocked and appalled at the desecration of mother's things, but we were half expecting that it would have to happen one day. Charlotte and I have already taken possession of most of mum's jewellery, and some of her clothes as well. Since she died, we've both been sharing the use of her more personal items, such as her hairbrushes, combs, perfumes and some of her make-up. It helps us to remember . . ."

Malcolm sensed that she was beginning to get a little upset just talking about it.

"Charlotte, do you have anything to add to what Michelle has told me?"

"Not really, daddy. Only to say that we are both truly sorry for our behaviour the other day. We've talked about it, and we are genuinely pleased to see that you are trying to move on from mum's death. The atmosphere at Oakwood has been, well, different, this past couple of days, a bit like it used to be. And it's good to see the Carters are so happy, as well."

Malcolm stood up from his chair and held out his arms, their words had touched him deeply, and found a raw nerve.

"Thank you girls, I was praying that you would say something like that. I'm so proud of you, that my words are beginning to fail me. I can feel a family hug coming on, come here you two . . ."

It was a rather pensive Malcolm that returned to finish his breakfast, retrieved from the hotplate, by the ever-attentive Carter. Sharon-Louise put her hand on his thigh under the table, and gently squeezed his leg. He looked up at her, his mouth full of his favourite smoked bacon and tomato.

"Is everything alright?" she whispered.

He swallowed hard and whispered back.

"Hmm, yes, I would say so, but it won't be if you keep on doing that. For goodness sake behave yourself, woman."

After breakfast, everyone retired to the lounge, and Malcolm had another small table brought in for George to set up his old tape recorder, and to lay out his paperwork. It was suggested, that as George was taking notes, he might like to effectively act as a sort of Chairman throughout the morning. Malcolm also suggested that Mr Cox might like to be present as well? He pointed out that he was as much involved with everything that had occurred, as anyone else present, and that he was probably confused and looking for some answers, as well? It was agreed that he should be asked if he wished to be included.

Sharon and Malcolm left to go and speak with him, returning some five minutes later pushing Jim in a comfortable wheelchair. The introductions made, and with Jim made fully aware of what was about to happen, it came down to Sharon-Louise to start things off. George suggested that as there was so much background to her childhood life, she might like to start with her earliest recollections and memories, while in the care of various foster parents, and the local authorities.

She struggled a little to begin with, for there were many gaps and painful experiences to recount. David found that he was able to fill in some of the missing detail, from memories of his conversations with Laura. George was also able to assist, by showing her e-mailed pictures of relevant documents, sent to his laptop that morning by Tony Williams.

For the first time in her life, Sharon-Louise saw her own Birth Certificate, together with those of her mother and father, and their Marriage Certificate, as well. It was a poignant moment, the revelations of her true identity, coupled with the death of her mother, was beginning to be a little too much for her to cope with.

David sensed it was the moment to give her a break, and for him to take up the narrative, so he launched into their first visit to Laura's house, to see her litter of puppies.

The morning wore on with Sharon-Louise and David alternately sharing the details of all their experiences over the past six weeks. Nothing was omitted. Each part of the story led into the next, and the principal in that particular episode gave their version of events, even

Edith, recounting the time that the two men had accosted her, at her home.

Carter served tea, coffee and biscuits mid-morning, and they took a break from it all. David rose to stretch his legs and was quietly casting an interested eye over the contents of the bookshelves when Malcolm came over for a quiet word.

"David, I've got to ask you about something that's been bugging me. Three times this morning, we've come to a part in someone's version of events that could do with a little more explanation or clarification, and you've said, 'Emily . . . Lets move on, and come back to that later,' or words to that effect. The rest of your family just nod and accept it, and then continue on without question. It is abundantly apparent that there is something about Emily that all the rest of you are aware of, but Sharon, Jim, and me, are all left wondering? Can I ask if we are to be given some sort of explanation, because there is a lot here that we are struggling to understand?"

"Malcolm, can we just leave Emily until we've all given our version of events, please. I promise you that I will tell you everything, and all will then become much more apparent. Sue and I have been struggling with our consciences on this one, believe me. I'm thinking that it's going to take more than just a few minutes for you to get your head around what we are about to tell you. So prepare yourself for a surprise, or two."

"It all sounds very mysterious, David, I'm intrigued. Incidentally, where is Emily? The twins have gone pony-trekking with my girls. They won't have taken Emily with them."

Malcolm saw David close his eyes for a few seconds, as if in thought.

"She's alright. She's with Sam and your three dogs in the feed store on the end of the stables."

"How do you know that, for God's sake?"

Not satisfied, Malcolm reached for the TV remote on the table, and walked over to a small monitor mounted on one of the bookshelves.

"The old byre and tack room are on a security camera, let's see if you're correct, shall we?"

The screen came to life and Malcolm flicked through the various security images until he found the one he was looking for. The picture showed Emily sitting cross-legged on a bale of hay. Arranged in front of her was Sam, the two Jack Russell terriers, and the black

Labrador. They were all sitting upright looking at her attentively as she appeared to be gesturing with her hands and saying something to them. Malcolm stared hard, "What is she doing, David?"

"My guess is that she's talking with them."

"Talking? As in speaking, like you and me, is that what you're saying?"

"Yes, that's it exactly. Emily is a remarkable child, Malcolm. Here, let me see if I can show you something. Tell me, is this security camera visible in the feed store?"

"Yes, as you can see, it's positioned behind and to her left, up in the corner."

"What would you say if I asked her to give us a little wave, then?"

"It's not wired for sound David, so I would think it impossible."

"Watch and wonder then, Malcolm."

Both men watched Emily as she stopped what she was doing, and turned her head to look in the direction of the camera. She gave a little smile, waved, and stared for a few seconds longer before turning away again.

Malcolm's jaw dropped and he looked at the monitor in total disbelief. "My God, how on earth did you do that? Can you do it again?"

David was laughing, "Probably, but I won't. What we have between us is not something that I would wish to reduce to some sort of cheap trick, Malcolm. It is far too precious for that. You are the first person outside of our immediate family to be given any sort of demonstration of Emily's powers. And if you thought that was clever, well, to coin a popular phrase, you ain't seen nothing yet, mate. So let's just leave this for the time being, shall we? Oh, and by the way, the little dog, the one you call Gemma, she apparently has a little ear infection or something, and is in a bit of pain."

"What? Oh, come on, David, how do you know that?"

"Emily just told me."

David smiled, swigged down the last of his coffee, and turned to walk slowly back to his seat. He could sense that Malcolm was staring, incredulously, after him.

They picked up the narrative again with Jim Cox painstakingly taking them through the firebombing of the B&B and Doris's death. It was heartrending for everyone, and Sharon-Louise was again moved to tears in comforting her father, as he finally succumbed to his grief. It took quite a few minutes before either of them was able to continue, so David filled in with some of the background information he had gleaned regarding Shaun Riley being suspected of several counts of murder.

George continued to tape record everything, as well as make pages of handwritten notes. With the third ninety-minute cassette just about to go into the machine, they had reached the point of Sharon-Louise's abduction from the hospital. She picked up the narrative again, describing in detail for the first time, her ordeal of being incarcerated in the bag and box trolley. Her vivid recollections of the claustrophobia, and the inability to breathe properly, all came flooding back, as did the image of the child's face that had brought her some comfort during her ordeal. She stopped in the sudden realisation of something . . .

"Oh, my God, it was Emily, wasn't it? Yes, of course it was, I can see her little face even now. It was definitely Emily that I was seeing in my mind. Well, how strange? I wonder what made me think of Emily at such a traumatic time?"

Malcolm was looking at David in askance. He smiled back and gave him a single nod and a wink.

Sharon-Louise went on to describe how she managed to escape from the bag and the mood began to lighten a little. Everyone sensed they were getting towards the end of the marathon session, although there were many aspects of it all that George would need to go over again, with each individual, in order to prepare detailed statements for the Police.

The events at Bleanaway Quarry were common to the three main principles in the narrative, and each was asked to contribute their own particular version of what had occurred, purely for the tape recording.

Malcolm checked his watch. It was one-thirty, and he got up from his chair to stretch his legs.

"Look everyone, what do you say to a breath of fresh air? How about a walk along the river, while Mrs Carter prepares a light lunch for us? I think we've broken the back of this, unless anyone wants to raise anything more? What about you, Mr Cox? You look as though you've got something on your mind."

Jim looked up, and his eyes came to rest on Sharon.

"I'm a little confused with this Sharon-Louise thing love. For the past twenty years, you've been our Sharon. Now, all of a sudden, you're to be Sharon-Louise. It's a bit of a mouthful, don't you think?"

"Dad, you can call me anything you wish, and that goes for all of you. Everyone in Weymouth knows me as Sharon, I was introduced here at Oakwood as Sharon, and until a couple of days ago, I didn't even know that my parents had given me any other name. Even my own mother has been calling me Sharon ever since I've known her, so it can't have meant that much to her, can it? Malcolm has said that he likes calling me Sharon-Louise, although this morning, even he reverted to Sharon, just the once. Oh yes you did, Mr Blackmore, so don't you go trying to look the innocent with me, my lad. 'Sharon, run ahead with the net,' you said, while dishing out your orders. Remembering now, are we, mister?"

She was waving the big school ma'am finger at him in mock chastisement, so he grinned and held up his hands in a gesture of supplication to her admonishment.

Yes, I noticed, my lad, so just you watch it in future . . . Anyway, getting back to what I was about to say. It really doesn't matter to me at all. I have no preference, and I will answer equally to both names. The choice is yours."

"Well said, Sharon," Chipped in David. "I shall be reverting to your original name, I think. However, I can see that Malcolm might be calling you something slightly more colourful in future, especially if you're to make a habit of returning all his best fish to the water, and scolding him, just for getting your name wrong in the heat of the moment."

Malcolm slipped his arm round David's shoulders as he too stood up to stretch his aching legs.

"Thanks, David, you tell her, mate. Us blokes need to be sticking together in the face of such adversity. Are you with us on this, George?"

"Oh no, please don't include me, Malcolm. In my house, everything is most definitely matriarchal. She talk, I listen. She cook and I eat. It's an altogether very satisfactory arrangement, isn't it Edith, my dear?"

They all roared with laughter at his wonderfully dry sense of humour.

Their planned walk in the autumn sunshine split the group into three. Malcolm and Sharon accompanied Jim and nurse Strong, at a deliberately slow pace. David walked ahead with George, while Sue and Edith had Emily and Sam to contend with. The short walk down to the river was enough for Jim, and after a few minutes rest, sitting on a felled tree trunk, he and his nurse were seen to be slowly making their way back up to the house again. Alone for a few minutes, Sharon took the opportunity to ask Malcolm about her father's medical condition, and his prognosis for recovery.

"I think your father is doing as well as can be expected, love. The burns are healing well, and hopefully, we should soon be able to cut back on the painkilling drugs a little, before he gets too dependent upon them. Nurse Strong will be seeing to all of that when I go back to work next week, and I'm hoping that you might like to be assisting her? Obviously, your presence alone, will raise his spirits considerably.

He seems to have come to terms with his wife's passing. This morning's little session was painful, but it will have helped him, just to talk about it. In the long term, well, we will just have to wait and see, I think. There will be some considerable scarring of his face and hands, and he may not regain the full use of his left hand in particular. That one received the most damage, I'm afraid.

This morning, I showed nurse Jacqui how I would like his hands dressed in future. It is important to separate the fingers before they begin to fuse together. Perhaps later, if Jim's up to it, I might be able to do something in regard to the scarring of his face, but it will entail transplanting bits and pieces of his own body tissue, which in itself, is painful, so he might not want to bother? Let's just let nature take its course, with a little help from us, and I'm fairly confident that Jim will eventually pull through this okay."

The phone in his pocket rang. He fished it out and hit the 'call accept' button. "Hello, this is Malcolm Blackmore, who's that please?"

Sharon faintly heard a man's voice on the other end of the phone.

"Oh, hello Charles, nice to hear from you again, how goes everything?"

Malcolm began to pace slowly backwards and forwards, answering and commenting monosyllabically, to what he was being told. The conversation went on for a couple of minutes, and Malcolm was clearly pleased with what he was hearing. Sharon was intrigued.

"Yes. No. Really? How much? Christ. That's good. Yes, of course . . . I don't know, Charles . . . No, just go ahead and do it, please . . . No, we have everything here . . . Okay Charles, we look forward to seeing you, cheers for now."

He broke the connection, and saved the caller ID to his phone book. He looked at Sharon, grinning like a Cheshire cat. He stepped forward and swept her off her feet, giving her a big spontaneous hug and spinning her wildly, round and round. Finally setting her back down again, and without giving her a chance to speak, he excitedly launched into the reasons for his actions.

"That was Charlie Ferguson, he's coming down tomorrow to stay for a couple of days on the excuse that he needs to take detailed statements from all of us."

"And is that sufficient cause for such a joyous reaction then, Malcolm?"

"Well, yes, he's a good guy, I've quite taken to him, actually. But there's some better news, as well. Apparently, in the furtherance of their enquiries, the Police had to open a floor safe back at Tiptree Farm. Inside, there was a large amount of money, all in used banknotes. Charlie's got to get it ratified, but it would seem that as you are now the owner of the property, it might all belong to you."

"Me? How can that be? How much are we talking about?"

"I can't remember the exact amount he said, but the big number was most definitely fifty-one thousand pounds and something."

"Oh my good God, Malcolm. Are you sure that this is right?"

"As right as I can be, love, I'm only repeating what I've just been told. However, don't be counting all your chickens just yet, there is a down side to this, as well. I've got to talk to my people, who are still assessing things, but apparently, there is a whole pile of bills and invoices that need to be paid rather urgently.

This is obviously out of the scope of his responsibility, but we did stress that the welfare of the animals was to take priority. To that end, Charlie suspected that the money might perhaps have been put aside to facilitate payment of the bills? He was asking if it would be in order to use it for that purpose? I told him that I didn't know. I suggested that once it's been cleared with his superiors, he goes ahead and uses some of the money as he sees fit. If he hands over what is required to my team, they will deal with it for you.

They apparently need to get some more feed in rather urgently, and the suppliers are demanding payment on the previous order, before they'll deliver again. Are you happy with that arrangement?"

"For goodness sake, Malcolm, how should I know? I have absolutely no concept of running a farm, but if my animals need feeding, then they must be fed. Is there enough money to buy what they need?"

Malcolm chuckled. "I would hope so, love. Fifty grand will buy an awful lot of grain and pig pellets, or whatever it is they are being fed."

"Do you think that there will be any money left over Malcolm? I'm worried about finding enough before all the bills start coming in. I can't be letting David pay for any of it, I owe him so much already."

Malcolm placed a hand on each of her shoulders and looked her directly in the eye to stress his words.

"Sharon-Louise Cox, will you please stop worrying your pretty little head over stupid things, like money? You're a property owner now, my love, and unless I'm very much mistaken, a rather wealthy one at that. So just be patient and let things take their course. Trust me when I say that it will all come right, very soon."

"Do you really think so, Malcolm? I've been wondering how I'm going to cope when all this is all over . . ."

"What do you mean 'all over.' What do you envisage happening that I don't? I thought that we might have some sort of a future here, together, at Oakwood. Am I being too presumptuous, or am I perhaps mistaken in your feelings toward me?"

She turned to face him again, reaching out to take his hands in hers. The words didn't come easy.

"Malcolm, you are the first man that I have ever had any true regard for. I have been so happy just being in your company, that I have to keep asking myself, 'is this for real?' With so much going on in my life, I am dreading the day that it all comes to an end. I can hear you saying, 'There you are Sharon-Louise, I think you can stand on your own two feet now. It's been nice knowing you, thanks very much, I'll see you around,' or words to that effect. If that were to happen, Malcolm, I don't think I could cope any more. You are not mistaking any of my feelings for you. I think I fell in love from the moment we first met, but it is difficult for me to see that we have a future together, as our backgrounds are so very different."

Malcolm released her grip on his right hand. Reaching up to gently caress her cheek, he lifted her chin and stooped slightly to kiss her tenderly on the lips. His voice was a husky whisper as he embraced her.

"You silly girl, I'm never going to be saying anything like that. You are the best thing that has happened to me since . . . well, you know. I have been making plans for us, and for some big changes at Oakwood. They all include you. I would hope that in the not-too-distant future, we might become a Mr and Mrs Blackmore? But we need to take one step at a time, please, Sharon-Louise. This is early days, and we are still getting to know each other."

He stood back and again rested his hands on her shoulders, looking into her face. Sharon had come to recognise that this was a gesture he commonly used to reinforce whatever he was about to say.

"There's an old maxim that says, 'marry in haste, repent at leisure,' and neither of us would want that would we? So, all this needs to be done properly, carefully, and only the once. From my point of view, there will be no going back on my commitment. Once it has all been put into place, that will be it.

There are quite a few considerations to take into account, not only in my own personal circumstances, but also in yours, as well. I think that, together, we can work our way through them all, and still come out with what we both desire.

Now, Sharon-Louise Cox, are you with me for the long haul, or not?"

"All the way, Mr Blackmore, all the way . . . Will you kiss me like that again, please?"

He didn't need asking twice.

Tony Williams sat in the Bournemouth Office of Thompson & McCall, Solicitors and Attorneys at Law.

He was seated at the desk of his son, his hands constantly wringing themselves together in obvious worry, as he spoke with his junior partner, and daughter-in-law, Lizzy Thompson. The cause for his concern was the mysterious disappearance of his son, Connor, who had apparently taken himself off somewhere, a week previous, and hadn't made any contact since.

Tony had listened to a tearful Lizzy as she had outlined Connor's sudden change of character, and of his depressive mood swings, just prior to his leaving. She was sure that there had been something deeply troubling him that he had absolutely refused to discuss, even with her. In desperation, she had turned to Connor's father, Tony, to see if he could throw any light on the matter?

For his part, Tony had seized the opportunity to leave his Fulham office, and come down to Bournemouth to stay with Lizzy for a few days. Unbeknown to her, he had scheduled a meeting with the family of his friend and colleague, George Lloyd, for the coming weekend. This was to be held at an address near Winchester, and involved a preliminary reading of the Last Will and Testament of Laura Dobson, to her only beneficiary. So far, everything had dovetailed together nicely.

On receiving Lizzy's invitation, he had quickly packed all the relevant case papers and documentation into his capacious brief case, thrown a few items of clothing into a holdall, grabbed his laptop, and driven down to their Bournemouth office.

Sitting there now, and watching the obvious anguish in Lizzy's face was difficult enough, but Tony knew that he was in possession of certain information, that if revealed, would in all probability, make things worse, not better, for her.

He was now wrestling with his conscience, for this situation had developed into one of the few times in his life when he really didn't know what to do for the best. On the one hand he could act the innocent, and try to comfort her as best he could. On the other, he could spill the beans, and give her the whole nine yards on his son's suspected complicity with IRA terrorism.

He decided to play it by ear for the time being. He was just as anxious to find Connor as she was. To that end, he would engage the services of his usual Private Investigation Agency, to see if they could trace any of his son's movements. He made the phone call, and arranged the meeting with representative from the Agency to outline the nature of the enquiry. It was scheduled for later that afternoon.

Lizzy thought that Connor might have been heading for Belfast, perhaps to meet up with his friend Marty, who had been helping him in his family's land title research? Together, they had checked his personal telephone directory, and found only a single number with the 028 Belfast dialling code, but a chance call had revealed it to be a 'number unobtainable.'

Tony noted that there were no mobile phone listings in Connor's directory. Lizzy was able to advise that all such numbers were on his personal organiser that went everywhere with him. A thorough search through the drawers of his desk and filing cabinet revealed nothing more of any significance.

They were seemingly at a dead end, already.


Lunch at Oakwood was a finger buffet of canapés, quiche, sandwiches and salad, that had been beautifully set out in the dining room. Quite apart from the chilled bottles of Chardonnay and Pinot Grigio in the ice bucket, and a small selection of beers and fruit juices, Carter was on hand to serve tea or coffee, and to take orders for anything else that might be desired.

Malcolm poured for himself one of his preferred German Lager beers, while Sharon-Louise sampled the excellent white wine, while studying the vintage labels on the bottles.

All the guests, having first freshened up after their walk, helped themselves to the food and drink. Malcolm was pleased to see them all, including Jim, were chatting amongst themselves, and appeared entirely at ease in the informality of the arrangement. He sidled over and whispered a word of praise and thanks to Carter, who characteristically, responded with a slight bow and beaming smile in light of such approbation.

"It's a pleasure, Mr Malcolm, sir. I shall pass on your appreciation to Mrs Carter."

"Where are the children, please, Carter?"

"They returned from their ride approximately half an hour ago, sir. Mrs Carter has prepared a similar buffet in the still-room, and I believe that they are all busy tucking into their food even as we speak."

"Are Charlotte and Michelle still taking good care of them, Carter? I don't want any mishaps this week."

"I'm sure they are sir, but you can be assured, that as far as is possible, Mrs Carter will be keeping an eye on what they are doing. Her only concerns at the moment are for the youngest child, Emily. She is very quiet, and is too young to join in with the boisterous games enjoyed by the others. She seems to spend a lot of time with the animals, sir. They have all quite taken to her, it seems."

"From what I have been told, I don't think you need worry too much about Emily, Carter. In fact, you might both find it of some interest if you left the security camera, sound and vision, on in the lounge this afternoon. You have my permission to eavesdrop on whatever we are all talking about."

"Yes sir, I understand, thank you, sir."

"Oh, and another thing, Carter. We'll need to get the vet to take a look at Gemma. I think she may have an ear problem? Will you arrange that for me, please?"

"Yes, Mr Malcolm. I will see to it immediately. I shall have to ask the vet to do a house visit, sir, as we are rather busy this week. I have also arranged for some extra help in the house, sir. There are three temporary housemaids, appointed by the Estate Management, arriving later today. They will be with us for the remainder of this week, sir. "

"As you see fit, Carter. I am content to leave all that sort of thing up to you. If you have a problem with anything, then please come back to me. One last thing Carter, and then I'll let you get on. Tomorrow morning, we will be receiving an additional guest. A Mr Charles Ferguson will be with us for a couple of days. Please have a single room made up for him, if you will. One of those on the first floor of the main house will be in order, I think."

Taking their drinks, Malcolm and Sharon set the example by making their way back into the lounge. The others took the hint and followed slowly on behind. Malcolm set about moving the seating slightly, so that everything would be within the view of the tiny security camera, disguised as a book volume, on one of the shelves. He waited until everyone was comfortably seated before making his little announcement.

"Listen up everyone, please. I've had a call from Charles Ferguson this lunchtime. He has been pleased to accept my invitation to come and stay with us for a couple of days on the excuse of needing to take detailed statements from some of us. George, I think that you are the best man to be organising this with him. I can foresee that these statements, if written longhand, will take up a lot of our time. Do you think that you could prepare statements for each of us, based on your notes and tape recordings?"

"I don't see why not. I was rather anticipating this. You are all going to be on hand to answer any little queries that may arise, so it should be fairly straightforward, Malcolm. However, I doubt that I could finish them all in two days. Even with Edith's help, our typing skills aren't that good."

"Okay, so how about if you dictated them onto an old-fashioned Dictaphone, we have one here at Oakwood. I could then arrange for them to be typed onto the proper stationery, scanned onto a word processor, for you?"

"That sounds like a better idea, Malcolm. It would certainly save me a lot of time."

"Right that's settled then, we'll get straight onto organising it after this afternoons little session. I'll ring Charlie later and let him know exactly what we're planning to do. I'm sure that he'll agree. Now, I think we are going to begin this afternoon by talking about Emily? Am I right David?"

David nodded taking his cue to start.

"Before I say anything more, I need you all to know that Sue and I have thought long and hard about this. We have come to the conclusion that you are to be regarded as friends, and people that we hope we can trust. Notwithstanding, we will still need you all to promise that what we are about to reveal to you, never gets repeated outside of these four walls. If that sounds a bit mysterious, then I need to point out that this is for Emily's sake, more than ours. We are only seeking to protect our daughter from exploitation. You will realise why, only after I have told you as much as we know.

I shall ask you all individually to make your promise to us. George and Edith already have some idea of what I am about to tell you all, but even they don't know the full extent of it yet. So Edith, you first, please. Do you promise not to tell anyone else about Emily?"

"Yes of course, David, she's my granddaughter, but isn't all this a bit melodramatic?"

"I'm sorry, Edith, but that's not how Sue and I see it. We genuinely fear for her whole future. George, what about you?"

"You have my promise, David."

"Sharon?"

"Yes, David. You have my promise, as well?

"Malcolm?"

"I promise never to reveal any of Emily's little secrets, whatever they may be, David."

"Thank you. What about you, Mr Cox?"

"Last time I made any promises like that, David, I ended up with a trouble-and-strife. But if it pleases you, then yes, I promise not to reveal anything about Emily."

"Right, well, I thank you all for making your promises, so here we go. Sue and I have somehow managed to produce what we can only describe as an exceptionally gifted child, a super-kid. We have both come to appreciate that Emily's little brain is nothing short of absolutely astonishing. We, her parents, are not even sure that we have yet grasped just what amazing power there is in that little head of hers.

Sue, perhaps you might like to tell us all a little about Em's early years?"

"Since the day she was born, I instinctively knew that there was something different about Emily. For instance, you all know and understand the bonding that takes place between a mother and new-born infant, and how a mother coos and whispers sweet nothings while cuddling her baby. Well, when I did it with the twins, it was a sure fire way to get them to go to sleep. Not so with Emily though, she would look me straight back in the eye. It was very disconcerting. I swear that she understood everything that I was saying to her. I even started to tell her things, as if I was speaking to another adult, or to David. She would look at me all the time that I was talking. I kind of sensed that whatever I was saying, was all being taken in, as if she knew, and understood, every word?

Emily hardly ever used to cry, even when she was teething. It really worried me. I would lie awake at night listening to her laughing, gurgling and chuckling away to herself. I would often try to creep into her room to see what she was doing, but she always sensed that I was there, and stopped to look at me as though I was somehow intruding into something.

I began to think that she might have some form of autism, and I voiced my concerns with David. I wanted to get her properly checked over, tested, just to be sure she was all right, but it never happened, did it David?"

"No. I persuaded Sue that we had a perfectly normal, beautiful child, and that we should go along with all her little extraordinary ways, while keeping a careful eye on her. We both noticed lots of little things that defied explanation. For instance, Emily would only eat certain foods that were put in front of her. So what's unusual about that, you ask? Well it took us a bit of time to work it out, but what she was eating amounted to an almost perfectly balanced diet for a child of her age. The twins will quite happily demolish a whole tub of ice cream, and then make themselves sick on chocolate gateaux, but not Emily. She might take a mouthful or two of each, but then shun the rest. Giving her a plateful of fresh vegetables, salad, and fruit is much more to her liking, isn't it Sue?"

"Yes, that's right. She will only eat what she needs, or that which we all know to be beneficial and nutritious. If you look at her, there's not an ounce of fat on her little body, but she is remarkably fit and well, seemingly able to shrug off all the normal coughs and sneezes that the twins bring home from school.

Another thing, David and I both noticed was that Emily was somehow able to let us know that she either needed her nappy changing, or that she was hungry, or thirsty, or something. We used to laugh about it, because we would both turn up at her cot-side, with the same thing in mind. It was really uncanny how often it happened, far too many times for it to be purely coincidental. Emily was definitely communicating her needs to us, in a way that we hadn't yet grasped. I could be anywhere in the house, and the thought that Emily needed seeing to, for something or the other, would just pop into my head. We talked about it, and I found it was exactly the same for David, as well."

Malcolm interrupted, "How old would she be when this was happening, Sue?"

"Probably six to eight months. She could only just about sit up unaided, by then. We had her potty-trained at twelve months. It was relatively easy, because she hated having a soiled nappy. I would have to say that Emily's physical development has been in every way, perfectly normal. In fact, if anything, she was a bit backward with her talking, but it seemed to come all of a sudden, didn't it David?"

"Hmm, that was all a bit odd, as well. Most children tend to use baby words when they first start talking. You know, 'bow-wow' for a dog, or 'gee-gee' for a horse, mama, and dada, that sort of thing. Not Emily though. As soon as she started talking, she was using all the proper words. Now, if you talk with her, she has a child's voice, and her pronunciation of some words needs correcting, but the very fact that these words are even in her vocabulary, leaves us wondering where she has learned them. Words like 'travelling' and 'interference,' are not even in the twin's vocabulary yet, but Emily used both words, in the right context, only a day or two ago.

I think you are all going to think we've both gone completely bonkers, if I tell you that we have come to the conclusion that Emily can already read a book, and not just any book, I mean really advanced educational textbooks and the like."

Malcolm gave a little chuckle. "How would you know that, David? Have you caught her reading Encyclopaedia Britannica, or some such volume?"

"No, that particular volume's not in our library, Malcolm. But we do have a complete set of Chambers Junior Encyclopaedia, and a couple of illustrated dictionaries. Then there's the family Bible, and all of Sue's accountancy reference books. We know that Emily's been into all of those. Does that surprise you?"

"It might suggest that she may have been fascinated by the pictures, David, but it doesn't mean that she's actually reading them, does it?"

David was becoming a little irritated at Malcolm's apparent scepticism.

"Alright, well let's put that aside for the minute. We'll just concentrate for the moment on what we know to be correct, and what we can prove to be right. After that, we'll move on to what Sue and I also suspect. Will that convince you, Malcolm?"

"Sorry David, I didn't mean it to sound like that. It's just that, like George here, I have to deal in factual evidence, rather than supposition and assumption. My apologies. Do carry on, please."

"Emily is telepathic."

David paused to let the significance of his statement sink in. To his surprise, nobody said a word, they were obviously waiting for him to elucidate further.

"What is more, she has taught Sue and me how to do it as well. Would you like us to demonstrate?"

Malcolm was the first to respond.

"Is this an example of what happened with Emily before lunch, David? I would be most interested to know how you did that."

"It's not a trick, Malcolm. I can communicate, telepathically, with Emily right now, if I so wish. I can also speak, telepathically, to my wife in the same manner."

"Go on then, David. Give us a little demonstration of your telepathic ability with Sue. Here, read her a passage from my newspaper, see if she can tell us what you are reading."

Malcolm picked up the paper and with a pencil, randomly circled one of the advertisements. He handed it to David, who looked at Sue, and she began to speak.

"Drives, patios, fencing, turfing, hedge cutting, pruning etc. Also drives, patios cleaned. Free estimates and then an 02380 Fawley telephone number. Look, David, is this really necessary? If these people are not prepared to accept what we are trying to tell them, why are we bothering at all?"

Malcolm grabbed the paper back from David and stared at what was written. He showed it to Sharon.

"My God, that was word perfect. How is it possible? Can you teach us how to do it, David?"

"If I could do that, I'd be worth a fortune, wouldn't I, Malcolm? So, no, I can't. I don't even know how I do it myself yet. I'm a complete novice at this, believe me. Sue and I can just about manage to communicate telepathically across this room, we might even manage if she was next door in the dining room, but beyond that, we'd both be struggling. So we're not quite ready to throw away our mobile phones, just yet.

Now Emily, is a different matter altogether. That little lady has the ability to communicate over vast distances. Try Godalming to Salisbury, for example. Not only that, but she can somehow project her whole being into the mind of someone else, to see, and simultaneously experience, what they are experiencing. Ask Sharon, she knows what I'm talking about."

Finding the ball in her court, Sharon felt obliged to say something, but in truth, she was finding everything equally as difficult to belief as Malcolm was.

"Well, it's true that when I was tied up in the sack and struggling to breath, I did keep getting this mental picture of a child. It was strangely calming and soothing in the circumstances. It wasn't until this morning, that I came to realise that the child's image was definitely Emily. I thought it was just a figment of my own imagination at the time, but in the light of what you're telling us now, David, I'm not so sure?"

"Did Emily perhaps speak with you, or was it only a picture in your mind, Sharon?"

"No, it was just her little face that I was seeing. Why do you ask, do you think she may have been trying to communicate with me, David?"

"I'm really not sure. Why don't you try talking to her, telepathically, see if she responds? You can never tell with Emily. We're fairly certain she talks with Peter and Rita, but they've grown up with it, and take very little notice. What about you George, have you tried it yet?"

"Well no, I have to confess that I haven't, but then again, this revelation is as new to us, as it is to the rest of you, isn't it Edith?"

Edith nodded her agreement. "Tell us how you do it, David, communicate telepathically, that is . . ."

David looked at Sue and sent her the message. 'Am I going too far?'

Sue answered, 'I'm not sure. Be careful, David. Emily might not take too kindly to it.'

David decided to sidestep Edith's question. He picked up on Malcolm's previous questions from a couple of days ago.

"Malcolm, you asked me how I knew that Sharon had been snatched from the hospital in Salisbury. I can tell you now, that it was Emily who told Sue, almost at the moment that it happened. She'd sensed it somehow, despite the fact that Sue and Emily were both in Godalming, some sixty miles away from Sharon, at the time.

You also asked how I knew that she was in a box with a sack over her head? Well Emily told Sue that, as well, and that Sharon was being carried in a vehicle that was heading further away from their location."

David's voice was beginning to go up a few octaves in his apparent frustration to prove his point, and Malcolm decided to placate him a little.

"Alright, alright, David, I think we're all pretty well convinced. Tell me, do you know what Emily is doing now?"

"Malcolm, I always know what Emily is doing. That is why Sue and I don't have to worry about her too much. Right at this moment she has just finished her lunch, and is going back outside with Sam to see the ponies. Do you want to meet Emily, and be properly introduced?"

"I would love to, David."

"I will ask her if she would like to come and join us."

They sat waiting in hushed expectancy, everyone eager to see whether or not David's telepathic message to his daughter would be responded to. The rattling of the big brass doorknob broke the silence. Sharon was nearest, so she hurried over to open the door.

Emily, holding lightly on to Sam's collar, walked boldly into the room and straight over into her father's arms. He picked her up, placed her comfortably into his lap, and gave her a little cuddle.

"Hello sweetheart, thank you for coming. There are a few people here that I would like you to say hello to. The lady that just let you in is Sharon, do you remember her from when we were on holiday in Weymouth?"

Emily looked across to where Sharon was sitting back down again. She smiled and wriggled herself down off of her father's knee. Walking eagerly towards her, she caught Sharon's eye. The words came into Sharon's mind just as clear as if they had been said out loud.

'Hello Aunty Sharon, it's nice to see you again. Are you all better now?'

The shocked and confused expression on Sharon's face left David and Sue in no doubt as to what had just occurred, even though neither of them had been party to Emily's first telepathic message to her.

Sharon held out her arms in the same manner as David, and Emily walked straight in, to receive a similar hug. Uncertain of how to respond telepathically, Sharon spoke her reply.

"Hello baby, it's lovely to see you again, and to be able to say thank you for helping me."

Sharon held up her bandaged fingers to show Emily.

"My hand still causes me a little discomfort, but I think it will be better very soon. Will you let me stroke Sam, please, Emily? I have missed him so much."

'Sam has missed you too. He says that he is sorry for biting you, Aunty Sharon. Would you like to come for a walk with us later?'

Sharon tried to 'think' her reply. 'Yes, I would like that very much, Emily.'

It obviously worked. Judging by the big smile on Emily's face, Sharon knew that communication between them had somehow been established.

Sharon couldn't get over how clear every word came into her mind. No wonder Emily didn't say very much, she didn't need to with a gift such as this.

Sam came to rest his head in her lap in the manner that he used to do. She fondled his ears and stooped to kiss his muzzle.

"Hello boy," she whispered, "It's good to see you again."

There were tears of happiness in Sharon's eyes as Emily climbed up onto the settee to sit beside her.

David spoke again. "Emily, the man sitting beside you is Malcolm. This is his lovely house, and he is daddy to Michelle and Charlotte. Would you like to say hello to him, as well, please?"

Emily turned to look at Malcolm, who, for a second or two, got the distinct impression that he was being subjected to her appraisal? Her tiny eyes met with his, and it seemed for an instant, that they looked right through him, boring their way right into his very being. It was an extraordinary sensation. The next thing that happened was even more so, for as the child held out her little hand to be shaken, she spoke to him without moving her lips.

'Hello, uncle Malcolm, I am pleased to meet you. I know that my daddy has been trying to tell you how he talks to me, so I thought it a good idea to teach you how to speak with me in the same manner. I have just tuned into your particular brain frequency, so that we can now communicate without talking out loud. If you just think your words, I will understand what you are saying.'

Malcolm could do nothing but stare incredulously at this tiny, remarkable, little girl child, with a seemingly perfect command of the spoken word. She had just taken over a part of his mind, of that he was certain, and now, she was teaching him something that he would have previously thought impossible. He 'thought' his first response to her.

'Hello Emily, I am very pleased to meet you. I don't know whether your daddy has told you, but I am a doctor of medicine. I try to help people who are ill, or injured, and make them better again. You have a quite remarkable ability which I think could be of great benefit in what I do. Will you speak with me again later, please?'

Emily smiled up at him. 'I wanted you to say that, uncle Malcolm. Yes, I will help you.'

To all the others in the room, the introductory exchanges between Emily and Sharon, and then with Malcolm, would have appeared to have been conducted in total silence. Only David and Sue suspected the reality of it, this being apparent on the faces of both of Emily's new telepathic acquaintances.

Her last introduction was to Jim Cox. But for some reason best known to Emily, she didn't see fit to include him in the same manner. It left David and Sue rather puzzled as to her reasons why?

Emily went over to her Nana Edith, and put out her arms to be picked up. To the others, especially Sharon and Malcolm, it was a gesture such as anyone might of expected from any normal child of that age, but after what they had just experienced with her, it seemed a little incongruous, somehow . . .

The room lapsed into silence for a minute or so, during which time the adults had time to think about what they had just seen. Malcolm was particularly intrigued, and for the first time began to appreciate David and Sue's concerns in regard to their little daughter's unique qualities. He began to explore the ramifications. Someone with the ability to see into the minds of others, and be able to silently communicate, as well? God almighty, if the politicians or military ever got wind of it . . . He shuddered to think of the consequences. David was definitely right to be worried. This was certainly going to need a bit of thought and careful handling.

As he rose from his seat and stretched his legs. Already, he had mentally resolved to try and further explore Emily's capabilities, if she would let him. He realised that her intellect was probably already far superior to his own, and she was only two years of age. He found it impossible to envisage a future for her, unless she was somehow shielded from the influences of the outside world? For that to happen, David and Sue would need as much as help and support as possible. Already, he found himself beginning to mentally revise some of his plans for Oakwood.

"Come on everyone, I think we've all just about had enough of this for today. Unless there is anything else on the agenda, George, I suggest we all take some tea, and then go outside for some fresh air? Perhaps we could join in with the children and drive a few golf balls, or fire a few arrows, or something."

George had the last word as he shuffled together his pile of paperwork.

"I just need to let you all know that I have spoken with Tony Williams, and he has agreed to come down and meet with us here, late on Saturday morning. There are still quite a few loose ends for him to tie up, but otherwise, he is ready and prepared to conduct a preliminary reading of Laura's Will for us. Is that arrangement alright with everyone?"

"That is excellent, George. Thank you for arranging it. Good news, eh Sharon? Come on, love, let's go and freshen-up a bit. I've got a couple of phone calls I need to make, as well."

He held out his hand to help her to rise. Sam reluctantly lifted his head from her lap as she ceased fondling his ears, and shuffled forward to get up from the settee. He looked round to locate Emily, and padded over to be at her side.

*I am sensing that there is some purpose and reason for your actions Emily, would you care to discuss it with me. Perhaps I might be of some assistance to you?*

*'Yes, Jo-jo, thank you. This has to do with my parent's future and in particular, their expressed concerns for my welfare. It has been a fortuitous development for this man, Malcolm Blackmore, to become their friend. My initial psychoanalysis of him has revealed that he is good and honest person. He also fits the profile of the sort of person that I was hoping to meet later in my life, someone who is philanthropically and altruistically motivated, rather than being preoccupied with the accumulation of personal wealth. It has all happened a little earlier in my development than I would have liked, but the opportunity has presented itself, and I cannot ignore it.*

*I have decided to take this man into my confidence, and to guide his thoughts into helping me to achieve what I desire for my own future. I have already planted certain ideas into his mind, which, should he choose to adopt them, I will help him to achieve.*

*I am aware that he has developed deep feelings of love and affection towards the lady, Sharon, and she, to him. It therefore seemed logical to include her in my plans, as well. I like Sharon, Jo-jo, for she is brave and resourceful, and basically a good and honest person, having learned by mistakes made during her previous hard life. I have* concluded that she will eventually become an ideal companion, or wife, for Malcolm Blackmore, and bring much joy into his life.

I think she might also be able to help me in my own physical development, Jo-jo. I am conscious of the fact that I still speak very much like a young child although my thoughts are very much more mature and advanced. I would like the lady Sharon, to become my personal life-coach and companion, someone able to assist with my social development. I would hope that as I progress through my childhood and into adolescence, she will be able to teach me the correct social airs and graces, associated with my physical development.

To initiate my plan, I have given them both limited powers of telepathy, so that they can communicate only with me. This is to my advantage, for it will serve to keep the receptors of their minds open to my subconscious autosuggestions, without either of them realising it.

I perceive that the next part of my plan to be the most difficult. My daddy is, by nature, a very cautious man and dislikes any change and disruption to the order of his life. It will take a lot of persuasion from Malcolm Blackmore to get my parents to enter into a joint venture with him. But if they do, and I shall be doing my utmost to influence the decision, it will ultimately entail my family moving permanently into this house.'

'It is apparent that you are giving this matter a lot of thought, Emily. I am surprised that you haven't seen fit to discuss it with me, before making the important decisions? I must again caution you against giving telepathic power to too many people, but I am pleased to see that you are heeding my previous warnings by limiting it to communication only with yourself. I think that this is very wise, but be aware, child, that these are very clever and resourceful people, and they may possess the inherent ability to expand upon it, despite your imposed limitations. In fact, I am sensing that they are already experimenting to that end, even as we speak.

Let us discuss further where you see your future life heading, Emily, for there are many of your years ahead of you before you become an adult person. What is it that you are striving to achieve, little one? You haven't told me anything about that yet'

'I am not yet certain where my destiny lies, Jo-jo, for there are still many factors for me to consider. Broadly speaking, I would hope to put my unique extra-sensory abilities that you have given me, toward benefiting humanity. As to how I am to achieve any of *this, presents its own difficulties. You have already taught me that the ability to guide another person's thoughts is a power that has to be used very carefully, and that I should examine and consider all the consequences before doing so. In this instance, I perceive that the man, Malcolm Blackmore, to be of a similar disposition, and I would wish to help him to achieve his aspirations, albeit to our mutual advantage. In order to gain his trust, I have been considering how I should demonstrate not only my ability, but also my good intent, Jo-jo, perhaps in this instance, you may be able to assist me?'*

*'What is it that you require of me, child?'*

*'My initial brain analysis of the elderly man, Mr Cox, revealed that he has a degenerative condition which we commonly refer to as dementia, Jo-jo. My limited medical knowledge is sufficient for me to know that he will soon begin to develop more obvious symptoms, and that his intellect, personality and physical condition will start to rapidly deteriorate.*

*This man is the lady Sharon's parent by adoption, and she has deep feelings of love for him. If it is possible, I would like to help this man in some way, but I seem to remember that, as yet, there is no cure for the condition. With your extensive knowledge in all things, Jo-jo, is there anything, as yet undiscovered on this planet, that will cure him?'*

*'The information you seek is no longer available, child. The condition you describe is linked to the aging process of nearly all the mammalian specie that inhabits this, and other similar worlds. There are numerous chemical substances that are purported to inhibit the progression of the disease, but the end is usually inevitable.*

*In other, more advanced humanoid civilisations, that no longer exist on this planet, chemical and herbal remedies facilitated some regeneration of the dead and damaged cells in the occipital and frontal lobe areas of the human brain, thus inducing retrogression. You will recall that there is evidence of this contained in your family Bible, Emily. Both Adam and Noah, amongst others, were purported to have lived in excess of nine hundred years before their death. Unfortunately, the information as to how this extreme longevity was achieved is not contained in any of my databanks, and the knowledge must therefore be presumed lost to mankind.*

*To help this man to stave off the debilitative effects of the progressive degeneration of his brain cells, it would be possible for me to reprogram certain other, little used, parts of his brain, encouraging them to take over the functions of the damaged cell areas. I can also stimulate the areas necessary to accelerate and expedite the healing processes associated with his burn injuries. But in order to achieve any of this, Emily, I would need to occupy certain parts of his mind, for the foreseeable future.*

*I am thinking that this man's unfortunate illness might prove fortuitous and beneficial to all of us. For me, it would be an interesting experiment enabling me to physically interact and communicate with you, and others of your kind, by means of all the normal human senses and speech. For the elderly, Mr Cox, who would be unaware of my presence in his mind, it would be of enormous benefit, a new lease of life, perhaps? Significantly for both of us, Emily, I would become a much more tangible and recognisable entity with which you can relate.*

*So, if after I have made a further assessment of Mr Cox's physical condition, and I find it to be viable, would you approve of such an arrangement?'*

*'It is not for me to either approve, or to disapprove, Jo-jo. I have asked if you could help this man, and you have responded in this manner. I trust your wisdom and judgement in all things, and if you consider that this is to be the best way to proceed, then that is how it must be. My own assessment of Mr Cox revealed that he is a very kind and gentle person who has suffered serious and debilitating injuries. He also grieves from the death of his wife. His immediate prognosis arising out of the onset of his dementia, will inevitably cause sadness and anxiety for the lady Sharon, with whom I would hope to become more closely acquainted. If you are able stave off, or prevent, any of that from happening, then I would have to approve. I do have some concerns though, Jo-jo. Perhaps you can reassure me before I agree to anything further?'*

*'What is it that troubles you, child?'*

*'Would your presence in his mind alter the man's character, Jo-jo? And what will happen to Sam when that part of you leaves his mind?'*

*'With no ill effects, Sam will simply revert back to being your pet and faithful companion, Emily. There will be no noticeable difference in his appearance or temperament.*

*As for Mr Cox, it is a little more difficult to predict, but as the pain of his injuries recede, his fitness will rapidly improve, and this will certainly make him become a much happier person. He is bound to be more active, and assertive, and will probably seek some form of occupational therapy to occupy his time. In this aspect, I can foresee that you will become instrumental, Emily. There may be other factors that are not apparent to me at present, child, but you can be assured that I will be taking particular care not to change any particular aspect of his psychology, unless I perceive that it is causing harm, or inhibiting what I am seeking to achieve. Does that answer your concerns, Emily?*

*'Yes, thank you Jo-jo. When will you start to put into effect the changes?'*

*'Just as soon as I've completed my assessment of the man's physical condition, and satisfied myself that everything I have outlined is possible, Emily. This is something that my kind have never attempted before.'*


"Nope, I'm getting nothing at all, Sharon-Louise. Read it again, love, think harder. Try looking me in the eye when you're ready to send. If David can do it, why can't we?"

Malcolm was getting frustrated, and Sharon bored, with it all. They were sitting ten feet apart, facing each other, and she had read the same sentence probably twenty times now, vainly trying to transmit its content to Malcolm, telepathically. She tried again.

"Have you done it?"

"Yes. I'm thinking the words as hard as I can, Malcolm. It wasn't this difficult with Emily, was it?"

"No, so why can't we do it now? Here, give me the paper, let me try sending something to you. No, on second thoughts, I'll send my own message. Tell me if you get this. Ready?"

"Yes, go for it."

"Did you get it?"

"No, nothing. What did you send?"

"There's no point in me telling you that, is there? Besides, I know you didn't get it, because my ears haven't been boxed."

Sharon laughed, "Lecherous beast. Come on, I'm fed up with this, Malcolm, we're obviously getting nowhere, let's go and find the others, shall we? Perhaps Emily might be able to help us later on?"

Charles Ferguson was barrelling down the M3 in his own beloved E-Type Jaguar. One of only three hundred models that were ever built, his limited edition two-seater convertible, was now finished in British racing green cellulose, and had a recently fitted, fully reconditioned, Janspeed-tuned, 4.2 litre, six cylinder engine under the bonnet. He was putting the car through its paces for the very first time.

Charlie loved his car. He had found it six years ago, languishing in a barn of a guesthouse, on the third day of a fortnights' salmon fishing holiday in Northern Ireland. Money quickly changed hands with the elderly owner, and he loaded the car, still covered in filth and chicken droppings, onto a hired car-transporter. Abandoning the remainder of his holiday, he immediately set off back home to London with his new toy.

The nut and bolt restoration and rebuild, had been painstakingly achieved, with no expense spared. Charlie cared little for the aesthetics of originality, for by the time he had finished, virtually everything on the car had been replaced with the very best options currently available. Even the interior, originally all black leather, was now duo-tone black and green Recaro sport seats, fitted with four-point seat belt restraints.

He was particularly fond of the chrome-spoked wire wheels with special-order Michelin tyres, the lettering picked out in white on the tyre walls. The only original features still remaining on the car was the Irish registration number plate, with its CFZ pre-fix letters, and the oversized, mahogany wood-trimmed steering wheel, now polished to perfection.

Travelling along at a comfortable seventy, he listened to the burble of the big engine at two thousand revs. The sound was music to his ears, and he smiled in self-gratification, in what he had achieved.

Charlie became aware of a Porsche Boxter driver, who had come up alongside to admire his car. The young man was now looking directly at him, from his position in the outer lane of the motorway. A quick glance at the other driver, and he received a thumbs-up for the car. Charlie smiled back, for the man was very good looking, and, judging by his slightly effeminate hairstyle, they might be of a similar persuasion? Charlie wished he had more time to explore the possibilities, but he was on his way to meet up with Malcolm Blackmore and David Morrison-Lloyd. The young man gave him a cheery wave, dropped the Porsche down a cog and roared away, leaving him with his thoughts.

Since receiving the invitation to stay at Oakwood with Malcolm Blackmore, Charlie had thoroughly researched his host's background.

Born 1965, in Dartmouth, where his father taught at the Royal Naval College, Malcolm Blackmore was educated at Rugby, and Oxford University. Now a Doctor of Medicine and a Fellow of the Royal College of Surgeons, he had joined the RNVR in 1995, but for what reason Charlie couldn't quite fathom.

Blackmore had married Lady Elizabeth Courtenay, a very wealthy young heiress, at Winchester Cathedral, in June 1990. There were now two children from the union, both pupils at a local private boarding school.

Why would a man with such a beautiful, wealthy wife, and two young children, want to spend so much time away from home, as life in the Royal Navy would surely dictate? His copper's nose was telling him that something was not quite right there, somewhere?

Charlie was astounded at the extent of the Courtenay family holdings, both in property and investments. It easily put them amongst the Sunday Times top twenty richest families in the United Kingdom.

Lady Elizabeth's tragic death was reported by a Times correspondent as, 'a great loss to many charitable organisations,' for her tireless fundraising work had benefited many of the smaller concerns, dedicated to helping with the rehabilitation of wounded ex-servicemen, and the welfare of their families.

Ever the cynic, Charlie always regarded such people with contempt and disdain. For it was easy to be generous if you were fabulously wealthy, and had nothing better to do with your money, wasn't it?

His personal view was that in this life, charity began at home. You looked after number one, made your own luck, created your own opportunities, and bugger all the rest. Nevertheless, Charlie was not averse, or too proud, to accept a freebie if it was on offer. He didn't mind occasionally kow-towing to their stupid whims, or even licking their arse, if it suited his purpose, as in this case. For who knows what the future might hold, especially in his dangerous profession? A friendly allegiance with the wealthy Malcolm Blackmore, might just prove to be both useful, and advantageous, at some later date?

He reflected on the thirty-six grand in readies, now contained in an envelope in his holdall. It would've come in very handy, but he was about to hand it over to that stupid tart, Sharon Cox, who in all probability, would want to waste it on clothes and make-up? It was a pity that it was Ahmed that had opened the safe and found the cash in the first instance, otherwise it might have surreptitiously found its way into his own coffers, with nothing more being said.

Charlie's thoughts turned to David Morrison-Lloyd. His interim report to his superiors had mentioned the veiled threat to go to the press with his story, but for some reason, Charlie had seen fit to play it down, somewhat, for he rather liked David. He'd had to report it, of course, just to cover his own back, but he made it clear that in his opinion, the threat had no real substance. To substantiate his view, Charlie had pointed out that David Morrison-Lloyd was ex-Special Forces with an exemplary Service record. As such, he surmised that he is far too principled, and patriotic a man, to ever consider such a drastic, and potentially damaging, course of action against the establishment comprising HM Government.

Outlining in detail, all the circumstances leading up to the incident at Bleanaway Quarry, and the vital intelligence that had been put forward beforehand, he stressed that the information he'd been given had a direct bearing on the success of the whole operation. He was therefore recommending that David Morrison-Lloyd be paid a sum equal to the original reward, put on offer by Monzer al Kassar, for information leading to the recovery of his stolen arms, and the apprehension of those responsible, now confirmed to have been members of an active IRA terrorist cell.

He suggested that the payment of the reward be conditional to his future silence, and to that end, he'd drawn up a suitable document for David's signature, a copy of which was attached to the report for approval.

As usual, his report and recommendations had all been accepted and approved without question. There only remained the problem of one, possibly two, members of the original terrorist cell that were still at large, and therefore perceived to be an ongoing threat to National security, and the delicate balance of the re-negotiated Irish peace accord.

In that respect, all his suggestions for dealing with them had come back stamped, 'Approved for action.'

Charlie was delighted at the prospect of spending some time with a few of his old mates over in Ireland.

In the mid-morning autumn sunshine, the tree-lined driveway of Oakwood looked resplendent in the shades of red and gold associated with the season. As the house came into view, Charlie whistled to himself as an expression of admiration, for it looked truly magnificent. A chocolate-box picture of a typically English, Georgian country Manor house, was the only way to describe it.

He slotted his car in between David's Mercedes and the now familiar Range Rover, both of which looked to be entirely in keeping with their surroundings. He was about to take his holdall from the boot when the butler appeared at the entrance to the house, and walked down the front steps to come over and greet him. Standing rigidly to attention and with the slightest respectful bow, Carter made his formal enquiry.

"Good morning, sir. Am I to assume that you are Mr Charles Ferguson?"

Charlie was already impressed. He thought that the age of such old-fashioned staff courtesy and formal address, was long dead and forgotten. The butler image was certainly far removed from his own Arab houseboy, Raki, who barely spoke any English and had to be taught everything with frequent beatings to help him remember. It crossed his mind that Raki was probably a lot cheaper though?

"Yes, that is correct. I'm here at the invitation of Mr Malcolm Blackmore."

"Thank you, sir. Welcome to Oakwood. I'm Carter, you are expected, and I am to show you to your room. May I take your bags for you, sir?"

"No, that's all right, thank you Carter, I can manage. Just lead on, if you would, please."

Carter led the way making small talk as they negotiated the sweeping open staircase up to the first floor landing. Opening one of the several doors with a flourish, Carter stood aside to allow Charlie to enter.

His first impression was that the large, light and airy, en-suite room, would not have looked out of place in any of the top London hotels, except for the expensive ornamentation. Comprised of pieces of fine pottery, porcelain figures, and some accomplished watercolour landscape paintings, they all served to compliment the lavish furnishings and decoration. It was apparent that someone with considerable artistic flair for interior design and decoration, had chosen, and carefully positioned everything, to its best vantage point.

The curtains gave a little flutter drawing Charlie's attention to the already open, double French windows. He walked out onto a small balcony that commanded a view down onto an adjacent stable block, and across an open meadow, to a distant river that sparkled in the morning sunshine. He stood for a minute watching Malcolm and David, who were alternately practicing their golf shots, aiming at three different length pins on a driving range. Their voices could be heard, but it was difficult to make out what was being said.

A movement from behind the stable block attracted his attention; it was a bright yellow, lofted tennis ball. Now he could hear women's voices, and laughter as well.

A quiet theatrical cough from behind reminded him that Carter was still present in the room. He went back inside.

"I'm sorry Carter, I was drinking in the views, and completely forgot that you were still here waiting."

"Quite, sir. Mr Malcolm and Mr David are out on the golf driving range. The ladies are enjoying a game of tennis. Mr George and Mrs Edith Lloyd are working together in the Library. I believe the children are all out riding. I shall shortly be serving morning coffee on the patio, sir. Mr Malcolm is aware that you have arrived and bids you to join him as soon as you have made yourself comfortable. If there is anything else that you require, sir, the house phone will connect you to Mrs Carter in the kitchens. Just dial zero, or nine, if you require an outside line. There are fresh towels in the bathroom; they will be changed daily by one of the housemaids. Lunch will be served at one o'clock; dinner at Oakwood is usually around six thirty to seven. Is there anything else I can do for you now, sir?"

"No, I don't think so, Carter. Everything seems just fine. I think I'll just freshen up a little before joining the others for coffee. Tell me, do you have a medium roast Columbian coffee, Carter? Coarse ground with a little cinnamon, it's my particular favourite."

"I'm not sure, sir. We certainly have a Columbian coffee bean, it's Miss Sharon's favourite, as well. The preparation however, is most definitely Mrs Carter's department. There's always a comprehensive selection of all the usual spices kept in stock, so please be assured, Mrs Carter and I will endeavour to find what you desire, or something very similar."

Carter backed out of the room quietly closing the door behind. He turned to walk along to the stairs, and was surprised to find Emily and Sam standing there, just behind him. The child appeared to be staring at the door with a slightly vacant look in her eyes, Sam too.

"Emily, what are you doing, child? There's nothing of interest for you up here. You and Sam should be outside playing. Come on, I'll take you back down to the playroom."

He held out his arms to pick her up, but she ignored him, turned around, and walked away without another word. He followed her slowly back along the passage, and down the staircase, watching her progress as she held lightly on to Sam's collar for balance, and they headed outside, toward the stable block.

Carter was already aware that Emily was an exceptionally gifted child in ways that he found difficult to comprehend, and the incident left him feeling a little uneasy.

He thought about Charles Ferguson, for he was fairly certain that it was he that was the object of Emily's attention. He wondered why this should be?

Carter prided himself on being a reasonably good judge of character. During his many years in domestic service, he had come across all sorts of people, and had developed an ability to make a fair assessment on whether a person was pretentious, or genuine, good or bad. His brief association with Ferguson had already served to give him the impression that the man was not the officer and gentleman that his dress and appearance purported him to be. Speaking with him, he had become aware of a certain evasiveness, a shiftiness, in his manner. He didn't look directly at you when he conversed, and he seemed to talk down, as if he was in some way superior? Carter didn't like that. He thought that it reflected an insincerity of character, and a trait that could usually be attributed to someone with bullying characteristics, or a vicious streak, perhaps?

He had also noticed how, on entering the guestroom suite, Ferguson's eyes had immediately fallen onto all the pieces of fine art and pottery, as if he was avariciously evaluating their worth? He concluded that there was something cold and calculating in the man's general demeanour.

He decided that, at present, he didn't have too much regard for Mr Charles Ferguson, and wondered why Mr Malcolm, himself usually such a good judge of character, had seen fit to invite him to Oakwood? No doubt the reasons would become apparent, but in the meantime, he decided to keep a close eye on the man.

*I am sensing the same as you child, this man has a ruthless and evil side to his character, but it doesn't necessarily follow that he means to harm you, or any of your family and friends. I think that it would be prudent not to trust him and also to alert your father as to your concerns.*

'*My father is already aware, Jo-jo, but I will do as you suggest and tell him again. The man is a policeman whose job entails catching criminals. There are no such people here, are there Jo-jo? So I cannot understand his intentions, or reasons for being here?*'

'*My initial assessment leads me to believe that the man was invited, and is pleased to be here. So far, I have detected nothing but goodwill and bonhomie in his demeanour, but his brain functions and thought processes are both complex and confusing, Emily. Outwardly, he wishes to appear to be of a friendly disposition, but I'm also sensing that in many respects, he has little regard for anyone other than himself. My conclusion is that this is a very devious and dangerous man who has been elevated to a position of authority within his profession. I sense that he will stop at nothing to achieve his aims, or whatever he desires should happen. Where this man is concerned, we will need to be very careful, child.*

Charlie showered and changed into one of his comfortable, light blue, Pierre Cardin sweatshirts, and a similarly branded pair of beige slacks. He chose a pair of Clarks Latch Dock, blue suede slip-on shoes, and selected his favourite Omega Planet Ocean wristwatch to complete his dress ensemble. With a final spray of Ferrari Red aftershave, and one last flick of the comb through his hair, he was finally satisfied with his appearance. He gathered together his wallet, pen and notebook, which he distributed into various pockets, and tucked the brown envelope full of cash, under his arm, before going down to find the others.

Following the sound of voices, laughter, and the delicious smell of freshly ground and percolated coffee, Charlie found his way to the Patio at the back of the house. Ever the one for making his presence felt, he emerged into the little gathering with a loud, "Good morning, everyone," thereby interrupting whatever conversations were taking place.

Malcolm rose from his seat to come forward and greet his guest with a smile and a handshake.

"Charles, good to see you again, glad you could make it. Come, I'll get you some coffee and introduce you to my other guests."

"Thanks Malcolm, but I think I already know everyone, and Carter is already sorting out my favourite brew of coffee for me, somewhere."

"Yes, I know. Coincidentally, it's exactly the same roasted bean that Sharon-Louise prefers. I've not tried it myself yet. Perhaps I'm missing out? I'll have a cup with you."

Had Malcolm been watching Charlie's eyes, he might have noticed the briefest flash of irritation and disappointment. In all honesty, Charlie knew that he would not have been able to differentiate any one particular coffee bean from another, or even from a cup of instant, for that matter. His request to Carter was all part of his pretentious attempt to slightly embarrass his host, from the outset, by requesting something he was reasonably sure wouldn't be unavailable, and thereby to gain a small psychological advantage. To now find himself second-fiddled by the same stupid tart that he was about to endow with a small fortune, he found both irksome, and demeaning. For no other reasons, other than the fact that she's a woman, in whose company he always felt awkward, and that she had innocently scuppered his little ploy, he found himself beginning to take an instant and unreasonable dislike to Sharon-Louise Cox.

"Strong and black, please Carter. Did you manage to find any ground cinnamon for me?"

"In the pepper pot, sir. My apologies for the container, but it is the best dispenser we could find."

Charlie smiled graciously. The small, insignificant admission, delivered with an apology, gave him the opportunity to be obligingly disparaging.

"Oh, I'm sure we'll manage, Carter. My thanks for your efforts."

Malcolm gave no outward indication that anything was amiss, and accepted a similar cup of the same beverage from Carter. He watched as Charlie added a small amount of cinnamon, but declined it for himself. Both men took a small sip, but it was not to Malcolm's liking, and he screwed up his face in disgust.

"Ugh, tastes like ditchwater, can I have some tea instead please, Carter?

Charlie laughed at his host's distress, and helped himself to a finger of homemade shortbread, which he dunked into the coffee without a second's thought. The biscuit proved to be delicious, so he took two more and placed them onto his saucer. He spotted Sharon talking animatedly with Edith and Sue. All three were similarly dressed in white short skirts and polo shirts. He begrudgingly conceded that they all looked very fetching, if one liked that sort of thing?

Excusing himself from Malcolm, he sidled his way over to the women who immediately ceased their conversation, as he came to stand in front of them. He started to speak while disdainfully looking them up and down.

"Good morning ladies, please excuse my intrusion, but I need to give you this envelope, Miss Cox. There is a receipt inside, which I would ask that you sign and return to me, after having verified the contents, if you please. I regret that I am not able to return your mothers jewel box. The Dorset Police have advised that they will only release it to a third party on production of a suitable letter of authority signed by you. I'm sorry, but it was the best that I could do in the circumstances."

Sharon had to put down her coffee to accept the envelope, and did so, politely murmuring her thanks. Charlie was pleased to see that she was obviously more than a little uncomfortable, and embarrassed, under his gaze, and she looked around for somewhere to put the package down. Without any more ado, he deliberately, and rather rudely, turned his back on them, and went over to speak with David and George. He could almost sense their indignant eyes burning into the back of his head as he walked away.

Smiling inwardly, he mentally notched up one more small success in the 'cause embarrassment stakes.'

"David, old chap, and George, isn't it? Nice to see you again, are you both well?"

"Hello Charlie, you managed to make it then?" David shook his outstretched hand and George, his hands occupied by a cup and saucer, merely nodded in his direction.

"Hmm, I've managed to wangle myself a couple of days, but I must be back in London by early PM Friday at the very latest. I'm off to Belfast for a week or so, from Saturday morning, and there's a lot to do before I go. Nice place Malcolm's got here, isn't it? I was watching your golf swing earlier, David, you look to be about as proficient as me. We must fix up a proper game while I'm here. Are you up for it, and shall we say a fiver a hole, to make it more interesting, perhaps?"

"I'd love to Charlie, but tomorrow is Doris's interment, and I'm to take Sharon and her father to London, so we'll be gone for most of the day. If you're to be away after lunch on Friday, that only leaves this afternoon or Friday morning, and I'm not sure we could get a course booking at short notice. How about we make a game of it on the range instead? We could have a three-ball with Malcolm, as well."

"Or a four-ball, what about you George, do you play?"

"Not for some years, Charlie. I have a bit of rheumatism in my arms and shoulders, so I tend to leave the game alone now. Can we talk shop for a few minutes, Charlie? I'd like you to cast your eyes over these statements that I'm working on."

"Let's leave it for the time being, please, George, I'm just getting into a relaxed mood. Can I suggest that you carry on along the lines we've already discussed, and in addition, provide me with a copy of the relevant tape recordings, as well? Then I can have them proof read by my office, who will make any necessary amendments, and send the transcripts back to you for approval and signature, before they're finally submitted. It's no big deal, really, George. Nearly all of this will be just for the records. I don't anticipate that any of it will ever be presented as evidence before anything but a Coroners Court, so the occasional bit of hearsay will be perfectly acceptable, just as long as the full circumstances, and the gist of the story, is adequately explained."

"Well alright then, Charles, on that basis, I think I can continue. My difficulty was in the complexity of some of the statements, and their background relevance to the sequence of events. To leave out any of the parts normally deemed irrelevant, or inadmissible, would leave gaps in the continuity, and leave one wondering how certain conclusions, and decisions, were reached. I estimate that I'm a little over halfway through the rough draught of the two main statements, those of David and Sharon, so I don't think I shall be anywhere near ready for you until the middle of next week, at the very earliest."

"No problem George, I shall be in Belfast all next week, so we can touch base when I get back. I'll give you a ring on your mobile number to see how you're progressing, a day or two before I return. It goes without saying that I'm very grateful for all this help, and that thought has just reminded me of something else. David, that little financial matter we discussed has been approved. If you give me your bank account details, the reward money will be electronically transferred, just as soon as I ring them through to my office. How does that sound?"

"Sounds like my lucky day, Charlie. A fifty-grand windfall is just what I would be praying for, if I thought that saying prayers would do any good. I'll go and get the details you need from Sue, can we do it now?"

"We'll see to it just as soon as I've finished my coffee, and just before I take some of it back from you on the driving range. I think you can afford a fiver a hole now, don't you?"

Malcolm, having relieved Sharon of her envelope and given it over to Carter for safekeeping, joined the group of men. He only caught the tail end of the conversation, but couldn't fail to notice the huge smile of delight on David's face.

"What's this you're all plotting, and did I hear someone mention a fiver a hole? And what's with the big grin, David? You look like the cat that just got the cream."

"That's the challenge, Malcolm, it almost seems a shame to take his money, doesn't it? As for my big grin, Charles has just confirmed that I'm to receive a substantial reward offered for information leading to the recovery of the stolen arms shipment, and the apprehension of those responsible, is that right Charlie?"

"That's it in a nutshell, David. There are a couple of pieces of paper to sign, and a certain file of evidence to be handed over to me in due course, but otherwise, the money's all yours."

"That's brilliant news, David. How much, if it's not too rude a question?"

"Fifty grand, more than enough to cover Sharon's treatment, and Doris's funeral expenses. Hopefully, the remainder will pay off my car loan, as well?"

"I don't think you need worry yourself with either of the first two, David. I've already squared up for Sharon Louise's treatment, and I'm anticipating that the funeral expenses will be more than adequately covered by the Cox's fire, and life, insurance claims. If we need to make any interim payment, Charles has just come up with some cash for Sharon-Louise, so we'll use some of that.

Incidentally, Charles, I would be most grateful if you could use your influence to speed up that enquiry for us. The insurance company won't entertain any sort of settlement until the police investigations are completed, and the Dorset Force do seem to be dragging their heals a bit. I can get George onto it, he is acting for Sharon in all her affairs now, but a bit of pressure from Scotland Yard might be better, don't you think?"

"Leave it with me Malcolm, I'll see what I can do. The life insurance will have to wait until after the inquest into her death, and that could take another couple of months, but I might be able to do something about the fire investigation. Now, come on, David, go and get those bank details for me, and then, with work out of the way, we can get down to some serious golf shots."

David hurried over to break the good news to Sue, and they were both seen to disappear off in the direction of their rooms. George excused himself, and with Edith, returned to his desk in the Library, leaving Malcolm and Charles to finish their beverages. Malcolm broke the slightly awkward silence between the two men.

"Thanks Charlie, that was good of you, the reward for David, I mean."

"It was nothing, he was entitled to it, Malcolm. In all honesty, it's me that should be thanking him. He's managed to clear up a case that I've been working on for nearly the whole of my police service. Apart from a few loose ends to tidy up, it's job done, and another big feather in my cap from the powers-that-be. There's no messy trial to pay for, and the reward money will come out of seized criminal assets, so everyone's a winner. Fifty thousand pounds is a small price to pay for what has been achieved, believe me . . .

I like David, Malcolm. As far as I can make out, he's an up-front, honest, sort of guy, and what you see is what you get. He obviously loves his family, and has made the most of what little he has. I take great pleasure in being able to help him along a little."

"Bravo, to that Charles, well said, mate, I like David, as well. In point of fact, he doesn't know it yet, but I am about to make him an offer that could potentially change his whole life. There are just a few more things that I need to put into place first, though, so mums the word for the time being, please."

"Yes, of course, Malcolm, it all sounds rather intriguing. Am I to be a party to your plans? Might I be of some further assistance, perhaps?"

"Possibly, Charles, possibly? Look, apart from George, who will probably be working, we're on our own tomorrow. The women are going off shopping, and David will be taking Jim and Sharon-Louise to Doris's funeral, so I'm anticipating that he'll be gone all day. Have a little think about what you would like to do. Golf, fishing, riding, shooting, sailing, all are on offer, and we can talk some more about my ideas. There might even be something in it for you, as well?"

The conversation lapsed back into silence until Malcolm made his excuse to get away.

"Will you excuse me for a few moments, please, Charles, I've just remembered that I needed to have a quick word with George."

Charles watched him out of the room. He found that he was quite surprised to be held in such high esteem by his host, and he immediately decided to back pedal on the embarrassment stakes a bit, at least until he knew what Malcolm had in mind.

He was very mindful of the fact that his own compulsory retirement age might prove to be a bridge too far, a difficult goal to reach, for his last bi-annual medical hadn't gone as well as he would have liked.

There were still more tests to be made, and he had been actively trying to put off the inevitable for as long as possible, but the facts still remained to haunt him daily. He had already been warned that the headaches and short spasms of blurred vision, might indicate a far more serious condition than the migraine headaches that he thought he was suffering from?

It now occurred to him that at this juncture, it might prove providential to have a top medical man to call upon if the worst-case scenario proved to be correct. Ever the cynical pessimist, Charles had already convinced himself. Shit happens, and his suspected condition only needed official confirmation, and he would, in all likelihood, be immediately discharged from his job on medical grounds. Of that, there was little doubt, for they don't let people with multiple sclerosis handle firearms, and there was no cushy desk job to be had in his particular, highly specialised, field of operation.

His thoughts were interrupted by David's return and they went off together to find a telephone.

# Chapter 10

Jim Cox awoke from the best nights sleep he'd had for weeks. He lay still for a few seconds wondering what on earth had happened to him during the night. He felt strangely different, somehow, much more sharp and positive, was that the right word? Nurse Jacqui Strong was fussing around trying to straighten up his bedclothes while chattering away incessantly. Very little of what she was saying was registering, for he was far too busy carrying out self-examination of all his wounds, while exploring a whole host of new sensations. He wondered how it was possible for all the pain associated with his burns, to have melted away during the night, they all felt so much better this morning.

He gently eased himself up the bed to be more upright, and was surprised to find that he felt little or no pain in the stretching of his damaged skin. He recalled that it hadn't been like that yesterday . . .

He tentatively reached up for the bed's electric tilt control suspended above his head. Jacqui saw what he was trying to do, and leaned across the bed to help him. He caught a faint whiff of her perfume and it stirred something deep inside his mind. It had been a long time since he'd found himself in such a close proximity to a lovely young woman. He saw the outline of her pants through the thin material of her cotton work trousers, and realised that it was too good an opportunity to let pass. His free, uninjured hand inexplicably found the sudden urge to plant a playful little slap on her pert little upturned bottom.

Jacqui shot upright in surprise, but her shocked indignation immediately melted when she saw the wicked little smile, and mischievous gleam in his eyes. Her admonishment was delivered rather tongue-in-cheek.

"Mr Cox, how dare you. What on earth has gotten into you this morning? We'll have no more of that sort of behaviour, if you please."

"Sorry lass, it was a kind of involuntary reaction that just got the better of me. I'm afraid a pretty girl's bottom is just too much of a temptation for any normal red-blooded man."

She was flattered, and decided that there was no real harm done, just as long as it didn't get to be an annoying habit. From a professional point of view, she knew that she must nip this in the bud before it started to interfere with her ability to do her job properly.

"I can see that I'm going to have to watch myself with you in future, my lad. You're obviously feeling a bit frisky and chipper this morning, and it's apparent from the gleam in your eye that you're on the mend. Now, we've a big day ahead of us, and I need to get you washed, shaved and dressed without fear of getting myself molested. Are you going to behave yourself, or do I need to go and get some handcuffs first?"

"I'm seriously feeling a lot better this morning, Jacqui, and the pain has subsided a lot. I'm feeling up to it, so can we try for a proper shower, instead of the usual sponge down. I promise to be on my best behaviour?"

"Let me have a look at those wounds first, Mr Cox, I don't want to be getting them wet before they've had a chance to heal properly."

Jacqui didn't hold much hope as she carefully removed the dressings from wounds that only yesterday, were still blistered and weeping. She looked in amazement at the transformation that had taken place in only twenty-four hours. Whatever was in that new ointment that Malcolm had told her to use, it was brilliant stuff. All the wounds had closed over with a new layer of healthy skin tissue, and although still a little swollen and inflamed, they were obviously healing very well. She could see no reason to deny his request for a proper shower; in fact it would probably prove to be positively beneficial for him.

"Come on then, Mr Cox, swing your legs out while I fetch your wheelchair, and we'll give it a go."

She turned her back on him to bring the chair over from the far corner of the room.

In one continuous movement, Jim threw back the bedclothes, and unaided, swung his legs out of bed and onto the floor. He brought himself straight up onto his feet and stood for a second or two experimentally transferring his weight from one leg to the other, gauging his balance.

Jacqui saw what he was doing and started to caution him against overdoing it, but he ignored her, and strode purposefully over and into his bathroom, not even bothering with his walking frame. She abandoned the wheelchair and hurried after him.

She watched in astonishment as the nightshirt came straight off over his head, and naked, he stepped under the cold shower, adjusting it to warm only after the cold jets of water made him gasp and give a little whoop of pleasurable joy. Standing with her arms folded, she watched as he soaped himself all over. He was obviously enjoying the sensation of his first proper ablution for many a long day. She marvelled as his vigorous attention to the area of his genitalia that started to bring about a partial arousal. 'My god, he's eighty-six, and still functioning' she mused to herself. She saw that apart from the scarring, his body, although now very thin, was still quite well-muscled. She concluded that Jim didn't look at all bad, considering his age, and wondered why she hadn't noticed any of this before?

He turned off the shower and stepped out onto the bath mat. She took the heavy bath sheet, reached up, and threw it over his head to land around his shoulders. For the first time, he was standing fully upright, and she realised that he was head and shoulders above her, and well over six feet tall. To preserve his modesty she moved behind him, and started to gently dry his back, but he was having none of it and stepped away from her to do it himself, with a lot more vigour.

"Do you want me to help you shave, Jim? You will need to be careful around the burned area of your face."

"I'm keen to give it a go on my own if you don't mind, lass. If I don't start doing things for myself, I might become too dependent and reliant upon you."

He paused for a moment to consider the implications of what he had just said.

"Christ, hark at me, what am I saying? There can't be too many chaps lucky enough to have a their own pretty little nurse to look after them, can there? I must be bonkers to refuse any such an offer?"

Jacqui laughed and watched as he wrapped and tucked the towel around his waist, and squirted some shaving foam into the palm of, what was, his bad hand. The transformation in him was little short of remarkable. It was difficult for her to believe that this was the same man that only yesterday was so pathetically weak and feeble, that he needed help with nearly everything.

She watched as with his safety razor, he removed the stubble from his face with the confidence of years of practice. She noted that he skirted his way round the badly scarred areas on the left side of his face, there would probably be nothing left to shave in that area anyway, she thought.

He threw some clean water into his face and gently towelled it dry before studying himself in the mirror for the first time. He didn't like what he saw, but realised he was going to have to live with it. At least he still had all of his senses, and that revelation suddenly hit him as well. He wasn't wearing his glasses, and yet he could see everything so clearly, something definitely wasn't right? He picked up the tube of toothpaste and looked at the small print in the 'directions for use.'

"Brush thoroughly at least twice a day or as directed by a dental professional." He breathed quietly.

The print was as clear as day to him. He looked again and read some more, uncertain of the reality of it. He squinted his eyes, blinked, and looked at them in the mirror. The pair of eyes that stared back at him are both clear, bright and blue, nothing like the ones he was used to seeing with his glasses on.

He knew now, that something miraculous had happened to him. He didn't know what, but he wasn't about to start questioning or complaining, that was for sure.

Jacqui was watching him closely, and noticed the slight look of confusion that had crossed his face. She couldn't understand why he was studying himself in the mirror, so intently.

"Are you alright, Jim? Do you want me to help you at all?"

"No it's alright, lass, I can manage. I've not used this particular brand of toothpaste before, I was just looking to see what the ingredients are."

"If you don't let me help you in some things, Mr Cox, I will shortly find myself being made redundant."

"Good Lord, I hadn't thought of that, lass. Tell you what, I won't say anything, and I'll continue to act the invalide for the time being. I've kind of gotten used to having you around, and I wouldn't like it to change just yet. Who knows, the very thought that you might be leaving me, could even bring about a serious relapse in my condition?"

They laughed heartily, each becoming aware of a slightly new understanding in their relationship with each other.

She waited while he thoroughly scrubbed away at his teeth before replacing the cap on the tube, and again looking at the small print as if to satisfy himself of something? He meticulously rinsed, dried, and put his toothbrush and toothpaste back into a glass tumbler. Then, from force of habit, she assumed, he wiped the sink round with the soiled hand towel. His mind seemed to be elsewhere, she thought.

She stepped forward, linked arms, and walked him slowly back into the bedroom.

"Am I to accompany you today, Mr Cox? You look as though you might be able to manage on your own."

"Too right you are, lass. Do you think that I would pass up the opportunity to show all my friends how fortunate I am to have such a pretty young lady to care for me? Have you ever been to a proper Cockney send-off with all the Pearlies in their finery, Jacqui?"

"No, tell me about it while I sort your clothes out for you."

He unselfconsciously dropped the towel off from around his waist and stepped into a clean pair of boxers that she handed to him. He sat down on the edge of the bed. watching as she sorted out the best of his white shirts and a black tie, which she draped over the back of a chair.

"David's parents will be there, they're a proper Pearly King and Queen, you know, just like Doris's parents were. We all went through the war together, and Albert and Josie Morrison have always been amongst our closest friends. I am so looking forward to seeing them again. I can promise you that my Doris, being properly laid to rest, will be the only solemn occasion in the whole day. David has given me to understand that before she goes, there's to be a bit of a wake, somewhere, with all her friends. Her coffin is to be transported in the traditional way, by a carriage and four, to the family plot in the City of London Cemetery.

As to what happens after that is anyone's guess, but I can't imagine that the people I know, will let her passing go without marking the occasion in the traditional way. If by the time we decide to leave, we're both still sober enough to remain standing, I shall be very surprised."

"I can't be taking too much of the drink, Mr Cox. I'm your nurse and you're my responsibility. I have to have a clear head at all times, so I'm sorry, but it's soft drinks only for me, at least until we get back. I might then be persuaded into taking a small glass of dry sherry with you, before we eat tonight."

He watched her taking his suits out of his wardrobe and examining them closely before apparently rejecting them again. She stood arms akimbo, staring at the wardrobe, as if looking for divine inspiration.

"Problem, lass?"

"You don't have a decent suit to wear, Jim. You've lost a lot of weight, and all of these suits are really dated. They'll probably hang on you, like on a scarecrow. We can get away with the shirt collar size, but I don't know about the suit. I'm going to see if Malcolm and Sharon can help."

"Hang on, Jacqui, I'm not sure about this, lets have another look first, shall we?"

"Jim, we don't have time to be messing about, this is serious. You can't be looking a scruff-bag at your wife's funeral, can you? Besides, you've me to consider as well now. I'm not going to be seen as the Aunt Sally hanging off the arm of some Wurzel Gummidge character, not by you, or anyone else. So think on, mister, if you want my company today, you will be smart, properly dressed, and well behaved. And that means no more bottom slapping, you hear me? Now get some clothes on, we need to speak to Malcolm."

Jim smiled at the colourful analogy. He was also rather fond of being bossed around by a forceful woman. She reminded him so much of Doris . . .

Their entry into the dining room, arm in arm, and with Jim in his bathrobe, walking unaided, and without bandages, caused everyone to stop eating and stare uncomprehendingly. Both Malcolm and Sharon quickly rose from their chairs to hurry forward and greet them.

"Good morning Mr Cox, Jacqui, will you both be joining us all for breakfast this morning?"

Sharon was already kissing her father's cheek in obvious delight at seeing him up and around.

"Hello dad. You're looking marvellous, what's happened? I can't believe the difference in you."

As soon as he spoke, she noticed that his voice was resonant and strong, much more reminiscent of his old self, and that old familiar smile and mischievous twinkle was back in his eye.

Jim undid himself from Jacqui's arm, but kept hold of her hand, giving it a gentle little pat as he spoke.

"Nurse Strong's ministrations are a tonic that certainly live up to her name, love. You wouldn't believe how much better I'm feeling this morning, and now we're quite looking forward to our day out together. But according to my lovely companion here," He patted her hand again, "I'm afraid there's a huge problem in my wardrobe department, and she's refusing to accompany me unless I look the part. We're rather hoping that Malcolm might be able to come to my rescue?"

Malcolm laughed, "I get the picture, Jim, and I'm sure we can sort something out for you. I'll just need to have a word with Carter, but please, come and join us all for breakfast, if you will."

Carter seated Jim next to Sharon, and Jacqui opposite him, next to Malcolm.

Sharon listened in amazement to her father's breakfast order of a small bowl of porridge, with a little added cold, skimmed milk, and honey, followed by scrambled eggs, with grilled tomatoes and a few mushrooms, on toasted wholemeal bread.

She had never known Jim to eat porridge before, nor to refuse fried eggs with bacon, sausage, black pudding and baked beans, if they were all on offer. His idea of a proper breakfast had always been full English, with everything, and to hell with the calorific consequences. She waited while Jacqui gave her order, and then she finished off the last of her own ham and cheese omelette, before quietly asking him,

"Is this the new healthy diet that Nurse Strong has put you on, then dad. I thought you hated porridge?

He looked at her blankly and whispered back,

"Do you know what, love, I have no idea why I ordered any of that. It just popped into my head as something I fancied eating. Same as now, I've forgotten to ask Carter for some fruit juice, but I can see there's some on the sideboard over there?"

"Hmm, sit tight, dad, and I'll get you a glass. Do you want orange or grapefruit?"

"No, you sit tight, I'll get it myself, love. I've been in bed far too long, and I need the exercise."

He grinned, and without giving her a chance to argue, he was up, out of his chair, and confidently striding across the dining room. Both Malcolm and Jacqui watched him a little apprehensively. He leaned toward her and whispered just loud enough for Sharon to hear as well,

"My God fathers, Jacqui, what have you done to him? I can't believe what I'm seeing. Only yesterday I was telling Sharon that she'd have to be a little more patient with regard the progress of his recovery. Yet this morning, here he is, prancing around like a young buck, and making my diagnosis look rather silly. Something quite remarkable has obviously happened, and it must be down to you?"

"Malcolm, I really don't know, I'm just as shocked as you are. When I looked to change the dressings this morning, there was absolutely no trace of any suppuration in any of his burns. They've all healed over since yesterday. At first, I thought it was the effects of the wonderful new salve you prescribed, but it's far more than that, isn't it? As you can see, he's so full of beans and self-confidence, it's like he's acquired a whole new mind-set overnight. I tell you, this morning, he's showered unaided, shaved himself, dressed himself, and I've even had to warn him to behave himself, after he playfully slapped my bottom."

Malcolm and Sharon immediately collapsed into stifled fits of laughter. It was infectious, and even Jacqui had to smile, so utterly ridiculous did it sound.

Jim came back to the table clutching a large tumbler full of fresh orange juice. He plonked himself back down into his seat, and couldn't fail to notice that the others all seemed to be grinning and staring at him. He reached up and theatrically felt all around his head.

"Have I grown an extra ear, or something? Why are you all looking at me like that?"

"Dad, nurse Strong is asking Malcolm for some personal injury compensation, and danger money, as well. You're really going to have to leave her bottom alone in future . . ."

Sharon couldn't keep a straight face any longer, and they all started chuckling, and then laughing uproariously, including Jim.

Charlie wasn't feeling so good that morning. As he dragged himself out of bed, the previous evenings over indulgence with Malcolm's twelve-year-old malt was reminding his head of its presence still in his system. He swallowed three paracetamol capsules, and drank two full tumblers of water in an attempt to re-hydrate himself. A long hot shower and a leisurely shave later, and the pain relief medication had kicked in, but the thought of a cooked breakfast still churned his stomach. As he dressed in his perception of smart country casual, he remembered that he'd agreed to accompany Malcolm to another nearby country estate for some skeet shooting. As far as he was concerned, it presented another opportunity for him to relieve his host of a few more pounds.

The thought brought a smile to his face, for yesterdays little golf competition on the driving range had already netted him forty pounds from David, and another thirty from Malcolm. It had been money for old rope, for he had lied about his handicap to gain an unfair advantage.

Looking at himself in the mirror as he carefully combed his hair and moustache, he thought about how he would need to go about it. He surmised that there was no way that Malcolm was going to be a better shot than he, for his job required him to practice with all weapons on the ranges on a monthly basis, and he always came away from authorised firearm user requalification, having scored a maximum.

To make it interesting, and to sucker Malcolm in, he would need to deliberately miss a few birds to start with, and then lay down the challenge. Not too much, say a hundred pounds, and win it by a whisker before offering a double or quits. He smiled again at the prospect.

Satisfied with his appearance, he glanced at his watch, it was just after eight, so he made his way down to the dining room. He passed Emily and Sam who were standing, as though waiting for something, at the bottom of the stairway. The child stared at him intently, her eyes seemed to be looking straight through him, and he found it uncomfortably disconcerting, for some reason. He stopped, stuck out his tongue and pulled a face, trying to frighten her. But apart from a small warning growl from the dog, they remained impassive, just staring, so he continued on his way without giving it another thought. They followed him into the dining room, where to his surprise, nearly everyone else was already near to finishing their breakfast.

Carter seated him on the same table as Malcolm and Sharon, where he was formally introduced to Jim and Jacqui. They waited while Carter accepted his breakfast order for a pot of his blend of coffee, and some fresh toast with Danish unsalted butter, if it was available. He couldn't help himself, it was yet another pretension, which he thought, might not be fulfilled, but, to his chagrin, Carter didn't bat an eyelid.

"You're the Policeman chap that was at my Doris's Service of Remembrance, aren't you?"

Charlie looked up into a pair of brilliant blue eyes that, like the child's, were looking straight into his own. 'What is it with these people, why do they all seem to stare so much?' he thought to himself as he answered.

"Yes, Mr Cox, I'm Detective Chief Inspector Charles Ferguson of New Scotland Yard, at your service. Please call me Charlie and accept my sincere condolences on your tragic loss, sir. Judging by the number of people present at the service, your wife, Doris, must have been quite a popular lady. I'm given to understand that she will be finally laid to rest in London, today. Is that correct?"

"It is, young man, and she will be buried with full traditional Cockney reverence. More to the point though, are the Dorset Police any closer to apprehending the scum that murdered her?"

The term, 'young man' was not one that Charlie was used to hearing, and it served to put him on the back foot. The question took him by surprise, as well. He had no adequately prepared reply, causing him to have to think on his feet.

"We believe that it is possible that one of the victims of the explosion at the quarry, might have been one of the same people that fled from your guesthouse on the night of the explosion, Mr Cox. Unfortunately, the situation is complicated somewhat, by the apparent lack of liaison between the two different Police forces, and the absence of any adequate forensics, from the scenes of crime team that attended the guest house explosion."

"Humph. Possibilities and might have been's, lack of evidence, none of it sounds very convincing does it, Mr Ferguson? What you really mean is that you've no idea who was responsible, isn't that the truth?"

Charlie was taken aback, he wasn't used to being spoken to in this manner. It was usually he that was the interrogator. He had to hold back his temper, remembering that he was dealing with an old man who had suffered the loss of his wife in tragic circumstances, and that he was a guest in someone else's house. He was being forced to eat humble pie, and he didn't like the taste of it. Dragging his eyes away from Jim's, and fiddling with his knife and fork in obvious embarrassment, he mumbled his reply.

"Unfortunately, Mr Cox, at this moment in time, I am reluctantly going to have to admit that your assessment is probably nearer the truth. However, the enquiry is still ongoing, and I am fairly confident that, in the not-too-distant future, there might be a breakthrough of some sort, that may allow us to . . ."

"Oh shut up, Mr Ferguson, you're prevaricating. Can't you at least be honest, and up-front with me? If there's no chance, then say so, man. All I'm after is a straightforward answer to my original question, and I'm getting all this bullshit. The answer is obviously a resounding 'no' isn't it? You've got your guns, and your terrorists, and that's all you care about, isn't it? The murder of my Doris was just an unfortunate circumstance in the lead up to the big issue. She became just another innocent victim in your little game, didn't she? I recall you coming into my guesthouse, claiming to be the long lost nephew of Laura Dobson. I didn't believe your story, and I sent you packing. Within twenty-four hours, Doris and I, are nearly blown to pieces in our bed. Now, I don't believe in coincidence, Ferguson, so try convincing me that you're not involved, somehow . . ."

Sharon, Malcolm and Jacqui had been following the conversation closely, amazed at the vehemence and level of intensity in Jim's verbal exchange with Charlie, who was looking ever more uncomfortable, aware that he was being turned into some sort of scapegoat.

Sharon reached over the table and took her fathers hand. Malcolm saw the gesture and felt that it was time to step in and say something to defuse the situation.

"Come on guys, let's not let this get too personal and spoil the day for all of us. I can see that it's an emotive and difficult situation for you both, and I wouldn't want it to get out of hand while you are both my guests here at Oakwood. Jim, why don't you let Carter show you to my wardrobe of clothes? You and Jacqui will almost certainly find whatever you need in there. Charles, if you'll excuse us, we'll leave you to enjoy your breakfast. Might I suggest we meet in the library in an hour, or so, when you're finished?"

Malcolm stood, taking Sharon's hand as he did so, and nodding to Jacqui to indicate that she should do the same with Jim. Charlie remained seated, saying nothing. They could all plainly see that he looked decidedly flustered and uncomfortable.

With the dining room now empty, apart from Carter, who had returned to begin quietly collecting together the soiled dishes, Charlie set about buttering himself a piece of fresh toast from the rack that had just been placed in front of him. He had consciously avoided having to look at Jim again. It was those eyes that bothered him. Like the child's, they seemed to be looking right through, and into his very soul?

Now alone with his thoughts, he took a bite of toast and a mouthful of coffee. It seemed to have no taste, and did little or nothing toward easing his mood. He noticed that the hand holding his coffee cup was trembling, and he could feel his damned headache returning. Inwardly, he was seething with anger and indignation at his humiliation, and his own inability to properly respond.

'Damn the man, what right did he have to put him on the spot like that? Who the hell does he think he is, anyway? Talking disrespectfully to a senior Scotland Yard detective? In the past, people would have died for less . . .'

He sensed another presence in the room and glanced to his right. He groaned inwardly, it was that bloody child and the dog again, just standing there in the doorway, staring at him, like before.

He pushed away his breakfast plate, got up from his seat, and left the dining room seeking sanctuary in the confines of his room, and with another big dose of paracetamol to boot.

*'The man, Ferguson, is angry and uncomfortable with himself, Emily. I am sensing that he is also very frightened, because he thinks that he has a terminal illness that threatens everything that he is. We must be careful not to push him too far and thereby provoke any violent reaction from him.*

*The antagonism from Mr Cox was an entirely unforeseen occurrence, Emily. There already exists a deep resentment in his mind for what happened to his wife. For whatever reason, he perceives that the man, Ferguson, is in some way to be held partially responsible.*

*I'm afraid that the simple alterations and adjustments I have made to the nuclei of his cranial nerves, to stimulate and speed up his recovery, have also served to make Mr Cox a much stronger and more assertive person again. It would be difficult to expunge this anger from his mind without bringing about another significant change in the man's character, for it is a basic human trait to seek revenge and retribution for any perceived wrongdoing against the person, is it not?'*

*'Do you anticipate that it will be any different when you begin to occupy other parts of his mind Jo-jo? Will you be able to influence or suppress the high levels of resentment and aggression, for it is not something that I am comfortable with?'*

*'These characteristics have yet to develop in your own mind, child, for you have yet to experience any personal wrongdoing from another. At some point in your life, it will happen, and inevitably provoke a reaction from you. It is how you react that makes you the sort of person that you will become. Study the two examples that we have before us, child. It will help you to understand what makes a person either good, or bad.*

*In answer to your question, I shall not want to interfere with any of the ventral tegmental area of the humanoid brain, for it controls many of the basic functions that determine Mr Cox's Character. We have both already perceived him to be a good and honest person, so it would be wrong to try and change any of that.*

*I am not yet sure if my partial presence in his psychogenetic being will have any significant affect upon him, or, how we are to continue to communicate without him becoming aware. These are problems that I have yet to address and overcome, Emily, but I can only do it while the basic functions of his mind are free from pain, and he is settled, and at rest. This may take a few more days yet, child, for I am finding the humanoid physical healing processes to be a little slow.'*

Malcolm sat on the corner of his bed next to Sharon. They watched in amusement as Jim, dressed only in his boxer shorts, stood patiently by, while allowing Jacqui to fuss over him in choosing the correct suit for the occasion. Fortunately, there was very little difference in their respective heights and sizes, so most of Malcolm's suits were a reasonable, albeit a little loose, fit on Jim. It really only came down a matter of choosing the right colour and style, something far better given over to the women, and there was no doubt in anybody's mind that Jacqui was revelling in it.

Malcolm took the opportunity to reflect upon the changes to Jim's physical appearance since his last examination, only about thirty-six hours ago. It was then that he had prescribed the new salve for the still suppurating burn wounds on his left hand, arm, and face. The healing process in the interim had been little short of miraculous, for there was no longer any need for dressings or pain-killing drugs. He made a mental note to check the ingredients on the ointment, but his experience led him to suspect that there must be more to this than was apparent. The man's whole demeanour had changed, as well.

The angry exchange with Charlie had been a lesson on how to verbally reduce someone to nothing. It had been impressive to watch, and he almost felt sorry for Charlie. Jim's verbal onslaught had left him floundering and lost for words. He'd been well and truly beaten at his own game. Malcolm's train of thought was interrupted by Sharon's sudden squeal of approval.

"That's the one, dad, it fits you perfectly. Double breasted, charcoal-grey worsted, with a darker grey pinstripe, just the right balance of smart and respect, and with a little bit of snap to it. You'll need a crisp, white shirt, black tie, dark grey or black socks, and black shoes. Do you have your gold cufflinks and tiepin here with you?"

"They were all in Doris's jewel box, love. I don't have any bling here, at all, unfortunately."

"You may take your pick from what I have, Mr Cox. You will find it next door, in my dressing room. Sharon will show you where."

Jim smiled wickedly. Avoiding direct eye contact, he calmly walked over and took Malcolm's right hand, pulling him easily to his feet. He stood deliberately close, and, feigning fatherly indignation, he brought his face near to Malcolm's to look him straight in the eye. Then, in a deliberately menacing tone, he posed the question.

"And how come my daughter knows so much about the content of your dressing room, young man? Is there something going on here that you do not wish me to know about, perhaps?"

The expression on Jim's face remained deadly serious, and there was a second or two when Malcolm looked decidedly uncomfortable, rather guilty, and lost for words. With the backs of his legs against the foot of the bed, he found himself effectively trapped, unable to step away, as he would have liked. From the corner of his eye, he saw Sharon come quickly to her feet, and even Jacqui started to move towards them, as well.

The timing of it had been perfect. Before anyone could intervene, Jim stepped away, still holding on to Malcolm's hand, the huge grin on his face said it all, and he started chuckling. He slapped his other hand on Malcolm's shoulder, and gently drew him forward into a fatherly embrace. He whispered into his ear,

"I've never seen her looking happier, lad, and I can't thank you enough for what you're doing for both of us.

I only ask that if this all falls through, you let her down gently, don't go hurting her, will you? She's all that I have now, and very precious to me."

He stood back, still looking in Malcolm's eyes for an answer to his question. Malcolm smiled and gave an almost imperceptible nod of his head and a squeeze of his hand. They released their contact, both men knowing that they had just come to a gentlemen's agreement. Where Sharon-Louise was concerned, there now existed a clear understanding between them.

Charlie lay on his bed with the curtains pulled, trying to shake off his headache, but it wasn't working, his mind was elsewhere. He reached for his special phone and hit speed-dial 1, then scramble, to connect with his Office.

The familiar voice on the other end merely said, "Good morning, sir."

"Give me the latest on McCue's movements," He demanded. There was the brief sound of shuffling paper.

"He is booked on a flight UA938 from Chicago, that is scheduled to land at Heathrow terminal 1, at 1115hrs tomorrow, sir. He has booked a connecting flight on LH6598, which will depart the same terminal at 1305hrs for Belfast International."

Charlie scribbled down the details into his police notebook.

"Right, change of plan. Get me on to the same flight, do whatever it takes, pull all the strings if necessary. I want to eyeball our target, and to make sure that he sees me, as well. Also, get on to our Belfast office. As soon as he lands, I want immediate twenty-four hour surveillance on his home and office. Put taps on all of his phones, and I want a full list of all of his known associates. I also want the name of anyone else that has been trying to contact him while he's been away. Have you got all of that?"

"Yes sir. Should I text you on this number for confirmation of your flight?"

"No, only if there's a problem, then you will call me direct. Otherwise, I'm to be deemed non-contactable. Is there anything else going on that I should know about?"

"Only that this operation has been given a higher priority rating, sir. It has been announced that the Queen is to make a state visit the Irish Republic in the spring of next year. With his previous track record, and so little known of his recent activity, Intelligence has identified our man as possibly being one of those that might actively wish to make things a little difficult for Her Majesty."

Charlie whistled in surprise. He couldn't recall the last time that a reigning British monarch had stepped foot on Irish soil. And to raise the security aspect to a higher level meant that the potential threat posed by McCue was deemed to be quite serious. He needed to think about this for a few minutes . . .

The voice on the other end of the phone brought his mind back again.

"Will that be all, sir?"

"No, let me run this past you, and then I want you to put it to the Operational Think Tank, for me. Switch on the voice recorder, now, will you please."

"It's on, sir. Go ahead."

"I'm thinking that with McCue being in America, he is unlikely to be aware of the demise of the rest of the terrorist cell, unless there is someone else, that we don't know about, that has already to put him wise. He probably won't yet be aware of the existence of the file detailing his part in the London bombings back in the seventies, either.

So how about we enlighten him? Make him aware, and see what his subsequent reactions might be? I'm thinking that a couple of our lads, perhaps posing as reporters from a national newspaper, might catch him at the airport and let it drop that such a file is rumoured to exist. They ask him to comment on the veracity, or something along those lines.

By then, I will have made sure that he will be aware of me watching him, although he won't know for certain who I am, but I will serve to become the focus of his mind and suspicions.

I'm anticipating that he will become panicked, and be so busy trying to avoid me, that he wont even notice any other surveillance measures, from another covert team. To us, he is a new target, and as yet, we have very little on his background. Who knows, his subsequent reactions might just give us a lead into his present activities, as well?

My initial assessment is that he will attempt to make contact with other members of the original terrorist cell to confirm the worst. When he does that, we've got him, otherwise all the evidence that we have becomes hearsay and purely circumstantial. As far as I'm aware, there is only one other person left alive who can substantiate and verify the contents of the file that will shortly be coming into my possession. That person is Connor McCall. He is the only other person involved with the original terrorist cell that we believe is still unaccounted for, with any degree of certainty. We have found no evidence to suggest that his body was amongst those killed in the quarry explosion.

In order to avoid any undue criticism, when we take McCue out, we will at least need something more concrete to satisfy our Irish counterparts that his demise was absolutely necessary in the interests of national security, theirs and ours.

Right, stop recording now. Pass the tape over to the Operational Commander immediately, please. I shall ring again at 0800 tomorrow for his comments, and a decision based on the ideas that I have put forward.

There is one last thing I want you to do for me. You will get on to the officer-in-charge of the Dorset Police investigation into the firebombing of the Weymouth guesthouse that led to the death of Doris Cox. I want all samples of the DNA, and any fingerprint evidence, that were found at the scene of the quarry explosion, to be compared with those found at the guesthouse. Any link, no matter how tenuous, I want to be informed of immediately. Give this a priority one rating. I want it done ASAP, and the results to be on my desk when I return from Ireland. Have you got that?"

"Yes sir, I'll get onto it right now. Will that be all, sir?"

Charlie broke the connection without even bothering to answer. He lay back on his bed, clasped his hands behind his head and closed his eyes. Step by step, he began to mentally run through all the logistical aspects of his proposals, his analytical mind looking for any potential flaws, or unexpected pitfalls.

Strategy, specialist personnel and equipment, other manpower, transport, weapons, and the timescale available for him to complete, in what would deemed to be reasonable. Each aspect was meticulously examined. This whole operation needed extremely delicate handling, for McCue was in a position of some considerable responsibility.

Charlie knew that he couldn't afford another fiasco like the David Kelly affair, back in 2003, or worst still, the recent, still unexplained murder of that weirdo, Gareth Williams, a GCHQ security embarrassment. Charlie had been assigned to deal with him, well before his mysterious, and still unexplained death.

Charlie had been severely criticised by the powers-that-be, for his part in the handling of both of those operations. The memories of it all going tits-up on both counts, still made him cringe.

This was what Charlie did best. The precise application of his thoughts to all of the minutiae of the operation would ensure that, as far as it was humanly possible to predict, everything would proceed as planned. His absolute confidence in his own ability to bring about a successful conclusion, served to clear his headache, and he went into his bathroom to throw some cold water into his face. He regarded himself in the mirror as he slicked his hair back into place. The altercation with Jim Cox was now put to the back of his mind for the time being. He felt that he was now ready to relieve Malcolm Blackmore of another couple of hundred quid, and was looking forward to it. Charlie smiled to himself at the prospect. He also remembered that he needed to speak to Malcolm about that his lost shotgun.

Under cover of darkness, and before the investigation had really got going, Charlie had easily located and recovered the gun from the shallows of the muddy stream. In its filthy state, he'd taken it home, stripped it down and thoroughly cleaned and oiled it, while recognising and admiring the perfection of the gun maker's craftsmanship. As he worked on the gun, his plans for it began to change. His original intention had been to return it to Malcolm Blackmore, fully cleaned and restored. But having recognised its beauty and considerable value, he'd fallen in love, and now coveted it. He wanted to keep it for his own.

In trying to justify to himself that he had any right to keep the gun, Charlie's warped mind examined all the options. He rather selfishly thought that, with his considerable wealth, Blackmore could easily afford to replace it. In all probability, he would have it heavily insured, and they, the insurance company, would be meeting the cost of replacement? Blackmore had mentioned its sentimental value, but Charlie chose to ignore that completely.

In reality, it was highly unlikely that he would ever be presented with another opportunity to acquire such a valuable gun. So now that it was in his possession, his intention was, that it should stay. It was to be a straightforward case of finders-keepers.

He carefully reassembled the gun and tested the weight and balance. Experimentally throwing it up to his shoulder a couple of times, he immediately realised that he would need to have it readjusted. The stock was slightly offset and a little too short for his liking. Charlie knew of a good gunsmith that owed him a favour or two, and might be able to sort that, and the modification of the serial numbers, for him. All done on the quiet, and for minimal expense, of course.

All things considered, Charlie concluded that with a new stock fitted, the gun's whole appearance would be altered considerably. That being the case, the risk of ever being found out was fairly minimal. He told himself that as long as he was sensible with its future use, nobody should ever be any the wiser. He carefully put his new acquisition away into his gun cabinet, locked it, and put the key back into its secret hiding place.

Malcolm emerged from his quarters into the hallway, still smiling to himself about how easily Jim had got him going. The apparent ease, at which he had pulled him to his feet, and the strength of his grip and embrace, reflected a quite staggering improvement in his physical, as well as his mental condition. He came to an abrupt halt as he nearly bumped into Emily and Sam. It was apparent that they were waiting for him. He spoke normally to Emily as he fondled Sam's ears.

"Good morning, Emily, and how are you today?"

The reply came back telepathically. 'Good morning, uncle Malcolm. Is it all right for me to call you that? It is how my parents refer to you when they talk to me, so it seems an appropriate form of address for me to use?'

Malcolm was tickled pink. He contemplated the tiny child standing in front, and looking up at him. He still found it difficult to believe that she was not only able to communicate telepathically, but also to converse in a manner more akin to an adult. He 'thought' his reply to her question, something still very new to him.

'Yes, of course, Emily, I am flattered that you see me in that regard. Is there perhaps something that I can do for you this morning? Why aren't you out playing with the others?'

He reached down to take her hand, and they moved over to sit on the bottom of the stairs. He felt the need to bring himself down closer to her eye level.

'I am finding that all the childish games become a little boring, uncle Malcolm. I would much prefer to read a book, and do something more educationally constructive.'

'So what's stopping you doing this, Emily?'

'My parents have told me that I'm not allowed to touch things that don't belong to me, and that would include your library of books, uncle Malcolm. Also, my diminutive size would preclude me from being able to reach some of the volumes that I would wish to read. I am seeking your permission to spend some time in your library, and to ask Carter to help me, whenever I find it necessary. I promise to be very careful with your books, uncle Malcolm. Please be assured, they are as precious to me, as they are to you.'

Malcolm found that she had tugged at one of his emotional cords. His extensive reference library was one of his most treasured possessions, but to be able to share it with this child was something he couldn't deny. He rose from his position, took her little hand and led her into the library.

'Where would you prefer to sit, Emily? I fear that my reading chair might be a little too big and awkward for you. Would you like Carter to bring a smaller desk down from the playroom for you?'

'That would be ideal, uncle Malcolm, thank you. A small stool positioned under the card index would help, as well. Will you kindly mention to my parents that you have given me your permission, please?'

'Yes of course, Emily. Is there any particular volume that you would wish to start with? Something to occupy your mind while we wait for Carter to sort out your seating arrangements?'

'If you are not joshing with me, and it is posed as a serious question, uncle Malcolm, then some of Darwin's works on the theories of evolution, might be appropriate. His Origin of the Species coupled with his Journal made during the voyage of the Beagle, might be just as good a beginning for me, as well, don't you think?'

The dry humour of it struck home. Malcolm burst out laughing and said out loud,

"Emily, that is priceless, well done, sweetheart."

Still chuckling, he moved over to one of the shelves. He removed both the requested volumes, adding The Descent of Man, as well. All three were first editions, their value inestimable, but he had no compunction in entrusting them to her care. He laid them carefully down onto the floor and watched as she knelt and opened the front cover of The Journal, briefly to inspect the frontispiece depicting Charles Darwin, before moving on to the Introduction.

He could see that she was immediately absorbed, and as Sam settled himself down beside her, Malcolm felt that it was time to leave them to it, but a thought suddenly occurred to him.

'Emily, just one last thing before I go, please,' She looked up from the book.

'I don't suppose that you have had anything to do with the remarkable improvement in Mr Cox's condition, have you?'

She smiled. 'I am pleased to hear you confirm that he is getting better, uncle Malcolm. It was only necessary to make a very small adjustment to his mindset, to encourage him to think a little more positively, and restore the natural balance of his mind. This in turn, enabled all of his bodily functions, and natural healing processes, to respond as they should. I cannot take all the credit for doing this, but I am aware that a change in him has been brought about.'

She immediately went back to reading her book, effectively ending any further conversation. Malcolm turned to leave, thinking about what she had just communicated. He kept repeating it over to himself, but found that he didn't quite understand the full meaning behind her words. He would have liked to ask her for further clarification, but somehow, this didn't seem to be quite the right moment?

Oakwood, that morning became a veritable flurry of frenzied activity as everyone readied themselves for their respective plans and destinations for the day ahead.

David decided to use the Range Rover, so that Sharon could get some experience behind the wheel of her new car. She didn't want to drive in central London, which suited David just fine, as he was well used to it, and knew his way around. Jim and Jacqui were quite content to take a back seat and be ferried around in comparative luxury. They were first to leave, amid the well wishes of all the rest.

Sue and Edith, for their shopping trip into West Quays, Southampton, were quite happy in David's old Mercedes. The chance for mother and daughter to spend a little money, and enjoy some quality time together, without having to worry themselves about anything else, was too good a chance to miss. They were next out of the drive.

The children, apart from Emily, were already in the saddle, and trekking their way down toward the river. The horses and ponies had become the number one attraction at Oakwood now, and the twins, under the guidance and tuition of Charlotte and Michelle, had already become quite competent and accomplished in their equestrian skills.

Malcolm breathed a sigh of relief, and went to find Charlie. He found him sitting out on the patio with another pot of coffee, and his nose into Malcolm's copy of the Telegraph. Malcolm slumped down into one of the comfortable wicker chairs opposite, and waited for him to acknowledge his presence.

After a few seconds, Charlie closed the paper and carefully tapped the pages back into line on the tabletop. He proceeded to fold it neatly in half, before setting it to one side. After pouring out a little more coffee and taking a sip, he finally looked directly at Malcolm, his face expressionless.

The two men regarded each other, each waiting for the other to speak first. Malcolm interpreted Charlie's silence as sign of his continued indignation following the run-in with Jim, but he wasn't about to start making any apologies for him, for deep down, he thought Jim had made a very good point. He broke the awkward silence though.

"The rest of the day's ours now, Charlie. Do you still fancy the skeet-shooting, or would you prefer to be doing something else?"

Charlie took another sip of his coffee, taking his time, as though considering the offer.

"Do you know that David's youngest is in your library with the dog? I just caught her messing around with some of your books."

"That will be little Emily then, Charlie. It's alright, I've given her my permission and I don't think she will be doing them any harm."

"You're more trusting than I am, then. I'm finding that there's something very odd about that kid, she keeps on staring at me for some reason. It's beginning to give me the creeps."

Malcolm laughed, "Detective Chief Inspector Charles Ferguson, of New Scotland Yard, finds himself troubled by a two-year-old looking at him? Come on, Charlie, you're losing it, mate . . ."

Malcolm was relieved to see the ghost of a smile flit across Charlie's face, as he too realised how ridiculous it must have sounded.

"You're right, I must be overworked, or something? But I'm not imagining it, am I? Does she stare at you, as well?"

Malcolm remembered his promise to David. He was not about to reveal anything about Emily.

"I can't say that I've noticed anything, Charlie. Emily is quite a sweet child, really. She's very quiet, well behaved, and she loves that dog to bits. They're virtually inseparable, you know. I expect she finds it difficult, not being able to join in and play with the others, because of the age difference? She likes looking at books, and it keeps her little mind occupied, so where's the harm? Besides, Carter will be keeping an eye on her, so I have no worries about her getting into any mischief."

Charlie had described it as 'staring,' but Malcolm suspected that he'd probably just had his mind scanned, if that was the right terminology for whatever it was that Emily was able to do? It crossed his mind that he should ask her why she found Charlie of particular interest, though? Perhaps she might already be aware of something significant that he had yet to find in the man? He watched as he drained the last of his coffee.

"Aren't you worried that she will damage your books, Malcolm? She's little more than a baby after all, and children have very little regard, or sense of value, for such things, do they?"

"I don't think that I have anything in my library that is of any great value, Charlie. They're mostly old reference books that we've accumulated over the years. I expect most of them are out of date by now, anyway. So, no, I'm not too worried on that score. Now what about these skeets, are you still up for it?"

Charlie stood up as he answered, and together, they started to move back through the house.

"Yeh, alright, come on then. I'm probably a bit rusty though. What have we got to shoot with?"

"I'm afraid that my gun cabinet is a bit lacking at the moment, Charlie. There's a couple of old 12 gauge Browning's that I only use for rough shooting. They're still serviceable, but you would have to say they've both seen better days. Then there's my 20 gauge Beretta Silver Pigeon, which I don't really get on with, and my Holland and Holland, which is my pride and joy, but that is still missing, of course.

Best we forget my guns, Charlie, the Club shoot will provide us with whatever we need, and it will serve to put us both on an equal footing to start with."

"Sounds fair to me. Look, I'm sorry that there's been no luck with finding your gun yet, Malcolm. I thought there was a good chance the search team might have located it for you. I'm advised that the forensic lads are nearly finished up at the quarry, and with any luck, they should all be leaving sometime this afternoon. When they're gone, it might be a good idea for you to go and have a poke around yourself, don't you think? After all, you know where it was last seen, so you're more likely to be able to work out where it went. You're going to have to get the site secured, anyway, so you might want to kill two birds with one stone, if you'll excuse the dreadful pun."

Malcolm chuckled and they paused in the hallway. "Give me five minutes Charlie, I need to change my trousers, make one phone call, and then we can go. Tell me, do I get to have a ride in your lovely E-type, or shall we take my four-wheel drive? No, on second thoughts, belay that and forget about yours, it won't like rough gravel tracks, will it?"

"Not bloody likely. That paint job, and the stainless exhaust system cost me a small fortune. Tell me, is there any sort of dress code for the shoot, Malcolm, or will these togs be alright?"

"It's nothing formal, Charlie, you look just fine to me. I shall book us a couple of rounds on the new Sportrap range, and try to ensure that we have it all to ourselves. That's settled then, I'll see you back here in five minutes."

The two men were in the car.

"So where do you see yourself in, say, five years, Charlie? Still chasing villains, or would you prefer to be engaged in something a bit less stressful, perhaps? How much longer have you got to work before you can draw your pension?"

As he spoke, Malcolm slowed the BMW to a virtual standstill to allow a farmhand, who gave him a cheery wave, to drive the last of his dairy herd across the road in front of him. Malcolm cast his eye over the animals as they all passed in front of the car, he recognised quality stock when he saw it. Their udders empty, the cows were eager to get back to their lush meadow grass, and the car was soon on its way again.

It gave Charlie the opportunity to think before answering. He wondered what was behind the question? Perhaps it was to be a job offer? So he suppressed the urge to tell Malcolm to mind his own business.

"Oh, I don't know, it's difficult to predict anything in my profession, Malcolm. My military service will count toward my Police pension, but I haven't taken any forecast on it yet. Due to my age, I shall be forced to retire in a little under four years, so I suppose I really should be making some plans. Why do you ask?"

"I have some big plans in the offing, Charlie, and I like to think that I'm a pretty good judge of character. As such, I prefer to surround myself with people that I know, and can trust to use their initiative. While I don't have anything concrete to offer you at the moment, would you perhaps consider working with me sometime in the future?"

Before Charlie could answer him, Malcolm slowed the car and pulled off the road to stop in the entrance to a field. The way ahead was blocked by a padlocked five-bar field gate.

"Step out of the car and indulge me for a few minutes, Charlie. There's something I want you to see."

The two men walked up to the gate, but Malcolm made no move to climb over, instead he leaned on the top rail, and waited for Charlie to ask the question, "Why have we stopped here?"

"This meadow belongs entirely to me, Charlie. Elizabeth and I bought it, as an investment, soon after we married, and I moved into Oakwood. It's called Twelve Acre Plot, for obvious reasons. Some years ago, outline planning permission was granted on it, when the local authority, Hampshire County Council, wanted to acquire the land to build a new waste incinerator plant. To cut a very long story short, there was considerable local opposition, mostly on environmental grounds, and a long protracted enquiry that finally led up to this site being rejected in favour of another, just down the road at Otterbourne. The clincher came about when The Courtenay Estate Management Company, commissioned a geological survey that showed there was a very real danger of water seeping down, and through to the river, to contaminate not only my stretch of fishing, but also some of the underground aquifers that provide much of the local domestic water supply to Southampton, and the surrounding district. It was highly providential, because it left us with this useful piece of land, upon which, outline planning permission for building, had already been approved.

Several years ago, my late wife, Elizabeth, came up with an idea on how to put the land to good use. First, she commissioned a feasibility study on a project that she had in mind, just to gauge the reaction from the planning people. When that all got the thumbs-up, she had some more detailed plans drawn up, and those too were submitted for further approval. She needed to be absolutely sure of everything, before making a start. The risk and investment dictated that once it got underway, there could be no turning back.

The plans for her project cleared all the various planning stages, almost completely unopposed, and at one time, it was all set to go. However, her sudden illness and untimely death, effectively put everything back on hold, which is the situation we are now left with."

Malcolm paused in his narration. He was unconsciously wringing his hands while gazing vacantly across the meadow. Charlie sensed that he still found her death somewhat difficult to talk about.

"I suppose you would have to call this miserable little bit of land, Elizabeth's field of dreams, Charlie. She's gone now, but that's no reason to preclude her ambition ever being realised, is it? The trouble is, until now, I've been so wrapped up in myself, and so full of grief, that I have completely neglected to carry on where she left off. She didn't say anything about it to me when she was ill, and I didn't think to ask her. But thinking about it now, I know that is what she would have wanted me to do, to finish the job she started, that is?

Well, things have rather come to a head now. The Estate Management has reminded me that unless I choose to proceed with it, the planning consent is due to expire very soon. If that happens, all of Elizabeth's work will have been in vain, her dream will never be realised, and it will all be my fault. I don't think I could live with that, Charlie."

"So what is Elizabeth's dream, Malcolm, you haven't said?"

"Sorry, Charlie. This is to be the site for, 'The Elizabeth Courtenay Memorial Hospital.' It will be a facility catering mainly for wounded service men and women. It is proposed to build a three-story, ninety-six beds privately funded, fully equipped, state-of-the-art teaching hospital. A trauma centre, of medical excellence.

All the plans and basic details have been thrashed out for some time, now. All the funding is in place, and now there is some additional pressure from the Coalition Government, who has somehow got wind of the project. In response to public pressure, they are keen to show that they are helping our troops. They are also seeking to get more private investment into the NHS, to relieve the already beleaguered budgets. So, it really comes down to me to be making the final decision. If I decide to press the start button, the diggers could be in here to begin work as early as next week."

"So what's stopping you, Malcolm?"

"Nothing really, except that it will be necessary for me to make some big changes at Oakwood, as well. I have yet to finalise exactly what they will be, and I really feel the need to discuss it with my girls, and get their approval before doing anything. I am, after all, going to be messing around with what amounts to their home, and future inheritance. I have to be sure that I am doing the right thing, and that is where I perceive there to be a problem. Things have not been right between us, since their mother, Elizabeth, died, Charlie. After she had gone, I found my own personal comfort in helping others. I immersed myself completely, and selfishly, into my work. But in so doing, I was completely forgetting about how my own children must be feeling. Too late, I realised my error, but the damage to our relationship had already been done. It was unforgivable of me, Charlie, so you will understand if I tell you, that right now, I'm feeling rather ashamed of myself. For as their sole remaining parent, I consider that I must have failed them at a time that they probably needed me the most?

Over the past couple of years, there has been a definite undercurrent of anger and resentment toward me. But again, I wrongly chose to ignore and overlook it all. I put their rudeness and bad behaviour down to their entering adolescence, and growing up into young adults. Too late, again, I realised my error. After the very recent events, which served to bring matters to a head, there was a frank and angry exchange of views made between us. It made me realise just how naive and blind I had been. If I'd just nipped it in the bud, as any normal father should, then I wouldn't be in the awkward position that I find myself in now?

On the good side, it would seem that we might now have cleared the air a little, and I'm hoping that we have at last managed to find some common ground upon which we can begin to re-build the bridges. But it has to be said, that this has largely been brought about by the influences of Sharon-Louise and David, entering into my life.

Sharon-Louise was good enough to offer me some unsolicited, but constructive advice, regarding my girls. I thought about it, and took on board what she said. It has served to bring me to my senses and realise the error of my ways.

David, in dealing with his terrible injuries, and this whole sorry mess involving the terrorists, has proved himself to be a clever, resourceful, and thoroughly trustworthy person, as you will no doubt agree? He too has been wholly inspirational to me."

Charlie merely nodded his approval, allowing Malcolm to carry on.

"Both have been patients of mine, so I feel that I know them, somewhat intimately, shall we say? I am well aware that they have both faced seemingly impossible adversities, both physical and mental. Their troubles were far greater than mine, and yet they both managed to overcome them, while demonstrated an extraordinary degree of courage and fortitude. What better character reference can there be for anyone?

I am going to need people such as these around me in the future, Charlie, and that is why, if I have my way, they will both figure largely, in all of my plans. I would like very much to include you in that, as well, should you so wish?"

"I'm flattered that you see me in the same light, Malcolm. But in what capacity would you envisage me working for you? I know little or nothing about business management, or medicine, for that matter."

"The most obvious positions that spring to mind would either be in personnel, or security, Charlie. Your particular field of expertise might prove invaluable in either respect. What do you think?"

"I think you should give me a couple of months to think about it, and to enable me to examine all my other options before I make any decisions, Malcolm. In the meantime, based on what you've told me here, this morning, I would urge you to go ahead and set things in motion. To me, it is abundantly apparent that this is what you really want to do, and you haven't yet put forward any real and valid reason as to why you shouldn't proceed. To quote an old cliché, 'you can't make an omelette without breaking a few eggs,' and that is how I see it. Your daughters might not like it, but if they love and respect you, they will understand your motivation, and will soon learn to live with it, you'll see . . .

Now, the day is a-wasting, so let's go and kill a few skeets, shall we? I've never shot, what did you call it, Sportrap? Yes, that was it. All my previous skeet shooting has always been English rules, standard down-the-line stuff, so, to avoid any embarrassment, you'd better explain the differences to me before we get there."

The Carters' stood together in the kitchen, he helping his wife with some of the food preparation, while watching Emily on the video monitor. He paused in his chopping of vegetables as the child set one book aside and picked up another. It was one that she had already looked at, and left open at a particular page. He concluded that she appeared to be either cross-referencing, or verifying something, when she put it back down again, and returned to the book she had originally been looking at.

He had been watching her with interest for nearly twenty minutes, as she slowly turned the pages of some large volume, open on the floor in front of her. Emily had soon abandoned the small desk he had painstakingly set up for her, it apparently being far too small to accommodate more than one volume at a time. It was evident, from the small up and down movements of her head, that she was looking at every page of the written text, for a second or two, before moving to the next. Carter was intrigued.

"Are you watching the child, Elsie? What on earth is she doing? I can't quite fathom it out, she can't be reading that fast, surely? It's not possible is it?"

They only ever used each other's Christian names when they were alone. She sighed and paused in her pastry making to gaze up at the monitor again.

"Well, she can't just be looking at the pictures, can she, David? If you look carefully at the book, you can clearly see that there aren't any. If you're that interested, why don't you go and speak to the child? Here, for goodness sake, take her a little drink of milk that she likes to have about this time of the morning, it will give you an excuse to go in there. Go on, Carter, away with you now, I can't be putting up with all these interruptions, I've far too much to think about without worrying about her, as well. If you really want to get in her good books, take a bowl of water, and a biscuit for the dog while you're at it. She'll love you for that."

It was an excellent idea, and he leaned over to give her an affectionate little hug and a kiss on the cheek, thereby bringing a smile back to her face.

Emily and Sam looked up as the library door opened, and Carter made his quiet entry, carrying a tray. He smiled at her and moved over to the table that Malcolm had set up for George to work on. Carefully moving some of George's handwritten notes to one side, he set the tray down onto the tabletop.

"Sam, here boy, I've brought you a nice drink of water, come on lad."

The dog looked at Emily who nodded her approval. He then padded over to Carter, his tail wagging, clearly pleased. They both watched as he gratefully lapped at the dish of cool, fresh water. Carter picked up a small glass of fresh, full cream milk, and a paper serviette for Emily. Kneeling down on the floor beside the child, he carefully set it down within her reach. Up until now, neither had spoken to each other, the only conversation had been directed to Sam. Carter looked at the assortment of books on the floor surrounding Emily.

"Are there any of these that you have finished with, miss Emily? Perhaps I can return some of them to the bookshelves for you?"

Emily pointed to the three Darwin volumes that Malcolm had given her to start with. Carter picked them up and looked at the titles.

"Ah, the great Mr Charles Darwin. I recall having the pleasure of reading these myself, Emily. I was a much younger man then, of course, but I found some of his theories and conclusions somewhat perplexing."

Emily turned to face him, her eyes looking straight into his. Her lips didn't move, but the words he heard in his head were as clear as a bell. What is more, they were not the words that one would normally associate with the speech of a small child.

'Which particular aspects of his work did you have difficulty with, Mr Carter? I have found in his writings, that all of his reasoning was quite logically drawn from the conclusive evidence he was presented with.'

Carter struggled to understand what was happening. In truth, he was merely trying to see if the child was actually reading the books, and if she had any comprehension of their content. Now, he found that he was being asked to comment on the content himself, in order to justify his off-the-cuff comment to her. He rose to the challenge, for he too, was well-read, and an educated man. He spoke normally, not yet understanding how to communicate telepathically.

"As an instance, Emily, I seem to recall that in the Journal, there is a paragraph or two under the heading of 'causes for extinction,' in which Darwin puts forward certain reasons, and conclusions, to account for the demise of a specie, thus allowing the rise to dominance of another, similar animal, living in the same habitat. His reasoning is sound, but he completely overlooks the phenomenon of global catastrophe? The catastrophic cataclysm, brought on by a meteor strike, is now generally accepted to be the most probable cause for the complete annihilation of nearly the entire Jurassic species, the dinosaurs that inhabited this planet. How can such a clever man have overlooked something so obvious?"

'Yes, I recall the chapter. It follows on from his geological explorations in Patagonia. I think you would need to remember, Mr Carter, that the Journal was written in 1834, and the existence of the Chicxulub crater in Mexico, was not discovered and verified until late 1978. My father's encyclopaedias contained only limited information on the subject, but they mentioned that there is evidence of forty, or more, similar sized craters, that is, ones with a diameter in excess of twenty kilometres, at locations that span virtually the whole of the globe. Do you not think that if the same knowledge had been available to Mr Darwin, he too might have speculated on the catastrophe of sixty-five million years ago, and drawn a similar conclusion?'

In his kneeling position, Carter's knees were beginning to ache, and he needed a few moments to think about what he was going to say next. The revelation of being spoken to, telepathically, by this tiny slip of a girl-child, was startling, to say the least. But to then hear her expounding on an academic argument, and on a subject that he had chosen to discuss, well, it was almost verging on the unbelievable?

Carter realised that he was already out of his depth in this discussion. He decided that to avoid further embarrassment, a tactical withdrawal was required. With a grunt at the effort that it took, he pushed himself back up onto his feet again.

"You make a good point, Emily, and I have to confess that I hadn't thought of that. You are right of course, the great man would indeed have taken it into account, had he known."

He theatrically pulled out his pocket watch to verify the time.

"My goodness, I need to get on with my work, Emily. I'm supposed to be assisting Mrs Carter with the lunch preparations. Before I go, I would wish to say that you have been communicating with me in a manner that I am finding rather difficult to understand. Nothing like this has ever happened to me before, and I am feeling rather privileged that you have taken me into your confidence in this way. Will you tell me, please, is it possible for me to communicate back to you in the same manner?"

'You can now, Mr Carter, for I have just enabled a part of your mind to receive my thought waves, and mine to receive yours. In future, you will only need to 'think' what you wish to say to me, and I will understand you completely. It will be the same for you, and nobody else will even be aware that we are talking with each other. In time, we may be able to increase the distance between us, but for the time being, let's limit it to being in each other's presence, shall we? You can try 'thinking' your reply to me now, if you wish.'

He formulated his considered reply before looking into her eyes.

'Thank you, Emily, this is an experience that I shall treasure.'

'Thank you, as well, Mr Carter. I anticipate that we will be doing this rather a lot in the future. Before you leave, would you be so kind as to pass me down some of Mr Blackmore's medical reference books, please. I can't quite reach high enough, and besides, they look a little too heavy for me to manage. The card index reflects two volumes of Dorland's Medical Dictionary, and also a Journal of the American College of Cardiology. I can see that they are located over there, on the second shelf from the top, next to the security camera. Can I start with those, please?'

Carter was chuckling to himself as he first replaced the three Darwin volumes to their proper place, and then lifted down the ones she had asked for. So much for the covert surveillance, he thought, there wasn't much that was missed by this smart little cookie, was there?

As he walked back towards the kitchens, he pondered on what had happened, and wondered what Emily had meant with her comment about, 'doing this a lot in the future?' The child was due to go back home with her parents on Sunday, wasn't she? In all probability, he might only see her again, if she was here on an occasional visit? Much as he would have liked it to be, there was very little chance of her ever staying at Oakwood permanently, so on what basis could she justify making the comment? It made no sense.

As usual, he found that the thought of her and the twins leaving, rather saddened him. With the presence of children in the house, Oakwood had seemingly come alive once more, like it used to be when Lady Elizabeth was still alive. He was aware that Elsie was feeling much the same, for she too was much happier when all the children were running around to annoy her with their playful antics.

Michelle and Charlotte seemed to have found a new lease of life in the company of the twins, as well. They had been teaching them how to ride. The four of them had become almost inseparable over the past week.

He and Elsie had seen the joy once again reflected in the fresh young faces of the two girls, and they had noticeably been laughing more than at any time since the Mistress, their beloved mother, had passed away. He pushed the morbidity to the back of his mind, telling himself that it didn't do to dwell on such things.

As he entered the kitchen, he heard the clip-clop of the horses and ponies out in the stable yard. The children were all returning from their morning ride, probably hungry, but it would take them a good twenty minutes to unsaddle and see to the animals. Next week, it would be he that would have to look after them again. He didn't ride, which was probably a good thing, he thought, as the horses might be grateful for the rest after all the activity this week? On Monday, the children would all be returning to school, Mr Malcolm would be going back to work, and the guests would all be gone. The old house would become awfully quiet, and very empty, once again. He didn't particularly relish the thought.

"Good morning gentlemen. My name is Simon, and I am to be your referee. Welcome to the New Forest Gun Club. Mr Blackmore, as a Club member, is already known to me, hello Malcolm, but I don't think we've yet had the pleasure, have we sir?"

The polite young man carried two gun cases, and two empty cartridge bags, slung over his shoulder. In his arms he carried a heavy looking cardboard box containing unopened boxes of cartridges. He thankfully placed his load down onto the flatbed of the electric powered buggy, and held out his hand to Charlie.

"Charles Ferguson, how do you do, Simon? Nice to meet you."

"Have you shot before Mr Ferguson, are you conversant with the general rules and safety procedures, sir?"

"I have, and yes, I am. Please call me Charlie, everyone does."

"Right, thank you Charlie. In that case I'll get straight on with it."

He unzipped one of the cases and extracted the gun, immediately breaking it to show that it was empty.

"Gentlemen. This is a twelve gauge, Browning Citori GTS, over-and-under, fixed action gun. The GTS stands for game and trap shooting. It is bog standard, with a single selective trigger, and a top tang selector, safety lever. The two identical guns that we shall be using today are both fitted with thirty-inch tubes, which are of standard skeet constriction. For our purposes, we have generally found these to be the most suitable. However, if you prefer to use something different, they can be changed for you in only a few minutes.

I am demonstrating the workings of the gun as I speak, but I expect that as experienced shooters, you are already familiar with all of this, I know that Mr Blackmore certainly is? So if you'll just bear with me, Charlie . . .

At a shade under eight and a half pounds, you would have to say the gun is a little on the heavy side, but it is well balanced and the recoil is minimal.

Mr Blackmore has ordered standard Remington two and three quarter inch, twenty-eight gram, number eight target loads, for you both to use, this morning. It is an excellent choice, they rarely give us any trouble.

Gentlemen, are there any questions on the workings or handling of the gun? If not, I will hand you one each, and we'll move over to the range."

Malcolm and Simon watched Charlie with interest as he was handed the gun that was being used for the introduction. The two were pleased to see that it was very obvious from the way that he first inspected and tested it for operation and wear, that he was used to looking at a gun that was new to him. They looked at each other a little apprehensively when he experimentally threw it up a couple of times to an imaginary target, for this was a blatant infringement of the basic safety rules. However, they both knew the gun to be empty, and his little demonstration served to show that he was well conversant with gun handling, so the minor indiscretion was overlooked.

Satisfied, the three climbed aboard the buggy and made their way down to a nicely set out Sportrap range, that was positioned facing north, on the edge of an open meadow. Standing atop the artificially raised earth embankment behind the range, Simon went into his prepared spiel, pointing out all the salient features as he was speaking.

"Gentlemen, can we first familiarise ourselves with the layout of the Sportrap range, which is a fairly new concept, and a fun way to enjoy clay pigeon shooting. You will see that the range is set out completely different from anything else that you may have used before. May I assume that by carefully observing the range as I point everything out, you will become conversant, and understand the layout?

As you can see, there are five caged, and numbered, firing points, which we commonly refer to as pegs. There are five traps, denoted clockwise, by the letters A to E, which are located at the points of an imaginary five pointed star. Trap E is located behind the shooting pegs, and will always deliver a variety of high-bird targets.

All of the traps are electronically operated, and will deliver the differing target, denoted by the card under the Trap letter. For example, you can see from the printed card, that the first trap to your left, trap A, will deliver birds from left to right, going away from the shooter.

You will appreciate that all the target birds take on a different dimension according to the shooters change of firing position, as in the normal DTL layout. But in Sportrap, it becomes much more accentuated and varied.

Today, there are only the two of you on the range, so we can vary things a little, to make it even more interesting and challenging for you.

Scoring is simple. To start with, all the birds will be delivered in simultaneous doubles, and you must take only one shot at each bird. If you hit the bird, it is called 'dead.' If you miss, it will be called 'lost.' Hence you will hear from me, 'dead pair,' or 'lost, dead,' or 'dead, lost.' Heaven forbid that I have to call, 'both lost,' because nobody wants to hear that, do they?

To start with, and as a little warm up, you will each shoot alternately, at five double targets, which I will nominate, one pair from each of the five traps. The full round will thus comprise fifty shots, ten from each peg.

In the event of gun, or cartridge malfunction, or anything else untoward, I will adjudicate according to English rules. Gentlemen, my unbiased decision is final, there can be no argument in any respect. If there are no questions, we'll move straight on to the matter in hand, and have a go at banging away at a few birds?"

Malcolm and Charlie looked at each other and nodded. Both were happy with the ground rules, and eager to get going.

"Are we going to make it interesting then, Malcolm? What about a hundred quid on the first round?"

"I'm still smarting from the few quid you relieved me and David of, yesterday, Charlie. But if you're happy to put that money back on the table, as well, I'll take your little wager."

"What, a hundred and thirty on the round, is that what you're suggesting?"

"No, let's put David's forty quid back in, as well. That'll be one hundred and seventy on the round, do we have ourselves a bet?"

Malcolm smiled and held out his hand to be shaken. Charlie eyed it suspiciously. This wasn't quite what he was expecting, Malcolm seemed pretty confident in his own ability, and Charlie hated the thought of losing.

Simon, standing silently watching, sensed the air of rivalry, and even a little undercurrent of antagonism. He'd seen Malcolm shoot many times, and knew that he was no pushover. This was going to be good.

Charlie was beginning to feel that he'd backed himself into a corner. To refuse the bet would cause him to lose face in front of Simon, so he rather reluctantly took Malcolm's proffered hand, thereby sealing the wager. Simon rose to the occasion.

"Gentlemen, there is a wager of one hundred and seventy pounds to the winner of the first round of five pegs. I will toss a coin to decide who will shoot first. Mr Ferguson, will you call, please."

Charlie won the toss, and nominated Malcolm to shoot first. He was aware that this would give him a slight advantage in gauging the flight of the birds before it was his turn to shoot. Malcolm counteracted this by electing to shoot from peg five, first. This meant Charlie would have to start from peg one, at the far end. For a right-hander, this was considered the more difficult peg to shoot from. Simon knew all of this, of course, and he smiled to himself at the already apparent gamesmanship tactics.

Malcolm emptied two boxes of cartridges into a shoulder bag, and put on the only items he had brought with him, his ear defenders and clear, safety glasses. Charlie did the same, but his were club issue items, supplied by Simon.

The two men went to take up their respective shooting positions in the cages of pegs one and five. Watched carefully by Simon, they loaded, and stood waiting, expectantly.

"Mr Blackmore to shoot first. From trap A, left to right, going away. Shooter will call when ready."

Malcolm took up his stance, left foot slightly forward, gun held at chest height.

"Pull." There was a clatter and the two clays took their flight. Both disappeared in a cloud of black dust, taken cleanly in successive shots, mid range.

"Dead pair," came Simon's call.

"Mr Ferguson to shoot. Trap A, left to right, going away. Shooter will call when ready.

Charlie had watched the flight of the first two clays. He realised that from his position the shot was slightly easier, in as much as with a slight breeze from his left, the clays appeared to be on a slightly converging course. Malcolm had needed to swing left to right through the shot, wisely taking the leading clay first. Charlie's shot required much less swing as the birds were going more away from him. He thought that if he left it just fractionally later . . .

"Pull." The clatter of the launcher sent the next two clays on their way. The pause seemed interminably long, but when the two shots came, almost simultaneously, both clays were cleanly broken at extreme range. Charlie had read it correctly and foreseen that at that range, they were almost close enough to be together in the same shot pattern. The second shot was therefore made much easier as almost no movement of the gun was required to achieve it.

"Dead pair," Came the call.

Charlie smiled to himself in satisfaction. He felt that he was going to be shooting well this morning.

"Mr Blackmore, trap B, incoming left to right, call when ready."

"Pull." This time it was easier for Malcolm, as both clays were coming towards him, and his shot required very little swing. Both birds were again taken mid-range, and disappeared cleanly in another cloud of dust.

The same shot moved to Charlie who took up his stance in readiness. For him, the shot required a slightly awkward left to right swing. With the gun on his right shoulder, he realised there was a constriction caused by the cage. There was a definite danger of the gun barrels colliding with the right hand upright post of the cage, before the shot had been achieved. He took a couple of experimental swings to gauge the shot. He was finding that there was no real comfortable position and stance. He was always going to be slightly off balance. He positioned himself as far forward, and to the left of the cage, as was possible. He wasn't happy with it, but it was the best he could achieve . . .

"Pull." The two birds came winging their way across the range. Swinging his gun up, Charlie sighted the leading bird and took his shot, but to his dismay it was the following clay that took only a slight hit, in trying not to collide with the cage, his swing had been too slow and his first shot had gone between them. He tried desperately to draw a quick bead on the other bird, but the inevitable had happened, and while the gun didn't actually make any contact with the upright, it was there, and in the way. He was unable to take the second shot.

"Dead, Lost." Came the call, and Charlie cursed under his breath. His only consolation was that Malcolm would be faced with the same difficult shot in a few minutes time.

"Mr Blackmore, trap C, incoming right to left, call when ready."

Charlie watched both birds disappear in another cloud of black dust. Malcolm Blackmore was proving himself to be a very competent shot, he thought. Perhaps taking his money wasn't going to be quite so easy as he had anticipated?

The same shot resulted in two more clays being reduced to dust for Charlie.

Trap D. Right to left, going away. This one resulted in a 'both dead' for each of them, but it was probably the easiest shot of all on the range?

"Mr Blackmore. Trap E, overhead, call when ready."

"Pull." The raised trap E was positioned on the earth bank behind both shooting pegs, so the high, fast-flying birds were already near mid-range before even the best of shots could sight them. Malcolm didn't miss, the first was taken cleanly, but the second bird, he only just managed to break. Charlie thought that it had probably been hit right on the extreme trailing edge by only one or two shot out of the pattern? It was the first bird upon which Malcolm hadn't scored a proper hit. It counted, of course, but only just. Perhaps the man was fallible after all?

Charlie took both cleanly, but after the first peg, he was one bird down to Malcolm's perfect ten.

Without saying anything to each other, they moved pegs. Malcolm went from peg five to the vacated peg one, at the other end of the line, Charlie, went next door into peg two. They were shooting side by side now, and this time it would be Charlie's turn to shoot first.

"Gentlemen, you will be presented with same sequence of birds, but on this leg, they will not be announced. Shooter will call 'pull' when ready, please. Mr Ferguson to shoot first."

Trap A's birds were again no problem for either of them. It was the trap B birds that Charlie had found a problem with. From peg two, the same shot was made much easier, and this time he took both birds cleanly.

'Right then, Blackmore, let's see how you get on with this one then?' he mused to himself. He stood back in his cage, well out of the line of fire in case Malcolm accidentally hit the post and discharged. There was always a danger of taking an accidental hit from some ricocheting shot. From his position, five metres along in the line of cages, he could only see the top of Malcolm's head and the ends of his gun barrels as he shot.

"Pull." Charlie watched both birds disappear almost immediately that they were launched. In unbelievably quick succession, they had been reduced to a cloud of black dust. He couldn't help but marvel, and heard himself calling out,

"Great shot, Malcolm," For indeed it was. Charlie's perceived nemesis, had become Malcolm's triumph.

Simon smiled to himself, for he too was impressed. It was only from his privileged vantage point, behind the guns, that he had seen Malcolm change from his right, and take the shot from his left shoulder. There were not many shooters able to do that, but then, he was aware that in skeet shooting, Malcolm Blackmore was a bit special, and this round really was comparative child's-play for him.

They both ended up with perfect tens from their second pegs, and from the third and fourth pegs, as well.

Simon knew that it was a very rare occurrence for anyone to shoot a maximum. Indeed, most of the experts were pleased if they managed to achieve anything over 80%. But so far, only the one bird had been declared 'lost,' and the two gentlemen were moving to the last peg of the round. It was obviously going to be a very close run thing, but all things considered, his money would have to be on Malcolm Blackmore to win.

Had he been able to place a bet, Simon would not have been disappointed. Both men scored another perfect ten on their last pegs, but once again, one of Malcolm's two high birds from the last trap, was an 'only just.' His second shot, the same as before, had resulted in only a slight deflection in the flight of the clay.

Both men descended from their respective pegs and came back to join Simon at the table.

"Gentlemen, my congratulations to you both. It has been a rare privilege for me to witness such a remarkable round of shooting ability. Regrettably, I have to declare a winner, and with a perfect 100% against Mr Ferguson's, extremely creditable, 98%, the winner of the round, and the wager, is Mr Malcolm Blackmore, my congratulations to you, sir."

Malcolm shook Simon's outstretched hand and turned to Charlie to do the same, but disappointingly, there was no sporting handshake to be forthcoming. Charlie was clearly very unhappy with the result.

"Is that to be it then, Malcolm, am I not to be given the opportunity of a rematch, a chance to redeem the situation? You are, after all, on your home turf, which gives you quite a considerable advantage, and there were a couple of those shots of yours that were a bit lucky. One of the last pair, I had strong doubts about. From my position, I didn't detect any sign of a hit. So I think it should justifiably have been called a lost bird."

Malcolm's eyes narrowed, this was not the sort of reaction he had expected of Charlie.

"Hmm, Simon called the hit, and I saw it deflect, as well. But I wouldn't like you to feel that I've been given any unfair advantage over you, Charlie. So, what are you after? Is it to be a straight forward double or quits, or shall we just forget this one, and up the ante to a really substantial amount, and shoot again? I'm sure Simon here, can come up with something a bit more challenging for us to shoot at. Am I right Simon?"

"Certainly, Mr Blackmore. If we use the present set-up, we can change the gun barrels to a modified choke. This will give a tighter shot pattern, or we can increase the speed of the birds, and vary the presentation as well. Failing all of that, the Club has only just come up with a really new, fun discipline, that requires exceptional speed, dexterity and ability, but we will have to move over to the other new Sportrap range, where the extra, hidden traps, have been installed."

He glanced at his wristwatch. "It's nearing lunchtime, so I'm pretty sure that it's free now, would you like me to check for you? It's only a phone call to the office."

"What do you think, Charlie? Are you up for a re-match on something completely different? This will be entirely new to me, as well."

"It sounds a bit more like my sort of thing, so let's give it a go."

Simon heard what was said, and he withdrew to make the phone call, leaving them alone. There was a distinctly awkward atmosphere of silence between them, each man feeling slightly aggrieved by the other. Malcolm broke the silence. Never one to sidestep a situation, Charlie's whole attitude was rankling him.

"So what about this little wager of ours then, Charlie? Am I to take it that you are not prepared to honour the first bet? Frankly, I am rather surprised, for as far as I can see, it was won quite fairly on the referee's decision?"

"I can see that there is a danger of us getting into an argument here, Malcolm, and that is not something I would wish. If that is how you see it, then reluctantly, I will certainly honour the wager. I was merely asking to be given the opportunity to redeem myself, while pointing out the advantages you had, and the disputed bird that awarded you the win. Is it really too much to ask of you, that in all fairness, we shoot again?"

"No, of course not, Charlie. But I question whether the word 'fairness,' as you choose to use it, has any real bearing on the matter? All right, we'll shoot again, only this time, it will be for another five hundred pounds. If I lose, I will pay you six hundred pounds in cash. If you lose, you will write me a cheque, made payable to the Help for the Heroes charity, and it will be for six hundred and seventy pounds, the full amount that I should rightly be entitled to. And before you say anything in response, Charlie, allow me to add that if you refuse this wager, I shall walk away from you, and take no further part, for I consider your present conduct to be highly unsporting, and not what I would normally expect of a gentleman friend."

The anger at this outrageous remark was immediately apparent in Charlie's eyes. He even took a threatening step forward, but Malcolm was unmoved and firmly stood his ground.

"How dare you speak to me like that, you jumped up, pompous, little prig. Why, I've a good mind to punch your bloody lights . . ."

He stopped himself mid-sentence, realising that despite the provocation, he had already overstepped the mark. Out of the corner of his eye, he had seen Simon returning, as well.

Simon, from a distance, had already seen that the two men appeared to be having a heated exchange, and even looked to be squaring up for a fight? Trouble on the shooting range was not something he particularly relished, for very obvious reasons. He saw that they were still eyeing each other malevolently, as he got to their sides. The atmosphere, he felt, could have been cut with a knife. Apprehensively, he attempted to defuse the delicate situation, by adopting a somewhat more cheerful, and innocent approach to the whole proceeding.

"Is everything all right here, gents? I've just got the okay for us to use the other range. It's just a couple of minutes drive over this way, so if you'll just gather your things together, we'll all make a move, shall we?"

"Everything is just fine, Simon. Mr Ferguson and I have just agreed to shoot for another five hundred pounds on top of the last wager, which we would like you to witness. We were just about to shake hands on it, weren't we, Charlie?"

Malcolm stood there with his hand outstretched. His eyes remained locked onto Charlie's, waiting for his response. The handshake, when it came, was brief and peremptory, rather than delivered with any sincerity. Charlie immediately, and rudely, turned his back on them and strode purposefully away. He left Simon looking to Malcolm for some sort of explanation?

"I'm sorry for my guest's behaviour, Simon. This is probably my fault. I seem to have badly underestimated someone whom I would have expected better of. I'll perhaps explain later. Best we leave it for now . . ."

"Gentlemen, for this discipline, which is completely new concept that has been devised by the Club purely for fun, like before, you will each shoot ten shots from each stand, or peg. For this particular program, your targets will be presented in a random sequence that will comprise four doubles, and two singles. The doubles will either be simultaneous pairs, or report pairs, where the sound of the gun being fired at the first target, will signal the launch of the second from the same trap.

The two single shots will be consecutive, and selected from any combination of those traps you are already familiar with, that is from traps A to E, and, or, from the five additional concealed traps, which can present either high pheasant, springing teal, or running hare. The hare, as you will appreciate, is a ground shot, and takes many by surprise. Are there any questions so far?

The first difference, you will notice on entering the cage. It is the addition of an illuminated red light, mounted immediately in front, and to the right, of you. While the lamp is illuminated red, it is not permitted to shoot, but you may load in readiness. You will also see that there is a big red STOP button, and a small digital black box. The box is a timer. It allows you to set the time between the trap releases. When you are ready, you punch in your desired time interval between targets, and press 'enter.' Your opponent will not know the figure you have decided upon, unless he has an accurate stopwatch running.

You may then call "pull" as normal, and from my position here, I will make the red light go to green, and set the timed sequence running. Three seconds will elapse before your first target will be released. It can be either a single, or a double, and come from any direction. You will not know what to expect, for none of the shots will be pre-announced. Are we all clear so far?

Both men nodded their understanding.

"Right, as if that is not difficult enough, your next targets will be automatically released on the preset time interval, decided by you, on the little black box. You must set your time at each peg. The maximum time allowed between the pairs of shots is fifteen seconds, and the minimum is five. Realistically, we have found anything less than nine seconds, is becoming quite difficult to achieve. Should you lose count of your shots, the lamp will go from green to red again, after your ten. Is that all clear?"

Both nodded again, and there was a bit of a grin on Charlie's face. Speed shooting such as this, was his forte. It was what he regularly practiced on the firearms handling courses, and on regular training days.

"In the course of a completed round of fifty shots, you will each have received exactly the same targets, but presented to you, in a different sequence. In the event of a tie on the round, the time factor then comes into being. The overall winner being decided by the shooter that completed the whole round in the fastest selected time.

Scoring will be exactly the same. You are permitted only one shot at each bird. The little microphone that I shall be wearing will record my voice, calling 'dead' or 'lost' and the computer will calculate the final scores. Other than all of that, normal English rules will apply. The shooter, in the event of a gun or cartridge malfunction, can use the STOP button. Hit immediately a problem arises, it will serve to stop the clock, and bring everything to an immediate halt, while we sort it out. Any range equipment malfunction, or the launch of a defective target clay, if not detected by the computer, will result in me doing the same thing from my handheld control.

Gentlemen are there any questions. Is there anything that you would wish me to go through again?"

"It would seem that a little pre-preparation is a key factor here, Simon. Are we permitted to set out our stall in readiness, so to speak, or do we have to delve for cartridges from our shoulder bags."

"Within the normal safety parameters, you are permitted to do anything you wish in order to speed things along, Malcolm. But it isn't always necessary to be going fast, to win the round. Many shooters have mistakenly tried to substitute speed, at the expense of accuracy, and paid the price. The highest percentage of hits will always win the round. Time taken, is purely a secondary factor. It is a point well worth bearing in mind. You can make things very difficult for your opponent by shooting to a consistently average time, while achieving a high degree of accuracy."

"What has been the average percentage of hits so far, Simon? Has anyone achieved the maximum yet?"

"On this program, there have been a quite a few perfect tens on the individual pegs, Mr Ferguson. But as yet, no one has come anywhere near a maximum score on the round. But having said that, it must be remembered that this discipline is completely new, and has only been running for a few weeks. We are still in the process of writing the computer software for it. The scores will undoubtedly improve, but we're still on a steep learning curve with it all.

I would say that a really good score, on this program, would be anything better than 86%, which is the highest posted far. Only three people, all Club members who have helped in the development of this discipline, have managed to achieved this figure."

There followed a few moments of silence while they each thought about the tactics of the challenge facing them.

"Gentlemen, if you are ready, I will toss the coin to see who is to shoot first. Mr Blackmore to call, please."

Malcolm won the toss and elected to put Charlie in first. He wanted to see his tactics, and to try and gauge the time being taken to achieve his shots.

Charlie picked up his two boxes of cartridges, broke them open, and without thinking, deposited them all into his shoulder bag, leaving the torn and empty boxes on the bed of the buggy. Malcolm watched, a little idea had already occurred to him.

Charlie pulled open the spring-loaded door, and took the single step up onto the non-slip, mesh covered wooden-plank floor of the cage that was peg 1. The steel door clanged shut behind him. He took a few moments to have a look at the construction of the cage before attempting to do anything else.

Painted bright yellow, and a full two paces deep, he estimated it to be and a little more than a metre wide. He saw that it had all been assembled from pieces of welded, square-section tubular steel. The heavily sheeted steel sides, and back door, came nearly to the top of his head. A piece of closely-woven heavy gauge wire mesh to the front of the cage, was welded to the floor rail, and to what looked like a piece of round scaffold tubing, formed a guard rail set at a couple of feet above the platform floor. The rest of the front was completely open to the shooter.

The aforementioned light, stop button, and little black digital box, were set out of the way, to the right of the cage, and mounted close together, on a piece of wood set flush to the top of the front tubing. He saw the red lamp was lit, and the LED light on the box was flashing a message, inviting him to enter a number of his choice, between five and fifteen, and then confirm by depressing the 'enter' key. Charlie thought for a second or two, and entered the number 11.

He looked around the cage for a hook, or some other convenient protrusion, from which he could suspend his cartridge bag, but there was nothing. Annoyingly, it would either have to remain on his shoulder, or be relegated to the floor at his feet. He decided on the latter, but first, tipped out, and arranged a neat line of ten cartridges, thereby making them easier to pick up, two at a time.

From a distance, Malcolm observed his preparation, and an idea occurred to him. He leaned over to retrieve one of the torn and discarded cartridge boxes, which he folded and slipped into his trousers pocket. He then proceeded to adjust the shoulder strap on his own cartridge bag to make it as short as possible.

Charlie bent to take his first load from the line of cartridges on the floor. In so doing, the barrels of the gun, held in his left hand, made contact with the front guard rail of the cage. He stopped, and rearranged the line of cartridges a foot further back from the front, and then tried it again. He was mentally running through everything beforehand, looking to eliminate any likely problems before they arose.

Next, he stood at the ready position and started counting to himself. He brought the empty gun up to his shoulder, took an imaginary swing, and brought the gun back down. He broke it open, stooped to pick up two cartridges, which he unhurriedly placed into the chambers before closing the gun and bringing it back to the ready position again.

He thought for a second or two, then re-entered the figure on the box. He'd changed it to 9.

Satisfied, he closed his eyes to focus his concentration, and took several long, slow, deep breaths. He carefully put on his ear defenders, adjusted his safety glasses, and took up his stance. He was ready . . .

"Pull." Out of the corner of his eye he saw the light go to green, and he started mentally counting. And one, and two, and thr . . . There was a clatter to his right, and trap C released two incoming, right to left. He took both cleanly, and went straight into his mentally rehearsed sequence. Step back while breaking the gun, the two spent cartridges ejected, but he saw them land in amongst his carefully arranged line on the floor dislodging a couple. 'Damn,' he thought, but smoothly picked up two more, placing them carefully into the chambers and closing the gun. He'd lost count, but stepped forward and was ready . . .

Almost immediately, there was another clatter, and a single came from trap B, incoming, left to right, the one he'd missed before. Not this time, though, he got it cleanly, but his shot immediately released a second from the same trap, which very nearly caught him out. He hurriedly sighted the bird, and brought the gun back for another short swing. His second shot was also a hit, but only just. There was no time to reflect, step back, gun open, pick up two cartridges, load, step forward, ready . . . Clatter, where? Then he saw them, two high birds from behind, gun up, but the birds were already mid-range and going away fast. His first took the leading bird, but his second shot missed completely. No time for recriminations, step back, break the gun, pick up two shells, load, and close the gun while stepping forward . . . The clatter came as he was still readying himself. A single running hare, left to right, going away, he took it cleanly, and not wishing to be caught out again, waited expectantly for a second, but it didn't come. Too late, he realised that it was only a single, and two valuable seconds had been wasted. He stepped back and broke the gun, picked up two shells, loaded, closed the gun, clatter . . . The second single shot was a springing teal from a concealed trap to his right. In his haste to get the gun up, the barrels struck a glancing blow on the cage front cross member, thereby messing up his timing and further delaying his shot. He got a shot, but he knew as he squeezed the trigger that it was going to be a complete miss.

'Damn and blast,' he muttered angrily to himself as he stepped back, broke the gun and picked up two shells to reload. He then had to reject one that he'd picked up, as it was a spent cartridge. It cost him another valuable second, and caused him to fumble with the reload. He was just about getting the gun closed, when the next clatter came. Trap D, right to left, going away, two birds, already halfway across the range before he could even get the gun high enough to begin to bear. Two shots, made in quick succession at extreme range, more by instinct than judgement, but both were hits, just about. Never mind, they counted . . .

Step back, break the gun, pick up two . . . but then he saw that the little light had thankfully turned back to red. He breathed a sigh of relief.

He kicked all his spent shells down the slit in the floor before picking up his bag to leave. It gave him time to reflect on his performance, which he knew, hadn't been good.

His mental analysis made him realise, only then, that in the heat of the moment, he'd reloaded unnecessarily between the two singles. And after having been clearly told during the briefing, that they would be consecutive shots . . . he cursed again at his own inattention and stupidity. That little error had cost him dearly in time, and had resulted in the second lost bird.

As he made his way back up to Simon, who was standing on the back of the buggy, he deliberately avoided any eye contact with Malcolm as they passed. Had he looked, he might have noticed the ghost of a little smile on his face. Malcolm had worked out that Charlie had been shooting on a time interval of either ten or eleven seconds. It clearly wasn't enough, and it had cost him dearly. He wasn't about to be caught out in the same manner and remembered what Simon had said.

"The highest percentage of hits will always win the round."

Malcolm wasn't about to commit himself to being in any hurry, at all. His whole strategy would rely on accuracy without burdening himself with the additional pressure of trying to achieve a quick time.

He entered the cage, and like Charlie, familiarised himself with the layout. He took his empty cartridge bag and looped the strap over the top of the front cross member, drawing it tight until the bag hung level with the rail top. Leaning over, he pushed the leather straps through two of the gaps in the mesh, to form little loops on the inside. These, he then locked into place with pieces of folded cardboard produced from his pocket. Next, he tucked the flap lid inside of the bag, so that it was out of the way, and pushed his fist down into the bag with a bit of weight behind it, to test that it was secure.

Satisfied, Malcolm carefully opened his first box of cartridges, taking particular care not to break the box. With the brass percussion caps all upright and facing towards him, Malcolm carefully placed the whole box into the bag. He extracted four cartridges from the box so that he could easily get his fingers down inside to get more. He thoughtfully entered a figure into the black box, loaded the gun, and stood surveying the range for a full minute. He was gathering his concentration. He finally donned his glasses and ear protection, and adopted a ready position, left foot comfortably forward, with the gun held at abdomen height.

"Pull" he watched the light go from red to green and mentally counted to three. His eyes and concentration were focused on the centre of the range. A clatter to his right sent two birds from trap D, right to left, and going away. With a slight twist of his body the gun came up to his shoulder to pick up their trajectory, and in quick succession both were reduced to a cloud of dust, just over halfway across the range.

Calmly and quite unhurriedly, and while keeping his feet absolutely still, he broke open the gun to eject. He reached down, extracted two cartridges from the box, placed them into the chambers and brought the stock up to close the gun. With his careful preparation, he was easily ready for the next shot, and even had to wait a second or two before it came.

His next target came from his left. Trap A, one bird, left to right, going away. He took it mid-range and his report immediately released another from the same trap. Resisting the temptation to move, he kept his gun held loosely in the same position, and it was there to take the second bird just fractionally further out than its predecessor.

As he calmly went through his reloading procedure, he knew that he had two singles and two more doubles to come. In readiness, he went back to focusing his concentration mid-range.

The muffled clatter of a hidden launcher sent a pair of springing teal skywards from his left. Notoriously the most difficult of targets to hit, he took both as they reached a height of about fourteen and fifteen metres, and just beginning to slow a little in their ascent. The hits were clean, and in quick succession.

Malcolm grunted to himself in satisfaction as he went straight into his reload. Six down four to go, and two of those were to be singles. Ready, he waited for the next bird.

The clatter from somewhere behind signalled a release, which he knew must be an overhead. The single high pheasant sailed into view, peeling away on the breeze from his right. He picked a spot a yard in front of the target and squeezed the trigger. He watched the clay fall to pieces, and tumble to earth at extreme range.

The wait for the second single seemed like an eternity. Malcolm kept the gun at chest height, the stock hovering just clear of his shoulder, all his senses focused mid range. Trap B, incoming, left to right.

It flashed through his mind that this was the awkward one, and the thought affected the swing of his shot. With no time to change shoulders, as he would have preferred, his inhibited swing picked it up mid-range. He squeezed the trigger and immediately had to bring the gun to an abrupt halt, to avoid hitting the cage upright with the barrels. He saw the clay deflect slightly downwards from its trajectory. The shot pattern must have just about caught the trailing edge, he thought. With a metallic clang, what was left of the clay collided with the base of one of the cages far to his right. He'd been lucky.

His concentration was rattled by the near miss, and he fumbled the reload, slightly. He was only just about ready when the final birds were released. Trap E, two overhead, slightly from his right, and curling away on the breeze. It was a comparatively easy pair from his position, and both were taken out cleanly.

Malcolm carefully retrieved his pieces of folded cardboard, which went back into his pocket. With his bag on the floor, and the gun propped upright in the corner, he was in the process of kicking his spent shells down the slit in the floor, when the cage door was flung open. It was Charlie and his eyes were everywhere. He was obviously eager to see how Malcolm had set out his stall, but with the cartridge bag now on the floor with the flap closed, there was nothing for him to see, and his face reflected his obvious disappointment.

"What time did you post on that one?" he abruptly demanded.

Malcolm smiled. "That's privileged information strictly between me and the computer, isn't it, Charlie?"

"Humph, well if you don't want to tell me . . . What about that second single, then? I hope you're not claiming it as a dead bird?"

"I didn't hear what Simon called for it, Charlie, but it was definitely a hit, I saw the deflection."

"Yes, well I didn't. He called it dead, but then he's your mate, so he would, wouldn't he?"

The door clanged shut as he made his way over to the peg 2 cage. Malcolm was left fuming with indignation as he picked up his things and went to join Simon.

"Bloody man, he's beginning to get right up my nose now, Simon. He's just accused you of favouritism. Can you believe it?

Simon clicked off his microphone and pushed it to one side of his face.

"That would be the number seven, single, that you just winged? He said as much to me, as well. Disputed the hit, but I clearly saw it deflect down towards the ground, and I told him so. He's just out to wind you up, Malcolm, trying to put you off your game. Take no notice, keep on shooting the way you are, and you'll win this bet, fair and square."

"I couldn't give a damn about the bet, Simon. It's the principle of it all that concerns me. In all my days, I have rarely encountered such rudeness and unsporting behaviour. The man is a senior police officer, and holds a position of considerable responsibility. It was only an hour ago that I was seriously considering making him an offer to come and work with me. God almighty, I'm glad I didn't. Tell me, how much longer before this round will finish, do you think?"

"A round is usually over in about fifteen to twenty minutes, Malcolm. Why do you ask?"

"Do you have the number of a local taxi company? If so, will you get one here for half an hour from now for me, please. The bastard's not travelling back to Oakwood in my car, that's for sure."

Simon grinned. "I'll get the office to do it in a minute, for you. I can't wait to see his face when you tell him."

Both men heard the 'pull' command, and Simon hurriedly had to go back to the matter in hand.

Malcolm watched as Charlie shot a perfect ten, but this time, he'd entered a longer time lapse between his shots. He'd settled down, and was shooting well, and that in itself now posed a bit of a dilemma.

Charlie, despite his near disastrous first peg, had set a good time advantage, but he'd obviously learned a lesson. So far, Malcolm still had the two-bird advantage, but he'd been lucky twice, so now, he couldn't afford to miss anything, otherwise it would all swing back to Charlie's time advantage. It was clearly going to come down to a question of accuracy, unless he could up his game a little? His thoughts kept harping back to Simon's advice, and he did a little mental calculation . . .

Charlie came away from peg 2 with a wolfish grin on his face. This time as they passed each other on the changeover, there was definite and deliberately eye contact. He too had worked out that Malcolm couldn't afford to miss anything, and he was going to do his damnedest to make sure that he did.

In the peg 2 cage, Malcolm carefully set himself up in exactly the same manner as before. His new strategy worked out, he entered a figure in the box, loaded, and stood back to survey the range. He was surprised at how much different it looked from this change of angle. At least there would be no more difficulty with the birds from trap B, for from here, it would be a far easier shot. He took a deep breath and focused his concentration.

'Pull.' The three seconds after the light went to green seemed like an eternity. His first two came from trap D, right to left, going away. They were taken mid-range, no problem.

Malcolm went calmly into his reload procedure, and was bringing the gun up to his ready position when the next two, overheads, were released. They too were reduced to about a hundred pieces that tumbled to earth. Working more purposefully now, Malcolm completed his reload, and was ready for the left to right single, from trap A. His shot reduced it to a cloud of dust, and he patiently held his position while waiting expectantly, for the second single. The time lapse seemed endless, but when it came, the running hare, from his right, was only fractionally away from his line of sight. The short swing and squeeze of the trigger came as the rolling clay hit a tussock of grass and leapt three feet into the air. Malcolm saw the grass tremble where the clay should have been, but with another little bounce it rolled slowly round in a circle to come to a halt sitting in clear view, as if to taunt him. It was a complete miss, and faintly through his ear protectors, he heard Simon calling it so.

With no time to reflect on his bad luck, he went straight into his next reload and was in good time to cleanly take the report pair from trap C.

His last two were springing teal from a concealed trap somewhere slightly to his right. Both were reduced to dust in quick succession.

Malcolm quickly removed his bag from the front rail, and placed it in the corner with the gun. He set about clearing away his spent shells, expecting at any moment to be interrupted by Charlie again, but it wasn't to be. Charlie was waiting for him with Simon, when he arrived back at the buggy.

"Just for the record, that sixth shot, the hare, was a miss. So purely for Mr Blackmore's benefit, will you confirm it as such, please, Simon. I wouldn't like there to be any misunderstanding about it later."

"I called it a 'lost' Mr Ferguson, as you heard, and I'm sure Mr Blackmore will concur?"

"It was a miss, Simon. The unbroken clay is sitting in full view, middle of the range. It's a bit off-putting, I think we should remove it before shooting the next peg."

"I'll see to it immediately, Malcolm, thank you."

Simon jumped down from the buggy and hurried down to the range. Malcolm seized upon the opportunity to play a bit of gamesmanship himself. He too could be particularly nasty if the circumstances warranted.

"There was really no need for that, was there, Charlie. The bird was called a loss, and it will be recorded as such by the computer. You are perfectly at liberty to play your silly little games with me, because I really couldn't give a damn. However, I take great exception when you start to question the integrity of the Club referee, who is after all, an innocent party to whatever is taking place between us. I have been a respected member of this gun club for more than twenty years, and I am finding your unsporting and un-gentlemanly conduct, here this morning, to be both embarrassing and totally unacceptable. As such, I am afraid that you will no longer welcome to the hospitality of my home. I will have Carter pack your things for you, and they will be ready, when the taxi that I have ordered, drops you back at Oakwood."

Malcolm watched with a degree of satisfaction as the suffusion of angry blood rose into Charlie's face. He was totally at a loss for words. His mouth began opening and closing in rage and indignation. With nothing but foul expletives, and little drops of spittle coming out, Malcolm calmly turned his back on him and reached over for his second box of cartridges. He caught a sudden movement out of the corner of his eye, and quickly turned back to face Charlie again. He now had the barrels of the closed gun held in two hands, as though it was a cricket bat, and had stepped forward as if he was about to play a stroke. Alarmed at his apparent intention, to use his head as the cricket ball, Malcolm brought his own, broken-open gun, to his front, in case he should need to use it to protect himself.

"Mr Ferguson, what on earth do you think you are doing? You will kindly put that gun down this instant, if you please. That sort of behaviour cannot be tolerated. I'm afraid I must disqualify you from any further shooting, and ask you to leave the club premises immediately."

From a distance, Simon had seen what was about to happen, and had sprinted up behind Charlie. He was just about to make a grab for the gun, but at the last moment, thought better of it. He didn't fancy wrestling with someone wielding a gun that might be loaded . . . His cautionary shout and timely intervention, was enough to bring Charlie back to his senses again. He stood for a few moments eying Malcolm with utter malevolence before throwing the gun down onto the floor of the buggy. He did the same with his bag of cartridges, spilling them out all over the place.

"Don't worry yourselves, I seem to have lost the stomach for it anyway. I'll tell you what, Blackmore, you can poke your hospitality up your arse, and your wager, too. It's not a good idea to make an enemy of Charlie Ferguson, as I'm sure you will eventually come to appreciate. I thought you were different, but now I find that you're just like the rest of your class. Rich little do-gooders, who think you're better than all the rest of us. You make me sick, the whole damn lot of you . . ."

# Chapter 11

The Boeing 747, which was flight UA938, from Chicago, taxied to a halt outside of Heathrow Terminal 1. Marty stifled a yawn, but stretched his arms and legs in readiness of standing up for the first time in seven hours. He had been wedged into a window seat with an elderly couple that, annoyingly, had slept for most of the flight. Not wishing to disturb them, he had thoughtfully remained seated, despite wishing to visit the toilet. Now, his need was getting more urgent, but he decided it could wait until he was inside the terminal.

With the walkway in place, the passengers slowly started to shuffle towards the exits, but three hundred people take quite a few minutes to disembark from an aeroplane, so Marty remained in his seat until the queue started to thin out, and people began to move a little faster.

The elderly couple vacated their seats and bade him a polite good day. He stood and reached up into the overhead storage locker to retrieve his sports holdall, which contained his two bottles of duty free Tennessee Rye whiskey, and four hundred American Lucky Strike cigarettes, as well as his passport and other travel documents. He checked that they were all correct, and that his duty-free goods were undamaged, then felt in the end pocket of the bag for his other mobile phone. It was an older, no frills, Nokia, that was not enabled for use abroad. He knew that it should have been replaced for a newer model years ago, but it had a phenomenal battery life, and the audio was a clear as a bell for his failing hearing. Marty liked to have things that stood the test of time, and proved themselves to be robust and reliable, so like an old friend, he nurtured it along. It was his personal phone, not for business, and he only used it when at home in Ireland or the UK. It had been switched off since he had departed for America, fourteen days ago, so he depressed the ON button, and entered his pin.

"Come along then, if you please, Sir. There are no prizes for being the last off the plane, you know. And I very much doubt that you'll be wanting to do the return flight, which is due to take off in a little under two hours from now?"

The smiling flight attendant stood in the aisle, pointedly looking at his wristwatch, while indicating with his other hand, the way to the exit. Marty realised he was almost the only passenger still left on board, but his attention had been distracted by his phone. It had flashed up fourteen missed calls, texts and voicemails. Someone was wishing to speak with him rather urgently, that much was apparent . . .

"Oh, sorry, yes of course, I'm ready now."

He held up his phone to show why he had been so remiss, and the attendant nodded in understanding.

"You'll not be making any calls while you're still on the plane, will you, sir? I'm afraid it's still not allowed, even though we've landed. Your calls will have to wait until you are in the terminal."

Marty thrust the phone into his jacket pocket, picked up his bag, and thoughtfully made his way off the plane. He'd just had that sudden feeling of dread, a cold shudder, like one gets if someone walks on your grave. Something had gone very wrong somewhere. Intuitively, he just knew it . . .

Charlie Ferguson stood just behind the two Customs and Immigration Officers that were checking the passports and visas of those arriving on flight UA938. He was smartly dressed in his three-piece, dark blue pinstriped suit. Legs slightly apart, he stood at ease, with both hands resting on the top of a rolled umbrella, held in front, with the tip resting on the floor between his highly polished shoes. He had chosen to wear a fashionable bowler hat, cocked at a jaunty angle, and pulled down slightly at the front, to hood his eyes. With his pristine white shirt and Irish Guards regimental tie, he looked every inch the city gentleman, or a retired, senior army officer, perhaps still active in some respect?

This pseudo-egotistical, James Bond, type image was precisely the impression that Charlie wished create and convey.

Looking down the queue, Charlie tried to pick out his man in advance, but the only photo of Martyn John McCue held on record, was his UK passport image, and already eight years old. It depicted a rather overweight, grey-haired individual, known to be in his sixties, wearing heavy spectacles, and sporting a neat little moustache, trimmed similar to Charlie's own.

He was therefore taken by complete surprise when he heard the Customs Officer use the name to address the clean-shaven, younger looking man, now presenting his passport for inspection.

"Mr McCue, good morning, sir. I see that you are travelling on an Irish passport, and entering the UK from America. Can I enquire as to the purpose of your visit, sir?"

The question was entirely unnecessary and superfluous. It was made entirely for Charlie's benefit and to capture his attention.

"I'm not staying in England on this visit. I have a connecting flight to Belfast City, so I have. It's due to take off in a couple of hours from now. Here's my ticket should you wish to verify the booking."

The man Charlie was looking at didn't look a day over fifty. Tanned, lean and muscled, he obviously looked after himself, and there was little doubt that he was very fit. He stood a little over six-feet tall, was clean-shaven, and not wearing glasses. His dark brown, naturally wavy hair, was greying at the temples and over the ears. It was neatly cut to a smart, medium length, and swept back at the sides. The voice was strong and resonant, well spoken, and reflecting only the slightest hint of an Irish brogue.

He was fashionably, and smartly dressed, in a dark green blazer over a pale yellow, open-necked shirt, and stay-pressed, fawn coloured, cavalry twill trousers. A heavy, gold choker chain hung loosely from around his neck, and served to compliment his suntan. Charlie had already noticed the gold Rolex that he wore on his right wrist, instead of the usual left, and the large, gold, monogrammed signet ring, worn on the middle finger of the same hand.

With expensive looking, highly polished, casual brown slip-on leather shoes to complete the ensemble, it would have to be said that he was very good-looking indeed, every inch a ladies man. His bearing and personality, in answering the questions being put to him by the Customs officer, had already conveyed an air of quiet confidence and self-assurance.

Charlie had the image of the photo on record, depicted in his mind. He was mentally comparing it to the man now standing before him. How was it possible to alter ones image so much? Looking closely, he began to see that with a little bit of theatrical hair dye, some facial padding in the lower cheeks, a false tache, spectacles, and, yes, there he would be, looking about three stone heavier, and twelve years older. Very clever . . .

Charlie had heard the Customs officer mention that he had produced an Irish passport. The photo Charlie had seen was from McCue's last UK passport renewal, so he must be in possession of two passports?

For the first time, their eyes met. Charlie held his gaze, looking to stare him down, and to put him ill at ease. He wanted McCue to remember his face, and to wonder who he was. The look that came back was not what he expected. It was one of complete disdain, exemplified by a slight sneer, as he finally averted his eyes back to the Customs officer, who was handing him back his passport and other travel documents.

As McCue walked away towards the exits, Charlie leaned forward to whisper into the Customs Officers ear.

"I want his luggage thoroughly searched, and ask your colleagues to put him to as much inconvenience as possible without causing offence."

The Customs Officer dutifully picked up his phone as Charlie set off to follow his target.

"Excuse me, sir, but I noticed that you came through the 'nothing to declare' channel, would you mind stepping over this way for a quick check of your baggage, please?"

Marty had been half expecting something like this. All the alarm bells in his mind had started sounding the moment he first saw the officious looking man standing behind the Customs Officers. He looked to be either a policeman, or perhaps military intelligence? Either way, as far as Marty was concerned, he was bad news.

With a shrug of resignation, Marty had no choice but to comply with the instruction. He placed his sports holdall, and wheelie suitcase, up onto the inspection table and stood back, thrusting his hands deep into his trouser pockets, trying to appear casual. He wasn't about to let any of these bastards nark him. For the time being, they were calling all the shots . . .

"Can you tell me, please, sir, is this your bag and suitcase, and did you pack them both yourself?"

Marty entered into the well-rehearsed Customs routine, and resigned himself to the indignity of having the entire contents of his bags neatly laid out onto the counter for inspection. He knew that there was absolutely nothing to cause him any embarrassment, and he was determined not to display any irritation. The Customs man, while examining everything, was trying to make small talk, asking apparently innocent questions in regard to his holiday, family, employment and anything else he could think of. Marty, answered everything as briefly as was possible, without being rude, or giving away any useful information.

At the bottom of his wheelie, the Customs officer found his bulging, black leather, document case. He pounced upon it, and made as if to open it for further inspection, but the zip closure was locked. He held it up and looked pointedly at Marty.

"Can I enquire as to the contents of this item, sir?"

"It's a document case. There are only files, and other confidential papers in connection with my profession."

"And what exactly is your profession, sir?"

"I work as a PA to a senior Minister of the Irish Government Assembly, so I do."

"Would you mind opening the document case for further inspection, please, sir?"

"The papers in that document case are of a confidential nature. I would be prepared to open the case if I can have your assurance that you will not be reading the content of anything contained within?"

"With respect, sir, you are in no position to dictate anything of that nature. It is for me to decide whether or not I should be reading anything. You are entering the UK, and for all I know, there might be plans to carry out terrorist atrocities contained in here. Now, I will ask you just once more. Would you please open this case for further inspection?"

Charlie was watching with interest on the overhead CCTV monitor contained in an adjacent office. He liked the innocently made reference to terrorism, but was disappointed to see that it didn't elicit any discernable response from McCue. He watched as he produced a small bunch of keys from his pocket and reluctantly unlocked the document case for inspection. Charlie would love to see the contents of the files, and an idea occurred to him. He picked up the phone to speak with the Customs Officer doing the examination. In response to his call, he saw him lift the phone, on the monitor.

"Swab it for drugs. I want you to find something. I need to see those files."

Like he had with the rest of the luggage, the Customs Officer routinely wiped a clean swab over a couple of the files and around the interior of the case. Within the sight and hearing of Marty, he placed the sample material into the analyser machine and pressed the start button. Expecting the sample to be clear, he was just about to surreptitiously depress the 'alarm test' to make it sound off, when the machine started bleating and flashing red of it's own accord. The indication was for a presence of cocaine within the sample.

Marty saw and heard everything, so there could be no argument, but he was both bewildered and totally dumbfounded. The Customs Officer returned to the table with a smug look on his face.

"I'm sorry, sir, but I have a reading for the presence of cocaine within this item. I'm afraid that it will be necessary to have a closer look at all the contents, and to X-ray the case itself. Before we go any further, can you tell me, please, do you use cocaine, at all?"

"No, of course not. I've never touched the stuff."

"Well, if that is the case, how then do you explain the presence of such a controlled substance, on the inside of your document case?"

"I do not have any explanation to offer, so I don't, apart from the obvious fact that other people have handled those files before I put them into my document case. Any contamination must have taken place before they ever came into my possession."

Even as he spoke, he saw that the Customs Officer was already on his phone. He heard him requesting further assistance with a 'positive for cocaine.' Marty began to feel more than a little apprehensive. With the phone back on its cradle, the Officer addressed him once again.

"One of my colleagues will be with you in a few moments, sir. I will then be able to conduct some further tests to locate precisely where the cocaine is present. Before I go any further, I am required to ask you if you have anything concealed about your person that I should know about? Please be aware that if you have, we will find it. At the moment, I have to inform you that you are being detained for the purposes of a physical search in order to ascertain whether or not you are in possession of any controlled substance, and on suspicion of attempting to import an illegal substance into the country. I must caution you that you do not have to say anything, but it may harm your defence if you do not mention when questioned, something . . ."

"Yes, yes, I know all that, so I do, and I understand completely. But please allow me to assure you that I am not a drug user, and I have absolutely nothing concealed about my person. Look, I fully appreciate the difficulty I find myself in, but I would urge you to please get on with whatever it is you need to do, using all speed."

Marty looked pointedly at his watch and held out his hands in resignation.

"Officer, I have a connecting flight to Belfast, which is due to take off in precisely one hour and thirty-five minutes from now. It is absolutely imperative that I am aboard that flight. Some of the papers contained in that document case need to be with my Minister before he leaves for an important conference this evening. I cannot stress strongly enough, just how important this is, and the extreme urgency of the situation. I am not exaggerating when I say that any delay could result in a diplomatic incident, and extreme embarrassment to my Minister, and the Irish Government Assembly, so it would."

"All in good time, sir, I too have an important job to do, and with a set procedure to follow, these things cannot be hurried. Rest assured we will do our best not to detain you any longer than is necessary, and your continued and complete co-operation, will certainly help matters along. Ah, here's my colleague now. He will stay with you while I conduct a few more tests on this document case. So if you will just bear with me for a few minutes . . ."

He watched the man disappear through a connecting door carrying his precious document case and contents. Marty could see the futility of trying to reason with the man. He had his job to do, and there was nothing more that he could say, or do, that would influence him in any way. There was nothing else for it, but to try and keep his cool, and sort out this sorry mess as quickly as possible.

He cursed under his breath, and wondered how it was possible for cocaine to be present in his document case? Thinking back, it was one of the young PA's of Senator George Mitchell that had handed him the bundle of files and dossiers, and he had put them straight into his document case and locked it. That was nearly a week ago, and since then, his case had remained unopened in his hotel room, while he enjoyed the rest of his holiday.

It was a fair bet that it was one of the Senators staff that had probably snorted a line of coke from one of the pages contained in the bundle? Damn them to hell for the trouble they had caused him.

He wondered if he should perhaps be making a phone call to warn his office, and the Minister, that he had been unavoidably delayed? He extracted both of his phones from his pockets in readiness.

"I'll take those, if you please, sir, and while we're waiting, it might be a good idea to remove all of your jewellery, and empty the contents of your pockets into this tray. Everything you have about your person will need to be examined before we can return it to you, and it will all save valuable time, in the long run."

He did as he was asked, and watched helplessly, as yet another Customs Officer came through to take his phones, and all his personal possessions away for further examination.

Charlie Ferguson couldn't believe his luck. When he issued the order for Marty's things to be routinely dusted for drugs, the last thing he expected was for it to come up with a positive result. He was now hurriedly photocopying the entire contents of the document case as the Customs Officer painstakingly dusted each sheet of paper for traces of cocaine. Charlie was getting impatient. Most of the paperwork he had looked at seemed to relate to proposed updates on The Belfast Peace Agreement, and requests for further financial support for the First Minister in the forthcoming Irish Presidential elections. The money to come from the American Ireland Fund, whatever that is? It all appeared fairly innocuous, but nevertheless, the information might be of some importance to someone, somewhere. So copies of it would all be sent back to London, for further appraisal.

It was obvious to Charlie that there was no significant amount of any drug to be found, and he didn't want McCue to know that his all his precious papers had been compromised. He came to a quick decision and addressed the Officer that had made the hit.

"Look, forget about looking for drugs, its fairly obvious that there's nothing much to be found here, so I want you to concentrate on doing a full body search on McCue instead."

"We would be doing that in any case, sir. But it is important that we follow the correct procedure, in case we find something more, and decide to prosecute at a later date."

"There will be no proceedings arising out of this, trust me, Officer, I know. I want McCue on his plane to Belfast, having first suffered as much humiliation and indignity, as it is possible to inflict, while still remaining within the scope of acceptable procedures. Do I make myself abundantly clear?"

"This is all highly irregular, sir, I shall need to consult with my senior officer before complying with any such a request, I'm afraid."

Charlie rounded on the man. Reaching into his pocket, he produced his warrant card, stepped forward, and waved it in front of his face. With as much venom as he could muster, he issued his next order.

"My authority comes direct from the Home Office, and supersedes the highest ranking Customs officer that you are in any position to consult. I am taking full responsibility in the handling of this matter, so you will do exactly as I ask, immediately, and without question. Now, go and do a full body search on Mr McCue, and make sure that he is made to feel as uncomfortable as possible, before boarding the Belfast flight that leaves this terminal at 1330. Any failure on your part, and by the end of the day, you will find yourself looking for other employment. Is that a clear enough order for you, Officer?"

The man gulped and took a step back. In all of his twelve years of service, he had never before been addressed in such a rude and overbearing manner. He looked around in bewilderment. All the other civilian staff and Customs Officers present in the room, had paused in their respective tasks at the sound of Charlie's slightly raised, and menacing voice. They were watching to see what was going to happen next. The unfortunate Senior Customs Officer was being forced to swallow his pride.

"Yes, sir. My apologies, I hadn't fully appreciated your rank and authority. I will see to it immediately, sir."

Flustered and hot under the collar, he thankfully hurried out of the room, eager to get away from this dreadful man, and the mocking eyes of his colleagues. Charlie passed the pile of documentation to another Customs Officer who was standing there gawking, apparently with nothing better to do?

"One copy of everything, and then repack it all in exactly the same order. You will thoroughly clean the case, as well. I don't want him stopped again when he gets to Belfast. Any questions?"

"Yes, sir. Sorry, I mean, no, sir. It will be as you ordered."

Charlie smiled to himself, and went back to his task. It felt good to kick arse occasionally. He picked up McCue's mobiles. Both were switched on, and had been enabled with their respective passwords.

On the old Nokia, he punched up the first of the 'missed calls,' and pressed 123 to listen to the voice mail. At the sound of the message being relayed, a broad grin slowly spread across his face, and he started making notes. His day was getting better by the minute . . .


Breakfast at Oakwood was one of quiet anticipation for Sharon-Louise, and her apparent preoccupation hadn't gone unnoticed by David and Sue.

"I'll lay odds that you're thoughts are on the preliminary reading of your mother's Will this morning, am I right?"

She looked up and smiled at David as he set his meal on the table and sat down beside her. He and Sue had noticed that Malcolm seemed to be having a rather one-sided conversation with Sharon, so at his imperceptible nod of approval, they picked up their breakfast plates, and re-seated themselves on his and Sharon's table.

"Well, am I right?"

Sharon nodded and set her knife and fork together on the plate in front of her. She pushed her omelette away largely untouched. Turning slightly in her seat to face toward him, she reached out to take David's hand, as it rested on the table. With her head bowed, the words came out in barely more than a whisper.

"I'm feeling frightened, David. Not in the sense of being scared, like of a ghost, but frightened of what I am about to be told with regard to my mother. Here I am, still struggling to get my head around her death, and now, it's as if I'm about to be shouldered with the additional burden of having to sort out all her affairs, as well. I spent most of last night lying awake in my bed. Again, I was thinking about the all those wasted years when we could have been a proper mother and daughter. Malcolm keeps telling me that I'm about to become very wealthy, and that I shouldn't worry my little head about it. He thinks that everything will sort itself out in the fullness of time. I'm sure he's probably right, but it doesn't stop me being apprehensive, yes, that's the right word, I'm not scared, I'm apprehensive, about my additional burdens of responsibility arising out of my inheritance."

David gave her hand a little squeeze, being careful to avoid hurting her now lightly plastered fingernails. He turned his chair round slightly to face her. He took her hand into both of his, and chose his words carefully.

"I think we all understand just how harrowing all of this has been for you, Sharon love, and I suspect that you are still reeling from the shock of it all? If there was anything else that any of us could do to ease your troubles, well, you know that we would, if we could. Unfortunately, coming to terms with grief, is a very personal conflict for everyone, but you will need to deal with it, before you can ever hope to move on.

From what I knew of your mother, I think you will find that there will be an efficient order to all of her affairs, and the transition, the handing over, from her to you, will have been thought out, well in advance.

Personally, I think that Malcolm is right. Everything will sort itself out in the fullness of time, of that there can be no doubt, for we cannot arrest progress, can we? Don't ever forget that George is going to be looking after all your affairs and interests now. Believe me when I tell you, that he's very good at what he does. Should he find it necessary to consult with you, in whatever matter you're discussing, you will only need to tell him what you would like to happen, and he will advise you accordingly. From there on, having reached a viable decision on the correct course of action, you can just sit back and let him get on with it, no worries.

As for your mother, we cannot turn the clock back, and it is too late for recriminations. Lara Dobbs was a quite remarkable and brave young woman, and Laura Dobson, her alter ego, even more so.

As far as I can make out, from the short period that I was privileged to know her, all the decisions that she ever came to in your regard, were always what she considered to be the best for you, at the time. Try to take comfort in the fact that in those years of happiness that you've had with Jim and Doris, you were also being watched over by your mother. Should there have been even the slightest hint that anything was amiss, I think she would have been there for you, just as any mother should.

Today, expressed in fiscal terms, we are about to find out just how much of a success your mother made of her life. I think she would want you to use your inheritance to make a fresh start. I would rather suspect that she would also like to see you carry on, where she has left off. Perhaps not in the same, slightly nefarious, vein that she chose to accumulate her wealth, but certainly in a manner that would not see everything that she has achieved, just squandered away. I think she would be pleased to know that you intend to put the fruits of her life's work, to some good use, don't you agree?"

Sharon nodded her assent, and reached with her other hand for her paper napkin.

"As for your feelings, can I suggest that you try putting your remorse and recriminations on the back burner, otherwise there is a real danger of them festering into some incurable canker of hatred and bitterness, for what you perceive to be all the wrongdoings perpetrated by your mother.

When I was in hospital, and struggling to come to terms with my own life crisis, a young soldier that had lost three of his limbs, and his sight, as well, gave me some similar advice. Greg, was his name, and I often used to sit and read the newspapers to him, or we'd be swapping yarns, like boys do. He liked to talk about his family. He had a wife, and two young children, that would regularly visit him. His injuries were truly appalling to see, but to the children, it didn't seem to matter, for the man left inside the wreckage of his body, was still their father. In particular, Greg would go on about all the help and support they were giving him on their daily visits. I was rather forced into doing a whole lot of listening when I was in his company.

At first, I was a bit sceptical as he outlined his plans for how he was going to cope with life, when he got out of hospital. But there was no deterring him, he had already come to terms, and accepted his terrible disabilities. Far from feeling sorry for himself, he was determined to overcome the terrible trauma of it all, and he knew exactly what he wanted to do with the rest of his working life.

Greg wanted to learn how to operate a computer. Even though he was completely blind, and had only three fingers left on the hand of his one remaining limb, he still thought that could do it. Can you imagine that?

I was discharged before he was, so I don't know if he ever managed it? Perhaps one day, I should take the time to look him up, and find out. I often think about him, especially on days when my legs are giving me some gyp. He serves to remind me of how much worse things could have been. Besides all that, I'd love to see him again, just to know how he's getting along.

Anyway, Greg's optimistic attitude was truly inspirational to me. His injuries were far greater than mine, yet he still saw a useful future for himself. It served to change my whole way of thinking. I followed his example, and I too found the solace, comfort, and support that I so badly needed. It was there for the taking, in the bosom of my family, but I had been just too blind, with anger and hatred, to see it.

With their help, I soon found all the anger and bitterness that I held toward my senior officers and the MOD, all the nightmares, and all the recriminations for the loss of my mate, Tommy Carr, and for what had happened to me, well, they all slowly started fizzling away into a series of bad memories.

When Sue announced that she was pregnant with the twins, I knew then, that I had finally made it. That was one of the happiest and most memorable days of my whole life, Sharon-Louise.

Speaking metaphorically, I suppose that in the end, I'd finished up with this dirty little pot filled with poison and nastiness, that I was finally able to relegate to the dustbin of bad memories, poor decisions, and missed opportunism. I cannot pretend to you that any of it was easy, it wasn't, but then I've also learned that nothing worthwhile in this life, ever is. There were so many times that I could just as easily have given up completely, and taken to the bottle, or something. But I didn't, and that is in no small part due to the love, support, and advice, that I was getting from my wife, and all the rest of my wonderful family.

So there it is, Sharon-Louise, I managed to get through it, but only with the help of all the people I hold most dearly, particularly the lady you see seated opposite, who to her credit, has never ever doubted me for one minute. God only knows why, I must have been an absolute nightmare at the time . . .

So now, you are similarly surrounded with people that love you, but they too will have problems. If and when they arise, they in turn, will need to be able to turn to you for help. The time will come when they will require a similar degree of love and support, to enable them to deal, and cope, with their own particular situations. It is the way of things. I like to call it, 'the circle of love and responsibility,' and I believe it to exist within every sincere, and loving family relationship, something that I am very fortunate to be a part of.

Here, at Oakwood, unless I am very much mistaken, lies not only your immediate, but also your long-term future. I think, like I have with Sue, that you will find with Malcolm, all the love and support that you will ever need. It will be there just for the asking, and it all comes unconditionally. So take heart, Sharon-Louise, for you are not alone in any of this. There is a good man sitting over there, and some very real friends here, that will always be there for you, should you ever need them.

Today, you will need to put on a brave face. So, it's chin up, shoulders back and chest out, girl, and put that lovely, wicked little smile back on to that pretty face of yours. Try looking upon today as being the first day of the rest of your life. As I said, you are about to learn the full extent of your mother's true regard for you. There is nothing to be frightened of, or apprehensive about, for even if you decided to give everything that you inherit to a charity, nobody would think any the less of you, would they? But I suspect that you're not about to do that, are you? You'll accept the challenge head-on, and fight it to your last breath, as we all know that you can. C'mon, Sharon-Louise, prove to us that you've inherited some of the stuff that both of your parents were so obviously made of."

Still holding her hand, he looked up into her face to see if his words had prompted any reaction. He was not surprised to see that the tears were once again rolling unashamedly down her face. In a friendly gesture, David leaned forward to offer a comforting embrace, and a shoulder for her to cry on. Sharon responded immediately, and with her head so close to his, she whispered her grateful thanks for his kind words of comfort and understanding.

For their part, Malcolm and Sue had been listening in rapt silence, as David waxed philosophical with his little biographical account of his time in hospital. Sue was truly surprised, for she had never heard him speak with such emotion about the period of time he spent recovering from his injuries. Nor had he ever mentioned before, the young man with the terrible injuries, that had so inspired him. To hear him speak of her personal commitment to him, in such tender, loving terms brought a lump to her throat together with a tear of emotional pride. It was Malcolm that broke the silence that followed.

"Well, there's not very much that anyone could possibly add to that, is there? Except to say that I have to agree with everything that David has just said. I too, remember Greg Harper, he was a quite remarkable young man. Sadly, I have to say that he later succumbed to his terrible injuries, David. He died from septicaemia, without ever leaving hospital. There were just too many particles of shrapnel left in his body for us to remove, and in the end we couldn't save him. I'm so sorry, David. Like you, he was SAS, and I thought that the Regiment might perhaps have kept you informed?"

David released his embrace with Sharon, and sat back with a stricken look upon his face.

"No, they didn't, but then that was probably my fault. I wanted nothing more to do with them after . . . Well, you know. Can we talk a bit more about this later, please Malcolm?"

"Yes, of course. Look, being as we all seem to have lost our appetite for breakfast, and we have a couple of hours to kill before Tony Williams is due to arrive. Can I suggest that we take a short drive up the road? There is something that I would rather like you all to see, and a little proposition that I would like to put to you both. You come too, please, Sharon-Louise. This project will involve you as much as anyone else, and it may help to take your mind off things for a while."

Connor McCall sat fidgeting in the lounge of the Park Avenue Hotel in Belfast. In the past week he had barely been out of his room, except to take his meals in the dining room, and for a late evening walk along Sydenham Avenue, a side turning just along the Holywood Road. Connor needed to regularly check on the lodging address of his friend Marty, to see if his car was back there yet.

On his last visit to Belfast, a year previous, he had been Marty's guest, and had been ferried around in his sporty little black, Mk1 Golf GTI, convertible. Marty had told him that he'd spent over two years and a small fortune in restoring the car, and Connor knew that it was one of Marty's most treasured possessions, so there was little likelihood of him ever parting with it. According to a friendly neighbour he'd spoken to, there hadn't been any sign of it car for some weeks now. The man had been out walking his dog, and on the third evening that they had passed each other, in Sydenham Avenue, he had wished Connor a good evening. Grateful for someone else to talk to, Connor had walked with him for a short while, and steered the conversation round to asking him if he knew Marty? The man declared that he had seen him around, recalling the distinctive little black open-top car, but he didn't know him personally, as he lived about ten houses further along the Avenue. He added that, on reflection, he couldn't recall seeing the car for some time, now that Connor came to mention it. Perhaps his friend had moved away?

The man had seemed perfectly genuine, so Connor had no reason to doubt what he said, but it left him feeling more than a little perplexed. The absence of Marty's car, coupled with the fact that he had failed to return any of his phone calls, and Connor too, was beginning to think that he must have left the area? But even if he had moved, it still didn't explain why wasn't he answering his phone, especially as Connor had left him so many messages stressing the extreme urgency in their establishing contact as soon as possible?

Meanwhile, one of the curtain-twitchers in Belmont Mews, a new development of houses that had been built just off Sydenham Avenue, had been having a veritable field day. The end-of-terrace house in the quiet cul-de-sac seemed to have been getting quite an abnormal amount of attention in the past day or so. This was definitely very odd, especially as the recent new occupant was known to be away. The wheelchair-bound, elderly spinster lady, Mary O'Hara, that lived opposite, in between her carer's visits, spent most of her day just reading her books of poetry, and looking out of her bay window curtains.

She had met the new owner, Mr McCue, back in the spring, on the day that he had moved in. He had seen her at her window, and had politely come over to introduce himself. On seeing her delicate situation, he had thoughtfully set about making her some tea. They had enjoyed a cup together, while in answer to her polite enquiry, he told her that he had a senior administrative position, and working for the Government, at Stormont Castle.

This information had caused her to form the opinion that he was a rather nice, respectable, bachelor-type of gentleman. He was so obviously well educated, and judging by his clothes and appearance, a man of some substance, as well. They had immediately struck up a bit of a friendship, and in time, his visits to her had become ever more frequent, usually for some tea and polite conversation.

It was all very civilised, and at his behest, she even began to use his Christian name, and he hers. To her great delight, Mary found him to be a very well read, and cultured gentleman. She took particular pleasure in reading to him some of her favourite pieces of poetry. Their conversations ranged over many subjects. Politics, religion, social problems, all were touched upon in some way, shape, or form, and she found that on many things, they were in complete agreement. Because of this, Mary soon began to find him rather attractive. She began to find that there was a degree of comfort to be found, in just being in his company.

Mary was under no illusions though. She thought at first that he was really just looking in on her out of sheer kindness, a neighbourly gesture, to see that she was alright. But as time went on, and his visits became ever more frequent, she really began to imagine that he might perhaps have been developing some sort of similar feelings toward her? She kept wondering whether he was now actively seeking to be in her company, or was she just deluding herself in that respect? Her physical disability, the result of infant poliomyelitis, was to her legs and lower body, and this had always stood in the way of having any meaningful relationship with a man. But it didn't stop her having the same feelings and desires as any normal woman. Now, in her twilight years, when the sexual aspect of a relationship was no longer that important, she still yearned for male companionship, and the good Lord had seemingly answered her prayers. Had the lovely Mr McCue been sent to perhaps fill the void in her hitherto lonely existence? Mary sincerely wanted it to be so . . .

Mr McCue had given her a new lease of life. Every time he went in or out of his house, she would be at her window watching for him. He would always look over to acknowledge her, usually with a smile and a cheery wave. She would return the acknowledgement with a thumbs-up gesture, delivered through the little viewing gap in her curtains. This small consideration on his part, served to make her day.

When he had told her, a couple of weeks previous, that he was being sent off to America for a fortnight, on important Government business, he had asked her if she would kindly keep a neighbourly eye on his property while he was away. She had readily agreed. Martyn was such a lovely, handsome man, and she was very flattered to be given the opportunity to respond to all his kindness. In truth, she had fallen completely under the spell of his charm, and would have done anything he asked of her. So to be of help to him in such a small, insignificant way, afforded her considerable pleasure, and it could be achieved by doing what she would normally be doing, anyway.

Now, to be able to report back to him, in minute recorded detail, exactly what she had seen, gave Mary a little thrill of excited anticipation. She had missed his company so much, that she had taken to marking off the days to the time of his expected return, on her calendar.

Today was the big day, and Mary could barely contain her excitement. She had dressed in her finest white silk and lace-trimmed blouse, and had put on her best heavy, royal blue, ankle length velvet skirt that served to hide the disfigurement of her legs. For the first time in many years, she had even applied a little makeup to her face. But when she regarded herself in her mirror, she thought it looked too obvious, so she removed it, and settled for just a little pink lipstick, a touch of rouge, and a dab behind the ears, of her lavender perfume.

Since her carer had left at around eight-thirty that morning, she had been at her window, patiently watching, and waiting for him. There wasn't much else going on in the Close today, and she found difficulty in concentrating on her reading. The warmth of the late-autumn sunshine, streaming through the net curtains onto her face, prompted her into putting her book aside, and closing her eyes for a few minutes.

In her little mind, Mary was picturing a man and woman. They were seated together, and looked so very comfortable in each other's company. She saw that they occasionally held hands and leaned affectionately toward each other, while talking and laughing heartily over some amusing little anecdote that the gentleman was relating. It was the twilight of a winter's afternoon, and they were about to share a pot of the finest Earl Grey tea. The chandelier lights twinkled off the highly polished silver teapot, as the lady removed the cosy, and set it to one side. She carefully poured the steeped brew through an antique, pierced, silver strainer. The amber-gold liquid, falling from the spout, tinkled musically into her fine bone china teacups that sat perfectly on matching saucers. These were the essential requisites to compliment both the tea, and the occasion.

Now, she was handing her gentleman his tea, and passing over the matching silver milk jug and sugar bowl. She waited while he added, and stirred in a little sweetener, before taking a little sip from his cup. He expressed his appreciation of the exquisite flavour, and she was seen to smile graciously at his approbation. With a little gesture of the hand, she invited him to help himself from a plate, upon which there was a dainty selection of quality biscuits and teacakes. All had been carefully chosen for his further delectation.

On the dining table, beside the tea tray, she saw there were two empty sherry glasses. It had been a slightly romantic little surprise gesture, made from her to him, as a winter warmer, and a little welcoming home treat.

The thought prompted Mary to awake with a start from her daydreams, and to manoeuvre her wheelchair over to her own rather sparsely stocked, sideboard drinks cabinet. She needed to see if she had enough of her favourite Harvey's Bristol Cream sherry, left over from Christmas . . .

Charlie was seated just inside the cabin door of the Boeing 737, that was flight LH6598, to Belfast International. From his privileged position, on one of the folding crew seats, he was facing all of the other passengers. They had all been seated and belted, in readiness for takeoff. The aircraft had remained on the stand, engines running, and the pilot, crew, and passengers kept waiting, now a little impatiently, for several long minutes. They didn't know why, but the crew had been forbidden to leave, without the last passenger being on board the aircraft. It was now only necessary for the cabin and ground crew to close the aircraft doors, and to have the walkway withdrawn, for the plane to be instantly ready for takeoff.

To the watching passengers, it was apparent from the way that the cabin crew were acting, that there was some consternation over the apparent no-show of the last passenger. There was also speculation that he must be someone of significant importance. For to be able to delay an aeroplane with everyone aboard, for so long, was almost unheard of. Intrigue and curiosity as to his possible identity, was rife.

With the crew visibly making anxious, and more frequent glances at their watches, the whole plane was aware that there was now a very real likelihood of the flight missing its takeoff slot, and considerable further delay. There began an ever-rising crescendo of audible murmurings of discontent from the passengers. Nearly everyone began vociferously urging the crew to shut the doors, and abandoning the last passenger, whoever he might be The stewardess stood from her seat, and was just about to urge a little more patience and decorum, when a man came rushing into the cabin behind her. The whole plane gave him a begrudging cheer, as in a bath of sweat, and with acute embarrassment, he took the last available aisle seat, indicated to him by the much-relieved stewardess. Almost immediately, the doors were slammed and latched shut, and the aircraft was manoeuvred away from the stand, to begin taxiing towards the runway.

From his position, Charlie was able to look directly at McCue seated just five rows away, down the aisle. Marty was sweating profusely, and busily trying to get himself comfortably organised while being urged to fasten his seatbelt. Emptying the contents of the plastic bag into various pockets, he had yet to notice the other man's presence.

For his part, Charlie had subtly altered his whole appearance since their deliberately engineered first sight of each other, back in the terminal. He had changed all of his clothes, and now wore a cheap, light grey, crease-resistant, two-piece travel suit, similar to those much favoured by travelling salesmen. Without any sort of head covering, Charlie had ruffled his mop of grey and ginger hair into a fashionably, untidy mess. With his formal shirt and tie removed, he now sported a more comfortable open neck, pale pink, Pierre Cardin polo shirt, and a heavy gold choker-chain similar to McCue's. Gone were the black socks and polished shoes, these were replaced with his pair of casual slip-on brown loafers, worn over socks of a colour to match his shirt. His whole appearance was to be regarded, as slightly camp, or even effeminate, a deliberate impression that he wished to convey.

With the addition of a pair of light, gold-framed and blue-tinted glasses, with plain lenses, Charlie hoped that he had changed his appearance just sufficiently enough, to cast a little shadow of doubt into McCue's mind, as whether or not he was looking at the same person that he had seen previously? Charlie buried his face into a copy of Men's Fitness magazine, trying to avoid any more direct eye contact with McCue, at least until the moment suited his purpose. Charlie knew that McCue was a dead man walking, but at the moment, like a cat playing with a captured mouse, he was thoroughly enjoying himself at the prospect of watching him squirm. Better still, he knew that before the *coup de grace,* there was a lot more fun to come . . .

Marty settled himself back into his seat and closed his eyes in a concerted effort to calm himself, and to try and bring his emotions back under control. The utter degradation and ignominy, he had suffered over the past couple of hours, was still painfully fresh in his mind, and one particular part of his lower anatomy.

His anger had known no bounds. Fuelled by the acute embarrassment at being forced into stripping naked, and then to have complete strangers examining, and probing, into the most private areas of his body orifices, had the effect of reducing his pride and self-esteem to virtually nothing. If he'd had a gun, he would, with no compunction, have shot and killed the whole damn lot of them.

He had no doubt that they were perfectly within their rights to do what they did, for every action was backed up, in writing, by an encapsulated piece of paper quoting the particular piece of legislation, which granted them the power to carry it out.

His frequent protestations of complete innocence had all been totally ignored, and he was forced into enduring the physical and mental torture of it all. Finally, when they had completely satisfied themselves that he wasn't some sort of drugs mule, and with no word of apology, they had urged him to get dressed as quickly as possible, so that he could board his next flight.

Various pieces of paper had been thrust into his hands explaining that on this occasion, no charges were to be preferred, but he was instead to receive a written, and verbal warning, for the constructive possession of a controlled substance, namely cocaine, a class A drug. Dire warnings were given as to the consequences, should he ever be found in possession of any sort of similar controlled substance in the future.

Most of what was said was now just a blur in his mind. It was with a feeling of great relief that he was urged to leave the Customs Suite, and to make his way, with all speed, to the relevant departure gate, where his flight was being held, pending his boarding.

Half-dressed, and with his shirt hanging out of his trousers, he ran full pelt, the entire length of the terminal, while carrying his blazer over his arm and clutching all his belongings, returned to him contained in a plastic bag. As he dragged his suitcase and holdall, it had careering from side to side, and occasionally collided painfully with his heels, as he ran. Stopping only for a minute to adjust his dishevelled state, and to hand over his baggage, to be placed in the hold, Marty finally boarded the aircraft that would take him to the sanctuary of his Belfast home.

"Would you like tea or coffee, sir?"
"Tea, please. Black, with a little sugar, would be nice."

Marty opened his eyes at the sound of her voice, and pulled himself upright. He reached forward and dropped the seat flap table, for the stewardess to place his cup upon. She poured his tea into a disposable cup, and put down single, sealed cellophane packet, containing two rich tea biscuits, and another two smaller packets of sugar granules. There was one UHT, long-life milk, together with a disposable plastic spoon and a paper napkin.

Before opening the packet, Marty examined at it all with obvious disdain. He detested anything deemed to be disposable. In his view, any sort of item designed to be used only once, and then thrown away, constituted a criminal waste of the world's rapidly diminishing resources. He was still reflecting upon this, and the other of his pet hates, packaging, as he struggled to tear open the cellophane bag at the point indicated that it should be opened. Try as he may with his fingers, the bag was steadfastly refusing to give up its contents. Marty's patience, already sorely tried that morning, was beginning to be tested, all over. He could feel the red mist rising.

'God Almighty,' He breathed to himself, 'Old people are expected to be able to open these damn things . . .'

He finally resorted to having to use his teeth on the corner of the bag. It was while he was doing this that his eye caught that of the man in the grey suit, looking in his direction. As their eyes met for the briefest instant, the man immediately averted his gaze back to his magazine, while sipping from his own cup of something. It struck Marty that he looked vaguely familiar, somehow, but he couldn't quite place him? He pensively stirred in half of the content of one packet of sugar, while surreptitiously taking another quick look at Mr grey-suit. He was definitely someone he'd seen somewhere before, but where? Marty took a sip of his tea, and screwed up his face in disgust. The attractive looking lady, seated beside him, looked in his direction. He thought that he needed to explain, and pushing his plastic cup away in a gesture of disgust. He struck up a little friendly conversation with her.

"My God, how anyone can have the unmitigated gall to serve this muck, under the guise of it being tea? It tastes absolutely bloody dreadful, so it does."

"Yes, I know, but if it's any consolation, my coffee is no better. I think it's all these convenience-catering packs that are to blame. There is no real taste to any hot beverage anymore, is there? Personally, I cannot wait to get home, and one of the first things that I intend to do, is to percolate some fresh-ground coffee beans for myself. I expect that you feel much the same about your tea, don't you?"

For the time being, Marty forgot all about the man in the grey suit. Talking with this friendly stranger was just the catalyst needed to help dissolve his anger and frustrations.

"Oh yes, but I have to confess to being a fairly recent convert to the pleasures of tea drinking. I have an elderly neighbour, who you would have to say is an absolute connoisseur. To be able to take tea with Mary raises the experience to a whole new level of pleasure, so it does. I shudder to think what Mary's reaction would be, were she to be offered a cup of this muck. It would probably induce her into having instant heart failure, so it would."

He chuckled at his own humour, but his comment had served to remind him that he'd missed her company. It would be good to get back home and to share a pot of Earl Grey, or Da Jeeling with her again. But in the meantime, he had the company of this rather charming lady, for the remainder of the flight.

David and Sue were in the library at Oakwood, with Emily in her father's arms. They were all looking at various schematic plans, and some of the artist's impressions of the proposed hospital development, that were spread out on the top of a large reading table.

After breakfast that morning, Malcolm, together with Sharon-Louise, had taken them to Twelve Acre Meadow. There, he had delivered much the same spiel as that given to Charlie the previous day. The only difference had been in not voicing his reservations with regard to the objections that might be raised by his daughters, in respect of any changes likely to be needed at Oakwood.

Malcolm's enthusiasm for the whole project was abundantly apparent from the outset, and they could all understand the urgency, and why he was now so keen to get things under way. But as he conducted them around the piece of land, describing in detail, and indicating exactly where each particular aspect of the development would be sited, they all began to wonder if he was perhaps going a bit over the top in his conducted tour of an empty field?

David, Sue and Sharon-Louise, were obviously all of a similar mind, and began looking to each other in bewilderment. Why, exactly, had Malcolm seen fit to bring them all here, and to find it necessary to go into so much detail? It was all very interesting, of course, but where, or what, was this all leading up to?

The bombshells came as they finally started walking back toward the car.

"So, tell me, what do you think of the whole project, then, David? How do you see it?"

"I think that the whole thing will be a testament to yours and Elizabeth's generosity, Malcolm, and I would wish you every success with it."

"So, would you and Sue care to be more actively involved with it all?"

"I'm sure that I speak for both of us, if I say that we would, of course, be happy to help in any way that you would care to mention, Malcolm. It would be a pleasure . . ."

"Good, that's more or less what I hoped you would say. So how about you come and work with me as my newly appointed Project Manager, then?"

The shock was enough to stop David in his tracks. He looked at Sue and telepathically sought her reaction. With a shrug of her shoulders, the return message indicated the need to know more, before committing themselves to anything, but, in principle, she wasn't averse to it.

"You're going to have to just run that past me again, in a little more detail, please, Malcolm. If I'm to understand what you are suggesting, I will need you, to convince me, as to why you think that I am the right man for the job. It has be said, that my knowledge of civil engineering is somewhat limited, and there must be many thousands of people far better qualified than I? You also suggested that Sue be involved, how do you see her role in this?"

Malcolm was obviously enjoying himself. In a friendly gesture he stepped between them and put an arm around each of their shoulders. They started slowly walking back towards the car again, talking as they went.

"I'm sorry to spring this upon you without any prior warning, David, but it was only yesterday that I finally made all the decisions that convinced me that I should proceed with the project. If I tell you that you do not need to have any more than a very basic knowledge of building work, and that your job would entail standing in for me in organising, and liasing, between the various architects, surveyors, contractors, etcetera, just to see that things run smoothly, would that put your mind more at ease? As for you being the right man, I need someone that I can trust completely. Someone that has already proved that they are basically honest, possessed of integrity, and that they are competent and resourceful. Without wishing to cause either off you any further embarrassment, these are all qualities that I have recognized to be abundantly inherent in you both. As for Sue's role, I am going to need someone with a head for figures, to oversee all the accounts during, and after, the build. I would hope that here, at Oakwood, Sue would be able to find the peace and quiet necessary, to resume her accountancy studies, and ultimately to achieve not only that qualification, but also another in business management. The hospital, when up and running, will need a Purser.

Look, there is obviously far more to this than the brief outline that I've just given you. So, back home, I've prepared for you both, a more complete job description, together with details of the salary that I would be prepared to offer. There are also a few suggestions as to the sort of extra help that I would be prepared to provide, should you choose to accept my offer, and re-locate to somewhere more local. For the time being, should you so wish, you are more than welcome to come and live here, at Oakwood. The twins will obviously need to go to a new school, but at that age, they are adaptable, and there are a couple of excellent choices for you to consider. In the longer term, I am offering, as part of the package, the same private educational opportunities that my own children receive, but all that is for you to decide, of course.

I appreciate that my offer is potentially life changing for you, and, as such, is far too much for you to be able to decide upon, without giving everything a great deal of thought and consideration. So, can I suggest that we adjourn back to Oakwood, and I will show you the plans, and give to you, in writing, everything that I have carefully prepared for your consideration? Please feel free to come and speak with me on any point that you feel needs further clarification.

As for you Sharon-Louise, besides my already declared wish that you should become the future Mrs Blackmore, I am not only going to need a hospital Matron, which is the position I envisage for Jacqui Strong, but also a hospital House Manager, as well. Yours, and possibly Jim's expertise in this respect, might prove to be invaluable?"

"Good Lord, Blackmore, is that your idea of a proposal of marriage? Offering a girl a plum job as part of the package? I sincerely hope that you're going to do better than that, mister?"

Sharon-Louise's light-hearted banter, delivered together with a playful little slap on the Blackmore derriere, then quickly followed up by a little kiss, was enough to put the smiles back on everyone's face.

Linking arms, they all made their way slowly back to the car, and Oakwood.


"So, all things considered, you like the look of this, do you, love?"

"On the face of it, well yes, but I'm not sure what the twins will think, David. Do you think that we should perhaps be asking them first?"

"What, ask them if they want to give up going to New Milton Junior School, and instead, go to, what was it called? Ah, yes, St Swithun's, a leading day and boarding school, it says here in the blurb? To give them the option of having to give up everything they have in New Milton, and instead, come out here to live in the country. Somewhere that they will have to suffer the hardship of living in the absolute lap of luxury, and instead of all their friends, have to put up with the company of Michelle and Charlotte, who will no doubt have to force them into going horse riding, swimming, playing tennis, sailing, golf, fishing . . . I don't see that they will possibly want to make the change, do you?"

Sue laughed, "Yes, alright, I think I'm persuaded on that score. But what about Emily's education, and then there's the taxi business that we've worked so hard for, are you ready to give that up, as well?"

"I still have a few bookings to fulfil, and I would have to notify the Licensing Officer of my change of address. But until the hospital project begins to become more of a reality, and needs more commitment, I see no reason why the two, shouldn't be run in parallel? Once I have sorted out all the contact numbers, it will be just as easy to work from here, at Oakwood, as it would from home, in New Milton.

If for any reason we find that this just isn't working for us, we will not have burned any bridges, and theoretically, we could step straight back again into what we already have. As for Emily, well why don't we just ask her?"

David turned to see that his little daughter, still in his arms, was regarding him intently. He realised that she had obviously been following his every word. He smiled at her lovingly, and took her little hand in his.

"So what about it then, little one? Would you be happy to come and live here?"

Her answer came back telepathically.

'Yes, daddy, I love this place, and all the people that live here. Mummy seems to be concerned about my education, so perhaps this would be an appropriate time for me to tell you both, what I think, and what I would like to happen in that regard. Is this to be allowed, please?'

Both David and Sue reverted to telepathy, the better to understand their tiny daughter. Still holding on to her hand, he carefully set her down onto the tabletop to stand at eye level, in front of them both.

'Bless your little heart, Emily. You do not need to ask our permission to tell us what you think, so please, go ahead and say whatever is on your mind.'

'Thank you, daddy, and you too, mummy. I think you have both realised by now, that I am slightly different from other children. Jo-jo has recently taught me how to organise my mind in such a way that I am now able to grasp enormous volumes of data. There is absolutely no limit to how much knowledge I am able to assimilate, for I have been assured by Jo-jo, that the learning capacity of the human brain is infinite.

I look around this magnificent library, and I see a whole wealth of knowledge just waiting there for me to access, and absorb into my memory. The only problem is, the more that I learn, the more I realise that there is still so much that I don't know about.

I have given the question of my future education a lot of thought, and I have concluded that by the time I get to be five-years of age, for you to have to make me go to school, will be like asking Professor Stephen Hawking, if he would like to learn to count up to ten. It will be an unnecessary, and totally ridiculous notion to even contemplate. The only area in my education, where I think I will need help and guidance, is in the area of my social, and physical development. To that end, if she will agree, I would like aunty Sharon to become my private tutor, and companion.'

Emily could immediately detect that her parents were both stunned at this seemingly rather silly idea.

'My goodness, Emily, you really have given this some thought, haven't you, sweetheart? I'm just a little curious as to why you think aunty Sharon might be the best person to teach you your social graces, though. How did you come to arrive at this choice?'

'I am the first to admit that I don't know many ladies, daddy, but I know aunty Sharon to be a very brave and clever lady, with the intelligence and ability, to better herself should she so desire. She is honest, loving, considerate, and compassionate, while still remaining what I have heard you describe as, 'a tough cookie, and very street-wise.' These are all qualities that would see her, quite comfortably, being able to mix into any company. And that is how, I too, would like to be. Besides, I anticipate that aunty Sharon will be here at Oakwood for the foreseeable future, as Uncle Malcolm has now recognised her potential as a marriage partner, with just the tiniest little bit of help from me, of course.'

Both her parents burst out laughing at this revelation, and Emily, still standing on the table, was left feeling slightly unsure of herself. Perhaps it would have been better if she'd not mentioned that?

'Emily Morrison-Lloyd, you are a scheming little minx. How can we ever hope to trust you, again? Have you been planning this whole thing all along, young lady?'

'I can only put the ideas or suggestions into a peoples minds, mummy. I regret that, as yet, I am still not able to directly influence any subsequent decisions that are made, but I'm working on it. I'm sure that it's possible.'

'Emily, that is very wrong of you. You really shouldn't be interfering in peoples lives, so.'

'But sometimes, mummy, people are just too blind to see the obvious, and a little help is all that is necessary to put things right, like with Uncle Malcolm, and Mr Cox. But if you tell me that it is wrong to help someone who is blind to the obvious, or needs to get better, then I will stop doing it immediately.'

'Mr Cox? Jim? What was it you did for him Emily? The sudden change in his physical condition has been quite remarkable. Are you saying that you are in some way responsible for that?'

'I cannot take all the credit, mummy, but it was only necessary to make the tiniest little adjustments to his mindset. This had the immediate affect of restoring the natural balance, and persuading his body to immediately start producing the natural body chemicals and solutions, so necessary to enable the healing processes to begin to work more efficiently.

His condition was causing much concern for aunty Sharon, so I asked Jo-jo if he could help him, and what you see is the result. I am hoping that Jo-jo will be able to teach me how to do it, restore the natural balance of a persons mind, that is. I don't think it is to be regarded as anything new, mummy. It's just another form of holistic psychotherapy, putting someone in the right frame of mind, to aid their own recovery.'

'Does uncle Malcolm know that you have helped to cure Mr Cox, Emily?'

'I think he has guessed that I might have had some influence in that regard, daddy. He asked me about it yesterday morning. I told him that I was aware of the changes, but couldn't tell him about Jo-jo, could I? He wouldn't understand, would he?

No doubt he will ask me about it again, and this gives me some cause for some concern. For if I am to be allowed to assist uncle Malcolm in his work, which is what I want to do, I may find it necessary to try and find another evasive answer. Jo-jo and I have always expected, that as time progressed, this might happen, so it is a problem we are both working on to find an acceptable solution. His continued existence here, with me, needs to be kept a secret for as long as possible.'

Both her parents stood before her thinking about the startling revelations of everything they had just been told. Emily, able to interpret their thoughts, was pleased to see, that they couldn't envisage any real harm in her little mind interventions, just as long as they were made for the right reasons, something she, herself, also thought to be right and proper. She waited patiently for them to say something more. The original question regarding her views on the family moving in to Oakwood, seemed to have been largely forgotten?

Her father finally addressed her in the proper way, voicing his admonishment, presumably to reinforce his words?

"Well alright then, young lady, you seem to have made your position abundantly clear in all of this, and your mother and I are left wondering just how much of a hand you might have had in deliberately bringing this about? In this instance, we are both grateful to you, and would have approved, only because from the family point of view, it presents a greater opportunity for us all. I am pleased to be able to tell you, that your wish is about to be granted. Your mother and I have decided to accept uncle Malcolm's offer, and for the time being, we are all going to move here, to Oakwood. But that still doesn't excuse what you have done.

In future, Emily, before you ever think of making any more such decisions, ones that would affect us all, you will see fit to consult with us, before doing anything. Your mother is quite right in saying, that to interfere in other people's lives, is very wrong. We would like your assurance that it will not happen again unless we know, and have sanctioned it, first. And that applies not only to us, but also to everyone else here, as well. Do I make our position abundantly clear, young lady?"

'Yes, father. I'm sorry if you think that I've done anything wrong, but my intentions were good, and the results would have to be regarded as moderately successful, don't you and mummy both agree?'

David smiled. He had to agree with her, but was not prepared to admit it. He reached out to take his little daughter back into his arms, and wondered how Sharon-Louise was going to react at being asked to become her companion and life tutor. He could imagine them becoming quite a formidable pair to reckon with.

Flight LH6598 touched down at Belfast International Airport exactly on schedule. Marty had spent a very enjoyable forty minutes chatting affably with the attractive lady seated beside him. He had learned that her name was Christina, and that she was a single lady in her early forties. She told him that she ran her own little import/export business, dealing exclusively in ladies shoes, from a boutique in the City, where she lived alone in the flat over the shop. Marty knew the location to be not too far removed from his Sydenham address, and they had gotten round to exchanging telephone numbers, with the idea of a future dinner date.

In relating to her his reasons for nearly missing the flight, he found she was entirely sympathetic, and even confessed to having had a somewhat similar experience herself, when going to Italy, a couple of years ago.

Their common experiences, had somehow served to unite them enough to want to take their brief association a step further, and Marty's previously foul mood, had swung completely the other way, he was now feeling particularly elated. Pleased with himself, at having unexpectedly pulled.

Together, they alighted from the aircraft and slowly made their way down to baggage reclaim, chatting like a couple of old friends, as they strolled along side by side.

Charlie Ferguson, on the other hand, was not so pleased. The last thing he expected was not to be noticed, or recognised, by McCue. He had watched in growing anger, as the cheeky bastard had started chatting-up the old tart seated beside him. McCue's whole attention had been focused on her for nearly the entire flight, and now, they were completely oblivious to him, even though he was ambling along only three yards behind, so obviously following, while listening to every word of their conversation.

Short of confronting him face-to-face, Charlie could think of no possible way of alerting McCue to his presence. Was the man bloody stupid, or something? How could he have failed to notice him? Charlie watched as McCue got his bags back almost immediately. Being the last to be placed in the hold, led to them being amongst the first to be removed. She was travelling with hand luggage only, so they were amongst the first passengers to start making their way towards Customs and Immigration.

Charlie was left waiting, and cursing the delay in the arrival of his own suitcase. He was forced into watching McCue and the woman go out of his sight. His biggest regret at the moment, was the possibility that he was going to miss McCue's reaction to the little surprise he had arranged for him in the Arrivals Hall.

"Shall we share a cab, Christina? I can have you dropped off at the boutique while on my way to Stormont, and the fare will be charged to my expenses."

"Thank you, Martyn, that is very kind and considerate of you."

Marty couldn't believe his luck. Christina was obviously warming to his company as with a radiant smile she slipped her free arm through his, to walk even closer together, much more like a proper couple. He didn't even realise that she was gently manoeuvring him into a small crowd of people that seemed to have gathered, and to the casual observer, might all have been waiting for something, perhaps?

But, as Marty and Christina merged into their midst, they all now began walking, as a group, away from the Customs and Immigration checkpoint.

Marty's passport had been given only the briefest, perfunctory examination, before both he and Christina had been waved on through, with no problem. Marty was a little surprised, and even breathed an audible sigh of relief. He had fully expected that Customs at Heathrow might have telephoned ahead, and that he might be detained again?

He and Christina, now in the middle of the group of twenty or thirty people, with more joining them, headed towards the double-door exit, that led out into the Arrivals Hall. As they emerged through the automatically opening doors, two men, both with cameras and handheld recording devices, pushed their way into the group in order to get to Marty.

"Mr McCue, Reporters from News International, can you tell us, please, sir, has your fund-raising trip to America been successful?"

Marty was taken completely by surprise, he wasn't aware that his trip had been such common knowledge. He carried on walking, now appreciating that Christina was gently urging him to do so, for some reason. Their cameras began flashing, and Marty held up his free hand to cover his face.

"I have no comment to make, thank you."

The other reporter was more direct and aggressive. Marty found the miniature tape recorder being thrust into his face as the man demanded,

"Are you a drug user Mr McCue? Is the First Minister aware that you snort cocaine? Have you been charged with possession, sir?"

Marty felt the red mist rising again. He wanted to drop his cases, and to take a swing at the man, but he was again aware of Christina urging him along. He heard her whispered order to say nothing, and to keep moving.

The reporter, on getting no apparent reaction from him, tried again.

"Would you care to give us a comment on the breaking news, that you were the one of the people responsible for planting bombs in London during the nineteen-seventies, Mr McCue?"

It was too much for Marty, despite Christina's insistence that they should keep moving, he came to an abrupt halt and whirled on the man, who was forced to step away as Marty lunged toward him.

"No comment, and if I see anything like that in print, your editor had better be watching for the imminent arrival of the biggest libel suit he is ever likely to see." He snarled.

"So the file that has been handed to the Metropolitan Police, detailing your part in the bombing operation is a complete fabrication, is it, Mr McCue? Are you saying there is no truth in it all? Can my paper print your absolute denial for you, sir?"

The crowd of people all seemed to be closing in around them now, and he and Christina were forced to start moving again. Marty wanted to stop and refute the allegation further, but to his discomfort and dismay, she was now squeezing the pressure point on the inside of his upper arm, just enough to cause him pain, and force him to keep moving along.

The two bogus reporters were left behind, disappearing into the melee of people that were following them up. Marty saw, and heard, one of them grunt in pain as he apparently fell to the floor. His companion stopped, and appeared to be trying to help, but he too suddenly found himself under a pile of people, that all seemed to be falling over them. Their equipment was smashed underfoot, and knees and feet inexplicably seemed to be finding heavy contact with particularly vulnerable areas of their anatomy.

By the time that two uniformed Police Officers arrived on the scene, the crowd had dispersed, and there was little to be done, except to call an ambulance for two injured men, who sat with their backs propped against the wall, looking thoroughly dishevelled, and very sorry for themselves.

A subsequent review of the available CCTV footage clearly showed that they had both been accidentally trampled after having fallen over in front of a crowd of people. It had all taken place in only a few seconds.

Marty and Christina had continued to be carried along by the crowd until they were safely outside, and almost in the clear. Marty, still effectively hidden from any camera view by the surrounding people, suddenly found himself being bundled into the back of a waiting, nondescript Belfast taxicab. Together with Christina, the pair were quickly driven away from the airport, to a destination as yet unknown to him. It took Marty a few seconds to collect his thoughts enough to ask,

"Am I permitted to ask who you are, and where you might be taking me?"

Christina was looking back over shoulder, through the rear screen, to check if anyone was following. She ignored his question and spoke to the driver instead.

"You can probably slow up a bit now, Brendon, I think we're in the clear? But just to be certain, pull off and put the car out of sight for a couple of minutes. Pick somewhere where we can watch this road, just till we see what the opposition are about. I don't suppose they'll be wanting to follow us, but we'll need to be sure where they're going, before we head for the meeting house."

The driver said nothing, but took the next right, turning the cab in a tight U-turn, and quickly slotting it into a vacant kerbside parking space, between two other parked cars. They sat in silence watching the traffic passing the junction.

"Look, I don't wish to appear overly pedantic, but would you mind telling me who you are, and what we're looking for? That little operation back at the airport, if engineered by you, was pretty slick, and I would like to express my gratitude for the way you dealt with those reporters, but I don't think it will stop them . . . ."

"They were not reporters, Martyn, they were Police, from a sub-section of the SIS, an intelligence-gathering, and problem solving division of MI5, which is laughably referred to here, as Provincial Security. It is a department run directly from Scotland Yard, and is hated by everyone, including our own Police hierarchy. We've been tipped off that there was also a man on the plane who is following you. His name is Ferguson, and he's a senior detective officer in the London Metropolitan Police."

Marty snapped his fingers, "Got him. Light grey suit, little moustache, slightly effeminate looking, sat facing me in one of the crew seats, am I right?"

"That's him, he followed us off the plane. He's really bad news, especially for you."

"Why would that be?"

"His job is to solve problems before they can get sufficiently out of hand enough, to cause embarrassment to the British Establishment. His methods are invariably to be regarded as permanent, shall we say. He's worked in the Province before, and caused us a lot of bother. The Ruling Council will be less than pleased to know that he's back again."

"Ruling Council? Am I to assume then, that you're . . . ?"

"It doesn't matter who we are, Martyn, it's probably best that you don't know, anyway. I was sent over to Heathrow to meet up with you, and to give you advance warning that there has been some certain unfortunate developments from your past, that have come back to haunt you. Suffice to say, we are on the same side. So for the time being, just do as we ask, and you will be okay."

"I have some correspondence files that have to be with my Minister before he leaves for a conference tonight. Can that be arranged, please, Christina? I assume that is your name, is it?"

"It will do for now. The Deputy First Minister has already been made aware of your situation. It was he who indirectly asked us for some help. You can deliver your files to Stormont just as soon as we establish that Ferguson is going to where we think. Just have a little patience, and bear with us, please, Martyn."

Charlie Ferguson's suitcase was one of the last to arrive on the carousel, and by this time, he was absolutely fuming. He snatched it up to throw it unceremoniously onto the baggage trolley, and hurry towards Customs and Immigration. Ignoring the snaking line of people in the queue, he went straight to the desk and barged rudely in front of a woman who was just about to show her passport. Flashing his warrant card and putting forward his passport for inspection, he addressed both the woman, and the Immigration Officer.

"My apologies, madam, but I'm a Police Officer on the trail of a suspected criminal, who has managed to get some way ahead of me. It is vitally important that I catch up with him before he gets out of the airport."

The Immigration Officer, refusing to be hurried, picked up his passport to compare the photograph. He looked pointedly at Charlie, and back again to the passport photo.

"This photo bears very little resemblance to your present appearance, Mr Ferguson. Would you just confirm your date, and place of birth, for me."

Charlie realised that he had taken pains to alter his appearance to confuse McCue, completely forgetting about how it would seem to anyone else. He felt rather stupid, now.

"Yes, of course, I'm Charles Windrush Ferguson, born 6th June, 1953, in Glasgow, Scotland. Look, Officer, my apologies again, but it is very important that I catch up with my suspect. I know I don't look very much like my passport photo, or possibly, your idea of how a Police Officer should look, and that is entirely intentional on my part. Believe me, there are very good reasons for making the subtle changes to my appearance, and for me being dressed in this way. Now, can I please be allowed to continue?"

"There are two gentlemen standing over to my left, also Police Officers, I think. I believe they might be waiting for you, Mr Ferguson? You may proceed. Good luck with catching up with your man."

Charlie walked quickly towards the two, tall, very smartly dressed, good looking, and fit young men. They stood side by side, their hands clasped behind their backs, watching him, with slightly bemused expressions.

Charlie didn't recognise either of them, and as he approached, he wondered why none of his usual Irish colleagues were not there to pick him up?

"Good afternoon gentlemen, I'm Detective Chief Inspector Charles Ferguson of Scotland Yard. I presume you've been sent to meet me?"

"Good afternoon, sir. DS Brody and DC Franklin. We are instructed to take you straight to your hotel to get you booked in. Also to advise that we shall be picking you up again at 0900, tomorrow morning, to take you to Belfast Police Headquarters at Knock. You have been scheduled in for a 1000 meeting with the Crime Operations Commander. He apparently wishes to speak with you regarding the present operation."

"Do you know the whereabouts of our target, McCue? He managed to get away from me at the airport. Has he left the airport complex yet?"

"We believe he has, sir, but we're not certain. Apparently, there has just been a bit of a fracas in the Arrivals Hall. We're given to understand that two of our lads have been taken to hospital for treatment. The COC is not going to be best pleased, as you can well imagine?"

"You mean you've lost him already? Christ almighty. Well, he needs to be found again, immediately. Who's in charge of the surveillance team? I need to speak with him, urgently?"

"I'm sure I don't know, sir. We're here just following orders, and right now, they are to get you to your hotel, and then up in front of the

COC, tomorrow morning. So shall we be leaving, please sir? The car is this way . . ."

Charlie was not a happy man, his seemingly well planned little operation appeared to have gone tits-up already. The news that McCue seemed to have given everyone the slip, and that he had obviously gotten some outside help at the airport, left him more than a little concerned. He was now in a car being taken to his hotel, with the only thing to look forward to being a meeting with some jumped-up uniformed, Northern Ireland Police Commander, who would no doubt want to know about everything. It was to be regarded as complete waste of valuable time. Sitting there, chewing the fat, instead of getting out and looking to locate McCue, and deal with him . . .

He leaned forward to speak to the two plain-clothed officers accompanying him. He'd already forgotten their names, but what did it matter?

"What's the name of this uniformed Commander, that wants to speak with me?"

"Crime Operations Commander, David Flanagan. His official rank is that of Deputy Chief Constable for the Province. Since the instigation of Patten, which is about when he was appointed, he does everything by the book, so you always know exactly where you are with him."

"That's good to hear. Tell me a little about his background, if you would, please. Is he good at his job?"

"He's very good, sir. He came to us as a Super' from the Garda Siochana, on a personnel exchange, and has been with us ever since. He's worked his way up through the ranks, and has been our COC since 2006.

He's a great bloke, very fit, regularly takes part in iron-man competitions. He has a black belt in several different martial arts, plus a degree in Criminal Law. He's reckoned to be the youngest, and second most highly paid Police Officer in the whole of the UK, our Chief being the highest.

Since confirmation of his appointment to the Police Service of Northern Ireland, in 2004, made by Chief Hugh Orde, Davey's made a real difference for us all, here in the Province. We all love him to bits, don't we Franksy?"

The other officer, the one driving, nodded and grunted his agreement. He carried on.

"The COC is very hands on, as well. He regularly turns up, completely unannounced, to do a night shift with the uniform guys, or to come out on a raid, with us. He just walks into any station in the Province, and sits in on a briefing. He doesn't interfere with the officer-in-charge of the operation, but will always join with him, and lead from the front. The very fact that he doesn't pull rank, take over, or throw his weight around, is much appreciated, and the men all love him for it. Experience has shown that he can be relied upon in any situation. He's not a man to get on the wrong side of, as many criminals, and a few corrupt Police officers, have found out to their cost."

"Is he married?" Charlie hoped that he might be of a similar disposition to himself.

"No, he's still single, but there's a whole queue of beautiful women out there, all just waiting for him to tip his cap in their direction. Am I right, Franksy?"

"That you are, Serge, that you are. Lucky devil can take his pick from the crop. What was the name of that American sort he had hanging off his arm at the last Christmas Ball? Wasn't she the daughter of some State Senator or Governor, or something?"

"What, Celine McCarthy, the blonde, all tits and teeth, is that who you're thinking of? I didn't know that she as well-connected, although it doesn't surprise me. Our Davey can certainly take his pick, so he can."

Their idle chit-chat continued, but Charlie had lost interest in the conversation. He sat back in his seat to ponder upon the identity and credentials of the young super-cop he was about to become acquainted with. He seemed to recall the name, David Flanagan, from somewhere, but couldn't quite recall where?

Cynically, Charlie had immediately categorised him as probably just another one of the Bramshill type whiz-kids, that all the Police Staff Colleges seemed to churn out in their hundreds, these days? Most of them seemed to be good at flying a desk, but are usually worse than useless in an operational capacity. To hear about one that was good in both areas of expertise, was highly unusual, as was a senior officer that was seemingly idolised by the lesser ranks under his command.

Charlie wondered why he wanted to speak with him? In the past, he had just met up with other officers in the SIS, and the PSNI Special

Branch, and they had all gotten on with the job in hand, with no interference. He weighed up his position, and, right at that moment, it didn't look too promising. He'd lost his man, was unarmed, on strange and hostile territory, with no apparent backup. Where were all of his usual old mates?

He was beginning to get a bad feeling about all of this, and, to top it all, could feel another of his headaches coming on.

"That's them," murmured Brendon, "The blue Ford Mondeo, do you want me to follow?"

"Please, Brendon, but only till we can verify which hotel he's booked himself into, and then its straight over to Stormont, for Marty."

Ten minutes later, they watched from a discreet distance as the car with Charlie Ferguson in, drove up to the front entrance of the Park Avenue Hotel in Holywood Road. He got out with his luggage and went inside. The car, with the two plain-clothed detectives, drove off and left him.

"Christ, he's only just around the corner from where I live, so he is . . ."

"I'm sure he knows that Marty, and that its the same hotel that Connor is staying in, as well."

"Connor? What, Connor McCall? What's he doing over here?"

"Haven't you checked your phone yet, Marty? Connor has been here for a week, waiting for your return. He's become part of the problem."

"My phones, Christ, I'd forgotten all about them. There's a whole list of missed calls for me to pick up."

He fished into his pockets and pulled out both of his phones. Christina reached over and snatched them from his grasp before he could do anything with them. She checked the missed calls on both.

"Sorry Marty, but are you saying that you haven't tried to access any of these calls yet, because someone has?"

"No, I haven't had a chance, what with being detained by Customs, and then being put straight onto the aircraft. Is it Connor that's been trying to get hold of me, what does he want?"

"This is indeed fortunate, Marty, you not having contacted Connor, that is. Now listen to me very carefully, this is very, very important. On no account must you try and make any contact with Connor, do you hear me? The Police have placed your home under surveillance, and we suspect that all your phones calls are being intercepted and monitored."

She looked at both of the phones and held up the old Nokia before giving them back to him.

"Turn this phone off, take out the SIM card, put it away somewhere, and forget about it. Use only your work Blackberry for the time being, and remember to watch what you say.

At the moment, Martyn, our sources are telling us that there is some sort of a file that has come to light. It apparently details the bombing operations that you were all involved with, while on active service, back in the seventies. We can only assume that because you haven't immediately been arrested while in London, that there is insufficient evidence to prefer any specific charges against you.

We suspect that they are now looking for you to give it to them on a plate. That incident at the airport we know was pre-planned. They are trying to spook you into doing something incriminating, like making contact with Connor for instance. That will then establish one of the links they are looking for. Any conversations you might have with him, will become a matter of record. It would all slowly come together until they feel there is sufficient enough evidence to act upon. It would then be curtains for you, I'm afraid, Marty."

"How do you know all this, where do you get your info from? Some of what you've told me must be classified, surely?"

"We have our sources, Marty. We found out about Lara's death from one of her relatives, a sister who lives in Londonderry. She is a keen Party member. Apparently, a solicitor had written to say that the house, in which she and her mother are living, is one that was owned by Lara Dobbs. The letter advised that it had been left to a daughter of hers, living in England, and that further correspondence would follow in regard to their continued tenancy. The family weren't even aware that Lara had a daughter, so it all came as a bit of a shock. Next, we were told by a different source, about a large amount of money being transferred from a bank account in yours, and Lara Dobbs' name. The police, and other security forces, in their fight against organised crime, regularly monitor this sort of thing, Marty. The movement of large sums of money, that is. Bank Staff throughout the Province, are duty bound to report any such transfers. But we usually get wind of it, as well, just in case we need to cover our tracks a bit. Incidentally, we are advised that you are still a signature on that account, so if you have any sort of paperwork in relation to it, destroy it all immediately. We already know that you've never tried to access it, at all, so don't go trying anything now. All the money that was regularly being deposited by Lara, now goes to her daughter. It's gone, no longer accessible, so that's the end of it. It's just a pity that we were not advised until it was too late ...

We had one of our solicitors pose as a Bank representative, to query the closure. In a little off-the-record chat with the solicitor handling Lara's affairs, he managed to find out some more of the background.

The solicitor let slip that he is the senior partner of a firm that includes the name McCall. We did some checking, and sure enough, it's Connor McCall, that we're talking about. Does the name Williams, Thompson and McCall, mean anything to you?

"That would be Connors father, then. His surname is Williams. Connor and his wife, Elizabeth, are junior partners in the firm, I seem to remember ..."

"You've got him, then. The odd thing is, he didn't seem to be aware that Connor was over here in the Province looking for you, so we kept quiet about it. It seems very strange that he should be here without the knowledge of the senior partner, his father, doesn't it?

Anyway, the information we did get, is all a bit sketchy and involved, but as we understand it, the active service unit that you were involved with back in the seventies, has been rumbled. Apart from you and Connor, we think that all the others are now dead. They either chose to blow themselves up, or were killed in some sort of shoot-out with armed Police. We think it might be connected with big explosion that took place in an old quarry, somewhere in Monmouthshire, South Wales, but we don't know for sure. It was all covered up by the Police, who put out a statement saying that it was some unexploded ordnance, left over from the war, that was accidentally detonated by some cavers."

"Oh my God. I can't believe it. That must have been at Bleanaway Quarry. We had our cache of arms hidden in a cave, there. You've already mentioned Lara, but Shaun, Michael and Dermot, are they all dead, as well? Are you sure? Like me, they've all got to have been in their sixties by now. I can't imagine there was much fight left in any of them?"

"As I say, Martyn, that's as much as we know. Connor, being over here and looking for you, has probably got something to do with it, so he has become an embarrassing problem that we are still looking to resolve. Leave him to us. He is obviously not aware of your new address, because he is still looking for your car, at your old lodgings. That's another thing, your little car is far too distinctive, so it must remain in your garage for the time being, in case he sees it. I suggest that you disable it somehow, just in case they wonder why you're not using it to go to work. It constitutes a slight deviation from your normal routine, doesn't it?

On no account are you to do anything other than to go home, and resume your normal life. Carry on with your daily work and leisure routines. It is very important that everything you do, must appear completely normal.

You must also assume that all your movements, phone calls, conversations, in fact everything that you do, will be under the closest scrutiny. You are going to have to be squeaky clean until this all blows over, or, we can sort something else out for you. You are amongst friends, Martyn, more friends than you ever imagined that you have. So don't you go doing anything stupid, and letting us down, will you?"

"How can I get hold of you, should I need to speak about something?"

"Try to avoid having to do so. But in an emergency, I suggest that you write it down on a piece of paper and wear a red tie when you go out. If we see that, someone will approach you and ask for a cigarette. Give him the packet of ciggies with your note inside. The answer, or reply, will either come through your letterbox with the normal post, or perhaps with a door-to-door leaflet distribution. Destroy anything written just as soon as you have read it. Burn it, and then flush it down the loo, but don't shred it, or just tear it up, things like that can easily be reassembled.

These are all worst-case scenarios, Marty. We will probably find that none of this will be necessary, but we have to have it covered, just in case. This man, Ferguson, is bad news. From what we know of him, he rarely gives up, and takes no prisoners. However, he is off his Manor, and about to learn that he is subject to a very different set of rules now. So we are fairly confident that his visit over here is not going to achieve anything, unless, that is, you do something really stupid, and give it to him on a plate.

This taxi is one of ours. Brendon will drop you off at Stormont to deliver your correspondence, and then take you home. This is where I get out."

She leaned forward and tapped the glass panel.

"Stop the car on the next junction please, Brendon. Look, I'm sorry, Martyn, but our dinner date will have to wait for another day. But I promise you, when this all blows over, it will happen. Bye for now . . ."

She kissed a finger and planted it on his forehead, and with that, Christina was gone, leaving him alone with his thoughts.

———*ΩΩΩ*———

In the mid-morning sunshine, Tony Williams drove his car, a brand new Lexus LS400h, saloon, up the beautiful tree-lined, driveway of Oakwood. He was not sure what to expect. George had casually mentioned on the phone that the house was rather nice, but it was understated, this was truly magnificent. The electric-powered hybrid car whispered to a halt on the gravelled parking area, and Tony stepped out to better admire the façade of the typically Georgian manor house. Almost immediately, the door of the house opened, and a butler emerged to greet him. Slightly bemused, Tony waited as he descended the steps and came to a halt in front, acknowledging him with a slight bow.

"Good morning, sir. Am I to assume that you are Mr Anthony Williams?"

"That I am."

"Then you are most welcome to Oakwood, sir. My name is Carter, and I am instructed to conduct you to the lounge, where Mr Malcolm Blackmore and his guests are taking morning coffee. If you would care to follow me, sir, I will show you the way."

They started to make their way towards the house, Tony falling in beside Carter, who carried his bulging briefcase for him. Carter enquired of him,

"Would you like some coffee, or perhaps tea, sir?

"Coffee will be fine, thank you Carter. Will Miss Sharon Roberts be present? It is she that I have particularly come to see."

"There is a Miss Sharon here, sir, yes, but I understand her surname to be Cox, now."

"Ah, yes, that would be the name of her adoptive parents. Thank you for correcting me Carter, you have probably just saved me from an embarrassing moment."

Carter opened the lounge door and ushered in Tony Williams. George stopped talking with Edith and Sue, put down his coffee, and stepped forward to greet his old friend with a big smile and a firm handshake.

"Tony, good to see you, old man, glad you could make it. It's all right, thank you, Carter, I'll introduce Mr Williams to Malcolm and Sharon."

"Very well, thank you, Mr George. I'll shall bring some fresh coffee for Mr Williams."

In a friendly gesture, George linked arms with Tony and started to guide him slowly to where Malcolm was talking with Sharon. He saw that as they approach, Malcolm had ceased talking, and was now waiting expectantly, to be formally introduced. George whispered quietly to his friend,

"So how are you, really, Tony? Our last meeting was very difficult for both of us. Have there been any more recent developments?"

"All in good time, George. Let's get through the matter in hand, shall we? I'll bring you up to date a bit later on. Is this the lucky lady?"

Malcolm and Sharon both heard his last remark as, with a smile, he held out his hand to her. She took his hand and regarded him in stony silence.

"This is Miss Sharon-Louise Cox, Tony. May I also introduce you to your host, Mr Malcolm Blackmore. Malcolm, this is my good friend, and colleague for many years, Mr Tony Williams."

The introductory handshakes completed, Tony found that it was he that was expected to take things forward.

"You know why I am here, of course?" He looked to see that they were both nodding their assent.

"That's indeed fortuitous, but at this juncture, I feel the need to point out that there is still a lot of work to be done in sorting out the affairs of the late Laura Dobson. She was a very well organised lady, but her estate is fairly complex, and involves several properties, bank accounts, and a quite comprehensive investment portfolio. As such, this mornings meeting can only be regarded as a preliminary affair, just to give you an outline of the general provisions of her last Will and testament."

Tony turned to look directly at Sharon, and reached out to take her hand again.

"There is only one beneficiary in all of this, and that is you, my dear. May I be permitted to say that you bear a startling resemblance to how your mother once looked, thirty-odd years ago? For that is how long I have had the privilege, and pleasure, to act for her in the care of all her personal affairs. Indeed, it was I that drew up her Will, only two years ago. I knew full well that it needed more work, but I didn't expect to find myself having to do it quite so soon. May I offer my deepest sympathy on your tragic loss, your mother was a quite remarkable woman?"

"Thank you, Mr Williams, that has been said about her several times before. But unfortunately, I was never given the opportunity to find it out for myself. You mentioned just now, that I might be a lucky girl? Well, believe me, I will take absolutely no pleasure in being in receipt of all her goods and chattels. If it were humanly possible, I would gladly give them all back, in exchange for some quality time spent in her company. Right at this moment, Mr Williams, I can feel nothing but anger towards her. She denied me my childhood, and has cheated and deceived me for a number of years, during which time, had I known the truth, she and I could have been a proper mother and daughter."

Tony looked stricken. The last thing that he expected was that his off-the-cuff reference to someone suddenly becoming very wealthy, would be misconstrued. He now realised just how crass his remark must have sounded to her, and he became contrite and apologetic.

"I am so very sorry, Miss Cox, I really didn't mean to cause you any offence. My comment, on reflection, was both stupid and uncalled for, given the circumstances. Will you find it in your heart to please forgive me."

Sharon withdrew her hand from his to use a tissue, and wipe a tear from her eye.

"Your apology is accepted, Mr Williams, I know that you meant no offence. It's probably me, being over-sensitive, as much as anything? This is a very difficult and emotional time, as you will appreciate?"

Tony bowed his head in a gesture of understanding. He looked troubled and uncertain, as if struggling to find the right words . . .

"Thank you, Miss Cox. I will endeavour to make the rest of the morning as brief and painless as possible for you. I don't think it will do any harm for you to know that I have never married, but I got to know your mother very well. The knowledge that she was a single lady, and despite the few years' age difference, has always led me into carrying a torch for Laura Dobson. Unfortunately, I considered that my professional relationship precluded me from ever making my true feelings known to her. If you will excuse my language, for I can think of no better way of putting it, life can be a real bitch at times, especially when things like this happen to us. If it is of any consolation, Laura's death has hurt me, as well. Much more than I can ever tell you. I too, feel cheated, but for different reasons entirely."

By the time he had finished speaking, Tony was head down, and finding it emotionally difficult to maintain his stiff upper lip. George, sensing this, stepped in to help his old friend. Taking his arm and with an understanding glance from both Sharon and Malcolm, he gently steered him away from them.

"We've set up a desk in the study for you to use, Tony. Come and get some coffee first, old chap, and I'll take you on through. Tell me, how are things going with Connor?"

Once clear of the others, George felt better able to speak.

"You sly old dog, you've never mentioned that you've ever had a soft spot for any woman, except for Mary McCall, that is."

"I am not a naturally gregarious type of person, as you well know, George. But whenever I found myself in the company of Laura Dobson, my heart would begin beating ninety-to-the-dozen. My mouth would go dry, and I frequently found myself completely tongue-tied. Try to imagine her looking like a younger version of Sharon Cox. Twenty-two, or three, maybe, short skirt and long legs, see-through blouse, absolutely stunning to look at, and there she is, sitting in my office, quite innocently discussing all her personal affairs with me.

Try to picture me also, for there was I, desperately trying not to stare at her crotch, while embarrassingly, trying to hide an enormous erection under my desk. In so doing, I'm sweating buckets of blood, and floundering around like a fish out of water. I'd often lose it completely. It didn't just happen the once. It was every bloody time, George, every time I saw her.

Over the years, she kept her looks, and, like Sharon here, matured into a naturally beautiful woman. I last saw her about two years ago, and I still found her devilishly attractive. Whenever I was in her presence, it was always the same, I just went all to pieces. Heaven knows what she must have thought of me as a man? I must have appeared to be a right Wally? For fear of rejection, I doubt that I could ever have found it within myself, to make any of my true feelings known to her. God only knows, George, it took an enormous amount of courage for me to just admit it to her daughter, let alone say anything to Laura, herself.

Now that she's gone, she will never know how I felt about her, will she? And for the second time in my life, due to my own bloody stupidity, I've allowed yet another opportunity for possible happiness, to pass me by. I'm finding that it's all rather sad, George, and I'm fast heading towards becoming a very lonely old man.

Just now, in having to make my apologies to Miss Cox, the moment just seemed to be right to let the truth about my feelings for Laura, be known. You are the first people that I have ever told."

George was chuckling sympathetically at his friend's uncomfortable admissions. Still seeking only to further lighten the mood, he led him back towards the table upon which Carter had just placed another fresh pot of coffee. He set out two cups and began to pour. Tony added a little cream, and gratefully sipped at his coffee. Their conversation effectively changed tack.

"That file you mentioned, George, where is it now, can I ask?"

"David has it, still. He was meant to pass it over to a senior Police Officer, yesterday, but the man was called away unexpectedly, so he's now waiting for further instruction."

"Do you think it would be possible for me to see it, George, just to satisfy myself as to the extent of Connors complicity?"

"That is not for me to say, Tony. Personally, I would see no harm in it, but you would have to ask David when he returns. At the moment, he and Malcolm's two girls, have taken the twins to have a look at their new school, St Swithun's. It's situated over the other side of Winchester. He should be back quite soon. I'm sure that he won't want to miss any part of your reading of Laura's Will. David became quite fond of her himself, towards the end, you know?"

"I'm not surprised. Laura was a very private lady, but when you did get to know her, she was really quite endearing. On a rather sadder note, George, I've just remembered that the Police called last evening to inform me that her body will be ready for release to her next of kin, on Thursday of next week. They will need to know details of the funeral arrangements. Does Miss Cox have anyone in mind, yet? I'll pass it on if she has. There are some last requests from the deceased that will need to be fulfilled in that respect."

"I don't think that it's even been discussed yet, Tony. As you know, I have been appointed to act for her now, so best leave it with me for the time being. I'll get back to you as soon as I have something arranged. We will need to get our heads together very soon, anyway. The handing over of the estate, and all that it entails will be no simple matter, I'll warrant?"

"On the contrary, George. In actual fact, the greater majority of the work is well in hand. I was just looking to buy a little more time. The bank accounts, and some of the conveyancing, need a little more work, but by the end of the month, most of it will just need signatures. It would help, however, if I were to be permitted to pass over the complete portfolio of investment shares, without my looking at them too closely. There is a lot of work to be done there, and it is a little out of my field of expertise. I would venture to suggest that it might best be put into the hands of an experienced broker to look at, before any firm decisions are made."

"I'll have a word with Malcolm Blackmore, he'll know of someone, no doubt. Shall we go through to the study and set out your stall in readiness, Tony, I sense that everyone is keen to hear what you have to say?"

—◦◦◦—

Charlie awoke that morning with the mother of all headaches, and a mouth like the bottom of a birdcage. The half empty bottle of Laphroaig single malt stood on his dressing table, with the remains of his last generous helping, still in the bottom of the tumbler. It served to remind him of the previous evenings over indulgence, mostly brought about by his frustrations. He closed his eyes and tried to rally his thoughts on what had been said the previous evening.

Charlie had spent much of it in the hotel restaurant and bar, hoping to recognise and identify, Connor McCall. He didn't want to make himself too obvious, otherwise he might simply have asked for him at the Reception desk. The other thing he didn't know was whether or not McCall was going to meet up with Martyn McCue, as he had requested in his phone calls? So for the time being, Charlie wished to remain completely anonymous to him.

Retiring from the bar to his hotel room, Charlie had set about ringing round some of his old pals, trying to get them to come out and give him some company. For whatever reasons, he found that many of his phone numbers were now unobtainable, but he finally tracked down his previous partner, and best mate in the Province, DI 'Razor' Sharpe.

Charlie was surprised to learn that he had taken early retirement, and now lived in Londonderry. They spent over an hour swapping yarns and remembering old acquaintances. Charlie soon found that nearly all of the old Special Branch lads had either resigned, been reassigned, or had similarly retired, mostly as a direct result of the massive reorganisation of the Police Service of Northern Ireland.

He also found out that the man he was due to meet later that morning, Deputy Chief Constable, and Crime Operations Commander, David Flanagan, had been responsible for instigating most of the changes.

Unlike the two young officers that he had briefly become acquainted with on the previous day, Razor's assessment of Flanagan, was somewhat less complimentary. The old regime, much to the distress of many long-serving officers, such as he, was dead. The new administration was dictated by the implementation of recommendations arising out of the Patten Commission Report. David Flanagan's responsibility and instruction, was clear and unequivocal. Every Police operation was to be within the Reports terms of reference. Razor went on to advise that all the stock phraseology would probably be wheeled out to him that morning. For Davey, as he was commonly referred to by most of the lesser ranks, was known to revel in its repetition.

"You see if I'm not right, Charlie. I'll lay odds on you getting his spiel on, 'effective, efficient, impartial policing' and something about, 'integrity not being negotiable.' Then, if you really get him going, you will hear all about his promise to, 'act with fairness, integrity, diligence and impartiality, to uphold fundamental human rights, and accord equal respect to all individuals.' All this rhetorical crap being part of the new Oath of Office, so it is."

"Jesus Christ, Razor, I hope that all the terrorist scumbags have taken the same oath? Talk about trying to do a job with your hands tied. How on earth did it all come down to this? Whatever happened to the old iron fist approach?"

"The Police over here are political pawns now, Charlie, that's how I see it, and I'm glad that I'm no longer a part of it. Less than a quarter of the electorate is Sien Fein, but they are demanding fifty per cent of a say in how Belfast and the Province is governed. Everyone here is bending over backwards to try and avoid any resurgence of the previous troubles, but with all the political and religious extremism, coupled with the Gaelic mentality, I for one, can never see it happening, Charlie. A United Ireland is just some Irish politician's whimsical pipedream, so it is. But, having said all that, just recently, it's been nice to be able to walk out on the streets of my hometown again, without too much fear of getting blown to pieces, or shot dead by the security forces. The majority of us are liking the peace now, Charlie, so we are. As for your man, Davey Flanagan, purely on that basis, I have to reluctantly concede that his approach to everything, is probably the best way forward for us all? So don't you go doing anything that might be upsetting him now, you hear what I'm saying, Charlie? I know that you're your own man, but things over here are very different now, and it wouldn't take much to upset the apple cart again. Who's your target, can I ask?"

Charlie would have liked to tell him everything, but aware of the security and confidentiality implications of his mission, he decided to keep quiet.

"Sorry, Razor, I'd love you to know, but I can't say anything, as I'm sure you'll understand. No doubt, in due course, you will get to hear about it, but until then . . ."

"No worries, Charlie. It's good to know that you are keeping your mouth shut. Be aware, even the walls tend to have ears over here. Good luck with your mission, Charlie, ring me again when it's all over, eh?"

"Cheers, Razor, enjoy your retirement, you lucky old bugger . . ."

As he swung his legs out of bed, Charlie managed a smile at the mental picture he had of his old friend. Naked, he headed for his bathroom. Half an hour, and a shit, shower, and shave later, together with a small handful of paracetamol rattling around his insides, saw him dressed, and heading down to breakfast. His headache had slowly receded to a dull ache, but his stomach churnings still persuading him that food was temporarily out of the question.

He settled for a fresh pot of strong black coffee, laced with some of the cinnamon from the silver pepper pot he had liberated from Oakwood. A single round of dry, brown bread toast, helped keep it down.

Strangely, for at first it had only been an affectation, Charlie found that he rather liked taking his coffee this way now? He looked around the fifty or more people in the dining room, vainly hoping to spot someone that might be Connor McCall. He finished his breakfast and set about scheming for a way to get the information he required from the Receptionist, without directly asking. He thought that if he were to phone the hotel and then ask to speak to Mr Connor McCall, while watching to see which room extension was selected by the Receptionist . . . ? It would take almost split second timing, and he would have to arrive at the Reception desk at the precise moment that she connected his call, but it was certainly possible, he thought.

Charlie strolled through into the Lobby and main entrance area, to get a better idea of the layout of the Reception desk. He looked to see where he would need to be standing, the best to see the call connected on the old fashioned switchboard. On the pretext of looking at various tourist brochures and leaflets, he moved around, getting a good idea of the layout. The only thing that bothered him was the presence of two Reception staff behind the desk. He concluded that he stood more chance of success if there was only one, but how? He was pondering this particular problem when a gentleman stepped up to the desk.

"Would you kindly prepare my bill for me, please, I shall be checking out tomorrow morning. I shall also need to book a taxi to take me to the City Airport. I'll need to be there for five-thirty, so shall we say a pick-up from here around five-ten, please?"

"Certainly Mr McCall, I will have your bill made up ready for when you leave. The Hall Porter will be here to process your account. Room two-eleven, isn't it?"

"Yes that's correct, thank you."

The Receptionist went into her normal routine, all smiles and charm,

"Have you enjoyed your stay with us, Mr McCall. Was everything to your satisfaction?"

He responded affably,

"Yes, I've been very comfortable thank you, but my business here is more or less concluded now, and I'm due back home, in England, tomorrow. You can rest assured that I shall certainly be using this hotel again in the future."

Charlie, standing only three paces away, saw and heard everything. The man's back was towards him, so he had yet to get a look at his face. He felt a tap on his shoulder, and turned to find that he was looking at one of the two officers from yesterday.

"Your car is waiting outside, Chief Inspector, so if you're ready, sir. It's best not to be late for the COC, he's a stickler for punctuality, so he is."

It all seemed to happen in slow motion. Charlie knew that McCall must have heard what was said. He cursed under his breath, and looked back at him to see if there was any visible reaction. He saw him stiffen, and look over his shoulder. For the briefest moment, their eyes met, and Charlie saw a look of absolute frightened horror pass across McCall's face. Without another word, he turned, and swiftly strode away, leaving the confused Receptionist talking to herself. Charlie watched him as he started to run towards the lifts. He turned to the rather surprised Receptionist, and produced his Warrant Card to identify himself.

"We are interested in the movements of that man. I heard him say that he is checking out tomorrow. If there is any change to that arrangement, you will ring me immediately on this number, please, miss."

He gave her one of his personalised cards. The Receptionist took the card and looked at it curiously.

"This is very important, miss. He's not considered dangerous, so you have nothing to fear. We just need to keep track of his movements. That is all. Will you do that for us, please?"

She nodded and put his card into a prominent position on her desk.

"He's not going anywhere, Officer, unless you say so, that is. We have his passport here, behind the desk."

Charlie gave her a big smile and expressed his thanks for her cooperation, before turning back to the young Officer, who was standing there looking a bit puzzled with it all.

"That was what you would call a piece of unfortunate timing . . . Sorry, I seem to have forgotten your name?"

"DS Ken Brody, sir. I'm sorry if I've just managed to put my big foot into something, here. It was completely unintentional, I assure you. Is there anything more to be done, sir? If it's important, we could go after him if you wish, but I fear we would be late for your appointment with the COC? With all the morning traffic, it's a good thirty minutes across the City, to Knock."

"Your apology is accepted Sergeant. I had just identified him to be one of the two men that I am after. The damage is done now, he knows we are here, and there's nothing to be achieved by chasing after him at the moment. I know what he looks like, and where he is to be found, so I think I'll just let him stew for a while. I just hope that he doesn't choose to go on his toes before I get the opportunity to speak with him. Lead on then, sergeant, if you will."

Connor McCall was well and truly spooked. He ran into his hotel room, slammed the door and went and hid in the bathroom. What he hoped to achieve by doing this was anyone's guess, but for him, it was seen as one more step towards the brink, or another nail in his coffin. After more than a week of extreme anxiety, waiting by the phone for contact from Marty, his mind was getting close to breaking point. He had daily, lain on his bed, allowing his imagination to run riot on the possible consequences of being taken into custody, and being charged with what? Conspiracy to cause explosions? Treason? Conspiracy to murder? The shame of it all, and what it would do to Lizzy and his father, was too much to even contemplate. He had even tried writing a letter of explanation to Lizzy, but the words just wouldn't come. He'd got no further than,

*"My dearest Elizabeth, I am so ashamed and sorry for what I have done . . ."*

But trying to pen the explanations had reduced him to a sobbing wreck. The abandoned letter remained on the writing pad. For the time being, Connor's highly emotional state was preventing it's completion.

He knew that the Police must be after him, but to find out that they had already managed to track him down to his present location, was his worse nightmare. He foolishly imagined that here, in Ireland, the land of his forebears, he might have found some sanctuary? But it obviously wasn't to be? Even they seemed to have forsaken him in this, his hour of need?

Sitting on his loo voiding his bowel, Connor was a bath of nervous sweat, literally shaking with fear and talking to himself incoherently. His deeply troubled mind was frantically considering his remaining options. Unfortunately, they didn't seem to amount to very much, at all . . .

"Take a seat, please, Chief Inspector, I'll be with you in just a minute."

Charlie sat himself down in the easy, office swivel chair, and for the first time, regarded the Crime Operation Commander of the Police Service for Northern Ireland. The first and most obvious surprise was to find that the man was of mixed race. Nobody had seen fit to mention that fact to him. Charlie spent the next minute or so, trying to determine the man's ethnic origins from his facial characteristics, alone. The best he could come up with was something south Pacific? Polynesian, or Maori, perhaps?

He looked resplendent in his dark green uniform, with silver insignia, crisp white shirt, and uniform tie. His cap, Sam Brown belt, and silver tipped swagger stick, sat together, neatly arranged, on a small folding table behind his seat. Charlie decided that he must be in his late thirties, and obviously very fit, judging from what little could be seen of his general build.

His office was very comfortably furnished. Thick, dark green carpet and dark wood panelling, with framed photographs, certificates, and awards, around most of the available wall space. By swivelling his chair round slightly, Charlie was able to see that apart from the door, the entire wall behind him was comprised of glass-fronted bookcases, and in the furthest corner to his left, sat a bulging trophy cabinet containing numerous cups, shields and medals. Apart from the small table, a coat stand, and one other seat, similar to the one Charlie was sitting on, the only other significant item of furniture in the room, was his huge desk.

The top, of highly polished mahogany, inlaid with silver tooled, dark green leather, was immaculate. The colour of the burnished wood seemed to match the man's complexion. That was how Charlie saw it, and he briefly wondered what he would be like as a sexual partner?

Charlie continued to watch as, with a pencil held delicately between his right thumb and index finger, he ran it quickly down a page of some typed report, before doing the same with the next page. He must be speed-reading, he thought. This was something that Charlie, himself, had never managed to master.

With a grunt, David Flanagan, flicked through the last few pages of the file before turning it all back to the first page.

For the first time, he lifted his eyes to look at Charlie. He regarded him only for a few seconds during which time Charlie felt that he was being completely appraised. Without any words of greeting or preamble, he tapped the file with his pencil.

"Chief Inspector, I have here a copy of your working file, together with all of your interim reports and recommendations, with regard to this current operation. It has all been forwarded from Scotland Yard at my request, and makes for some interesting reading.

My initial reaction is that you have been very fortunate up until now, as most of the information you have gleaned, seems not to have come from any good Police work on your part, but from sources related to other enquiries. Specifically, the West Midlands Regional Crime Squad's ongoing investigations into the murders of three prostitutes, and, the as yet undetermined number of people, all believed to be terrorist connected, that died in an explosion in some Welsh quarry. Then there is the information from this man, David Morrison-Lloyd, from whom you have apparently obtained some sort of file of incriminating evidence. Unfortunately, I don't appear to have anything relating to that file, here in front of me. So my first question is, where is that file now. Do you have it with you?"

"No sir. I haven't yet had the opportunity to collect it from Mr Morrison-Lloyd. It was due to be handed over to me on the day before I came to Ireland, that would be Thursday, but other unforeseen circumstances rather prevented me from collecting it from him."

"Would it be possible for you to verify, by making a phone call, that he still has it in his possession, Chief Inspector? Wherever he is located, I can probably arrange for it to be picked up from him by a Police courier. I need to see that file before making any further decisions with regard to this operation."

Charlie fished into his pocket for his phone.

"Bear with me a moment, if you will, sir. I'm sure I can speak to him."

Charlie found that his hands were shaking slightly, and that he was feeling uncomfortably warm. He tried to appear outwardly calm, but somehow knew that he was failing. Scrolling down his list of contacts, he found what he was looking for, and hit the call button. To his relief, it was answered almost immediately. He put the phone on loudspeaker, and placed it on the corner of the desk in front of him.

In answer to David's tentative 'hello,' for he clearly hadn't recognised the caller's ID, Charlie tried to sound cheerful and friendly.

"David, my boy, its Charlie Ferguson, are you free to speak?"

"Hello Charlie. Just let me pull over, I'm hands-free in the car with the children at the moment, but I don't like talking while I'm driving. Hang fire for a minute, I'm just getting off the carriageway . . . There, we're okay now, Charlie, what can I do for you?"

"I'm after that file, David, do you have it with you?"

"Well, not right now, Charlie. It's at Oakwood awaiting your instruction. I'm sorry we missed each other on Thursday, Malcolm said that you'd been called away unexpectedly."

Charlie breathed a little sigh of relief. The potential for having to deliver some embarrassing explanations had been averted. He heard himself saying,

"David, if I can arrange for a Police courier to come to Oakwood, would you be there to hand the file over? That would probably be later this morning, or early this afternoon, at the latest."

Charlie looked at David Flanagan for his approval of the arrangement, and received a nod of assent.

"I see no problem with that, Charlie. We're just on our way back to Oakwood now. Am I to presume that you'll be ringing me back to confirm the arrangement?"

"That I will, David. Many thanks for your help, old son, I'd love to chat a bit more, but I'm in a rather important meeting at the moment."

Charlie broke the connection and looked at the COC, expecting some approbation.

"Where exactly is this Oakwood address? Which force area is it, Chief Inspector?"

"I have the full address and postcode here, sir. Its near Winchester, in Hampshire."

Charlie was consulting his notebook and scribbling down the details onto a piece of paper passed to him for the purpose. David Flanagan managed a little smile for the first time as he passed it back over.

"Hampshire is Alex Marshall's patch."

The COC pulled out his own mobile phone from the top pocket of his tunic. After consulting his own list of contacts, he depressed the call button, and put the phone to his ear. Charlie could hear it ringing.

"Hello David, this is a pleasant surprise, what can I do for you this lovely morning. If it's another race you're after, I'm afraid that I'm far too busy, and besides that, you're too good for me."

The COC chuckled, "Hello Alex, its good to hear your dulcet tones again. Long time no see, old friend, how goes it with you?"

Charlie listened as the two men continued to exchange initial pleasantries before finally coming to the point.

"Alex, I have a little bit of a problem that I think you can probably help me with? There is a file of paperwork located at an address, not too far removed from your Headquarters building, in Winchester. That file needs to be on my desk, here, at Knock Police Headquarters, in Belfast, just as soon as is humanly possible. It would seem to be vital piece of evidence that has come to light, relating to an operation we have ongoing over here, even as we speak. Would you kindly arrange for the file to be collected from the address that I am about to give you, and for it to be taken straight to Southampton Airport, there to be put on the next available flight to Belfast. I will arrange the easy bit, at this end, just as soon as I know which flight it is on. Can you do this for me, please, Alex?"

"I don't see any problem with any of that, David, but I shall expect a little drink from you at the next ACPO get-together. I shall instruct that the file is sealed into one of those one-off document bags, and that it is addressed to you personally. How does that sound?"

"Excellent. Thanks, Alex. Here are the details of the man with the file, and the address where it is located.

He painstakingly passed over the information, spelling everything out phonetically, and then having it all read back to him, to ensure that it was correct. Satisfied, his last request was to have the courier ring him back on his personal mobile number, with the flight details.

He broke the connection and looked at Charlie, his expression, being one of pained sufferance.

"Frankly, none of this would be necessary, Chief Inspector, if you had seen fit to bring the file with you in the first place. I am rather surprised that you have treated such a potentially vital piece of evidence, with so little regard. Tell me, have you actually seen, or examined, any of the content of this file yet?"

"Not yet. Sir, but I am aware of much of the content. I'm told that it's comprised mostly of old newspaper cuttings, with sketch plans, and handwritten details of how, and who, carried out each of three London bombing operations, way back in the nineteen-seventies."

"And all this information has been collated and written by this woman, what was her name? Ah yes, Lara Dobbs, later to become, and also known as, Laura Dobson, and who is now dead. Is my understanding of the circumstance correct, Chief Inspector?"

Charlie was beginning to feel decidedly uncomfortable again. He didn't like the direction the conversation was going. This damned, uniformed super-cop, who at the moment, was talking down to him, as though he was some errant probationary Constable, was now suggesting that in relation to the gathering of evidence, he had ridden roughshod over fundamental police procedures and practice.

Charlie knew that technically, the COC was right, and he was in the wrong. It is a vital piece of evidence, and he should have seized the file at the earliest opportunity, but the true significance of it, at that time, had not been apparent. It was too late now, and he was powerless to do anything about rectifying his error.

The sweating was getting worse, and now he had pins and needles in his hand. He could feel that his headache was returning with a vengeance. He desperately needed to try and retrieve something from the situation.

"I fully appreciate that with her death, it would be difficult to substantiate anything in the file, sir, but may I respectfully point out that there are other, very important considerations that have been identified."

"Such as what, Chief Inspector?"

"Such as the perceived threat that this man, Martyn McCue, might pose to the Royal visit next year, sir. We know very little about his present activities, except that he is a PA on the staff of the Deputy First Minister. And we are all aware of the Ministers previous record with the IRA terrorists."

"That is because no one at Scotland Yard saw fit to consult with our local intelligence sources, Chief Inspector. Martyn McCue is a well-respected person now, almost a leading figure in the Belfast community. I know him personally, in point of fact. When your request for full surveillance measures first appeared on my desk, I was rather surprised, but I went along with it, only because it had been rubber stamped, 'approved for action' by one of your own Operational Commanders. I also authorised yesterday's fiasco at the airport, against my better judgement, I hasten to add. As a direct consequence of that operation going wrong, I now have two of my plain clothes officers on sick leave, having achieved absolutely nothing . . . blah, blah, blah . . ."

And so it went on, but Charlie had heard enough, he was no longer listening. He hated being the brunt of any form of criticism, especially when it came from someone who clearly had little idea of what he was talking about. Charlie knew that during his service, he'd felt more collars than this jumped-up little prig could ever dream of, and yet he had the bloody audacity to sit there lording it over him. Didn't he appreciate that it was due entirely to the incompetence of his own men, that the carefully contrived plan had failed, and McCue had been allowed to get away?

The red mist had reached the top, and was boiling over now. Charlie could feel the pent up anger about to burst out of him. He couldn't allow this unwarranted tirade to continue, without having his say. He might well regret it later, but with his track record, he was confident that his own senior officers would back him to the hilt.

He could contain himself no longer, and stood up with the intention of smashing his fist down onto the desk top in front of this stupid prat, who was still droning on incessantly. Strangely, as much as he tried, he found that his right hand and arm, was refusing to leave his side, and the words of anger and ridicule, that he so desperately wanted to hurl into the face of this idiot, already seemed to be coming out of his mouth in an unintelligible, garbled mess of spit and dribble. His voice was refusing to function properly, but the realisation only became apparent, as, clutching at the corner of the desk with his left hand, his right leg gave way from under, and he sank slowly to the floor.

He was vaguely aware that the COC was kneeling down beside him, supporting his head, and calling out his name. Charlie felt that his head was about to burst. His vision was closing in. The edges of darkness were creeping in on him from all sides. He just needed to close his eyes for a few moments to rally his thoughts . . .

# Chapter 12

From her window, through the net curtains, Mary had watched the Belfast black taxicab draw to a halt outside of Martyn's house, opposite. She saw him alight from the rear, and collect his luggage from the boot, placing it on the footpath. He went to the driver's window, and she watched him say something before shaking hands with the man. She thought it curious that the driver hadn't bothered to help him with his luggage, nor had she seen any money change hands for the fare? She concluded that Mr McCue must know the driver.

The taxi spun around in a tight turn and drove off. Mary waited with a beating heart for Martyn to look over to her window as he always did. Her hand hovered ready to gesture for him to come over. The bottle of sherry, and two polished schooner glasses, stood ready on the silver tray, waiting for him to pour.

Martyn watched the cab disappear out of the Close. His mind was full of the events of the past few hours. He fumbled his keys out of his pocket, and turned to look at the front of his house. Christina had told him that surveillance measures had been put into place, he wondered what form they took.

He started by looking for anything out of place, or different. At first glance, everything seemed normal. He noticed that the grass had been cut, and the border hedges trimmed. Then surprisingly, saw that all his windows looked nice and clean, but apart from that . . .

He remembered Mary, and turned to look over to her window. The curtains were immediately lifted and he saw her pale little hand gesturing for him to come over. He pointed to his cases and held up his hand with five fingers spread. Her single 'thumb up' indicated that she understood.

Martyn let himself in, stepping over the pile of mail on the mat. He kicked it all aside for the minute, and closed his front door. The inside of the house was totally silent, cold and uninviting. His granddaughter clock in the hallway had stopped its friendly tick. He opened the front and pulled up the weights to set it going again. Resetting the time by turning the hands through to the required hour took a few minutes, for he needed to allow the clock to chime the hours in between, but it afforded him more time to think.

His old-fashioned style house phone was on the wrought iron wall bracket, beside the clock. He picked up the receiver and listened to see if there was any discernable change to the familiar dialling tone. Satisfied that there wasn't, he was about to replace it, when another thought occurred to him. He carefully unscrewed the mouth section and exposed the wiring connections inside. In truth, he didn't really know what he was looking for, but he had seen them do it in films. As far as he could tell it looked completely normal, so he put it back together again and replaced the receiver. Looking around for other ideas, he surmised that surveillance measures had probably gotten a lot more sophisticated by now?

He carried his case and holdall upstairs and dumped them on his double bed. Opening the wheelie case first, he located the flat, cake tin inside. To his dismay, the cellophane seal had been removed and it was apparent the tin had been opened, probably by Customs, he thought. A quick examination of the contents revealed the blueberry pie inside, to be still intact. He carefully replaced the lid, and remembered that he had forgotten to pick up a carton of double cream on his way home. Damn and blast, his little surprise for Mary was spoiled now. Mary . . . Oh my God. He glanced at his watch. Ten minutes had elapsed since he'd arrived home. She would be waiting for him. Leaving the pie on the bed, he bounded down the stairs two at a time.

Two hours later, with a schooner of sherry, and three cups of delicious, Jade Ginseng Oolong Chinese green tea, inside of him, Martyn felt that he was now cognizant of every single occurrence that had taken place in the Close, since he'd left for America. Following his initial greeting and the inevitable small talk regarding his trip abroad, Mary confessed to having missed his company. Then, feeling slightly embarrassed at being so forward, she had quickly changed the subject completely, and presented him with two foolscap sheets of paper, detailing exact dates, times, and descriptions of people who were strangers, that she had seen in the Close. There were notes as to what they appeared to be doing, and even details of their vehicles. It was all beautifully hand-written in her lovely, neat, copperplate script writing, and Martyn likened it to a work of art, worthy of being framed, he thought.

Her attention to detail had been really quite staggering. More so, when she had insisted on going over every single entry verbally, and in even greater detail than what was written? He allowed her to carry on, uninterrupted, to the end.

"Mary, I don't know what to say, my dear. A simple 'thank you' barely seems adequate. I am pleased to say that everything at home appears to be in good order, but had it not been so, I'm sure that all your detailed notes and observations would have helped considerably. I really am very grateful for everything you've done for me, and most appreciative for this lovely welcoming home. Perhaps I should consider going away more often?"

He saw that she was responding with pleasure, and basking in his words of praise. He decided to make a little token gesture and arose from his seat to walk over and stand in front of her. With one foot slightly forward of the other, he performed a theatrical, deep flourishing bow, before gently taking her hand in his, to kiss the back.

"My sincere thanks for everything, dear heart, and long may it continue . . ."

The words he had chosen to accompany his bow were meant to be light-hearted, but had he known that such physical contact on her hand, was sufficient to set her little heart all a-flutter, he might perhaps have thought twice, before doing it?

In Mary's estimation, their personal relationship had just taken another significant leap forward.

David pulled his Mercedes into the car park area at Oakwood. The presence of the new hybrid Lexus indicated that Tony Williams had arrived. He spent a couple of minutes walking all round, and admiring the car, while the children, Charlotte and Michelle, together with the twins, were still in his own car. They were still talking excitedly amongst themselves about St Swithun's School. All the way home, David had listened to Malcolm's girls extol, and enthuse, on their own years spent at this particular school, prior to moving on the Canford School.

The twins, on being told that they would be moving into Oakwood to live, had been jumping for joy at the prospect. However, when it was pointed out that they would need to change school, it had rather taken some of the shine off their enthusiasm.

Malcolm had separately let it be known to the girls, that he had invited David and his family to come and live at Oakwood. He was both relieved and pleased with their enthusiastic approval of this arrangement.

He had very briefly started to give them his reasons for doing this, but on reflection, decided to hold a full family gathering, a little later on, the better to outline and explain all of his plans.

For his part, David had a quiet word with Charlotte and Michelle. He was seeking for them to reassure the twins on their change of school. Both girls had responded admirably, for they had truly spent many a happy year at St Swithun's, and indeed, would have wished to continue their education there, but for the wishes of their mother, who had been a pupil at Canford.

David and the twins were really impressed to see the girl's old Headmistress embrace them both, and with a genuine interest, ask after their progress at Canford. To David, it reflected a caring environment if the teachers were able to react in this way to their former pupils.

Peter, however, was soon disappointed to learn that he would not be eligible to attend this school, as he had already reached the boys upper age limit of seven years. David could see that the prospect of being separated from his sister, for the first time, was being received with mixed feelings, at the moment. He knew that there was some remedial work to do here, but for the time being, he wanted to allow a little time for the idea to sink in.

Rita though, with encouragement from Malcolm's girls, was full of enthusiastic anticipation at the prospect of being a pupil at a boarding school. David thought that she would fit in really well, and without the necessity of having to compete constantly with her brother, be better able to concentrate on her studies?

He felt the need to talk this through with Sue, before coming to any firm decisions, but had now identified that it had become a matter of priority to find a suitable school placement for Peter. He surmised that they needed to find somewhere that he would be happy, and open to equal opportunity to that of his sister.

David smiled to himself as he watched the children all exit his car and scamper off to get changed, the game plan being to get the horses saddled-up and ready for an afternoon ride. The subject of schooling was instantly forgotten. The horse riding was obviously a far more important consideration.

He thought how nice it was to see how well the four of them had all bonded together in only a week. Malcolm's girls, according to their father, were absolutely over the moon with the prospect of having Peter and Rita coming to live with them, and even Carter had commented on how much happier they had both been, which was also very gratifying. At the moment, everything was looking very rosy, but David could see that there were a few obvious problems looming up ahead.

He locked the car and decided to head for the kitchens to beg a cup of coffee out of Mrs Carter, and to advise Carter of the expected arrival of a Police courier to collect the file.

Reverting back to his train of thought, he wondered how long it would be before the age differences in the children, led to inevitable friction. Michelle and Charlotte, physically, were already young ladies, that was very apparent. Little stunners too, he thought. As is the natural way of things, he expected that it would very soon be boyfriends, parties, clothes, hair and makeup, that would be replacing the horses, as their main leisure activity. He wondered whether the girls would still see Peter and Rita in the same light?

Rita, he had noticed, was just beginning to acquire some slightly broadening curves to her boyish figure, and she was conscious of the fact that her breasts were already budding. Apparently, she'd been proudly showing them off to her mother, and her brother, as well?? This, of course, had led to Sue voicing her concerns. It had happened only a week or two ago, and David had initially found it to be rather amusing, but had recognised there was an obvious problem, and had been pondering on how best to deal with it?

He and Sue had immediately agreed that it would soon become necessary to stop the pair of them sleeping in each other's beds, as was frequently the case, at present. There was no real harm in it now, of course, it was all quite innocent, and still very natural for them to want to cuddle up together. They had been doing so since birth, after all . . .

He thought that Michelle and Charlotte might perhaps have noticed something, and inevitably pointed out the more sexual connotations of their close relationship? But so far, it obviously hadn't happened.

The fact that Peter might now have to attend a local state school, and travel daily, while his sister would be a boarder, and only come home at weekends, would seem to offer a partial solution to a delicate situation? The next logical step, would be to allocate them separate bedrooms, and there were plenty going spare at Oakwood. The thought cheered him up no end, for David liked a simple life. He strolled into the kitchen area.

"Hello, Mrs Carter, can I be a nuisance in your domain, and make myself some coffee, please?"

She had her hands in the pastry bowl, and jumped slightly at his sudden intrusion.

"Oh, Mr David, you startled me, sir. Please, go right ahead, you will find everything you need in the stillroom just behind you. Would you like me to do it for you, sir?

"No, that's all right Mrs Carter. I only want a cup of instant, and I think that I can just about remember how to do that."

He walked around behind her to fill the electric kettle, and noticed that the security monitor was not displaying any images. David knew that it was usual for her to be keeping an eye on Emily while she worked. He tried a bit of telepathy to see if he could locate her, but to no avail.

"I presume everyone is in the study with Mr Williams, Mrs Carter, but I don't seem to be able to communicate with Emily. Do you have any idea where she might be?"

"Emily and Sam have gone for a walk with Mr Cox and Nurse Strong, Mr David. Carter tells me they are out in the back paddock playing a game of padder tennis, and throwing a ball for Sam. It's refreshing to see her out in the fresh air, getting a bit of exercise and enjoying herself, instead of having her little nose stuck in some musty old book all the time."

"I rather tend to agree with you Mrs Carter. Sue and I have noticed that she's rather taken to being in the company of Mr Cox, over the past couple of days. I hope she doesn't wear him out too much. His health has significantly improved, but young children can still be very tiresome at times."

"I shouldn't worry too much on that score, Mr David. Carter says that Mr Cox is out there running around like a spring lamb. We wonder where he is getting all his energy from, because we wouldn't mind having some of it ourselves?"

David finished making his coffee and came to stand in front of her, watching as she expertly rubbed in the ingredients in the preparation some sort of pie crust pastry.

"I suppose that Malcolm has mentioned to you, that we are all coming to live here at Oakwood, has he Mrs Carter? Sue, me, and the children, that is . . ."

The smile that accompanied her reply was evidence of her obvious delight at the news.

"He hasn't told us officially yet, but it comes as no surprise, Mr David. Emily said nearly as much to Carter, a couple of days ago, when they were in the library together. Can I say that we are both delighted at the prospect of having you all. Oakwood is a house that seems to come alive only when the children are here. We both hate it when they're all away at school, and we're left here on our own with only the animals."

David smiled to himself and mused quietly to himself, "A couple of days ago? But that's not possible? Sue and me, we only decided ourselves just yester . . . day? Oh, I see . . . Cunning little minx, she's been up to her little tricks again. I wonder what she's up to with Jim, now? Whatever? It seems to be doing them both a power of good at the moment . . ."

He finished his coffee, and while rinsing his cup, remembered that he needed to speak with Carter regarding the courier. The thought reminded him that Charlie should have rung him back by now, but he did mention that he was in some sort of important meeting? Probably delayed?

"Mrs Carter, if you see him before I do, would you kindly advise Carter that there will be a Police courier calling here very soon to collect some paperwork from me. Just in case I'm not to be found in the Study, I'll keep my phone switched on so that he can call me, if necessary. I'm to be found in the study, where I thought I'd like to go and sit in on the last of Mr Williams reading of the Will."

"Certainly, Mr David. They've been at it for well over half an hour, so they must be getting down to the nitty-gritty's by now? I do hope that it is all going well for Miss Sharon. Carter tells me that the poor love has been stewing on it for a few days."

"Thanks, Mrs Carter. I'm sure it will all work out just fine, for her. Sharon has got to cope with this, and the up-coming funeral of her mother, as well. The only thing that we can do, is to give her all the support that we can offer. She is a strong and resilient character, as we all know, but there is also a much softer, and gentler side to her nature, that is obviously more vulnerable. It's a pity that Malcolm can't be around this week, he has rather become her rock, so to speak. I think it might be good idea, if Sue and I can arrange to take her mind off things, perhaps by getting her involved with doing something else? I must remember to talk to Sue about it . . ."

David carried the thought in his mind as he started to make his way from the kitchens through to the Study. There was certainly a lot of work that needed to be done down in Weymouth. It would take quite some time to pack up Laura's collection of *objets d'art,* and bring them all back to Oakwood. Then there was the house, and all her other things to sort out. Doris's jewellery box still needed to be collected from the Police Station, and hadn't Malcolm mentioned that both Tiptree Farm, and Bleanaway Quarry, needed to be made secure again? Perhaps a trip to each location might afford Sharon the opportunity to lay a few ghosts to rest? It would also facilitate a better appraisal with regard to any practical arrangements that needed to be put into place, for the future security of each property.

Yes, it made good sense to be doing all of these things before the Hospital project really got going. He and Sue had planned to go together, and pack up all their clothes and personal belongings back in New Milton, this week, but it might be better to let her go with Sharon, instead?

No, on second thoughts, it was better that he be the one go to the Farm and Quarry. It was going to need a practical mind, and the application of a skilled pair of hands, if the buildings needed to be made secure with whatever materials were available on site. The girls couldn't be expected to do that. He smiled at the fond memory of Sue, bless her heart, attempting to hammer in a three-inch nail.

'Who's the bloke crying in the corner? Why, he's the carpenter, darling . . .'

Notwithstanding all the work that needed doing, the children's schooling arrangements must be regarded as the most urgent, and pressing problem. That needed to be sorted before anything else.

He arrived at the door of the study, and paused for a few seconds, listening to what was taking place inside. He was just about to enter when he remembered the file. It was upstairs in his bedroom, best fetch it now, he thought, and tiptoed away from the door. David bounded up the stairs, two at a time, and burst into his room. Taking one of two large brown envelopes from the top drawer of his bedside cabinet, he carried it over to his bed. Inside of the substantial, A3 sized, reinforced envelope, was the file. He very carefully tipped the it all out onto the bed to verify the contents.

Everything inside the file, was by now, well known to him. He and George had spent many a long hour, repeatedly going over it all. David knew that there was only one single sheet of paper that made any direct reference to the involvement of Connor McCall. But to remove it was virtually impossible, for his name was written in the centre of a handwritten line of text, on the second of a three-page handwritten plan of action. The plan related to the bombing of the Swiss Cottage Tavern, and then the North Star Public House.

All other references to Connor in the folder, were made just using his initials. On that basis, 'CM' might refer to anyone with similar initials.

David turned up the relevant page, and stared at it thoughtfully. On impulse he undid the treasury tag and removed the whole handwritten document from the folder. He took it over to the dressing table, where Sue had all her makeup, and laid it open on the glass top, at the second page. Carefully identifying the exact spot on the page where Connor's name appeared, he reached for Sue's nail varnish remover and opened it.

One dab, and the acetone would mix with the ink and probably render that part of the text virtually illegible. His hand, with the brush loaded, hovered over Connor's name for several seconds, but his conscience wouldn't allow him to carry out the final act.

He and George had long debated the involvement of Connor, recognising the folly of youth. They looked to see if it was possible that he might have been acting in all innocence? Their final conclusion was that this was highly improbable. There must have been a degree of guilty knowledge, *mens rea,* George had called it, given the gang's frequent prior visits to all the establishments that eventually were targeted for bombing.

Neither David, nor George, knew Connor personally. It was only George's concern for what all this was doing to his good old friend and colleague, Tony Williams that even prompted any sort of discussion on the matter. They had both realised that they had it within their power to remove the document from the file, and by so doing, completely remove all evidence of Connor McCall's involvement with the terrorists. This would effectively mean that a guilty man would go unpunished for his crime, albeit one that was committed thirty-six years ago, when he was just a rather stupid, impressionable youth. Was it morally justified to help him, for the sake of Tony Williams, now? That was the crux of the matter, and the dilemma they both faced.

His decision made, David replaced the file in the envelope and sealed it down.

With an envelope tucked under his arm, he thoughtfully made his way back down to the study. He was still pondered as to whether he'd got it right when he got to the door?

He paused, listening. It would seem that he had arrived at just the opportune moment. Tony Williams appeared to be getting close to summing up, he thought.

"Of the three properties in the Northern Ireland Province, two are leased to immediate family members of the deceased.

Numbers thirty-one and thirty-three Cuthbert Street, is in the Gobnascale area of Londonderry. The property is comprised of two, two-bedroomed terraced houses that have been knocked through into one. They are currently under occupation by two ladies . . ."

David opened the study door and quietly made his entry. He mouthed an apology to Tony, who paused while David occupied a vacant chair next to Sue. He then continued to read from his notes.

"Currently under occupation by two ladies, Mrs Ann O'Hare, and Mrs Sandra McBride. I believe these two ladies are the mother, and younger sister of the deceased. It is specified that their occupation of the property, be allowed to continue, until such times as they either voluntarily choose to vacate, or they reach the end of their natural life. The ownership of both properties are to be transferred to Miss Sharon Cox, with the added proviso that she be responsible for the land and outbuildings at the rear, which extends over . . . blah, blah."

David was already finding it somewhat boring, and his mind drifted back to his own immediate problems. He pushed aside any more thoughts to do with the file on his lap, and concentrated on what they were all planning to do in the coming week.

In an effort to help bring about Emily's expressed wish, that Sharon become her life companion, he and Sue had planned to ask Sharon if she would kindly baby-sit Emily, while they packed up their old home in readiness for the move to Oakwood. It would seem to present an ideal opportunity for them both to become better acquainted? It was good that Emily had rather taken to the company of Jim Cox, perhaps it might help Sharon to accept Emily, if she could see that her father was . . . The thought suddenly struck him. Emily and Jim? Of course, that was what she was up to . . .

"I'll bet that little madam has had it all planned for a long time?"

He realised he was talking out loud to himself. Tony Williams paused again at the sound of his voice, and David felt slightly embarrassed.

"My apologies, sir, I didn't mean to interrupt. I just remembered something important . . . Please carry on."

Sue reached out and took his hand in hers. Telepathically, she asked if everything was okay? He replied in the same manner, advising that they needed to talk some more about Emily's little mind games.

Meanwhile, Tony Williams was picking up the threads of his notes again.

"Where was I? Ah yes, the property, number six, Derrymore Road, Craigavon. This is a substantial four-bedroomed, semi-detached house, in a very picturesque location, overlooking Lough Neagh. It is currently occupied by a Mr and Mrs Michael Dobbs, and their two children. I have established that Michael Dobbs is the deceased's nephew, and is therefore a second cousin to Miss Sharon Cox. The exact details of the relationship are here, but, for the moment, I propose to move on.

There is a small additional income derived from this property, which amounts to approximately £500 per annum. Mr and Mrs Dobbs occupation is subject to a similar lease, and rent arrangement, to the previously mentioned property, in Gobnascale. However, Mrs Dobbs has been permitted to operate two rooms of the house as a bed-and-breakfast facility. Profits from the venture were shared with the deceased. I understand it to be a very loose, family, arrangement, based largely upon trust, with no written agreement.

Ownership of this property is also to be passed to Miss Sharon Cox, with similar provisos as outlined for the previous property. I don't see that there is any necessity for me to go over all of those again. So, once again, I propose to move on.

43, Marlborough Avenue, Weymouth, was the home address of the deceased. Ownership of this property, together with the entire contents, that is to say all the furniture and fittings, together with all personal goods and chattels, is to be passed to Miss Sharon Cox. There was the small matter of a second mortgage. My client left instruction that, in the event of her death, the outstanding amount be settled from monies currently held in savings. This instruction has now been fulfilled, but I am awaiting the final paperwork and return of the deeds, necessary to bring the matter to a final conclusion. I will come back to that in more detail, in a minute.

There are two other properties, namely, Bleanaway Quarry, near Brecon, in South Wales, and Tiptree Farm in Gloucestershire. I am instructed that ownership of both is to be passed to Miss Sharon Cox.

The deceased was also the Managing Director and Company Secretary, of the company, Close Roadstone & Tarmacadam Ltd. The day-to-day business operations were controlled and operated by the two other Directors, Michael and Dermot Close.

Records from Companies House reflect the head office to be the premises at Bleanaway Quarry, and the deceased has always submitted all annual accounts from that address. There are currently two other depots, belonging to the Company, that are still operating. One is based near Swansea, and the other, near Bristol. I have spoken with the respective Managers of each, advising that the Close Brothers, Dermot and Michael, were believed to have perished in an accidental explosion at Bleanaway Quarry. Enquiries are still in hand to establish the precise ownership of the business, as there doesn't appear to be any last Will and Testament in respect of those two gentleman. It would appear at this stage, that the brothers were orphans, with no known living relatives. If it can be established that they have indeed died intestate, then best title will eventually come back down to you, Miss Cox. But such matters usually take some time to sort out.

Both depot managers are now awaiting further instruction pending the results of my enquiries. They are happy to continue trading, as each depot is structured to operate completely independent from Head Office. It would seem that the Close brothers, having appointed reliable and competent managers, were more than happy to just let them get on with it, with as little interference as possible? Off the record, I have concluded that this is a very sound and lucrative little business, Miss Cox. From a letter that I received only yesterday, the offer of a management buy-out has already been intimated. This option would seem to be a very distinct possibility? Should you so wish, we can, perhaps, discuss this later, in a little more detail, Miss Cox?"

Sharon merely nodded her understanding, thereby prompting Tony Williams to continue.

"Tiptree Farm is another very successful, and potentially lucrative pig rearing business. The deceased solely owned the property, and the business. But unfortunately, there seems to have been a considerable lack of adequate supervision. Just recently, there is clear evidence of some rather creative book keeping, that has allowed the man responsible for the day-to-day running of the business, one Shaun Riley, to embezzle a considerable amount of money. I understand that the Police found in excess of fifty thousand pounds in a floor safe at the property, and that this money has already been passed on to you, Miss Cox?"

Tony paused to allow Sharon to confirm that this had happened, and she quietly nodded her agreement. This prompted Malcolm into pointing out that some of the money had already been used to pay outstanding bills for animal feed. Tony paused to make several small pencil notations in the margins of his prepared notes.

"Very well, but I am also advised that there is an outstanding VAT demand in the sum of . . ." He consulted another page in his file. "Ah yes, here it is. £12,366.48p For my part, and in order to avoid late payment charges, I have advised HMCR, that the owner of property and business, has died. This has bought us some more time, but as the business is now yours, Miss Cox, and it is remains a problem that needs addressing as a matter of urgency."

Both of the businesses are generating considerable profits from which the deceased received a percentage share at the end of each financial year. The actual amounts seem to have varied according to any planned improvements or expansions, but as an example, last year, the deceased received seventy three thousand pounds from Close Roadstone, and a further thirty one thousand, from Tiptree Farm. Both figures are gross, and before tax. I have the other figures here for previous years, as well, but there is little to be gained by going over them all at this stage.

There are now only two matters remaining. The deceased's portfolio of stock and share investments, and monies that were held in her bank accounts.

Mr Lloyd has kindly agreed to help me with the handling of the share portfolio. There is a considerable amount of work involved in transferring ownership of the shares over to Miss Cox.

However, based on the share price index published last weekend, I calculated the total share values to amount to nine hundred and seventy-six thousand pounds. That figure, of course, was a simply and quick calculation, arrived at by multiplying the number of shares by their stated value. It takes no account of any brokerage charges, or any other fees, that may be incurred in the transfers of ownership.

Finally, there is the matter of monies that were held in the bank accounts. I have consolidated these down as far as possible to my own Client account. Subject to agreement on the figures, I am in a position to be able to transfer some of the money, into your nominated bank account, as soon as is convenient, Miss Cox.

Your mother was a very tidy and orderly person, who found it expedient to conduct all her business affairs from four different bank accounts. Two with the Bank of Ireland, a savings account, and a current account, and two more, with differing banks, needed to administer each of her two other businesses.

I have prepared a detailed breakdown outlining the sources from where each amount of money came, but I need to point out that there is considerably more money, which will need to remain in the business accounts. In my calculations, I have detailed these figures, the ones relating to the business accounts, on separate sheets for you. I need to point out that these are fluid accounts that are subject to change on a daily basis. They can only be closed, and a final figure arrived at, as and when, you decide on the final disposition of the businesses to which they relate.

I have not had the opportunity to carry out any up-to-date valuation of the businesses. At this stage, I do not consider it to be necessarily within my terms of reference. I have based all my figures from copies of the last annual accounts submitted to HMRC.

Basically, I have used my power of attorney to close the deceased's two personal bank accounts held with the Bank of Ireland. Anything that I identified as 'spare cash,' for want of a better term, I have gathered together, and transferred into my Client account. Would you like me to briefly go over the figures, or would you prefer to look them over privately, Miss Cox?"

"These people are all my friends, Mr Williams, I have no secrets from any of them. Please carry on, there is no necessity to enter into detail, or to be too specific. George and I will want to go over it all again later."

"Very well, Miss Cox, thank you. Moving swiftly on then, the sum of money that I am in a position to transfer over to you, after a rough calculation to cover death duties, probate, legal fees, and other related deductions, amounts to one point eight-seven-five, million pounds. He handed her several sheets of paper with the number highlighted in red at the bottom of a long column of figures, that detailed his calculations. £1,875,000

Sharon sat there dumbfounded, just staring. She was trying to picture in her mind just what that amount of cash would look like, if it were stacked in piles of banknotes, on a table? The image wouldn't come. She felt Malcolm gently squeeze her bad hand to attract her attention. She looked up into his eyes and saw that he was trying to offer her a smile of reassurance. She shook her head at him almost imperceptibly, and looked back to Tony Williams as he started to speak again.

"I have rather erred on the side of caution in coming to that total, Miss Cox. When everything is finally settled, I anticipate that the final calculations will probably take the bottom line figure to well in excess of two million pounds. Can I ask if you have any questions at this stage, please, Miss Cox?"

Sharon bit her lip, there were hundreds, but this was probably not the most appropriate time to be asking him for more details of her new found grandmother, aunt and cousin? For her, the biggest thing to be announced so far. Sharon had already decided that she was going to have to visit Ireland to meet with them. They were her family, there was no other way. She found herself asking,

"Do you have a copy of your notes that I can perhaps refer to later, Mr Williams? There is rather a lot for me to digest and to think about, and I really feel the need to discuss everything with Malcolm and Mr Lloyd, in order to get my head around it all."

"Yes of course, Miss Cox. Please be aware that the provisions I have outlined, here, this morning, are to be regarded as just the very basic outline of your mother's Will. There is still much work to be done, but you can rest assured that George and I will be working together over the next few weeks, with your best interests paramount in all of our considerations. Please feel free to ask me about anything you not sure about."

The study door opened to interrupt the proceedings. Carter waited for everyone to look his way.

"My apologies for the intrusion, sir, but there is a Police Officer, a motorcycle courier, who wishes too speak with Mr David."

David stood up and waved the brown envelope in explanation to Malcolm and Sue's questioning looks.

"Thank you, Carter. He's come to collect this, I believe. Charlie Ferguson rang me about it, earlier."

Had he looked back as he left the study, he might have seen the stricken look on the face of Tony Williams who immediately guessed what was in the brown envelope, but was powerless to do anything about it. George wasn't, however, and he quickly excused himself from the gathering to hurry after his son-in-law. He caught up with him in the hall, where the uniformed Police officer stood waiting expectantly. George caught hold of David's arm to arrest his progress.

"David, can I have a quick word, in private, please."

David allowed himself to be steered into the library, George shutting the door behind, as they entered.

"Sorry, my boy, but am I to assume that you are about to hand the file over to the Police?"

"George, we've been over all of this. I thought that we'd both agreed that there was no reason why we shouldn't? Have you now changed your mind, or something?"

"David, please. I know that I really have no right to ask this of you, but only this morning, Tony asked me if he could see the file, in order to gauge the extent of his son's complicity. We both know the evidence is conclusive, but I genuinely fear for what it would do to Tony, to see his only living relative dragged through the Courts, for some stupid mistake he made thirty-odd years ago. Tony is a good man, David, he really doesn't deserve to be humiliated by . . ."

David interrupted, "It was a mistake that ruined the lives of God knows how many people, George. Don't ever forget that, will you?

Tony Williams's feelings are not to be the primary consideration here, are they? It is whether or not it is right for Connor McCall to be brought to justice for what he did? And who are we to be making that decision? Charlie Ferguson says the file needs to be in Belfast ASAP, so we don't have time to debate this anymore. Trust me, I think that I'm doing the right thing here, George. It may not be what you, or I, would like, but it is what my own conscience tells me is correct."

Without giving him the chance to say anything more, David opened the door and walked over to where the Police Officer was standing.

"Sorry for the short delay Officer, we just needed to check that it was all there. This is the file of paperwork that you've come to collect."

George came to stand beside him, and they watched as the envelope was placed inside a one-off sealed document case. The name of some Police Commander was printed on a label that was inside the case, and visible to the outside, only through the clear polythene window. David finally had to sign his name over the seal to complete the package. Hopefully, the next person to open it would be the recipient?

Together, they watched the officer's bike roar off down the drive, with the file securely locked in the pannier of his motorcycle. David put his arm around the shoulders of his rather forlorn looking father-in-law, and started to lead him back inside.

"I'm sorry, George, I had to do that. When I was upstairs getting the file, I thought exactly the same as you. Tony Williams doesn't deserve to be humiliated and treated this way. But to avoid it happening, posed a moral dilemma for us both, one that we would have to live with for the rest of our life. In consequence, I have rather taken the cowards way out, and sidestepped the issue completely. The decision as to whether Connor should be punished for his crimes rests with someone else, not us."

He reached into his back pocket and produced a small brown envelope.

"Why don't you give this to Tony Williams, but only after you have pointed out the seriousness of his son's crimes. He's his father, after all, George. And if Tony is as good a man as you think, he will want to do the right thing. So let him decide on the correct course of action. Let the decision be on his conscience, not yours or mine. What do you think?"

George took the envelope from him and saw that it was sealed down. He waved it as he spoke.

"Is this what I think it is, David?"

"Yes, George. It must have somehow fallen out of the folder, unnoticed, before I handed it over. Alright?"

"Yes, my boy, I understand completely. Thank you, thank you, from the bottom of my heart . . ."

In an uncharacteristic gesture of gratitude and affection, George turned to embrace his son-in-law.

Connor knew that he desperately needed to pull himself together and start thinking logically. He pulled out his cell phone, switched it on, and sat down on the edge of his bed, staring at it, as over twenty missed calls pinged up. He was seriously contemplating ringing his father and asking him for some help, but that would entail telling him all the reasons why. The same thing applied to Lizzy, she too would want to know everything, for sure. He remembered that Lizzy had some family, a brother, Brian, who lived somewhere in Belfast. Apart from Liz sending him unacknowledged Christmas and birthday cards, there had been no direct contact between any of them, since he and Lizzy's gypsy style wedding, thirty-odd years ago. He recalled that at the time, Brian Thompson, himself a good Catholic, had voiced his disapproval of the heathen ceremony that the couple had chosen to enact, in order to cement their relationship, but that was another story from a long time ago. Connor hoped that he might perhaps have forgotten, or even forgiven, their little falling-out, by now?

Thinking about Brian, Connor doubted that he would even be able to recognise the man, after all this time, but at the moment, he was the only person he could think of, that might be able to help? Connor riffled through the pages of his file-o-fax, looking for an address or phone number for him. He finally found an address.

76, Beechmount Avenue, in the Ballymagarry suburb of the city, but he had no phone number.

Connor thought about his next move. After all this time, it would be a bit much just to turn up on his brother-in-law's doorstep, unannounced. No, probably better to try and get a phone number, and ring him first? He'd noticed that there were telephone directories down in Reception, but that would mean having to explain his hurried, and rather rude departure, when the Receptionist had been talking to him earlier? And then there was that policeman to consider, as well, where was he? He thought he'd heard the other man say that there was a car waiting outside, so in all probability, he'd gone off somewhere? Perhaps they weren't after him after all? They hadn't made any attempt to apprehend him, so, was it purely a coincidence that they were there? Was that too much to hope for?

Connor headed back into his bathroom to throw some cold water over his face, trying to focus his thoughts into more logical, and calculated, thinking. His deeply troubled mind was full of pessimism, but he knew that if he was going to do anything, it needed to be done now, rather than later. He scribbled down Brian's address on a piece of hotel stationary, and thrust it into his jacket pocket. Slowly opening the door of his room, he peeped outside. The corridor was empty and quiet, so he exited his room and tiptoed his way along to the stairway, shunning any use of the lift.

He waited by the stairway door for the hotel Reception area to start emptying of people, before plucking up the courage to approach the desk again. The same Receptionist eyed him curiously as he came to stand in front of her again. Connor felt that he owed her an explanation for his previous bizarre behaviour.

"I'm sorry that I had to leave so suddenly, just now, miss. I was taken short, and only just made it to the loo. I must have picked up some sort of tummy bug, or a virus infection, or something. Can you perhaps direct me to a local chemist shop, please?"

For a spur-of-the-moment effort, Connor felt quite pleased with himself. It sounded really quite genuine.

"I'm sorry to hear about that, Mr McCall. There is a small selection of pharmaceuticals to be found in the Tesco Express Store just across the road from here."

She waved her arm in the general direction that he should take. He nodded his understanding and produced the piece of paper from his pocket.

"Thank you, my dear. I'll just pop over and see if I can find myself something suitable. In the meantime, do you think that you could look in your local telephone directory, for me, please? See if there is a listed number for this person. I'll be a few minutes over the road, so I'll ask you again, when I come back. Is that alright?"

She looked at the writing on the paper, recognising the local address.

"Certainly, Mr McCall that will be no problem, sir."

Connor made his way out of the hotel exit into the fresh air. After the relative disasters of the morning, which seemed to have come to nothing, so far, and with the ghost of a plan, he was beginning to feel slightly better in himself. Just being outdoors in the fresh air, was enough to induce a feeling of freedom, a kind of release, from the mental constraints of his immediate troubles. He took a few deep breaths, and with nowhere better to go, headed over towards the Tesco Store, thinking to buy himself another bottle of brandy, and some lemonade.

He was completely unaware of the fact that two different people were watching him from a discreet distance. Both watchers were themselves unaware of the presence of the other. Neither were Police, and their particular interest in Connor, was for completely differing reasons . . .


The preliminary reading of the Will now over, everyone went to freshen up, then to reconvene in the dining room, for a rather late, buffet lunch. It was inevitable that whilst eating, the group would separate themselves out into little cliques to quietly discuss the implications of the Will, and to speculate on what Sharon should be considering with regard to her newfound wealth.

Tony Williams and George Lloyd took themselves over to a quiet corner for a more professional discourse on how they could best help each other in the coming weeks, and to exchange written details on what had already been proposed. It was during this period that Tony's mobile phone gave a shrill ring to announce an incoming call. He took it from his waistcoat pocket and looked at the caller ID. George saw a look of irritation at the interruption, and then one of surprise and anticipation cross the face of his old friend, as he realised who was calling.

"You'll have to excuse me for a few minutes, please, George. I really must accept this call . . ."

Tony got up from his chair and walked towards the dining room door, apparently seeking a little more privacy. George watched him exit the room. He had been looking for an opportune moment to steer the conversation around to the envelope that David had given him. His intention was to deliver it into Tony's hands, together with a personal observation on the need to be doing the right thing, delivered from the moral high ground, perhaps?

"Hello, this is Tony Williams, do you have some news for me?"

"Good afternoon Mr Williams, this is Caroline at Southern Central, yes, I do have some good news for you. Are you free to speak?"

"Yes, yes, please tell me that you've managed to locate Mr McCall, for me."

"I have one of our private investigators on the other line even as we speak, Mr Williams. He is at a location in Belfast, Northern Ireland, and is currently watching a man we believe to be Connor McCall. The purpose of this call is to find out from you, if there are any further instructions, now that he has been located?"

"What's he doing at the moment?"

"Just a moment Mr Williams, I will need to speak on the other line."

Tony could vaguely make out that there was some sort of question and answer type of conversation taking place. He heard the receiver being picked up again.

"Mr Williams, Mr McCall is alone. He has just come out of a hotel, and has walked across a couple of roads to enter a local supermarket. Our investigator, at this moment, is following him from a discreet distance pending your further instruction."

"Are you absolutely certain that it's Connor?"

"Investigator Grogan has copies of the photographs you supplied, and has verified that Mr McCall has booked into the hotel using his own name. I think we can be as certain as it is possible to be, Mr Williams. What do you want us to do now?"

Tony had to think on his feet. He needed to get over there just as quickly as was humanly possible. In the meantime . . .

"For the time being, I want you to continue to keep tabs on his movements, for me, please. I am going to try and arrange an immediate flight to Belfast. If I can do this, I will come back to you with the details, so that we can work something out at that end. Is that alright?"

"I can see no problem with that, Mr Williams. Keep a watching brief until we hear from you again. It will be as you instruct, sir."

"Thank you."

Tony broke the connection, his mind in a whirl. It came as no real surprise to find out that Connor was in Belfast. Liz's suspicions had been correct. His friend Marty lived there. He'd studied at Queens

University, and much of his family research had been carried out using the Belfast Library archive records, so he must be very familiar with the City?

For probably the twentieth time since he had disappeared, he tried ringing Connors mobile number again, but his phone was still switched off.

He wondered if he should ring Lizzy and put her in the picture? She would have to be told eventually, of course, but if he left it to the last minute, it would lessen the chances of her being able to tag along. Tony wanted to speak to Connor, alone. Deep in thought, he made his way back to where George was waiting patiently for him.

"Is everything all right, old son, you look as though you lost half a crown and found a tanner?"

"They've located Connor, George. He's in Belfast."

"Connor? Why, is he missing, then?"

"He went missing over a week ago, George. He didn't say anything to Lizzy, or me, just packed a few things and took off, somewhere. We've been worried sick about him, thinking that he might be contemplating doing something really stupid."

"I'm guessing that you've told him about the file then, Tony? Despite your solemn promise to me . . . ."

"I'm sorry George. Connor is my son, my only living relative, I had to warn him."

"What, warn him that the Police were coming for him, and that he's about to be arrested and charged with conspiracy to murder? What on earth were you thinking of, Tony? What did you imagine that he would do, for God's sake? You've probably pushed him over the edge? Belfast is where that senior detective, Ferguson, from Scotland Yard, was headed for only yesterday. It's too much of a coincidence, don't you think? He's probably after Connor."

"George, I need to get to Connor first. Perhaps I can talk him round before he does anything stupid? I need to book a flight from the nearest airport, which I'm thinking is Southampton? Do you have a phone directory here, please?"

George reached into his pocket and pulled out the brown envelope.

"Tony, just listen to me for a minute, please."

He eyed the envelope in George's hand, wondering what was coming next.

"Contained in this envelope, Tony, is the only document from the file that makes a direct reference to Connor McCall, by name. All other references, are made by using his initials, only. So theoretically, they could be anyone with the initials CM.

David and I, well, we only came to this decision, just before he handed over the file to the Police, this morning. We've agreed that this particular document is best given over to you. David has suggested that, as Connors father, you are the person to decide on any subsequent course of action?"

He took the envelope and saw that it was sealed down. He was tempted to open it, but dreaded the contents.

"George, I don't know what to say. Should I be reading this now?"

"I don't think that at this juncture it would be of any help, Tony. Save it for when you are on the plane and have more time to think. You have some very difficult decisions to make, old friend. But, come on, first things first, let's get you on your way to Belfast . . ."

Crime Operation Commander David Flanagan sat at his desk and contemplated the small collection of personal effects that had just been removed from the body and clothing of the late Chief Inspector Charles Ferguson. The man had died in his arms, right here in his office, after having apparently suffered a massive stroke, or cerebral embolism. Using CPR techniques, he had fought for fifteen minutes to try and keep him alive, but to no avail. Even before the arrival of the paramedics, who took over from him with their more sophisticated equipment, it was very obvious that the man was already dead.

The body had been taken away now, but death has a peculiar, lingering smell about it, that defies the efforts of most proprietary brands of air freshener. Like so many experienced Police Officers, David Flanagan was no stranger to death, but never before had he been so personally involved with the final moments of the deceased person. The experience had left him very shaken indeed.

It was true that from the moment he first clapped eyes on Ferguson, he'd taken an almost instant dislike to the man. He'd recognised that here was yet another example of the older, more corrupt, regime of police officers, whose methods were frequently questionable, as in this case. He reflected on the fact that he seemed to have spent an inordinate amount of his service, in trying to rid the PSNI of these dinosaurs, and their flawed, do anything to get a conviction, mentality.

He picked up the dead man's Police pocket book and flicked through the pages to the latest entries. His initial reaction, on reading the almost illegible scrawl, was one of disgust. There were no headings to denote any day, date or time, that each note was made, or where, and how, it was acquired. As such, he knew that under scrutiny, all the entries would become inadmissible as evidence.

If this pocketbook had belonged to any ordinary police constable, he would have found himself on an immediate fizzer, a disciplinary charge, for failing to keep a proper record of his duties.

The last notations appeared to be a record of conversations relating to some telephone messages. He concluded that it must be those made by the man mentioned by Ferguson, someone named Connor McCall. He tried to piece things together, but without the mysterious missing file, none of it was making much sense at the moment. He flicked back through the pages of the pocketbook again, stopping as a list of names caught his attention. It included the names of Marty McCue and Connor McCall, together with Lara and Ryan Dobbs, Shaun Riley and Dermot and Michael Close. There was no indication as to the significance of the entry, or anything to denote a reference of any sort. Clearly, the only person to whom it made any sense was now on his way to the public mortuary.

He tossed the pocketbook back down onto his desk and picked up the man's wallet. Davey never liked looking through another person's private possessions, it always seemed to be like taking an unwarranted intrusion into their personal affairs. Charlie Ferguson's bulging wallet reflected exactly that. Apart from several hundred pounds in cash, and the usual debit, credit and loyalty cards, there were dozens of scraps of paper with scribbled down names, phone numbers, and addresses. Once again, most of it was absolutely meaningless, except to the wallet's owner.

Charlie's phone, still sitting on the corner of his desk, announced an incoming text message. He picked it up and recognised it as being a Blackberry Smartphone of standard Metpol Issue. Ignoring the incoming text message, he scrolled down through the list of numbers until he found what he was looking for. He hit the call button and put the phone to his ear.

"Good afternoon, sir, how may we help you, today?"

The voice on the other end was obviously expecting the caller to be Chief Inspector Charles Ferguson.

"Good afternoon to you. This is Commander David Flanagan of the Northern Ireland Police Service. Put me through to your Operational Commander, please?"

There was a few seconds silence on the other end of the line while the surprised recipient of the call tried to work out what he should do next. A stranger calling in on DCI Ferguson's phone, and asking for Opscom? There was definitely nothing in the Manual of Guidance to cover this one, that was for sure . . .

"Excuse me asking, sir, but can I enquire as to the nature of the call. The Operational Commander is very busy at the moment, so could I perhaps arrange for a ring-back in a few minutes."

"No, that is not acceptable. The nature of the call is somewhat delicate, so I will hold for him. Can you give me his name, please?"

"The Operational Commander for today is Chief Superintendent Julia Fox, sir. If it's urgent, I can page her for you, but she is in a staff meeting at the moment."

David smiled to himself, Julia was well known to him.

"No, it's rather urgent, but nothing that can't wait for a few minutes longer. Please have her call me back on this number, if you will, and be sure to give her my name. We're old acquaintances."

He broke the connection and carefully propped up the phone against his computer monitor. He tapped his fingers pensively on the desk top, while looking to see if there was anything else he might have overlooked?

After a few moments, he reached for the internal phone, and dialled up the CID office extension number.

"CID, DS Brody speaking. How may I help you?"

"Hello Ken, would you come up to my office as soon as is convenient, please. I need to speak with you."

"Two minutes, sir. I'm just finishing my briefing, and getting my lads out on their assignments."

Three pairs of eyes watched Connor, clutching his supermarket carrier bag tightly to his chest, as he made his way back towards the hotel entrance.

He was trying to rally his thoughts, for his mind was still in turmoil. He needed to get out of the hotel and into hiding, that was his first priority. Then, he needed to contact Marty. That was his second. Marty would know what to do for the best. He would almost certainly have some sort of contingency plan already in place, possibly an escape route of some sort, for just such an eventuality? If he could just persuade Brian to let him stay at his place for a few days, but he would need a pretty convincing story. Lost or stolen wallet, together with all his cash and credit cards, perhaps? That might work, but it all sounded a bit lame. Brian was no fool. He would wonder why the hotel bill couldn't be covered, by making a couple of phone calls? No, it was definitely going to need something a little more convincing than that.

Connor waited patiently for the Receptionist to finish speaking with another guest. Had he been more alert, he might have noticed the rather attractive, middle-aged woman that had followed him in, and was now standing a few yards away to his right, apparently browsing through the tourist literature.

"Ah, Mr McCall, I think I have found what you were looking for, sir. Here it is, Mr and Mrs B.Thompson, 76, Beechmount Avenue, that was the address, wasn't it? I had to do it from memory. I seem to have mislaid the piece of paper that you gave me. It's probably here amongst all this paperwork, somewhere . . ."

Connor took the piece of hotel notepaper from her, and looked at the telephone number. The woman, standing to his right, scribbled something onto the corner of one of the leaflets, then folded it in half, and popped it into her handbag.

"Thank you, that looks to be right. Can I provisionally book two extra covers for dinner tonight, please? I'm anticipating having these people here, as my guests."

"Certainly, Mr McCall, no problem, sir."

"And may I have my bill prepared and ready for this evening, please. I don't want to be messing around too much early tomorrow morning. Oh, and I shall need to have my passport back now. I will need to be showing it to someone as proof of identity, this afternoon. You can take my credit card details now, if you wish."

The Receptionist considered his request for a second or two. She knew that she had no right to deny him, but in the light of the Police being interested in his movements? Offering his credit card details ensured payment of his account, and he had, after all, just booked two people in for dinner tonight, so perhaps it would be in order? She would cover herself by phoning the detective, and putting him in the picture.

"Your passport is in the hotel safe, Mr McCall, I will just need to go and fetch it for you, sir. Just give me a couple of minutes."

She went through the door behind, marked 'staff only.' The woman, the one that had been browsing the leaflets, tagged herself onto a family group that was exiting the hotel main entrance. She kept her face looking down and away from the CCTV camera, mounted just above the revolving doors. Once outside, she separated from them, and almost unnoticed, walked across the road to enter the rear of a waiting, non-descript, Belfast black taxicab.

Connor, re-united with his precious passport, hurried up to his room. He needed a stiff drink, and to make a telephone call.

Glass of brandy in one hand, he picked up the telephone receiver with the other, and dialled 9 for an outside line. Having checked for a dialling tone, he carefully punched in the number he had been given by the Receptionist. The connected call was answered almost immediately.

'You have reached the messaging service for Brian and Sarah Thompson. We're sorry, but we cannot take your call at the moment, but if you would care to leave us your name and number, we will get back to you.'

Connor waited for a few seconds to hear the beeping tone before delivering his message.

"Hello Brian, hello Sarah, this is Connor, Lizzy's husband. Look, I'm over here on business for a few days, and I thought it would be nice to meet up with you, and catch up on some old times. I'm staying at the Park Avenue Hotel in Holywood Road, room 211. I've provisionally booked two extra places for dinner tonight, and I would be delighted to see you both. Sometime around six-thirty for seven, would be good, it will allow us time for a little aperitif in the bar, before we eat. Can you give me a call back on this number to confirm, please?"

There were three other telephone calls routed to the office of David Flanagan that afternoon. The first was from the hotel Receptionist who got no reply on the phone belonging to Chief Inspector Charles Ferguson, so she left him another text message, backed up by a voice mail advising him of the latest developments concerning Mr McCall.

The second call was from the Hampshire Police motorcycle courier, giving details of the Southampton to Belfast flight, BE996, advising that the urgent package for Commander David Flanagan was safely on board the aircraft.

The last call was from Chief Superintendent Julia Fox to her friend, and colleague of old, David Flanagan.

"Hello David, I don't suppose you were calling to tell me that you were coming over here especially to take me out to dinner tonight?"

"Not tonight, I'm afraid Julia. By the time I get finished here today, I'll have done something close to a twenty hour shift, so I'll be no good to man nor beast, let alone a very attractive brunette with a penchant for men in uniform. Can I take a raincheck on it though? I do have some leave coming up soon, and a couple of tickets for the Royal Ballet, in the pipeline."

"I'll look forward to it, David. Those tickets for Covent Garden are as rare as hen's teeth, unless you are fortunate, or rich enough, to carry some clout. Tell you what, if you're coming alone, you can stay at my new flat in Chelsea. You've not seen it yet, and I've just finished redecorating the spare bedroom. It's yours for the asking. So, if your call isn't a social one, it must be business. What can I do for you, Commander Flanagan?"

"Thanks for that Julia, but I might be about to spoil your day. I've got some bad news, I'm afraid. It's to do with your man, DCI Charles Ferguson. I'm sorry to have to tell you that earlier today, he suffered a massive stroke and died, right here, in my office."

"Oh my God, David, how awful, for you. I was wondering why you were calling on his phone? What can I say? Charlie was a bit of a legend in these corridors. I have to confess that I didn't know him personally. He worked in some sort of specially created section of either MI5, or 6. To be honest, David, now that I come think about it, I really don't know who he took his orders from. If you were looking to get him replaced, you would probably have to go straight to the top, and talk to the Commissioner himself. I know that sounds rather callous, but I assume that is what you are phoning for, isn't it?"

"No, not really, Julia. I'll make no bones about the fact that I resent Scotland Yard sticking their nose into our affairs, and sending their people over here to do a job, that we could, in all probability, better handle ourselves. I don't like to speak ill of the dead, but this buffoon, and I choose the word carefully, together with his cock-eyed plan of action, has already caused two of my officers to be put onto extended sick leave. Someone over there has rubber stamped one of his reports 'approved for action.' If their decision was based on evidence contained within the working file, a copy of which, I have right here in front of me, I have to say that I am struggling to find anything substantial enough to justify any action, within your definition of the word. In my view, there is still a lot more legwork that still needs to be done, before we can get anywhere near to proving any wrongdoing by the man he was after."

"I'm sorry, David, but as I say, I'm not the person you should be talking to. My responsibilities as an Operational Commander, is loosely confined to what happens here, on the streets of the Capital. Charlie Ferguson worked nationally, and for people whose sole aim was to identify, and try to head off perceived problems before they arose.

His section would also resort to methods, and tactics, that you and I would normally regard as being outside the scope of any normal Police procedures and practices. He didn't take any prisoners, if you get my meaning? I have absolutely no idea what he was working on, but it would rather have expected that it was something connected with counter-terrorism, or serious, organised crime. In my office, it was recently rumoured that Charlie had finally cracked a case that he'd been investigating for nearly the whole of his service. I know for a fact that a huge quantity of illegal firearms has recently been recovered, but any more than that, I can't tell you, David, and that's not because of anything official, it's because I just don't know." "Yes alright, Julia, thanks anyway. I'll do as you suggest, put a confidential report together, and send it up to Sir Paul for his attention. Perhaps now that Ferguson's dead, someone over there might just take another look at this, and realise the need for a little more, proper, common sense Police work?"

As he broke off the connection, there was a polite knock on his office door before it was opened slightly.

"Come in, Sergeant Brody, take a seat, please."

He waited a few seconds while his Knock Police Station, CID Sergeant, made himself comfortable.

"I suppose by now, what happened in here this morning, is fairly common knowledge around the whole of the station, is it, Ken?"

"Yes sir, bad business, to be sure. But nothing like that can be kept a secret for very long within these walls, so it can't?"

"Off the record, Ken, what did you think of DCI Ferguson? You met him a couple of times. Picked him up at the airport, and again this morning. Did he have much to say for himself. Please speak freely, this is strictly between us?"

"Well, I don't really know, sir. A bit full of himself, I suppose, and perhaps even a little eccentric? Franksy and I both thought the same. He was dressed up like a poof when we met him at the airport, said he had good reason to be, although he didn't say why. Whatever it was that happened at the airport yesterday, the incident that put our two SIS blokes out of action, well, he seemed to think it was our fault that it all went wrong. Even blamed us for losing his target. Franksy and me, well, we didn't have much idea what he was talking about, so we didn't. He asked a lot of questions about you, though, sir. But that would be right after we told him that you wanted to see him. Then there was a little incident in the hotel reception area this morning. Some bloke, a hotel guest, I think, who appeared to be in a hurry to get away from us? That was very odd. Mr Ferguson told me that it was one of the men he was after. I offered to go after him, but your man said that it could wait till later, said that he knew where he was, and wanted to let him stew for a while. Those were his exact words."

"Did you get a name for this man, Ken?"

"The Receptionist called him, Mr McCall, I think, sir."

"Ah, that would explain why Mr Ferguson insisted on being booked into the Park Avenue, instead of our usual accommodation. What did he look like, this man, McCall?"

"Sixtyish, heavy build, medium height, grey hair, I didn't see too much of him, sir, he took off like a frightened jackrabbit when he clapped eyes on Mr Ferguson and me."

"Would you recognise him again, Ken?"

"I think so, sir."

Ken Brody watched his Commander as he thoughtfully tapped the file in front of him with a pencil. He seemed to be trying to come up with a plan of action.

"Ken, I want you to take over on this operation for the time being. We will need to keep a containing brief pending further instructions from Scotland Yard. The surveillance measures that we have put in place on McCue will remain, and in the meantime, find out as much as you can about this man McCall. There is a single reference made to him in Mr Ferguson's pocketbook. His first name is Connor, Connor McCall.

We will need to keep an eye on his movements, contacts, that sort of thing. So I suppose you had better get DC Franklin in on it, as well. It's a bit late now, so jack it all up to start from tomorrow morning. Round-the-clock surveillance on him, as well, please. Here, take this with you. It's DCI Ferguson's working file. Run yourself off a copy of everything, and then return it to me immediately. If you read it through, you will be just as wise as me, at this moment in time.

I think this one is to be regarded as highly sensitive and confidential, Ken, so everything will be on a need-to-know basis, is that clear?"

"Yes, sir, but I shall need to brief Franksy, surely?"

"Just the bare bones of it then, Ken. I have no idea of what we might be getting into, just yet. So you are to report anything significant back to me, direct, is that clear?

"Yes sir."

"Good man. One last thing before you go, Ken. There is a package, a file of paper, that relates to this operation. It will be arriving on flight BE996 from Southampton, which is scheduled to land at City Airport, at 1725, today. The package is addressed to me, and I have left instruction for it to be deposited at the Airport Police Office, pending collection. See if you can get uniform to send a traffic motorcyclist to get it. Tell them that the officer is to deliver it back here to me, personally, just as fast as his bike will go. If you stress that aspect, I don't foresee that there will be any argument. Those lads just love roaring around the city on blues and twos, don't they?"

Ken Brody grinned and nodded his agreement. No wonder they all loved this guy . . .

"I suppose we had better collect Mr Ferguson's personal effects, and pay his hotel bill. Ask them if they would be prepared to send the account in to me, here. I can then authorise it out of one of our budgets. If not, pay cash, and I'll authorise an immediate refund from petty cash, for you. Is that alright, Ken?"

"Yes sir, no problem."

Jacqui Strong sat on the terrace, cup of coffee in hand, and watched in amusement, as Jim playfully picked up little Emily to swing her wildly around. Both man and child were enjoying themselves immensely, that much was apparent. Emily's squeals of delight, mingled with the Jim's deep, throaty laugh, were enough to bring a smile to anyone's face. He had been trying to teach her how to catch a tennis ball, but the child's hand-eye coordination was not yet sufficiently developed enough to enable her to master the task. Now, every time she dropped the ball, he would playfully chase after her, to pick her up and swing her around again, much to her absolute delight.

As she watched them play, Jacquie reflected upon the continued rapid improvement in Jim's physical condition. She was beginning to feel a little superfluous to requirement. It was difficult to believe that only ten or twelve days ago, he might have been regarded as being close to death's door. She had to keep reminding herself, that the man she was supposed to be nursing was an octogenarian. The wheelchair that had been used, when he was first brought to Oakwood, was now relegated, and gathering dust, in one of the basement storerooms. She had also noticed that his whole attitude and general demeanour had, over the past few days, undergone yet another significant change, and it all seemed to coincide with his developing relationship with little Emily.

To say that they were good for each other would be an understatement. They were becoming almost inseparable. The child seemed to spend hours sitting in her little chair, apparently reading books, with Jim occasionally breaking off from whatever he happened to be doing, to come over and explain something to her. To Jacqui, their often whispered, conversation was almost unintelligible. But then, she wasn't to know that normal conversation was only used, when she was in a close proximity. Most of the time, they were communicating with each other, telepathically.

Jim hadn't fully understood what was happening to him, either. He only knew that he hadn't felt as good as this, since he was a teenager, and he saw no good reason to question why. He was determined to make the most of it. His mind was sharper, his reactions quicker, and his whole body almost seemed to be retrogressing back to how it was thirty-odd years ago. He wondered what his beloved Doris would have made of it all? Her memory brought a smile back to his face and he realised that the feelings of pain and anguish, associated with her death, were already slowly receding from his thoughts.

Only this morning, after he finished shaving, he stood looking at himself in the bathroom mirror. Was it his imagination, or is the musculature of his chest, shoulders and arms, looking a little more defined? It prompted him into remembering how he once looked, fifty years ago. He thought that with a few sit-ups and stomach crunches, he might even be able to re-achieve the six-pack stomach he'd once had, and been so proud of, when in his twenties and thirties?

There and then, on the tiled bathroom floor, he experimentally tried a couple of sit-ups, and found that he could still do it. He rose easily to his feet and pinched the couple of inches of unsightly, loose fatty tissue that hung around his midriff. The mere sight of it was enough for him to resolve that he would try and make it disappear. Optimistically, he had his eye on nurse Jacqui, now . . .

'Diet and exercise' is the key to weight loss and a healthy body, he recalled from something he'd read somewhere. And, 'If you look good, it will make you feel good,' was another cliché in the same vogue.

The diet side of it was easy, for just lately, he'd found that he had developed a healthy eating fad. All the previous cravings for huge portions of all things sweet, and fatty, were no longer with him. He just didn't fancy them anymore. Mediocre portions of fresh fruit and vegetables, more fruit juices and a lot less alcohol, eat only when you're hungry, and then a little and often . . . Where the hell had all this come from? He had no idea, but it was fast becoming integral to his newly adopted lifestyle.

Emily coming into his life was another stroke of good fortune. Doris, being unable to bear any children, meant that he had never experienced the immense joy to be found in sharing their company.

A few days ago, the child, herself, had begun it all, by actively seeking to be his companion. She and Sam had found him early one morning, sitting out on the terrace, after breakfast, chatting with Jacqui and Sharon. As with any normal child she had calmly walked over to Sharon, and held out her arms in the usual gesture of a child wishing to be picked up by someone. Sharon had, seemingly without thinking, picked her up and placed her onto her lap. Jim saw Emily snuggle down into her fond embrace, all quite natural, and perfectly normal, for a two-year-old. The dog, Sam, had settled down contentedly beside Sharon's chair, head on paws, in a protective, watching mode.

What Jim didn't see or hear, was the silent telepathic exchange that had already taken place between the child and Sharon, as she had picked her up.

Their three-way, adult, conversation had continued on for a few minutes, with Jim slowly becoming aware that the child was looking at him wide-eyed. For an instant, he allowed his eyes to similarly focus onto hers. An idea, no, it was more than that . . . It had been a request, from her, had popped into his mind.

In response, he had held out his arms as an invitation that she should come over to sit on his lap, instead. Emily sat up, looked knowingly at Sharon, who gave her a little smile, and proceeded to set her back down onto the ground again.

Jacqui and Sharon had both watched as Emily presented herself to Jim, who carefully picked her up, and placed her astride his knees, to face him. Sharon knew what was about to happen, but Jacqui had absolutely no idea.

A look of complete surprise was seen to pass briefly across Jim's face.

"And hello to you, too, little one. How did you do that?"

All Jacqui saw was the child smiling, while looking fixedly into Jim's eyes. A look of intense concentration appeared on his face, and lasted for several seconds, until, with a little laugh, he pulled her gently into his chest, to give her a grandfatherly hug.

Sharon knew that telepathic communication, between Emily and her father, had just been established.

The knowledge gave her a feeling of reassurance that only served to increase the already strong bond of affection that she herself, had developed for the child. Malcolm had already told her, that Emily was in some way contributory to her father's quite remarkable healing progress. This knowledge, coupled with her own recent experiences, had led her to conclude that just being around Emily, was sufficient enough to make good things happen.

Little did Sharon know that it was all part of Emily's, and the alien's plan? And, that for the very first time, a proper, physical contact, of a human nature, had been established between Emily, and her guardian alien, a part of whom, now existed as an integral part of Jim's cerebral physiology. Their first human touching had taken place when Jim had lifted Emily up onto his knee.

The communication problem, previously perceived by the alien, had been overcome in the simplest way. He had slowly, and carefully, taken complete control of the parts of the brain that dealt with all the humanoid's involuntary and automotive bodily functions, without interfering in any way, with those that controlled the man's character.

Identifying many of the more serious cerebral faults, and degenerative inconsistencies, mostly relating to the mammalian aging processes, he had immediately set about putting them back into good order.

By subtly re-routing the minute electrical brain impulses away from the dead and damaged cells, and through other, little used areas of undamaged tissue, he was able to bring about an immediate heightening of the five human senses. Then, by stimulating other areas, he encouraged more of the bodily production of natural chemicals, to be carried by the blood supply to the areas of damaged bodily tissue, thus stimulating the healing process even further.

Another slight adjustment to the mind-set, served to suppress the humanoids unhealthy natural cravings for certain foods. Like he had with Emily, he began the process of encouraging his host into self-regulating his own dietary and calorific intake, taking in only what was necessary to keep his body fit and healthy.

By achieving all of this, he knew that he was slowly correcting the host body's most basic functions. In time, there would be a natural purging of cholesterol from the arteries, thus improved the blood circulation, and thereby placing less strain on the heart.

Eating the right foods, in moderation, brought about an immediate improvement to the digestive tract, and other associated vital organs, such as the liver, kidneys and pancreas. It would all serve to make the person feel so much better in himself, and to want to do more exercise, thus stimulating the respiratory system.

Such monitoring and fine-tuning of everything, was proving to be a constant, on-going process, mainly due to his host body's advanced years. Nevertheless, the alien persevered, for there was no other option available to him. He had to make this humanoid body work more efficiently, if it was to be the vehicle within which, he was to achieve his original purpose for remaining on this little planet.

In so doing, the alien considered that he was not only rendering assistance to his host, but also moving one step closer to achieving his desired wish. To be able to physically interact, share, and experience all the emotions, that up until now, had been suppressed and denied to him. In particular, he sought to find and understand the one the humanoids called, love. For this is by far the most powerful of them all, and the least understood, by all of his kind.

The alien had begun to recognise, that this emotion, in all its many forms, was the singular driving force that dictated virtually everything that the human's did for each other, in their relatively short lifespan. It was the one factor that his kind had previously failed to identify, and comprehend, in all their previous encounters with humans.

He knew that the others, for the first time in their existence, were beginning to communicate. They were closely monitoring the knowledge that he was acquiring, and questioning the implications, and reasons, for one of their kind seeking to assume a physical existence once again.

Connor's frequent refills from the brandy bottle inevitably led to him into falling into a drunken sleep. He completely failed to hear his bedside phone ringing. The call, from his brother-in-law, Brian, was to advise that they would not be able to come to dinner that evening, due to a previous arrangement, but could they perhaps meet for lunch, tomorrow? On getting no reply, it was assumed that he had gone out, so this message was left with the Receptionist to pass on to Connor when he returned.

Private Detective Pete Grogan had been sitting patiently in his car all afternoon. He was watching the front of the Park Avenue Hotel. His last sighting of the target had been at 1103 that morning, when he had followed him back from the supermarket. After more than five hours, he was bored out of his skull. Constant references to his wristwatch did little to help, it only served to remind him of how long he had been sitting idle.

The only incident of any real significance, had been the arrival of two plain-clothed Police Officers at precisely 1507hrs. Almost immediately he saw them, he'd pegged them for what they were. The Ford Mondeo car, with its additional radio aerial, and their general appearance and demeanour, was always a dead giveaway.

They had entered the hotel, stayed inside for precisely seventeen minutes, and emerged carrying a holdall and a wheelie suitcase. He saw both items loaded into the boot of their car before they drove off again.

He'd logged it all into his observation notes, for no particular reason other than to relieve the boredom.

At 1610hrs, his office rang to order him to go to City Airport to meet flight BE 996 from Southampton. The flight was scheduled to land at 1725hrs, and had on board, the client, Mr Anthony Williams. He was ordered to then take his direction and instruction, according to the expressed wishes of this very important client.

Pete Grogan, not wishing to leave his target unobserved for any longer than was necessary, calculated that if the flight landed on time, it would take at least an extra thirty-five minutes for the passengers to clear baggage, customs, and immigration. So, allowing himself half an hour to get to the airport, and then to find a parking space, he would have to abandon this observation point at 1730hrs, at the very latest.

He was praying that nothing would occur in the meantime, to mess up his plan. Get the client re-united with the target, and then, with a bit of luck, it might be possible to wrap this one up, and to start heading back home again sometime tomorrow? He hoped so, it was his wife, Caroline's, birthday on Monday . . .

The need to empty his aching bladder was sufficient to bring Connor out of his drunken stupor. It would have been around the same time that Pete Grogan was leaving to fetch his father from the Airport.

Glancing at his wristwatch, and the nearly empty bottle of brandy, he cursed his own stupidity and shut his eyes for a few more minutes. He needed to pee, and to get himself together for his evening dinner date with Brian and Sara, although at this moment, the thought of eating anything was enough to turn his stomach over. Carefully pushing himself upright from the bed, he rose unsteadily to his feet to shed his trousers, and stumble over towards his bathroom to relieve himself.

Standing there over the pan, with his seemingly endless stream of urine tinkling its way into the bottom, he realised that Brian hadn't yet rung him back to confirm the evening arrangement. Perhaps he should ring him again? He looked again at his watch, it was coming up towards six. He calculated that they were probably already close to leaving home in order to get to the hotel for six thirty? Connor finished urinating and turned on his shower. He thoughtfully shrugged off the rest of his clothing, to step naked under the power jets. The cool water made him gasp, but it served to revive him.

An invigorating scrub later, he stepped from the shower to wrap a bath sheet around himself. He was feeling a whole lot better now. Rubbing his wet hair with a towel he came back through into the bedroom just as his phone gave out a soft, purring ring. He picked up the receiver and put it to his ear.

"Ah, Mr McCall. There are two people, a man and a woman, down here in Reception asking for you, sir."

He glanced again at his watch, it was only six-ten. Damn and blast, they were early.

"Thank you, would you ask them if they would like to order a drink from the bar, for me please. I shall be down to join them in ten minutes."

Pete Grogan stood patiently waiting in the Arrivals Hall of George Best Belfast City Airport. According to the flight information board, BE996 from Southampton, landed at 1735hrs, ten minutes late on its scheduled ETA. At 1810hrs, the board flashed up 'baggage arriving,' so he reckoned on about another five minutes before he got Mr Williams.

He looked again at his makeshift name board, an A5 sized sheet of paper torn from his notepad with the clients name handwritten in black biro. It wasn't good, but it would have to suffice. Twenty minutes to get back to the hotel again, and after that, who knows? He wondered if there was another Belfast to Liverpool car ferry that he might get on that evening? If there was, he could comfortably be back home in Poole, by lunchtime tomorrow. He rang his wife to give her an update on things.

Meanwhile, a uniformed Police motorcyclist was busy signing for an urgent package that had arrived on the same flight. The Constable's explicit instruction, from his Sergeant, was that it be personally delivered only into the hands of Commander Davey Flanagan, at Knock Police Headquarters, and with all speed . . .

Connor scrubbed his teeth and applied a little of his Old Spice aftershave. He straightening his knitted tie, and regarded himself in the mirror. His Harris Tweed jacket and fawn corduroys, were not the most appropriate dress for dinner, but it was the smartest togs he had left available. All his other clothes were either soiled, screwed up, or in need of some remedial attention with a smoothing iron.

For the first time, he wished Lizzy were there with him to help. Never mind, he'd already made up his mind that if Brian and Sarah couldn't help, he would have to go back home tomorrow and confess everything. There was nothing else for it.

He pocketed his wallet and hotel key card, and quietly let himself out of his room. Dreading that he should come face to face with that policeman again, he took the stairs instead of the lift. He opened the door at the bottom and stood for a few seconds looking around at the people in Reception. He saw nobody that he immediately recognised.

"Excuse me, I'm Mr McCall, room 211. You rang me about fifteen minutes ago to say that my guests had arrived. I don't see them anywhere, do you know where they might be, please?"

"The two people sitting at the corner table, Mr McCall. They're the ones that were asking for you."

He looked across in the general direction indicated. A rather attractive looking, well dressed, middle-aged blonde, woman, together with a slightly younger man, were looking back at him, expectantly.

"But they're not my . . . Yes, alright, thank you."

Puzzled, he made his way over to where they were seated. They both stood up as he approached the table.

"Good evening, my name is McCall, I understand that you have been asking for me?"

The woman extended her hand to be shaken as she replied.

"Good evening Mr McCall, my name is Christina, and this is Brendon. We are associates of Martyn McCue, who he has asked to see you."

"Oh my God, Marty? I've been trying to get hold of him for over a week, now. Where is he?"

"Yes, we know you have, Mr McCall. May I call you Connor, Mr McCall? We are all on the same side here, and we usually only refer to each other by our first names?"

"Yes, of course, but why hasn't Marty returned any of my calls?"

"Telephones calls are notoriously easy to monitor and trace here in the Province, Connor. The Police and Security Forces have just about everything covered, so we tend not to use any identifiable mobile phones for the more sensitive calls. Martyn has currently been moved into one of our local safe houses. We have a car waiting outside to take you to meet with him, so shall we go?"

"I can't, I have two people meeting me here for dinner tonight. I can't be letting them down, can I?"

"Ask the Receptionist to make your apologies, Connor. With any luck, if you keep your meeting with Martyn brief, we could have you back here for seven-thirty."

Minutes later, Connor was recorded on the CCTV leaving the hotel with a man and a woman, both of whom had kept their faces averted from the camera.


Pete Grogan watched the elderly, overweight gentleman emerge into the Arrivals Hall and pause to look around. His name board proved unnecessary, Pete recognised him for what he was, and made his approach.

"Mr Williams?"

A look of relief appeared on the old chap's face. "Yes, are you the private detective?"

"Pete Grogan, sir. Did you have a good flight?"

"It's been a hectic day, Mr Grogan. The flight was noisy, cramped, and thoroughly uncomfortable. The food abominable, and the cabin crew, surly and objectionable. I'm tired, hungry and thirsty. So, in answer to your question, no, it wasn't a very good flight."

"I'm sorry to hear that, Mr Williams. What exactly would you like to do now then, sir?"

"I would like you to take me to wherever my son is, please, Mr Grogan."

"Your son? I'm sorry Mr Williams, I hadn't appreciated the relationship between you and Mr McCall. My office hadn't advised me of that fact."

"That's understandable Mr Grogan, I hadn't advised them, as such. They think that Connor is my business partner who is apparently suffering from a mental breakdown. Can I ask where he is located?"

"Mr McCall is staying at a rather nice three-star hotel, the Park Avenue, not too far from here. When I left to come to meet you, he was still inside, where he's been all afternoon."

Pete looked at his watch for effect, and stooped to pick up the single piece of hand luggage, a holdall.

"But that was a little over an hour ago, now. My car is parked over this way, sir, so shall we go?"

Connor sat in the back of the black, Belfast taxicab with Christina. The driver, Brendon, obviously knew his way around the City, as he took several rat-runs to avoid the worst of the early evening traffic congestion. At least, that is what Connor surmised. The real reason was slightly more sinister. Brendon was seeking to avoid the many traffic regulation cameras sited on all the main City routes.

Christina, sitting beside him, seemed to want to chat.

"Do you know your way around Belfast City, Connor?"

"Vaguely, I studied politics, history and law at Queen's, back in the seventies, but the City has undergone many changes since those days. Unless we are close to any of the more recognisable landmark buildings, I think it would be easy for me to get lost now."

"Have you not hired a car for yourself while you are here?"

"No, I left my old Morris Minor back in Southampton airport. I was thinking that my visit to see Marty would only take a couple of days, never expected to be over here for more than a week . . . Tell me, does Marty know that all of our previous operations have been compromised by some sort of file that details everything?"

"He does, and we are already aware of the existence of this file, Connor. We are currently engaged in what you would call, a damage limitation exercise. That is why Martyn is temporarily in one of our safe houses. Are you aware that the Police are looking for you, as well?"

"There's one currently staying at my hotel, but I'm not sure that it's me he's after. No direct approaches have been made to me yet, but I don't believe in tempting providence. I was planning to get on an early flight back to Southampton tomorrow morning."

"Have you booked your flight, Connor?"

"Yes, I'm getting picked up from the hotel at five-fifteen in the morning."

"And what will you do when you get back to England? The Police will still be looking for you."

"I don't know. Just go home, I suppose. I've nowhere to hide. Short of catching a flight to some third world Republic, with no extradition treaty, I'm stymied. For me to flee the country would require a lot of money, and I'm not a rich man. I'd rather hoped that Marty might be able to help me out in some way?"

Christina sat back and appeared to be pondering the problem, so Connor left her to think in silence while he tried to work out exactly where in Belfast, they were heading.

Christina was indeed thinking about Connor's future, but not in any way that would serve to benefit him. The ultimate decision had been left with her to make, and the man, by his own admission, had just become too much of a liability. He had to be taken care of. Permanently.

Police traffic motorcyclist, Constable Phil Emmett, the latest recruit to the Road Crime Unit, stowed the Commander's precious package into the pannier of his new 1200cc BMW bike. He donned his safety helmet, and fastened down the acrylic visor. Noticing the first spots of rain appearing on the surface, he cursed his luck. His waterproof over-suit was in his locker back at the station. He'd removed it from the pannier to make room for the package. He eyed the darkening sky to the west, and reckoned he had about ten minutes before the heavens really opened, best get a move on. Astride the bike, he pulled on his gauntlets and hit the starter to bring the big engine to life.

"He's just leaving with the baby."

The message was relayed from the telephone of a man dressed in the overalls of an Airport Maintenance Operative. He was standing on the roof of the Terminal building, and had been keeping ob's on the Constable's bike since he'd arrived. He watched as it roared off up the road, on flashing blues.

"He's just gone out onto the Bypass, and is heading down towards the roundabout."

He broke the connection, took off his overalls, and put them into an airport duty-free plastic carrier bag. Smartly dressed in a suit and tie, the man descended from his vantage point, and headed over to the short term car park. His part of the operation had been successfully completed.

Constable Phil Emmett loved his bike. The exhilaration and adrenalin rush gained from merely twisting open the throttle, and experiencing the application of raw power being translated into speed, was for him, the ultimate buzz. He smiled to himself. Better than good sex, he'd reckoned to his mates. Most of them tended to scoff and disagree with him, questioning the sort of women he was consorting with?

He reduced speed without braking, bringing it down from eighty, to a comfortable third gear, twenty-five, to negotiate the complex roundabout system at the end of the A2 Sydenham Bypass. The road surfaces were now wet, as the falling rain steadily got worse. Traffic was fairly light, and the street lighting had just come on early, in response to the rain-cloud gloom. Phil indicated left and steered the bike onto the A55 Holywood Road. A brief burst of acceleration up through the gears, before letting it drop back again to a comfortable fifty-five, for the slight left hook onto the Parkway. No brakes, all done on engine speed and gears alone, his Advanced Course Instructor of two weeks ago, would have approved.

He now had a couple of miles of dual carriageway with very little traffic. Positioning the bike in the outer lane, he wound the throttle wide open, smoothly climbing up through the gears. The big BMW engine, singing its delightfully throaty song, was music to his ears. A quick glance down at the speedo saw the needle hitting 110mph. The deflected rain from the bike windscreen, pelted into his visor, and he could feel it uncomfortably blowing up under his helmet and soaking into his shirt collar. He hunched his head down a little lower, holding on to his speed, although there was still more there to be had.

He saw a builder's truck with a trailer attached, waiting at the Garnerville Drive junction up ahead, its right indicator flashing. Phil's foot moved to cover the back brake and his fingers extended to rest lightly on the front brake lever. He let his speed fall off fractionally, while watching the wheels of the truck, always the first indication that it was moving. He was having a nasty premonition.

The single car in the nearside lane, the only other vehicle between his bike and the truck, passed it by and he saw the wheels of the truck slowly begin to turn as it moved forward across carriageway.

His footbrake and handbrake came on hard almost simultaneously, and he felt the rear tyre immediately begin to lose grip in the wet, the bike started snaking around underneath him.

Feathering his braking to regain control, Phil knew that it was a lost cause, there was no way that he could bring the bike to a halt in the distance left between himself and the truck, which by now, had completely blocked the two lanes of the carriageway ahead. It all flashed through his mind, the emergency dismount procedure.

"Bleed off as much speed as possible, and if there was no other alternative, get off the damn thing. Lay it down and throw it away. Lie flat on your back and take your chances with the road surface. Whatever you do, don't hang on to the bike, you'll always come off worst."

He could hear the Instructor's words being hammered home under the general heading of, "Oh, shit!"

Phil allowed his bike to come round sideways while keeping the front wheel steering into the skid. Textbook stuff, practiced on the skid pan in a car. Doing it on a bike though, was a slightly different matter . . .

Fifty, forty, thirty, the yards melted away almost as fast as he could say them. Somewhere between thirty and forty, and with the bike still doing over fifty, he laid it right down and felt himself make contact with the tarmac. Now, he was grateful for the rain. The wet tarmac allowed him to slide along on his leathers, with far less friction. He still had the presence of mind to spread-eagle himself, to keep from going into a roll.

The bike smashed into the side of the truck hitting the rear wheel before bouncing forward into the fuel tank. The fibreglass fairing and plastic side panels all disintegrating on impact.

Phil, sliding along on his back, narrowly avoided the front wheels, passing just under the front bumper of the truck. He finally came to rest after his right shoulder made hard contact against the kerbstones of the central reservation. He felt his right collarbone snap just momentarily before losing consciousness, as his helmeted head, thrown sideways, made a similar heavy impact.

Following traffic came to a stunned halt, and witnesses stated that three men quickly got out of the truck. One went to tend to the injured Police Officer. One was busy on his mobile phone, while the third seemed to be pulling at the smouldering wreckage of the bike, now jammed under the fuel tank side of the truck. What he was actually doing was surreptitiously allowing a plastic drinking bottle, produced from under his hi-vis jacket, to empty itself of two litres of petrol into the middle of the mangled bike engine. He made sure that it formed a puddle all around the wreckage of the bike, and under the fuel tank of the truck as well. His very last action was to surreptitiously flick a cigarette lighter on the edge of the fuel puddle, before hastily scrambling out of the way of the resultant conflagration.

With a huge whoosh, the whole of the back of the truck was instantly ablaze. The load, comprised of old timber and roofing felt, immediately added its weight to the blaze, sending thick, black, acrid smoke, right across both carriageways of the Parkway. Everyone realised the potential for the lorry fuel tank to explode, and immediately retreated to a safe distance.

The driver of the lorry, later to be hailed as a hero, carried the unconscious Police Officer over his shoulder to a point considered to be out of the danger zone. All three men then took to closing off the road completely for safety sake. The evening traffic quickly backed up, hampered the arrival of the Fire and Rescue Service, and giving the fire much longer to burn. By the time they managed to get some water onto it, there was little left of the motorcycle that was recognisable. Phase two of the operation was complete.

Pete Grogan and Tony Williams were almost unaffected by the traffic hold-up. Their car was stationary for only a few minutes, mainly due to the rubber-necker's backing up the traffic, as they gazed over at the huge pall of black smoke drifting over the Holywood Road from the direction of the Parkway.

Ten minutes later, Pete Grogan pulled the car into the hotel car park, and carrying his holdall for him, accompanied his client into the hotel Reception area.

"I would like to book a room for the night, please."

"Certainly sir, do you have a reservation?"

"No, I'm sorry, I don't. Is it a problem?

"I don't think so, sir. Was it a single or double room that you require, and how long do you anticipate staying, please?"

"Single room, and just for the one night."

"Is the other gentleman not with you then, sir?"

"Other gentleman? Oh, you mean Mr Grogan here. I'm not sure, just a moment."

Tony turned to Pete Grogan.

"I'm sorry, Mr Grogan, I'd rather assumed that you were booked in here already. Where are you staying? What are your plans now?"

"That depends on you Mr Williams. I am instructed by my office to comply with your wishes. If you consider that my services are no longer required, I should be heading off back home, sir."

Tony thought for a few seconds before turning back to the Receptionist.

"Would you just confirm for me that you have a Mr Connor McCall staying here at the moment, please?"

"I'm sorry sir, we are not allowed to divulge the names of other guests. You will need to speak with . . ."

He interrupted her, raising his voice an octave.

"Mr McCall is my son, miss. It's a perfectly simple question, and a straightforward answer would be appreciated. You are placing me in some difficulty. If my son isn't staying here, then there is no point in me staying either, and I will take my custom elsewhere. This establishment would not be my first choice of accommodation, so, are you to answer my simple question, or not?"

The chastened Receptionist, rather than lose the business, decided to ignore protocol.

"We have a Mr McCall staying with us, yes, sir."

"Thank you." Tony extracted his wallet and turned back to Pete Grogan.

"My thanks to you, Mr Grogan, I see no reason to detain you any further. Perhaps you would be kind enough to accept this small consideration as a token of my sincere appreciation for your efforts?"

He held out his hand to be shaken, pressing a couple of large denomination banknotes into Pete's hand in the process. They quickly disappeared into Pete's trouser pocket. Elated, he bade his client a very good evening, and hurriedly left before he changed his mind.

"Now then, miss. Which room is my son's?"

She pointedly consulted the guest list, for his benefit only. She already knew which room Mr McCall was in. He had, after all, been the subject of her attention for much of the day.

"Room 211, sir, but he's not in at the moment. He left the hotel in the company of a man and woman, around six twenty-five this evening. We are expecting him back shortly, though. He has booked two extra covers for dinner tonight. Can we complete your check-in, please, sir, assuming that it is your intention to stay with us, that is?"

"Yes of course. Can I have a room close to my son's, please. And when he arrives back, don't tell him that I'm here, I want it to be a little surprise for him."

"The closest that I can get you is three doors further along the corridor, sir. Room 214. Dinner is now being served in the Dining Room. The bar is over there, through the archway. Breakfast is between 0700 and 0930. Will there be anything else you require, sir?"

"Nothing that I can think of. Tell me, do you perhaps know the names of the people that my son went out with tonight?"

He got his wallet out again. Sensing a reward, the Receptionist quickly looked about her desk and produced a piece of hotel stationery. She passed it over to him.

"He may be in the company of these two people, Mr Williams. Mr McCall asked me to find a telephone number for them earlier today. He also mentioned that they were to be his guests for dinner tonight."

Tony looked at the paper. He recognised Connors handwriting and the names, Brian and Sarah Thompson, Elizabeth's brother, and his wife. Yes, of course, it made perfect sense for him to be looking them up again. The Receptionist was not to be disappointed as another banknote swiftly changed hands.

Tony made his way up to his room with a feeling of great relief. He would soon be re-united with Connor, his only living blood relative. Now, with the only damning piece evidence safely in his pocket, he had it within his power to make everything all right for him, again. In his minds eye, he pictured a joyous father and son reunion. Perhaps they might even partake of a few celebratory drinks together, before they headed off back home tomorrow. Their troubles were definitely all behind them, now. In Connor's presence, he would ritualistically reduce the document in his pocket, to a small pile of ashes. That would be good.

Tony was very was tired, and felt the need to freshen up. His thought he would then go down to the bar and get himself a large scotch and soda, and perhaps a club sandwich of some sort, while he waited for Connor's return.

Meanwhile, Connor had been taken to an area of the City that he vaguely recognised from his days as a student. In those happier times, when he and Lizzy had spent many an hour in the local public houses, attending political meetings and debates, listening to the rantings of some of the fanatical local nutters.

"This is the Falls Road, isn't it, Christina? I seem to recognise some of this as my old stomping ground. As a student, I had lodgings in Donegal Road."

"You're right Connor, this area of the City still has a very strong following for us. We are just about to drop you off. From here, you can make your own way."

"What, you're not coming with me? Where will you be? How will I contact you to take me back to my hotel again?"

Brendon turned the car left, off the Falls Road and into St James's Road, before bringing it to a halt.

"Right Connor, listen to me carefully. If you don't get this right, you will not get to see Martyn, do you understand what I'm saying?"

"Yes."

"When you get out of the car, you will walk slowly back to the junction. I suggest that you try to make it look as though you've perhaps had a few too many to drink. There is a pedestrian crossing that is monitored by a traffic regulation camera. You will use it to cross over to the other side of the Falls Road. Once there, you will pause for twenty seconds, while looking up at the shop fronts. Is that clear? You will stop, and count slowly up to twenty. This is to enable the person watching, to get a good look at you. His name is Dominic, and he will also need time to get down from his vantage point, and prepare to meet with you.

You will then walk slowly along to the next road junction. When you get to the corner, there is a taxi office. Look slightly to your left, and you will see a pair of heavy, galvanised steel, gates on the other side of the road in Rockmount Street. You will see that they obviously serve to access the rear of the four large derelict houses on the Falls Road. You are to walk over and go through those gates. If the coast is clear, Dominic will have just unlocked them for you. So after you have entered, you will relocate the padlock and fasten it behind you. Are we all clear, so far?"

"Yes."

"Right, you will walk twenty yards along the alleyway, to the second gate on your right. It serves as the back entry to a large, white-painted building. Go through that gate and close it, quietly, behind you. You will find yourself in a small, covered courtyard area. There, you are to wait until Dominic comes out from the building to meet with you. You will identify yourself, and if he is satisfied, he will then take you to see Martyn. Is that all clear?"

"Yes, I think so."

"Right, repeat it all back to me, then."

Connor painstakingly did as he was asked.

"Alright then Connor. When you've finished with Martyn, a telephone call will be made to let us know that you are ready to be picked up again. You will be accompanied back as far as the steel gates. Walk back over to the taxi office premises on the corner. We will pick you up from there, alright?"

"Yes. Thank you."

"No problem Connor. It goes without saying that you will try to do all of this, unobserved, please. We don't want the location of one of our precious safe houses to be compromised in any way."

Connor nodded his understanding of the situation. He waited while Christina made a telephone call. She said only three words before breaking off the connection.

"He's coming now."

Connor got out of the car into the miserable falling rain. He pulled up his jacket collar and screwed up his face against the weather.

In response to her call, the man, Dominic, got up from his easy chair, and took up his position at the first floor window of the derelict house. From a gap through the shutters, he had a clear and unobstructed view of the pedestrian crossing. With the aid of a pair of cheap binoculars, he watched the man slowly cross over the Falls Road. He needed to size him up, and to satisfy himself that he would recognise the man, when they met again, in a few minutes time.

He was being very well paid for this little job. The whole plan was his, so he couldn't afford to be making any mistakes.

As the man slowly started to make his way towards the taxi office, Dominic pocketed his binoculars, and quickly descended the creaking staircase to the ground floor, to exit the building via the back door.

Walking quietly across the darkened courtyard, he took up a position behind the first gate that led out into the rear alleyway. He stood silently in the pouring rain, listening and concentrating all his senses on to what was taking place on the other side of the gate.

He glanced at his wristwatch; it was a little after a quarter to seven. His night shift at the Milltown Cemetery Crematorium was due to start in three hours. He had plenty of time . . .

Connor stood at the road junction looking around. The need to move slowly was allowing him time to think. The huge picture of the revolutionary socialist, James Connolly, 1868-1916, of Sinn Fein Trade Union Dept, seemed to be looking down at him. It was painted as a mural directly onto the brick wall of the corner building, opposite.

Try as he may, Connor couldn't now remember the significance of the man, who he recalled was executed by firing squad, and subsequently martyred for his beliefs. He looked along the graffiti covered wall, topped with razor wire, a depressing reminder of the more recent turbulent history, associated with this area of Belfast City. 'End British rule,' was emblazoned in large, black spray-painted, block capitals. It took him straight back to those days of heated student debates during the seventies. Evenings when the literati gathered to discuss popular and controversial issues such as this. He and Lizzy had proudly regarded themselves to be associate members of that unique little clique of educated people, who loved the cut and thrust of a good debate. He was reminded of the seedy little spit-and-sawdust types of establishment that they chose to frequent. Often they would have to sit and listen, unimpressed, to some fanatical extremist, attempting to rally support, by spouting off with a load of rehearsed, clichéd, rhetorical rubbish. They really enjoyed seeing such people reduced to being little more than a highly embarrassed, gibbering idiot. Often, all that was necessary, was a single unexpectedly difficult and searching question, to which there was no prepared stock answer. He and Lizzy had spent many hours thinking up and formulating such questions.

Back in the good old days, there was always a dank, smokey, depressing odour to the City. Connor took a deep breath, and decided that seemingly little had changed over the intervening thirty-odd years.

Crossing diagonally over the road, Connor stood with his back to the galvanised steel gates. He had noticed that they were indeed unlocked, beckoning him to enter. He waited while a car came up Rockmount Street to the junction, there to pause briefly, before going left onto the Falls Road. He was fairly sure that the driver, a young man, hadn't even noticed him. He looked all around, there was nobody else in sight.

A gentle push with his backside caused the gate to swing inwards with a loud squeal from the un-oiled hinges. Dominic, who lived in the first house past the gates, had purposely left them that way. It was part of his alarm system.

Connor quickly slipped into the alleyway and turned to push the gate shut again. The noise from the hinges put his teeth on edge, and in the deathly silence, sounded horrendously loud. He pushed over the sliding latch and replaced the padlock left hanging open on the wire. It snapped shut with an audible click. Connor turned to look up the alleyway. It was almost pitch dark, the only light coming from the offset street lighting at his end. He paused for a few seconds to allow his eyes to become accustomed to the gloom. With one hand on the wall to his right, Connor started to make his way slowly along the alley, feeling his way with his feet, trying to avoid the puddles, while steadying himself with his outstretched hand running along the wall.

Dominic, from his hiding place behind the gate, heard the squeal of the gate hinges, and then the snick of the lock being replaced. With his ear held close to the woodwork of the gate, he faintly detected the sound of slowly moving footsteps on the gravel. A faint scuffle, only inches from his ear, caused him to hastily draw back. Connors outstretched hand had just passed across the woodwork. Dominic counted the footsteps up to five, and then silently opened the gate. In the darkness he could just about make out the dark shape of a man. He reached into his pockets and drew out two items. The first was a powerful Maglite torch, the second, an eighteen-inch length of cycle inner tubing, tightly packed with wet sand, to make a cosh.

He moved swiftly up behind the shadowy figure, grabbed a shoulder and dragged the person around. He immediately switched on the torch to shine it into their face, knowing that the light would dazzle whoever it was.

"Who are you, and what do you want?" He demanded. His cosh was held at the ready.

Connor had nearly shit himself. It took him a second or two to recover enough from the shock, to be able to answer.

"Jesus Christ, you scared me half to death. I'm Connor. Christina brought me here to see Marty."

"Good. I'm Dominic. Sorry, my friend, but we can't be too careful. Go through the next gate on your right, it's not locked."

He shone the torch to indicate the location of the gate, three or four paces ahead. Relieved, and with his heartbeat still striving to return to normal, Connor did as he was asked. The gate opened to a gentle push and he stepped forward into the dark courtyard, aware that the man, Dominic, was following close behind. He still hadn't any idea what his chaperone looked like.

It was dry in the covered courtyard. The rain pitter-pattered noisily on the corrugated plastic roof sheeting over his head. In the darkness, there was a sound of running water away to his left somewhere. He shook himself of the loose raindrops, and while attempting to wipe his face dry with his handkerchief, he turned to see where Dominic was.

In the deflected torchlight, Connor saw that he was turning the key in the gate to lock it behind them. The dim outline revealed Dominic to be a man of quite huge proportions. He turned to face Connor again and indicated ahead with the torch beam.

"Through that door over there, it should be open."

Connor turned and took a step in the direction indicated. It was his last. He felt his jacket collar being grabbed from behind an instant before the cosh came down onto the back of his head. It was delivered with just sufficient force to render him unconscious, without breaking the skin of his skull. Dominic wanted no blood.

Gently lowered his limp body to the ground, which was covered over with a piece of blue, reinforced plastic sheeting, Dominic gave a grunt of satisfaction for a job well done. He turned Connor onto his back.

In such a manner so as to illuminate the area, he propped his torch on top of a few bricks, then went to fetch a sports holdall he had previously stored in the far corner of the courtyard. Starting with his shoes and socks, he set about removing all of Connors clothing. It took him only a minute or two, for this was something that Dominic was well practiced, and particularly adept at doing. Next, he located in the holdall, a glasses case. It contained a hypodermic syringe filled with a lethal dose of heroin. The solution was double the dose, and five times the acceptable strength. Kneeling to his task, he flicked at Connors arm to locate and raise a vein. He then carefully administered the injection. From that moment on, Connor was a dying man.

Replacing the syringe into the glasses case, he put it into his jacket pocket. The next item to come from the holdall was a little digital camera that had been given to him specifically for the purpose. Standing astride Connors chest, Dominic took two close-up portrait type photographs, of his face. Then by turning his head first one way, and then the other, two more, profile pictures. The camera then joined the glasses case, in his pocket.

His next task was to carry out a careful inspection of Connor's whole body. Dominic was looking for any scarring that might indicate evidence of any major surgery. He paid particular attention to the chest area, in case there might be a pacemaker, and the hips, looking to see if they might be artificial replacements.

Satisfied there was nothing untoward, Dominic loosely tied Connors wrists and then his ankles, together as he was shown how to do in a previous employment, when he was an Undertaker's Assistant.

He shuffled and rolled Connor over to align his body to one edge of the plastic sheet, and then proceeded to wrap it tightly around him, twice rolling him over, to form a parcel. The overhanging ends of the sheet were folded back over, and tied securely around the ankles and neck, to complete the package.

His last task was to fetch a huge wheelie suitcase from the same corner that he had stored the sports holdall. Laying it open on the ground beside Connor, he lifted his feet until he was able to get his backside over the edge of the case. It was then a simple task to lift and manoeuvre the head end in, as well. Turning Connor onto his side in the case, Dominic forced his body into the foetal position, thus enabling him to close, and lock, the suitcase. He stood it upright and wheeled it around in a circle to test the balance, weight and handling. Connor weighed nearly fourteen stone, 195lbs. This was over three times the recommended maximum gross weight for the suitcase. Dominic carefully applied lifting pressure to the handles. The case handles creaked and groaned in protest, but they held. He hadn't far to go, it would have to do, he thought.

He roughly folded Connor's clothes, and put them all into the holdall, adding the camera from his pocket. All of Connor's personal belongings, his wallet, watch, pen, wedding ring, gold cuff links and tie pin, his hotel and car keys, they all went into a clear plastic bag, and were placed in the side pocket of the holdall.

Dominic had paused for a few seconds to admire the gold Patek Philippe Calatrava wristwatch. He thought that it was probably worth three times what he was getting paid for this little job, but then Christina would certainly know that, and he wasn't prepared to risk anything where she was concerned. Besides, whatever else he might be, Dominic wasn't a thief.

He shone the torch around to see that there was nothing he might have overlooked then glanced at his own wristwatch again. It was nearing seven-fifteen. The first part of the job had taken him less than twenty minutes. Now, he had to dispose of the body in such a way as to make it completely untraceable.

Dominic Schwedler's grandfather had been a white Afrikaner, whose family had fled their small coffee plantation in Kenya, to escape the Mau Mau uprising during the nineteen-fifties. They had finally settled in Belfast where his father had found regular employment working as a Mortuary Attendant, in the Royal Victoria Hospital. Converting to Catholicism, he had married a local girl, a nurse, working in the Orthopaedic Unit.

Dominic was born in 1968, soon after the couple had bought their little two-bedroom house in Rockmount Street. As a child, he had listened to the conversations between his parents. They always seemed to revolve around deaths, or terrible injuries, sustained by people they knew, or had known, during the Troubles, as the sectarian and political turmoil came to be known. Both of his parents were pro-active IRA, and loyal *Sinn Fein* supporters, and with typical Gaelic mentality, Dominic merely continued to follow their example.

On leaving school, he wasn't exactly well qualified for anything, so it was inevitable that Dominic should wish to follow in his parent's footsteps. He was a big lad, and quickly found employment with a local undertaker, initially as a junior pallbearer, but there was always the promise that, eventually, he would be trained as an Assistant to the Embalmer. These had been some of the happiest days of his rather macabre life. Without showing any emotion, he had even assisted in the embalming of his own parents, now dead for the past nineteen years.

The Undertaking Company had folded following the death of the owner, and that is when Dominic had found his job with the Belfast Corporation's Crematorium in the Milltown Cemetery. He had now worked there for over twelve years, and was in charge of the three-man night shift. Dominic knew the job inside out, and this included all the nefarious ways with which to exploit his privileged position.

The night shift at the Crematorium usually dealt with the backlog of bodies that accumulated as a result of the totally inadequate facilities for dealing with them. Belfast City, together with it's growing urban sprawl, now numbered a population approaching 700,000 people. Like so many large cities, there was a huge drugs and alcohol related death rate. Poverty and unemployment led to widespread depredation, and inevitably fuelled the rise of the drugs and crime syndicates, who fought with each other for supremacy.

The City mortuaries were stuffed full of bodies awaiting disposal. Generally, these people were the dregs of society, drug addicts and alcoholics, people who had finally succumbed to their addictions. Many had lost everything, and had been forced into living rough, on the streets. They became the down-and-outs, with no fixed abode. Then there were the forgotten ones, the elderly, whose relations had no time, or money, to support them when they were alive, let alone pay for a funeral at their passing. The City nursing homes were God's waiting rooms, filled to overflowing with them.

The evening and night shifts were expected to process as many of these poor unfortunates, as it was possible for them to handle. There were no complications where they were concerned. No ashes to be collected, no services of remembrance, no grieving relatives to placate.

One after the other, they were loaded onto the motorised trolleys and fed into the retorts. The barest details, their name, where known, their sex, and most importantly, their weight, were entered into the programmable logic controller, via the touch screen. Having entered the required details, the operator, with a touch of the 'start' button, would set into motion the computerised crematory processes.

The temperature inside the retort chamber would need to be something between 1050 and 1150 degrees Celsius, to facilitate a successful cremation process. The time it would take would vary according to the size, and density, of the particular body in the retort, but this aspect was all monitored and controlled by the computer. Generally, it would take approximately ninety minutes to reduce an average sized male to a pile of charred bones. These would then need to be pulverized in the cremulator, a crushing process that took a further twenty minutes. The final result would be about six pounds of human ashes. Finely crushed bone fragments, with the consistency of coarse sand, that could be distributed over consecrated ground.

Dominic was the man in charge of the night shift. It was he that would be supervising everything. He would rotate the tasks so that each of the team took a turn at loading the retorts, clearing and collecting the bone to be crushed, and operating the cremulator, while sifting out the gleanings. Small fragments of gold and other precious metals, not removed from the body before cremation.

At some stage, usually while one of the others was on meal break, and it was his turn to load, he would slip one extra body into the system. He would give it a false identity by 'doubling-up' on one of the other retorts. An illegal process whereby it was possible to cremate two smaller bodies together as one. This would create one extra identification tablet to keep the records straight. As long as he was the one to unload, on the other side of the retort, after cremation, nobody would ever be any the wiser. By eight o'clock tomorrow morning, the end of the night shift. Connor McCall's body will be reduced to just another pile of human ashes.

Easy, like taking money for old rope. Dominic had done it several times before . . .

He wheeled the suitcase to the end of the alleyway, and quietly unlocked the steel gates. He looked outside to check there was no one around. Dominic's old Volvo Estate car was parked just outside of his house. He unlocked and lifted the rear tailgate in readiness. Wheeling the suitcase to the back of the car, he placed it up against the big rear bumper. Shunning the use of the vulnerable handles, and in one easy movement, he hefted it from the bottom, up into the back of the car. Quietly closing the tailgate, he re-locked the car, and went back for the holdall.

Five minutes later, Dominic delivered the holdall and contents, to the lady waiting in the Belfast black cab, parked just inside St

James's Road. There was no conversation, it was unnecessary, for there was nothing to be said. In exchange for the holdall, he received an envelope full of tatty, used, and untraceable banknotes, pounds sterling, and euros.

Tony Williams sat contemplating the remains of his third large whiskey and soda. He was the only one left in the bar, now, and the steward was trying to look busy by polishing all the tabletops. He wanted to get rid of his last customer and close-up for the night. He took the initiative.

"Can I get you another, sir?"

"Eh, what?" The question brought Tony out of his thoughts. "No, I don't think so, thank you. I think I'll be retiring to my bed now, it's been a long day."

He drained his glass, stood, and picked up the small brown envelope, replacing the three handwritten sheets of paper, before returning it to his inside pocket. He glanced up at the wall clock as he made towards the exit from the bar. It told him that it was just on ten forty-five.

Taking the lift to the first floor he walked slowly along the corridor. Pausing outside of room 211, he tapped gently on the door. Tony already knew that it was a futile gesture, made more in hope, than anything else. He had been watching the hotel entrance area all evening, awaiting his son's return. Unless he had come in via a back entrance, or fire escape, there was no possible way that he could have failed to see him. After a minute of repeated knocking on the door, he trudged disappointedly along to his own room.

As he went through his bedtime ablution routine, Tony surmised that Connor and the Thompson's must have been making a night of it? Probably a nightclub or casino, he thought. Their reunion would have to wait until breakfast, now. Putting all thoughts out of his mind, he put his head on the pillow, and went out like a light.

At eleven-thirty that evening, the Night Porter admitted a gentleman bearing a remarkable resemblance to Connor McCall. Wearing his clothes, and having the same height, build, and hairstyle, the CCTV camera was not able to discern any noticeable difference. The Porter had never met Connor before, so he wouldn't have known him, anyway. As he came into the Reception area, the man produced his room key card, as proof of his identity.

"Good evening, Porter. I'm Mr McCall, room 211. Could you just confirm for me, please, that there is a taxi coming at five-fifteen, to take me to the City Airport?"

The Porter consulted the desk diary.

"Yes, that is correct, Mr McCall. There is also a telephone message for you here, as well, sir. It's from a Mr Brian Thompson, who called earlier this afternoon."

He handed the man a folded telephone message sheet, which he read. Screwing it up, he handed it back to the Porter to be discarded.

"Thank you, Porter, but I was already aware of that. Tell me, is my bill prepared. I don't want to be messing about too much in the morning?"

"It is, sir. Do you want to be paying it now?"

"If I may."

The Porter handed him an itemised bill, which he appeared to check through very carefully. Satisfied, he reached into his inside jacket pocket for his wallet.

"Yes, that seems to be perfectly in order, thank you. I have already given you my credit card details, but I have now decided to pay in cash, instead. I have five hundred Euros, and the remainder will be in pounds Sterling. So if you would kindly do the calculation for me, please . . ."

The man waited patiently as the Porter worked it all out. He then passed over the required amount rounded up to the nearest pound over the total, adding a generous tip for the man's troubles. He wanted to ensure that he would be well-remembered. The man then bade the Porter a polite goodnight, before making his way up to room 211.

Tony Williams awoke with a start. It took him several seconds to work out exactly where he was, and why he was there. He looked at his watch. It was seven thirty. Dragging himself out of the comfortable warmth of his bed, he padded into his bathroom. He turned on the shower, allowing it to warm up while he stood patiently, trying to relieve himself. The tinkling of the running water seemed to act as a psychological encouragement for him to pee. Like so many men of his age, Tony had an embarrassing prostate problem that sometimes made it difficult for him. One day, he would need to seek some medical advice about it . . .

He had no toilet bag, so had to make do with the totally inadequate little pieces of soap, and sachets of shampoo, supplied by the hotel. He wished he had his own razor, as well. The little disposable one had barely touched his chin when it snapped off at the head. He was forced into abandoning any idea of a shave completely. He hated facing the world with a day's growth of beard on his chin. He always thought that it reflected a slovenly attitude.

He had a clean vest and pants, shirt and socks. All the rest was the same as he'd worn the day before. He used one of his dirty socks, with a little bit of spit, to restore a shine to his slightly scuffed shoes.

Satisfied that his appearance was the best that could be achieved in the circumstances, he let himself out of his room, and headed for Connor's. He rapped hard on the door of room 211. There was no reply. Perhaps he had already gone down to breakfast? He made his way down to the Dining Room, and then to Reception.

The Receptionist, the same one who he had spoken to yesterday, had only just started her shift. She remembered her generous elderly guest, and greeted him with a beaming smile.

"Good Morning, Mr Williams, how may I help you?"

"Would you be so kind as to buzz room 211, for me please. I can't seem to locate my son anywhere, perhaps he's overslept, or something?"

The Receptionist looked at him a little confused. She checked her computer screen, and then the desk diary.

"I'm sorry, Mr Williams, but Mr McCall checked out earlier this morning. The Night Porter confirms that a taxi we booked for five-fifteen, to take him to City Airport, picked him up on time. Didn't he mention anything to you last evening?"

"I never saw him. I waited up for him, but when he hadn't returned to the hotel by eleven o'clock, I went to bed. Tell me, do you still happen to have the telephone number of the people, the Thompson's, that you looked up for my son yesterday?"

"I can certainly look it up for you again, sir. A Mr B. Thompson, wasn't it?"

"Yes, that's correct. Brian and Sarah Thompson, 76, Beechmount Avenue, Ballymagarry. Here's the piece of paper you gave me."

"If you'll bear with me for a few moments, Mr Williams, I'll find it again for you, sir. I just need to get my desk organised and see to this gentleman first. Can I help you, sir?"

Tony Williams stood back from the desk to make way for another man who had come up behind him. He saw the man open his wallet to identify himself, and clearly heard the conversation.

"Good morning, miss. Can you tell me, please, is there a Mr Connor McCall in the hotel, I need to speak with him?"

The Receptionist looked from one man to the other, unsure of what she should say, or do, next. Everyone seemed to be interested in the mysterious Mr McCall? She was getting fed up with being pestered . . .

"Look, I have no idea what is going on here, but as I've just told this gentleman," She indicated to Tony, "Mr McCall checked out early this morning. He booked a taxi to take him to City Airport. The Night Porter processed his bill, and has confirmed in the desk diary that he was picked up on time. That is as much as I can tell you."

The man looked at Tony.

"Good morning, sir. I'm Detective Constable Franklin, Belfast Police. Would you care to identify yourself and tell me exactly what your interest in Connor McCall is, if you please?"

"My name is Tony Williams. Connor McCall is my son, and business partner. I am trying to get to speak with him before he does anything stupid. I fear that he is suffering from some sort of mental breakdown. He left home in England over a week ago, without telling anyone where he was going, or the reason why. It's not like him, at all, and I'm very worried."

"Sorry, sir, but did you say Mr McCall is your son, and that your name is Williams?"

"McCall was his mother's maiden name. It's a long story, but that is the name he chose to keep. The reasons are irrelevant, believe me. Why do the Police want to talk to Connor. What has he done?"

"Nothing in the Province, as far as we know, sir. We were rather hoping that he might be able to help us with our enquiries into another incident, the details of which, I am not at liberty to disclose."

Franksy realised that he was getting himself into deep water. He was under expressed instructions to keep everything under a tight wrap until they were sure of what they were dealing with. His only reason for asking for McCall that morning, was to identify his target. Franks didn't even know what he looked like.

"Shall we go and find somewhere a little quieter, sir. I shall need to take some more details from you? Then I'll do a few checks to try and establish where Mr McCall might be now. We can help each other, here . . ."

An hour later, Franksy was on the blower to his Sergeant, Ken Brody.

"He's gone, Sarge, back to England, I've just checked with the Airport. He checked in on flight BE985 to Southampton, that took off at 0650 this morning. His flight will have already landed over there by now. I've got his father here at the hotel. He's beside himself with worry, reckons McCall was having some sort of a nervous breakdown. He's just checking out to go after him. What do you want me to do now?"

"Just stay there with the father for the time being, Franksy. I'll need to talk to Davey on this one. I'll get back to you as soon as I have anything more . . ."

"Yes, sir. I've just finished speaking with Customs and Immigration at Southampton Airport. They have him on their CCTV, going through at 0822 this morning. He wasn't checked specifically, but then there was no reason for them to do so, was there? What are your instructions now, sir. Franksy is still at the hotel where McCall's father is checking out. I don't think that there's any mileage left in this one for us now, sir. Shall I be calling him back in? I could really do with him here this morning. We're a bit snowed under with other work."

Commander Flanagan was smiling to himself. This was the best news he could have wished to hear. Absolute confirmation that the man was officially seen to be leaving the Province, and further, that he had been positively identified as arriving back in England.

"Yes alright, Ken. I see no point in detaining the father. He's a solicitor, so we're not about to get anything much out of him. Call DC Franklin back in, and put everything back on hold for a few days, just in case something else crops up from our surveillance on McCue."

"Yes, sir."

The phone went dead. Ken slowly replaced the receiver, a thoughtful expression on his face. How did the COC know that McCall's father was a solicitor? He couldn't recall reading that fact anywhere in the file . . .

"Christina?"

"Yes. Hello, Davey."

"I'm just calling to say, well done. I'm due to meet with the Deputy First Minister at a civic function this evening. Can I assure him that the immediate problem has now been fully resolved?"

"Yes, we think so. How's your man?"

"Broken collar bone, slight concussion, and a few minor grazes. I understand that he's keen to be back at work. I've told his Sergeant to put him on light duties. He'll be alright, I'm sure."

"Glad to hear it. And the file?"

"What file?"

There was a chuckle on the other end of the line before it went dead.

# Chapter 13

Sunday at Oakwood hadn't started too well. Malcolm had planned to take Sharon down to the river for an hour or two's fishing before breakfast. She had been very quiet and preoccupied since Tony Williams' hurried departure, and Malcolm was keen to lift her mood and get a smile back on to her face again.

The atrocious weather conditions had immediately put paid to their fishing. A deep Atlantic depression had moved in during the early hours, bringing with it a band of heavy rain that was falling like stair-rods. Ordinarily, Malcolm would have donned his waterproofs and coped with the conditions, but the occasional flash of lightning convinced him that, in the interests of self preservation, it perhaps wasn't such a good idea to be waving a wet, carbon fibre fishing rod, around.

Ever the one to make the best of a bad situation, Malcolm persuaded Sharon to join him in his bed. Their lovemaking had been slightly lacking in the usual fervour, but for her, it served as a release for some pent-up emotions. Now, in their post-coital relaxation, the couple lay comfortably in each other's arms, quietly talking things through, and making plans for the week ahead.

Sharon expressed her intention to accompany her mother's body back to Ireland, on her own. Her mother's last wish was that, with the minimum of fuss, she be finally laid to rest close to her place of birth. There existed a small family plot within the Londonderry City Cemetery.

Sharon intended to make first contact with her aunt and grandmother, by telephone, later that day. There was a need to discuss with them, who exactly should be invited to the funeral service. Not perhaps the best way to make contact with ones family for the first time, was it? Malcolm understood her concerns.

Breakfast was a leisurely affair. The bad weather conditions were forecast to persist well into the late morning before showing any signs of abating. Malcolm took the opportunity to ask everyone, including the Carters', if they would like to join him in the lounge, where he would outline and confirm his plans for the immediate commencement of the Elizabeth Courtenay Memorial Hospital.

He made his presentation, and there then followed a long period of discussion from which the children, now thoroughly bored, excused themselves in favour of one last horse ride, before the prospect of returning to school the next day.

Malcolm then sprang another surprise, by calmly announcing that he had just asked the Estate Management Company to initiate urgent negotiations to purchase a nearby, recently vacated, residential retirement home premises.

Grey Gables, as the house is named, is situated a little further along the road from Oakwood, and stands within a mile of the hospital development. He considered that it was too good an opportunity to pass up. Reading from his notes, he gave them a brief description of the property.

The three-storey, Portland stone, building had originally been built as an Edwardian gentleman's country house residence. Standing in formal gardens extending over three acres, there was an additional seventeen acres of arable land and paddocks, some with stabling, that had fallen into disrepair due to lack of use. The curtilage of land extended right down to the river, on the other side of the road, and immediately below the road bridge, that was the southern boundary of Malcolm's stretch. When acquired, it would provide another two hundred and eighty yards of valuable riparian fishing rights. They all smiled knowingly to each other at this piece of information, for it clearly had significant influence in Malcolm's decision to seek purchase of the property.

The main house had originally been built with six large bedrooms, but in the late sixties, when it was converted to a retirement home, it had undergone sympathetic and tasteful extensions using similar building materials. With the addition of a new wing at either end of the building, and enlarged kitchens leading out onto a south facing sun terrace at the rear, it now boasted a total of eighteen bedrooms, most of them en-suite, and still comfortably furnished with all the basics.

Like Oakwood, Grey Gables is now a grade two listed building, and although structurally very sound, and generally in very good order, the design and layout of much of the interior, had apparently failed to meet all the new stringent rules and safety regulations that governed buildings being used solely for the care of the elderly.

His discreet enquiries had revealed that because of the prohibitive cost of making all the necessary alterations, and the strict planning constraints as to the buildings future use, the consortium that owned the property, now considered it to be a bit of a white elephant. He had correctly surmised that they were probably very keen to sell, and for a simple, quick transaction, it might be available at a hugely knocked down price? He had, accordingly, left explicit instruction with the Estate Management Solicitors to the effect that no matter what it took to acquire, a signed, 'sale agreed' document, was to be on his desk by the end of the coming week.

He had stressed the degree of urgency by pointing out that if the vendors got wind of the commencement of the hospital project, there might well be a significant hike in the selling price. It was a good point, and while everyone agreed with him, it prompted some further discussion. David questioned whether or not it might be better to perhaps delay the commencement of the building project, until firm agreement on the purchase had been reached? Malcolm though, was adamant. Nothing was going to delay the start of the hospital, for in that respect, time was not on their side. He then went on to explain his reasons for wishing to acquire the property, even though everyone had already worked it all out for themselves.

Besides being an excellent investment, and a substantial addition to Oakwood, he thought that, initially, the house might be used to accommodate not only the extra staff now needed to help the Carters at Oakwood, but also many of the essential personnel that were soon going to be working on the hospital project. Long term, he could foresee the house would eventually become a nurse's hostel. He also envisaged that much of the land would be put to good use, in providing fresh, organically grown produce, for use in the hospital, and hostel, kitchens.

His reasoning was sound, and it effectively ended any further discussion on the subject. The Carters took the opportunity to excuse themselves from the gathering in order to catch up on their work.

George and Edith had already agreed to stay on at Oakwood for another week. George's intention was to complete the draught statements, and then to help Sharon with the funeral arrangements. Edith wanted to assist Sue and David in packing up their home in New Milton, and to help with getting the twins settled into their new schools.

After discussion with the children, it was agreed that for the time being, Rita should be a day pupil at St Swithun's, at least until she had made a few friends, and felt comfortable with the prospect of becoming a boarder. David and Sue had very few concerns in her regard, she was as keen as mustard.

Surprisingly, it was Peter who was proving to be more of a problem. There just wasn't a school for boys of his age, of a similar calibre to St Swithun's, anywhere within the immediate locality of Winchester. After much discussion and deliberation, it was decided that Peter should be offered the chance of becoming a boarding pupil at the Hordle Walhampton School, near Lymington, in the New Forest.

Both parents agreed that it was vitally important that their children be given equal opportunity, and access to the best education that they could possibly afford. After another brief discussion with Malcolm, who had re-confirmed his previous offer of private educational facilities for the children, the decision was made. For David and Sue, all that was needed was to convince Peter, that this was the best thing for him.

To that end, they planned that Sue would take Rita to St Swithun's for enrolment, while David took Peter to Walhampton. Both parents doubted that it would be possible for their children to be able to start school immediately, as there was the obvious necessity to fit them out with their respective uniforms, and other, yet to be identified, essential requisites. It was hoped that after all the introduction and admission formalities were complete, they could all meet up again for a shopping trip either to Southampton or Bournemouth. David and Sue both recognised that with the minimum of fuss, there was a need to get the children settled, and back into full-time education, as quickly as possible.

David, always looking to identify the possible difficulties, pointed out that in the long term, it would be onerous to have to drop off, and collect Peter from the school each day. But as they had already planned to go to New Milton to pack everything up, certainly for the next week, it wasn't going to be all that difficult. Ultimately, both parents identified the need was to get Peter settled into a school where, above all, he would be happy. In trying to discuss it with him, they both sensed that for some reason, there was some degree of reticence, to become a boarding school pupil.

David asked Charlotte and Michelle to talk to the twins some more. This time to extol upon the virtues and advantages to be found in a boarding school environment. The girls didn't need too much encouragement, for the reality was, that they wouldn't have it any other way. David listened in as they spoke to the twins.

Charlotte took the lead in explaining that they both regarded school to be their place of learning. Out of necessity, a disciplined environment, where they were expected to get their heads down, and devote the majority of their time to study, whilst being ably assisted by the teachers, who were always on hand to assist.

For them, it made coming home during the usual school term breaks, and very occasionally, for a weekend, an absolute delight. It was regarded as a time to temporarily set aside the school routines, and, with homework projects completed, to be able to do whatever took their fancy. Coming home to their own rooms, made them much more appreciative of everything they possessed, as well.

Michelle pointed out that boarding pupils always seemed to do better than their day school counterparts. To be a boarder was far better, she said, for there were no pressures associated with having to travel backwards and forwards to school each day. For her, the weeks between school holidays always seemed to fly by. It was after all, only four or five weeks, that they were away, and then it was half term again, and possibly, a week spent back at home. She added that it was great fun to find oneself temporarily outside of any parental guidance and control. She thought that being given the opportunity to make some decisions for herself had prompted her into acting more responsibly. Charlotte agreed with her.

David smiled to himself. He thought that this might have been said more for his benefit than anything else? He remembered some of his own wild, dormitory parties, and recalled that he certainly hadn't been acting responsibly, when to satisfy a dare, and a small wager, he had climbed up onto the roof of the girl's dormitory, to hang a pair of frilly pink knickers over one of the chimney pots. He wondered what sort of similar mischief a bunch of teenage girls could think up?

Even after the little pep talk, Peter still remained unconvinced. He just couldn't bring himself to share in his sister's obvious enthusiasm to become a boarder, and couldn't understand why she was choosing to attend a school that would effectively split them apart? He had already tried to get her to persuade their parents to let them both attend Walhampton, a co-educational establishment, rather than St Swithun's, an all-girl's school, but Rita was having none of it.

Emily lay awake in her bed listening to her brother and sister's whispered bickering on the other side of the room. Little disputes between the pair were fairly commonplace, but on this occasion, she sensed that there was far more, a much deeper rift developing, and it was in danger of threatening all her carefully laid plans. Rather than transmit her words telepathically, she got out of her bed and went over to her sister's, climbing in beside her.

Telepathic communication between Emily and her brother and sister, had long been established, but was rarely used. Peter always seemed to resent Emily's frequent attempts to join in with their conversations and activities. Emily sensed that the main reason for this was due to their age difference, and also because of her extraordinary mental capabilities, which Peter couldn't quite come to terms with. Unlike Rita, he absolutely refused to accept that his little sister could be cleverer than he. She was only two years old, after all . . . Rita shuffled over to make more room for her little sister.

"Sorry, Emily, are we keeping you awake?"

Emily chose to answer her telepathically, so that Peter couldn't hear what was being said.

'Not really, Rita, but I was listening to you and Peter arguing. I don't like it when you do that, it frightens me.'

'Peter doesn't like it because I'm going to a different school, Em. He wants us to be together like we always have, but I don't want to, anymore.'

"Why not, Rita?"

'I really don't know, Em. I just feel that I'm getting fed up with always trying to do everything better than Peter. I'm growing up into a big girl now, and I feel that I want to be with other girls of my own age. Peter thinks that because I don't want to go to the same school, I don't love him anymore.'

'Can I tell you what I am sensing, Rita?'

She put her arms around her baby sister to give her a little cuddle, and they snuggled down into the bed together. Rita had always been closer to Emily than Peter. They both understood that it is not in a boy's nature to outwardly express their feelings for each other in the same way that girls do.

'Yes, of course, Em. Tell me what you think.'

'I am sensing that Peter is frightened of being on his own, Rita. All your life, you and he have done everything together. Now, you are telling him that you don't want it to be like that anymore. He is confused, Rita, and he doesn't understand your reasons why. I think Peter needs to be reassured that we both still love him.'

Peter was watching his two sisters, and he understood the silence.

"I know that you two are talking about me over there. What are you saying?"

Rita reverted back to normal speech.

"Me and Emily think that you're too scared to go to school on your own, Peter."

"Scared? Who says I'm scared? That's rubbish. I'm not scared of anything. And what would she know anyway, she's only a baby?"

"If you're not a little scaredy-cat, Peter, then why are you so against me not wanting to go to the same school as you? It doesn't make any sense. Mummy and Daddy have already told us that it will only be for two years, and then we will both be going to the same school as Charlotte and Michelle. It's not my fault that St Swithun's doesn't allow boys of your age, Peter, and I really liked everything that I saw when we visited the school, yesterday. Besides all of that, I was just telling Emily that I'm growing up now, and I feel the need to be in the company of girls of my own age. It doesn't mean that I've stopped caring for you, Peter. Emily and I both love you, you know that, but you can be a real pain, sometimes. I think it will do us both good to be apart for a few days each week."

"I'm not a scaredy-cat, Rita, so don't dare call me that again. I don't like it, you hear? Anyway, Mum says that there are boys, and girls, at Walhampton. So what's the difference?"

Peter was whining, now, and Rita detected that the argument was almost won. She raised her voice an octave to deliver what she considered to be her final word on the matter.

"There are boys there, Peter. That's the difference. I don't want to be going to a school where there are any boys. We are being given the choice, Peter, and I want to go to an all-girls school. Now, Emily and I want to go to sleep. You can come and cuddle up with us if you want."

And that was how their parents found them in the morning. The three children all snuggled up together in a single bed, with Sam lying at the foot, keeping an ever-watchful eye.

The Belfast City flight BE997 into Southampton, landed at 1930hrs, five minutes late on its scheduled arrival time. Just as soon as airport regulations dictated that he was allowed, Tony Williams was on the phone to his daughter-in-law, Lizzie, for an update on Connor. She answered his call on the first ring.

"Is he home yet?"

"No."

"Have you heard from him? Has he phoned?"

"No. I've been here beside the phone all day, waiting . . ."

Tony could detect from the tremor in her voice that she was overwrought and very close to tears.

"I'm still at the airport. I'll check around the car park to see if his car has gone. If it's not here, I'll see if the car-parking people are able to tell me when it left. Chin up, Liz, at least we know that he's back in England. Have a little think, see if you can come up with somewhere he might have gone. I'll call you back if I find out anything at this end."

Tony deposited his luggage into the boot of his own car before walking around the whole of the Southampton Airport Car Park, up and down the rows of all three storeys. There was no sign of Connor's car, so he made his way to the office.

"Yes, mate, what can I do for you?"

"I was wondering if you could help me, please. I've been looking for my son's car. It's a maroon Morris Minor Traveller, the old 'woody' type. Do you know what I mean?"

"Yeh, I know the one. Lovely old car. I was admiring it only the other day. It's been here for a week or more. It's parked up on the far side of the first floor, as I remember."

"I don't think that it's there now. I've just walked all around the car park looking for it. I'm fairly certain that my son arrived back here on this morning's early Belfast flight. Do you think that it would be possible to check your security cameras to see exactly when it left for me, please? I would be ever so grateful . . ."

"Unless it's deemed to be urgent, we're not supposed to do that, mate, it's against the rules. Is this some sort of an emergency, perhaps?"

"My son might be suffering from a nervous breakdown. So, yes, you could say that."

Tony produced his wallet from his breast pocket and carefully extracted a crisp, new, twenty-pound note. It hadn't gone unnoticed, and had the desired affect.

"In that case, let's see what we can do for you, sir . . ."

"The security cameras picked him up leaving the airport at 0842 this morning, Liz. He paid for his parking using his debit card, so it must have been him. The pictures on the camera are a bit fuzzy, but it was clear enough for me to see that it was definitely Connor driving. So, if he's not come home, where on earth could he have taken himself off to now, do you think?"

"I don't know, dad. I've been racking my brains trying to think. He's got lots of friends in the local gypsy community, but I can't imagine that he's gone over to see any of them? Why would he, anyway? What's he running away from, dad?"

"Liz, I'm afraid that I might just know the answer to that one, my dear. Look, I'm coming over to stay at yours for a few more days. I'll explain everything when I get there, but you might not like what I'm about to tell you, so you had better prepare yourself for a bit of a shock."

Monday morning at Oakwood was decidedly hectic. Malcolm, anxious to avoid the worst of the motorway traffic on his journey to the clinic, near Aldershot, was the first to leave.

To ease the pressure on the Carters, Sharon volunteered herself to take Charlotte and Michelle to school. She thought that the one-hour journey time would give them all an ideal opportunity for a little frank exchange of views. For her part, and in order to get the girls on-side, Sharon felt that she first needed to commend them both for their excellent efforts in managing to keep the twins entertained and occupied over the past week. Malcolm had said as much to her only that morning, but as he wasn't there to deliver the message himself, she thought that she would do it for him.

After dropping the girls at Canford, Sharon planned to go on to Weymouth to spend some time, alone, packing, and sorting through some of her mother's things. She felt the need for some time to herself, for there was some serious thinking to do.

Her first phone call to her newfound relations in Ireland, made the previous evening, had been a little awkward, to say the least. Following the initial introductions, her elderly grandmother, obviously ignorant of the recent events and circumstances, had rather thoughtlessly, started to ask her many quite personal, and upsetting questions. This was not at all what Sharon had expected, and she was quite taken aback. Out of respect, she had held her tongue, but found it very difficult to answer her politely. It became apparent from the tone of her grandmother's voice, that for some reason, there was a strong undercurrent of resentment toward her. Her antagonistic attitude had put Sharon very close to tears again, necessitating that she cut the call short.

Her questions regarding who should be invited to the ceremony had remained unasked. Sharon thought that having allowed the dust to settle, she might perhaps give it another try, and call again, later that day. This time, out of necessity, she would try and get things off on a better footing. The last thing she wanted was for there to be any bad feeling at her mother's funeral service.

Sharon also wanted to call in at the police station and collect Doris's jewellery box for Jim, who had given her the necessary written permission.

Unusually, all the children had chosen to breakfast together in the dining room that morning. Charlotte and Michelle, for the most part, were excitedly discussing matters relating to their father's plans for the purchase of Grey Gables.

Their previous afternoon's ride had prompted them all into making a little exploration of the land adjoining the old house. They too, had liked what they had seen, especially the extra paddocks and stabling, for which they had very different plans and ideas to those of their father. They couldn't wait to find out what progress had been made in the acquisition. On the run down to the end of term, they had already worked out the exact number of weeks and days to the commencement of the Christmas holidays, and had begun making tentative plans for Christmas, accordingly.

For the twins, there was an air of anxious anticipation. Peter was strangely quiet. He seemed to have, at last, come to terms with the fact that he and Rita were going to go to different schools. It was, however, abundantly apparent that he still wasn't over-enamoured with the idea. Rita's jibe, accusing him of being a scaredy-cat, had hit home. It had hurt his pride, and effectively stopped all his bickering. His male ego damaged, Peter now felt that he had to prove that he was more than an equal to his sister's perceived challenge to his superiority. His mind was made up. He'd show her . . . Anything she could do, he would do better.


The big old house slowly lapsed into comparative silence as everyone started to depart for his or her different destination. This was the time that the Carters' both hated. Having seen to all the animals, Carter tidied himself up, and served morning coffee to George and Edith, both working quietly in the study, and then to Jim and nurse Jacqui, who together, were looking after Emily, in the library.

Jacqui Strong set her book aside to take a sip from her coffee. A little chuckle from Jim prompted her to look up, and then to spend the next few minutes contemplating with interest, the interaction that was taking place between the man and child. He was comfortably seated at the reading table with Emily on his knee, and they were both intently studying the diagrams contained within some sort of medical textbook. For most of the time, there was no audible conversation to be heard, but it was very evident from the way that they were reacting with each other, that some form of communication was taking place. Jacqui already suspected that this might be some form of telepathy, but never having seen or experienced anything like it before, she found it very difficult to comprehend.

She took another sip of her coffee, and fondly considered the man that was supposed to be her patient. She recognised that there had been yet another hugely significant change in his health and personality over the past week, or so. As his physical condition had continued to rapidly improve, and he had become much more attentive towards her. Her female intuition detected that, despite his age, Jim was wishing to take their relationship into something beyond what it was now. Thinking about it, she wasn't averse to his little advances, in many ways, she found that it was really quite refreshing to be treated like a lady in the old fashioned way. The little things, like polite, attentive, conversation, and having the door opened for one. To be properly seated at a table, and having a strong, comforting arm to hang on to, when out walking. These all served to make her feel quite special.

Jacqui thought about her previous sexual encounters. She knew that there was nothing wrong with her sexuality, but up until now, she had never found a man that was truly able to satisfy her. As such, she had rather given up on men altogether . . . Unless, that is, the right man happened to come along.

Since the incident in the shower, when she had witnessed him becoming aroused, she had found herself waking up during the night to some really quite vivid sexual fantasies, in which Jim featured as the sole object of her desires. At first, she had dismissed the whole idea as being preposterous, totally unprofessional, and absolutely out of the question. But as time progressed, and with the dreams frequently recurring, she had been prompted into re-examining the possibilities.

Any affair that she entered into with Jim, would, out of necessity, have to be kept totally discreet, of course. She shuddered to think what the others would say if they ever found out. In the worst-case scenario, it would probably lead to her being instantly dismissed from her job? On the other hand, Malcolm Blackmore, had perhaps left himself open to somewhat similar criticism, in respect of his relationship with Sharon, she still being his patient? Perhaps, in the circumstances, he would understand and sympathise with the delicate situation, thereby persuading him into turning a blind eye? Could she rely on him seeing that way? It was a huge risk to take, for she loved working for him, in this way.

On reflection, it would definitely be better if their relationship were kept totally discreet. She would need to speak to Jim about it, before they entered into anything more meaningful.

The revelation suddenly hit her. Had she just made up her mind that she was going to have an intimate, sexual, relationship with a man who was certainly old enough to be her grandfather? She had . . .

Reaching thoughtfully for her coffee cup again, she became aware that both Jim and Emily had paused in whatever they had been doing, and were both now looking directly at her. There was a twinkle in Jim's eyes, and there was that affectionate, cheeky smile, that he usually reserved only for her.

He looked directly into her eyes, and Jacqui likened it to having a burning light that seemed to shine directly into the deepest recesses of her mind. After a second or two, she heard his voice, but she was absolutely certain that his lips hadn't moved. The words she heard, were those of tender reassurance.

Jacqui might have thought that the decision that she had just come to, had been all hers to make. Strictly speaking, it was, but then she was totally unaware that her mind, and her decision, had been ever so subtly, manipulated. The suggestion as to her intended course of action, had been subconsciously introduced, and her natural reticence to accepting the affections of a much older man, suppressed, and made to appear less of a consideration. In reality, her mind had been made up for her, and she never really stood a chance . . .

*'Can I ask what is happening, Jo-jo? Why have you just established telepathic contact with this lady?'*

*'I'm not sure that I have a simple answer your question, Emily. Since I took control of parts of this human's brain, certain things have been happening that I am struggling to comprehend. There is an area of this man's psyche over which I have absolutely no control. He is finding the company of this woman to be both pleasurable and exciting, and I am interested to see where this might lead. Rather than try to suppress any of these very powerful urges, I have decided to go along with them. As for my establishing telepathic communication; this woman is this man's constant companion, and physically, I have become a part of him. She has already worked out that there is telepathic communication taking place between us, Emily, and I am sensing that she is beginning to feel somewhat excluded. There is a danger, that if this is allowed to continue, it might cause her to terminate her relationship with him. Do you understand, child? This*

*is very much an adult characteristic that I can only liken to the bond
of affection that exists between your own parents.'*

*'Are you telling me that Jim loves Jacqui, Jo-jo?'*

*'Yes, Emily, I think that is exactly what I am trying to convey to
you. Jim loves Jacqui, like mummy loves daddy.'*

*'And like I love you, Jo-jo. Yes, I understand.'*

She slowly stood up in his lap, and for the first time, wrapped her
little arms around Jim's neck in a tight embrace. Her simple action
induced a whole multitude of emotional feelings within his being,
and in those few moments, the alien within, began to find that which
he had been seeking to acquire . . .

The house phone on the corner of George's desk interrupted his
dictation. He reached to answer it.

"I'm sorry to bother you, sir, but there is a policeman asking if it
would be possible to speak with you."

"That's alright, Carter. Put him through, please." There was a
slight pause as the call was connected.

"Hello, who is that, please?"

"Good morning, sir. This is Detective Sergeant Ahmed Suffajji,
of the West Midlands Regional Crime Squad. Am I speaking to the
solicitor, Mr George Lloyd?"

"You are. Good morning, sergeant. What can I do for you?"

"Sir, I am given to understand that you are preparing some witness
statements in regard to the incident that occurred on Saturday 16th
October, at Bleanaway Quarry, in South Wales, is this correct?"

"It is. I have been liasing with Chief Inspector Ferguson of
New Scotland Yard. I was rather expecting that it would be he, that
would be contacting me again, next week. How may I help you,
sergeant?"

"Sir, there has been some rather unfortunate recent developments
that dictate that the statements you are preparing, should now be
passed directly over to me, instead. New Scotland Yard have, only
this morning, directed that I assume full responsibility for bringing
this enquiry to a conclusion. To that end, would it be possible for
me to come and speak with you, personally? I would appreciate the
opportunity to examine your work on the statements, just to ensure
that they will all meet with our particular requirements."

"The statements are nowhere near to completion yet, sergeant. I am still in the process of dictating their content in readiness for typing. My arrangement with Mr Ferguson was to forward them all to him, together with copies of all my tape-recorded interviews with the witnesses. His Office would then proof read, and make any corrections they deemed necessary, before returning the documents back to me for approval, and final signature. It is an arrangement that we found mutually acceptable, and I see no point in changing it."

There was a pause on the other end of the line while the information was being digested.

"I see no problem with that arrangement, Mr Lloyd, except that the statements should now be sent to my office instead of Mr Ferguson's. In point of fact, they are such important and sensitive documents, that I would be much happier if they were not entrusted to the inconsistencies and irregularities associated with the Royal Mail. Can I perhaps arrange for them to be collected from you by a courier, instead?"

"Yes of course, sergeant. If you give me your contact phone number, I will advise you when they are ready for collection. You might also ask Charlie Ferguson to give me a ring, please, just to confirm the change in our original arrangement."

There was another, slightly longer, pause on the line. George assumed that the sergeant was sorting out a contact phone number, but the silence was lasting longer than he felt comfortable with.

"Are you still there, sergeant?"

"Yes sir, I'm sorry for the delay, I was just thinking. Look, this is very awkward, and, I'm sorry, but there is no easy way to tell you. I'm afraid that Mr Ferguson collapsed and died, in Ireland, some time over the weekend. The exact details are still a bit sketchy at the moment, I'm awaiting a copy of the official report, but I'm given to understand that he might have suffered a massive stroke."

"What? Charlie's died? Oh my God, how awful. He was here, with us, only last Thursday. He seemed to be in perfectly good health, then."

"Yes, sir, I know. He'd told me how much he was looking forward to taking a short break. But these things tend to happen when we least expect, don't they? Charlie was a good friend, and respected colleague of mine, for many years. He was assisting me in my murder enquiries, not because he was ordered, but for no other reason other than that was what he had chosen to do. To give up his time, and to come and help me to shed some new light on my murder investigations, that were fast running out of lines of enquiry. It was typical of the man. He was a totally dedicated, professional police officer, of the very highest calibre. I make no secret of the fact that the events of Saturday 16th were entirely unexpected. And coming on top of a protracted triple-murder enquiry, it created a whole mountain of extra paperwork, that we could well have done without. But having said all that, I feel rather privileged to have been instrumental in helping to solve a case, that had bugged Charlie for nearly all of his Police service. It's a great pity that he isn't around to help square things up, and to see his job through to its ultimate conclusion."

He gave a little laugh before adding,

"But then, that was Charlie. He has frequently told me how much he hated doing all the damned paperwork associated with the job. In point of fact, I'd be prepared to lay odds that he's up there, somewhere, and probably having a good laugh, at my expense. It would be just typical of the crafty old devil, to have engineered this, on purpose? Coupled with your offer to do all the witness statements for him, it must have sounded to Charlie, like all his Christmas presents were going to arrive two months early? I'll bet he just loved you for that, Mr Lloyd. I'm certainly going to miss him."

"Yes, I'm sure you will, sergeant, but can I urge you to let me have that contact number, please. As much as I sympathise with what has happened to Charlie, I really need to be getting on with my work."

"Yes of course Mr Lloyd, my apologies, sir. I will give you my personal cell phone number, it's far easier than trying to get me through our switchboard. If you're ready, the number is 07779865669, and my first name is Ahmed. Do you have any idea when you might be ready to get back to me?

"Probably by the end of next week, sergeant, but before you go, perhaps you could tell me something? Would you happen to know if Charlie ever got the file that was sent over to him by my son-in-law? A police courier picked it up from here on Saturday last. It was addressed to some Northern Ireland Police Commander, named Flanagan, I think. The file contained material of an extremely delicate nature, relating to the background of this case. I would hate to think of the consequences of it going astray?"

"I'm sure I don't know, Mr Lloyd, but in view of what you've just told me, I'm persuaded that I should make some enquiries in that regard. Just give me the details again if you would, please sir. As much as you can remember . . ."

For Sharon, the journey down to Canford, with Charlotte and Michelle, couldn't have gone better. Far from being the expected confrontational situation, she was surprised to find that the girls were being quite polite and respectful toward her. Since the incident down on the river, where she had overheard the angry, exchange with their father, Sharon had hardly spoken a word, to either of them. She considered that Malcolm had effectively put the ball into their court, and it was up to them to make the first move towards building a more amicable relationship. She also assumed that Malcolm might have advised his girls of the change in his personal relationship with her, but couldn't be sure. She and Malcolm certainly hadn't made any secret of their mutual affection for each other, and anyone with a modicum of common sense would surely have realised that their relationship was a lot more than being, just good friends. Sharon decided that she would try dipping her toe, to test the water . . .

To Sharon, who felt that she was being excluded from their conversation, it sounded as though the girls were quietly discussing their father's intended purchase of Grey Gables, and their plans for the run-down stable block. They were occupying the rear passenger seats of the Range Rover, and she thought she heard her name being whispered. She put on her best smile,

"What are you two rascals plotting back there? Did I hear one of you mention my name?"

There was a little embarrassed giggle from Michelle, who answered for both of them.

"Sorry, Sharon, we were just about to ask if you could do us a little favour?"

"A favour? Well, I suppose that rather depends on what it is, exactly? Try me . . ."

"Assuming that Daddy manages to buy Grey Gables, we would like him to allow us to use the stable block and three of the paddocks."

"I don't see any real problem with that. Why don't you just ask him? I can't imagine he will say, no."

"We spoke to him briefly, last night, Sharon. He came to wish us goodnight, and thanked us for helping out with Peter and Rita, last week. As he was in a particularly good mood, I gave it a try. He laughed and said it was far too early to start making any firm plans, but said that any spare land would probably be put to over to arable use, to support the new hospital. How many carrots, cabbages and potatoes will he need, for goodness sake?"

It was Sharon's turn to have a little smile. She was imagining a veritable vegetable mountain.

"Your father hasn't discussed any detailed plans with me yet, girls, so I really don't know what he has in mind."

It was a blatant lie on her part, but she wanted to see where this was leading before saying anything more.

"Always assuming that his acquisition of the property is successful, and I don't for one minute, see it as a foregone conclusion, why do you need any extra stabling. Surely there's enough at Oakwood?"

"You don't know my daddy yet, Sharon. When he sets his mind on doing something, nothing will be allowed to stand in his way. By the end of this week, Grey Gables will be a part of Oakwood, you see if I'm not right."

"Well alright, Michelle, I'm willing to concede that you probably know your dad, better than I, but you still haven't told me why you want the extra stabling, unless you plan on getting more horses, that is?"

"You've got it in one, Sharon. Yes, we are planning on getting some more horses, if daddy will let us? Well, they're ponies actually, Welsh cobs. The parents of a school-friend of ours, breeds them. Charlotte and I would like to get into carriage driving, and show jumping. She wants to do the driving, I want to jump."

They all laughed at the way she put it over.

"What exactly do you want me to do then, Michelle? You and Charlotte are the apples of your dad's eye, and, due to your efforts over the last week, probably flavour of the month, as well. Why do you think he would refuse you?"

"Having two sets of stables, nearly a mile apart, will mean having to take someone on to look after them. A groom, or stable hand, which, in turn means wages and accommodation, not to mention insurances. We will need to show that the expense can be justified before he will agree to anything. Daddy can be a bit tight in that respect, Sharon. He's quite prepared to spend millions on the hospital project, but if we ask him for a few thousand from our inheritance, it's like trying to get blood from a stone."

"So how will you justify the expense? What do you have in mind?"

"Lessons. Charlotte and I are both sufficiently equine trained, and qualified, to be able to offer riding lessons to other children, wishing to learn how ride and look after horses. Mummy made us do our BHS Assistant and Intermediate Instructors, when we were learning. We think that teaching would be a good weekend and holiday pastime for us all. I'm including Peter and Rita in this, as well. We're pretty certain that they will want to become actively involved, in some way."

"I'm sure they will, and I'm pleased to hear you say that, Michelle. Am I to presume that you want me to try and put in a good word for you, then?"

"Please, Sharon. Daddy will listen to you. He's been very different with us, since you've been around. Whatever it is that you do for him, please don't stop, he's so much happier now."

"Which brings me to mention that your dad and I have just become what you would call, an item. How do you feel about it? Please be honest, frank, and open with me, Michelle, I won't take exception to anything that either of you might wish to say. If we are to be living under the same roof, and sharing the same table, we mustn't be afraid to say what we think to each other."

"We've guessed as much, Sharon, you and daddy, that is. Charlotte and I were really quite shocked at first, especially as daddy had only just specifically told us, that there was nothing going on between you. But having talked about it, and seeing daddy looking so happy again, I think we are now quite pleased for you both. Daddy told us all about the terrible things that have happened to you, and about your inheritance. Congratulations, by the way, you must be very pleased?"

Sharon decided not to go down that road, again. Things were going quite well at the moment.

"Thank you, Michelle. Yes, it is a bit of a relief to be solvent once again. Perhaps I'll feel better about it all when my mother is finally laid to rest on Thursday, and the inquests into the circumstances of hers, and Mrs Cox's death, is out of the way. Much like yourselves, I need to be able to put it all behind me, and try to move on, but it can't happen until everything related to their death, is out of the way."

Sharon's comment effectively brought an end to that part of their conversation. The girls, from their own bitter experience, appreciated exactly what she must be feeling, but could think of no adequate words of comfort to offer. Changing the subject completely, Sharon asked,

"Tell me what you think of little Emily. Neither of you have mentioned her yet?"

Watching in the rear view, Sharon saw the girls look at each other. Charlotte answered her question. "Well, to tell the truth, Sharon, we're not quite sure what to make of her. She is, after all, only a toddler, and neither of us have ever had any experience of being with very young children. She likes to try and join in and play with Peter and Rita, but we've noticed that Peter, in particular, seems to ignore her? No, that's not the right word . . . He seems to keep her at arms length, if you see what I mean? It's almost as if he finds it awkward to be with her? We can't quite make it out. She's certainly a little sweetie, very quiet, and well behaved, and daddy seems to be quite taken with her. He even lets her look at all his precious books. We were never allowed to do that at her age, for goodness sake. We would need to ask his permission, even now. And have you noticed her piercing brown eyes? The way she sometimes stares at you? It's almost feels as though she's looking right through you? We've found it to be a bit creepy. Why are you asking about Emily, Sharon? Have you noticed anything peculiar about her, perhaps?"

Sharon had a little smile. Remembering her promise, she wasn't about to reveal Emily's little secret, but it was interesting to hear that the girls were not yet aware of anything radically different about her.

"No particular reason, really, Charlotte. She just seems to have become rather fond of my dad, just lately, and he loves her to bits, as well. The pair of them always seem to have their heads stuck into one of your dad's books, or they can be heard quietly whispering to each other, about heaven knows what? I've never seen my dad act like that with any other child before. Tell me what you think of him, my dad, I mean."

"Oh, Mr Cox is lovely, great fun to be with. He's been telling us all about how his house got bombed during the war, and some really quite dreadful, and amusing stories, relating to some of the people that have stayed in his guesthouse. We both think that he's sweet on Jacqui, his nurse."

Sharon laughed at this little revelation.

"If you're right, Charlotte, and he is, it would be a bit of a miracle if he could manage anything. He's eighty-six, for goodness sake."

"Just you watch how he looks at Jacqui, Sharon, see how he treats her. Always seeking to be the absolute gentleman. If a boy looked and acted with me like that, I'd be absolutely delighted, but I'd have one hand hanging tightly on to my knickers, that's for sure."

Sharon and Michelle roared with laughter. Any ice between them had definitely been broken, now . . .

The remainder of the journey to Canford continued in much the same, light-hearted, mood. Their arrival at the school was well ahead of the normal rush hour, so Sharon was able to drop the girls off right outside of their de Lacy dormitory.

"Shall I be picking you up on Friday? If so, what time?"

"Sorry, Sharon, but Charlotte and I won't be coming home on Friday, and probably not for a few weeks yet. We both have an awful lot of schoolwork to get through, and we really need to get our heads down. Besides, it's only since mum died that we've had special dispensation to go home on the occasional weekend to see dad. We both found that, apart from the horses, there was very little for us back at home, so we've reverted back to staying over for several weeks at a time, sometimes for the whole half term.

If we want to come home for any reason, we usually ring the house in the week before, and Carter arranges for us to be picked up, but the school doesn't really like us doing it. Thanks for the lift, Sharon. Take good care of daddy for us. I've told Peter that he and Rita can ride Tara, but not Totsy, she can sometimes be a little bit frisky with strangers. They're not to go anywhere beyond the confines of the back paddock. Will you keep an eye on them for us, please? We'll ring you next weekend for an update on how things are progressing, and we can have a little catch-up on the gossip. Is that alright with you?"

"Of course it's alright, you silly thing, I shall be looking forward to it. Come here, you two, give me a little hug before you go . . ."

Sharon was left to her thoughts as she continued her drive down to Weymouth. She was quite surprised at the girls' decision not to want to come home at the weekend. There was to be quite a lot going on at Oakwood that week, and she rather thought that they would want to be part of the decision-making?

She hadn't let on, but Malcolm had already mentioned that one of the new staff that had been appointed by the Estate Management, was a young groom and stable lad, who would take over care of the horses from Carter. He would also be expected to lend a hand with some of the routine garden maintenance.

He'd told her that he'd received a slightly amusing phone call from the Estate's Personnel and Human Resources Manager, who'd seen fit to consult with Malcolm, before sending the new lad over. This was rather unusual, as domestic staff appointments were solely their responsibility, and usually conducted to the highest standards. In consequence, he had questioned her reasons for first wishing to speak with him?

She explained that she thought there was rather a delicate matter for him to consider. The new stable lad is named Miguel, and is a Portuguese national. He is only just twenty-years-old, and a student of modern languages, who has been granted a working visa while he continues his studies in this country. He is definitely to be regarded as a very fit, good-looking young man, with a rather charming and magnetic personality.

Her concerns were in regard as to what effect this might have on Malcolm's two daughters, whom she considered might be at an impressionable age, perhaps?

Malcolm, far from sharing her concerns, was delighted at the prospect of having some young blood around the place, but refrained from telling her as much. He thanked her for her consideration, and asked her to confirm that the lad had been appointed on the usual three-month trial basis, just to ensure that he would fit in with the routines at Oakwood. Any perceived problems could then be addressed and resolved at his first work appraisal interview, prior to granting his confirmation of appointment, and contract of employment.

Sharon knew that Malcolm always liked to conduct these interviews personally, usually after consulting with Carter, who was effectively in charge of all Oakwood's domestic arrangements, including the disposition and conduct of staff.

He'd told Sharon that after he had ended the phone call, he'd had to smile to himself, for he too, was thinking of the effect that a handsome young man being around the place might have on his girls? Charlotte in particular, for in many ways, she was so like her mother, but he didn't elucidate any further in that respect, so Sharon was left wondering as to exactly what he meant? He also told her that he'd thought about it for a while, but eventually concluded that he was not to be overly concerned. He trusted his girls enough to think that they were both sensible, and would want to avoid doing anything that might cause him any embarrassment, especially if he nipped it in the bud, and delivered a stern warning to that effect, right from the outset. That was his intention, and he asked her for her views on the matter. He went on to say that he didn't wish to appear too high-handed, and moralistic with them, but on reflection, perhaps there might be grounds for some concern?

They had quite a long discussion, and Sharon realised just how ignorant he was in regard to both of his daughter's sexuality. He didn't even know if they knew the facts of life, or if either had ever had a boyfriend. It had simply never been discussed, and he assumed that the school took care of all that sort of thing. Sharon was appalled at his attitude, but held on to her tongue. She kept reminding herself that this man is, after all, a very highly qualified doctor and surgeon, and he had never thought, or couldn't bring himself, to discuss matters of a sexual nature with his own children?

Sharon had realised that there might be some rather delicate work for her to do, here. However, Charlotte's hilarious comment, about hanging on to her knickers, at least proved that she was sexually aware. Sharon wondered if she and Michelle were still virgins? She wasn't, at their age, but for entirely different reasons.

She and Malcolm had moved on to discussing some of his plans, should he acquire Grey Gables. He'd already expressed his intention to completely refurbish the derelict stable block, so she was aware that he had radically different ideas for it's future use, to those of his girls? She could foresee that unless she could persuade him to change his mind on a few things, there might be some trouble looming up on the horizon? Malcolm's stated intention was to use the buildings to house agricultural machinery, and the land, to grow organic vegetables. Enough, he hoped, to supply both of the houses, and the hospital. Sharon wondered if there was sufficient land available to make it possible to do both? To avoid further friction, there was a need to accommodate the girl's wishes, as well.

She rather liked Michelle's ideas, and wouldn't mind signing up to become one of her first pupils. Riding was something she'd always fancied having a go at, and with Michelle teaching, it might serve to further the bonds of friendship between them. Yes, that was the way to go, Malcolm would definitely see the sense in that, surely? She remembered that she'd promised to ring him, this, and every other, evening, just for a little chat about their respective days, and any significant developments that might have arisen. If she put Michelle and Charlotte's ideas to him, tonight, and give her reasons for wishing to support them, he'd have plenty of time to think about how to come to a compromise.

Sharon found that her mind kept harping back to Michelle's suspicions about Jim and Jacqui. Thinking about it now, she realised that he was indeed acting with Jacqui in precisely the way she described. But the whole idea that it could ever lead to anything was too ridiculous to even contemplate, surely? There was the little bottom-slapping incident to consider, and Jacqui herself had mentioned that she'd caught him doing sit-ups on the bathroom floor. He'd told her that he was keen to get himself back into good shape again, but for what purpose? Perhaps the old boy did rather fancy his chances? As to what Jacqui's reaction might be to his advances, she could only guess. On reflection, she could see no harm in whatever might be taking place between them, so she fondly whispering him good luck with his amorous endeavours. If he was happy, then so was she.

The man who was impersonating Connor sat in front of the dressing table mirror in his room at the Lyndhurst Park Hotel. With the death-mask photograph, taken by Dominic, propped up in front of him, he carefully positioned the small grey, hairpiece, and combed his own hair over it, to blend in. Satisfied that he'd got it right, he cemented it all into position with a strong, weather resistant gel spray. To complete the transformation, he finally glued into position the artificial, bushy, grey eyebrows, and added the distinctive small brown facial mole, to the middle of his left cheek. After one last comparison with the photo, he was satisfied that his general appearance would now stand up to casual scrutiny. It would be difficult for anyone to spot that he was wearing theatrical makeup.

Humming quietly to himself, the man carefully repacked all his make-up back into an expensive, leather, gent's toilet bag, before putting it into the bottom of his own overnight holdall. To avoid any cross contamination of minute traces of make-up, he was being very careful to avoid anything of his, from coming into contact with anything of Connor's. Hopefully, this would be the last time he would have to do this, for wearing make-up all day was very uncomfortable, and one had to be very careful not to do anything that might inadvertently spoil the effect. As a second rate, bit-part actor, he'd been doing this sort of thing for most of his working life, so it had become second nature to resist the temptation to scratch one's head, or wipe the nose with a handkerchief. Things that we all do, often without thinking.

Following his departure from Southampton Airport, he'd driven around the locality, carefully seeking suitable locations to complete the last phases of his elaborate subterfuge. His instructions were to establish beyond any reasonable doubt, that Connor McCall had returned to England before disappearing completely. And so far, everything was going exactly to plan.

Last evening, using Connors name, he had booked himself into a single room for three nights. He produced Connor's passport and credit cards as proof of identity. Thankfully, the hotel receptionist hadn't bothered to compare his image with the passport photo, too closely. He was aware that it was human nature not to appear overly suspicious of a friendly person, so he had handed her the passport at the same time that her attention was being slightly distracted by their conversation. It had achieved the desired result.

For the Register, which she filled in for him, he gave Connors home address in Downton, while telling her that although he lived locally, he had never fully explored the area. He had decided to spend a couple of days doing a bit of walking over some of the forest tracks and bridle paths. Could she recommend any nice routes, perhaps? Was there any tourist information available? She was answering his questions as she worked. After only a cursory glance at Connor's passport, she had photocopied the document before handing it back. He was profuse in thanking her for the helpful information, and she responded with a big smile by saying that she was only too pleased to be of assistance. Without giving it a second thought, she had accepted his credit card details to guarantee payment of the bill, and stapled them to the photocopy of the passport.

He spent the rest of the afternoon, and much of the evening, in the hotel bar, chatting to the barman, Larry, who, to relieve himself from the attentions of this stupid, egotistical, Irish twat, recommended that he treat himself to a nice steak dinner, from the evening grill menu. From what he knew of Connor, the man was sure that he had parted with sufficient information, to make it easy for the barman to recall speaking with him, if necessary.

His last task, before leaving his room to go down to breakfast, was to unpack all of Connors clothing and personal effects, and to spread them around in the drawers, and available wardrobe space.

His file-o-fax, passport, mobile phone, house keys, wallet, containing some cash, and all of his credit and debit cards, was all sorted, and went into the room safe, contained in the wardrobe. He locked it and pocketed the key. No sense in making anything too easy . . .

Despite wearing latex gloves to avoid leaving any fingerprints, he wrinkled his nose in disgust at some of the soiled underwear. Most of this, he left in the Tesco carrier bag, in the bottom of which, was a receipt for a bottle of brandy and some medicinal product, bought in Belfast. A nice touch, he thought.

Using a damp bathroom hand-towel, that he knew would be changed that morning, he set about wiping off the glass top of the dressing table, then bedside table, and any of the areas around the doors and light switches that he might have inadvertently touched. Finally, to ensure that the bedding was changed, he dribbled half a cup and the dregs, from his morning coffee, onto both the top, and bottom sheets. In a few minutes time, he would report to reception, that he'd had a little accident, and apologise for any inconvenience.

Taking one last thoughtful look around to see if he'd forgotten anything, he remembered the bathroom. He removed his own toiletries from the glass shelf, replacing them with those belonging to Connor. He flushed the loo, and still using the dampened hand-towel, wiped all around the toilet seat, the wash hand basin, and then the shower tray, all of which he had used during his short occupation of the room.

Finally satisfied with everything, the man shrugged himself into Connor's tweed jacket, and felt in the pockets. He found the car keys. After a moments thought, he added them to the other items in the safe.

Connors distinctive little car, the Morris Minor, he'd parked out of sight from the main road, at the rear corner of the hotel car park. It was locked, and empty of all items of a personal nature in relation to both Connor, and himself. Although he'd been careful to wear latex gloves when driving, he still carefully wiped down the steering wheel, handbrake, gear stick, and instrumentation panel, using a yellow duster found in the car. He then brushed off the faux-leather, driver's seat and foot-well area, to remove all traces of any hair or clothing fibres from the car. Satisfied that it was as clean as he could get it, he effectively abandoned it where it was. He had no plans to use it again.

Sitting on the foot of the bed, he changed his socks, putting on a pair of his own cotton rich, with non-elasticised tops. He pushed his feet into Connor's brown, brogue shoes. They felt loose and comfortable, because they were half a size too large for him. He thought how nice it would feel, to remove the make-up, and be able to get back into some of his own clothing once more. Not long now . . .

Leaving his packed holdall in the bottom of the wardrobe, for he would return to this room just once more, he made his way down to speak to the Receptionist about his soiled bed, and then to enjoy a full English breakfast, enough to sustain him for the rest of the day.

Tony Williams had overslept. He woke up with a thumping headache, and it took him a few seconds to remember exactly where he was. He recalled that he and Liz had sat talking, discussing Connor, until well into the early hours. They had shared the whole of a bottle of single malt before retiring, and this was probably the reason for much of the discomfort that he was now experiencing?

He dragged himself out of the bed and made his way slowly across the hall, and into the bathroom to relieve his aching bladder, and to brush the layer of fur from his teeth. After swilling down a couple of paracetamol caplets, he set about attacking the growth of beard with his electric razor, but the resonance of the little machine coursing uncomfortably through his brain, hastened its task to a premature completion. He thankfully repacked it back into its little leather case.

Why-oh-why, did he do this to himself? He wondered. From previous experience, he knew that there was rarely any solace to be found at the bottom of a whisky bottle, yet at times of stress, it is usually the first thing that everyone reaches for. He leaned over to turn on the shower, adjusting it to the right temperature before kicking off his pyjama bottoms to step into the bath, and under the refreshing jets of water. He lathered himself all over, using a 'just for men' shower gel, from off the shelf. He assumed it was Connor's, and his name caused him to wonder how Liz would be with him this morning?

Yesterday, he'd hardly had time to step in through the front door, when she was demanding to know exactly what he meant by his comment about 'knowing the answer to that one' What was he keeping from her? She was demanding to know the whole truth about Connor, no matter what it was.

He had seen that she was over-wrought with anxiety, and with the realisation that she might have been kept in the dark about something, she was incandescent with rage, as well. In all the years that Tony had known her, he'd never seen his daughter-in-law quite so angry. As he sought to placate her, he was already beginning to regret his decision to come and stay with her for a few more days. He feared that when the whole story came out, the situation with her would probably become even more turbulent and difficult? He thought it highly unlikely that she would understand, let alone sympathise, with Connor's predicament? He'd definitely needed a drink to get him started. Preferably, a very large one . . .

Armed with the whisky bottle, a bucket of ice, and two glasses, he had sat her down and pulled up another chair to sit facing her. Foregoing lunch completely, they had spoken for almost two hours.

Step-by-step, beginning with George's unexpected phone call of nearly a month ago, and omitting nothing, he took her through everything that he knew. She frequently questioned everything she was being told. At precisely the right juncture, he produced from his pocket, the damning pages from the file of evidence. The ones that George had given over to him only the day before yesterday, he stressed.

He waited patiently, watching, while she read it through several times. He could see that she was having difficulty in digesting the content into her already troubled mind. He had yet to tell her, that part of his reason for being there that week, was to administer the final affairs of the document's author . . .

Liz, though, was very astute. She wasn't about to be bamboozled, or misled, by his deliberate attempt to try and lead her into thinking that he hadn't yet been given the opportunity to make her aware of Connor's involvement and complicity with the terrorists. She quickly pointed out that he'd known about the existence of this document from the very outset, his first meeting with George Lloyd, and certainly when he came down to see her at the beginning of last week. So why hadn't he told her about it before? Why had he let her stew for so long?

Tony was cornered. He was forced into admitting that, for the sake of the love he felt toward his son, he had been trying to smooth things over, without having to tell her anything. He tried to justify himself, by pointing out that her present reaction, was precisely what he had foreseen happening, and was therefore part of the reason why. It was a lame excuse, and he knew it. So, in a sincere gesture of supplication, he offered her his abject and deepest apology for what he now realised, was a serious error of judgement on his part. He begged her forgiveness.

Liz said nothing, but looked pointedly at him for a full half minute. She got up from her seat and disappeared into the kitchen. He could hear the rattle of plates, and the various cupboards being opened and closed. Liz was obviously preparing some food, and, he assumed, using the time to mull it over?

Ten minutes, saw her returning with two ploughman's lunches, and a pot of fresh ground coffee. Tony gratefully accepted the food. Not having eaten anything since breakfast, he was very hungry. They ate in silence, but Tony kept looking at her. He sensed that Liz was building up to something, and looking for the right words, perhaps? She set her empty plate aside and poured the coffee.

"He's not your son, you know?"

"What?"

"Connor, he's not your son." She pushed a steaming mug of coffee across the table to within his reach.

"Why are you telling me this now, Liz? Are these just sour grapes, to try and get back at me? Because if that is what it is . . ."

"No . . . Well, yes, I suppose so, but you don't seem surprised?"

"I'm not. I suppose that I've suspected as much for many years, but I chose to ignore it. I had an affair with his mother, Mary, so there was always the possibility that it could be right. Thomas and I, well, let's say that we both shared her charms, and, by one or the other of us, Connor was the result. Son or nephew, does it really matter? Either way, he's my only living, blood relative. If he goes, apart from yourself, I shall have no one."

She was quiet for a few moments. His complacency and acceptance was not what she had expected. She was looking for someone upon whom she could vent her anger. She tried again . . .

"I knew all about the affair with Mary. Connor told me."

"So how long have you known for certain, that he wasn't my son, Liz?

"Since we were law students, together at Queen's. After a few drinks, he used to boast to his mates about the stupid old uncle, who thought he was his dad, and was paying for everything for him. It was Mary that put him up to it in the first place. She told him to go and find you, and what to say. She said that it was her way at getting back at you, for what you did. He made me promise never to tell you."

"So why now, Liz? What's changed your mind?"

"Finding out just how much of an evil, devious, murdering rat, that he really is, I suppose? I think that if Connor walked back in through that door, right now, dad, I'd kick him straight back out again. I think that as far as I'm concerned, our marriage is over. As from this moment, we're finished."

She got up from her seat and put on her old waxed jacket and gumboots. Walking out into the kitchen, he heard her expressing her immediate intention.

"I need to see to the animals . . ."

Tony just sat there, effectively stunned to silence. He'd always believed their union to be rock solid, built around their love for each other, their common interests, and the slightly eccentric lifestyle that they chose to lead. Her anger was apparent, and he vainly hoped that her words might just be something she'd blurted out as a result of it. A spur of the moment, hurtful remark, directed more towards him, than Connor, perhaps? It was difficult to believe that her love for Connor could turn to hate, so very quickly. And that she was prepared to cast everything aside, just like that?

In truth, he was beginning to feel that now this was all out in the open, Connor was probably lost to him, as well? He'd come to the reluctant conclusion that his son, with the balance of his mind disturbed, probably intended to do away with himself? He could think of no other rational explanation for his present conduct. With a sigh, he heaved himself forward in his chair and reached for the bottle. He poured another two large whiskies, took one, and sat back again.

Swilling the amber liquid around in the tumbler, he stared at it in quiet contemplation. In his mind, he would have wished to remonstrate with Liz, to try to make her be more reasonable. If nothing else, Connor had surely been a good and faithful husband to her, for more than thirty years, or so he assumed? Tony realised that any interference on his part, might be misconstrued. In consequence, he found that he was apprehensive, and even a little frightened of saying anything more to Liz for fear that he might effectively, drive a wedge between them? That being the case, in his own pathetically lonely, little existence, he would truly have nobody left to turn to. The dreadful thought prompted him into draining his glass in one gulp.

The whisky bottle on the table seemed to be sending out another invitation, but he resisted. Instead, he heaved himself to his feet, put on Connor's old waxed jacket, and went outside to find Liz. On the way out, he resolved that any further conversation in regard to Connor, would have to be entirely at her instigation. But also remembered that he still had to tell her all about Laura Dobson. Did he dare mention his true feelings towards the woman? He decided not . . .

The simple act of rounding up the animals, and putting them all to bed, was sufficient to help calm her down, so easing some of the tensions that existed between them. As each animal was put into its particular stall, byre, pen or coop, he watched as she whispered soothing and comforting words, while seeing to all their material needs. She always finished off with some affectionate patting and stroking, before wishing each of them goodnight, by name. There was an obvious rapport between her, and all of her charges, they revelling in her loving attentions.

Finally, with the last of the setting sun on their backs, they leaned together on the wall of the farrowing pen, watching in amusement, the antics of the little micro-piglets, clambering over each other, until they were all lined up, eyes closed, and snuffling contentedly while hanging on to the teats of the sow.

He dared to reach out and put a comforting arm around her shoulders. She responded by leaning slightly closer, and resting her head onto his shoulder.

"Connor used to like doing this, as well . . ."

She had spoken quietly, so as not to disturb the piglets, he assumed. His lawyer's mind recognised that it was a statement of fact, and invited no response, so he remained silent.

"What do you plan on doing next, dad? About finding Connor, I mean?"

He paused for a while before offering her any answer. Instead, he posed another question.

"Do you want me to find him, Liz? Given what you said about your marriage being over?"

It was her turn to think before answering.

"Not for me to take him back, I don't. I meant every word of what I said. The knowledge of what he's done has killed anything, and everything, that there ever was between us. He's deceived us both, dad, for forty years, or more. I could forgive him for all the lies that he made to you, for they have obviously done you no real harm. But to find out, now, that I've been married to a murderer . . . How could I ever bring myself to come to terms with that? It goes against all my principles. However, I would still like to know that he is safe. I also need to know that he will be brought to justice, and be properly dealt with for his crimes. He cannot be allowed to get away with committing murder, dad, no matter how long ago it was. Please, tell me that I'm right."

Tony paused to consider her words.

"Can I suggest that we go indoors, Liz? There's still quite a bit more to this that you really need to know about. When I've told you everything, I will offer you my opinion, and then perhaps we should sleep on it, before you give me yours. Between us, we should then be able to come to some agreement in regard to what happens next. Do you approve?"

They both took a shower and undressed ready for bed. She, curled up on the sofa in her dressing gown, and he, similarly attired, in the easy chair opposite. Sharing the remainder of the whisky bottle, their conversations and frank exchanges, took them all evening, and well into the early hours, way beyond their usual bedtime.

Tony, dressed casually, and feeling slightly better for the medicine, made his way through to the sitting room. He was surprised to find Liz curled up on the sofa, with a duvet wrapped around her. She was fast asleep, and he saw that she was already fully dressed. A quick glance out of the window confirmed that the horses, goats and chickens, had already been turned out into the paddocks, so she had obviously been up and around for some time? He tiptoed past her into the kitchen and felt the teapot. Even under the cosy, it was barely lukewarm. Probably hours old, by now, he thought. He emptied it out, and put the kettle on again. The remains of the bread from last night's ploughman's, popped under the grill, soon provided two chunky pieces of toast. He selected two nice-looking large, brown eggs, and set them on to boil.

"Morning, dad."

He jumped, startled by the sound of her voice. She was standing in the doorway with the duvet draped around her shoulders. He thought she was looking decidedly bleary-eyed and dishevelled.

"Morning, Liz, I was just about to bring you a cup of tea and some breakfast. Boiled egg and soldiers, is that alright?"

"Thanks dad, but no thanks. I'm not feeling very hungry."

"Come on, lass, you've got to eat. It isn't much. A bit of breakfast and a nice shower will make you feel much better. Set you up for the day. Go and lay the table for me, the eggs will be another two minutes."

It was precisely at this time that the man impersonating Connor, his doppelganger, was finishing his own substantial breakfast. There was nothing wrong with his appetite, and with a long day ahead, he was rather keen to get on with the completion of his meticulous arrangements. He drained the last of his coffee, and, out of habit, gathered his breakfast dishes together into a neat stack. Unlike Connor, he had a tidy mind.

The receptionist looked up as he approached the desk. She gave him her best smile, although inwardly, she was wondering what the hell he wanted now? The Irishman was becoming a bit of a pest, what with his soiled bedding, and his endless, stupid questions about forest walks.

"Hello again, Mr McCall, how may I help you this time, sir?"

He detected a note of irritation behind her painted smile, the precise reaction he wished to create.

"I was wondering if you had a bus timetable, or if there's a bus service that goes to this place here, perhaps?"

She looked at the point he was indicating to on his Ordnance Survey map.

"That would be Bolderwood, Mr McCall. It's an arboretum. I seem to recall that it's very pretty, and a popular destination for walkers, such as yourself. As for a bus service to take you there, I'm not sure that one exists? There is a Tourist Information office in the town car park, or better still, a camping shop only just up the road, literally only two minutes walk away. I'm sure they will be able to advise you far better than I can."

He deliberately tried to look a little crestfallen.

"I was thinking of heading out there on the bus, and then walking back. It looks to be about ten miles, would that be about right, do you think?"

"I really don't know, Mr McCall, I'm not a walker. Why don't you try asking in the camping shop, as I suggested. They're very nice people in there, and well used to handling inquiries such as yours. Now, if you don't mind, sir . . ."

He gave her a moment's look of irritation before turning on his heel to walk away. She watched him heading towards the lift. 'Stupid man,' she was thinking, 'Why doesn't he just walk to Bolderwood? That's what he's supposed to be here for, after all.' With a slight shake of her head, she went back to her morning paperwork. He was dismissed from her mind, forgotten, for the time being.

He walked into his room and was pleased to see that while he was having breakfast, the chambermaids had already changed his bedding and tidied around. With a grunt of satisfaction, he set about his final arrangements. Retrieving his holdall from the bottom of the wardrobe, he set it onto the bed.

Next he extracted Connor's writing pad from the drawer of the bedside cabinet. He opened it to the page where Connor had written, *My dearest Elizabeth, I am so ashamed and sorry for what I have done.*

He gazed thoughtfully at it for a minute or two, before tearing out the note, and one other blank page from the pad. Turning the pad over, he rested the blank page on the back. Then, using Connor's own gold, ballpoint pen, he wrote, *Please forgive me* while attempting to emulate the same handwriting style. He did it several times over, each time comparing his own effort to copy Connor's writing on the original. He knew that he would only get one shot at this, so it had to be right first time.

Finally, satisfied that he'd got it right, he added the three words to Connors original note. He held it up to the light and studied it closely. Not at all bad, he thought. It would take a handwriting expert to see any difference. As a final flourish, he signed it *Con x* and added a cross for a kiss. Nice touch?

Screwing up the piece of paper upon which he had been practicing, he put it into his jacket pocket for later disposal. He carefully put the original note back inside the pad, and left it on the dressing table.

He was about to leave the pen as well, but on second thoughts, he clipped it into the inside pocket of his jacket. It was made of gold, and matched the cufflinks and tiepin he was wearing. Together, they were probably worth quite a few euros, so why leave them for someone else? Besides, a man about to commit suicide would hardly be likely to leave such things behind, would he? He looked at Connors watch. He wasn't aware that Connor's Patek Philippe had been replaced with a similar looking, cheap, Seiko quartz, before the bag of belongings were passed over to him. It still told the same time though. Nine-thirty. It was time for him to get going.

Carrying his holdall, the man walked out of the hotel, crossed over the main A35, and stepped straight into a waiting taxi that had just pulled up outside of the fire station. Twenty minutes later, it dropped him off at Southampton Parkway Railway station. He paid the fare and immediately made his way to the toilets. It was time to for him to change back to being himself. The whole elaborate subterfuge had, at last, reached it's conclusion. His very last act, when he got back to his home in Belfast, would be to burn any of Connor's clothing that he'd worn.

He hoped that all his carefully contrived plans would be sufficient to convince everyone that Connor McCall had either got lost, or had deliberately taken himself off to commit suicide somewhere in the depths of the New Forest, a not too uncommon occurrence.

Tony finished his breakfast, and some of Liz's as well, spreading large dollops of her delicious homemade marmalade over the last two fingers of toast left on the side of her plate. He wiped his fingers on a paper serviette before pouring the last of the tea from the teapot, to top-up and refresh his own cup.

Breakfast had been conducted largely in silence, and now, Liz sat before him, her shoulders still draped with the duvet. Judging by the look on her face, her thoughts were obviously miles away. She looked a picture of dejection, with her hair an uncombed, tangled mess, and very noticeable dark bags under her eyes. He thought that she might have been crying?

"What, if anything, did you have planned for today, Liz?"

It was a question intended more to break the silence than anything else. She dragged her eyes round to give him her attention.

"Nothing. I don't feel up to going in to the office. I'm just going to attend to the animals. The stables need doing, and the farrowing pen, as well. Then there's a whole load of housework and washing that I need to see to. What are you intending to do?"

"I really need to get on with some of the work that I'm doing in conjunction with George Lloyd. I may find it necessary to go back to my office, at some stage, but I was rather hoping that I could use yours, instead?"

"Yes, of course."

"Liz, I've decided to get back in touch with that detective, Mr Grogan, from Southern Central, again. I want to put him back on the case. I can't bear not knowing what's happened to Connor. What do you think?"

She regarded him in silence for a few long seconds, as if mulling it over.

"Do what you like, dad, I'm past caring any more. I hope the bastard rots in hell, for what he's done."

The vehemence with which she came out with it, left him in no doubt that any further discussion was not to be advised. He drained his teacup.

"That's settled then. I'll give their office a ring in a minute, see if I can't get it all jacked up for today. Would you like me to pick something up from the supermarket for dinner tonight? I notice we've run out of bread."

"Just bread and milk, dad. We've got a freezer full of meat and vegetables. I'll knock up something nice for us for tonight, that's a promise. Look, I really feel that I need to be saying sorry, or something. Now that I've had time to think about it, I've realised that you thought you were acting with the best of intentions? But I need you to promise me that there will never be any more secrets between us, dad, no matter what the future may hold. It looks like its just going to be you and me from now on, and I need to feel that I can trust you to be honest and up-front with me. Besides that, I don't want you to go. I would really appreciate having your company around here for a while longer. What do you say?"

He could see that her lips were beginning to quiver, and that emotion was getting the better of her. He felt awkward, but moved forward in her direction, with his arms outstretched. His intention was to take her hands into his, and to try offering a few words of comfort. Instead, she fell straight into his arms, and started sobbing her heart out. Tony instantly felt that he was right out of his depth and comfort zone . . .

Using her mother's house keys, Sharon let herself in through the back door of 19, Marlborough Avenue. She stood for a minute eyeing the old, pine, kitchen table. The mere sight of it was sufficient to remind her of the horror and revulsion that she still felt toward her own mother and Shaun Murphy for what they did to her. It would take a very long time for all the bad memories of this place to dissipate from her mind, if indeed, that were possible? She ran her tongue over her repaired teeth and flexed the nearly healed, broken fingers of her left hand. They were a constant reminder, and still gave her some painful discomfort.

It was at that moment that Sharon decided that she must sell the house. She realised that she could never bring herself to live there with Jim, as she had once considered. There were just too many ghosts.

Shrugging herself out of the morbidity, she rinsed out the electric kettle, refilled it, and set it to boil. She'd brought with her some milk, which she went to put into the fridge. However, on opening the door, she was knocked backwards by the overpowering stench of rotting food. Quickly opening all the doors and windows, and after bringing in a plastic dustbin from outside in which to dump everything, she set about her first, and most odious task of the day. With a bucket of bleach and soapy water, she worked quietly and methodically, cleaning everything until it sparkled. It gave her plenty of time to think.

Now that her decision on what to do with the house was made, she had a specific goal to aim for. It must be cleared of clutter, cleaned, decorated, and readied for inspection by potential buyers. She tried to remember if Tony Williams had set a valuation on the property? He assumed that for probate purposes, he must have, but any recollection of his mention of it, wouldn't come to mind. George could handle the sale for her. She would instruct him to sell it cheap, preferably to a nice young couple looking for their first home. With vacant possession and in good order, she was sure it would be snapped up almost immediately.

As she moved on to clearing out the larder, she thought how good it felt to be doing something constructive again. Living in the lap of luxury at Oakwood, was all right for a short time. It was a bit like taking an extended five-star holiday, but she was not sure that she wanted to live like that on a permanent basis? She definitely needed a daily challenge, something to occupy her mind, and this sort of thing was what she liked doing best. It set her to thinking more about Malcolm's plans, should he acquire Grey Gables.

He'd said that it would ultimately become a nurse's hostel. How many bedrooms was it? Eighteen? And most of them doubles? She didn't know whether the people staying there would be expected to cater for themselves, but on reflection, that probably wouldn't work. Except for the kitchens, there would be no adequate cooking facilities in any of the rooms. Fire Regulations would certainly have precluded that. So Grey Gables would need to be staffed with a chef, and one or two kitchen assistants.

Then there was the laundry to consider. That number of people living under one roof, created a whole lot of bedding and towels that would need to be changed on a regular basis, not to mention their own personal laundry items. The new hospital would no doubt have some state-of-the-art facility, of course, but would Malcolm want to be using that? Probably not. This meant employing additional staff to handle the laundry, and then more to do the cleaning, as well. The place would need to be run like an efficient guesthouse, she thought. Rooms cleaned, beds made, meals prepared, and a suitable charge levied to cover all the expenses. Everything that she, herself, was used to doing.

Her mind was made up. The hospital House Managers job, that Malcolm envisaged her doing, could go to someone else, better suited. Sharon had set her sights on becoming Housekeeper at Grey Gables, preferably, with her dad helping. That would be good . . .

The morning flew past, and at last she felt that her work in the kitchen was more or less complete. Sharon stood back and surveyed the results of her efforts. Apart from the windows, which she would tackle as a separate task, sometime later, the place was spotlessly clean. All the cupboards and drawers were emptied, and the entire contents now sorted into three separate piles of black bags. The largest pile, was of items bound for the tip. Then came those intended for the charity shops, and lastly, the single remaining bag, sitting on the pine tabletop, contained the very few items that she had decided to keep. She moved all the bags out into the garage, before making herself a brew.

Walking through to the sitting room with her mug of tea, she paused to pick up the pile of mail and leaflets from the doormat. Sharon sat down on the sofa, mug in hand, and with her free hand, started sorting through the letters. A couple of utility bills that she would pass over to George, a lot of obvious junk mail, which she would tear up and recycle, and a letter from the Bank of Ireland. What's all that about? She wondered. Setting her mug of tea carefully onto the table, she opened the letter. It was from the Manager confirming closure of her mother's current account, and politely requesting an explanation as to why, after so many years, she had chosen to cease banking with them? What's the matter with these people? She thought. Surely they must know that the account holder has died? That's the reason for the account being closed, for goodness sake . . . What the hell, give it to George to sort out. Get him to write a snotty one back.

The last letter in the pile had a partial, handwritten, address on the envelope.

Laura Dobson, ?? Marlborough Avenue, Weymouth, Dorset. There was no house number or postcode, but the local Post Office had still delivered it correctly. Puzzled, Sharon opened the A5 sized envelope.

Inside was a brochure for a Swansea based, Good Care Group retirement home. The blurb said it was for people suffering with dementia. Tucked inside the front cover was a short, pencil-written note, on a page that had obviously been torn from a book. The handwriting was spidery, and from a shaky hand. It read,

*Dear Lara, I hope you get this, I just wanted you to know where I am. It is nice here, they look after me very well. Did you read about the explosion at the quarry. I hope Dermot is all right. If you are in contact with him*

*would you tell him that I am here, please. There is no answer on his phone any more. They think that I have got senile dementure and that I have lost my memory. They all call me mister Ireland. You cant come and see me otherwise they will know something. They fixed up my face a bit, but it hurts a lot and still looks a horrible mess.*

*Good by for now, thank you for helping me, love, Michael xx*

She read it through twice. The envelope was dated only three days ago. It was obviously from Michael Close, of the Close brothers. Sharon knew for certain that Dermot Close was dead, she had seen his body at the quarry. She also knew that it had been assumed by the Police, that Michael Close was one of the people up in the cave, killed when the explosion occurred.

The Police knew that at least one, or possibly two people, had been blown to pieces, and their bodies instantly incinerated by the extreme intensity of the blast. Enquiries to establish any positive identities were still ongoing, but David had told her, that Charlie had admitted, the exact death toll would probably never be known. The Police had no idea who they were looking for, as none of the victims had ever been officially reported missing by their families.

Sharon pondered on what, if anything, she should do now? Her thoughts were a turmoil of indecision. She assumed that she was now the only person that knew for definite that Michael Close was still alive? With everyone thinking that he was dead, she was about to inherit, what was, his share of a nice little business. Malcolm had suggested that he might award the contract for supplying all the stonework for the internal floors and work surfaces of the new hospital, to Close Roadstone. The company would only need to show that they were in a position to be able to meet all the specific requirements. He had assured her that the contract was worth in excess of a million pounds, and if handled correctly, would possibly be the making of what was expected to eventually become, her business.

She realised that if she released this rather unwelcome piece of information, it would immediately throw all of that into confusion. Sorting it all out could take months, even years?

Reading the note again, she also realised that Michael Close was effectively trapped where he was. He was obviously only pretending to be suffering from amnesia, and was quite anxious that this deception should continue, by virtue of not wishing to have his true identity revealed.

Then, he was telling Lara that she should not try to contact him for fear that they would be suspicious. Another obvious indication that he would wish it to remain that way. He mentions that he was being well treated, and that it was nice where he was. He had also received treatment to some sort of facial injury, so he was being medically well cared for, as well. More justification for saying nothing, perhaps?

On the moral side, Sharon knew that she should be turning him in to the Authorities. They would probably go and arrest him immediately. After questioning, he would be charged, and in all probability, incarcerated for several months in some sort of secure medical facility to await trial. There would then follow one of those long, protracted affairs, all conducted at the taxpayer's expense. So, not much to be gained there?

He was obviously unaware of her mother's death, and that of his brother, so should she perhaps advise him of the truth? And what good would it do, if she did? At the moment, he was reasonably happy in his ignorance. He must also be aware that the Police were after him, hence his reason for wishing to remain anonymous and hidden. That being the case, he couldn't ever dare to reveal himself, for fear of being arrested.

Sharon came to the conclusion that she should destroy the note, and say nothing to anyone, but then, she would have to live with her conscience. Could she do that? She thought about it.

This guy, after all, is one of a bunch of terrorists who indiscriminately bombed and murdered innocent people, including her stepmother, Doris Cox. Did she owe him anything? Most definitely not. Did he deserve any mercy? No. Was it justified for her to take everything from him, in this way? Why not? The bastard deserved to be made to pay, and she would personally ensure that all of his money would be spent helping others, far less fortunate. With that sort of justification foremost in her mind, she could definitely feel more comfortable with her decision.

Sharon angrily ripped the note and brochure into tiny pieces, and relegated it all to the waste paper bin. With that simple action came the resolve that Michael Close was effectively dead. He should therefore be put out of her mind, completely.

Her next task was to try talking to her grandmother again. She apprehensively reached for the house phone, and consulted her diary for the number.


Tony sat in the Bournemouth office of Thompson & McCall with detective Pete Grogan, seated on the other side of the desk. Pete was being briefed in regard to Connor's disappearance, taking notes and asking pertinent questions. Tony Williams' problem was trying to decide just how much he should tell him? Did he need to know, for instance, that Connor was under the impression that the Police were after him, and in all probability, didn't want to be found?

"So let me see if I've got this right then, Mr Williams? After I dropped you off at the Park Avenue Hotel, on Saturday, despite the fact that he was staying there, you never actually got to see your son, is that correct?

"Correct, yes. He wasn't in his room, he had left with a man and a woman, but the Receptionist thought that he would be returning shortly, as he had booked two extra covers for dinner. She gave me this piece of paper. It's Connors writing, and the names of his brother and sister-in-law, his wife's brother, that is."

"Are these the people who he left with, and the ones who were supposed to be meeting with him for dinner, then?"

"Presumably, but I never saw them. I was waiting for Connor in the reception area, and then the bar, all evening. He hadn't returned by the time I decided to turn in. That would have been around eleven, as near as makes no odds."

"Have you spoken to this Mr & Mrs B.Thompson, to find out if they actually saw Connor that evening?"

"Brian and Sarah? No, I never thought to. I'm sorry, Mr Grogan, but when the Receptionist said that he'd left the hotel with a man and a woman. I naturally assumed it was them."

"Well, it would be a good place to start, don't you think, sir. They might be able to shed some light on all of this? Do you have a phone number for the Thompson's? There's nothing on this piece of paper."

"I don't, but Connors wife Liz, will have it. Just give me a minute if you will."

Pete Grogan watched and listened as Tony Williams rang Liz. The few minutes gave him time to think and reflect upon a few things. This was certainly the most unusual misper case that he had ever dealt with, and he had the distinct impression that there was a lot more to it, than he was being told.

Tony scribbled the phone number down on the same piece of paper that bore their address, and with a smug look of satisfaction, he pushed it over towards Pete.

"Why are you giving it to me, sir? Surely, the phone call would be better coming from you? Why not do it now, while I'm still here? You never know, we might even be able to clear up this whole thing, here and now. They may even know of your son's present whereabouts?"

Tony considered his suggestion for a few seconds, and glanced at his watch.

"Brian and Sarah will probably be at work by now, but it's certainly worth a try . . ."

He dialled the number, and Pete could hear it ringing at the other end.

"Hello, this is Sarah Thompson speaking, who's that, please?"

"Hello, Sarah, this is Tony Williams, Connors father, how are you?"

"Oh, hello, Mr Williams. I'm feeling a bit poorly at the moment. I've got a bit of a heavy cold, as you can probably hear? This is a bit of a surprise, we haven't spoken for years. What can I do for you?"

"Sarah, I'll cut straight to the chase, I'm urgently trying to get hold of Connor. He's over in Belfast conducting some personal business, and his phone has gone on the blink. I've just established that he checked out of his hotel yesterday, and he's obviously moved on to somewhere else, without letting us know where. Am I correct in thinking that you and Brian had dinner with him on Saturday evening? And did he happen to mention where he was going, next? This is very important, Sarah, otherwise I wouldn't be troubling you in this way."

"It's no trouble, Mr Williams, but I'm afraid I can't help you very much. We haven't seen anything of Connor. He phoned here on Saturday morning, while we were out shopping. He left a message on the answer-phone inviting us to come to his hotel, the Park Avenue, for dinner, that evening. Unfortunately, Brian and I already had a prior engagement, so we couldn't make it. Brian phoned the hotel to speak with Connor, but he was out. He left a message with the Receptionist to give to Connor, suggesting that we could meet with him for Sunday lunch, instead. Connor never got back to us, to confirm, though. That's about as much as I can tell you. Have you tried phoning his friend, Marty? He might know something? Connor wouldn't come to Belfast without looking up Marty, that's for sure."

"We don't have his phone number, Sarah, and we don't have an address for him, either."

"We know Marty McCue, socially, Mr Williams. He's a bit of a high profile character in Belfast, now. But he always talks to us about Connor, whenever we see him. He works at Stormont Castle, so you might be able to get in touch with him if you went through their switchboard, and perhaps told them that it was urgent? Other than that, I don't know what else to suggest."

"Yes, alright then, Sarah, I'll give it a try. I'd love to chat with you some more, but right at this moment, I really need to be getting in touch with Connor. Many thanks for your help, my dear. Give my regards to Brian, if you will. Bye for now."

Tony hung up without giving her another chance to speak.

"Did you get all that?"

"Mostly. Who's this friend of his, Marty?"

"Someone Connor went to university with. They've been friends for close to forty years."

"And he works out of Stormont. So are you going to give him a try then, Mr Williams?"

Pete could see that his question had posed a huge dilemma, the body language said it all. The old guy was sitting there wringing his hands, and judging by the worried look on his face, he was obviously struggling to come to terms with something? He let the silence hang, waiting for Tony Williams to come to a decision about what to say next. Pete watched him slowly reach into the inside pocket of his jacket to extract a brown envelope, which he pushed over the desk in his direction.

"You had better read this first, Mr Grogan, and then I'll endeavour to answer some of your questions."

Pete pulled three, handwritten, foolscap-sized sheets of paper from the envelope, and spent the next five minutes reading them through.

"Is this for real, Mr Williams? Where did these originate?

"Yes, they're definitely for real, as you put it. The originator was a woman named Laura Dobson. She was one of the gang of IRA terrorists that committed the atrocities you see mentioned before you. That is her handwriting, beyond any doubt. I knew her, you see . . ."

"You're talking about her as though she's dead, Mr Williams?"

"That would be right, as well, Mr Grogan, as are most of the other people mentioned in that document. They're all dead now. All except Marty McCue, and my son, Connor, that is."

His lip began to quiver and he hung his head, staring into his lap. His hands still wrung at each other on the desktop. Pete gave him a minute to pull himself together.

"This man, McCue. You said he worked out of Stormont Castle. What does he do, exactly?"

"As I understand, he is a Personal Assistant to the Deputy First Minister, Martin McGuinness."

"Bloody hell. I'm not much on Irish politics, Mr Williams, but isn't he the one who's just recently announced that he's to be an Irish Presidential candidate, or something?"

"One and the same, Mr Grogan. One and the same. I looked up his background on the net, and by his own admission, he was a leading member of the Provisional IRA at the time of these bombings. So he might even have been directly instrumental in authorising their perpetration?"

"And do you suppose that he knows about this document, Mr Williams? Because if something as scandalous as this was to ever fall into the hands of the national press, they would have an absolute field day. The adverse publicity would certainly be sufficient to completely scupper his ambition of ever becoming Irish President, that's for sure."

"We must assume that he does know, Mr Grogan. I would think it reasonable to assume that his loyal and trusted PA would have alerted him immediately the existence of this document came to light, don't you agree?"

"I do, Mr Williams, and it beggars the question as to what lengths the First Minister might be prepared to go in order to head-off a political disaster? Tell me, who else knows about this document? And how did it come to be in your possession?"

"That's quite a long story, Mr Grogan, but as we appear to have time on our hands, and I'm paying for it, I will tell you everything I know. As to where we go after that, you had better tell me? I'm beginning to feel decidedly uncomfortable, and way out of my depth with all this. Would you like some tea?"

David, Sue and the twins arrived back at Oakwood late that afternoon. They were all exhausted from dragging around the shops buying school uniforms and the like. The children scampered off excitedly to find their Nana Edith, to show her their new laptop computers, and to get her assistance in setting them up, ready for use. Sue went to take a shower, David went to find George in the study.

"Ah David, my boy, you must have read my thoughts, I need to speak to you. I've received some rather disturbing news, today. Sit down, and I'll tell you about it."

"Me too, dad, but you go first . . ."

"I had a phone call this morning from that Arab Police Sergeant, The one that came to my house that evening, what's-his-name, Ahmed something. You know who I mean?"

"Yes, Dad, Charlie Ferguson's side-kick, Sergeant Suffajji, Is that right?"

"Sounds right, yes. Anyway, he told me that Charlie Ferguson had suffered a massive stroke, and had died. Can you believe that?"

"What? Charlie's died? Are you sure, Dad?"

"Of course I'm sure. That's what he said, David, I wasn't mistaken, if that's what you're thinking?"

"No, of course not. Sorry Dad, I didn't mean it to sound like that, it just came as a bit of a shock. Did he ring you just to tell you that, or was there something else, as well?"

"Only that he's now in charge of clearing up all the paperwork relating to the Police enquiries, and that these statements should now be forwarded to him, instead of Charlie Ferguson. Why do you ask? Is there something else, then?"

"I'm not sure, dad. I had a phone call, as well, but mine came through to me from Charlie Ferguson's mobile phone. The bloke on the other end said he was that Police Commander Flannagan, the one that the file was addressed to. He said he was using Charlie's phone so that I could see that the call was genuine, but he didn't say anything about Charlie having died."

"So, what exactly did he want then, David?"

"He wanted to know if we had made any copies of the file that we sent over to him. I asked him why? And he told me that the one we sent, had been accidentally destroyed in a vehicle fire. Can you believe that? Because it all sounded a bit far-fetched to me . . ."

"What did you tell him?"

"I told him that we hadn't, of course."

"And his reaction was?"

"One of minor disappointment, I would say. He didn't seem overly concerned though, which is probably just as well, in the circumstances."

George looked puzzled.

"What circumstances, David? What are you talking about?"

David grinned. "Apart from the three original pages of the document that we passed over to Tony Williams, the whole damn file was a copy. The original is still upstairs, contained in an envelope, which is in the drawer of my bedside cabinet. When I thought that I was going to give the original file back to Laura Dobson, I ran off a copy of everything on your photocopier up at Godalming. It was to be a form of insurance against any double-cross on her part."

"I don't understand, David. Why didn't you send the original over to Charlie, as you were asked?"

"I don't know, Dad. It was a spur of the moment decision that I made only just before the courier arrived to collect it. I knew that Charlie would see that it was only a copy, so I put a note on it telling him of my intention to hand him the original, personally, the very next time I saw him. It's a very sensitive, and potentially valuable piece of documentary evidence, dad, as I'm sure you'll agree?"

George nodded, and thought for a few seconds.

"So what are you going to do with it now, David?"

"Probably just sit on it, for the time being. There's only you and me that know I've got it, so let's keep it that way. If nothing else happens in relation to its existence, I'll eventually pass it over to Sergeant Ahmed So-far-so-good, for disposal as he sees fit. What do you reckon?"

"At the moment, I don't think anything, David. I'm still trying to get my head around any possible implications. But on the face of it, your decision, to keep hold of the original, would seem to have been fortuitous. I can foresee that you might have a problem in explaining your actions when you finally do decide to part with it? But let's cross that bridge when we come to it. Alright, we'll do as you suggest."

Sharon sat on the edge of her mother's bed. She had been in the process of turning out all of her clothing from the wardrobe and chests of drawers, when, from down the back of the tallboy, she came across what she assumed was, a long forgotten plastic carrier bag. It contained lots of old photographs, and other pieces of paper, that had obviously been of some significance to her mother.

Her original task instantly forgotten, Sharon set about examining everything much more closely, and laying it all out on the bed. Wherever possible, she sorted everything into a rough, chronological order.

Her mother, meticulous in nearly everything she did, had, in most instances, dated and captioned many of the photos, naming the people depicted, and where the particular picture had been taken.

For the first time, Sharon was finding images of her grandmother, her aunt, and other cousins or relatives, whose existence, she wasn't aware of. The latest pictures of her grandmother were all dated, July 2005, and had been taken at her eightieth birthday gathering. Obviously a very big affair, judging by the number of people, she thought.

Her grandmother, in her imagination, a typical old lady seated in a fireside chair draped in a shawl, while doing her knitting, was seen to be anything but. The pictures showed her up on a dance floor and doing an Irish jig of some sort with a whole group of young people, all identified as family, by the caption; *Mum at her birthday ceili, showing up the grandchildren*

Sharon studied the photo using a magnifying glass fetched from her mother's bureau. There was an obvious, and quite startling family resemblance, with her mother, and, she realised, with her own image, as well. She smiled to herself. Despite the fact that her second, and most recent telephone call to her grandmother, hadn't gone as well as she would have liked, her first meeting with her was certainly going to be an interesting prospect. There could be no denying that she was her mother's daughter . . .

The fading light caused Sharon to glance at her watch. She was surprised to see that it was nearly five.

"God, where's the time gone?" she muttered to herself, and slightly flustered, hurriedly started to pack all the photographs and pieces of paper back into the carrier bag, with the intention of heading off back to Oakwood. She cursed her stupidity for not keeping an eye on the time. The rush hour exodus from Weymouth probably meant adding an extra half an hour to her journey, so that meant sometime after seven before she got back? Better ring Carter and let him know she would be late for dinner. She paused for a moment, an idea had occurred. Why bother going back to Oakwood at all? If she remained here, in her mother's house, she could have another couple of hours at this. Then, treat herself to some of Weymouth's finest fish and chips, together with one of her mother's nice bottles of Chardonnay that she'd found in the larder. A nice hot bath, curl up on the sofa for a bit of telly, and a chat on the phone with Malcolm. Closely followed by an early night, and an even earlier start again tomorrow morning. Perfect, but was she forgetting anything? Yes, ring George to find out the final arrangements for Thursday and Friday. She abandoned her task and went downstairs to use the house phone.

Pete Grogan sat in the Bournemouth office of Southern Central Securities, and regarded his wife and business partner, Caroline, on the other the other side of the desk. They were carrying out a case review and discussing the missing Connor McCall. She was reading a photocopy of the document.

It was her birthday, and the eve of their silver wedding anniversary as well. With a family party planned, the very last thing they wanted was to be stuck in the office, but as always, work had to come first.

Pete and Caroline, both ex-CID Police Officers from the Met, knew the importance of commencing their enquiries as early as possible, so that everything was all still fresh in people's minds. Pete, reading from his notes, had outlined as much as he knew regarding Connor's involvement with IRA terrorism. He then showed her the photocopy of the handwritten document, in which, Connor was specifically named. Caroline read it through several times. They both understood the implications of it ever falling into the public domain. This case had the potential to be the biggest thing that either had ever worked on, both during their Police service, and in private practice. She put the document down and looked up at her husband. He took it as his cue to comment.

"This whole thing smells of something very fishy to me, love. Let me tell you what I think, and you tell me if I'm wrong . . ."

From past experience, Pete had learned to respect her woman's intuition, and with her different way of looking at things, they made a good partnership.

"Go on then, but if you're going to tell me that he's gone on his toes with the intention of doing himself in, then I would have to agree. That's what it looks like to me."

"I think that is precisely the conclusion we are supposed to come to, love. I'm thinking that Connor McCall is already dead. Eliminated, expediently taken out, call it what you will. I think that his body is still over in Ireland, somewhere, and that this is all a ploy to make everyone think that he's come back over here with the intention of committing suicide."

"Why would you want to think that? Where's your evidence?"

"That's where I'm struggling. At the moment, I don't have the slightest scrap of anything, it's just my nose telling me that this stinks of something decidedly fishy. I reckon that, like us, the big political noises in Northern Ireland have recognised the danger that Connor McCall posed, and they've already taken the appropriate steps. Think about it, love. If he had died, or disappeared, in Ireland, there would have to be enquiries made to trace him. Or, if a body were ever found, there would be an inquest. That would lead to the Police asking lots of awkward questions to this other bloke, McCue, and it would probably come out as to why he was over there in the first place?

His father, Tony Williams, is a solicitor. He's not daft, he knows the significance of that document, and he will likely have produced it to the Police. Shit hits fan . . . But if it can be shown beyond reasonable doubt that McCall left Ireland, and that he came back over here, before disappearing, then there's no case to answered over there. It's very nearly perfect."

"So, assuming that you're correct, and I don't for one minute concede anything yet, what do you intend to do now? How do you see it progressing?"

"We need to carry out the clients wishes, and try to find him, or, if my hunch it right, at least find the person that was pretending to be him. Then, we work backwards from there. My guess is that he won't have gone too far to affect the disappearance, probably somewhere local to Southampton? In fact, see if you can find out if anyone booked a last minute flight back to Belfast, or Dublin, from Southampton Airport, in the last forty-eight hours. It might just give us a starting point. Meantime, I'm going to start ringing round some of the smaller hotels and guesthouses listed in Yellow Pages. It found him for us in Belfast, so let's hope it will work over here, as well.

Come on love, we've still got another hour before we need to get off home, so let's make a start. We can pick it up again in the morning, if necessary."

Peter lifted the heavy saddle off of Tara, and with a grunt at the effort, slung it over the wooden saddle horse. He began wiping it clean and applying neat's-foot oil leather dressing as Charlotte, whose saddle it was, had demonstrated. Meanwhile, Rita led the pony away to her stall, and started to give her a vigorous brush down. The twins had taken turns at riding Tara around the paddock while attempting to put into practice the basic dressage skills that Michelle had been trying to teach them. Each vociferously criticised the other when recognising the most obvious faults, but this had inevitably led to disagreement and argument, now they weren't speaking to each other, again.

Things hadn't been right since the decision for them to attend different schools. Both had been granted the rest of that week to get their uniforms and essentials sorted out, before starting school after the following weekend. Now, with everything ready, both children were full of anticipation, and the extra week of enforced holiday, was not appreciated. Without the company of Charlotte and Michelle, both of whom the children now looked up to for guidance, there was an ever-increasing air of impatience and intolerance toward each other. It had not gone unnoticed by Sue and David.

Rita, now impatient to get away from her brother completely, had persuaded her parents to allow her to step straight into being a boarder, instead of starting as a temporary day-pupil as they originally envisaged. She pointed out that with her new mobile phone, she was in touch, and able to speak with them if she felt uncomfortable with anything. She promised to ring every evening to let them know she was all right.

Peter, not to be outdone by his sister, reluctantly asked for the same consideration, but only after his first visit to the Walhampton School, when he had recognised another lad of his age that lived nearby to their old address, in New Milton. At least there was someone else there that he knew, and it made things slightly easier . . .

Their parents were equally full of trepidation for what they felt, was effectively splitting up their family. Both recognised that it was inevitable, and ultimately, very necessary. It had to happen at some point in their children's life, for they were both growing up. But at barely nine-years-old, they are still very young? Was this fair? They discussed it at length, while desperately trying not to let any emotive issues cloud their judgement.

In the end, it was Rita's change of attitude that led them to conclude that this was the correct course of action to adopt. Physically, she was obviously on the verge of entering into puberty, and, although she probably didn't appreciate it herself, it was the changes in her own hormones that were affecting her state of mind, with regard to her brother. In particular, her expressed wish to be in the company of girls of her own age, with no boys present, to spoil everything. Sue could recall a similar period from her own childhood, when she felt much the same.

Both parents knew that it is generally accepted that girls begin to mature a couple of years in advance of boys. This would perhaps explain why Peter couldn't understand why his sister was no longer seeking to be with him, all of the time? They both understood that the feeling of rejection, must be a particularly hard concept, for someone so young, to be forced into accepting, and to try to come to terms with. Would he perhaps understand better, if they sat him down and tried to explain? They thought not. If he thought that his sister was, in any way, more advanced than he, it might only serve to alienate him further.

In time, they both knew that he would reach the same psychological crossroad, and then perhaps, he would come to better understand his sister's present feelings? They hoped so, for the discord between them was painful to see.

In the meantime, they also knew that Peter was a fighter. Where his sister was concerned, he would never let his true feelings reveal any perceived weakness in his dominance over her. By insisting that he too wanted to become a boarding school pupil, he had already demonstrated that he was prepared to meet the challenge, head-on. His, and Rita's attitude, invoked a deep sense of pride from their parents.

Carter, dressed in his Wellington boots and warehouse coat, headed out to the stables. His normal routine, when the girls are at school, usually dictated that the horses and ponies be fed, watered, and settled for the night, before dinner was served. He reflected on how much he disliked this particular aspect of his duties, and how long he had been pushing the Estate Management to employ a stable lad, come general dogsbody, to look after the animals, and help keep the place tidy, under his direction. There was so much that needed doing, to bring it all back up together again.

Tomorrow, his wishes would be fulfilled, and this would likely be the last time he would be required to do this onerous task. Carter had been advised that the new stable lad, Miguel, was to be arriving early tomorrow morning. His imminent arrival had posed a slight problem in regard to his accommodation. Normally, extra staff, usually house, or chambermaids, would be allocated a room in the servant's quarters, on the top floor of the main house, where they shared bathroom facilities. With three young women already up there, Carter thought it was entirely inappropriate to be putting a young man in, on the same floor. Quite apart from the obvious implications, and the possible consequences, it was essential to maintain harmony amongst the staff. Having any extra male staff at Oakwood, was highly unusual, and Carter couldn't even recall the last occasion, so there was no previous example to follow. In consequence, he and Elsie, after much discussion, decided to allocate one of the first floor rooms from their suite, in the West wing of the house. This would allow Miguel an easy access to the stable block, via the rear fire escape stairway, and avoid the necessity of him having to use any part of the main house. He would take his meals with the rest of the staff, in the stillroom annex.

Carter met up with Peter and Rita, just as they were just closing, and padlocking, the stable doors.

"It's all done for you Carter. Me and Rita, we've just finished feeding and watering all the animals, for you."

"Thank you, master Peter, but on a point of grammar, young sir, it should be Rita, and me."

He looked a little puzzled.

"Why should it be you and Rita, Carter?"

Carter laughed. "No sir, it was your form of address, that I was seeking to correct. You said, me and Rita. To be grammatically correct, what you should have said was, Rita and me."

Peter looked even more confused.

"Never mind, master Peter, I'm grateful to you both, for your efforts. I shall just need to check that nothing has been forgotten, otherwise, I shall not be able to sleep easy in my bed tonight. From tomorrow, the care of all the animals will be the responsibility of the new stable lad. His name is Miguel, and he comes from Portugal."

"Does he speak English, Carter? Apart from *ola* and *adeus,* which I think means, hello and goodbye? I don't know any other Portuguese words."

"Bless you, miss Rita. That will be a very good start, don't you think? Miguel, I'm given to understand, is a student of modern languages. His résumé, which I was reading only this morning, says that he can speak French, Spanish, Italian and English, as well as his own language. In addition to his normal daily work here at Oakwood, he will be going to college for two days a week to study for an A-level English qualification. I think we can safely assume that his English language skills will be the equal of you and I, but I'm not sure about young master Peter, here?"

Carter playfully ruffled his hair. "If you use bad English to Miguel, master Peter, I'm sure that he will be correcting you, the same as I. Me and Rita, indeed . . . In my day, that would have earned you a slap on the hand with a ruler, young man. The correct form of address is to say, Rita and I, or, Rita and me have just finished feeding the horses for you . . . At least, I think that's right? There, you've got me at it now, you young rascal."

Peter and Rita were laughing together again. For the moment, their differences were forgotten.

# Chapter 14

Pete and Caroline Grogan steadily worked their way through the list of hotels and guesthouses in the Yellow Pages Directory for Southampton and the New Forest. Gambling on Pete's assumption that the man they were looking for, would not have gone too far from the airport, they decided to concentrate first, on checking with those establishments within a fifteen mile radius, and to the west of Southampton. The New Forest.

Half an hour into their task, and Caroline hit pay dirt.

"Lyndhurst Park Hotel, Linda speaking, how may I help you?"

"Oh, good evening, I wonder if I might speak to Mr McCall, please?"

"Is Mr McCall a guest with us? Do you have a room number, for him?"

"No sorry, I don't."

"Just one moment then, please. I will just need to check the guest lists. Ah yes, here we are, room 120, I'm just putting you through."

Listening intently to the phone, Caroline snapped her fingers at Pete to attract his attention. He looked up at her beaming face, and her excited thumbs-up to indicate her success. But disappointingly, there was no answer to the call. After a full minute of it ringing, she hung up.

"Well, there's a Mr McCall staying in room 120, of the Lyndhurst Park Hotel. But as to whether he's our man, your guess is as good as mine?"

"And how many other McCall's have you ever come across, Caroline? It's got to be him. I wonder if he's still there?"

Pete was looking at his watch, and Caroline could see that he was contemplating going straight over there.

"Forget it Grogan. It's my birthday, and tonight's our family party. I should already be at home preparing food, and setting the table. And then it's you and me, in the hot tub, with a large glass of champers, before everyone arrives. So, whatever it is that you're cooking up, it can wait til tomorrow morning. I'm not having you gallivanting off on some wild goose chase tonight, my lad, and that's final. The only place you're going is straight home, with me. C'mon, get your backside into gear, Mr Grogan, we're out of here in one minute."

Pete smiled to himself. It's never a good idea to argue with the cook . . .

The mobile phone in Sharon's pocket purred to an incoming call. She set her fish and chips to one side and wiped her greasy fingers on a tissue before extricating it from her pocket. A quick glance at the caller's ID put an immediate smile onto her face.

"Good evening, Dr Blackmore, I thought you'd forgotten me. How's your day been, so far?"

"Hello, lovely lady. Hectic, is probably the right adjective, what about yours?"

"Oh, you know, hair, manicure, facial, shopping for a new wardrobe. All on your credit card, of course. It's damned hard work for a girl to keep herself looking good all of the time. I'm absolutely exhausted."

Malcolm chuckled. "I'm just about to cancel my card. You already looked good enough to me, and I can't have you wearing yourself out, especially if it's at my expense."

"Tight wad. I knew you'd say that, so I got in first, and spent right up to your credit limit."

"Good God, woman, have you bought the whole damn boutique?"

"Not yet, but I'm working on it."

"Where are you exactly, I can hear voices and what sounds like traffic in the background?"

"I'm sitting on a public bench on the old waterfront at Weymouth, and I'm eating some of the best tasting fish and chips in the world, straight out of the wrapper. It's a beautiful evening, very mild and not a breath of wind. I'm watching all the little fishing boats chugging around in the harbour. With the lights glistening on the water, it's all very pretty, Malcolm. I just wish you were here to share it with me."

"I wish I was there, as well. Although I'm not sure about eating fish and chips out of the wrapping paper? It's a bit primitive for my liking."

"You don't know what you're talking about, Blackmore. With a generous splash of vinegar, and a little salt, it's the only way to eat fish and chips. Served up on a plate, they don't taste half as good. It must be all that mollycoddling you get back at Oakwood that prevents you from sampling one of life's most delightful, simple pleasures? Believe me, mister, you've not lived until you've tried this, especially if you wash it down with a bottle of your special lager. That's the only thing I'm missing here. They don't allow anyone to drink alcohol while on the streets in Weymouth."

"So, how about a compromise? I'll ask Mrs Carter to fry us two large pieces of cod, or haddock, in some of her delicious beer batter. And together with a generous portion of nice crispy chips, we wrap it all up in newspaper, grab a bottle or two of what you fancy, and we head off for our own little picnic, down on the river? The spot where you released Elmo, would be nice. They'll think we've both gone stark staring bonkers, of course, but what the hell, who cares? What do you say, lovely lady?"

"It's a date, Mr Blackmore. Next weekend, when I get back from Ireland."

"Ah, that might be a bit of a problem, love. I'm probably not going to be back at Oakwood until the end of next week. I'm duty-rostered over the coming weekend, I'm afraid. That was one of the reasons I was ringing you. Sorry, lovely lady, but I'm needed here."

"Oh, not you, as well? Charlotte and Michelle are not coming home either."

"Yes, I know, but that's not unusual, they sometimes stay away for several weeks at a time."

"Never mind. It won't take that much to organise, let's put it on hold until the right opportunity arises. While we're discussing the girls, Malcolm, they've come up with a little scheme, which on the face of it, sounds like rather a good idea. I've been asked to have a word, and try and persuade you into seeing your way clear to letting them . . ."

Malcolm interrupted with what sounded like, exasperation?

"Oh, here we go, again. Little minxes have put you up to doing their dirty work, have they? What is it this time, and how much do they want from their inheritance?"

Sharon was quite shocked. "Is there any point in me talking with you any further, Malcolm? You seem to have already made up your mind that anything they might want to do, is totally out of the question. I hadn't realised that I was getting myself into some sort of family, or parental, disagreement, here? That being the case, I shall say no more."

"No, sorry, Sharon. I'm the one that's out of order, I shouldn't have used that tone, I apologise. It's just that they always want to be dipping into their inheritance fund, for anything that takes their fancy. Their mother would never allow it, on the grounds that they need to learn, and understand, the value of money. She would never sanction anything she deemed to be unnecessary, or frivolous. Last time, it was the latest, most expensive, I-pads that were the new, must have, essential. And only because all their school pals had them. I finally capitulated, and they got them for Christmas, last year. Damn things came to nearly a thousand pounds each. Can you believe that? Tell me what it is that they want now?"

"What they are asking for rather depends on whether there has been any progress made in acquiring Grey Gables, Malcolm. So is there any news?"

"I'm given to understand that the Estate Management Solicitors, and whoever is doing the negotiating on our behalf, have arranged a meeting with the vendors, for tomorrow. I'm optimistic that we can come to a mutually amicable, and binding agreement, before the conclusion of that meeting. That is my expressed wish, but what has it to do with what we are talking about?"

"They want to take over the old stable block, and to use it as a teaching facility for riding and carriage driving. They see it as a way of earning themselves some money, but it will obviously need a bit of funding to get it off the ground. Personally, I see it as quite enterprising, and I wouldn't mind signing up to be one of Michelle's first pupils. It would certainly be a step in the right direction with regard to me establishing a good relationship with them both. So, just have a little think about it, Malcolm, will you, please?"

"Well, I have to confess that starting a little business, was not what I was expecting. When are you going to be talking to them again? I'm sure they'll be wanting to know my decision?"

"Michelle said she'd ring me over the weekend."

"Well alright. Assuming that we do manage to acquire Grey Gables, you can tell her that I am not wholly averse to her, and Charlotte's, little idea, but I want to see some detailed plans on what they would wish to do, when refurbishing the stables. I shall need to know how much additional land they will require for their facility, and some projected figures with regard to the actual cost of getting it all up and running. I want to see a realistic estimate of how much time each of them would envisage devoting to teaching, just to ensure that it doesn't interfere with their education. I would also like to see a projection of how much they would both expect to earn from it. In short, Sharon, I want to see them deliver a proper little business plan, before I make any final decision.

That should give them something to think about, and afford me, a little bit of breathing space. If they do manage to come up with something realistic, it will at least demonstrate to me, that they will have thought about it from every aspect. It will also serve to bring home exactly how much it will all cost. What do you think?"

"I can see where you're coming from, Malcolm, but are you seriously expecting their little enterprise to turn a profit, because if you are, I don't think that's at all fair? They're not budding entrepreneurs, just a couple of enterprising kids, trying to justify to their father, as to why they want to buy a couple more ponies."

"I wasn't aware of the extra ponies, but now that I come to think about it, it's an obvious necessity. The livestock we currently have, is totally inadequate, and unsuitable for carriage driving, if that's what Charlotte is planning? I rather suspect that you might have inadvertently, sussed them out, here? I need to be satisfied that this is not just a ruse to spend money on a couple of ponies that have taken their fancy. You can tell them that as well, if you like."

"You're a hard man, Mr Blackmore, but I will pass on your wishes."

"No, I'm not really, love. I just don't want them running away with the idea that they've got me twisted around their little fingers, even if they have. They usually manage to get their own way in the end, it's just become a bit of a game, wearing me down to the point that I finally capitulate. They'll probably find they've got two more ponies and a big bundle of cash in their Christmas stockings, but don't you dare tell them, you'll spoil it all . . . Changing the subject completely, have you spoken to George about your mother's funeral arrangements yet?"

"We had a long chat this afternoon. It's all arranged, do you want me to run it past you?"

"You can if you like, are you happy with it all?"

"I'm not sure 'happy' is the right word, Malcolm, I'm very apprehensive about meeting my aunt and grandmother. I'm sensing an undercurrent of resentment, and antagonism, there somewhere. I learned today, that they've not invited anyone from anywhere outside of Londonderry, only immediate family.

I can't say very much, because that's basically, what my mother's last wishes are. But I'm not sure she would have wanted the Dobbs side of the family to be totally excluded?

George has organised for mum's coffin to be flown over to Belfast International, from Bristol Airport, on Thursday. I'm to fly from Southampton to Belfast City, there to be met, and driven, by the Funeral Directors, to The City Hotel in Derry. I'm booked in for two nights, Thursday and Friday.

Mum's coffin will be in grandmother's house overnight, and I'm invited to come and pay my last respects in the traditional way, whatever that means? The funeral service will be short and sweet, conducted at the graveside, in the cemetery, on Friday morning. After that, I shall play it by ear.

I've hired a car, a Ford Focus, and I intend to drive myself back to Belfast, probably calling in on the Dobbs family, at Lough Neagh, on the way. I have an open ticket, so either a Saturday, Sunday or Monday return flight, will do, depending on how I'm received by the Dobbs's. It's a guesthouse, so I might be tempted to stay for a night or two, if it's convenient.

George says I'm to ring Carter when I know which flight I'm on. He will then arrange for me to be picked up from the airport. That's about it, really. I don't suppose for one minute that everything will go as smoothly as I would wish it to, but I live in hope . . ."

"It all sounds reasonable, love. I hope it goes well for you. Be sure to ring me, won't you. I might not be able to take your call immediately, but I'll get back to you as soon as I can. Tell me, did George happen to mention anything about Charlie Ferguson?"

"No, why should he? Has something happened?"

"It would seem that Charlie collapsed and died, sometime over the weekend. A stroke, I'm told."

"Oh, my God. I'm so sorry, Malcolm. You quite liked him, didn't you?"

"Well, let's just say that I once had a degree of respect for him. Latterly, my opinion of his character took a bit of a tumble, and we parted on slightly less than friendly terms. I don't wish to speak ill of the dead, Sharon-Louise, but he was not the man that I at first thought him to be."

"Well, now that you've come to mention it, I can tell you that, we girls, all thought him to be a bit of a creep. We came to the conclusion that underneath all that false charm, there lurked a homosexual woman-hater. Edith used the word, misogynous, and after she finished explained the meaning, Sue and I both thought it described him exactly. You didn't see how he was with us, when he came to Oakwood last week, Malcolm. Horrible man, I shan't be mourning his passing, that's for sure . . ."

"Why didn't you say something? I would have sent him packing, sooner than I did."

"He was there at your invitation, Malcolm, as were we all. I'm pleased to hear you say you sent him packing, though. Do you want to tell me about it?"

"I'll save it for another day, love. Look, I've got to go and scrub-up, I'm due in theatre in ten minutes. I'll ring again about this time tomorrow, hopefully, there will be some positive news on Grey Gables by then?"

"And that's another thing I need to discuss with you, Malcolm. I've been thinking about the staffing and organisational requirements that you're going to need, to get Grey Gables up and running as a nurses hostel."

"Save it, love. Let's just take one step at a time. Tell me about your ideas when we've got something a little more definite. I really must go now. Love you."

The phone line went dead leaving Sharon with her thoughts, and half a portion of, now cold, fish and chips, which she reluctantly fed to the ever-ravenous harbour seagulls. She looked at her watch and was surprised to see just how long they had been talking. Starting to stroll back towards Marlborough Avenue, caused her to remember the nice bottle of Chardonnay in the fridge. A nice deep hot bath with a large glass, or two, of one of her favourite chilled white wines, would seem to be just the ticket? It prompted her into quickening her pace a little.

The next morning, Pete Grogan pulled his car into the car park of the Lyndhurst Park Hotel. It was six-fifteen, and not yet daylight. The previous evening's family get-together, had gone on well into the early hours, and he'd had very little sleep. Even when he did finally get to bed, his mind was still working in overdrive. It was uncommon for a case to be bugging him this much.

The car park was nearly full, indicating the hotel must be fairly busy. Unusual, he thought, considering how late in the year it was? Pete's early arrival was timed to try and catch whoever was impersonating Connor McCall, hopefully, before he had a chance to leave. The first thing he needed to do was to establish the correct identity of the man.

Pete locked his car, and took a little walk around the car park. He found the distinctive maroon, Morris Minor Traveller, tucked away in a far corner. It was covered in dew, which meant that it had been there all night, and had not yet been driven, this morning. With a smile of satisfaction, he left the car untouched, and made his way towards a side entrance, meant for staff only. The door wasn't locked.

Unobserved, Pete found his way up to room 120, where he gave the door a polite, but firm, rap with his knuckles. With his ear to the woodwork, he could detect no discernable response. He tried again, a little louder this time. Nothing.

Pete pulled a thin piece of flexible plastic from his wallet, and inserted it in the gap beside the lock. By carefully manoeuvring it around, he managed to slip the latch. Stepping inside the room, and quietly closing the door behind, he stood for a few seconds, orientating himself. In the dim light coming through the curtains, he could see that the bed had not been slept in, so he dared to switch on the light. He stood with his back leaning against the door, whilst replacing the piece of plastic back into his wallet. All his senses were on heightened alert. The air conditioning had been turned off, so there was no sound, only a faint smell of body odour to indicate a fairly recent presence in the room. There was something else as well, a chemical, perfume-ish, type of smell, but he couldn't quite put his finger on what it was. His eyes scanned around the room, noticing only that there was some soiled clothing on the end of the bed, a pair of dirty socks. Why? That sort of thing would normally be tucked away, out of sight, so as not to embarrass the maid.

Slipping on a pair of latex gloves, he pulled from his pocket a small ultra violet light. He then commenced a systematic and thorough search of the whole room. Under the light, it soon became apparent that all of the surfaces had been wiped over with a damp towel or cloth. The light clearly highlighted all the dried smears on the glass dressing table top, where it had been wiped. It was here, that the chemical smell was at its strongest. He put his nose up close to the mirror and sniffed again. Hairspray of some sort? Yes, definitely that, but also something else as well? He tried to recall what makeup Caroline used, the smell was definitely something familiar. With his head in that position, his eyes spotted something that had slipped down the back of the dressing table and had become trapped against the wall. It looked like a piece of thin card. He carefully fished it out with two fingers, and turned it over in his hand. The realisation of exactly what he was looking at caused him to take a sharp intake of breath. Three differing facial views of a man whom he recognised as being Connor McCall. A positive link was now established. He looked closely at the images, and felt increasingly apprehensive.

Pete carefully put the picture into a small, sterile, plastic exhibit bag, a few of which he always carried. He sealed it down and carefully placed it into the fold of his wallet for safekeeping. His attention was drawn to the writing pad that he'd pushed aside, to get closer to the mirror. Using the end of his biro pen, he flipped it open to the first page. The short, handwritten note, was there for him to read.

Pete was now in a bit of a quandary. He knew that the correct thing to do would be to alert the local Police, but he might then have a bit of awkward explaining to do, with regard to his presence in the room. To remove the pad, and the photo in his wallet, was deemed to be interfering with a potential crime scene, and he briefly considered replacing them.

He thought through the sequence of events that would occur when McCall was inevitably reported missing to the police. In all probability, some junior, uniformed officer, would come blundering around in this very room, and any evidential value attached to these items, might potentially be lost, or overlooked, in the initial stages of enquiry.

The photograph alone was sufficient enough to confirm his previous suspicion. He was now convinced that Connor McCall had somehow met his demise elsewhere, and that all of this was an elaborate plan designed cover up his murder. There was no way that he could get the handwriting checked and verified without taking the pad away, so that factor alone, dictated that it was going to have to go with him. The same criteria applied to the photo in his wallet, it needed some careful forensic examination, a task that he was not prepared to trust to anyone else.

That thought caused him to pause for a few minutes, just to think about what evidence he'd got so far. What he really needed was some irrefutable forensic. A fingerprint was the most obvious thing, but where to look? He would have liked to get into the room safe, but it was fitted with a heavy, Yale type lock, and the key was nowhere obvious.

Pete went back into the bathroom, the most likely place to find what he was looking for. He looked all along the glass shelves and even in the rubbish bin. He settled for a shiny paper wrapper from a bar of soap, and the small glass tumbler in which stood a small tube of toothpaste and a toothbrush. Holding the tumbler up to the ultra violet light, he could see a couple of reasonably good prints on the surface of the glass. He put the soap wrapper in the glass, before placing both items into one of the plastic bags provided for the disposal of sanitary towels. The package went into his jacket pocket. With one last look around to see if there was anything else he might have overlooked, Pete turned off the light, and exited the room. Peeling off his latex gloves, he thoughtfully made his way back down to the reception area.

He walked up to the desk, which was unmanned, and rang the bell for some service. After nearly a minute, the Night Porter appeared, bleary-eyed, in answer to his second ring. Pete produced his ID card. It was deliberately designed to resemble a Police Warrant Card. He gave the man a quick flash, before returning it to his pocket.

"Good morning. My name is detective Grogan, and I am wishing to speak to one of your guests, a Mr McCall, whom I am given to understand, is in room 120. I have just been knocking on the door of that room, but I am not getting any reply. Is there any way that you can confirm if he is in there, for me? Please. His car is outside in the car park, so he can't be far away, can he?"

"I can try ringing his room extension, sir, but it is only six thirty, and it might not be appreciated."

"Do it, please, just to check. I did knock fairly hard on the door, so I'm fairly certain he's not in there. Don't worry about upsetting him, I will accept full responsibility for any potential repercussions."

Pete watched as the Porter went through the motions of doing as he was asked.

"There's no reply, sir. He's either a very sound sleeper, or it's as you say, he's not there."

"All right, that being the case, can you check to see if he was here for dinner last evening? I presume that guests are required to identify themselves before being served?"

"Yes, sir, but I don't have that paperwork to hand, it won't have come through from the dining room yet.

Look, sir, I am just the Night Porter, and I'm not sure that I should be doing any of this, it's all highly irregular. Would you mind just waiting for a few more minutes? The regular Receptionist is usually here for about a quarter-to-seven, and she may be able to help you further?"

Pete made a point of consulting his wristwatch while trying to look peeved.

"Tell me, are you familiar with this man, McCall? Would you recognise him, if you saw him?"

The Porter was looking at the guest lists on the computer screen.

"No sir, I don't recall that I've ever seen him. It says here that he booked in on Saturday for three nights only. Bed, breakfast and evening meal. He ate in on Saturday, and had a breakfast yesterday morning, but that's as much as I can tell you, I'm afraid."

"Do you have a pass key? Can we have a quick look inside his room? If I tell you that there is some concern with regard to this man's mental state, and that he might be considering suicide, would it make any difference?"

"I'm sorry, sir, I'm not comfortable with any of this. I must insist that we wait for someone with more authority to make decisions such as that. Would you like me to call for one of the management staff to come and speak with you? That's the best I can offer, I'm afraid."

"So what happens if a guest loses their key-card? How do you gain entry in those circumstances?"

"We have a master key-card, sir, but in these circumstances, I do not feel justified in using it. Please, let me call someone from management, for you . . ."

A door opened behind him and a young woman, carrying a sheaf of paperwork, came through into the reception desk area. She eyed Pete, perhaps sensing trouble?

"Morning Jim, is everything alright?"

"Ah, Carol, thank goodness you're here. This gentleman is a detective, and he is inquiring about one of our guests, Mr McCall from room 120. Can you help him, please?"

She gave Pete one of her big smiles.

"The Irishman? What's he been up to? Probably boring the pants off someone, I expect?

Pete reciprocated her smile, and held out his hand to be shaken.

"Detective Pete Grogan. Good morning, Carol, I'm pleased to meet you. I take it you're familiar with our man, then?"

She took his hand in a gentle handshake as she answered,

"You could say that, yes. What's he done?"

"Nothing yet, as far as I'm aware. He's been reported missing by his family, and there are some concerns as to his state of mind. Pressures of work, that sort of thing. My office rang early last evening, and established that he was booked in here. I've been sent over this morning, to speak to him. His car is parked outside, and we've been trying to raise him, but we can't get any reply from his room. I was in the process of trying to get Jim, here, to use the passkey, just to check and see if he's alright."

"You think that he might have committed suicide in his room. Is that what you're saying, Mr Grogan?"

Pete needed to keep it going without causing undue alarm.

"I think it would be a good idea for us to check, before jumping to any conclusions, Carol. The fact that we can't raise him, should give us some cause for concern, don't you agree?"

She thought for a few seconds. "Yes, I think you're right, Mr Grogan. Come on, we'll do it now, while Jim is still here to watch the desk. Can you give us five more minutes, Jim?"

He nodded and handed her the master key-card. It was attached to a long piece of neck-chain, which she put over her head. Pete followed her over to the lift.

"Tell me Carol, how did you know that Mr McCall was Irish?"

"I'm not very good with accents, Mr Grogan, but Mr McCall's was about as Irish as it is possible to be. Very pronounced, even to the point that he was sometimes difficult to understand. Larry, in the bar, said much the same thing."

"Really? That's interesting . . . And why did you think he was a bore? You said that he might have been boring the pants off someone?"

The lift arrived and they stepped inside. The doors closed, and she hit the button for the first floor.

"It is not my place to speak ill of our guests, Mr Grogan, but Mr McCall was a real pain in the butt. Rather too full of himself, what with all his stupid questions about Forest walks, and bus routes. And then there was yesterday's incident of his soiled bedding. The Chambermaid had to replace both his mattress and duvet, after he spilled coffee into the middle of his bed. How does one manage to do that?"

The lift stopped, and she led the distance along to room 120. Pete was still mulling over the reasons for soiling the bedding, when she halted at the door. Key-card in hand, she was clearly reluctant about inserting it into the lock. She reached a decision, and knocked loudly on the door. They waited.

"Look, Mr Grogan. I'm not very good with this sort of thing, dead bodies, and all that. Would you mind doing this, while I wait outside? We only need to know if he's in there, or not. So just one quick look around, please."

Pete smiled in unspoken understanding. He took the key-card from her grasp and lifted the chain from around her neck. He already knew that he wasn't going to find anything, so he made a show of wrapping his hand in his handkerchief before inserting the key card.

"Fingerprints," he said quietly, and she nodded her understanding. He opened the door, reached round to switch on the light, and stepped inside. She placed her foot against the bottom of the door to prevent it from closing. She watched him look briefly into the bedroom, and then the bathroom, pausing only for a few seconds at each. He came back, extinguished the light, and they stepped outside, shutting the door.

"Nothing. He's not here, and his bed hasn't been slept in. Some of his personal belongings are still dotted around, though."

She breathed a loud sigh of relief, and with her hand held high on her chest, took a deep breath.

"Oh, thank God for that. I was dreading that you might find something horrid."

They stood in silence for a few seconds. She could see that he was thinking.

"He booked in for three nights, you said. So when, exactly, should his room be vacated?"

"Officially he has until tomorrow lunchtime, but what should we, the hotel, be doing now?"

"Nothing yet, I guess. His car is still outside, and it's quite possible that he's spent the night elsewhere. Can we check to see if he was in to dinner last night? And can I see the address that he gave for the booking registration? Has he paid in advance for his room?"

"Let's get back down to my desk, Mr Grogan. The answers to all your questions will be readily to hand down there. Besides, Jim needs to get off home. Poor man, he's just done a ten-hour nightshift."

"I think it might be a good idea for me to be taking a statement from you, Carol, while all this is still fresh in your mind. I have a bad feeling about this one. I think we'll be finding a body somewhere, and the Coroner will certainly want to know all the background. I think I'll have a word with your barman, as well. What was his name, again?"

"Larry Gardner, but he won't be on until tonight, though. His shift is from six to eleven thirty, or until the last guests vacate the bar."

In the lift, Pete produced from his pocket, a small brown envelope containing the original photograph of Connor McCall, the one he had been given by Tony Williams, when the enquiry was first initiated, nearly a fortnight ago. He handed it to her, deliberately choosing his next words.

"Tell me, Carol, is this a close image of our Mr McCall?"

She studied the photograph for several seconds, holding it up to catch the light in the lift. They reached the ground floor, and together, walked slowly across the foyer towards her desk. Still holding the picture, she paused, and leaned towards him. She held up the photo and started to point things out with her finger.

"I would say that it's a pretty close resemblance, but that's definitely not him, Mr Grogan."

"In what way is it different then, Carol? How can you be so sure?"

"His ear lobes, for a start. Look here, this picture is of a man with quite distinctive lobes to his ears. Mr McCall barely has any at all. His ears are like a single, even, fold of flesh all the way around. Nowhere to hang an earring from. Us girls, we tend to notice such things. And then there's his chin. McCall's chin is quite a bit more pointed than that, and his lips are thinner, his mouth a bit smaller. This picture is of a similar looking person. The mole on his cheek, the bushy eyebrows, even the hair all looks similar, but it's definitely not the Mr McCall that is staying here with us. Who is this person, anyway?"

Pete took the photo back from her, and carefully replaced it back into the brown envelope. He didn't offer her any immediate answer to her question, for he was thinking, 'there lies the sixty-four-thousand dollar question, Carol, because the photograph I have just shown you, is of the real Mr Connor McCall.'

Her insistence interrupted his train of thoughts. "Mr Grogan?"

"Huh, oh, sorry, Carol, I was miles away. What was it you said?"

"I asked you who the man was in your picture?"

"Oh, just someone who closely resembles Connor McCall, as you have just confirmed. Can we go and find a cup of coffee, and have a bash at that statement, please Carol?"

Clutching his two precious kitbags, and an old, Portuguese army haversack, the young man alighted from the rear of the rather tatty looking Winchester licensed taxicab, that pulled up in the lane outside of Oakwood. The driver had made no attempt to offer him any assistance with his luggage, but now, still seated in the driver's seat of the car, he held out his hand for payment.

In his ignorance, the young man had previously agreed a price of forty pounds for the journey from the railway station. He wasn't to know, but it would have been a lot cheaper to do it on the meter. He took the last of his money from his wallet, a tatty, red, fifty-pound note, and passed it over. The driver looked at him, and the young man felt that something else was expected? He smiled, and made as if to shake hands with the driver.

*"Muito obrigado, meu amigo.* Thank you."

"No problem mate. Have a nice day."

The driver ignored his offer of a handshake, and instead, carefully flattened out the corners of the banknote before slipping it into the his wallet. He put the car into gear, released the handbrake, and made as if to drive off. The young man dropped his bags, and slapped angrily on the roof of the car.

*"Hey, hey, hey, da-me minha mudenca, e um recibo, por favor."*

The driver stopped the car moving, and looked questioningly at him. He theatrically shrugged his shoulders to indicate that he didn't understand. The young man switched to English.

"You will give me my change, and a receipt, please."

"Sorry mate, you should have said. In this country, it is usual to give a tip for good service."

"I am sorry, senhor, but I cannot afford such luxury. Now, my change, and a receipt, please."

The driver was considering remonstrating further, but the young man looked as though he might be able to handle himself? Not to be outdone, he picked up his bag of change from the door pocket, and sorted out a handful of coins, which he dumped unceremoniously, into the expectant hand. He took down a pad of taxi receipts from behind the car sun visor, and scribbled an amount into the total column. He tore it off and thrust it out of the window, allowing it to fall to the ground at his feet.

Without another word being spoken, the driver sneered at the young man, before burying his foot on the throttle to accelerate the car away up the road.

Left standing in a cloud of acrid, diesel smoke and fumes, the young man stooped to retrieve the precious receipt, and then his bags, from the muddy puddle where they had landed. He pocketed his change, and then slapped his bicep into a raised fist. In the traditional gesture of anger, he added his shouted curse at the fast disappearing taxi.

*"A variol em você, filho de um porco . . ."*

Miguel Pereira shouldered his heavy load. It was comprised of virtually everything in the world that he owned. As he started the long walk up the drive, to the place that he expected to be calling his home, for at least the next two years, his anger at being so rudely treated was soon lost in the unexpected beauty of his surroundings. He paused frequently to rest, and to admire the carefully tended, mature gardens.

Changing his grip on his handle-less kitbags, he realised how just how inefficient and unsuited for purpose they really were.

Back in Portugal, in his hometown of Agueda, his widowed mother now lived in what she proudly regarded as, retirement. Following the tragic death of his father, from bowel cancer, he and his mother had struggled to keep the farm going. She had insisted that he continue with his education, but it meant that he had to spend evenings and weekends doing all the heavy work around the farm.

Their plight had not gone unnoticed, and the avaricious *funcianarios de governo local,* the local council, had started to put pressure on his mother to give up the place, by offering her money, and alternative accommodation in the town. Eventually, she had been worn down, and pressured into parting with their small farm and vineyard, for only a fraction of it's true value. The land was needed to make way for proposed urban redevelopment, it was said. But three years later, it was still a derelict demolition site.

At the time, Miguel had been too young to fully understand what was happening. But as he watched their family home being razed to the ground, while he was left dealing with the tears of his still grieving mother, he had become full of hatred. In consequence, he now harboured a burning desire to somehow seek revenge and retribution, against the perpetrators of this outrage, the members of the local town council.

Left with no means of support, and with little, or no, prospects of good employment, Miguel had been forced into abandoning his college education, and to face the prospect of having to leave home.

So as not to be any further burden on his mother's fast dwindling, and meagre finances, he had boldly announced his intention to leave the country completely, and while continuing his education, to seek gainful employment abroad, in England, perceived by him, to be the land of milk and honey?

His mother had tried to persuade him not to go, but even she could see that their financial position had become untenable. She finally relented, and together, they began to pack up all of his things.

To save money, he had been grateful for the use of the kitbags. His mother had removed them from under the mattress of her bed, where, stored flat, they had served to help support the sagging middle.

She told him that they had belonged to his late father, and his father before that, so they were to be regarded as valuable family heirlooms. Now that they were entrusted into his care, it was his responsibility to look after them. But, heirlooms or not, it didn't make them any easier to carry . . .

He wondered why his father, or his grandfather, both practical men, hadn't seen fit to throw them away, long ago? Awkwardly clutching one under each arm, he thought it might be a good idea to stitch a couple of handles onto the heavy canvas sides, and in so doing, make them a lot easier to handle? Yes, he would do that at the earliest opportunity.

A car coming up the drive behind, interrupted his thoughts. He hastily stood to one side to allow it to pass. He watched, apprehensively, as it drew to a halt just ahead of him. A man, smartly dressed, got out, and came round the back of the car, to where he was standing. There was a big, friendly smile on his face, and Miguel was relieved to see that, as he approached, he held out his hand to be shaken.

"Good morning, young fella. Unless I'm very much mistaken, you must be Miguel, am I right?"

Miguel dropped his bags, and took the man's hand in a firm handshake, returning the smile.

"*Sim, senhor, eu sou Miguel.* Pardon me, sir, I forget myself. Yes, I am Miguel Pereira, at your service."

"Pleased to meet you then, Miguel, I'm David Morrison-Lloyd, and I live here at Oakwood. Throw your kit in the boot, lad, and I'll give you a lift up to the house. It's not far, but you look to be struggling?"

Seconds later he was being whisked along in a beautiful Mercedes, he wished his mother could see him.

The car pulled up outside of the house and Miguel got out of the front passenger side. He stood in the open car door, gazing spellbound at the magnificent house before him. The man that owned it must surely be someone *muito importante? Talvez, o governador provincial?* He thought.

The door of the house opened, and another, much older, and equally smartly dressed man appeared. He must surely be the owner, Miguel thought, and he bowed respectfully in his direction. The man gave him the briefest friendly smile, and slight bow, in return.

"Ah, Carter, I've just come across this young man walking up the drive. This is our new stable-lad, Miguel, I believe."

As he spoke, David was already lifting his heavy bags from the boot of the car. Without saying anything, Carter merely snapped his fingers, and pointed to indicate to the lad, that he should be doing that task for himself.

*"As minhas desculpas, cavalheiros,* Sorry, I forget myself again. My apologies, gentlemen. My mind, it was not here. I am overwhelmed, a little, I think?"

David smiled in understanding, and handed him his rucksack together with one of his kitbags. Carter moved down the steps to take the other bag.

"There are two phone messages for you, Mr David. Mr Malcolm and Miss Sharon would both wish you to return their calls. They say that your mobile number is not being answered, for some reason?"

David fished in his pocket for his phone and looked at it. There were four missed calls.

"Damn thing's still on silent mode, that's why, Carter. I've forgotten to switch it back over after the meeting I've just been to. I'll ring Malcolm immediately.

"Thank you, sir."

Carter put one hand on the young man's shoulder, and started to lead him towards the side gate. David paused, watching as Carter effectively, took him under his wing. He heard the first pearls of wisdom being delivered, and wondered how many times Carter had given this same spiel?

"Now then, master Miguel, let's be getting you sorted out, shall we? Come this way, lad, and I will show you to your room. My name is Carter, and that is how I would wish to be referred to. I am the butler, here at Oakwood, and I am in overall charge of all the staff. There are just three rules that will govern your work while you are here, young man, so I shall first tell you what they are, and then give them to you in writing, together with a list of the daily tasks that you will be expected to complete. Are you paying attention?

*"Sim, senhor Carter."*

"Good. Well, if you will kindly stop gazing all around for a few minutes, I will begin . . .

Rule one. If you want to know anything, you will ask me. And preferably, in English, if you please.

Rule two. If you are not sure about how something should be done, you will ask me.

Rule three. If someone else asks you to do anything that is outside of the scope of your normal duties, you will ask me, or tell me, first. Are we all clear, so far?"

*"Sim, senhor.* Sorry, sir. I mean, yes, Mr Carter."

"Excellent. If you follow those three simple rules, you will be taking direction from me, in all matters relating to your duties, and we will be getting on very well, together, won't we, Miguel?"

"Yes, Mr Carter."

"No, Miguel, it's just Carter. Not, Mr Carter. In this house, that form of address is reserved for the master, Mr Malcolm Blackmore, who you will refer to as, Mr Malcolm, sir. The same applies to his guests. While they reside here at Oakwood, you will be polite and respectful at all times, and address them in a similar manner. Now the ladies, you will refer to as . . ."

They went through side gate and out of David's hearing. He thought that he would have liked to hear the rest of Carter's strict code of conduct, something he recognised as being essential to the smooth running of the house.

David hit Malcolm's speed dial number, but only got his messaging service, so he called Sharon instead.

"Hello David, thanks for ringing back, I expect you're busy?"

"Never too busy to speak with you, Sharon-Louise. How's Weymouth this morning?"

"A bit mizzly and overcast, at the moment, David, but I can see that there's some blue on the horizon. The reason I'm ringing, David, is with regard to my mothers car, the Nissan, here on the driveway. I just tried to start it, and the battery's flat. I don't suppose it's been used for over a month?"

"What do you want me to do then, Sharon? I'm here, fifty miles away, and fresh out of magic wands . . ."

She immediately rose to his facetious remark.

"Really? And there was me thinking you might still be flying around while wearing your usual blue spandex suit, and red pants, outside of your tights?"

He chuckled, "It feels that way, sometimes, love."

"Seriously, David, I need to get the car back to Oakwood. With Grey Gables looking to become an imminent reality, we're going to be needing a little staff run-around, and the Nissan will fit the bill perfectly, don't you think?"

"I think it's an excellent idea, Sharon-Louise, but what does Malcolm say?"

"To get David to organise it . . ."

"I rather thought as much. Yes, alright, leave it with me, and I'll get something put into place. When are you off to Ireland? You've got the only set of house keys for your mum's house."

"Thursday morning, but I shall be back at Oakwood for Wednesday evening to pack my things. If we can't do it before then, it will have to wait until next week, I suppose?"

"That might be better. The rest of this week is looking a bit hectic, at the moment. I really should be helping Sue and Edith with packing up all our stuff, but Malcolm keeps loading me up, as well."

"Next week it is then. Perhaps you and I could do it between us, and combine it with a trip up to Bleanaway, as well? The Police have just sent me yet another reminder about the place being insecure."

"We'll have to see, Sharon-Louise. Malcolm told me yesterday, that the diggers are coming in early next week to begin breaking ground for the footings, apparently, as a matter of urgency. We need to show that the building project is underway. Something to do with the imminent expiry of planning consent, he said. I'm still in the process of trying to organise better site access, and all the contractor's facilities. That's where I've been this morning, and now I've got planning meetings scheduled for tomorrow, and Friday, as well. Incidentally, did you know that Malcolm's not coming home this weekend?"

"Yes. Apparently he's been duty rostered. Oakwood will be fairly quiet, I think. Charlotte and Michelle won't be home either. I'm not planning to be back from Ireland until Sunday at the earliest, and George says he's got to go back home on Saturday. So, apart from my dad and Jacqui, it looks as though you, Sue, and the children, will have the place to yourselves? Changing the subject, David, what's the story with Charlie Ferguson? Malcolm didn't seem to know very much at all, except that he suffered a stroke."

"That's all I know, as well, Sharon-Louise. You know, it strikes me that there's something very odd about all of this? What with Connor McCall going missing, and now Charlie's sudden death. I can't tell you why, but I'm getting the distinct feeling that we've not seen the end of it, yet. I sincerely hope that I'm wrong, but I wouldn't be too surprised if it all came back to haunt us once more?"

They spoke inconsequentially for a few more minutes, but Sharon didn't really know what to say. She already knew that David's instincts were definitely correct, and in talking about it, she had been unintentionally reminded about the significance of note from Michael Close. Now, it had begun to prick at her conscience.

Meanwhile, Pete Grogan's mind was still working in overdrive. Caroline, on the other end of the phone, was aware that he only got like this, when his copper's nose told him that he was on the trail of something big. She listened carefully as he related everything he'd got so far, jotting down the salient points, and clarifying things, as he spoke.

"So I think it would be a good idea to ring round all the taxi companies local to Lyndhurst, and to ask if any of them picked up a man from anywhere near here, and took him to the airport, at any time yesterday? If we strike lucky, we need to know what name was used for the booking, and at what time he was dropped off?

Next, we need to check the Southampton Airport passenger lists for yesterday's flights to Belfast or Dublin. We're probably looking for one, middle-aged man, travelling alone, possibly, a last minute booking? I'm going to get a statement from the Receptionist, here at the hotel, and then try to persuade her into giving me the Barman's address. He, apparently, was talking with our man, all evening, in the bar. Have you got all that, love?"

"I have, but before we go any further, I think we will need to speak with the client. Our remit is to find his missing son, and as far as I can see, we've gone about as far with that, as is possible. You might be about to get into doing more work than we are likely to be paid for. He might not want us to take this any further, Pete, so just you hang fire until we've spoken to him, and got the okay."

"Caroline, we can't just let this go, now. The trail is red hot. Try phoning him, if you must. You've got to persuade him into letting us carry on. My instincts are telling me that this has the potential to be absolutely enormous. I'm talking about a murder that has quite possibly being instigated, or sanctioned, by a leading Irish political figure."

"Yes, well, you don't know that for certain, and it looks to me as though you've got no real concrete evidence, as yet. So far, it's all circumstantial and just your suspicions and theories. Perhaps you'd like to suggest how am I going to put it to Mr Williams? I can't just ring him up and say, 'Oh, by the way, our enquiries lead us to believe that Connor McCall, your son, has been murdered.' Christ, Pete, the shock alone, will probably be sufficient to give the old chap a heart attack? For the time being, and only because we have nothing more pressing, I am prepared to go along with your train of thought. I'll do the enquiries you suggest, and let's see what we come up with, when you've done the forensics. After that, we go no further unless the client is put fully in the picture, and it his express wish, that we proceed. Is it a deal?"

"Deal. Ring me back as soon as you get anything, Caroline, I'm already halfway to the airport should my presence be required over there in person. I've got a good feeling about this one, love, I reckon it could turn into the big break we've both been looking and waiting for?"

Miguel had unpacked his belongings, changed into his work-issue clothing, and now sat at the staff dining table, tucking into his first proper meal since leaving home, nearly a week ago. The deliciously simple lunch, of a meat and vegetable broth, served together with freshly baked bread, and a selection of fresh fruit, was being well received by all the staff.

Carter had formally introduced him first, to Mrs Carter, and then to the three, slightly older women chambermaids, that now sat opposite him, and were laughing and giggling amongst themselves.

Acting in the customary Portuguese way, he had taken their hand and bowed politely and respectfully to each one, as they were named to him.

*"Prazer em conhecê lo.* Pleased to meet you . . ."

At first, he had felt slightly embarrassed by their rather obvious lascivious remarks that were being whispered between them, immediately after Carter's back was turned. But slowly, he began to turn things to his own advantage. By simply pretending not to fully understand what they were saying, he found that their comments to each other were becoming ever more outrageous. He began to enjoy himself by responding with an occasional smile, or by raising his eyebrows in mock surprise. He took to openly flirting with his eyes, especially toward the rather pretty little blue-eyed blonde, whose name he recalled, was Susan. He'd already noticed that beneath her pale green, cotton work suit, comprised of a lightweight Breton style fisherman's smock, worn with matching trousers that were supported at the waist by a drawstring, she wore very little else underneath. Her pert little breasts were certainly unfettered . . .

Slim, muscled, and standing a little over six feet tall, with his black hair, brown eyes, and a swarthy complexion, Miguel, knew that most woman found his Latin looks to be rather attractive.

Since the age of sixteen, when for his birthday, his father secretly arranged that he lose his virginity to the wiles of a much older woman, he had certainly never found himself to be short of female company. She had kept the rather well-endowed young man in her clutches, and her bed, for over a week. The time had been well spent, for after the first frantic and frenzied fumblings associated with his inexperience, she had patiently set about teaching him how to pace himself, and how to address some of the finer points of how exactly, to pleasure a woman. He'd been a willing pupil, and had learned well.

As yet, not having read the six-page document given to him by Carter, Miguel was totally unaware of the strict rule forbidding staff indulging in any sexual liaisons while working at Oakwood. In his ignorance, he was thinking that, given time, and the right opportunity, he stood a very good chance of getting his leg over with Susan.

"Carter says that you speak French as well, Miguel. Are you good at French? Do you give lessons?"

The others giggled. He was not so naïve as to be totally ignorant of the sexual connotation. He smiled at the question, which had come from the loudest one, Karen, whom he thought might already be in a lesbian relationship with the other woman, Joyce? He gave her his best smouldering look, and answered her in a husky, sexy voice.

*"Oui, madame, que mon francais est excellent. Aimeriez-vous de practiquer avec moi, peut-être?"*

"Oo blimey, lover-boy. I don't know what you just said, but yes please, whatever it is . . ."

The others burst out laughing. Miguel had turned to look directly at Susan as he had spoken. He suspected that she alone might have understood, and he wasn't disappointed. She had clearly caught the meaning, and now, under his very pointed gaze, he could see that she was visibly blushing.

To his utter disappointment, Carter arrived back on the scene to break up their little gathering.

"Come on, you lot. Time's up, let's all be getting back to work, then, shall we? Karen, I want you and Joyce to give the master's suite a really good seeing to this afternoon. He and miss Sharon will be away at least until this weekend, so we can use the opportunity to change the curtains and drapes to the heavier winter ones. But before doing that, I want you to shift all the furniture around, so that we can shampoo the carpets. It will have several days to dry out, and be nice and fresh for their return.

Susan, it's your weekend off, are you planning on leaving Oakwood?"

"Yes, Carter. I shall be going back home to Charmouth, to see my mother."

"Very well, I've noticed that your work standard has been particularly good this week. As a small thank you, I am extending your time-off. You have my permission to leave on Friday, after lunch, if you so wish. You will not be expected to be back here, at Oakwood, until midday, on Monday. Is that clear and acceptable?"

"Yes Carter. Thank you."

"You, master Miguel, will come with me, and I will introduce you your particular work areas. You will need to put on your boots and boilersuit, for the tasks that I have in mind for this afternoon."

As they departed, Miguel gave Susan a smile, which she coyly acknowledged by parting her lips with the tip of her tongue. Her meaning was unmistakeable, and he definitely knew that he was on a promise.


"This room is the tool store and workshop, Miguel. Responsibility for keeping everything in here in good order will be part of your duties. There are only two keys for this door. Here is one for you, I have the other. For health and safety reasons, this door is to be kept locked at all times that the workshop is not being used. There are young children living in the house, Miguel, and we don't want any accidents, do we?"

"No, senhor Carter."

Miguel stood looking around. At the far end he could see numerous tins of paint, and associated paraphernalia, all stacked untidily on shelves that went from floor to ceiling. The huge wooden workbench stretched all along the wall to his right. It was fitted with several vices, and the top was littered with tools of every description. Two broken wheelbarrows, three old bicycles, an ancient Honda moped, and a whole stack of assorted gardening tools, and equipment, took up nearly all the rest of the available floor space. The whole place was in a shambles.

"I apologise for the state of things in here, Miguel. It has long been on my list of tasks, to get it all put back into good order, but I never seem to have found the time."

Carter experimentally switched the light switch on and off, it didn't work.

"I will get an electrician in to fix it for you, Miguel. It's probably only a fuse, or a bulb, that's required. In the meantime, I would like you to make a start in sorting everything out. Anything that you consider to be broken beyond repair, put to one side for later disposal. Items to be repaired, stack separately. The hand tools all need to be cleaned and sharpened, and then put somewhere readily to hand.

This workshop is to be almost entirely your domain, Miguel. Somewhere in here, you will find virtually everything that you will require to enable you to do your work. So how well this room is kept, will become a reflection of your character and efficiency, will it not?"

"Sim senhor Carter, I understand."

"Excellent. Right, shall we go and look at the stables then? Tell me, Miguel, the résumé in your CV says that you are experienced in taking care of horses and ponies, but can you ride, as well?"

"Sim senhor. For all of my life, I have been working with animals on our farm. We use the horses for everything. I have been riding since I am *criança pequena,* a small child."

They were walking towards the stable block, when, at the very far end of the paddock, two children were seen to be riding tandem on a pony. Their antics had caught Miguel's attention, and he stopped to watch. Carter saw where he was looking, and immediately voiced his disapproval at what they were doing.

"Would you go and call those two young rascals, please, Miguel. That's Peter and Rita, two of Mr David's children. They have permission to ride the pony, but not two-up, like that. I shall need to be delivering a rather stern rebuke, I think."

Miguel turned, put his fingers to his lips, and let forth with a very loud piercing whistle. The children were seen to bring the pony to an immediate standstill, and one of them guiltily jumped down from off the hindquarters of the animal. Carter smiled and gestured for them to come.

"You might want to teach me how to do that, as well, Miguel . . ."

They watched as the rider dismounted, and the pony was slowly walked back the whole length of the paddock. The two miscreants could clearly be seen to be arguing about something.

"They're probably trying to think up some sort of excuse for their behaviour, Miguel. Do you think they might have harmed the pony?"

"No, senhor Carter. The animal looks very fit, and is quite capable of carrying two small children. My only concern would be if one of them should fall off, for neither of them is wearing a safety helmet."

"By golly, you're right. They both have proper riding hats, so there is absolutely no excuse."

They walked the rest of the way over to the yard, and waited for the hapless pair to arrive. They finally came to a halt in front of him, heads bowed. Tara recognised Carter, and started to nudge at his pockets for her usual titbit. Her attentions were knocking him slightly off balance, thereby inhibiting his ability to rise up to his full height, and deliver his dignified reprimand. Miguel stood just behind, his hand covering his mouth to hide the fact that he was desperately trying to keep a straight face.

"What on earth do you two young reprobates think that you are doing? When Miss Michelle gave you permission to ride her pony, do you think that she meant that you should both be up on Tara's back together? And where are your riding hats? They are meant to be protecting your head. Well, master Peter, what have you to say for yourself?"

"We're sorry Carter. We didn't think we were doing any harm, it's a bit of a pain having to take turns all the time. And the hats are very hot and uncomfortable to wear if you're not actually riding."

"So that is what you would wish me to pass on to your parents when they come to visit you in hospital, is it, Peter? That you thought it was alright to ride without a helmet, because it's a little uncomfortable, and that you encouraged Rita to do the same?"

"I never encouraged Rita, she . . ."

"She was up behind you when you were the rider, and in control, Peter. Yours is the responsibility."

The children looked crestfallen. They both knew that if Carter told their parents, it would effectively put an end to their riding. Carter let the moment hang, allowing the silence to press home the point.

"Clearly, you cannot be trusted to act responsibly, so, in future, you will not be allowed to ride unless you are properly supervised. Do you understand?"

Peter looked at him forlornly, and mumbled their acceptance of the situation. "Yes, Carter."

"Fortunately for you both, this will not be too difficult to organise. Allow me to introduce you to Miguel. From this moment on, in Michelle and Charlotte's absence, responsibility for looking after the horses and ponies will be wholly his. Therefore, if either of you wishes to ride, you will ask Miguel if it is convenient for you to do so. As before, you will only have permission to ride Tara within the confines of the paddock. Now, there are the added provisos, that you are to be suitably attired, and under his direct supervision at all times. Is that clear to you both?"

They both answered him, gratefully accepting the added restrictions, in return for their future good behaviour. Rita visibly brightened up and stepped forward to greet Miguel. This was the moment she had been waiting, and practicing for. She held out her hand,

"Olá Miguel, meu nome é Rita."

Miguel smiled, recognising her effort. He gently took her hand, bowed, and kissed the back.

*"Olá perca Rita, tenho o prazer de conhecê-lo. Voce fala Português?"*

He smiled again as the slightly disappointed look of bewilderment crossed her little face.

"I replied to you, hello, miss Rita, I am pleased to meet you. Do you speak Portuguese?"

"Oh no Miguel. So far, I have only learned that one little sentence, but I can say 'goodbye' as well."

"Well, let us hope that you and I will not need to say *adeus* for some time, shall we Rita?"

Peter, not to be outdone, stepped forward and offered his hand. He tried to copy his sister.

"Hola Miguel, I'm Peter."

Miguel shook his hand firmly.

*"Coma você faz, o jovem senhor?* How do you do, young sir?"

"I'm very well, thank you. Will you be teaching us how to ride properly, as well? We think we're doing it right, but Michelle is not here to tell us, and we keep arguing."

Miguel looked questioningly at Carter, who shook his head imperceptibly.

"I regret that in my country, our riding style is a lot different to how you ride in England, Peter. I am not sufficiently conversant with what you have already been taught, so I would not wish to confuse anything that you might have already been told. I think it would be better if I only observe, just to see that you don't hurt yourself, or the animal."

Tara had moved forward on the halter and was now sniffing inquisitively at Miguel. He gently offered her the back of his hand while leaning forward to breath into her nostrils. They did this for a few seconds before she seemed to accept him. He reached into his pocket and produced a small titbit for her. Presenting it on the palm of his hand, the children saw that it was a Polo mint. Tara took it into her mouth and immediately started salivating from the corners. She began gently nudging him, clearly looking for more. He stroked her muzzle, gently pushing it away from his pocket.

*"Não, voce não está recenbendo mais ainda, mina beleza,"* he whispered into her ear.

Carter and the children watched enthralled, as Tara seemed to understand him completely, and stepped away, not bothering him any further. It was Rita that posed the obvious question.

"Tara's an English pony, Miguel. How come she can understand Portuguese, as well?"

"Tara understands my thoughts, Rita, and I understand hers. I can sense what she requires from me. From now on, as long as I treat her well, she will do as I ask. Won't you, *mina beleza,* my beauty?"

He scratched her forehead and fondled her ears, while taking the halter from Peter's hands.

"Our little sister, Emily, can do that, as well, Miguel. She can talk with the animals."

Peter had heard enough. Where Emily was concerned, he was having none of it.

"That's just plain silly, Rita. Em can't talk with animals, nobody can, its' not possible. Tell her Miguel."

"I'm sorry, Peter, but I have to say that you are wrong. There are some people that do have a special way with animals, and I am fortunate to be one such person. I look forward to meeting your little sister, Rita. Why isn't Emily out here, riding with you? Where is she now?"

"Probably in the study with uncle Jim, reading some boring old book, of some sort. She can't ride yet, Miguel, Emily isn't old enough. She's only two."

He was tying the halter to a hitching rail in readiness for removal of the saddle.

"My father, he teaches me how to ride as soon as I am able to walk, Rita, so if Emily wishes to ride, she should be encouraged. Come along, master Peter, I am doing your task. You and Rita prepare the stall with some fresh bedding, while I will lift off the saddle for you. Then you can show me how well you can clean everything, while Rita demonstrates how to give Tara a good brush down."

Carter stood back and watched on in silent approval, as the children, eager to please, immediately set about their allotted tasks. He was impressed with the ease at which Miguel had already endeared himself to the twins, and how they were both so keen to do his bidding.

He reflected on the fact that in the past few minutes, Miguel had adequately demonstrated that he did indeed have a natural ability with animals, and with children, as well, it would seem? So far, the young man's easy-going, almost unassuming, personality was everything that he would have hoped for, and he found that he was already developing a liking for him. He thought that it was time to extend to him, the courtesy of trust and responsibility. He placed a hand on his shoulder to attract his attention.

"I have other things to do, Miguel, so I am going to leave the children to introduce you to the other animals. I don't think that I need to tell you anything in regard to their care. I am quite happy to leave everything up to you. However, you need to know that the other pony, Totsy, and the two horses, Bess and Bella, have not been out of their stalls today, and their bedding will need refreshing, as well.

If you do decide to let them out to graze, Miguel, miss Michelle insists that they must be brought back in before dark. You will find that Totsy will be no problem, and Bess will usually come quite easy. Bella though, can be a bit naughty, and likes to have a little run around before finally submitting to the halter. I have found that a little tit-bit usually helps to persuade her, but unfortunately, she now tends to look for it as being her entitlement. Are you okay with all of that?"

"Yes, Mr Carter, *obrigado, senhor.*"

Carter smiled, overlooking the incorrect form of address. He was beginning to quite like the occasional little bit of Portuguese being thrown into the conversation. He could envisage that as everyone got to know Miguel, and with his very likeable character, very soon, the whole house would probably be at it?

He walked back to the kitchens muttering to himself, *'obrigado, mina beleza'*—'Thank you, my beauty' His first three words in Portuguese. He quickened his pace in anticipation. It was a good one to go and try out on Elsie.

Sharon-Louise decided to take a short break from her sorting out. The cupboard under the stairs was proving to be particularly challenging. It was obviously the place where her mother had stored all those items that were either seldom used, too good to throw away, or which might come in handy one day?

With the thought of keeping anything that might be of use at Grey Gables foremost in her mind, she had been pondering the fate of three rather ancient looking, but still serviceable, electric fires, and several boxes of perfectly good sets of chinaware, tea and dinner services. There was also several boxes of assorted hand tools, and a couple of battery-operated drills, which, she thought, her father might like, as all his precious tools, ones that he had accumulated over the years, had been lost in the fire.

She struggled to lift the heavy cardboard boxes, eventually realising that she would need to repack them into smaller loads, so that she could manage. That meant a trip to the local shops for more cardboard boxes. A cup of coffee first, though . . .

She sat at the dining room table with her steaming mug of coffee, and a couple of her mothers chocolate digestives. Sitting in the middle of the table was her mother's laptop computer, its tiny blue flashing corner light, caught her attention. It was apparent that it had been left switched on for God knows how long? She pulled it in closer, and did an experimental double-tap on the pad. The screen immediately burst back into life. Sharon-Louise studied the page before her, identifying it as one from her mother's Irish banking file. Her attention captured, all thoughts of doing any more sorting out, was immediately forgotten. She backtracked to the file headings, and pondered the list, vainly trying to make some sense of her mother's complex filing and accounting systems. She wondered why there were two sub headings marked Derry A, and Derry B?

She called up the first one. It related to bank transactions on another Lloyds Bank account, held in the name of S & K McBride Investments. Sharon was puzzled. She recognised that the S probably referred to her aunt Sandra, her mother's sister, but as to who the K might be, she had no idea?

From the pages contained within the folder, it was clear that her mother had, for many years, been handling all of her sister's finances, as well. Sharon worked her way through all the different pages of figures, some of which were absolutely astronomical. It was apparent from some of the annual totals that her aunt Sandra, and whoever 'K' might be, was very well off, indeed.

Sharon remembered that her grandmother, in a previous conversation about flowers at the funeral, had mentioned that they would not be able to afford too much, as they were largely reliant on state benefits. Interesting? Why would her grandmother wish to lie about such a thing, unless she herself had something similar to hide?

She called up the Derry B file. Not surprisingly, it was found to be structured in much the same way, but related to yet another account, this time with Barclays Bank, and in the name of AOH Holdings and Investments. It didn't take a genius to work out that the AOH probably referred to her grandmother, Anne O'Hare, and that her mother had been complicit in setting up and running this one, as well.

It was clear that until very recently, reasonably large sums of money, usually several hundred pounds at a time, were being transferred in and out of both accounts. Try as she may, she couldn't track down exactly where the money was going, or from whence it came. She suspected that the information she was looking for was probably stored on one of the CD's, in the carrier bag? But in order to access it, she would need to understand her mother's intentionally complicated system of accounting.

Sharon-Louise concluded that both of these accounts had developed into a small scale money laundering operation, probably with the sole purpose of cheating the Benefits Agency? She suspected that the main source of income to be from the sale of stolen dogs, and puppies, to which had been attributed a false pedigree, but it would need further proof and verification for her to be sure. She sat back in her chair, sipped her coffee, and started to give it all some serious consideration.

These people, her aunt and grandmother, were living in a property that was now rightfully hers, and for which, she was solely responsible for all the upkeep, and maintenance.

George had already pointed out that under the present arrangement, her ownership of the property was a liability that was costing her considerably more than she was receiving in rent. Not being in possession of the full facts, i.e. her aunt's and grandmother's enhanced financial status, his best advice had been for her to consider abrogation of her responsibility, by disposing of the property completely.

He had pointed out that by far the biggest drawback, was the fact that her aunt and grandmother were both sitting tenants, with a legally binding Tenancy Agreement. With the current economic climate forcing the housing market into further depression, even if a buyer for the property could be found, their true value was unlikely ever to be realised.

George had even suggested that in the long term, it might be better to consider transfer of the ownership by making them a present of the deeds, suggesting that it could be construed as a gesture of goodwill towards her family. Sharon-Louise had rather liked that idea, and was fully prepared to go along with it. But now, faced with the unwarranted antagonism she was getting from her aunt and grandmother, and her discovery of their hidden wealth, things had subtly changed.

She reflected on the fact that it was her mother's dying wish, and specified in the terms of her will, that they should continue paying her only a pepper-corn rent for the privilege of living in her house, and that it should remain that way, at least until the property was vacated, or until they died.

Sharon now felt that she wasn't happy with any of this. Her mother, in handling the affairs of both her aunt and grandmother, was obviously aware of their considerable wealth, and yet she still saw fit to allow them to live for virtually nothing, in a property that she herself, had maintained. Why would she choose to do this, it made no sense at all?

On impulse, she reached for her mobile phone. Her call was answered immediately.

"Good afternoon, Sharon-Louise, what can I do for you today, my dear?"

She glanced at her watch, realising that she had been nearly two hours staring at the computer screen.

"Hello, George, are you busy? If you've got time, I've a couple of questions for you, but I can just as easily call again later, if it's an inconvenient moment?"

"Well, you're talking to me now, Sharon-Louise, so try me."

"Its to do with the Tenancy Agreement that my aunt and grandmother have on Cuthbert Street. Tell me George, do we have a copy?"

"No, but it won't be any bother to get Tony Williams to email, or fax one over. What's the nature of your query?"

"I was wondering if there was any provision written into the agreement, that would allow for any sort of service or maintenance charges to be levied?"

"I'm not sure, Sharon-Louise. These agreements tend to be fairly standard documents, and I would have expected that Tony Williams, in drawing it up, might have adapted something similar. That is what I would do in the circumstances. What's the problem?"

"It's not really a problem, George, just a little idea that I have. I've decided not to part with the deeds just yet, but instead, try and make the property pay its way. Would you kindly get a copy of the original Tenancy Agreement, and check to see if there is a clause relating to service and maintenance charges? If there isn't, I would like you to slightly amend the document, to include one that will allow a charge, the amount to be decided by the landlord, to be levied. Then, under the guise of the Agreement needing to be transferred into my name, I will take copies of the amended documents over to Ireland with me, for signatures."

She could hear George chuckling on the other end of the phone.

"I take it you like my little idea then, George?"

"Sharon-Louise, its brilliant, and I love it. I can't think why I never thought of it myself. But can these people afford it, do you think? I'm given to understand from Tony Williams, that the original reason for drawing up the peppercorn rent agreements, was because they live entirely on state benefits. It is not for me to question your reasons, but do you feel that it is morally justifiable to be burdening the taxpayer into paying for any of this?"

"I don't think that will be the case, George. Obviously, until I've been over and seen for myself, I can't say anything for definite. But I've just been looking at my mother's computer, and I've just discovered that my aunt and grandmother are not as poor as they would have us believe. In fact, they're both in possession of some rather large, almost certainly undeclared, sums of money. So let's just proceed with the plan, and see what happens, shall we? If it doesn't work, we can always revert back to plan A."

"Do you want me to do the same with the Derrymore Road, property, as well, Sharon-Louise? Getting the agreements put into your name is something that would certainly need addressing at some stage, so why not do it now?"

"Yes, alright George, do that, then."

"I'll get onto it immediately as we don't have much time. You said you had a couple of questions, my dear. What's the other one?"

"It follows on from the last, George. If I knew that people living in a property belonging to me were using it to pursue some form of criminal activity, am I in any way liable?"

"That's a difficult one Sharon-Louise, and a lot depends on the particular circumstances. Perhaps it might be better if you qualified your question a little further, and tell me what's on your mind?"

She went on to voice her suspicions, and they spoke at length with regard to her legal responsibilities.

"In conclusion, Sharon-Louise, and to safeguard yourself, why not put another additional clause into the Tenancy Agreements, one specifically forbidding the property being used for any illegal or immoral purpose. In the event of non-compliance, you could even make it grounds for eviction.

In my experience, when people are signing a document that they are eager to lay their hands upon, they rarely take the time to read all the small print. As long as this new Agreement looks very similar to the old, I doubt that you will have any trouble getting the required signatures."

By the time that she finished her phone call, Sharon-Louise felt a lot more confident in being able to face up to her aunt and grandmother, should she find it necessary.

The phone in Pete's pocket purred to an incoming call. He was uncomfortably seated on a bar stool and having to work while resting on the end of the reception area counter. The detailed statement from Carol Short was taking a long time to formulate, due to the frequent interruptions. There was apparently nobody else available to temporarily relieve her from her duties, so they were endeavouring to complete it, in between her doing everything else. He looked at the caller's ID and pressed the 'accept' button.

"Caroline, what have you got for me?"

"It would seem your hunch was right, Pete. Yesterday morning, a Waterside taxi picked up a man, fitting Connor's description, from outside of the fire station, which is right opposite the Lyndhurst Park Hotel. The cab was booked for 0930, the night before, in the name of Curtis. The driver dropped him off at Southampton Parkway Railway Station, just after 0950. He was in the office when I called, so I spoke to him personally. He told me that the man came across from the direction of the hotel, and that he spoke with a broad Irish accent. He paid in cash.

Next, I checked with the Airport, and it seems that just after 1015, a middle-aged man by the name of Charles McGuigan, obtained a last minute booking on the 1305 Flybe flight to Belfast City. I'm told that the check-in desk will have a photocopy of his passport details on record, but you will have to speak to one of their managers to obtain a copy. Pete, I've had to pull in quite a few favours from Airport Security, just to get this far. You're going to have to grease a few palms to get what we're after, they don't like giving out any information, these days."

"I'll be on my way over there in about an hour, Caroline. Who's my point of contact?"

"I spoke to their Head of Airport Security, Pete. He works for Seimans, who handle all the internal surveillance equipment. His name is Dave Cranshaw, and he's ex-the job. He's your best bet, I reckon."

"Okay, I've got that. So, you're the one with a finger on the button, where do you see us going from here then, love?"

"I'm already working on trying to get an address for anyone named Charles McGuigan living in Belfast, Pete, but there's something else that's been bugging me. Why did our man ask to be dropped off across the road from the airport, at the railway station? The only thing I can come up with is that he wanted to change his clothes, and to resume his own identity. Think about it. When he left the hotel, he was still posing as Connor McCall, but when he checked in for his flight, he had to use his own passport. The chances are he removed his disguise, and probably changed into his own clothes, as well. It's a bit of a long shot, but while you're over there, it might be worth checking to see if any of the railway station security cameras managed to pick him up before, and then after, he changed his appearance?"

"Good thinking, and he might even have dumped the clothes somewhere? Let's hope that the rubbish bins haven't been emptied yet."

"Pete, hold fast, and listen-up for a minute. I need to remind you of our earlier deal. I'm prepared to give this enquiry the rest of today. After that, I must insist that we go no further until we've spoken to the client. I think that we've already gone way beyond our original brief, and I'm not prepared to do anything more without his expressed wish that we proceed, and get his signature on the bottom of a new contract. This is our living, Pete, and we don't work for nothing. I know what you're like. One whiff of the slightest scent, and you're off like a bloodhound, usually with me being dragged along behind on a short leash."

"Okay, ring him now, Caroline. If possible, try and fix up another meeting for tomorrow morning. Tell him that it's time we had a case conference on this one. At some stage, he's going to have to officially report Connor McCall as missing, to the Police, and now, seems as good a time as any. Meanwhile, I'm going to finish up here, and then chase down those bits and pieces you've just uncovered over at the airport. Ring me back immediately if you turn up anything else significant. Well done, love. Put my dinner on the hot-plate, will you, please. I've just remembered that I still need to talk to the barman here at the hotel, and he won't be starting work until six.

Miguel, alone in the stables, was busy grooming one of the horses. By humming to himself, and whispering little words of affection, he'd established a rapport between himself and the animal, and it stood quietly by as he worked, listening to his voice and obviously enjoying his attentions. He sensed a slight change in the behaviour of the animal, a tensioning of the muscles, an awareness of something. He paused in what he was doing, and without turning round, probed with his mind for the reason.

This was a gift that he'd discovered that he possessed as a child, a sort of sixth sense, for such things. His mind detected another human presence, and he seemed to be receiving a message, requesting his attention. He slowly turned his head.

The small girl child, and her dog, were standing just outside of the stall, watching him work. He hadn't heard them enter the stables, and had no real idea of how long they had been there, watching. There was no need for any introduction, he knew immediately who she must be. He smiled and turned toward her.

*"boa noite, miss Emily, eu presumo?"*

The dog remained closely at her side as she came forward, offering her little hand to be shaken. Her lips didn't seem to move, but the words were so clear that he thought he must be mistaken.

"Yes, good evening, Miguel. I am pleased to meet you. This is Sam."

He took her hand, bowed politely, and gently kissed the back. He fondled Sam's ears, his mind already detecting the animal's friendly nature, and it's obvious devotion to the child.

"My sister, Rita, told me that you had arrived. She also said that you could talk to the animals, so I have come to see for myself. I have sensed that you possess the gift, as well."

He stared at her uncomprehendingly. The words he was hearing were clearly coming from her, but she wasn't actually speaking. The horse, Bess, stirred behind him and slowly came forward, lowering her head as she came closer to the child. The animal positively dwarfed her diminutive little figure, but she was totally unafraid, and reached up to stroke her muzzle and to breathe into her nostrils.

"Hello, Bess, is he looking after you and treating you well, then?"

He sensed, rather than heard her words to the animal, for again, her lips hadn't moved. The horse gave her a little snicker in response. Miguel became aware that the other animals had all moved to the front of their stalls and were intently watching the child as she continued to talk with Bess.

"Well, that's good then, isn't it, girl. Here, I've saved you a few little pieces from my dinner."

He watched as she unwrapped her little handkerchief to reveal a few slices of carrot, which she placed on the flat of her hand as an offering. The horse, using only her lips, gently drew them into her mouth before briefly chewing and swallowing. The animal, seeing there was no more to be had, then gently rubbed her muzzle on the side of the child's cheek in a gesture of obvious affection. Miguel had never seen anything like it before. As yet, he hadn't used any English, but she had understood. He tried again.

*"Você fala português, Emily?"*

"No, Miguel, I cannot speak your language, but I'm finding that I can understand your thoughts."

Once again the words were in his mind, but her lips hadn't moved. How was this possible? He was thinking in his own language.

"Miguel, I understand your question. I have sensed that you already possess a latent telepathic ability, so try opening your mind, and just think your words to me. In this way, we should be able to communicate with each other in a similar manner. Please look into my eyes for a few seconds, and I will try to help you. He did as he was asked, and for the briefest moment, felt that her bright brown eyes were looking into his very soul. She broke their momentary gaze, and he took a step away from her, holding his hands to either side of his forehead. He was aware that something in his brain had just subtly changed.

*"Meu Deus, Emily, o que você acabou de fazer comigo?"*

Emily gave him a little smile in understanding, and came forward to take his hand in reassurance. They sat down together on a bale of straw.

"Don't worry, Miguel, I haven't done anything nasty to you. I have just slightly enhanced the thought receptors of your mind to make it easier for you to communicate telepathically with me. In time, and with a little more practice, you will find that this will work with the animals, as well. Now, try asking me something by just thinking your question to me. It doesn't matter which language you use, I will understand, but I regret that for the time being, I will have to answer you telepathically, in English. My spoken communication skills are still developing."

Intrigued, Miguel tried thinking his next question in his own language.

*"Você fala para outras pessoas dessa maneira, Emily?*

Her answer came back immediately.

'Yes, Miguel. I speak to nearly all the other people that live here at Oakwood, in this manner. I find that it is much easier for me. As yet, the communicative skills of all the others are somewhat limited, and they can only talk telepathically, with me. In time, I expect that they will probably learn how to speak to each other in this way. My parents can already do it, but so far, they are the only ones.'

He found the telepathic concept came easy, and immediately fell into its use, only this time, he thought in English.

'And can they speak with the animals, Emily, like you and me?'

'No, Miguel. The gift we have, is something very special. I think we were born that way.'

'You understand my language, Emily. Will I be able to similarly understand the language of another?'

'I understand your thoughts, Miguel, not your language. The thought patterns of a person are similar, whatever language they speak. If you were unable to understand English, I doubt that we would be able to communicate as we are. You will need to find someone who speaks a different language, one that you are not familiar with, just to test your own awareness. I have been able to do this since my birth, Miguel, so while it appears very strange to you, it is all perfectly normal for me. I have already sensed that within your mind, there are many undeveloped aspects of a unique nature. I am sure that with application, it will be possible for you to develop these into far greater understandings, but I regret that I am unable to tell you what they are, or to teach you how to do it. You can only find this out for yourself. I am but a child, and my brain is still developing. So I too, still have very much to learn.'

'Such wisdom, coming from one so young, is difficult for me to grasp, Emily. I cannot doubt what you say, for you have just opened my mind in such a way, that I would have previously thought impossible. For that, I thank you. I am not sure how to proceed in seeking further enlightenment, but you have certainly been inspirational, and I feel the need to start applying myself into trying to discover some of these undeveloped aspects that you say I possess. Any guidance you can offer in that respect, might prove to be helpful.'

Emily sat quietly thinking for a few moments, her eyes staring ahead at nothing in particular. Miguel sensed that she might be seeking guidance herself, but from what source, he couldn't fathom. She finally spoke again, but her words seemed to be something being relayed from some other person.

'The knowledge that you seek is already within your character, Miguel. In all things, you must endeavour to see beyond that which is apparent. Picture in your mind how you would envisage something should be, and then strive toward making it so.

Never accept that anything is impossible, or unchangeable, for it isn't, and your belief in your own ability will be sufficient to bring about all the necessary changes.

You must put aside any feelings of malice that you may harbour towards another, for such feelings will inhibit the clarity of your thoughts.

Restructure your mind in such a way that you seek out only that which is right and proper.

Look for the good in everyone that you meet, and learn by their example.

By applying these five basic principles for life, in everything that you do, you will acquire enlightenment, Miguel, thus enabling you to offer similar guidance to others.'

Miguel stared at the small child. Emily had delivered everything in such a way that there was absolutely no hesitation in any of her words. He instinctively knew that they must have been formulated, and come from somewhere other than her own little mind. He also thought that he might have read something very similar to this, somewhere before?

'I think you will need to repeat all of that, Emily, so that I can write it down.'

She looked up at him, and gave another of her disarming little smiles.

'No, that will not be necessary, Miguel. It has just been stored into the memory banks of your mind. If you disbelieve what I say, try repeating it all back to me.'

He did as he was asked, and to his absolute astonishment, found that he'd got it word perfect.

'You have given me much to think about, Emily, and I would be interested to know how you implanted that knowledge into my mind. Can you teach me how to do it, for I am here to study your language, and will need to be sitting exams in the future?'

'I can teach you how to restructure your mind to enable the greater assimilation of knowledge, Miguel. Would you like me to ask uncle

Malcolm if you can use the library for your studies. It's a good place to work, and I could be there, with you, to help?'

'This is my first day here at Oakwood, Emily. I have yet to prove myself, and to meet all the people that live here. I think it might be better to wait for a little while, before I ask for any such favours.'

'As you wish, Miguel. Unfortunately, I've got to go now. I can sense that my father is calling me to come back into the house. We will talk again tomorrow. Good night.'

With that, she stood up and walked straight out of the stall, with the dog, Sam, falling in at her side. Miguel, left with his thoughts, watched her out of the stable block. Picking up the curry-comb to finish his grooming of Bess, he experimentally sent another telepathic message after her.

'*boa noite, um pouco.* Good night, little one, *e obrigado.* '

'No thanks necessary, Miguel, I've enjoyed our little chat. Good night.'

Such was the immediate reply that came back to him. Now, he had to believe that communication by mental telepathy was very much a reality. Otherwise, he might not have believed what had happened to him during the last half an hour. He tried reciting the principles for enlightenment once again, pausing between each one to fully comprehend the meaning behind the words.

Experimentally, he pictured in his mind, Bess, standing before him with her coat gleaming, and her tail and mane combed out to perfection. He rolled up his sleeves, and vigorously set about making it so.

Fifteen minutes later, having just finally applied a small amount of hoof dressing to make them shine, he stood back to admire. He found that the work had been hard, but enjoyable, and the reward was to see the animal as he had pictured it in his mind. But was this enlightenment, or just a satisfactory awareness of a job done, to the best of ones ability? He was still pondering the question when Carter came quietly into the stables to tell him that his dinner was about to be served. Miguel sensed his presence.

"By golly, lad, you've done a magnificent job there. I've never seen Bess looking so good. I wish Miss Michelle were here to see her, she would be absolutely delighted."

Miguel smiled and bowed very slightly in his direction, basking in his praise.

"*Obrigado,* Senhor Carter. I have been talking with Emily."

"Ah, and how did you find the experience, Miguel?"

He paused to consider his reply.

"Both interesting and enlightening, Senhor Carter. Emily is an exceptionally gifted child."

"Yes, we know. How did she speak with you, Miguel. I mean, was she talking normally, or was she . . . ?"

"Communicating, she called it, Senhor. And the child is able to read my thoughts, even though I am thinking in my own language. I am asking myself, how is this possible?"

"Can she? Well, that's another revelation. I rather suspect that even her parents are not aware of that one? Mind you, Emily is only two, and I don't suppose that she has ever met anyone that speaks a different language before? So she might not have even known, herself? Did she ask you to 'think' your conversation with her?"

"Sim, Senhor. It is a very strange sensation, is it not? The child is able to speak *como um adulto.*"

Carter chuckled to himself. That was another little phrase to add to his new list.

"Not nearly as strange as the knowledge that your thoughts are no longer your own, Miguel. Come on lad, finish up here, your dinner is nearly ready. Mrs Carter has made for us, a delicious fish pie, tonight."

He quickly packed everything away, and made one last check of the animals before dousing the lights. Carter placed a friendly arm around his shoulders, as they slowly made their way back towards the house. Their topic of conversation was Emily, and Carter, believing that Miguel had been admitted to her little clique of privileged people, told him everything that he knew about her. He also made him repeat the promise, never to reveal to anyone else, what he had been told, explaining the reasoning.

As they removed their boots and walked into the kitchens, he could hear Susan's laughter, and was reminded of his plan to tempt her into his bed. The first principle came back to him again.

'Picture in your mind how something should be, and then strive toward making it so.'

But then it occurred to him that this was in direct conflict with the fourth.

'To seek out only that which is right and proper.'

What he had in mind for doing with Susan, would far better be described as highly improper . . .

He smiled at the humour of the thought, but it left him suddenly wondering if Emily was able to read what was in his mind, all of the time? He realised that in future, he would need to be a little more careful and circumspect with what he was thinking about.

Sharon-Louise's evening call from Malcolm came as she was languishing luxuriously, in her mother's bath, with a glass of chilled Chardonnay. The trill of her phone, perched ready to hand on a stool beside the bath, served to interrupt her simple pleasure. She looked at the caller ID and pressed the 'accept' button. Reluctantly, she then found it necessary to sit up from the deep warm water and bubbles, to avoid getting it wet.

"You really do have an annoying knack of choosing the most inopportune moments, Blackmore."

"Really? Let me guess. Toilet, bath, or hands in the sink?"

"Number two. Were your ears ringing, perhaps? You were just in my thoughts, it seems ages since I last saw you."

"Ah, she misses me, that's somewhat gratifying, because I'm missing you, as well. How's it going, I'm presuming that you're still in Weymouth?"

"Same as yesterday. I've been at it all day, and just about broken the back of it, now. Most of her stuff, I've already taken round to the local charity shops. I've still got to do a couple more trips to the tip, and then there's a whole carload of various bits and pieces that I thought might come in handy if we get Grey Gables. Is there any more news on that score?"

"Yes, it's all looking very promising. After a morning of negotiation, a broad verbal agreement was arrived at early this afternoon. A price has been agreed, and I'm given to understand that our legal eagles are drawing up some sort of document, ready for signatures, in the morning. I'm told that we've bought every last nail and pane of glass, from chimney to cellar floor, including the entire contents, as well."

"And is that what you wanted, Malcolm?"

"Hobson's choice really, love. The vendors were really keen for us to take everything, and save them the trouble of clearing the place out and putting it all into storage. We don't really need any of it. The Estate Management already has a huge store of household equipment and furniture, more than enough to furnish Grey Gables. However, to keep everything moving sweetly along, I've agreed to the purchase. At the earliest opportunity, I shall want you and your father to get in there and make a proper assessment of everything. You know what the place will be used for, so, as far as I can see, it just needs adapting for purpose."

"You're trying to make it all sound very simple, Malcolm, and I just hope that you're right. What's the deadline on this?"

"Probably two weeks, maybe three? We've Christmas looming up on us, don't forget. Certainly by the beginning of the New Year, I would hope to see the place being ready for use. The first of the German engineers will be arriving on site to oversee the installation of all the underground services pipe-work and footings by then. They will require some comfortable accommodation, and Grey Gables, quite apart from being a whole lot cheaper than a Winchester hotel, is also damn sight more conveniently located."

"What about staff, Malcolm? I tried to speak to you about it yesterday, but you had to go and scrub-up."

"I've already given it some thought, love, and it's difficult to know exactly how many people we are going to need, until we've made a proper assessment of the place. Facilities, and all that sort of thing. That's why I need you and Jim in there, ASAP. I'm assured that actually getting the right staff, at short notice, will be no problem. The Personnel and Resources Manager says that she's got a list of good people standing by, just waiting for a suitable position to arise, with us."

"Well, alright Malcolm. So given that everything goes to plan, tomorrow? Where exactly are the keys to Grey Gables, and how soon could we get in, to make a start?"

"Good question, and I must confess that I really don't know. I'll get onto it immediately, thanks love . . ."

"Malcolm, I shall be back at Oakwood by tomorrow afternoon. If the keys are somewhere local, ring me immediately they're available for collection, and I'll get them picked up. I'll also brief my dad on what you want. No, on second thoughts, you do it. I'm sure he will want to respond to any request coming directly from you. Do you think he's well enough?"

"Jacqui says that he's as fit as a fiddle, and looking for something constructive to occupy his time. So, I don't see that this will do him any harm at all. I will caution him against overdoing the physical, though. I shall also ask Jacqui, in her future capacity as hospital Matron, to help him, by casting an eye over the nursing hostel aspect, that we have planned in the long term. What do you think?"

"I think that you seem to have covered everything, for the time being. I also think that I need to get out of this bath, the skin on my toes has gone all wrinkly, and the water is beginning to go cold. So if you don't mind . . ."

"Yes, alright, sweetheart, I know when I'm not wanted. I'll be in touch tomorrow. Love you, byeee . . ."

The mid-morning meeting between Southern Central Securities and Tony Williams, by necessity, took place at Lizzie McCall's home at Downton, on the borders of the New Forest.

Tony had completely failed to convince Liz that she should accompany him to Bournemouth for the meeting, so he reluctantly had to asked them, both Pete and Caroline, to come over to Downton.

As they made themselves comfortable, Liz served coffee and biscuits, but then made no secret of the fact that she no longer cared a damn about her husband, or anything that might have happened to him. Her intransigent attitude made the whole meeting a rather tense and difficult affair.

More for the benefit of Tony Williams, than Liz McCall, Pete set about presenting a detailed verbal report on his investigation and findings, so far, endeavouring to answer any questions, as they arose. Tony listened as Pete voiced his suspicions regarding the true identity of the man that had returned from Northern Ireland in the guise of Connor McCall. Even as he was speaking, Tony's solicitors mind was already seeking the evidence needed to support any such suspicion, or assertion, and he was quick to pose the questions.

Pete first produced his statement taken from Carol Short, in which she described the man, purporting to be Connor McCall, who had stayed at the Lyndhurst Park Hotel. Pete pointed out her observations regarding the obvious differences in the ears, and the more pointed chin, to those in the photograph of Connor that he had shown to her. She also mentions that the man spoke with an Irish accent.

Next, he came up with a rather grained and slightly blurred photograph of the man driving Connors car, when it left the airport car park. He explained that it was an enlargement of a still photograph image, lifted from a video recording. But it was sufficiently clear enough to see, that the man in the drivers seat, definitely had no lobe to his right ear.

He then showed them the statement from the barman, Larry, who said that the man who claimed to be Mr McCall, from room 120, had spent nearly all evening in his bar, and, had spoken with a very broad Irish accent. On three pints of Guinness with Irish whiskey chasers, he ran up a bar tab of nearly eighteen pounds, to be charged to his name. He showed them a photocopy of a bar bill, that had been initialled CM, but the handwriting was definitely not Connors.

Asked how he knew, Pete showed them the original note, which he'd found in the writing pad, on the dressing table of room 120, and was now sealed into a clear plastic wallet.

He passed it to Liz first.

"Can you please look carefully at the note, Mrs McCall, and first of all, tell me if that is your husband's handwriting?

She took it over to the window and studied it for nearly half a minute, before bringing it back.

"I would say that some of it is Connor's writing, but I'm certain that the signature is definitely not his."

"How can you be so sure?"

"That's easy. Connor hated having his name abbreviated, and he would definitely never sign himself in that manner. I'm not sure about the bit that says 'please forgive me' either. The s, the f, and the g, don't look quite right."

"I'm glad you noticed that Mrs McCall, because I came to the same conclusion. Am I correct in assuming that your husband was right-handed?"

"Yes, he is."

"The last phrase, the one you refer to, was written by a left-handed person. Under a magnifying glass, one can see that the pen was pushed over the paper, rather than pulled, as it would be by someone using his, or her, right hand. I also have the writing pad from whence that sheet of paper came. On the back cardboard cover of the pad, there are some faint impressions of the same phrase having been written several times, as though someone had practiced writing it, first."

Tony Williams had been listening very carefully, and he now took another look at the photo of the man in the driving seat of Connor's Morris Minor. He conceded that Grogan was right . . .

"So, apart from the now rather obvious and compelling doubts that you have discovered, Mr Grogan, can I ask what conclusions are to be drawn from all of this?"

Pete looked at Caroline. On their way over to Downton, it had been agreed that she should be the one to give them their suspicions, breaking it to them as gently as possible. She took up the reins.

"Mr Williams, Mrs McCall, I think we need to examine the reasons for Connor going over to Ireland in the first place. Pete and I have discussed this, and we both agree that with his past having come to light, and in the belief that the Police were after him, he went with the sole intention of contacting his friend and accomplice, Martyn McCue, presumably to warn him? Whether any actual contact was established, we don't yet know. In fact, Connor spent a whole week in Ireland, and we don't know anything about his movements, except that he stayed at the Park Avenue Hotel. It's safe to assume that he didn't spend the whole week in his room, so what exactly did he do?

To find out, we would first need to get hold of a list of all his phone calls, both incoming and outgoing, for the period. There is an outside chance that Connor's mobile, might still be amongst his belongings over at the Lyndhurst Park Hotel. So a good starting point would be to get everything back from over there."

"He wasn't answering his mobile, Mrs Grogan. Liz and I both tried on numerous occasions."

"The fact that he wasn't answering, doesn't necessarily indicate that the phone was not being used, Mr Williams. In the circumstances, he might not have wanted to speak with either of you. The bogus suicide note reflects that he might have been considering writing to you, instead. I believe that the genuine part, is the beginning of a difficult letter that he was trying to put together."

She handed them the note again, before continuing.

"You will see that it begins on the top line of the page, as would a letter. If it were a short suicide note, surely, it is reasonable to assume that any normal person, would begin writing further down the page? I certainly would. However, we digress. Let us get back to Connor's reasons for being in Ireland. If we assume that he did manage to make contact with Martyn McCue, what do you think his reaction might have been? Connor, suddenly turning up on his doorstep, and with the Police hot on his tail, was probably not something he would have relished? We know that McCue holds a position of some responsibility, on the staff of the Deputy First Minister, a man who has recently announced his intention to be an Irish Presidential candidate. The last thing that he would want is any sort of scandal or adverse publicity, especially if there is any sort of tenuous link to his previous terrorist activities. If you were in his position, what action might you take to prevent such a potentially catastrophic occurrence? Mr Williams, I'm asking, what would you do, sir?

"Well, I suppose I would do everything within my power to try and prevent it from happening."

"And how far might you be prepared to go with that, sir, given that you are in a position to be able to get such things taken care of, without sullying your own hands?"

"Your question is purely hypothetical, Mrs Grogan. It overlooks and ignores the integrity of the person being asked to make the decision. What might be perfectly acceptable to you, might be equally abhorrent to me. You are asking me to make a judgement on behalf of someone else, with whom I'm not even acquainted. For those reasons, I feel unable to comment. I would strongly urge you to cease posing hypothetical questions, try to remain factual, and please, come to the point."

"Yes alright, Mr Williams, my apologies for trying to put you on the spot, sir. Pete and I have come to the reluctant conclusion, that Connor might have met his ultimate demise, while over in Ireland. We suspect that this whole thing is an elaborate ruse to try and lead us all into believing that he returned to this country, before taking himself off somewhere to commit suicide. We are ninety-nine percent certain that the man you see in that picture you are holding, is not your son. We do have some more forensic tests to carry out, but we are both as sure as it is possible to be, that we are right.

We do have some idea as to who the man in the photo might be, but there are a whole lot of further enquiries that would need to be undertaken, probably necessitating another visit to Ireland, to establish his true identity, and his reasons for coming over here?"

"Are you both saying that you think Connor might have been murdered, just to keep him quiet?"

"Yes, Mr Williams. That is exactly what we're saying. Here, take a look at this, if you will."

Pete produced a clear cellophane packet. It contained the three-dimensional photographic images of Connor's face, the ones he had found down the back of the dressing table in room 120. Tony looked at the picture.

"This is Connor. What is this? It looks like one of those images the Police use in their criminal records?

Pete ignored his question for the moment.

"Take a closer look at the eyes, will you Mr Williams, tell me what you see."

Tony took the photo over to the window where he used his glasses as a magnifying glass.

"His eyes appear to be only half open, as though he is very drunk, or nearly asleep."

"Do they look a bit watery, as well, Mr Williams?"

Tony looked again.

"Well yes, I suppose they do. Is there any significance to this, Mr Grogan? You haven't said where this picture came from."

Pete related exactly where he had found the photograph.

"It is my belief that this is a death-mask picture of Connor, probably taken by his killer, standing over him. If you look at the background, it appears that Connor is lying on of those reinforced plastic sheets. As for the eyes, they tend to appear that way in death, Mr Williams. I think you are holding a picture of Connor that was taken immediately after his death. The man who was impersonating him was probably using it for reference."

Tony studied it again before offering it to Liz. She declined to look. He handed it back to Pete.

"In which case, the Police will need to be informed immediately, Mr Grogan. My friend and colleague, George Lloyd, has the name and contact number of the chief investigating officer. If my memory serves me well, his name is Ferguson, but I'll just give George a call to verify that its . . ."

The mention of the name caused Pete to suddenly sit upright in his chair, and interject.

"Ferguson? What Charlie Ferguson? Are you sure, Mr Williams?"

"Yes, why? Do you know him, Mr Grogan?"

"I know of him, the man's a bit of a legend with a reputation for never having given up on any enquiry. Detective Chief Inspector Charles Ferguson, of New Scotland Yard Serious Crime Squad, at least, that is what it was known as, when I was in the force. Was he the man that followed Connor over to Ireland?"

"I'm fairly sure that it was, Mr Grogan, but George will know for certain. Should I ring him?"

"Not just for a minute, Mr Williams, we need to have a little bit of a rethink, first."

"Why? Is there a problem?"

"Charlie Ferguson was reckoned to be one of an elite squad of difficult problem solvers. They were rumoured to work outside of the scope of normal police methods. Whatever that meant, nobody really knew, but the very fact that he might be involved, sheds a whole new light on things."

"I'm afraid you've lost me completely, now, Mr Grogan. Would you care to elucidate?"

"As I just said, Mr Williams, Charlie Ferguson's role, is as a problem solver. He works directly for the establishment, all those faceless people, that we know to exist, and who dictate government policy, despite what the politicians would have us belief. If the establishment identified Connor McCall as being a potential embarrassment, it is quite possibly that it was they who ordered, and arranged, for his disappearance? If that is the case, there will be no point in reporting him missing, or voicing any of our suspicions. They will simply not want him to be found. The local Police would probably go through all the motions, and make all the usual enquiries. They might even organise a search of the Forest, but we already know that there is nothing here to be found, is there?"

"I'm not sure that I'm in total agreement with everything you've said, so far, Mr Grogan, but your views are certainly compelling. The trouble is, where do we go from here?"

"That would rather depend on whether you, and Mrs McCall, are interested in getting to the bottom of it all, Mr Williams. If you are content to let it rest, then by all means go through the motions, and simply report him as being a missing person.

If, however, you do decide to continue with this enquiry, I would suggest that, at this stage, you delay making the report. I would also ask that you go over to Lyndhurst Park Hotel, taking with you some appropriate identification, and that you recover all of Connor's personal possessions.

His bill has been pre-paid on his credit card, up to midday today. So you have a little over an hour before incurring anything extra. I would think that a simple phone call to the Receptionist, Carol Short, letting her know that you are on your way, might perhaps buy you some additional time, should you require it? The ball is firmly in your court, now, Mr Williams, what do you want to do, sir?"

"For the moment, Mr Grogan, and before I make any further decisions, I want the opportunity to discuss all of this with Elizabeth, my daughter-in-law. She is Connor's wife, and I note that she has remained very quiet through all of this. I can also see that she is more than a little upset by what you have told us.

In my own mind, I felt, or rather suspected, that my son might already be lost to us, but in the absence of any real proof, I have said nothing to Lizzy.

However, for the time being, Mr Grogan, I am prepared to accede to your request. Liz and I, will arrange to go to Lyndhurst and fetch his things. I will give you our decision before the end of today."

"Thank you, sir. Can I ask that you both wear a pair of these gloves when handling Connor's personal effects, and when driving the Morris. There is just an outside chance of some fingerprints having been left by the man impersonating Connor."

As he and Caroline rose to take their leave, Pete gave them two pairs of latex gloves from his pocket.

"All things considered, I think that went quite well, wouldn't you say, love?"

Pete and Caroline were in their car, and on the way back to the office. She had been unusually quiet.

"I'm not sure, Pete. I've got an uncomfortable feeling about all of this, even more so, now that we've discovered that Charlie Ferguson is involved, as well."

"Did you know him, love."

"Not personally. Like you, I only knew of him. The Serious Fraud Squad Offices, where I worked, were on the floor below where his are located. I used to occasionally see him in the lift, coming and going, and I would nod to him, just as a passing acquaintance, but he never ever spoke to me. I got the distinct impression that he had some sort of a grudge against women police officers. Some of the other girls said much the same thing. We didn't like him, at all. When he looks at you, there's something very cold, calculating, and downright unfriendly in those eyes. The very thought of him, is still sufficient enough to make me want to shudder."

"He's a good copper though, Caroline, you've got to give him that, at least. There aren't many blokes in the force that are able to boast a near one hundred percent detection record."

"Hmm, there were a few in my squad that wouldn't agree with you, Pete. I've heard it said on more than one occasion, that Charlie liked to jump in towards the culmination of an enquiry, and thereby try to steal some of the glory."

"Okay, so putting his shortcomings aside for the minute, love, what do you reckon he was doing over in Ireland, then?"

"I think you've got it absolutely right, Pete. Quite apart from Martin McGuinness, think of the damage that a scandal such as this, could have been caused to the fragile Irish Peace Accord. If Ferguson was sent over by the powers-that-be, under strict instruction to get it sorted, this could well be part of his scheme. Has that thought occurred to you?"

"Well no. It hadn't."

"No, I thought not. Well think about this, then. If Tony Williams does agree to this investigation continuing, you, Mr Grogan, will be sailing our little ship into some pretty dangerous and murky waters. If the establishment have it within their power to commit one murder to cover things up, what's to prevent them from committing another, or even two more? Personally, I would prefer to live long enough to draw my pensions, wouldn't you?"

Pete was saying nothing. He hadn't even considered that aspect, but quickly concluded that Caroline's assessment, was probably correct?

"And another thing, Grogan. Even if you do manage to get to the bottom of this, what are you going to do with it? You can hardly get the establishment to listen, can you? Can't you hear them saying it now?

'It will not be in the public interests to prefer charges against anyone, and drag it all through the courts.'

The usual get-out . . . You do appreciate that if we are right, Pete, this comes down to organised crime and corruption, being condoned and perpetrated, by those supposedly there to investigate and prevent it from happening in the first place? Ask yourself, Pete, what chance do you think we stand? Now, let me answer for you. No chance, or a dog's chance, at best . . . You see if I'm not right. In the end, this will all prove to be for nothing, and it might even have the potential to get us both killed, for our trouble."

"So are you saying that we should pull out, and do no more, Caroline? Because I don't think I could let this go now, even if the client doesn't want to pursue it any further. I wouldn't be able to live with myself. I'd always be wondering . . ."

She was silent for a few minutes, while they both pondered the consequences of carrying on.

"We could always sell it all to a Sunday newspaper, Caroline. I wouldn't mind betting that they'd be willing to pay an absolute fortune for a story like this, even if we only gave them what we've got so far."

"And that would be the end of our little business, as well, Pete. Client confidentially being breached, we would probably both find ourselves on the wrong end of an expensive lawsuit. He's a solicitor, don't forget. Come on, let's put this to bed, for the time being. I'm hungry, and rather fancy a bit of Chinese. Let's go and try that new place in Boscombe, your treat . . ."

"No dad, nothing's changed. I still feel the same, and don't give a damn about what's happened to him. As far as I can see, this news of his death should allow us to breathe a sigh of relief. It's saved us both from the embarrassment of having to deal with all the inevitable publicity, that would have arisen out of his arrest and trial. I can fully appreciate how you must feel, but personally, I want nothing more to do with any of it. The only reason I'm here now, is to get the car. Half of it is rightfully mine, and I love driving it around. All the rest of his stuff will be heading straight for the tip, just as soon as I can get around to sorting it all out. I want him out of my life, completely, utterly, and totally."

They were in Tony's car, on the way to Lyndhurst, and he was sounding her out on the delicate subject of pursuing the investigation further.

"So can I presume that you would have no objection, if I were to instruct the Grogan's to keep at it then, Liz? I don't want to be doing anything that would cause you any more distress, my dear. If you tell me to let it drop, then that will effectively be the end of it, I promise."

"Alright then, dad, I'm saying it. I want you to let it drop. When we get back, talk to the Grogan's, find out exactly what they would expect us to do next, with regard to reporting him missing. I don't suppose for one minute, that they will want to become involved with any formal police enquiries, so as long as we aren't compromised in any way, just do as they suggest. After that, I don't want to hear another single word about Connor. His name will be taboo, whenever I'm around."

"And what about me, Liz? Am I to be similarly excluded, merely because I'm related to him? I have to say that I wouldn't want that to happen. You're all I've got now . . ."

"Dad, that will never happen. In fact, I was going to suggest that you give some thought to retiring, and coming to live down here, with me, permanently. I'm sure that between us, we could make it work."

Tony was slightly taken aback. Coming so soon after Connor's disappearance, the most obvious thought was that she was seeking someone to take his place? He needed time to think this through, and, he surmised that she needed to take more time, possibly to grieve, and to reflect on the loss of her husband?

"Liz, I have work commitments in London, that will take me well into the spring of next year, before I can even consider making such a move. I thank you for the invitation, and I will give it some serious consideration. Shall we see how we get on together, between now and the New Year, and then talk again? We are neither of us in the first flush of youth, and I would be the first to confess to being very set in my ways. In consequence, you may find that I'm just too difficult to live with? Similarly, I haven't lived in the company of a woman since Connors mother, Mary, and that was sixty-odd years ago. So, I too, might not find it to be to my liking."

"You will be staying up to, and including, Christmas and the New Year, won't you dad? I don't think I could face being alone over that period?"

"What about your family, Liz? I'm referring to your brother, Brian, and his wife, Sarah. Don't you have any contact with them anymore?"

"No, not really, dad. They're both strict Catholics, and thoroughly disapproved, when I renounced my religion to marry Connor. I send them a Christmas card every year, but I never get one back."

"Connor was in touch with them, you know. I spoke with Sarah when I was over there. He'd invited them both to come and dine with him at the hotel. They couldn't make it, due to some sort of prior engagement. They left him a message requesting that he should get back to them, but he never did."

"Really? Well, I am surprised. None of us have spoken to each other since our wedding, thirty-odd years ago. I wonder what he wanted, Connor, I mean?"

"Why don't you give them a call and speak to them. I have their phone number if you want it."

"I'll think about it, dad. I would like to speak to Brian again, we were very close when we were children.

I cant help thinking that it might be a bit awkward after all this time, and I would hate to feel rejected."

"You'll never know unless you try, Liz. Who's to say that Brian might not feel the same way about you?

People's attitudes tend to change as they get older, and wiser. Unfortunately, they also tend to get much more stubborn, as well, like me . . ."

She looked at him and gave a little smile of understanding.

# Chapter 15

Sharon, luxuriating in the air-conditioned warmth and comfort of the undertakers Mercedes stretched limousine, watched the urban sprawl of Belfast slowly give way to the more picturesque Irish countryside. As it slid past, in a veritable blur of motorway speed, the miserable, cold, damp conditions were giving rise to pockets of mist that hung in the hollows and valleys. It served to severely inhibit her visibility of the surroundings.

In a couple of day's time, Sharon reflected that she was going to have to do the return journey all by herself, and she was endeavouring to memorise the route that the driver was taking. She looked again at the writing pad that rested in her lap, and with a slightly shaky hand, added Templepatrick, to her short list of significant motorway landmarks.

So far, since exiting the Belfast City Airport, she estimated that they had probably travelled twenty-odd miles, and virtually all of it had been on dual carriageways, and now motorway. All she had jotted down so far, was A2→M3→M2 Newtownabbey→Templepatrick(A57)

'Well, I can understand it, even if nobody else can,' she muttered to herself.

Already, Sharon was beginning to regret her decision to do this alone. She didn't exactly feel frightened, but coupled with the dubious expectations of the first meeting with her aunt and grandmother, it was all giving rise to further apprehension. She wished that Malcolm, or David, were there to hold her hand, and offer some welcome reassurance.

Through the intervening glass partition, she could hear that the driver was talking to someone on his hands-free, but with his broad Irish accent, she couldn't quite make out the gist of his conversation. He did appear to be in a most unholy hurry though, that the car speedometer was hovering at just over ninety.

With very little other traffic, they continued along at this breakneck speed for another ten or fifteen minutes, before the driver began to let the car slow down to a much more sedate, and welcome, sixty.

Looking up ahead, Sharon saw that they were coming up behind another slower moving, coffin-carrying, hearse. As the driver brought their car into the same lane to take up station behind, she correctly assumed that this must be the one containing the body of her mother.

It was proving to be a very poignant moment, and caused Sharon to begin to well up inside. In her heightened emotional state, she sentimentally told herself that, Mum, for the very last time, was going home, to be back, once again, in the bosom of her family.

With that, all the memories of the last couple of months started coming back to haunt her. She reached into her handbag for a tissue to dab her eyes. She decided that none of this was going to be easy, and to be able to face up to the next couple of days, she desperately needed to get a grip of herself . . .

In the early hours of that same morning, Jacqui had awoken with a start. At first, she thought that she might have heard the sound of someone quietly moving around, either in her room, or in the passage outside? She listened intently, but soon realised that she must have only been dreaming again. This time though, everything about her dream was still so fresh, and vivid, in her mind. She felt that it was the most realistic, and erotic dream, that she had ever had. So much so, that she even began to wonder if it might have been something more?

She recalled that as she fell asleep, her mind had pictured a man. It had been Jim, standing there, naked, beside her bed. She had reached out a hand, inviting him to join her. She had felt that as he moulded himself to her form, and had snuggled back into his embrace, she had felt his arousal nestling against her bottom.

In her dream, their subsequent lovemaking had been something wild and passionate, each giving their mind and body to each other in a total commitment to the shared fulfilment of the moment.

She fingered her lips, imagining that they felt slightly tender and bruised from the passion of their kissing. Had it been more than a dream? She still wasn't sure, but as she examined herself further, there, between her legs, was the familiar wetness, and coupled with it, the strong and urgent sensation she felt in her loins. It was ample evidence of her extreme arousal. Her mind was also telling her that her nipples and breasts felt as though they had been gently rolled, tweaked and kneaded. She recalled that in her dream, she had knelt astride him, grinding her sex down onto his engorged penis. He had reached up, cupping a breast into each of his hands. With his gentle probing fingers, massaging and caressing her most erotic zones, he had succeeded in prolonging the moments of her ultimate ecstatic pleasure, expertly inducing her into further, delicious, multiple orgasms. Each time that he sensed she was nearing another climax, he had reached down to firmly grasp her hips and buttocks, holding her tightly against him, while thrusting himself up, and into her, to his very limit. He had been practically insatiable, and she likened it to being held astride a wild, uncontrollable, stallion as she felt him bring about his own throbbing climax, deep inside of her.

She buried her head in her pillow, trying to smell for his now familiar male muskiness, but it wasn't there.

Her emotions were reaching boiling point, and she threw back the duvet to head for her bathroom.

'Oh God, I cannot stand this anymore. I am fast becoming a lascivious and shameless woman, miserable in her frustrations. I have just got to do something about it . . . ' she told herself.

Jacqui threw off her sweat-soaked nightdress and panties, to stand naked in front of the full-length bathroom mirror. She ran some tepid water into the sink, and commenced to wash herself all over with a perfumed, soapy bath sponge. She paid particular attention to the area of her sex, her wicked thoughts trying to imagine how his mouth and tongue might feel when applied to that region of her anatomy? No man had ever done anything like that before, but some carnal instinct was telling her that it was about to happen. She vigorously brushed her teeth, and quickly ran a brush through her hair. Finally she sprayed on a generous application of her favourite Chanel No5, which she usually kept only for special occasions.

Shunning all thoughts of putting on any more night clothing, and with the sole aim of making her intentions so obviously apparent, she apprehensively tiptoed over towards Jim's bedroom. The door had been left ajar, and she slowly pushed it open to step inside. In the moonlight, she could make out the shape of him, lying prone on top of the bed, the duvet was already thrown open, and she saw that he was awake, and holding out his hand to her, in a silent invitation.

"Jim, I need you . . ."

"Don't say anything, lass, I've been waiting, and longing for this moment. Come to me."

Elsewhere in the big house, two other people were also wide-awake.

Miguel, unfamiliar with his surroundings, was listening to the deep stentorian snores that were emanating from the Carter's bedroom, situated further along the corridor. He too, was harbouring carnal thoughts, but his were directed toward the pretty little housemaid, Susan, and what she might be able to do, to help him get to sleep. He resisted the temptation to masturbate, and, with a sigh, punched his hard pillow into a more comfortable shape for his head.

Trying to put her out of his mind completely, he thought that tomorrow, he would try moving the furniture around in his room, so that his bed was aligned north/south, instead of east/west, as it was now. Back home, he had read somewhere, that it was all to do with ley-lines and the magnetic field of the earth. He hadn't completely understood the reasoning, but found that when he tried, it had seemed to work, for him.

His mind also kept harping back to thoughts of little Emily. He was still puzzling over the reasons for her having given him, what she had termed, 'The basic principles for life.' He had repeated them to himself a dozen times over, now, and could see the wisdom and reasoning behind their application to all things, but why should he have been seemingly singled out to receive them?

In an effort to get her to answer his question, he tried several times to establish another telepathic connection with the child, but so far, he seemed to have failed.

Emily, too was wide-awake. Her mind had detected that something wonderful was happening for two of the people she held most dear, Jim and Jacqui. She couldn't understand exactly what was occurring, in her child's mind, she was content in the knowledge of it being a very adult thing.

She also recognised a certain similarity in Miguel's attraction toward the housemaid, Susan. She told herself that as daddy loves mummy, Jim now loves Jacqui, and Miguel wants to love Susan.

Perhaps she should try to help him? Then she remembered her parent's sternly delivered warning with regard to her interfering in other people's lives. Perhaps she should consult with them first, as she had promised to do?

In his efforts to establish telepathic contact with her again, she had also detected Miguel's probing thought waves. She remembered Jo-jo's warning, and declined to answer him, for fear that his already strong telepathic ability, might become a nuisance to her. She decided that to keep his unwanted thoughts at bay, she would respond to him, only when it suited her purpose.

Jo-jo, now speaking through Jim, had told her, that like he had with the man, Ferguson, he had brain scanned Miguel and had detected, some really quite exceptional and unique mental capabilities. He thought that he was a good person, and, with the right help and guidance, the young man had the potential to achieve far greater things. He had urged Emily to take him into her confidence, and to immediately set about helping with his re-education. It was from he, that the five principles had come. Miguel wasn't to know it, but they had been offered, merely to test his ability and resolve.

A little after midday, the hearse, negotiated its way onto a small estate of terraced houses. After a couple of turnings, it started to make it's way slowly up the steep hill between the mirror image rows of small, quite pretty, little identical houses, that comprised Cuthbert Street, Londonderry.

Sharon, in the following car, was counting off the odd numbers, on the front doors to her left, trying to pre-judge where numbers 31 and 33 might be? She could see some of the curtains twitching as the two magnificent black limousines slowly made their way past. Behind, people were starting to come out of their houses, and follow the little cortege, either in curiosity, or respectful welcome, she knew not which? The street was strangely empty of vehicles. They had passed only two small cars, parked nearer to the junction at the bottom end, as they turned in. She wondered if all the usual parked cars might have all been deliberately removed, pending their imminent arrival?

Looking around, she thought that the area looked clean. There was no litter, the houses had been brightly painted, and most appeared to be well cared for. Sharon had seen only one 'for sale' sign, usually a good indicator as to the popularity of any small community, such as this.

The coffin-carrying hearse drew to a halt outside of the last two houses on the left. Only then did Sharon recall Tony Williams having mentioned that they were 'end-of-terrace.' Sharon's car pulled in behind, and she remained seated in the back, waiting to see what would happen next. A couple of people stared in at her through the tinted, offside door window. Feeling slightly uncomfortable, she reached up and pulled a black veil down from her hat, to cover her face, thereby hiding herself from their gaze.

For the funeral, Sharon had treated herself to a very smart, black, two-piece jacket and slim-line skirt, cut just above the knee. She had tried it on in the boutique, and worn with a pair of comfortable black patent leather, three-inch high-healed shoes, she thought it made her look tall, slim, and tastefully, very elegant. The neat little black velvet hat had been the boutique owners own, and was only on loan to her, for the occasion. It sat rather neatly and comfortably slightly to the back, and left side of her head, allowing her red hair to cascade down over her right ear. The addition of the veil, lightly stitched under the front rim of the hat, had been nothing short of inspirational. Yet another idea from the boutique owner, it could be worn either thrown back over the top, or worn over her face, as now. Her mother's pure white, Irish silk blouse, the same one she had worn at Doris's Service of Remembrance, and a pair of lightweight black ribbed tights, completed the ensemble. She carried a small, black, rolled umbrella, and a slightly large Mulberry Bayswater, black leather handbag, necessary to carry the new Tenancy Agreement documents that she had brought with her, without the need for any further bending or folding.

Sharon watched as the doors of nearly all the houses opened, and more and more people poured out onto the street. Most, she saw, were dressed in respectful black, and they stood back, whispering and watching, as events slowly began to unfold. Her driver got out and came to open the offside door, offering his hand in a polite invitation, that she should step out of the car. Sharon purposely remained where she was, thereby creating the impression that she was deciding whether or not, to accede to his request.

This was to be her moment, her entry, and she was going to make damn sure that she got it just right. She hadn't yet seen any sign of her aunt, or grandmother, coming out to greet her, as they rightfully should. So she would make them all wait for her, instead.

The front door of number 33 finally opened, and her grandmother, black shawl, and walking with the aid of a stick, she noticed, stepped out, to look around the small crowd of people gathered around. She graciously acknowledged one or two, with a slight nod of the head, and they acknowledge her in a similar manner. Her gaze finally came to rest on the car with Sharon still inside. Sharon then caught sight of her aunt Sandra. She was standing in the doorway, leaning on the doorframe, fag-in-hand, and looking decidedly much the worse for wear, scruffy, and apparently uninterested. Sharon was forced to conclude that there was very little respect being shown for her mother from that quarter. She wondered why?

Shuffling her bottom across the seat, she took the hand of the driver and swung her legs round, while keeping her knees tightly together. Sliding forward to place her feet firmly on the ground caused her skirt ride up, thereby exposing a small amount of thigh. She allowed herself to be assisted into a standing position, from which she rose to her full height, there to pause, and haughtily look around.

It was a perfectly executed manoeuvre, conducted in the style of Lady Diana Spencer, who had perfected it into a fine art.

Sharon allowed her eyes to come to rest on the rather diminutive looking figure of her grandmother. She was pleased to see that she was a full head and shoulders taller, and that she was also struggling to look beyond her veil, to see her face. Sharon walked slowly forward to come to a halt three paces in front of her. The old lady stood with both hands resting on top of her walking stick, waiting . . .

Sharon placed her handbag on the ground at her feet, and slowly reached up with both hands to throw back her veil. She slowly raised her head, and eyes, to look directly into those of her grandmother.

The reaction that this produced, more than exceeded her highest expectations. There was an audible gasp from the crowd, and her grandmother's jaw was seen to drop, as if in sheer disbelief of who she was looking at?

That morning, using an early photograph she had found, for reference, Sharon had restyled her hair and applied her mother's make-up, exactly in the style used by her mother, when at her age. The resemblance, even she had to admit, had been quite remarkable. They might even have been taken for identical twins.

Sharon, calmly and confidently, held out her hand to be shaken.

"Good afternoon, grandmother. My name is Sharon-Louise, and I am your granddaughter."

The old lady recovered her composure. She ignored the invited handshake, and summoned up her reply to be delivered with as much vehemence as she could possibly muster, in the circumstances.

"The look of you, child, is telling me, that this is so. But you're my granddaughter in name, and looks only. I don't know you, and I have no wish to. You're English, and a complete stranger to me. Sharon-Louise, why, even your very name, is an abomination. Your grandmother, on your father's side, Louisa Dobbs, was a nothing but a whore, and traitor to the cause, so she was. Cast out by her own family and all those that knew her. You are here today under sufferance, and only to see my daughter, your mother, laid to rest. After that, I shall never want to see you darken my doorway again."

Sharon took it all unflinchingly. She had been half expecting this sort of reaction, and had even considered her response. There was no way that she was going to allow herself to be browbeaten into submission be this vindictive old crone. She stepped forward, threateningly, and spoke quietly, so that her words would not carry to the crowd.

"I am sorry that you feel that way, grandmother. But I don't think that here, and now, is a very good time to be getting embroiled in any personal family differences. Your daughter was never to be regarded as a very good mother to me, and I can quite see where she might have inherited it? She has, however, left to me, what is to be regarded as a small fortune, perhaps in some recompense for the error of her ways? Do I need to remind you that the houses that you, and aunt Sandra are living in, now belong to me? They are mine to dispose of, in any way that I see fit. So if it is your wish to remain living here, I will thank you to kindly keep a civil tongue in your head, when addressing me, in any future conversation."

The anger flashed into the old ladies face. Nobody had ever dared to speak to her in this manner before.

"They should have been mine, the houses, and everything else as well, you have no right . . ."

"On the contrary, grandmother, I have every right. I can even give them to Michael Dobbs, if I so wish. Perhaps he might prove to be a better landlord for you?"

She had played a hunch, rightly guessing that there was no love lost between the Dobbs, and the O'Hare's.

"You wouldn't dare, lady. By God, I would have you hunted . . ."

She stopped herself mid-sentence, realising that the crowd was overhearing her raised voice. She brought it back down to a something a little above a whisper.

"Under the terms of my daughters Will, it clearly states that we shall be allowed to continue living here on a peppercorn rent. I have her solicitors letter to that effect, so I care not who is the landlord is, so I don't."

"Words, grandmother, just words. You do care, I can see it in your face. The thought of having to ask a Dobbs for anything, rankles, doesn't it?"

Sharon realised that the crowd around her were slowly closing in, either to better hear their conversation, or more alarmingly, to begin to join in, perhaps? She was beginning to feel threatened now.

"Grandmother, do you not think that this has gone far enough. I apologise and withdraw my threats to you. Despite your harsh words to me, I have no wish to cause you any embarrassment, or distress. I am prepared to honour my late mother's last wishes, and as a gesture of good faith, I will even get my solicitor to write to you, and reconfirm the terms of your Tenancy. But I fear it will have to wait until the paperwork is all sorted out, and everything is transferred over into my name. I hadn't expected that I should be faced with having to air our differences in public, like this, and I have to confess to feeling more than a little embarrassed by it all."

Her words of contrition seemed to strike just the right chord. The old lady was left with nothing to say that might enhance her position any further. She stood there staring defiantly at Sharon.

"Grandmother, do you think that we should let the undertakers remove the coffin from the hearse, and take it inside? If you will then just allow me a few minutes to pay my last respects to my mother, I will take my leave, and bother you no further. I have no wish to carry any of this bad feeling over to the funeral service, tomorrow. What do you say?"

The old lady stood contemplating her request. In the eyes of everyone present, and to maintain her respect and standing in the community, she had to be seen to be doing the right thing. She made her decision, and with a curt nod to the patiently waiting undertakers, she pointed her stick, first at the coffin and then to her front door.

With nothing more to be said, they stood back and silently watched as the coffin was carried indoors to be set up on trestles in the front parlour of the house. Sharon dared to go and stand beside her grandmother as this was happening. She wanted her to catch a whiff of her mothers very distinctive Dior perfume, the only one she had ever used.

The undertakers, their task complete, for the time being, emerged from the house. Sharon beckoned to her driver and spoke to him, so that her grandmother could hear what was being said.

"There has been a slight change of plan. Would you kindly allow me ten minutes, or so, to pay my last respects to the deceased, and then take me to my hotel, please driver?"

"Certainly ma'am. That will be no problem at all."

Sharon looked at her grandmother, who indicated that she should follow her inside the house. The parlour had been cleared of all other furniture, except for a table upon which there was a selection of drinks and a few glasses. The coffin, now draped in the Republic of Ireland's, green, white and orange flag, stood in the middle of the room. Her grandmother stood in the doorway, watching, as she went to stand at the head of the coffin. Sharon looked at her pointedly.

"Am I not to be allowed the common dignity of saying my last goodbye's without an audience, grandmother? Here, you might like to spend the next few minutes looking over the new Tenancy Agreements, before I leave. If you and aunty Sandra would care to sign them, I can take them back with me. You will see that they are similar to your previous agreements, and that I have already signed my part. There is one copy for each of you, and one each for you to sign, date, and return to me."

She produced the three A5 sized envelopes from her handbag, and held them out. The old woman eyed them suspiciously, making no effort to take them from her. Sharon shook them impatiently.

"Well, do you want them, or not? I have given you my word that your peppercorn rent arrangement will continue, so what are you waiting for? I came over here to Ireland with the very best of intentions, but it is you, grandmother, that has made everything so very difficult for me. After I consult with my solicitor, I might yet be persuaded into changing my mind, who knows? So, we can either do this now, while I'm still here, in which case it would immediately become a legally binding agreement in my name, or, you can await my convenience to get them sent through the post, at a later date. The choice is yours, grandmother, for I care little, either way."

She took the envelopes, and left the room, quietly closing the door behind herself. Sharon breathed a sigh of relief, her stomach felt as though it was turning somersaults, let alone churning . . .

"So this is your immediate family, is it, Mum? Well, I can't say that I'm too impressed."

She was whispering as she moved over to slightly part the heavy drapes that covered a window. Putting her eye to the tiny gap she had created, she saw a man working in the back yard. His back was to her, and he was on his haunches, carefully putting a basket full of tiny pups, back into one of a bank of glass fronted kennels, or pens, that he had just finished cleaning. She could see that stacked three high, they bordering as much of the garden, as was in her view. Judging by the number of illuminated infrared lights, the greater majority of them appeared to be occupied?

She noticed that there was a manhole cover lifted, presumably to dispose of the faecal waste, mixed in with wood shavings, that was being used for bedding. Water from a garden hosepipe was running into it. Probably necessary to help it along and prevent blockages, she thought, but being on top of a steep hill, as they were, would certainly help it along.

The man stood up and turned round. He was looking directly at her, and the realisation caused her to guiltily step back, allowing the curtains to fall back into place. She cursed her own stupidity; surely he must have seen them move? Sharon went back to the head of the coffin. The time had come to say her last goodbye to her mother.

She clasped her hands and rested them on the coffin top. Hanging her head, she whispered her last words.

"Well mum, this is it, I guess. Things between us have never been quite what either us would have liked, have they? But then, that's life, and I have learned that it can be so cruel, sometimes. Now, I shall never know what your expectations of me might be, you have never been in a position to tell me, so I can only guess. I know that you might not like some of what I'm about to do, but then, we have very differing ideas of what is right and proper, don't we?

David thinks that I should be 'putting the fruits of your life's work to some good use.' He has a lovely way of saying these things, and has been of great comfort to me. I gather that you and he became rather close, as well? He was certainly very upset, when you were so cruelly taken from us.

It's a pity that you never had the opportunity to properly get to know Malcolm, the man that I'm going to marry. I'm sure that you would have grown to love him, as much as I do. I'm also sure that you will be happy in the knowledge, that with Malcolm, I have a whole new life ahead of me, now, mum.

It occurs to me, that in a weird, twisted, sort of way, I suppose I have you to thank, for bringing it about in the first place. If you, and that animal, Shaun Riley, hadn't put me in hospital, we would never have met. It's strange how something so good, can come out of something so evil, isn't it? Mind you, I still think that if we could just turn the clock back, and rewind the last three months, in hindsight, things could have been oh so very different between us.

I hope you don't mind me not being present when you are laid to rest, tomorrow, mum. I'm obviously not welcome around here, and these people are entitled to pay their last respects, just as much as I am.

Grandmother has seen fit to grant me these last few minutes, to be alone with you, and it is only right that I leave her to grieve in the way that she chooses, without me being there to cause her any further distress.

I don't know if you had any great expectations with regard to our meeting, mum, and I came over here with a completely open mind. But to find myself being publicly harangued, and totally rejected, was the last thing that I expected from my own grandmother. I think that there are probably far too many skeletons still lurking in the cupboards, to prevent us from ever to finding any common ground. This has come as a bitter disappointment to me, for I was so looking forward to being part of a proper family. Perhaps I might have better luck with my father's side? I am planning on going to meet Michael and Vera Dobbs, for the first time, tomorrow. I'm quite looking forward to . . ."

She paused as the door of the parlour was slowly opened. The man that stood looking at her from just outside, was the same one she had seen in the garden. He gave her a little reassuring smile.

"I'm sorry to be intruding, so I am. If you're requiring a little longer, I can come back again in a few more minutes. The grandmother is asking me to see if you're ready to leave yet? Some of the neighbours are waiting outside, as well, do you see?"

He stood there looking highly embarrassed, fingering the brown envelopes that he held in front of him. Sharon calmly met his gaze.

"And you are?"

"Kian McBride, I'm told that I'm you're cousin. Your aunty Sandra is me mother. I'm her eldest son."

From where she was standing, Sharon returned his smile and held out her hand to be shaken.

"Hello Kian, I'm Sharon-Louise, I'm very pleased to meet you."

His smile grew, and she caught a glimpse of lovely set of clean white teeth. He ducked his head to get under the doorframe, and moved further into the room to take her hand. Sharon saw that he was enormously tall, and proportionately built, which tended to belie the fact.

Up close, he was a veritable giant of a man with clean-shaven, open, friendly face, green eyes, similar in colour to her own, and with his unruly mop of fair auburn hair, she felt an instant liking for him. His huge hand took hers in a strong but gentle grip, to be pumped vigorously up and down for a few seconds. He would be a dead ringer for the pantomime part of the BFG, she thought, as she looked up and into his smiling, friendly face.

"The grandmother said you to be a stunner, miss, and for once, she wasn't kidding me."

He laughed at his own awkward forwardness.

"She said I'm to be giving you these, as well. She says they're all signed and dated, as you asked."

He handed her two of the envelopes, and she put them back into her handbag as she spoke.

"Thank you for the compliment, Kian, you're quite a handsome man, yourself. Tell me, are you married?"

"Oh no, miss, I just take care of me mother, and the grandmother, so I do. Me mother says that I'm not cut out to be a ladies man, so she does."

Sharon began to realise that Kian was not quite the ticket. Apart from his enormous size, he looked to be completely normal, but there was very obviously something missing, up there, in the attic department . . .

"I'm just about finished here, Kian. Will grandmother and aunt Sandra be coming to wish me goodbye?"

The smile disappeared from his face and he took on a more pained, embarrassed, sort of expression.

"I'm thinking not, miss. They have asked me to see you out of the house. I'm sorry, so I am."

"Not to worry, Kian, it's not your fault, is it? Will you be so kind as to see me safely to my car, then?"

The smile immediately came back to his face.

"Oh, miss, it would be my honour, so it would."

To his immense pleasure, she stood close and linked arms with him, and they moved out of the room and to the open front door of the house. There, a large crowd of people were all talking amongst themselves, and presumably waiting their turn to come in and pay their last respects? Sharon was surprised at the very obvious high esteem that her mother must still have been held, even though she had no longer been a part of this tight-knit community, for some twenty-odd years.

They all went silent as she and Kian, still arm-in-arm, stepped out onto the pavement. He merely had to glare at the people standing in their way, for them to shuffle apart, and allow clear passage through to the waiting car. Sharon could almost feel the animosity of the crowd, being directed toward her, and was grateful for the protection she felt, by hanging tightly on the arm of the man at her side.

The driver quickly opened the car door for her, and she and Kian stopped beside it.

"Thank you very much, Kian. Come here, big man, and bend down a little for me. I would like to kiss your cheek, if I may be allowed?"

He stooped toward her as he was asked, and in the usual gesture of parting friendship, Sharon bussed him on both cheeks. He visibly blushed as she did so.

"Kian, this little card has my address and telephone number on it. Should you ever find yourself in need of a friend, I shall be there for you, just as you have been, for me, here, today. I'll not forget this, big man."

She tucked her card into the top pocket of his old tweed jacket, and gently patted his chest, while adding,

"Keep it safe, and always remember me when you look at it. Goodbye Kian, I hope that one day, it will be possible for us to meet again. Oh, and for what it's worth, I think that your mother is wrong. You can be a ladies man, if you want to, that is. Somewhere out there, is just the right lady, and she's just waiting for you to come along and make her very happy. You must take the time to go and find her."

She kissed the tip of her finger and pressed it to his lips before lowering herself into the car. He gently shut the door behind her.

As the car moved silently away, Sharon resisted the urge to look back. Had she done so, she might have seen him waving his fond farewell to her. Tears of joy were rolling unashamedly down his cheeks. In only five minutes, she had effectively stolen his heart.

'S & K McBride. So now I know who the 'K' is, and he probably doesn't even know how wealthy he is,' she thought. She opened her bag and extracted the two new Tenancy Agreements. They had both been correctly signed and dated. She smiled in satisfaction as she replaced them. How long should she wait before springing her nasty little surprise? Should she ruin their Christmas, perhaps? Or maybe wait until the New Year, and then hit them with it? There was absolutely no doubt that the back gardens were being used as a puppy farm, but was this, in itself, illegal? She wasn't sure, but George will certainly know.

What was really needed was evidence of some deception arising out of the sale of the pups. False pedigrees being attributed, perhaps, like her mother used to do. She decided to take a further look at some more of the records held on her mother's computer. If she could track down some of the owners from previous sales, she might find evidence of something there? And then there were the people that were supplying the pups, as well. There must be a record of their names and addresses held somewhere, surely?

All this was going to take some time to sort out properly, and time, was not something she was going to have, what with Grey Gables needing to be reorganised. Perhaps she should pass it all over to someone else to look at, instead? But to what purpose? What exactly was she seeking to achieve out of this?

She was still thinking about it, as the car pulled up outside of her hotel. The driver carried her small suitcase from the boot of the car, up to the reception desk. He waited, standing slightly to one side while she verified her booking.

"Good afternoon, my name is Cox, I believe I have a reservation with you?"

The Receptionist looked at her computer screen.

"Ah yes, here it is madam. A double for two nights, is that correct?"

"It is, but there is to be a slight change to that arrangement. My itinerary has changed, and I shall now only be staying for just the one night. Can you tell me if my Hertz rental car is here yet, please?

"It is, madam. The blue Ford Focus is parked just opposite of the front entrance. Here are the keys for the car, and this is your room entry key card. You are at the front, overlooking the river as requested. Room 205 is on the second floor. Turn left out of the lift, and then third door on the right. Will you be dining in tonight?"

"I shall, thank you very much, and all being well, I shall be taking breakfast before checking out, mid-morning tomorrow."

"Thank you, madam. Please enjoy your stay with us."

Sharon turned to her driver from the undertakers. Passing him an envelope from her handbag, she thanked him for his trouble.

"A pleasure to be of service, ma'am. Thank you very much indeed."

Fifteen minutes later, she was languishing in a hot, bubble bath, a chilled glass of Chablis resting on the side. She felt relieved that that the day she had been dreading for so long, was finally over.

Back at Oakwood, following their night of intense passion, Jim and Jacqui were acting like a couple of love struck teenagers, a factor that hadn't gone totally unnoticed by David, Sue, and even Carter. They had no idea of exactly what had taken place, of course, but it wasn't that difficult to make an educated guess.

The couple had entered the dining room arm-in-arm. Jim had made his customary fuss over ensuring that she was properly seated, before taking his own seat, beside her. They normally sat opposite each other.

Sue, with her woman's intuition for such things, couldn't help but notice that Jim appeared to be particularly attentive toward her this morning, and that Jacqui was reciprocating by giving him little knowing looks, accompanied by rather coy smiles.

All the signs were definitely there, she decided. Overnight, their personal relationship had taken a significant step forward. Sue saw that Emily was looking over in their direction, as well. Using telepathy, she asked,

'Emily, I can see that there something different between uncle Jim and nurse Jacqui, this morning. Do you know anything about this, young lady?'

Her little daughter looked up into her mother's eyes, and gave her one of her disarming smiles.

'Jim loves Jacqui, mummy. Like you love daddy . . .'

'Is this anything to do with you, Emily? Have you been interfering again?'

'No mummy, I promised I wouldn't. This is what Jo-jo wants.'

Sue went back to her breakfast thinking about what Emily had just told her. She never for one second disbelieved her daughter. If Emily says that she wasn't responsible, then that is how it is, no question.

The thing is, Emily hadn't made any mention of Jo-jo for quite some time now, and both she and David had thought that perhaps he was no longer as much a part of her psyche, as had been previously apparent? Hearing his name being mentioned again, and in this context, left her now wondering.

Why would Jo-jo want Jim to love Jacqui? And what did she mean by, 'like mummy loves daddy?' What on earth was going on in that tiny head of hers, now?

Sue took another mouthful of cornflakes, and again, looked across at Jim. There was little doubt that apart from the scars, he was now fully recovered from the injuries he had sustained in the fire. In fact, he looked an absolute picture of health, considering his age. She reminded herself that he was in his eighty-sixth year. Was it possible for a man of that age to still be sexually active? Looking now, at how Jim was acting with Jacqui, she had to believe that it was.

She wondered what it must have been like for Jacqui to make love with a much older man? Did she have to coax him along, or even help with a flagging erection, in some way, perhaps?

The thought caused her to reflect upon her own sex life. She looked fondly at David, whom she considered to be an exceptionally good lover. He is certainly more than enough for her . . .

Apart from during the period when he first came out of hospital, and they had to rediscover everything, he had never had any such problems. In fact, if anything, his age and experience had made things in that department, even better.

He looked up from his newspaper and caught her looking at him. He gave her a cheeky smile.

"I know exactly what you're thinking, woman, but you'll have to be patient, I've a long day ahead me."

"Well, I'm sure I don't know what you mean, sir. But don't be too late home tonight, will you, please."

They both chuckled, and as he got up from the table, he came round to kiss her neck just under the ear, and to give her hand an affectionate squeeze. He knew what kissing her neck like that, did for her . . .

Sue went back to finishing her cornflakes, again, but now, with a sparkle of anticipation in her own eyes. She caught Emily's telepathic message, and looked up in surprise. She had obviously been cognizant and fully aware of everything that had just taken place between her parents.

'Like mummy loves daddy.' Was Emily, telling her mother, that she understood the physical side of love? With that revelation, came yet another for Sue. For as far as she could make out, the only reason for Jo-jo to want Jim to love Jacqui, would be if he were now part of Jim's psyche, as well?

The more she thought about it, the more it made sense. It would also serve to offer some explanation in regard to Jim's quite remarkable recovery. Somehow, he was being helped by Jo-jo, from within . . .

She looked over and found that Jim had turned in his chair, and was now looking directly at her, instead.

*'Your deductions are quite correct, Mrs Morrison-Lloyd. It is, of course, within my powers to expunge this knowledge from your mind completely, but I am persuaded by Emily, that I should, instead, take you into my confidence. In exchange for your total discretion in this, I am granting you limited access to speak with me, on certain matters only. I shall not be specific as to what these are, you must discover for yourself. I can also promise that I shall endeavour to see that no harm will ever come to anyone, arising out my presence here amongst you. Do we understand each other?'*

*'Yes, I think so, but am I really talking with you, Jo-jo?'*

*'You are indeed, Mrs Morrison-Lloyd.'*

*'My name is Sue, but then, you already know that, don't you, Jo-jo? Emily has already assured me that you know everything. I would appreciate you addressing me as Sue, in future, though. Can I ask who exactly you are, and where you have come from, Jo-jo?'*

*'You may ask, Sue, but on your timescale, it would take a full day for me to give an adequate answer to your question. You have already worked out for yourself, a quite considerable amount of who, or what, I might be, and I can tell you that, so far, all of your deductions have been correct. I shall always be a part of your daughter's psychological being, for I was there at her birth, I have been with her ever since, and I have promised that it will remain so, for as long as she wishes it to be. In return for her unconditional love, I offer her only help and guidance, in all that she would wish to achieve.*

*The very small part of me that is now Mr Cox, is more tenuous. It is largely dependent on whether I am able to continue to nurture and sustain this frail human body of his. It was Emily's wish that I should help him in this way. Unfortunately, I am finding that the degenerative aging processes will eventually overcome even my capabilities, and I may then have to seek some other alternative host, to enable my humanoid interaction to continue.'*

*'What exactly is your purpose for being here with us, Jo-jo?'*

*'At the moment, Sue, I am living my purpose for being here. And the emotional experiences just seem to get better and better, as for example, with my relationship here, with Jacqui. Between us, there has developed a new happiness and a love, the like of which surpasses anything I could have previously imagined possible.*

*Humans have a simple phrase that is common to all languages. 'Love is what makes the world go round.' Astrophysically, this is totally incorrect, of course. But if applied more philosophically, it's meaning perhaps becomes more apparent? Having given this much thought, I have concluded that this saying can be attributed to the ancient Chinese Yin and Yang, complementary principles, whose interaction is thought to maintain the harmony of the universe, and everything within.*

*In identifying the principles of Yin and Yang, I believe the philosopher to be referring to the power of love, and its direct opposite, that being, hate. These are humanoid traits of character that I have found to be inherent in all of you, but in vastly different proportions, dependent on the mind of the individual.*

*When taken as a whole, these differences tend to cancel each other out, and in so doing, create a balance for everything. Thus, we have people that you refer to generally, as being either good, or evil.*

*There is another which says, 'Love can move a mountain.' Once again, you would have to say, a physical impossibility for any human. But who first coined the phrase, and what message was he trying to convey?*

*My purpose for being here, Sue, is to find out about such things, and wherever possible, experience them for myself. All the knowledge that I seek, is here, within you all. I see it every day in the way that you choose to interact, and help, or hurt, each other.*

*I would hope that my continued presence here, amongst you, will help to promote and nurture the Yang positive principle, that of your continued love for each other, conquering all.'*

Sharon's evening call to Malcolm, was largely taken up with her detailed recollection of the day's events. She vividly recounted and recalled, the undercurrent of pure hatred she had felt from her grandmother, and the community in general. Then she went on to tell him of the gentle kindness and consideration, extended by her slightly simple-minded cousin, Kian.

"I tell you Malcolm, he put every single one of them to shame. It is obvious to me, that the poor man has been brainwashed by his evil mother, and grandmother, into thinking that he is of little use, except as a sort of slave to their demands. I would like to help him to try and achieve greater things, but I fear that he is totally under their control. I can only hope that he gets back in touch with me."

"You gave him your card, you said. Do you even know if he can read?"

"My God, Malcolm, I never even thought of that."

"Well, you're going to see Michael Dobbs tomorrow. I dare say he will know of Kian, he might be able to tell you more, perhaps?"

"Hmm, we'll see. Anyway, enough about me, how was your day?"

"All things considered, quite good really. I received an unexpected telephone call from Holland and Holland the gun makers, late this morning. It was to do with my lost gun, the one that went missing at Bleanaway Quarry, you remember?"

"Yes, of course. What about it?"

"Well, it would appear to have been found, but in very odd circumstances, you would have to say. My gun was apparently offered for sale, as part of a job lot, to a dealership somewhere in west London.

Fortunately, the owner, recognising that mine was something exceptional, phoned Holland's to check the serial number before buying. They of course, were able to tell him that the loss had been reported, and that an insurance claim was pending.

The Police were called in, and they arrested a young Iraqi man, when he came back to get his money. Apparently, he had claimed that the guns were his, and that they had been given to him, but he wouldn't say who by. I spoke to the Police, and it has now been established that he's an illegal immigrant who was living rough, in some squat. They've got him in custody, it seems, and are endeavouring to get to the bottom of it, now, even as we speak."

"And your gun, where is it now? Will you get it back, Malcolm?"

"I would hope so, love. The Insurance Company hasn't paid out on it yet, so technically, I think it still belongs to me?"

"Why don't you get George onto it, he'll sort it for you, Malcolm."

"I have my own solicitors for that sort of thing, love. But your reasoning is sound. So, yes, I'll do that, thanks very much. Oh, by the way, I've asked your dad to take a look around Grey Gables for me. It's practically ours now, subject to the usual red tape being all in order. David will be getting the keys from a local estate agent, tomorrow morning. I've asked Jim to get six rooms up together, and to let me know what items we need to get everything up and running, pending guests at the end of next week."

"Next week? Who are we expecting?"

"Well nobody, actually. But there's nothing like meeting a deadline to motivate someone, is there."

"Oh, that's a wicked thing to do, Malcolm. He's eight-six, remember?"

"Yes, and the old fraud is apparently bedding his nurse, as well. David had me in stitches telling me all about it this morning. Can you imagine it? Jim and Jacqui Strong, for goodness sake?"

"It's old news, I'm afraid Malcolm. Michelle told me as much, when I took the girls back to school, on Monday."

"What? Are you kidding me? Why am I always the last one to know what is going on under my own roof? But if it's true, then I'm surprised at Jacqui. It's got to be regarded as highly unprofessional."

"What, as in like you and me, then, is it?"

"No, of course not. We're different."

"Oh, really. When exactly did I cease to be your patient then? Answer me that one, Mr Blackmore. Was it before, or after, you seduced me?"

"As I remember it, lady, it was you that enticed me into your bed, wasn't it?"

"Yes, and I seem to recall you kicking and screaming against it, shouting the odds at me, because it was all so unprofessional. I wish you were here with me now, my lad. I'd soon show you how to be highly unprofessional."

She could hear him laughing heartily on the other end of the phone.

"Now just you listen to me, Mr Blackmore. This is my dad we're talking about, here. If he and Jacqui Strong have managed to find comfort in each other's company, it is to be applauded, not ridiculed in this manner. What they choose to do, in private, is none of our business, unless it interferes with anything else, that is. They are no different to you and me, and I would soon take exception if I thought people were talking about us, in this way. Now promise me that you will say, and do, absolutely nothing in that regard. In fact, I would prefer it if you offered them both separate accommodation at Grey Gables. He and Jacqui can become your unpaid house sitters for the time being."

"Hey, that's a damn good idea, Sharon Louise. You can then have their vacant suite. Its identical to mine."

"That's not why I suggested it, Malcolm, but your idea does have some appeal. Isn't there a connecting door between the two master bedrooms?"

"Oh yes, so there is. Do you know, I had completely forgotten all about that?"

"Yes, alright, I'm sure you had. The thing is, though, how will we ever decide which of us keeps the key?"

"Toss a coin, arm wrestle, biggest fish on the next trip down to the river? You choose, I'm easy."

"Yes, I've heard that said as well, mister. I'll give it some thought between now and when I get back. Look it's gone seven thirty, and I haven't eaten all day. They finish serving in half an hour, so I'm going to love you, and leave you, to hotfoot it down to the dining room. I'll ring same time tomorrow. Bye sweetheart, catch you later . . ."

The journey from Londonderry to Gawley's Gate, Craigavon, using the in-car satnav, was all done with surprising ease. After only two hours, Sharon pulled the Ford focus off the Derrymore Road, and onto the front driveway of number six. She stopped the engine, and sat in the car for a minute, just looking at the large, grey-fronted, detached house. She noticed that the roof was divided down the middle, indicating that at some time in it's life, the house had been two, that had been converted into one. It all looked very clean, tidy, and well presented, but there was no sign to indicate that it was a Bed and Breakfast establishment. She wondered why?

The front door opened, and a tall, slim man, of about her own age emerged into the glass porch. He was carrying a small boy of around two or three, in his arms, and was followed out by another little girl of about six or seven, who shyly hid behind her father's legs. As they walked out, towards the car, the first thing that Sharon noticed was that they all had ginger, or red hair, and green eyes, just like her own.

Sharon got out and stood in the open door of the car. A few paces apart, and for a few seconds, they stood and regarded each other.

"You must be Michael?" She finally managed, holding out her hand to be shaken.

"That I am. I'm sorry, please forgive my manners, I can see that you are definitely Sharon-Louise."

He put the child onto his other hip and took her hand, holding it while their eyes met.

"This one in my arms is young Paul, and the one, between my legs, is Kathy. Come on, you two, say hello to your aunty Sharon-Louise. She'll be wanting to stay with us for a couple of days."

The children both hid their faces from her.

"Sorry, they're a bit shy with strangers, but as soon as they get to know you . . . Where's your bags? Come and meet Vera. I expect you'll want to be freshening up, your room is all ready for you."

Sharon allowed herself to be ushered into the house, and into the front sitting room. She put her case on the floor, and Michael divested himself of young Paul from his arms. The child ran straight into the arms of the rather petite, and pretty little blonde woman, as she came into the room.

Despite her large heavy glasses, that magnified and accentuated, a pair of bright blue eyes, she had an attractive, very open face, and a lovely smile that revealed overly large incisor teeth. Sharon's immediate impression was that she looked like a little chipmunk, or squirrel, and the rather unkind thought caused her smile. Sharon held out her hand to be shaken.

"Hello, Vera, I'm pleased to meet you."

The next surprise for Sharon came in the form of her lisp. It was very pronounced, probably caused by what Sharon now termed as her buckteeth? And she was obviously very self-conscious about it, poor girl.

"Hello, Sharon-Louise. You are welcome. Please be making yourself at home."

She had taken Sharon's hand, and even bobbed a respectful little curtsey as she spoke. Her words came accompanied with a cloud of minute spittle that glinted in the rays of the afternoon sunlight. Sharon thought it to be almost surreal, and was desperately trying to stifle the urge to laugh. It was Michael that broke the ensuing few seconds of awkward silence. He picked up her suitcase and made for the door.

"Come on Sharon-Louise, I'll show you to your room. Will you be eating with us tonight? At this time of the year, I'm afraid there's not much around here by way of good eating establishments. You would need to be travelling either back up to Antrim, or into Belfast City itself, to find anything anywhere near decent. Vera is a good cook, though. What with the children, who tend to be a bit fussy with their food, we keep it quite simple. It's a meat and tatty pie tonight, and I think she's done us a sherry trifle, as well."

He was talking over his shoulder as they went upstairs.

"Sounds good to me, Michael. I've brought with me, a couple of bottles of wine that will go rather nicely with that. Do you and Vera like wine?"

"Vera does, but I'm a Guinness man, myself, Sharon-Louise. Don't let me stop you, though, I've plenty in the garage."

He opened the door of a very comfortably furnished double bedroom. Placing her suitcase onto the bed, he showed her the small, en-suite toilet and shower, and waxing lyrical, pointed out the lovely view over the Loch. Sharon listened to his patter, politely waiting for it to come to an end.

"Michael, shall we drop the Louise? I'm quite happy with just being called Sharon. It's a long story, but it's been like that for most of my life, and I'm not even sure that I'm comfortable with it, myself, yet?"

"I presumed that the Louise part of your name must have come from our grandmother, Louisa Dobbs? If you're interested, Sharon, I can show you all the genealogy. It's part of my work, and I've studied it all. It's a fascinating story, and I can tell you that we both come from a very dubious, and shady past."

"Part of your work? What's your job then, Michael?"

"Officially, I'm on the staff of the City Librarian, at least, that's what it says on my contract of employment. It also says that I am supposed to work out of the Linen Hall Library, where they hold all the genealogy and social history records. Unofficially, I'm also called upon to do a lot of work for the City Archivist, at The Public Record Office of Northern Ireland, over on Titanic Boulevard. What with all the cutbacks, we're desperately short staffed, so I tend to have to fill-in on high-days, and holidays."

"Do you like what you do, Michael?"

"I've been doing it all my working life, Sharon, that would be since I graduated back in ninety-five. I'm not much good at anything else, using my hands, I mean, so I have to like it. The pay scales are pretty abysmal, and Vera, bless her, has to work part-time, as well, just to keep our heads above water. That's why we do a little B&B on the side. We don't have any official planning, so we can't advertise the fact. All our clientele is dependent solely on repeat business, and word-of-mouth recommendation. I understand that the house is yours now, are you planning on changing anything?"

"Apart from attending my mothers funeral, that is one of the reasons that I'm over here, Michael. To meet you, and to see what needs doing to the house. As far as I can see, it all looks to be in fairly good order? Perhaps you might like to show me round, in a minute? We can make a list of anything you feel needs attention. Then, you can tell me all about my shady past. How does that sound?"

"Great. It's a lovely afternoon, Sharon. Let's forget the conducted tour just for now. How do you fancy a walk along by the Loch, with the children? We've got a little Springer spaniel, and she needs a walk, as well. Her name is Chelsea, and she's as daft as a brush, but very loving. She lives in her kennel out the back. Vera won't have her indoors because she leaves dog hair all over the carpets. We can talk as we walk, I feel that I need to work up a bit of an appetite."

"It just so happens that I packed my walking shoes in anticipation. Have I told you that I used to run a proper little B&B for my stepparents down in Weymouth, Michael? Perhaps we should see about getting you made legal? I confess that you, operating like this, worries me a little. I'm the owner of this house now, and the penalties can be pretty harsh if you get found out, you know? And it might even put your job on the line, as well? Don't worry about the expense, I'll pay for it all, it's my responsibility, after all's said and done."

"Gee, thanks, Sharon. That would be a weight off of our minds, I can tell you. I also have it in mind to convert one of the outside buildings into a one of those French gite, types of accommodation. Would you care to have a look, and tell me if you think it's viable?"

"I will certainly look, Michael. But, on reflection, you must promise me not to be doing any more B&B until you get all the proper certification through. That has got to be your first priority. What with planning approval, it will probably take several months, so get on to it immediately. Do you have any bookings?"

"Nothing till Easter, Sharon."

"Well, let's hope we can get it all sorted before then. Otherwise, you will have to cancel out. Is that clear, Michael? I cannot afford to have my good name sullied, in any way. I have a responsibility to my fiancé, who is a very important man, back home in England."

He looked a bit sheepish.

"We were planning on Vera's parents coming to stay for a week over Christmas, Sharon. Knowing how we're fixed, they usually like to pay their way. Vera will be devastated if you say that they can't come."

"Just as long as you accept no payment, Michael, there will be no objection coming from me. You might like to discuss the nature of the gift they choose to give to the children, though. If you explain, I'm sure they'll understand?"

"Ah, Yes, I see. Thank you, Sharon."

"No problem. Now, if you'll just give me a minute to slip into an old pair of jeans, we can get that walk."

"Yes, of course, sorry Sharon. Downstairs when you're ready. Would you like a coffee, or something, before we go?"

"Strong, black, and with one sugar, please, Michael."

As they walked down through a gap in the road fencing, Michael explained that their walk would take them for several miles along the picturesque shoreline of Loch Neagh. The children were already scampering along ahead, playing at jumping over puddles, and throwing sticks for the dog. Chelsea seemed to be determined to make herself as wet and muddy as possible. Sharon laughingly pointed out the problem they were going to have when they got back.

"No worries, I'm sure she does it purposely? She knows that when we get home, I'll simply be putting the garden hose on her, before giving her a vigorous rub down with an old bath towel that we keep for the purpose. You'll see, she absolutely revels in it, so she does."

"Is she one of grandmother's dogs, Michael?"

"Good God, no. I would never be lowering myself to buying anything from that evil old bitch, I hate her, so I do."

"I sense that you're about to tell me why, Michael? But how about you start somewhere way back, and tell me why we come from a such a dubious and shady past, as you called it?"

"For that, Sharon, we would have to go all the way back to the mid-eighteen hundreds, and our great, great, great, great, grandparents, twice removed. It is from their genes, that we have probably inherited our red hair, and green eyes.

In the wake of the great potato famine, history reflects that Irish people were resettling anywhere that they could find work, Sharon, and our ancestors were mostly fishermen. Desperately poor people, working with nets and boats, they harvested the enormous quantities of salmon that annually enter the Foyle estuary, and make their way upriver to spawn. The Foyle system is still one of the most prolific salmon spawning rivers in the world, you know. Thousands of tons are still caught and processed every year.

Records reflect that the Dobbs' and the O'Hare's originally settled in a little village named, Saint Johnston in County Donegal, There, they all lived together in one, or two, tiny little fisherman's hovels. Thatched cob cottages, with peat and driftwood fires, on which to cook, and provide their only source of warmth. At night, they all slept on straw mattresses, laid on the bare earth floor, all huddled up together.

Their diet was probably limited to fish, mixed in with any source of vegetable protein that could be found. The milk cow was too valuable to slaughter for meat, and sheep, goats, and pigs ate far too much vegetation, to be kept on tiny pieces of rented land. Beer and pochene, a fiery drink made from fermented potatoes, was what they drank. But it was evil stuff, and reckoned to addle the brain. Eventually, those that weren't killed at sea, probably only lived long enough to die of disease, or alcoholism. One's life expectancy was very short indeed, in those days, Sharon.

I suppose that in a small community, and we're probably talking about as many as four, or five, interrelated families, of anything up to ten in each. We would have found that, despite their shortcomings, they were all God-fearing Catholic people, ruled over not only by the landed gentry, but also by the local Priest. They were living in a time when contraception, as we would understand, was not only taboo, but probably yet to be properly perfected? Almost certainly, to avoid unwanted pregnancies, they relied upon old crones, such as grandmother O'Hare, to provide secret concoctions of herbs, probably sold, or bartered for, at extortionate rates. Because of this, interbreeding and incestuous relationships, were known to be rife, and I have even managed to uncover several, going back through our own genealogy. I'll show you our family tree later, if you're interested."

Sharon laughed, and linked arms with him.

"Are you trying to tell me that I'm some sort of genetic throwback, Michael?"

"No, you can make up your own mind about that, after I finished. But I'd be willing to gamble that you've already come across one? Did you get to meet Kian, yesterday?"

She stopped in her tracks.

"Oh Michael, that's a dreadful thing to say. Kian was the only person to show me any consideration while I was there. I understand that he's missing a few essential brain cells, but why do you think he's . . ."

"His father, Verne O'Hare, was a huge man, as well. He was head of the family, and our great grandfather, who married Sheila Dobbs, herself already a second cousin to him. Their offspring, Sara, would be your grandmother. When only nineteen, and unmarried, she gave birth to your mother's sister, Sandra, then your mother, Lara, was born soon after. Then came James, but he's dead now. Their father turned out to be Louis, the son of another of Verne O'Hare's conquests, this time, his mistress, Katrina Dobbs. She was a war widow, whose husband had been a cousin of Verne O'Hare's. Desperate for someone, she had taken up with Verne's sister's boy, her nephew, but he was unable to support her properly, so she prostituted herself with Verne.

Sandra got herself pregnant, and had to be quickly married off to one Calum Riley. This was to cover the scandal of her claim that her grandfather, Verne, had raped her. Incidentally, did you happen to notice that she too has red hair and green eyes?"

"Well no, I was never introduced, so I never actually got to speak with her. Her hair looked grey to me."

"Hardly surprising. She was already an alcoholic when my father died, and Vera and I moved to here, now eight years since. Anyway, after giving birth to Kian, who is autistic, I don't think aunt Sandra ever got over it, Sharon. She's always been a pathetic character, and besides Kian, has had four other children, all with different fathers. There are a whole tribe of grandchildren, far too many to even try to recount.

Finally, to cap it all, Katrina, remarried to yet another Dobbs, the youngest brother of her dead husband. They had a daughter, Louisa, who never married, but my father, Colin, and your father Ryan, were both her children. Louisa Dobbs is our grandmother, on our father's side.

Imagine then the horror of your grandmother finding out about her daughter, Lara, your mother, having taken up with Ryan Dobbs, a lad who, because Louisa is her half sister, was in fact her nephew, once removed. Do you get the picture, now?"

"I think so, but you would have to show me the family tree for me to fully grasp it all. What happened with Louisa, then. Grandmother called her a whore and a traitor to the cause. What was all that about?"

"It was always suspected that she was having an affair with some English lecturer, while she was studying at Queen's University. Despite being already married, he became the father of her children, my father and yours. Mary O'Hare found out about it, and told the

Catholic Priest that she was bedding a Protestant for money, to pay for her education. Louisa's position and social standing in the community slowly became absolutely untenable, and she was hounded out, a broken, disgraced woman. Working as a shop assistant, she found lodgings in the slums of Belfast, which is where our father's were brought up. Grandma Louisa died of cancer, when I was only five, and I only have vague recollections of the tall, lovely looking lady with red hair and green eyes. She looked a lot like you, come to think of it. I've got some old pictures at home, remind me to dig them out and show you.

My father worked in the shipyards until his death, Sharon, but I have absolutely no idea of what happened to yours. He seems to have disappeared completely. I can't find any record of him, whatsoever."

She tucked her arm tighter, and drew herself in slightly closer. A chill breeze had started to come off the water.

"Would you like to know, Michael, because I can take it up from there, if you like? Would you also like to hear the story of my life, because it is equally as harrowing, I can assure you. I've spent most of my childhood in care, so I've never known what it's like to be part of a family. You are probably all I've really got, now, apart from Kian, that is. Apart from you, he is the only other person in my family that I would now be prepared to put myself out for.

It might also help me a little, if I offloaded some of my recent past onto someone else that I feel that I can trust? Shall we turn back now? I'm getting a little cold, and my part of the story should just about get us back in time for tea . . ."

It was precisely as she predicted, and they were just walking up the drive, as she started to relate her recent discovery of exactly how much money was involved with the puppy farms and related sales. They set about preparing to give Chelsea a shower, while still talking.

"Your grandmother also owns a small, farm premises, situated a couple of miles out of town on the A6. I went out there once, and it's all part of her puppy breeding business. She's got nearly the whole of her family, and quite a few of her neighbours helping to run it all, now, Sharon. I'm afraid that you've only just uncovered the tip of the iceberg."

"But what does she do with all the money? Michael? Her personal fortune is considerable, but my own mother had managed to achieve more than that, just working on her own."

"They're Republican Catholics, Sharon. IRA supporters. Where do you think the money is going?"

"Are you kidding me, Michael? These people are supposed to be unemployed and drawing state benefits."

He shrugged his shoulders in resignation. That's how it is, Sharon. Unemployment in the Province is currently running at around ten percent of the population. This is not to be regarded as a true figure, of course, because it has been massaged by the politicians. But there's little that anyone can do, is there."

"Why not? Doesn't anyone ever report them to the Benefits Agency, for example?

He gave a little chuckle at the naivety of her remark.

"Not if they want to keep their kneecaps, they don't. Over here, being a grass, is a sure-fire way to finding yourself in an unmarked, early grave. Violence, extortion and corruption are a way of life, Sharon. We all have to live with the horrors of it, every day of our life. The majority of Irish people still hate the British, but realise that without them, the Province would be immediately be going bankrupt. So they do the other thing, and milk it for all its worth. Everyone's at it, from the politicians and police, all the way down through all the social scales, till we get to the dregs of society. The pimply-faced hooded, youths, seen loitering on the street corners, while looking for some poor innocent, to roll, for their next fix.

The offer of money-for-nothing is just too good to turn down. It also frees up other monies to pour into their election coffers, and provides funding for what they term as, direct action politics."

"I presume you to mean terrorist atrocities?"

"Call it what you will, Sharon. We both know what I mean."

They stopped talking while he gave Chelsea a very vigorous rub with the towel. Sharon and the children watched on in amusement, as the little dog kept slipping away from his grasp, to turn herself around, and then immediately come back for more. He fed her, filled her water bowl, and put her back into the spacious caged enclosure, that contained her cosy little kennel. Chelsea was settled for the night.

Sharon found that Michael's words had struck a chord with her, and the ghost of an idea was beginning to form in the back of her mind. Now, she needed to refine it into a more detailed plan of action.

Elsewhere in the Province, it was the night of The Deputy First Ministers Presidential Election Campaign Ball, being held at Stormont Castle. All the local dignitaries and politicians were present including the Police Commander David Flanagan, and his lovely escort for the evening, Police Superintendent Julia Fox of New Scotland Yard, whom it was rumoured, had flown over just to be there for the evening.

In the usual manner, the guests waited in line to be introduced to their host, a lengthy process as it involved over three hundred people, and he had a gracious word or two, for every single one . . .

Way down the line was Mr Martyn McCue and his escort, who was simply listed as Christina. For Martyn, this evening was a personal triumph, as he had been advised by Christina, that according to her most reliable sources, he was no longer subject to any Police surveillance, and it was therefore safe and acceptable for him to slip back into his more normal way of life. It had been a difficult couple of weeks for him, living on tenterhooks, as he had.

Martyn had noticed that there had seemed to be a little more gardening activity in the Close, than was normal. And, according to Mary, his house had received yet another unsolicited trial window-clean, from the same company as before.

Mary herself, on the evening of the ball, had insisted on helping him dress for the occasion. She had fussed over repressing, starching, and then personally retying his bow tie, to her idea of perfection. The addition of a tiny Shamrock picked from her garden, and affixed through his jacket lapel buttonhole, in her eyes, was the final touch of elegance to complete his outfit.

She had clapped her hands in pure excitement, as she had draped her father's pure white silk scarf around his neck, and offered him the loan of his lightweight black Burberry cape, with its distinctive red satin lining, to carry over his arm, should it rain.

Martyn had graciously accepted, but quickly discarded both, leaving them in the care of his driver, before arriving by official car at the venue. It had pleased Mary to see him leave with them, so she was kept happy . . .

He had to wait only a short time for Christina to be picked up from her address, and he didn't get a proper look at her, until they arrived at Stormont, and he helped her from the car. She looked absolutely stunning in her figure hugging, emerald green, off-the-shoulder full-length gown. With her shoulders covered by a pure white faux, Arctic fox, fur stole, she carried an emerald and pearl studded Gucci leather, clutch bag finished in the same tangerine shade of her leather, as her stiletto healed shoes. The overall effect was meant to tastefully compliment the colours of the Republic of Ireland Flag, and it certainly drew a few admiring looks from the other ladies present, who wished they had thought of the idea. The tiny emerald and gold Shamrock pendant, worn nestling just above her ample cleavage made Martyn regret having discarded his own little natural one, but it was too late now, he was about to be formally introduced to his boss. His turn finally came, and he gave a polite and respectful bow, as his hand was taken in a firm grip.

"Ah, Martyn, nice to see you, thank you for coming. I've had a quiet word on your behalf, and I'm assured that you will be troubled, no more. Have a good evening.

"Christina, my dear. Nice to see you again. May I say that you look resplendently beautiful tonight. My thanks for your continued sterling efforts. Your loyalty and dedication is very much appreciated.

She had bobbed a little curtsey, and he held her hand for only as long as he was speaking. His release meant that she had been dismissed, and should immediately move on, to make way for the next in line.

Feeling slightly miffed, she and Martyn made their way into the gathered throng of people before them. The itinerary suggested that guests were expected to socially mingle, while being served by waiters carrying trays of delicious little French *hors d'ouvres* and *canapés,* with a selection of aperitifs.

It was during this period that Martyn and Christina happened to pass close to where Commander Flanagan, was talking with a few people. He looked up and their eyes met for only the briefest moment, but it was enough to convey both recognition, and polite acknowledgement, between he and Christina.

Sharon's own evening meal was a rather more informal affair. Vera's meat and tatty pie, served with fresh home baked bread and butter, was probably every bit as tasty and nutritious, as the exotic courses being served at Stormont. The chilled South African pinotage rosé was, as she had predicted, a perfect accompaniment, as was Michaels dark, creamy Guinness. The adults and Kathy, had all finished their first course, and Sharon and Michael were watching Vera trying to coax a little more food into young Paul, sitting beside her in his highchair. As a time filler, Michael suddenly remembered that he was going to show her some photographs. Excusing himself from the table, he quickly bounded upstairs, shortly to return with a small album. He moved his chair round to be closer to Sharon, and cleared a bit of space on the tabletop.

"Here we are, this is a picture of our grandmother, Louisa. The two boys are your father, Ryan, he's the smaller one, and my father, Colin."

Sharon gazed at the picture, and for her, it was like looking in a mirror. She recalled the look of shock and incredulous horror she had seen on the face of her other grandmother as she had lifted her veil, yesterday. Now, she understood why.

"Michael, just give me a minute will you, please?"

Sharon went upstairs and quickly adjusted her own hair and make-up to that she had worn the day before. She put on the hat and veil, and the black jacket as well, before making her way back down to where they were waiting. Little Paul, seeing the black veil over her face, started to whimper, and held out his arms to be picked up.

"It's alright sweetheart, it's only aunty Sharon playing a little game," Vera lisped as she sought to comfort him. She looked daggers at both Sharon and Michael.

"I'm sorry Vera, I didn't think, I just wanted Michael to see this."

She looked at him and slowly lifted the veil, as she had with her grandmother. Her eyes stared into his.

"My Godfathers," He exclaimed. "I'd have given my right arm to have seen the old cow's face, when you did that to her. She must have thought that her sins had come back to haunt her. Look at this, Vera?"

He held up the photograph of Louisa, for comparison. The similarity was quite remarkable, even down to the black hat and dated hairstyle.

"Did you do this on purpose, Sharon? How did you know?"

For little Paul's sake, Sharon quickly removed it all, and shook her hair back into place.

"No, Michael, I was trying to copy this picture, that I have of my mother."

She went to her handbag and got it out to show him. He compared the two together.

"But these were taken what, eighteen? Even twenty years, apart? They both look to be around the same age, wouldn't you say?"

"I would have to agree with you, yes, Michael. But do you think that its coincidental, or was my mother perhaps trying to prove something, as well? I don't suppose we'll ever know, now."

"Not unless the old cow lets on, we won't. I'll bet this was like a slap in the face with a wet kipper, when she first clapped eyes on you, yesterday?"

They all laughed at his turn of phrase.

Sharon spent the next few minutes looking through the rest of the photograph album while Michael explained each one. Vera retired to the kitchen to fetch the trifle.

"Is it possible for me to have a copy of some of these, Michael. I only have this one picture of my mother, and this tiny one of my father, contained here, in my locket?"

"Sure, it's no problem, Sharon. I can either email them to you, or we can go upstairs, and print them off when we finish here. I've got a photo quality scanner/printer in my office."

"You have an office here, then, Michael?"

"Yes, it's quite often possible for me to conduct my work from home. I can just as easy do it from here as in one of the offices at the Library, or Records. A computer, and the work that is to be transferred, is all that is needed. It saves me an hour and a half, or a fifty mile round trip, to and from work. And when I'm not using the office, Vera helps out by doing the same thing, part-time. It's a win-win situation, both for us, and our employers, the City Council. I'll show you in a minute."

"Are you telling me that you have access to all the public records, from right here, in your home, Michael?"

"Yes, but no more than anyone else would have. The only difference being, that out of necessity, I can still access them, while the rest of the public can't. As with all computerised files, the art lies in being able to find your way through all the masses of data, to find exactly what you are looking for. Vera is particularly good at it, probably better than I, if the truth be known, aren't you, my love?"

She smiled and while passing over a generous helping of trifle to Sharon, nodded her tacit agreement. A few minutes passed in comparative silence, while they ate. Finally, as Sharon, the last to finish, placed her spoon and dessert fork neatly in the middle of her plate, Michael asked,

"What's on your mind Sharon? I can almost hear the cogs whirring, from here?"

"Only the gist of an idea, Michael. It has to do with what we were talking about earlier. I have it in mind to try and bring an end to grandmother's little empire of misery and cruelty. I want to destroy it completely. I was thinking that if I were to hire the services of a private investigator, and get him to look into all that she is doing, would you be prepared to offer him some assistance, by using only your knowledge and expertise? I don't want you, or Vera, to feel at all pressured, or obliged to do this, and if you decide to say no, I will understand completely, and say no more about it."

"What do you have in mind Sharon?"

"We would need to work out the all the details of how to go about it, of course, but I'm thinking of bringing pressure to bear, so that funds from her nasty little enterprises, perhaps find their way into contributing towards some much more worthy causes. Do you get my drift?"

He chuckled at the thought. Encouraged, Sharon went on.

"Here, in my handbag, there is a CD. It was one of my mother's, and contains, what I believe, to be a list of transactions relating to my grandmother's little empire. Back home, there are eight other similar ones, that I haven't even looked at yet. Would you and Vera, care to have a quick look at the one I've got with me, and tell me how you think we might use the information that's on it?"

They looked at each other and shrugged, both silently agreeing that it will do no harm to just to look.

While Vera went about getting the children ready for bed, Sharon made her usual evening call to Malcolm, but this time kept it short, on the excuse of being in company.

Next, she made a call to George, asking him to find out about the Private Detective Agency that Tony Williams had used. She stressed that she needed a contact phone number, as she needed to consult with them immediately. For the time being, she declined to give George her reasons for requiring the details, stating only that she was seeking his advice about something. Reluctantly, and feeling slightly excluded, George said he would phone her back, just as soon as he had the required information.

Apart from George's returned call, that came ten minutes later, all the rest of the evening was spent with the three of them delving into the information contained on the CD, and what else they were able to glean from it. They then went on to discuss how best to go about using what they had, to the best advantage. The most obvious need was to avoid revealing from where, or from who, the demands they had in mind, were being originated.

Sharon likened it to being a modern day Robin Hood type of situation, robbing the rich of their ill-gotten gains, to give it over to the rather less fortunate, and deserving causes.

Michael thought that with the use of computers, what Sharon was proposing was perfectly feasible, but he had some doubts as to the legality of it all. Sharon promised to talk it through with her solicitor, George.

And so it was. On the run down to Christmas, all the people in Emily's little world were all going about their daily business, while endeavouring to realise their hopes and dreams.

Those closest to her, her parents, settled into their new positions, working with Malcolm Blackmore. David found that his job as Hospital Project Manager, often had him working twelve, and fourteen-hour days. He soon came to realise that his job title would better have been described as Personal Assistant, and General Dogsbody, to Malcolm Blackmore, who, on a daily basis, still insisted on being advised and appraised of every single little detail, and decision. Notwithstanding, David still found that he thoroughly enjoyed what he was doing. The hospital could visibly be seen, to be rising from the ground, and he found a great sense of job satisfaction, and achievement, in helping with its creation.

Sue, with the twins off her hands, set about her accountancy studies, with a renewed vigour. She often shared the library for hours on end, with her tiny daughter as sole company. Invariably, they were both to be found with their heads stuck in a book, of some sort. Emily's thirst for knowledge was insatiable, and she was quickly working her way through nearly every volume, that wasn't a work of fiction.

Much to the relief of their parents, the twins quickly settled into their knew schools, and when home at weekends, even found a hitherto undiscovered respect for each other's privacy. Thankfully, their constant bickering had now ceased, although there still existed a spirit of fierce competition, in virtually everything that they did together. David and Sue realised that this was something that would probably accompany their children's relationship all the way through adolescence, and even into adulthood. Was it such a bad thing? They thought not . . .

Jim and Jacqui made the move from Oakwood, into what was previously, the House Managers apartment at Grey Gables. Together, they took over the complete running of the place, only drawing on additional staff from Oakwood, as and when, more help was required. Their happiness, together, was apparent for all to see.

Miguel and Susan, now cognizant of the prohibition on staff liaisons, restricted themselves to meeting in secrecy, somewhere away from Oakwood. Usually, it would be on their days off, which they always requested to be the same. From this, Carter suspected that there was something going on between them, but as they were both excellent, and highly valued workers, he now regarded them as an integral part of the household. So, he and Elsie, while cautioning them into discretion, were prepared to turn a blind eye, just so long as their relationship caused no disruption to the harmony, and smooth running of things.

Sharon, on her return to Oakwood, with the idea fresh in her mind, immediately set about planning the demise of her grandmother's little empire. She spent many determined hours on her computer, patiently trawling through all her mother's files, and financial records. By cross-referencing them with other archive files, and by making copious notes on all her findings, she eventually began to positively identify the names and addresses of some of the main suppliers and dealers, involved with her grandmother.

These, she would mark down as potential 'targets,' and allocate to them, a unique file reference number.

In small batches, all the known details of the targets, together with a detailed record of their previous transactions, would be upload onto another CD, and post it on to Michael and Vera, together with her observations, and anything else thought to be relevant.

In this way, no traceable, sensitive data, was being sent between computers, something that Michael and Vera, for security reasons, had absolutely insisted upon. Very slowly, it all began to come together, and, having selected six of the most likely targets, as their first candidates, a more detailed plan of action was formulated. It was all set to be put into operation, early in the New Year, when Pete would travel back over to Ireland, to make a start.

None of them had any idea of the size of the hornets nest, they were about to disturb. Otherwise, they might have had second thoughts?

Sharon found herself being drawn more and more, into Emily's company, but was totally unaware of the fact, that this was all part of Emily's plan. As such, she was equally ignorant of the subtle little mind manipulations, and suggestions, that she had been receiving. Everything that Emily did, had an underlying purpose, and these suggestions were being introduced to help and encourage, Sharon, into developing a deeper bond of affection, toward her little charge.

For her part, during their time spent together, which by now was almost on a daily basis, Emily undertook to keep Sharon delightfully entertained, with her telepathic exchanges, and constantly enquiring mind.

With very careful and selective guidance, Emily began helping Sharon to further enhance, and develop, her telepathic skills. She did this with the full knowledge that eventually, with practice, she would be able to pass some of it on to Malcolm, and they would learn to communicate telepathically, with each other.

In Emily's view, this would help to further strengthen the bond of love, and trust, between them. Like it had with her own parents.

At weekends, when Malcolm was home, Emily tended to leave Sharon to enjoy his company, without any interference. She already understood the need to afford them their privacy, but was both pleased and delighted, when Malcolm himself, sought to be in her company, albeit usually, to discuss certain medical matters with her.

Emily, though, was quick to realise that he was seeking to gain information, which she was reluctant to disclose. This was because it indirectly involved Jo-jo, and the part of his being, that had taken over Jim's psyche. She knew that this was something that Malcolm would never understand. So, much to his frustration, she invariably sidestepped, or avoided, answering many of his more probing questions.

Malcolm had still not forgotten her exact words, in relation to Jim Cox. When Emily told him that she had managed to, "make a small adjustment to his mindset, to encourage him to think more positively, and restore the natural balance of his mind. This in turn, enabled all of his bodily functions, and natural healing processes, to respond as they should . . ." The whole concept had left him struggling to understand.

As a consequence, Malcolm had spent many hours pondering how this had been achieved? Indeed, if he hadn't witnessed it for himself, he would have previously thought it to be totally impossible.

He had even sought the professional opinion, of a colleague trained in clinical psychology. When Malcolm asked if he thought the hypothesis was feasible, he too, was somewhat sceptical. They had discussed it at length, and had come to the conclusion, that in order to achieve it, there would probably be a requirement for some form of voluntary hypnosis? Firstly, to enable the suggestion to be implanted, and secondly, for the patient to subconsciously respond, in the desired manner. That then posed the question of how such a suggestion should be worded? He doubted, that merely telling someone that they needed to be more positive about getting better, would be sufficient enough, to achieve anything significant. In the end, the psychologist had dismissed the whole idea, as being unworkable. But Malcolm knew differently . . .

Once again, he was forced into reconsidering Emily's quite remarkable mental capabilities. Apart from the telepathy, of which, he was now an active participant, there was the incident when Sharon was kidnapped. Even though she was sixty miles away, Emily was able to paint a vivid picture of exactly what was happening to Sharon, even as it was occurring. How on earth was that achieved? Malcolm couldn't even begin to speculate, but equally, he was determined to find out, one way, or another . . .

To that end, he had decided to ask her parents, if they would allow him to introduce her to one or two of his patients, who were suffering from severe post-traumatic stress syndrome. A common legacy arising out of people having been caught up in the dreadful horrors of conflict, and war. Often, it was possible to attend to the physical injuries, but the mental aspect, could rarely be addressed to the same degree of success. He was therefore keen to see if Emily could make use any of her unique powers, and perhaps help them, in some way?

So, for the time being, all was well in Emily's little world. But unbeknown to her, and the others, there were a few dark clouds lurking beyond the horizon.

At a secure, residential care home facility, in South Wales, a lonely old man, with a horribly disfigured face, spent his days wondering what had become of his brother? He also failed to understand why Lara hadn't responded to his letters? He was sure they were being sent to the right address?

In his frustration, he had come to the conclusion that there was nothing else for it, but to go and find out for himself. With that in mind, he had already set about plotting his escape.

Pete and Caroline Grogan, after several meetings, had accepted Sharon's rather peculiar brief. Together, they had travelled over to Craigavon to meet Michael and Vera Dobbs, for a full case conference on their intended plan of action. It had been an interesting long weekend, and both couples found a developing degree of respect, and friendship, toward each other.

Since then, Pete had been back in touch with Tony Williams. After explaining that he had, other, long-term enquiries, to conduct in Ireland, on Sharon's behalf, he had sought to be re-engaged by Tony.

He outlined his desired wish, to conduct follow-up enquiries on seeking to trace the man who had impersonated Connor. Pete confessed that the unsolved case had been bugging him, and that this was just too good an opportunity to pass up.

The same could definitely be said for Tony Williams. For having some time to dwell upon it, he too was now harbouring a similar desire. The need to establish the truth about what had happened to Connor?

So, on receiving Pete's little proposition, he was inwardly delighted, and had readily agreed and accepted.

Tony, having given the matter some thought, decided not to say anything to Lizzy about it. Despite his promise not to harbour any more secrets, he was fearful of causing her further distress, or giving grounds for any more bad feeling. He very much doubted that their rather tenuous, developing, relationship would stand the strain? And, as she was now his only living relative, he was naturally anxious, not to lose her.

The alien, having found true love with Jacqui, was now preoccupied in experiencing all of the emotional and physical delights, arising out of his intimate association, with her. In consequence, Emily was finding that her interaction with him, was becoming rather less than it had been. While she was still able to make telepathic contact, and speak with Jo-jo, if she so desired, she was no longer finding the necessity.

Even so young, Emily was able to recognise that it was largely her own attitude, that was bringing about the slight changes in their relationship. There still existed that deep bond of love and affection, between them, but she was now much more able to think for herself, and to make her own plans, and decisions, without the need to constantly seek his advice, guidance and reassurance. Consequently, Emily was becoming far less reliant on his continued presence in her everyday life.

The alien also recognised that Emily was growing up, and while still keeping a watchful eye, he was quite content to allow her education, and personality, to develop quite naturally, without too much interference from himself. True to his promise to Sue, he was always going to be there, to watch over, guide, and protect Emily, but to what extent that would be, he could not even begin to predict . . .

**To be continued**